NAYRA and the DJINN

Iasmin Omar Ata

VIKING

WHAT
ARE
DJINNS?

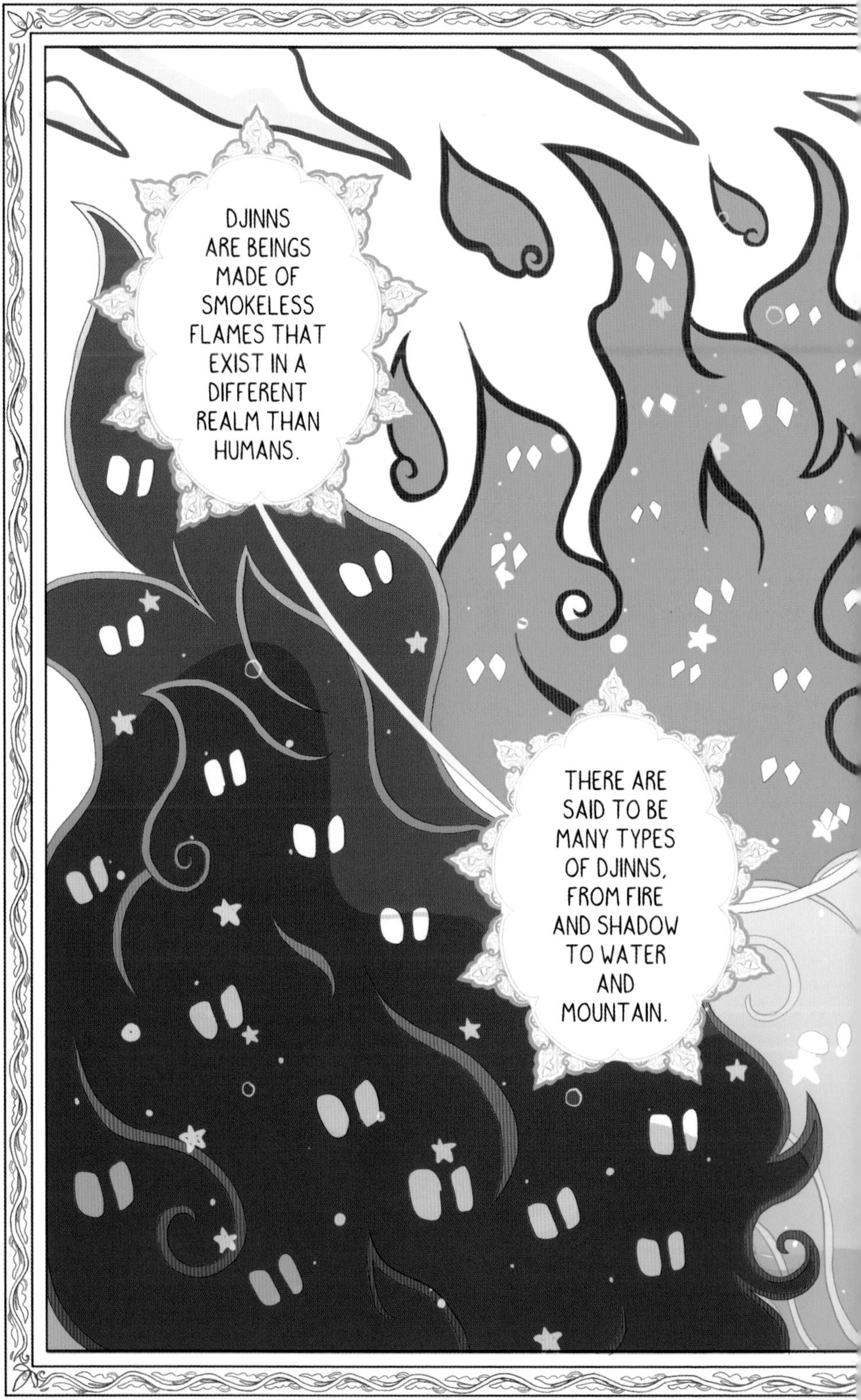
DJINNS ARE BEINGS MADE OF SMOKELESS FLAMES THAT EXIST IN A DIFFERENT REALM THAN HUMANS.
THERE ARE SAID TO BE MANY TYPES OF DJINNS, FROM FIRE AND SHADOW TO WATER AND MOUNTAIN.

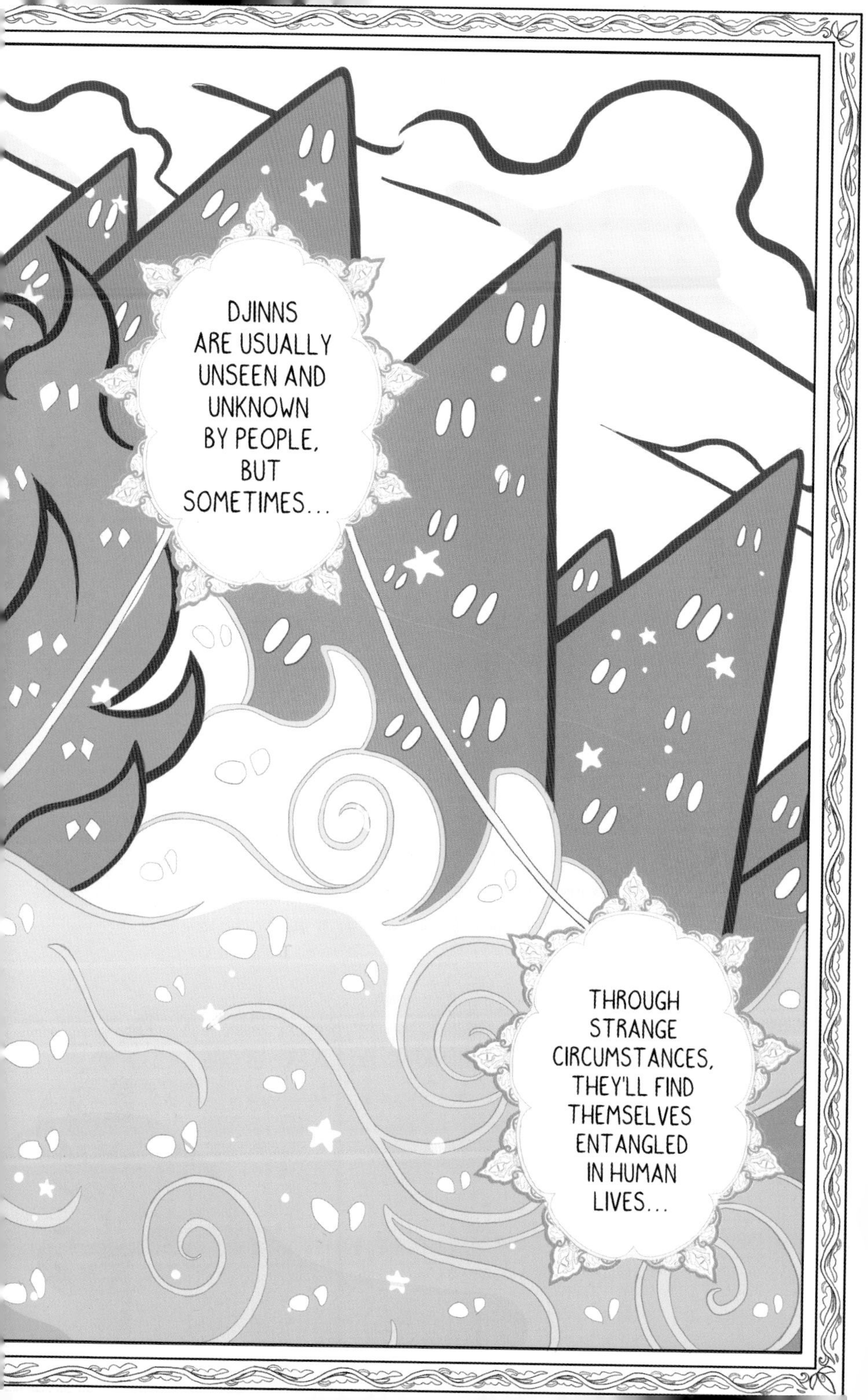
DJINNS ARE USUALLY UNSEEN AND UNKNOWN BY PEOPLE, BUT SOMETIMES...
THROUGH STRANGE CIRCUMSTANCES, THEY'LL FIND THEMSELVES ENTANGLED IN HUMAN LIVES...

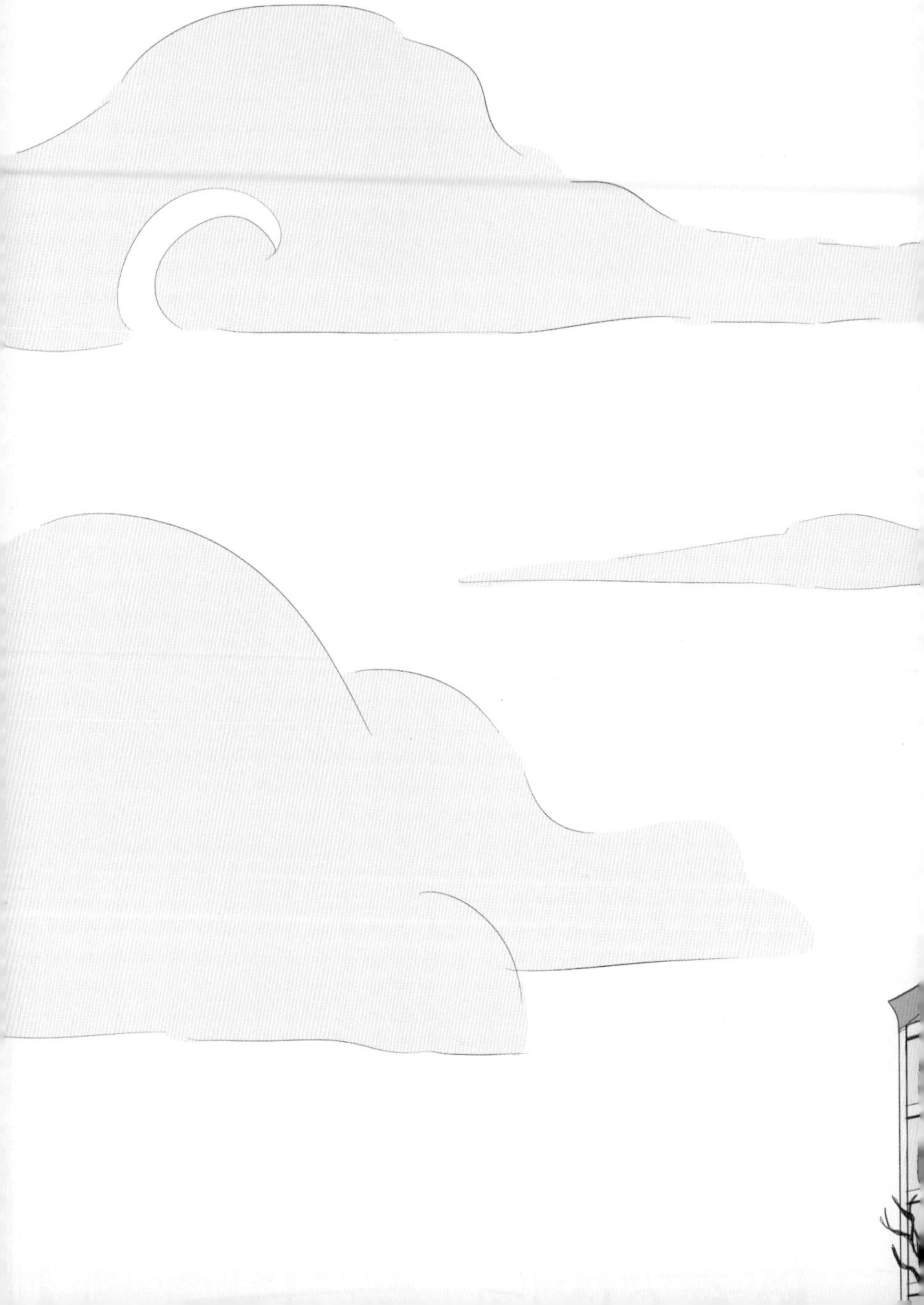

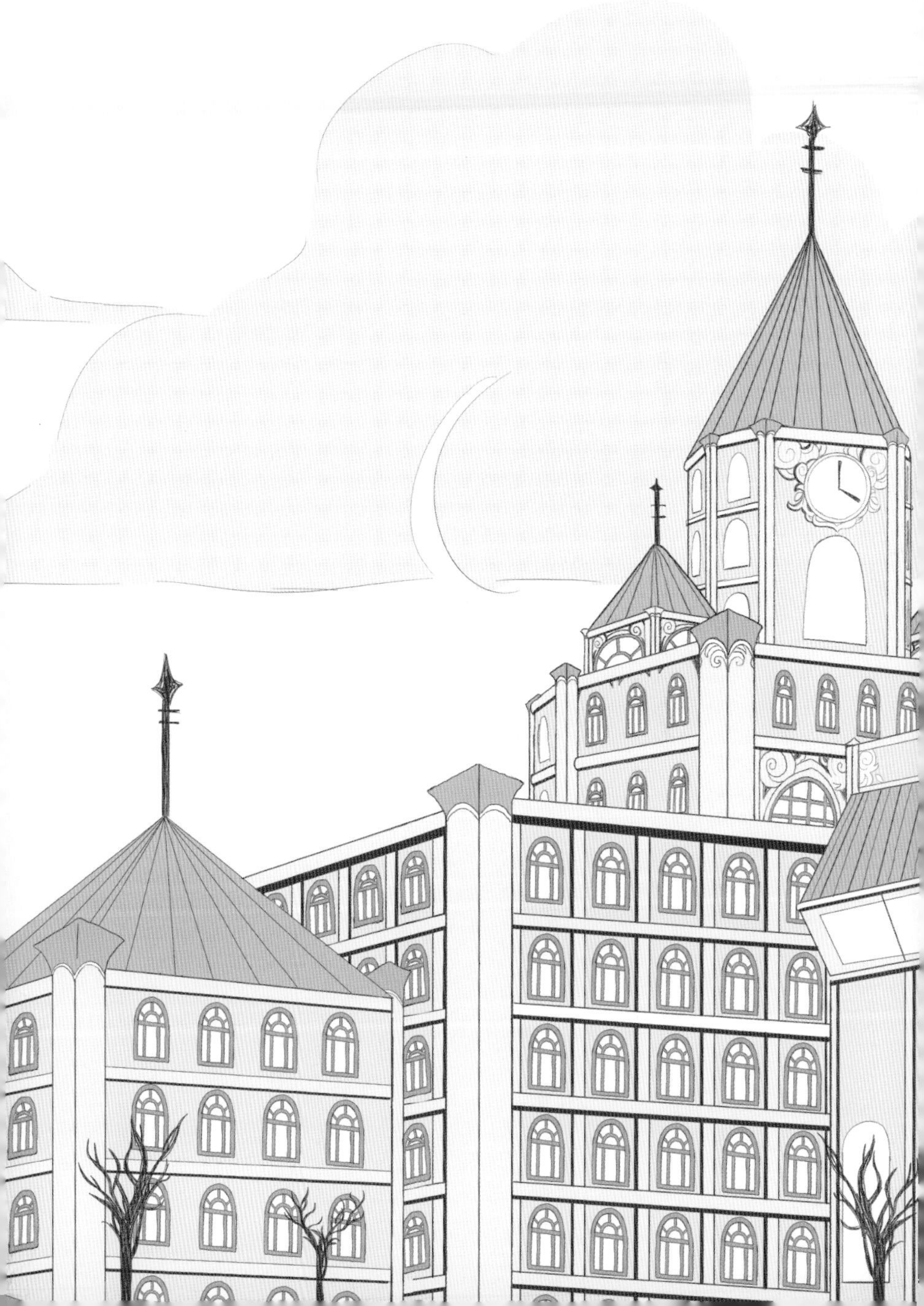

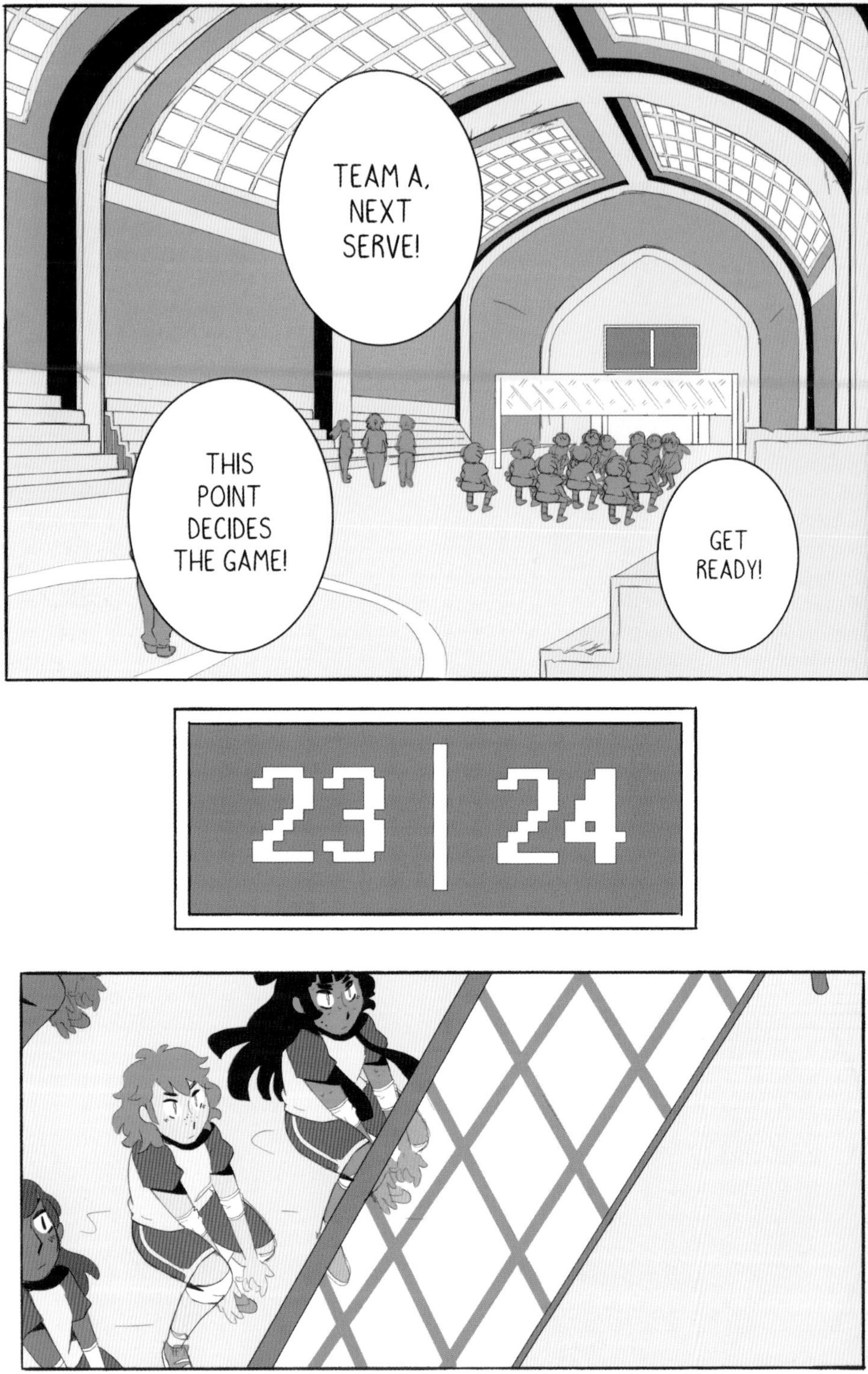
TEAM A, NEXT SERVE!
THIS POINT DECIDES THE GAME!
GET READY!
23 | 24

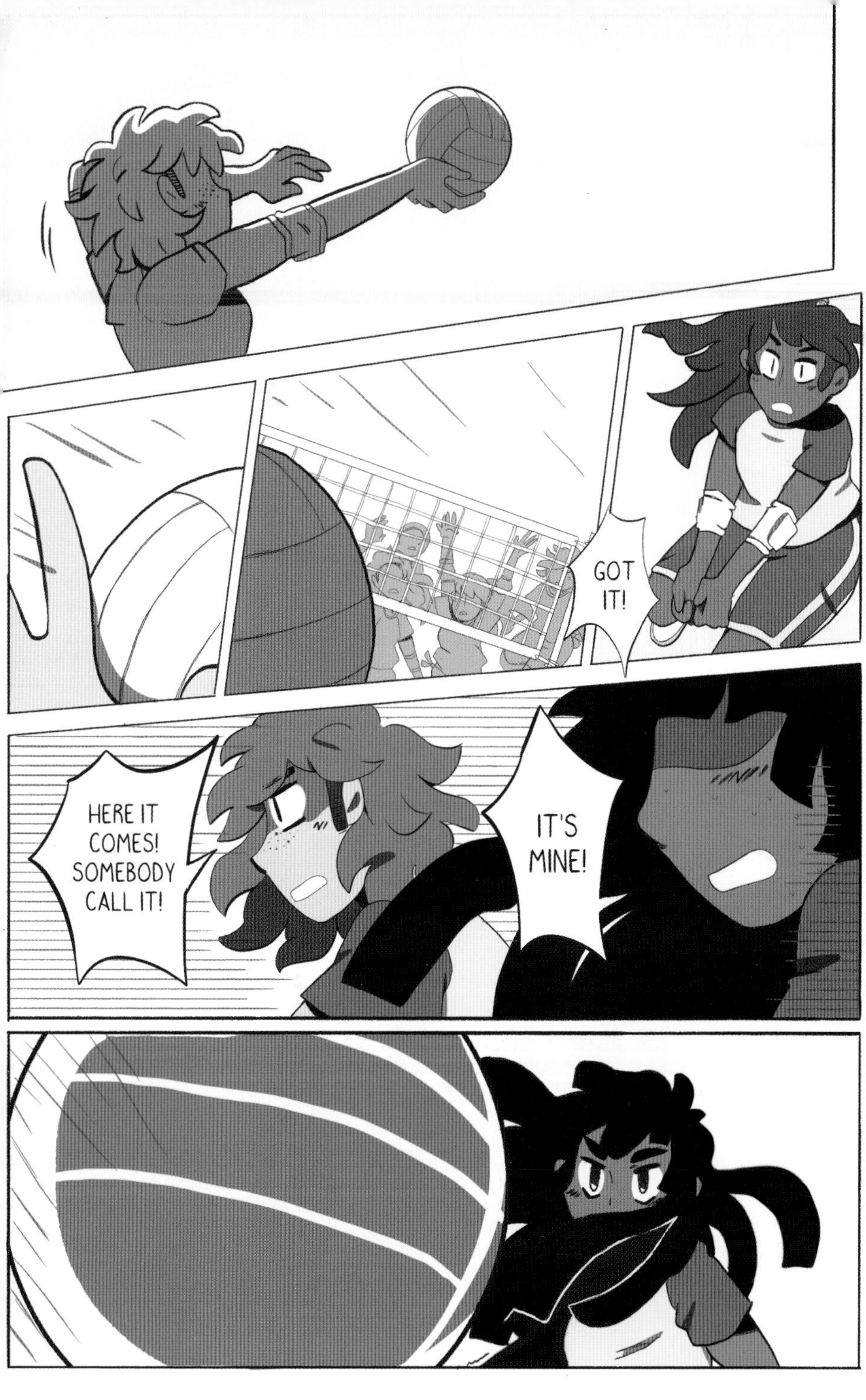
GOT IT!
HERE IT COMES! SOMEBODY CALL IT!
IT'S MINE!

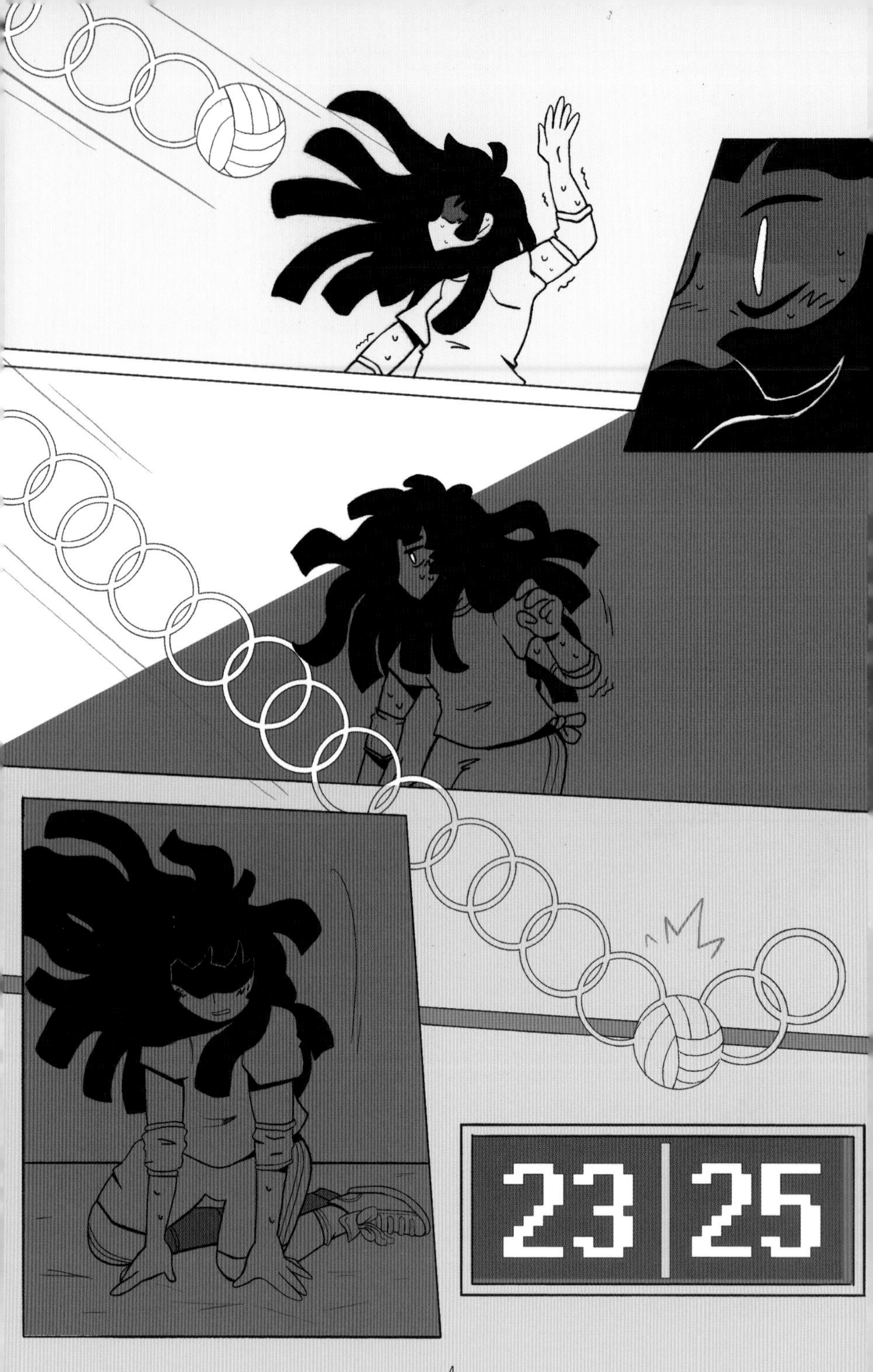
23 25

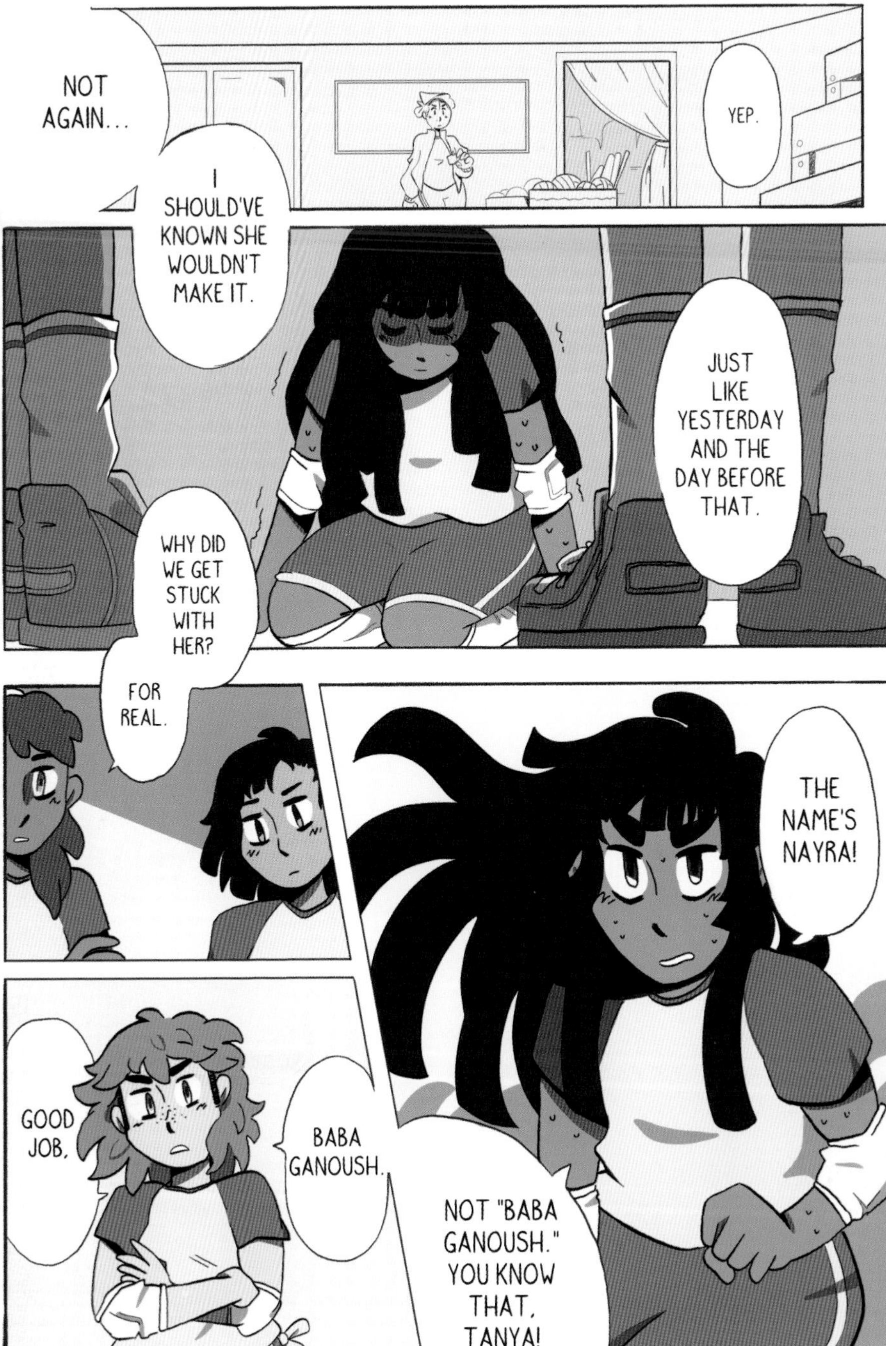
NOT AGAIN...
YEP.
I SHOULD'VE KNOWN SHE WOULDN'T MAKE IT.
JUST LIKE YESTERDAY AND THE DAY BEFORE THAT.
WHY DID WE GET STUCK WITH HER?
FOR REAL.
THE NAME'S NAYRA!
GOOD JOB,
BABA GANOUSH.
NOT "BABA GANOUSH." YOU KNOW THAT, TANYA!

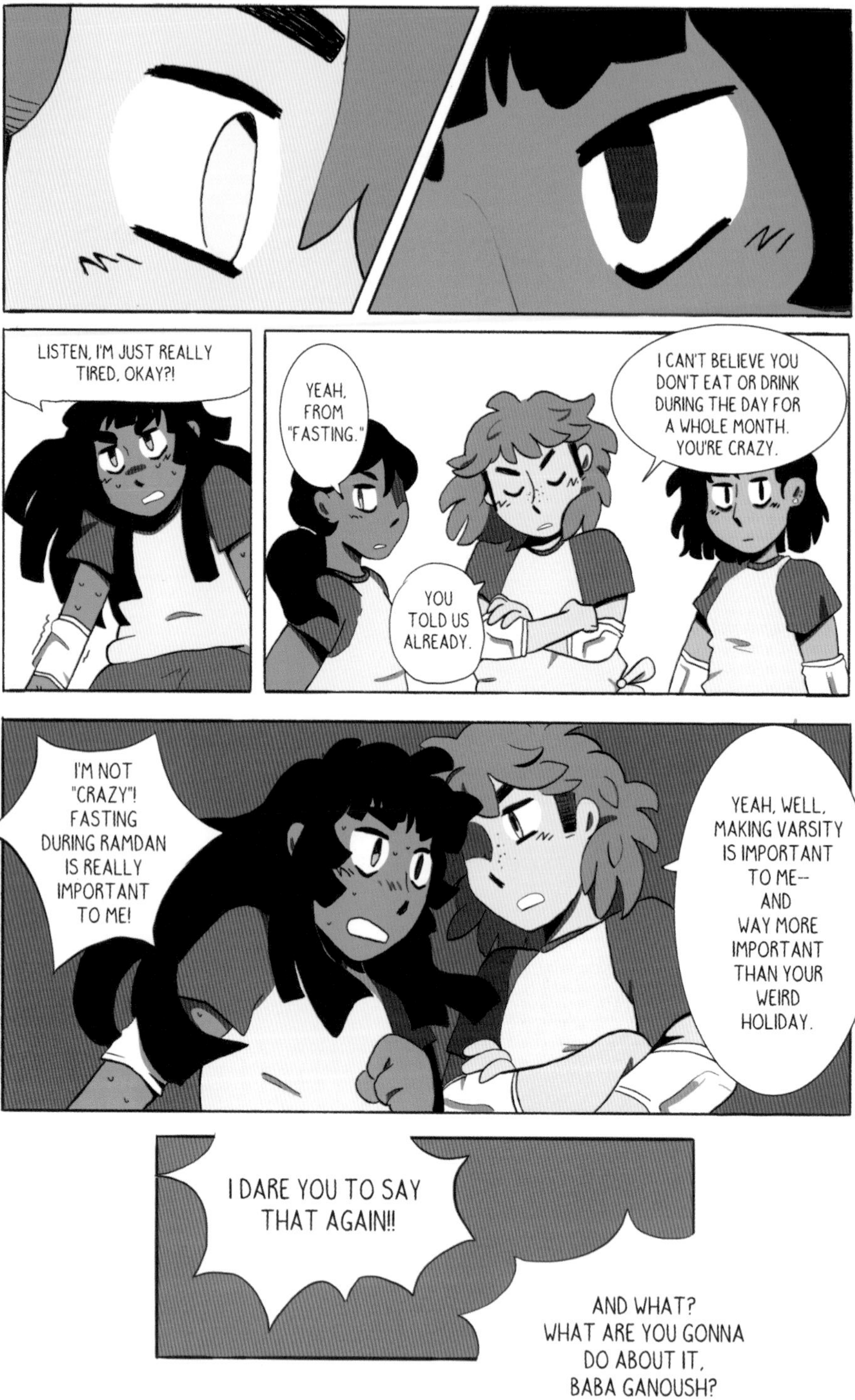
LISTEN, I'M JUST REALLY TIRED, OKAY?!
YEAH, FROM "FASTING."
I CAN'T BELIEVE YOU DON'T EAT OR DRINK DURING THE DAY FOR A WHOLE MONTH. YOU'RE CRAZY.
YOU TOLD US ALREADY.
I'M NOT "CRAZY"! FASTING DURING RAMDAN IS REALLY IMPORTANT TO ME!
YEAH, WELL, MAKING VARSITY IS IMPORTANT TO ME-- AND WAY MORE IMPORTANT THAN YOUR WEIRD HOLIDAY.
I DARE YOU TO SAY THAT AGAIN!!
AND WHAT? WHAT ARE YOU GONNA DO ABOUT IT, BABA GANOUSH?

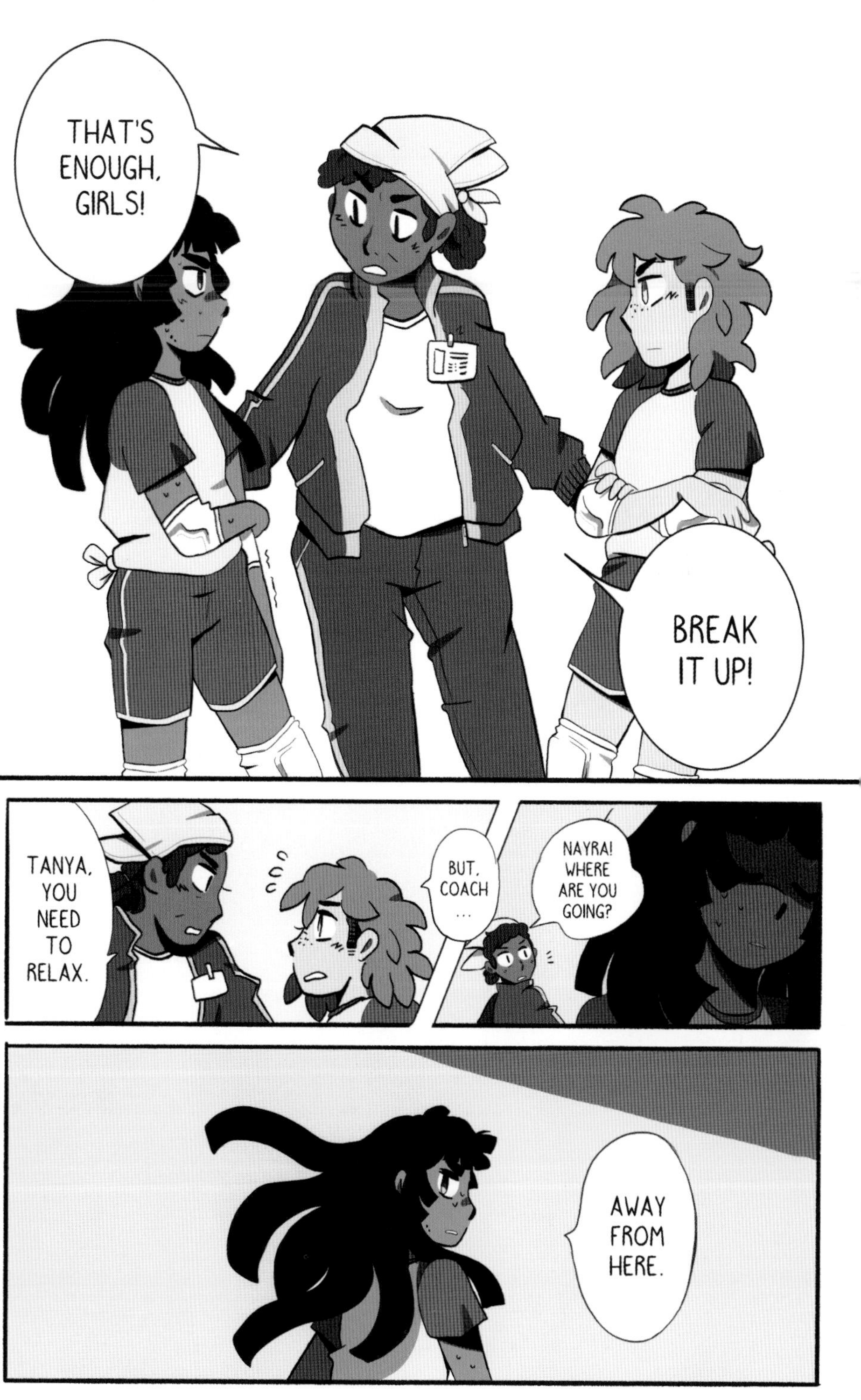
THAT'S ENOUGH, GIRLS!
BREAK IT UP!
TANYA, YOU NEED TO RELAX.
BUT, COACH . . .
NAYRA! WHERE ARE YOU GOING?
AWAY FROM HERE.

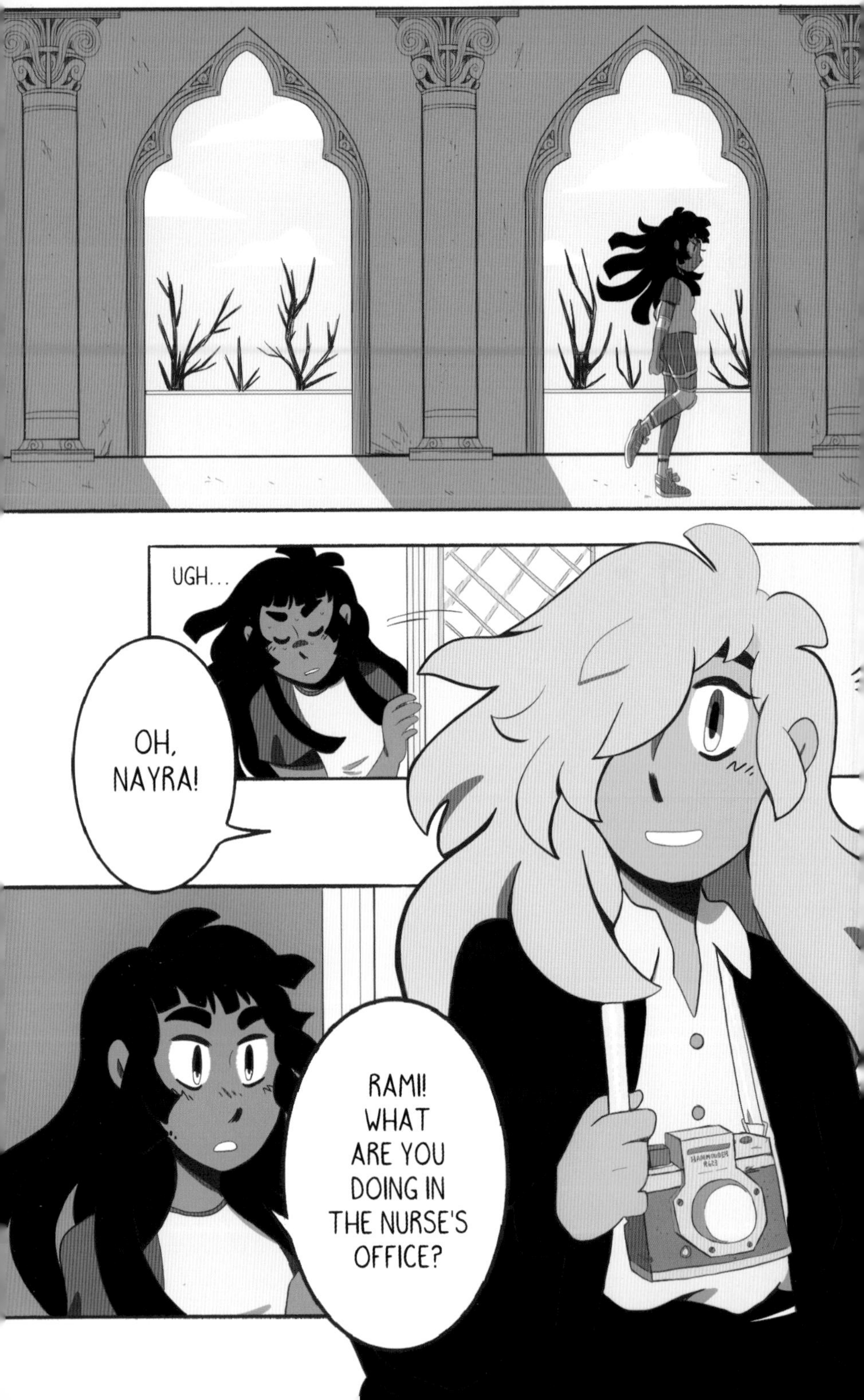
UGH...
OH, NAYRA!
RAMI! WHAT ARE YOU DOING IN THE NURSE'S OFFICE?

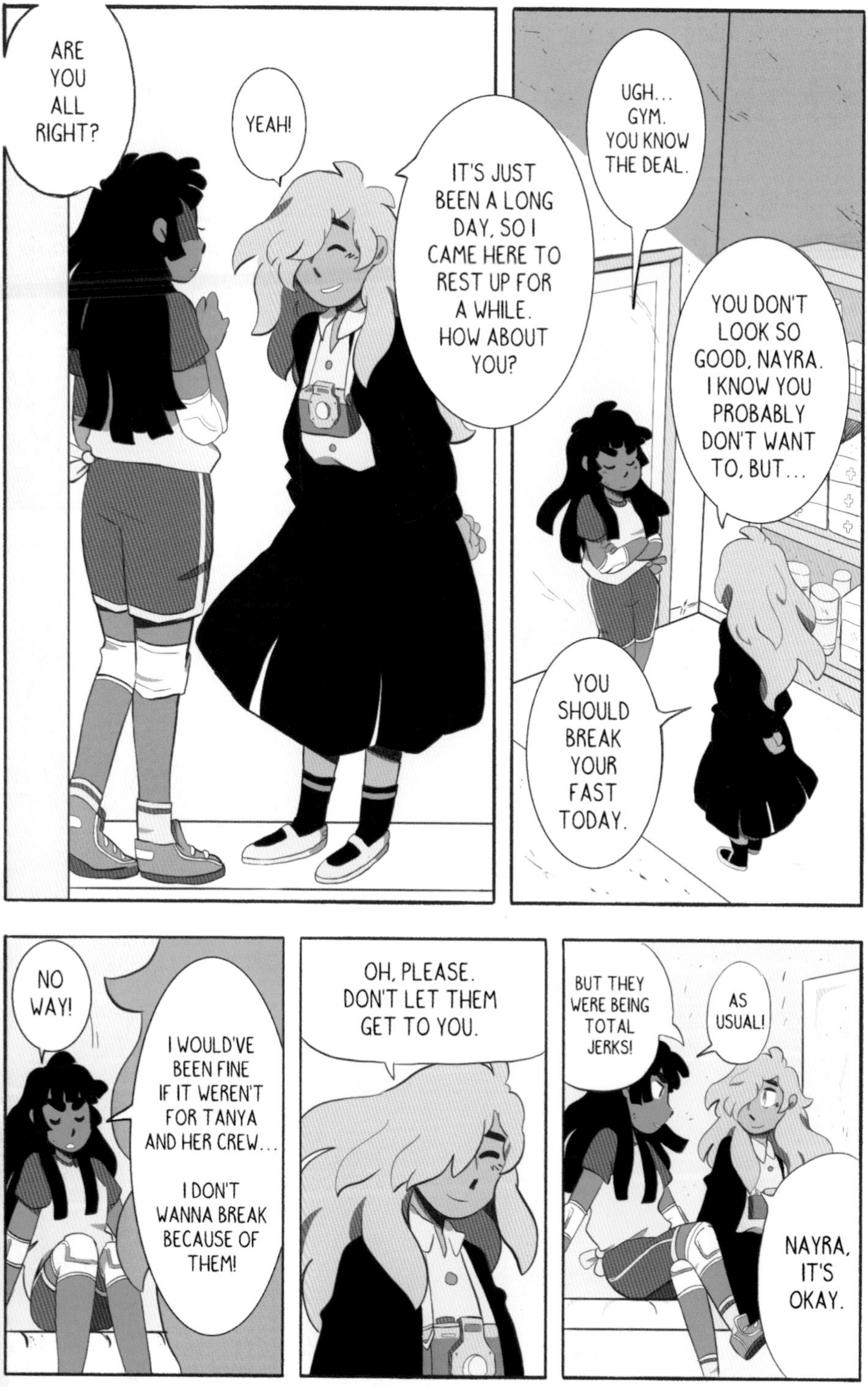
ARE YOU ALL RIGHT?
YEAH!
IT'S JUST BEEN A LONG DAY, SO I CAME HERE TO REST UP FOR A WHILE. HOW ABOUT YOU?
UGH... GYM. YOU KNOW THE DEAL.
YOU DON'T LOOK SO GOOD, NAYRA. I KNOW YOU PROBABLY DON'T WANT TO, BUT...
YOU SHOULD BREAK YOUR FAST TODAY.
NO WAY!
I WOULD'VE BEEN FINE IF IT WEREN'T FOR TANYA AND HER CREW...
I DON'T WANNA BREAK BECAUSE OF THEM!
OH, PLEASE. DON'T LET THEM GET TO YOU.
BUT THEY WERE BEING TOTAL JERKS!
AS USUAL!
NAYRA, IT'S OKAY.

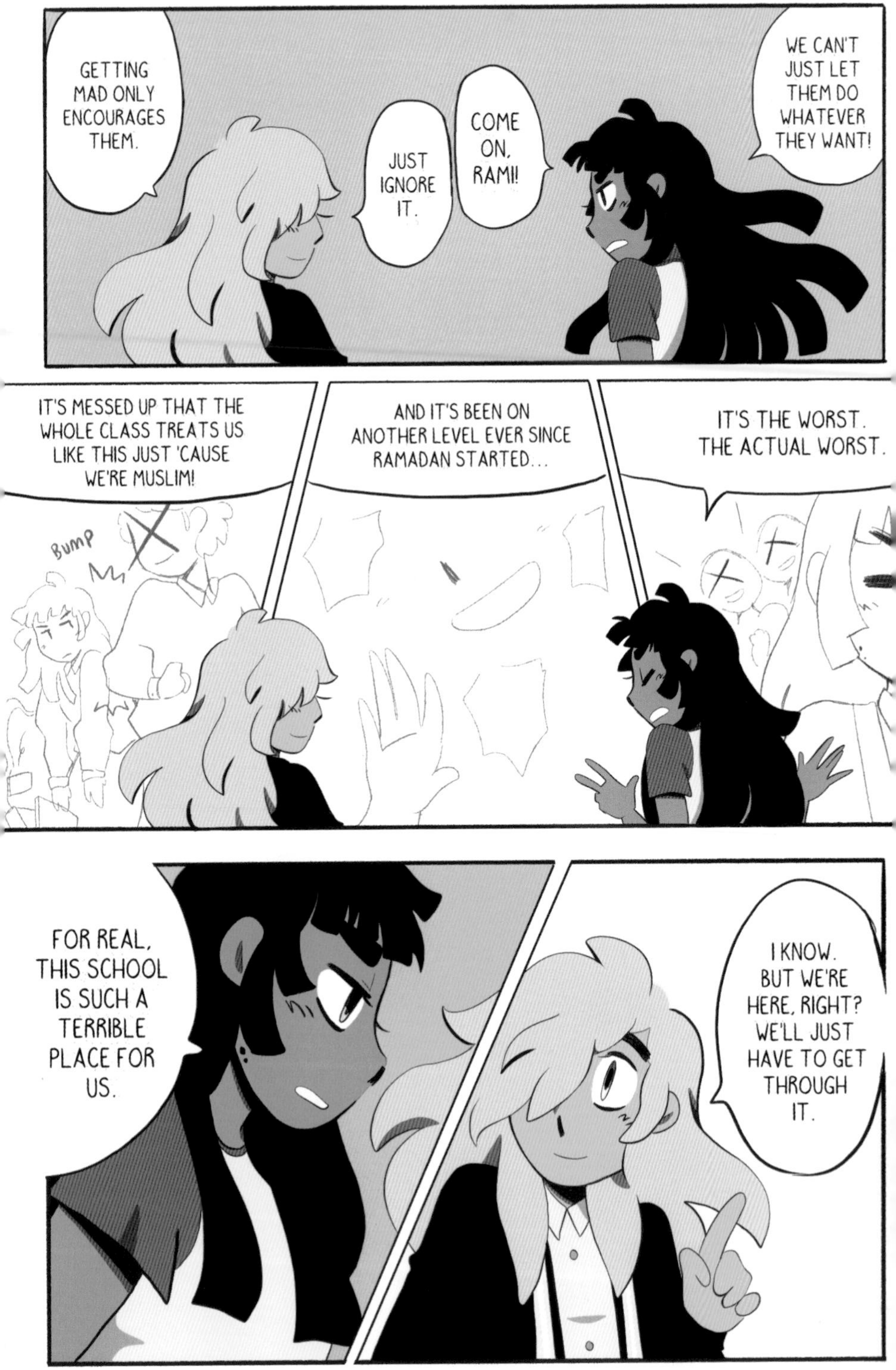
GETTING MAD ONLY ENCOURAGES THEM.
JUST IGNORE IT.
COME ON, RAMI!
WE CAN'T JUST LET THEM DO WHATEVER THEY WANT!
IT'S MESSED UP THAT THE WHOLE CLASS TREATS US LIKE THIS JUST 'CAUSE WE'RE MUSLIM!
BUMP
AND IT'S BEEN ON ANOTHER LEVEL EVER SINCE RAMADAN STARTED...
IT'S THE WORST. THE ACTUAL WORST.
FOR REAL, THIS SCHOOL IS SUCH A TERRIBLE PLACE FOR US.
I KNOW. BUT WE'RE HERE, RIGHT? WE'LL JUST HAVE TO GET THROUGH IT.

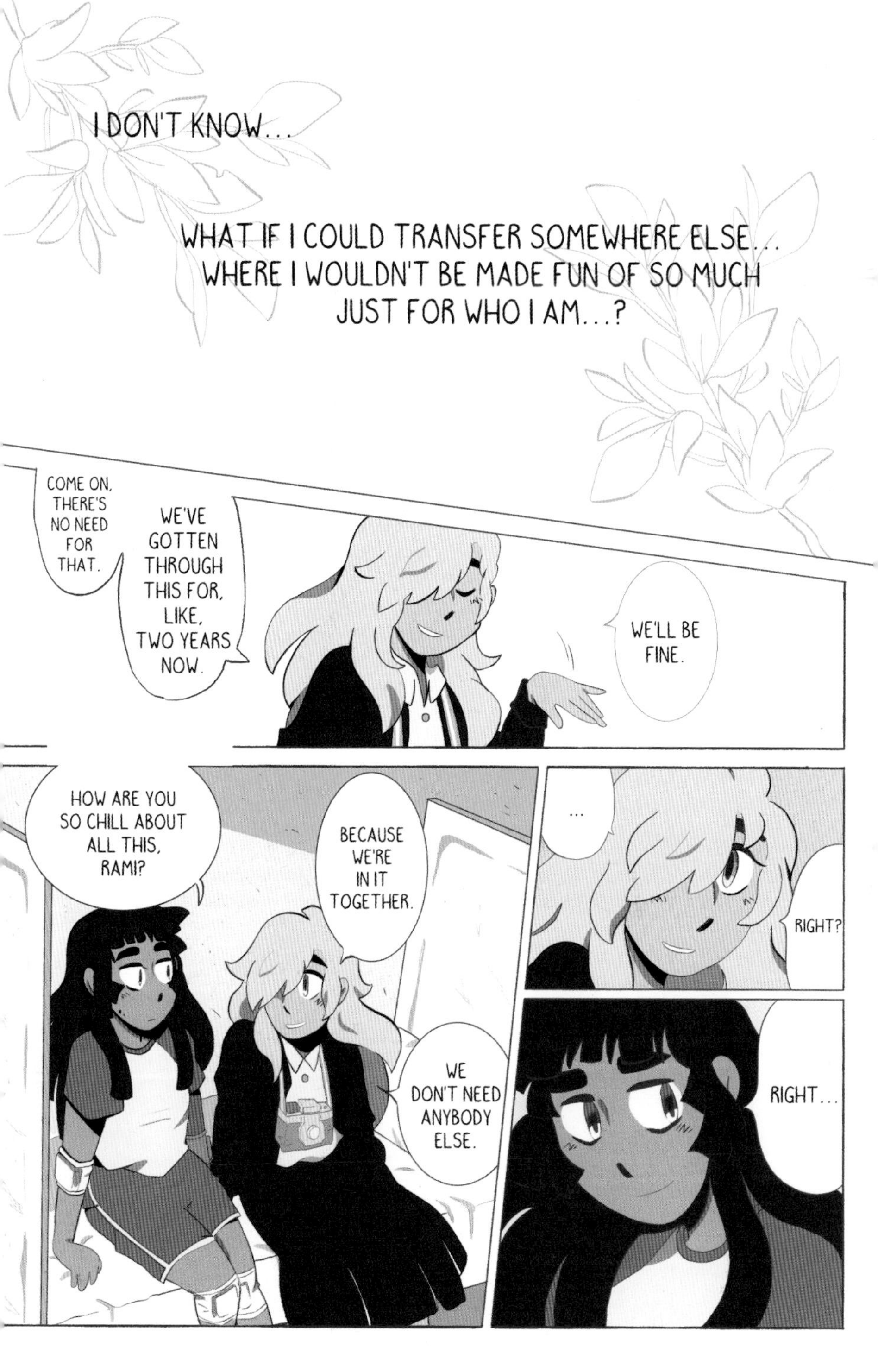
I DON'T KNOW...
WHAT IF I COULD TRANSFER SOMEWHERE ELSE... WHERE I WOULDN'T BE MADE FUN OF SO MUCH JUST FOR WHO I AM...?
COME ON, THERE'S NO NEED FOR THAT.
WE'VE GOTTEN THROUGH THIS FOR, LIKE, TWO YEARS NOW.
WE'LL BE FINE.
HOW ARE YOU SO CHILL ABOUT ALL THIS, RAMI?
BECAUSE WE'RE IN IT TOGETHER.
WE DON'T NEED ANYBODY ELSE.
...
RIGHT?
RIGHT...

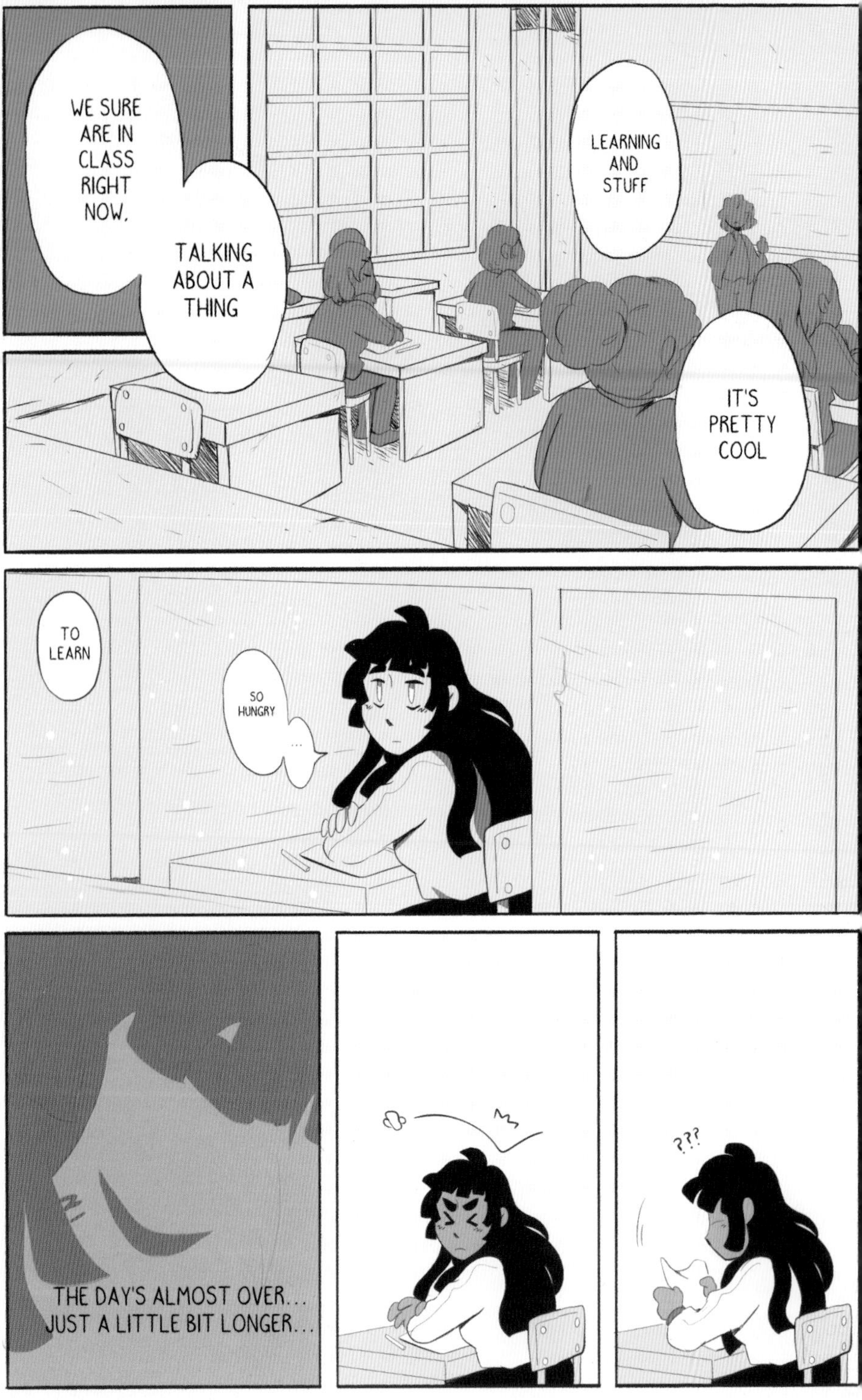
WE SURE ARE IN CLASS RIGHT NOW,
TALKING ABOUT A THING
LEARNING AND STUFF
IT'S PRETTY COOL
TO LEARN
SO HUNGRY
...
THE DAY'S ALMOST OVER... JUST A LITTLE BIT LONGER...
???

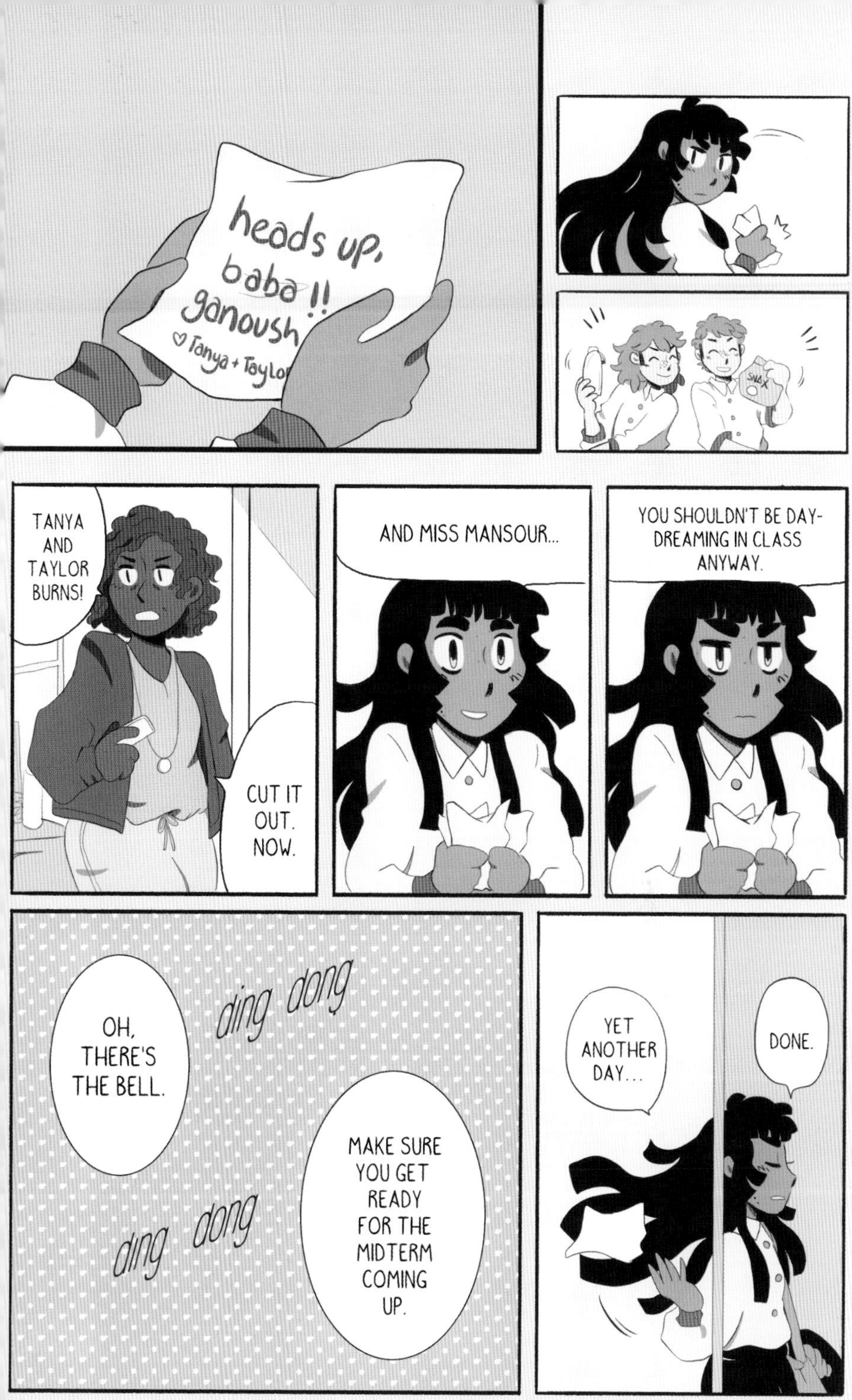
heads up, baba ganoush!!
♡ Tanya + Taylor
SNAX
TANYA AND TAYLOR BURNS!
CUT IT OUT. NOW.
AND MISS MANSOUR...
YOU SHOULDN'T BE DAY-DREAMING IN CLASS ANYWAY.
OH, THERE'S THE BELL.
ding dong
ding dong
MAKE SURE YOU GET READY FOR THE MIDTERM COMING UP.
YET ANOTHER DAY...
DONE.

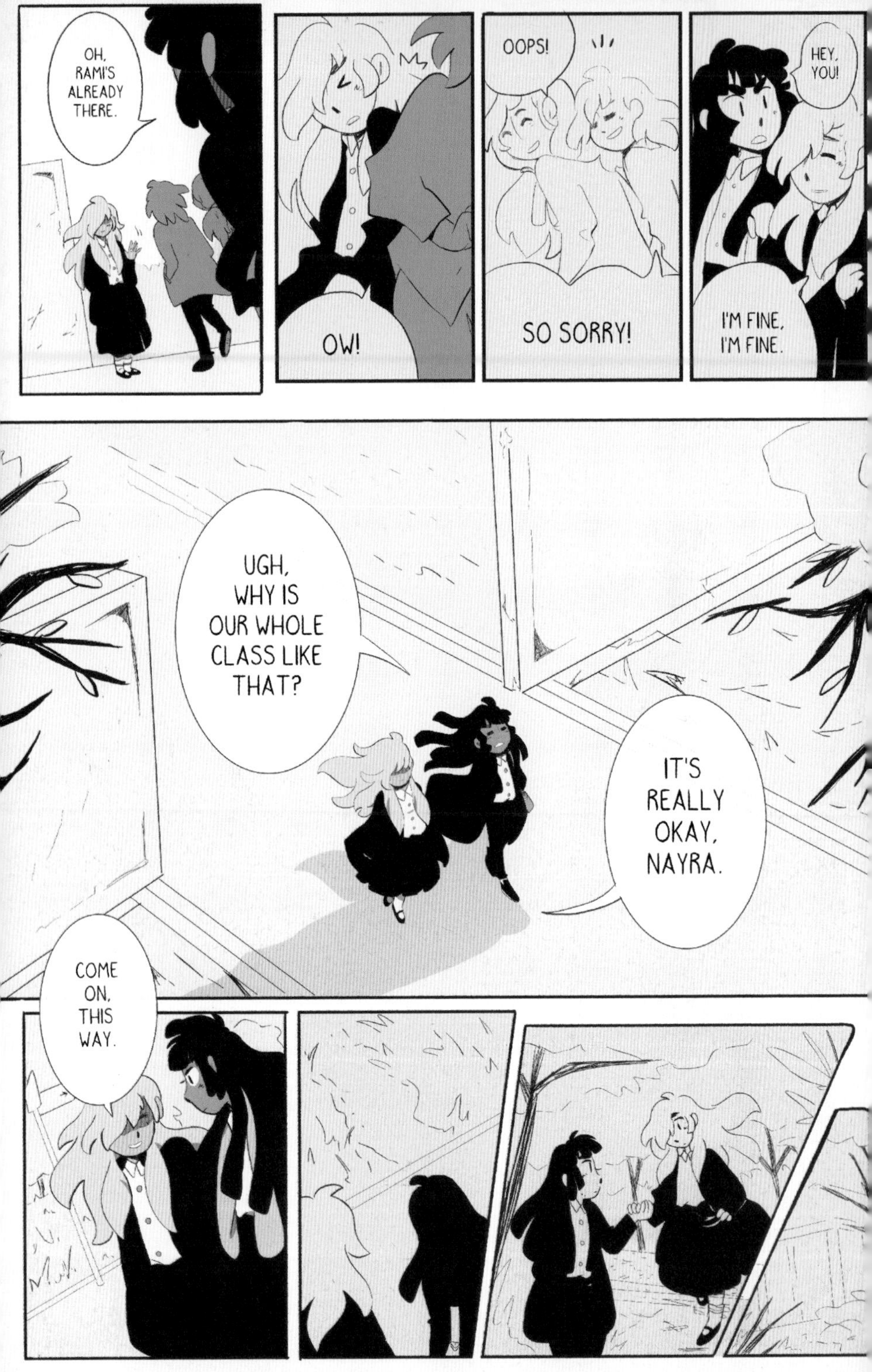
OH, RAMI'S ALREADY THERE.
OW!
OOPS!
SO SORRY!
HEY, YOU!
I'M FINE, I'M FINE.
UGH, WHY IS OUR WHOLE CLASS LIKE THAT?
IT'S REALLY OKAY, NAYRA.
COME ON, THIS WAY.

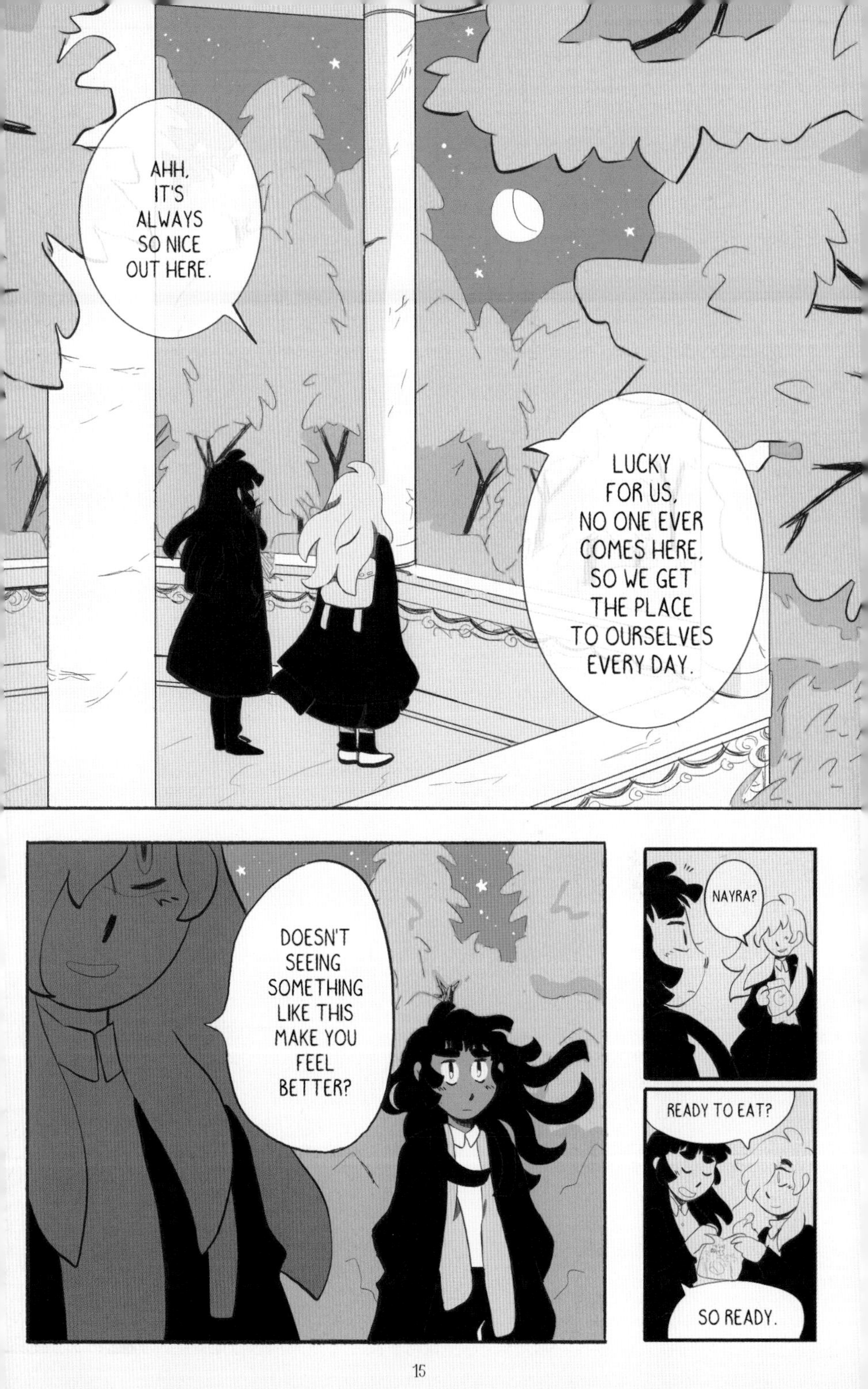
AHH, IT'S ALWAYS SO NICE OUT HERE.
LUCKY FOR US, NO ONE EVER COMES HERE, SO WE GET THE PLACE TO OURSELVES EVERY DAY.
DOESN'T SEEING SOMETHING LIKE THIS MAKE YOU FEEL BETTER?
NAYRA?
READY TO EAT?
SO READY.

How to break fast.

Step 1:
Say "Bismillah Al-Rahman Al-Rahim."

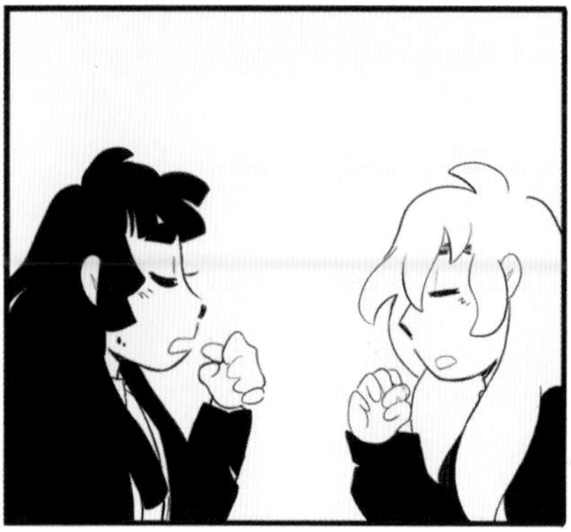

Step 2:
Eat a date fruit.

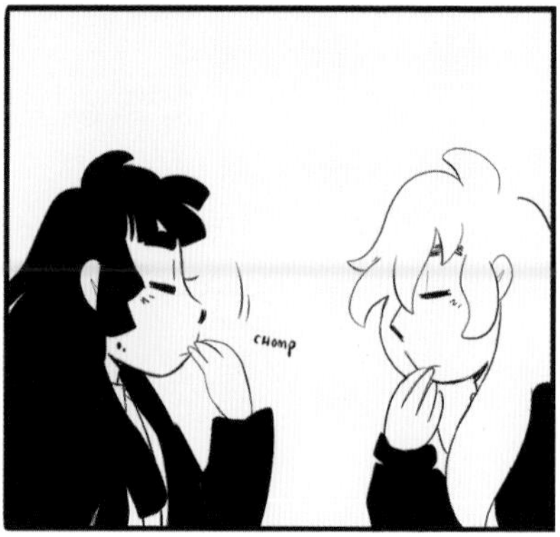
CHOMP

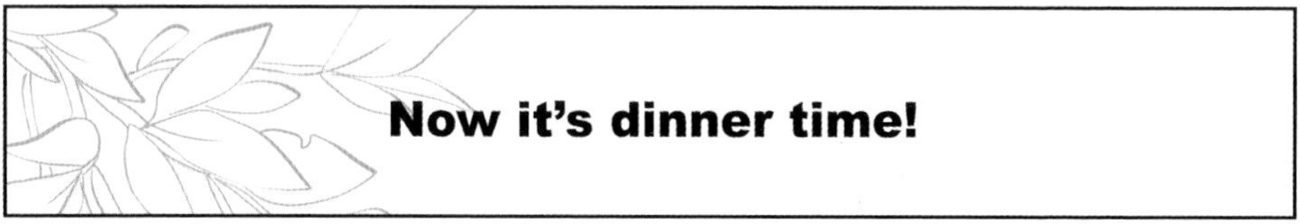
Now it's dinner time!

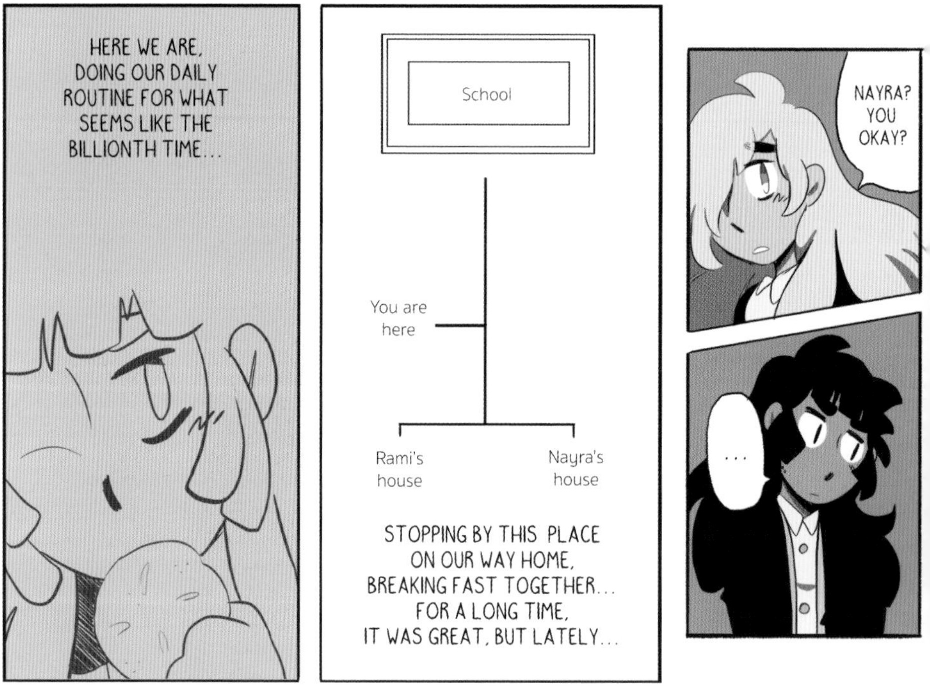
HERE WE ARE, DOING OUR DAILY ROUTINE FOR WHAT SEEMS LIKE THE BILLIONTH TIME...
School
You are here
Rami's house
Nayra's house
STOPPING BY THIS PLACE ON OUR WAY HOME, BREAKING FAST TOGETHER... FOR A LONG TIME, IT WAS GREAT, BUT LATELY...
NAYRA? YOU OKAY?
...

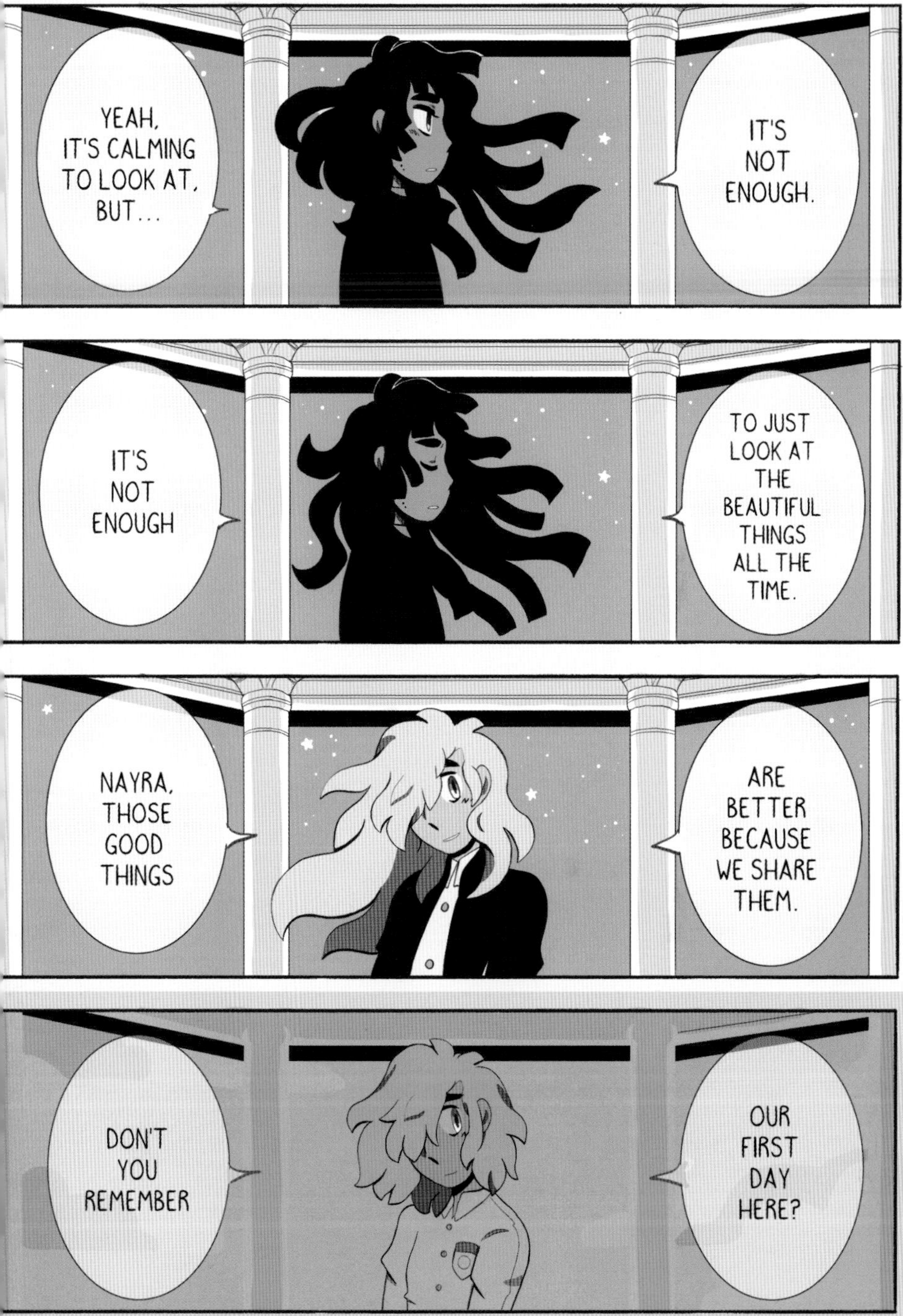
YEAH, IT'S CALMING TO LOOK AT, BUT...
IT'S NOT ENOUGH.
IT'S NOT ENOUGH
TO JUST LOOK AT THE BEAUTIFUL THINGS ALL THE TIME.
NAYRA, THOSE GOOD THINGS
ARE BETTER BECAUSE WE SHARE THEM.
DON'T YOU REMEMBER
OUR FIRST DAY HERE?

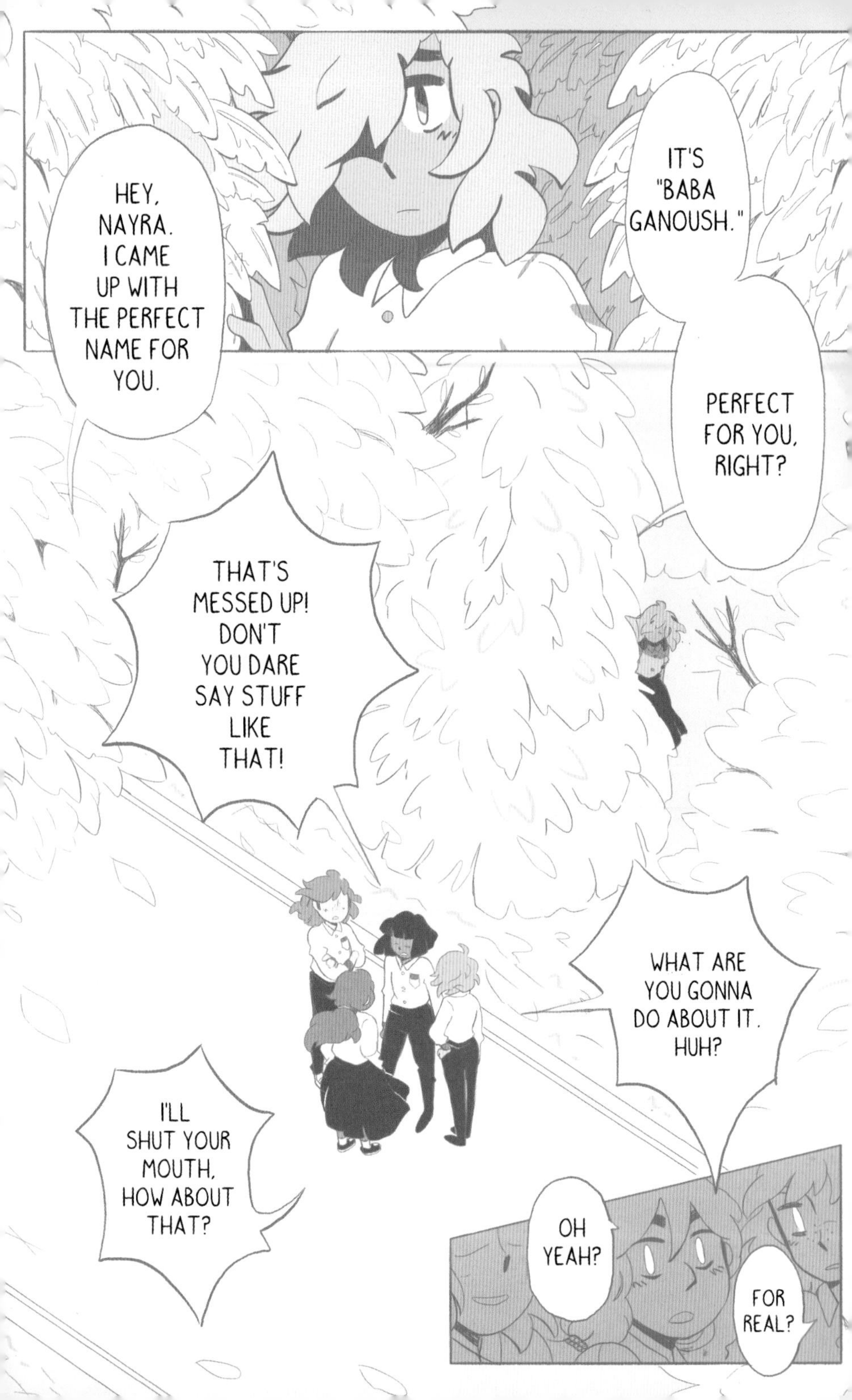
HEY, NAYRA. I CAME UP WITH THE PERFECT NAME FOR YOU.
IT'S "BABA GANOUSH."
PERFECT FOR YOU, RIGHT?
THAT'S MESSED UP! DON'T YOU DARE SAY STUFF LIKE THAT!
WHAT ARE YOU GONNA DO ABOUT IT. HUH?
I'LL SHUT YOUR MOUTH, HOW ABOUT THAT?
OH YEAH?
FOR REAL?

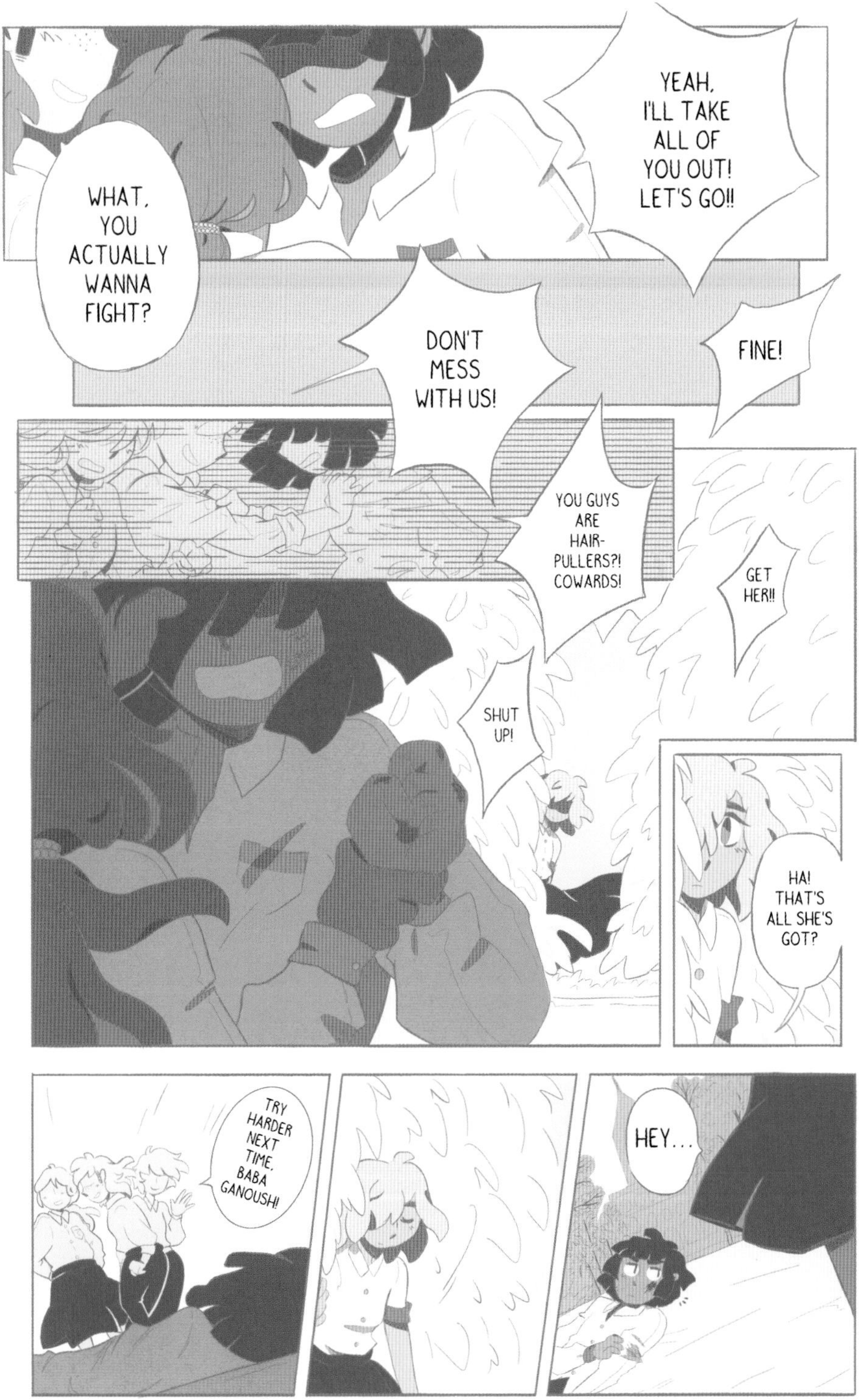
YEAH, I'LL TAKE ALL OF YOU OUT! LET'S GO!!
WHAT, YOU ACTUALLY WANNA FIGHT?
DON'T MESS WITH US!
FINE!
YOU GUYS ARE HAIR-PULLERS?! COWARDS!
GET HER!!
SHUT UP!
HA! THAT'S ALL SHE'S GOT?
TRY HARDER NEXT TIME, BABA GANOUSH!
HEY...

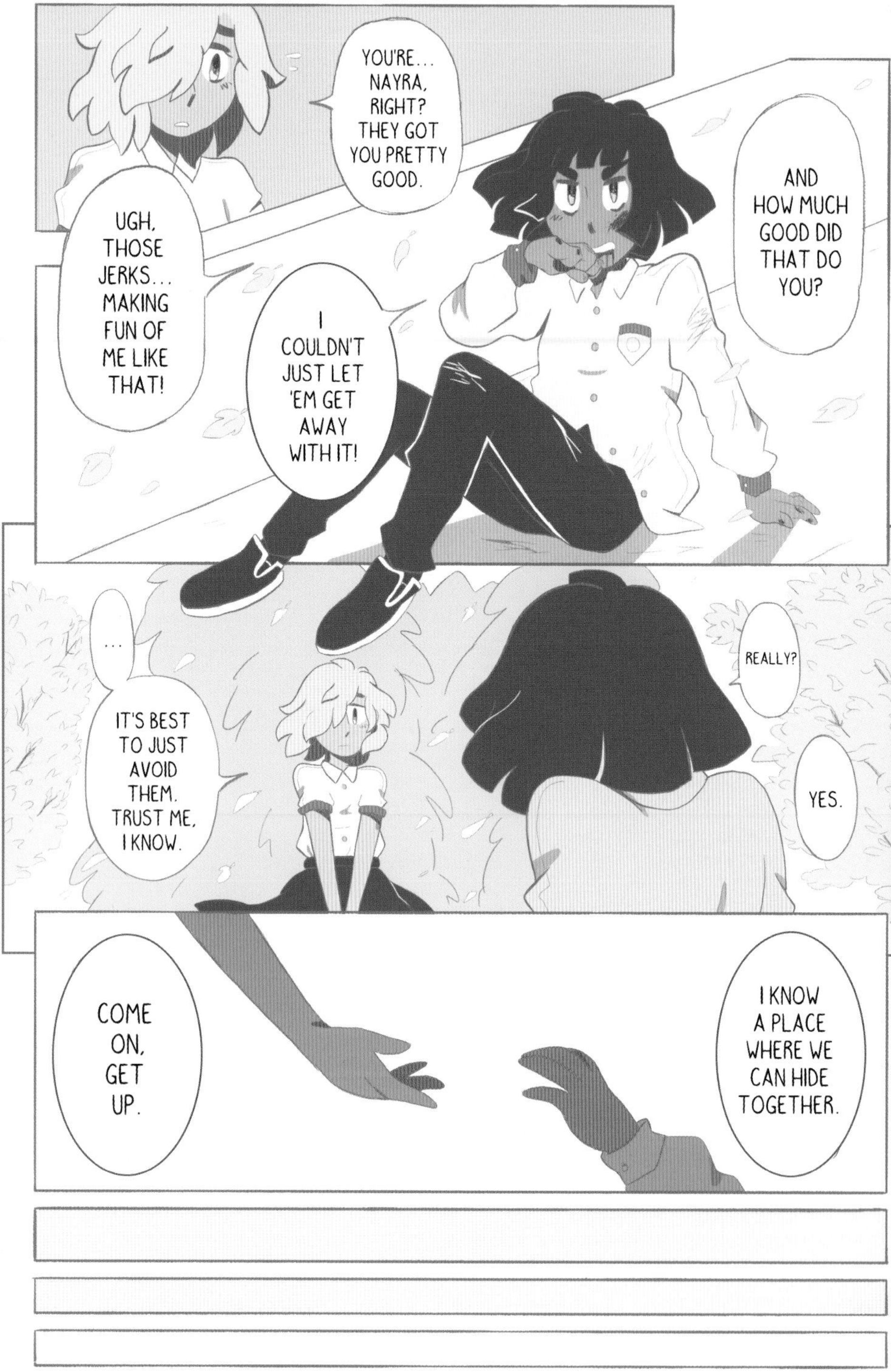
YOU'RE... NAYRA, RIGHT? THEY GOT YOU PRETTY GOOD.
UGH, THOSE JERKS... MAKING FUN OF ME LIKE THAT!
I COULDN'T JUST LET 'EM GET AWAY WITH IT!
AND HOW MUCH GOOD DID THAT DO YOU?
...
IT'S BEST TO JUST AVOID THEM. TRUST ME, I KNOW.
REALLY?
YES.
COME ON, GET UP.
I KNOW A PLACE WHERE WE CAN HIDE TOGETHER.

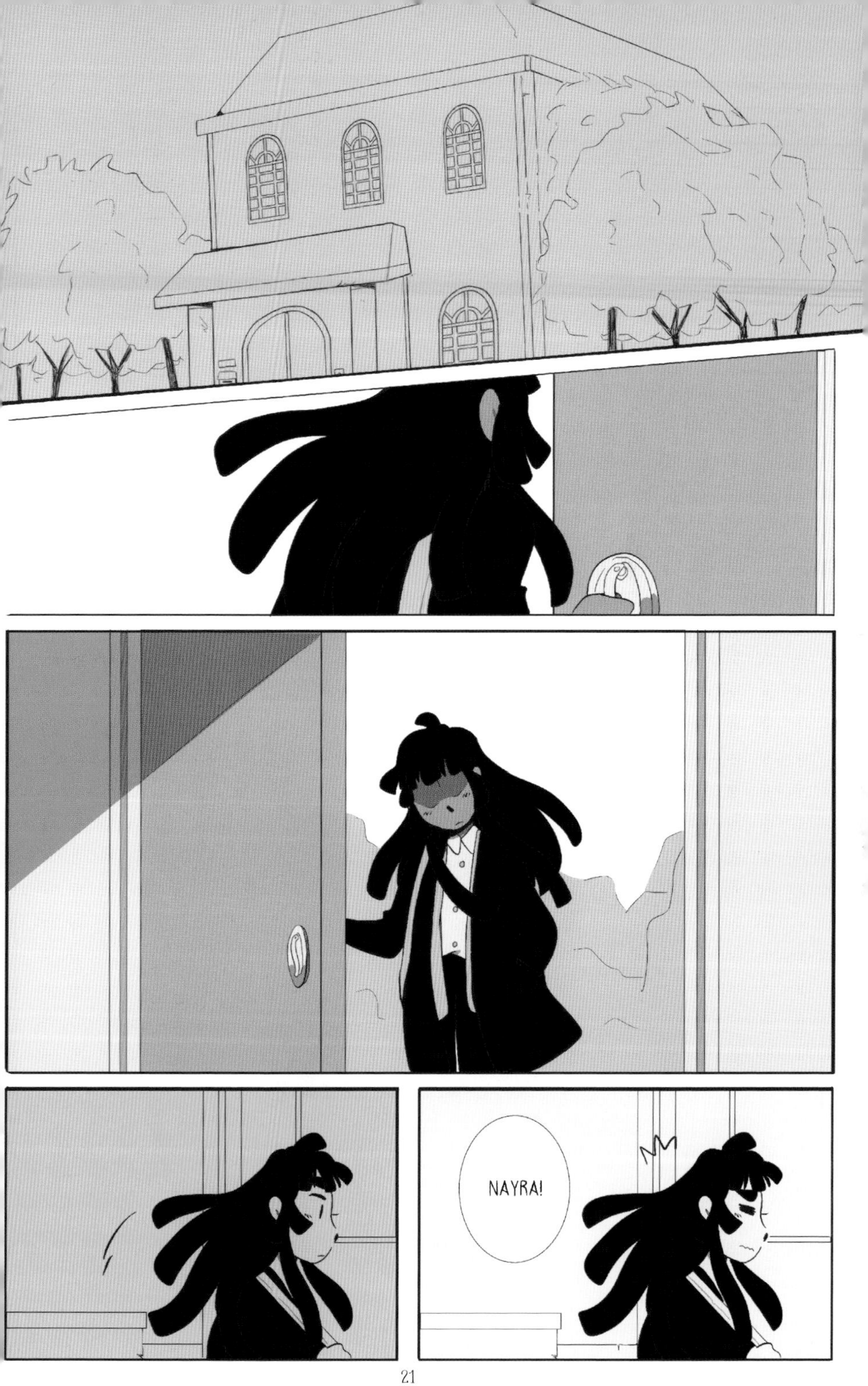
NAYRA!

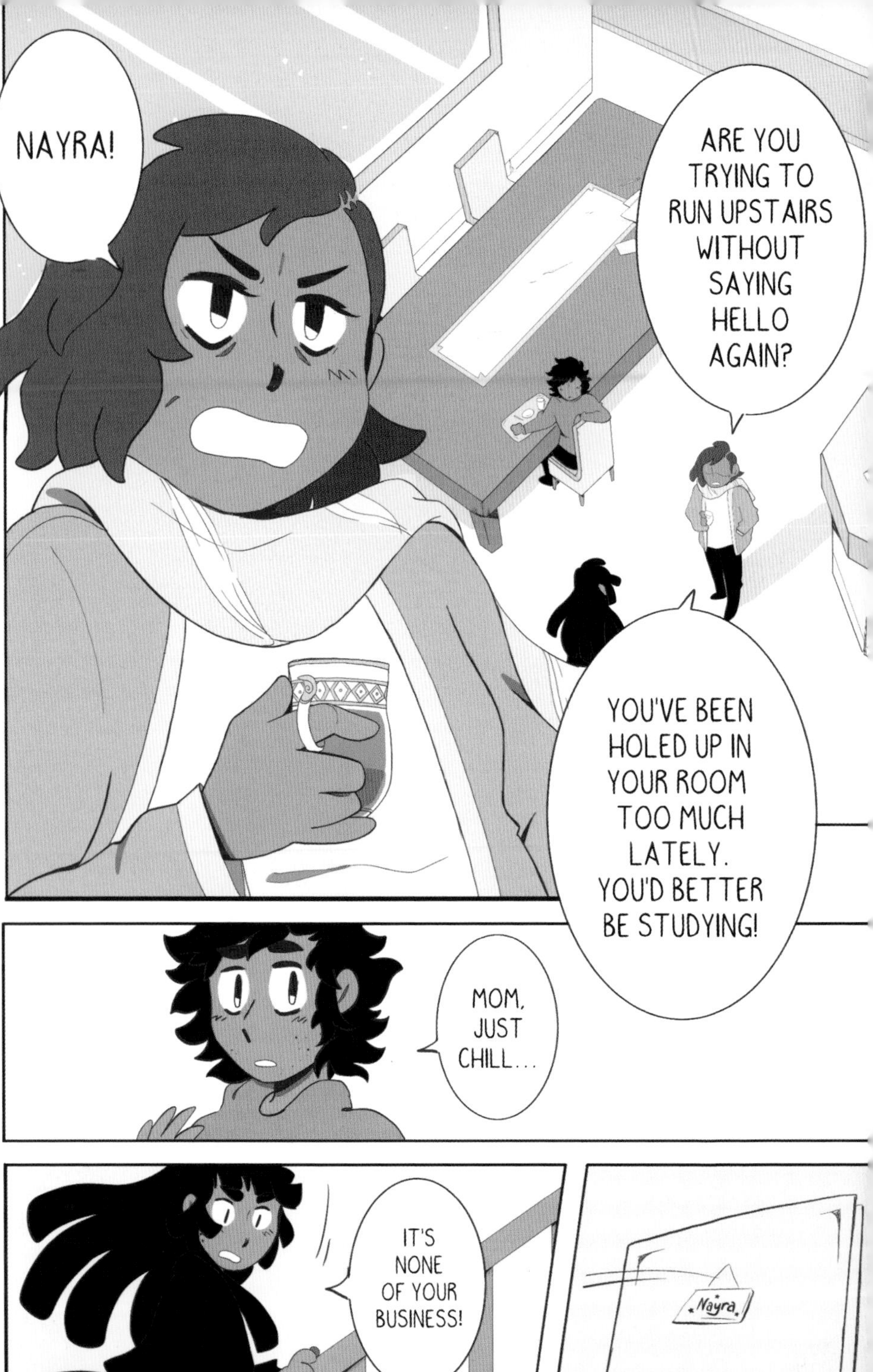
NAYRA!
ARE YOU TRYING TO RUN UPSTAIRS WITHOUT SAYING HELLO AGAIN?
YOU'VE BEEN HOLED UP IN YOUR ROOM TOO MUCH LATELY. YOU'D BETTER BE STUDYING!
MOM, JUST CHILL...
IT'S NONE OF YOUR BUSINESS!
Nayra

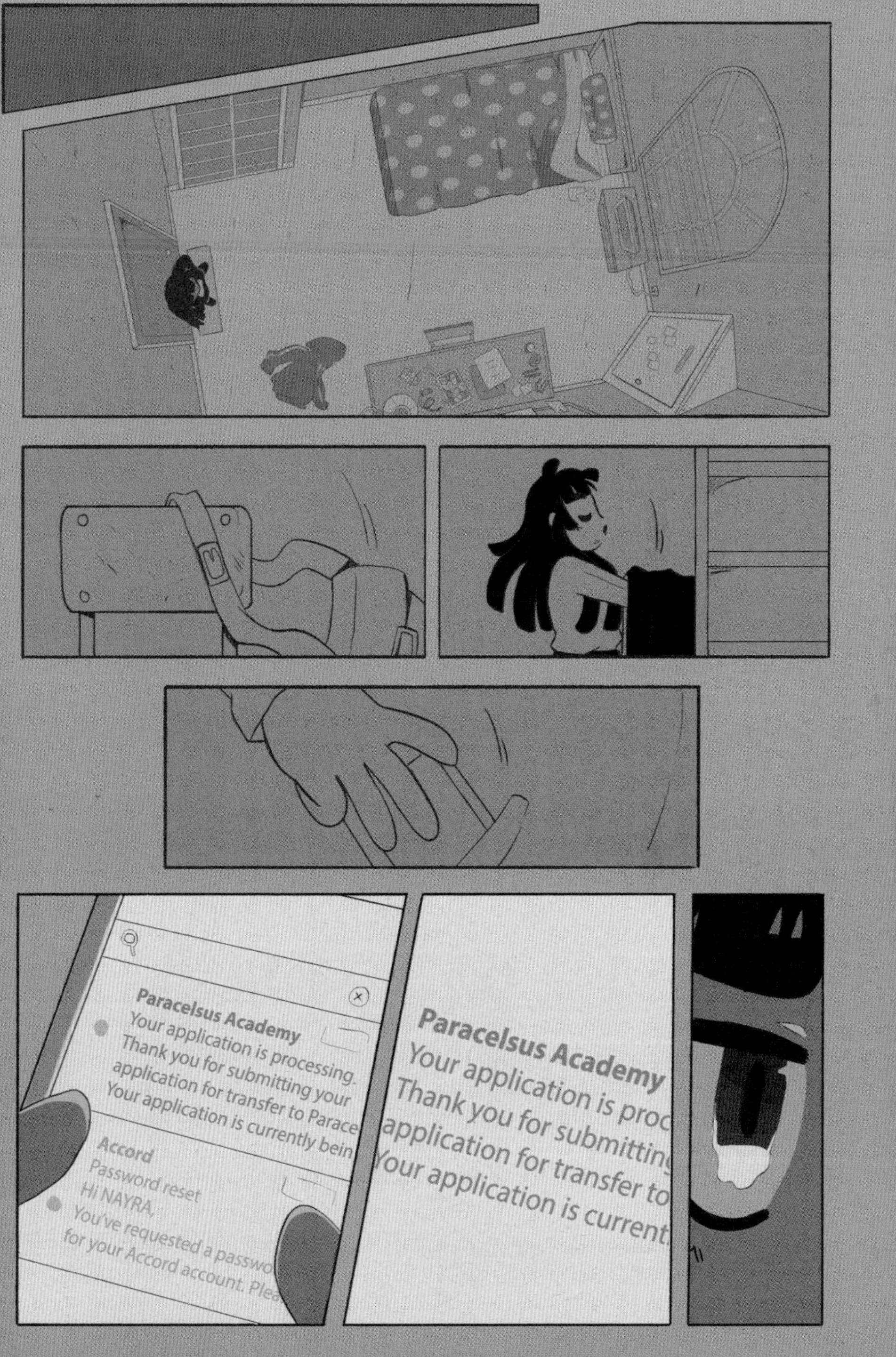
Paracelsus Academy
Your application is processing.
Thank you for submitting your
application for transfer to Parace
Your application is currently bein
Accord
Password reset
Hi NAYRA,
You've requested a passwo
for your Accord account. Plea
Paracelsus Academy
Your application is proc
Thank you for submitting
application for transfer to
Your application is current

SIGH

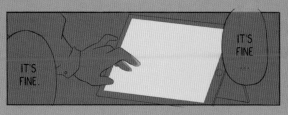

IT'S FINE.

IT'S FINE ...

3/xx RAMADAN

#M-A-digital-archive-project

Welcome to the channel! This is a group for Muslim Americans dedicated to digitally archiving our cultures' folklore, as oral tradition begins to become obsolete. Please read the channel guidelines before posting. Thank you!

Channel

Text servers
welcome
announcements
general
anime/games
food-pics
discourse
channel requests

Voice servers
general
just chatting
link mondays
tuesday streams

43 users online:
@star__rod
@mmarlenaa
@0000000
@namudarki
@__f_almasi
@boringprofile
@wwwhhattt
@rishiiii___
@amira_nasser

LOTS OF PEOPLE TODAY!

LOOK AT THAT.

@star__rod: what's up everybody
@rishiiii___: finally eating!!!
@boringprofile: me too. i was dying today.
@__f_almasi: same. i skipped gym, couldn't deal.
@__f_almasi: it's too hot down here.

THEY ALL SEEM SO NICE...

MAYBE I SHOULD TRY—

@mawdi_saudi: I hate when you're hungry all day, but then when you finally get to eat, you only eat 5 bites, and you're full.
@namudarki: i'm at home with my family.
@namudarki: my taita is here, and she's telling lots of stories about djinns.

...NAH. NEVER MIND.

@wwwhaattt: namu, your grandmother's a hakawati, right?

...00000: a what?

@namudarki: it's like, a really good traditional storyteller sorta. like folklore and stuff. and yeah, she is. she was pretty well-known overseas before we moved out here.

@namudarki: th... ask her about this... it here, since she...

@boringprofile: thi...

@namudarki: she's told me before that djinn hakwatis exist too, but i don't think i really believe that. anyway, here's some of the stuff she told me today!

WHEN I WAS LITTLE, MY FAMILY USED TO TELL ME ALL THESE STORIES. GHOULS, QARINAHS... AND DJINNS. THEY ALL SEEMED SO COOL AND MYSTERIOUS... SO DIFFERENT.

I KNOW I'M OLDER NOW, BUT STILL, WHENEVER I THINK ABOUT ALL THIS STUFF, I FEEL A LITTLE LIGHTER.

LIKE I DON'T HAVE TO FOCUS ON ALL THE COMPLICATED STUFF THAT KEEPS HAPPENING LATELY...

25

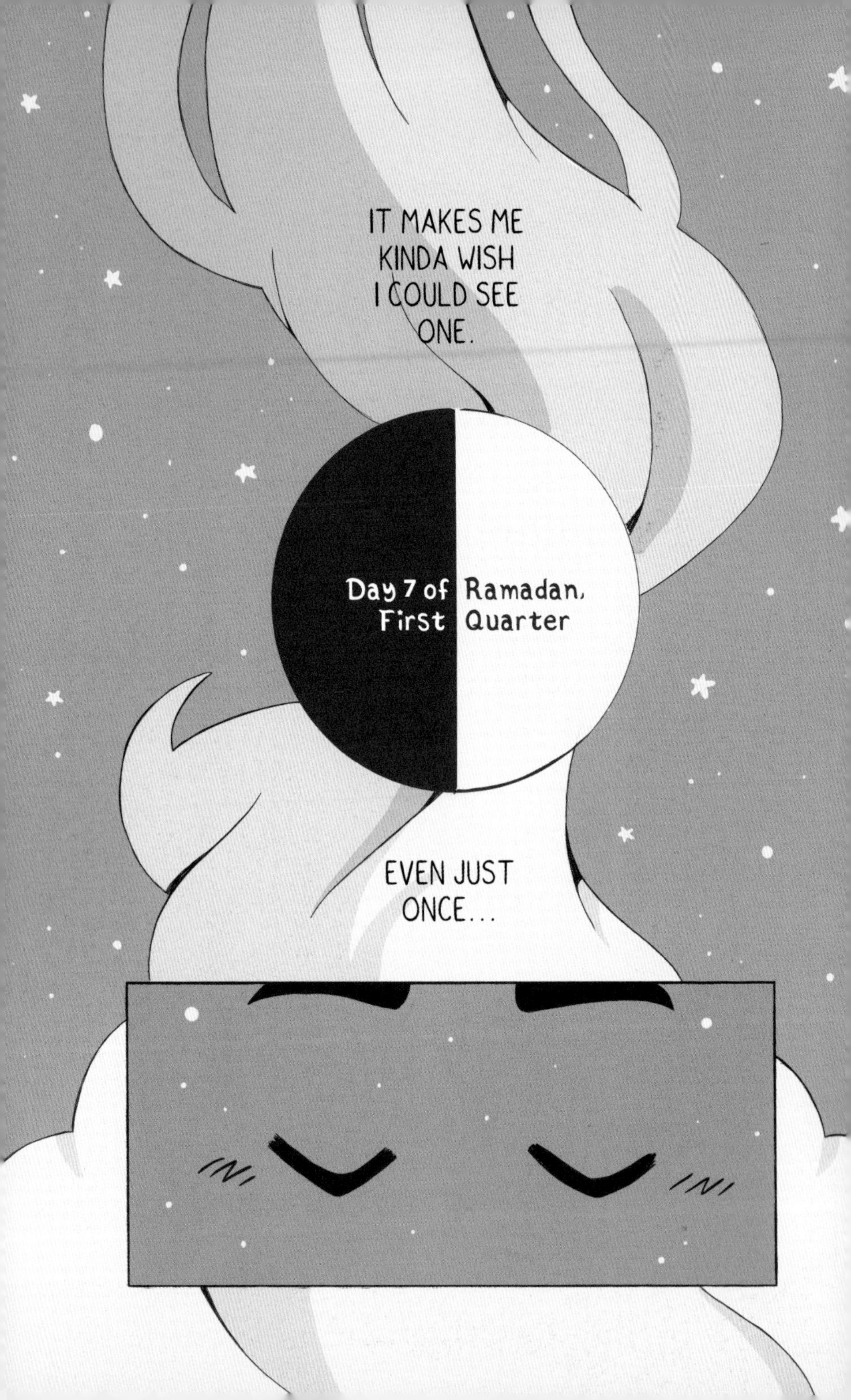

IT MAKES ME KINDA WISH I COULD SEE ONE.
Day 7 of Ramadan, First Quarter
EVEN JUST ONCE...

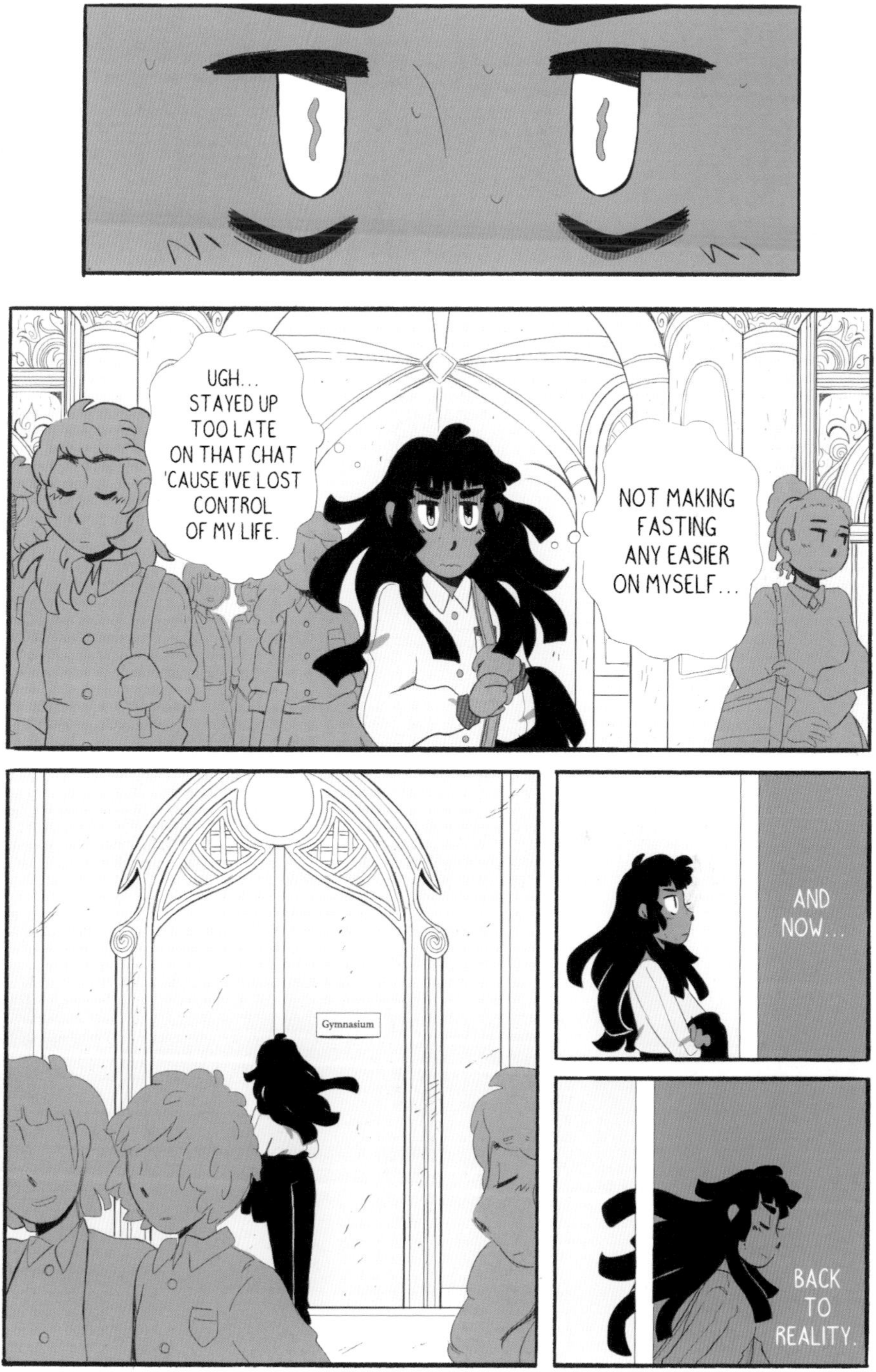
UGH... STAYED UP TOO LATE ON THAT CHAT 'CAUSE I'VE LOST CONTROL OF MY LIFE.
NOT MAKING FASTING ANY EASIER ON MYSELF...
Gymnasium
AND NOW...
BACK TO REALITY.

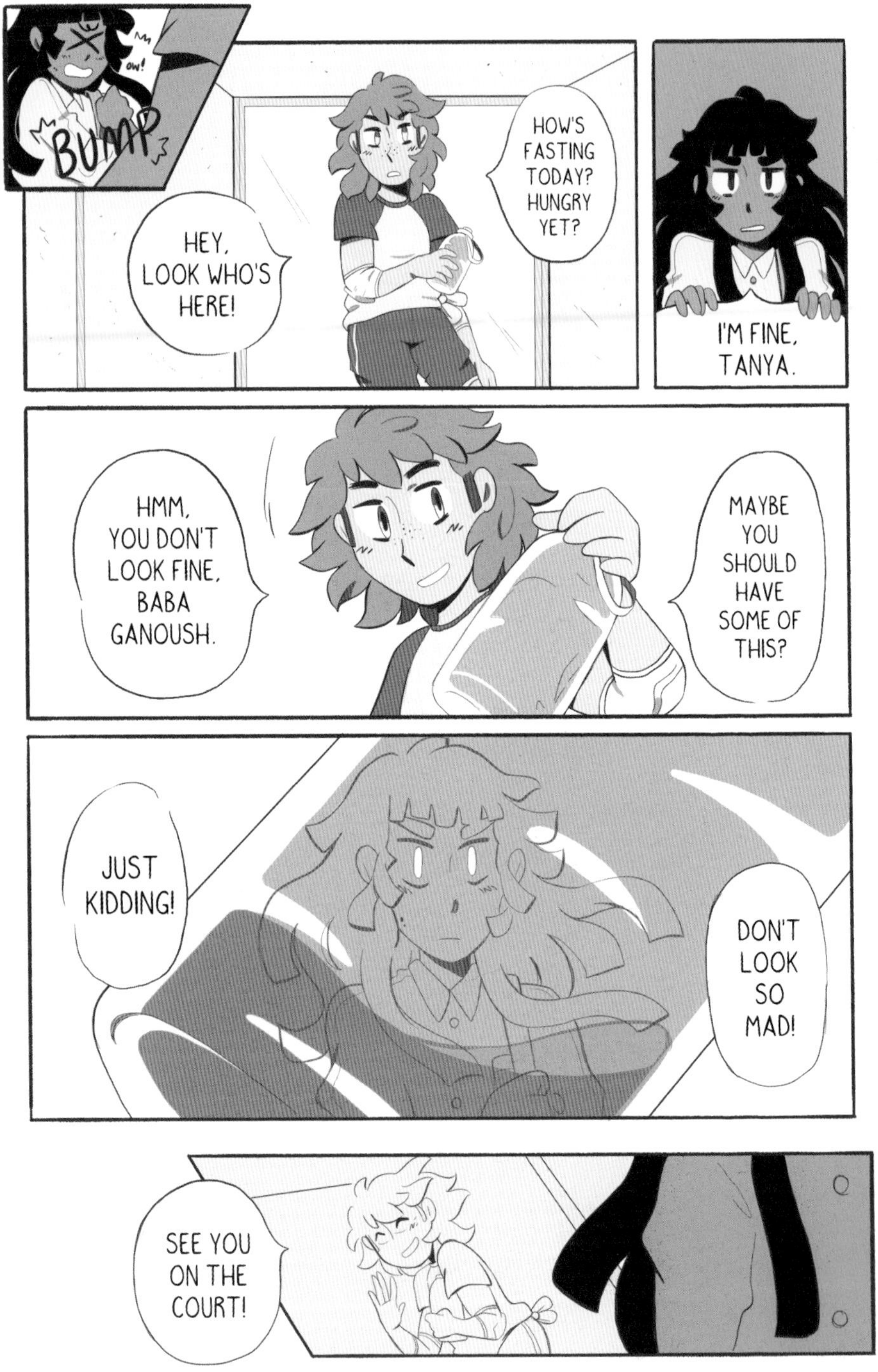
ow!
BUMP
HEY, LOOK WHO'S HERE!
HOW'S FASTING TODAY? HUNGRY YET?
I'M FINE, TANYA.
HMM, YOU DON'T LOOK FINE, BABA GANOUSH.
MAYBE YOU SHOULD HAVE SOME OF THIS?
JUST KIDDING!
DON'T LOOK SO MAD!
SEE YOU ON THE COURT!

REALLY NOT FEELING THAT TODAY...

_rod: what's up everybody
i___: finally eating!!!
gprofile: me too. i was dying today.
masi: same. i skipped gym, couldn't deal.
masi: it's too hot down here.

HMM...

MAYBE

JUST ONCE

I CAN TOO!

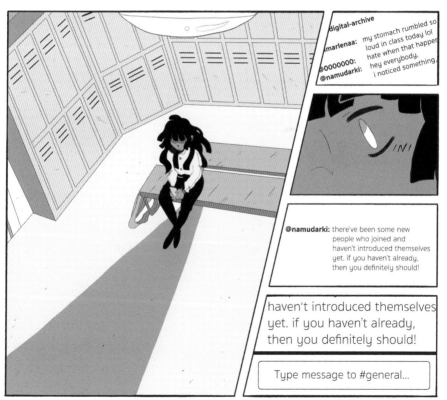

digital-archive

marlenaa: my stomach rumbled so loud in class today lol hate when that happens
@0000000: hey everybody,
@namudarki: i noticed something,

@namudarki: there've been some new people who joined and haven't introduced themselves yet. if you haven't already, then you definitely should!

haven't introduced themselves yet. if you haven't already, then you definitely should!

Type message to #general...

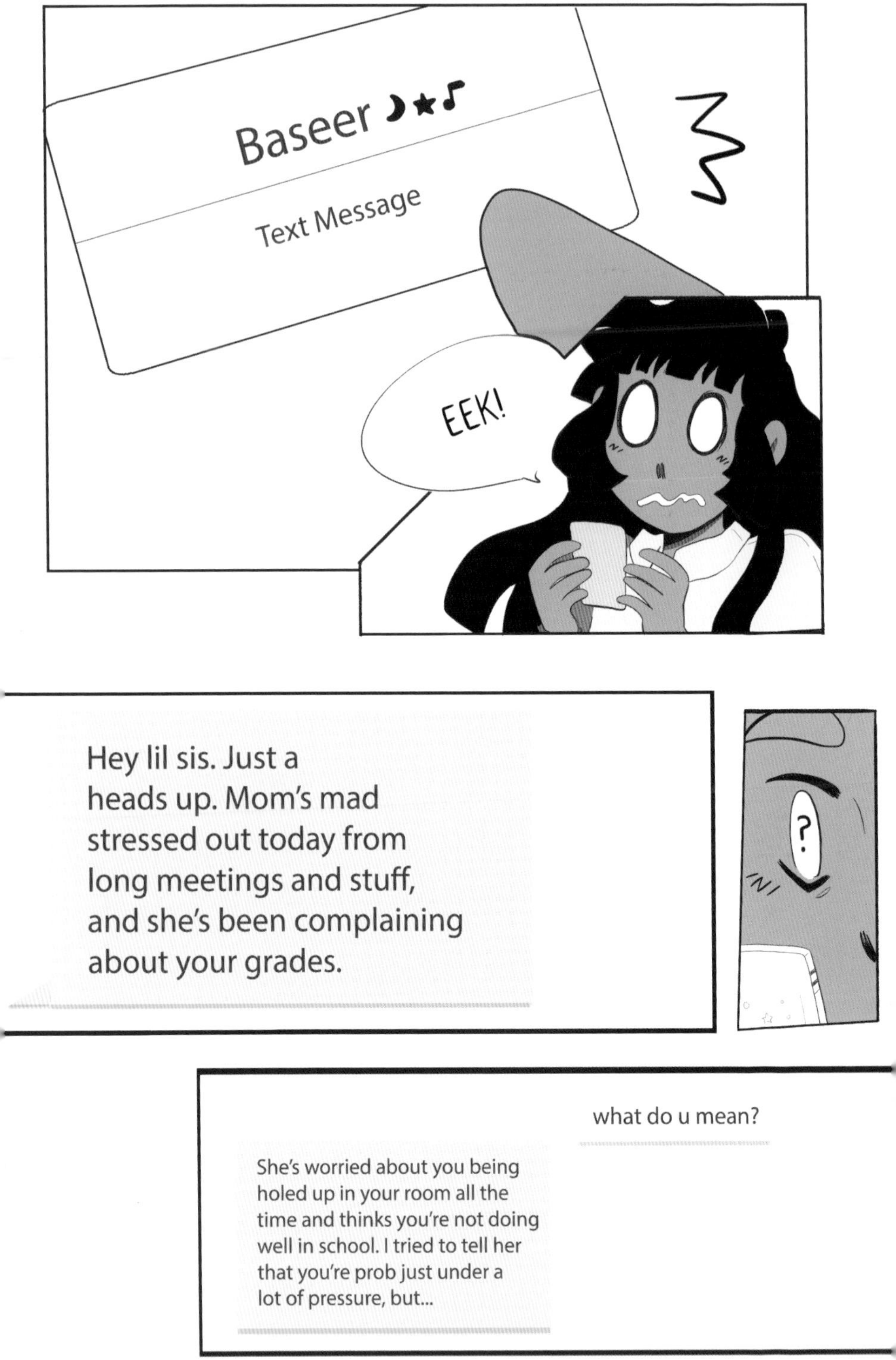
Baseer
Text Message
EEK!
Hey lil sis. Just a heads up. Mom's mad stressed out today from long meetings and stuff, and she's been complaining about your grades.
?
what do u mean?
She's worried about you being holed up in your room all the time and thinks you're not doing well in school. I tried to tell her that you're prob just under a lot of pressure, but...

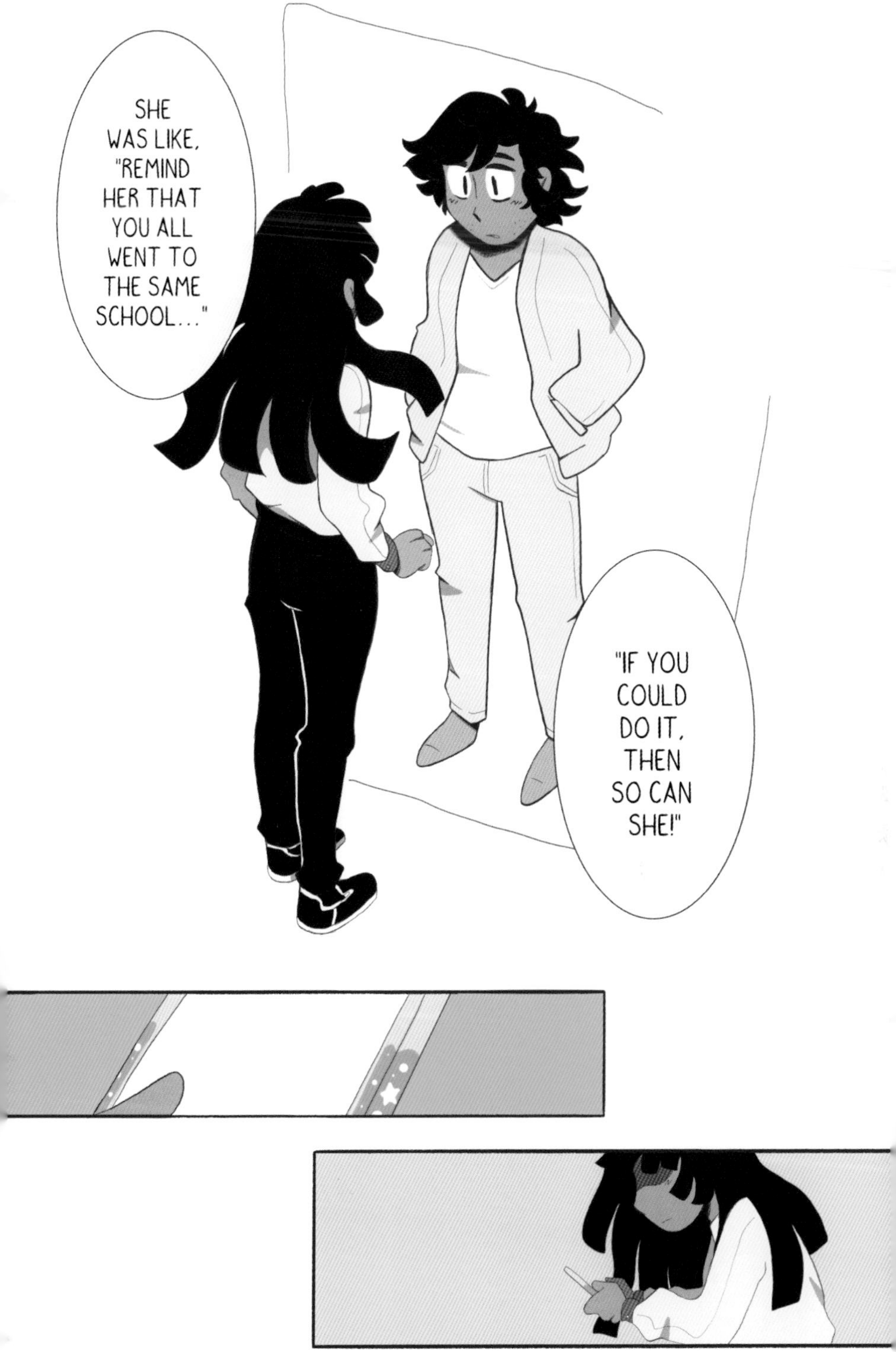
SHE WAS LIKE, "REMIND HER THAT YOU ALL WENT TO THE SAME SCHOOL..."
"IF YOU COULD DO IT, THEN SO CAN SHE!"

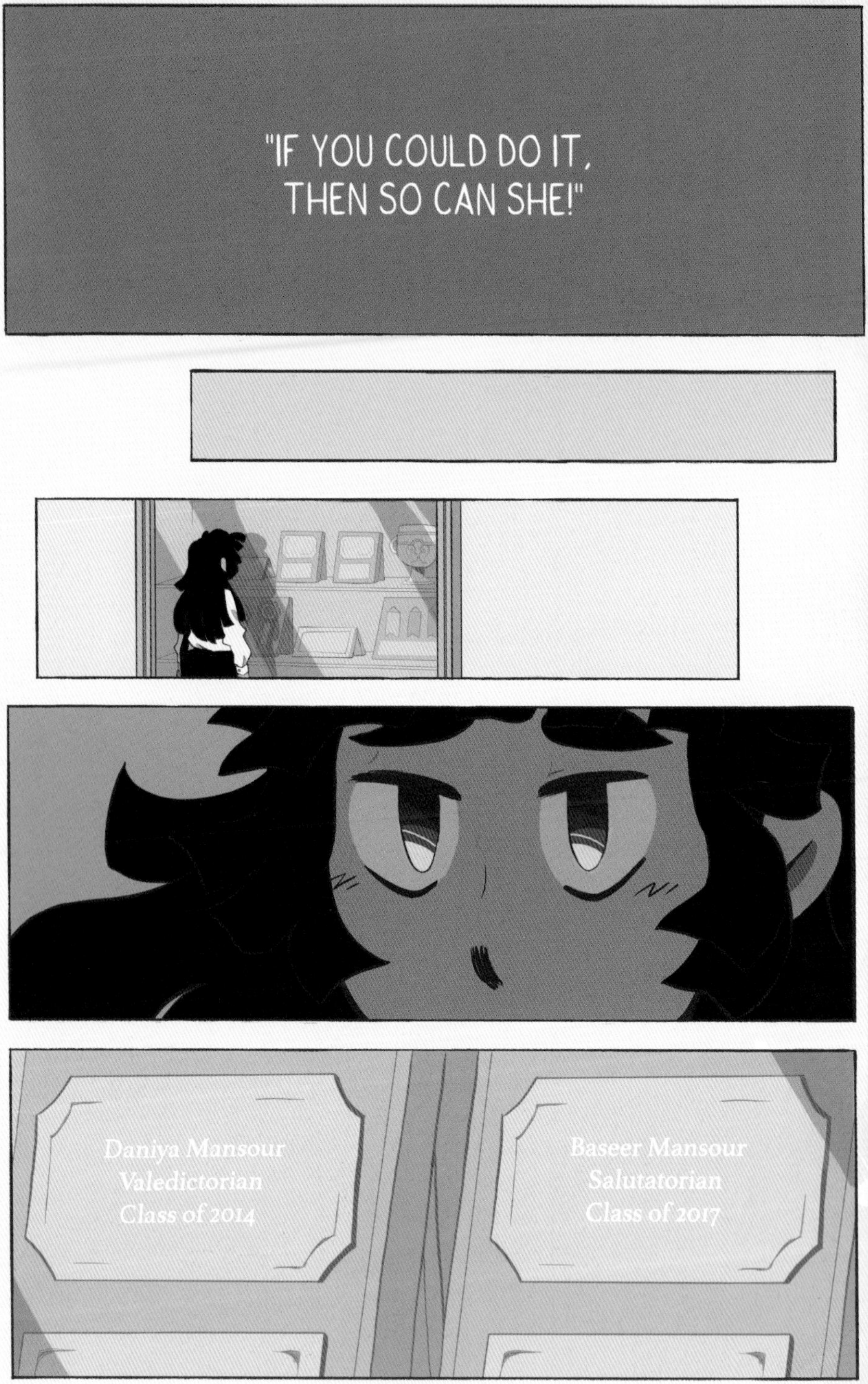
"IF YOU COULD DO IT, THEN SO CAN SHE!"
Daniya Mansour
Valedictorian
Class of 2014
Baseer Mansour
Salutatorian
Class of 2017

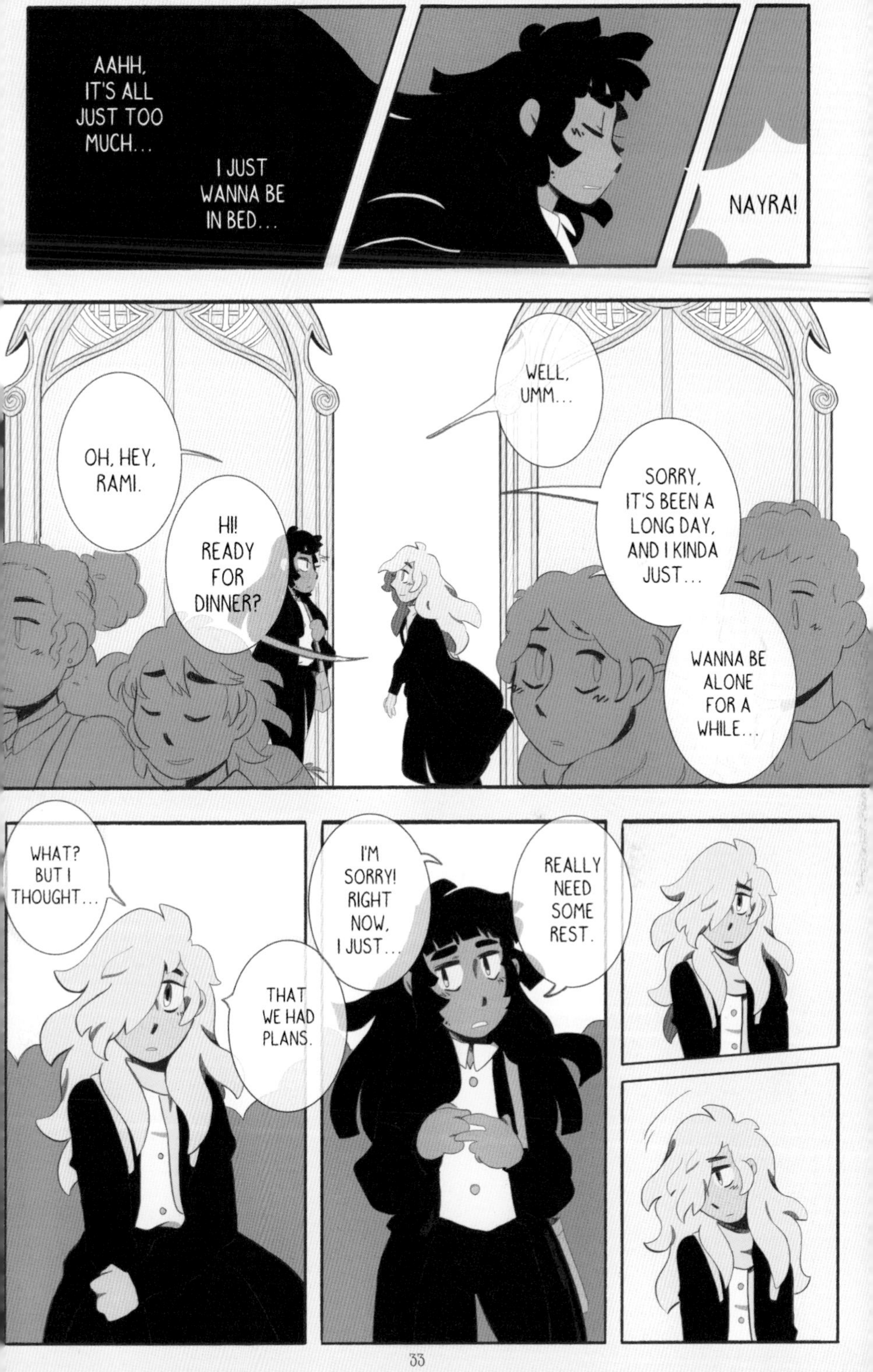
AAHH, IT'S ALL JUST TOO MUCH...
I JUST WANNA BE IN BED...
NAYRA!
OH, HEY, RAMI.
HI! READY FOR DINNER?
WELL, UMM...
SORRY, IT'S BEEN A LONG DAY, AND I KINDA JUST...
WANNA BE ALONE FOR A WHILE...
WHAT? BUT I THOUGHT...
THAT WE HAD PLANS.
I'M SORRY! RIGHT NOW, I JUST...
REALLY NEED SOME REST.

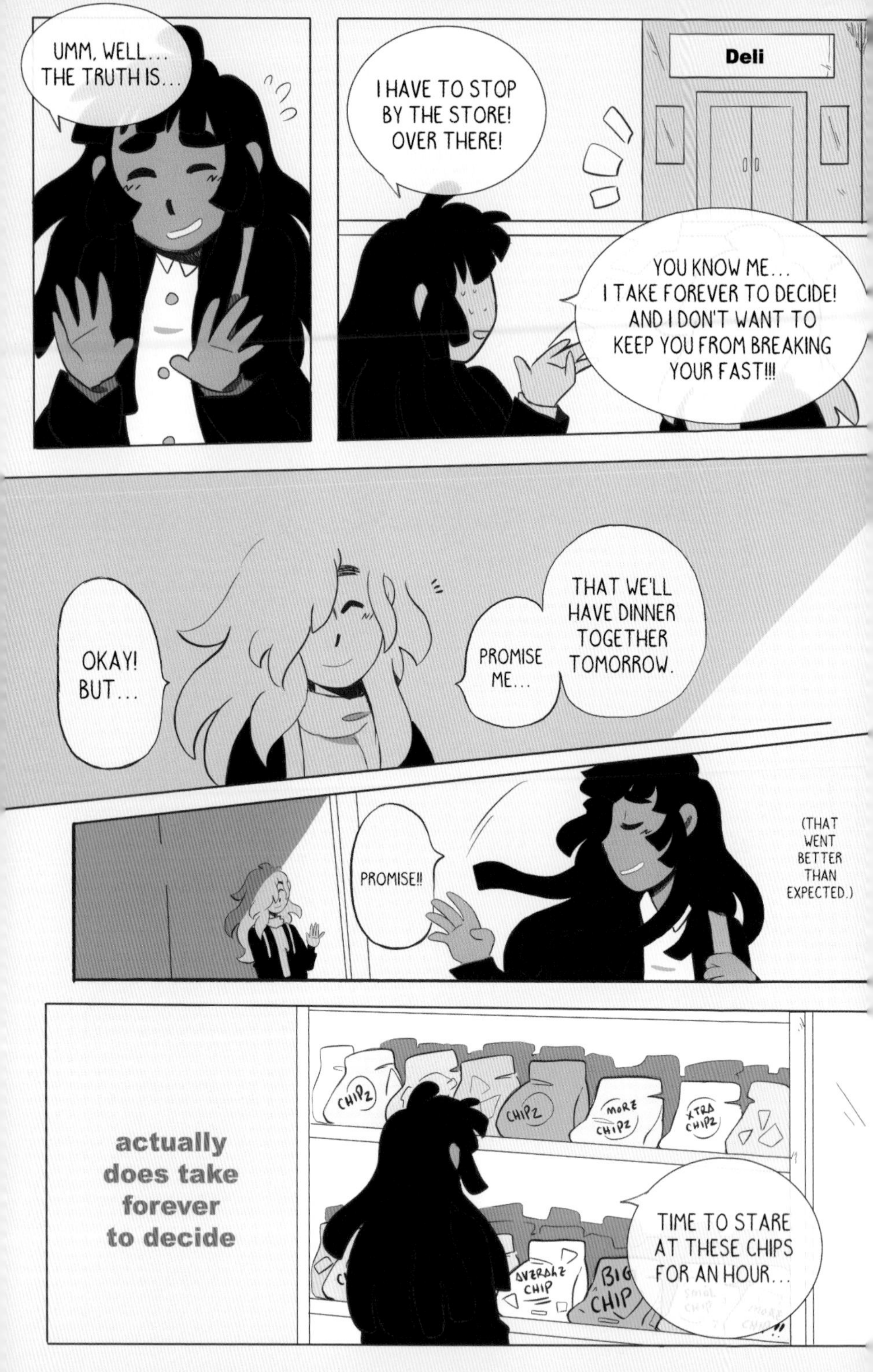
UMM, WELL... THE TRUTH IS...
Deli
I HAVE TO STOP BY THE STORE! OVER THERE!
YOU KNOW ME... I TAKE FOREVER TO DECIDE! AND I DON'T WANT TO KEEP YOU FROM BREAKING YOUR FAST!!!
OKAY! BUT...
PROMISE ME...
THAT WE'LL HAVE DINNER TOGETHER TOMORROW.
PROMISE!!
(THAT WENT BETTER THAN EXPECTED.)
actually does take forever to decide
CHIPZ
CHIPZ
MORE CHIPZ
XTRA CHIPZ
AVERAGE CHIP
BIG CHIP
TIME TO STARE AT THESE CHIPS FOR AN HOUR...

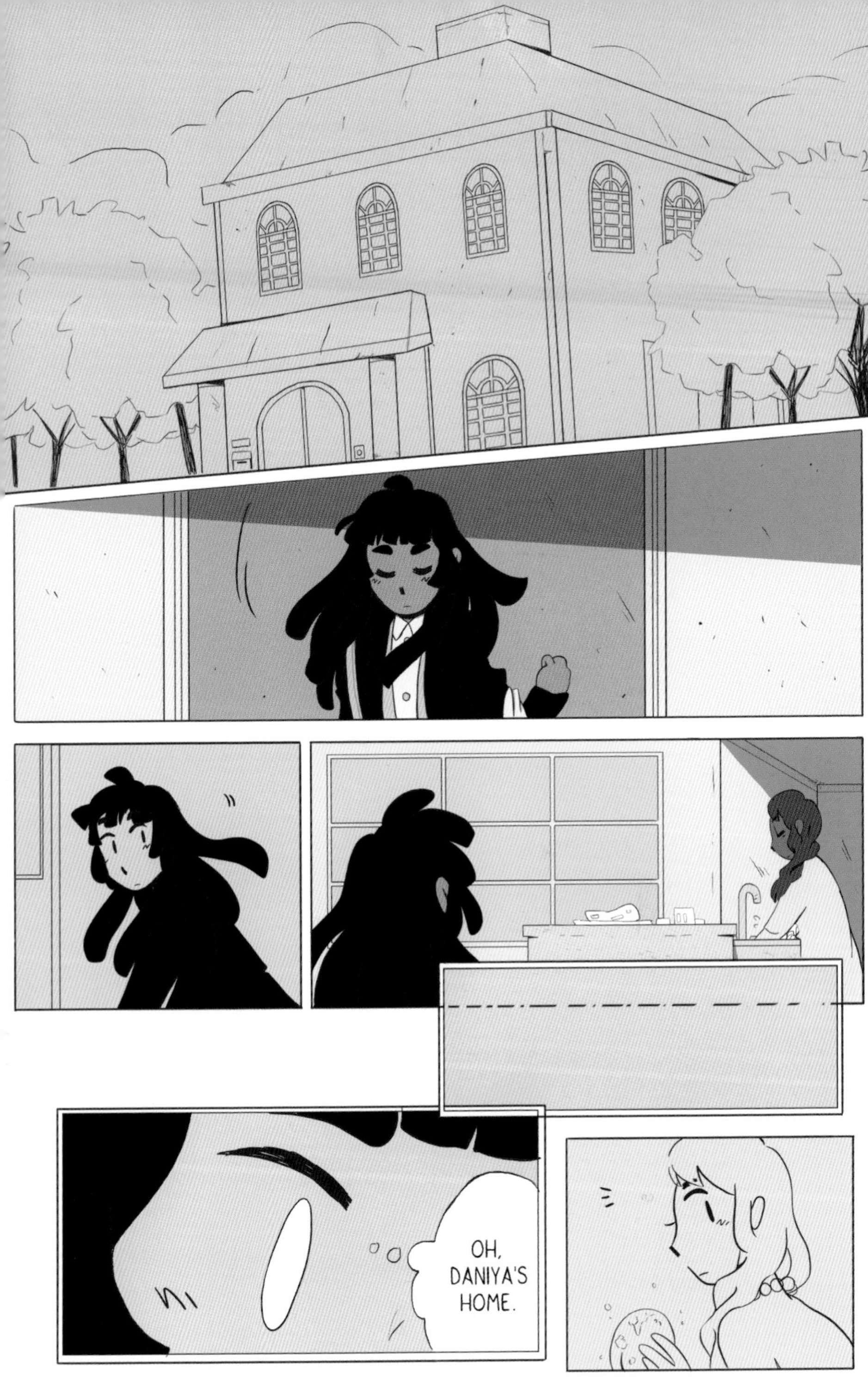
OH,
DANIYA'S
HOME.

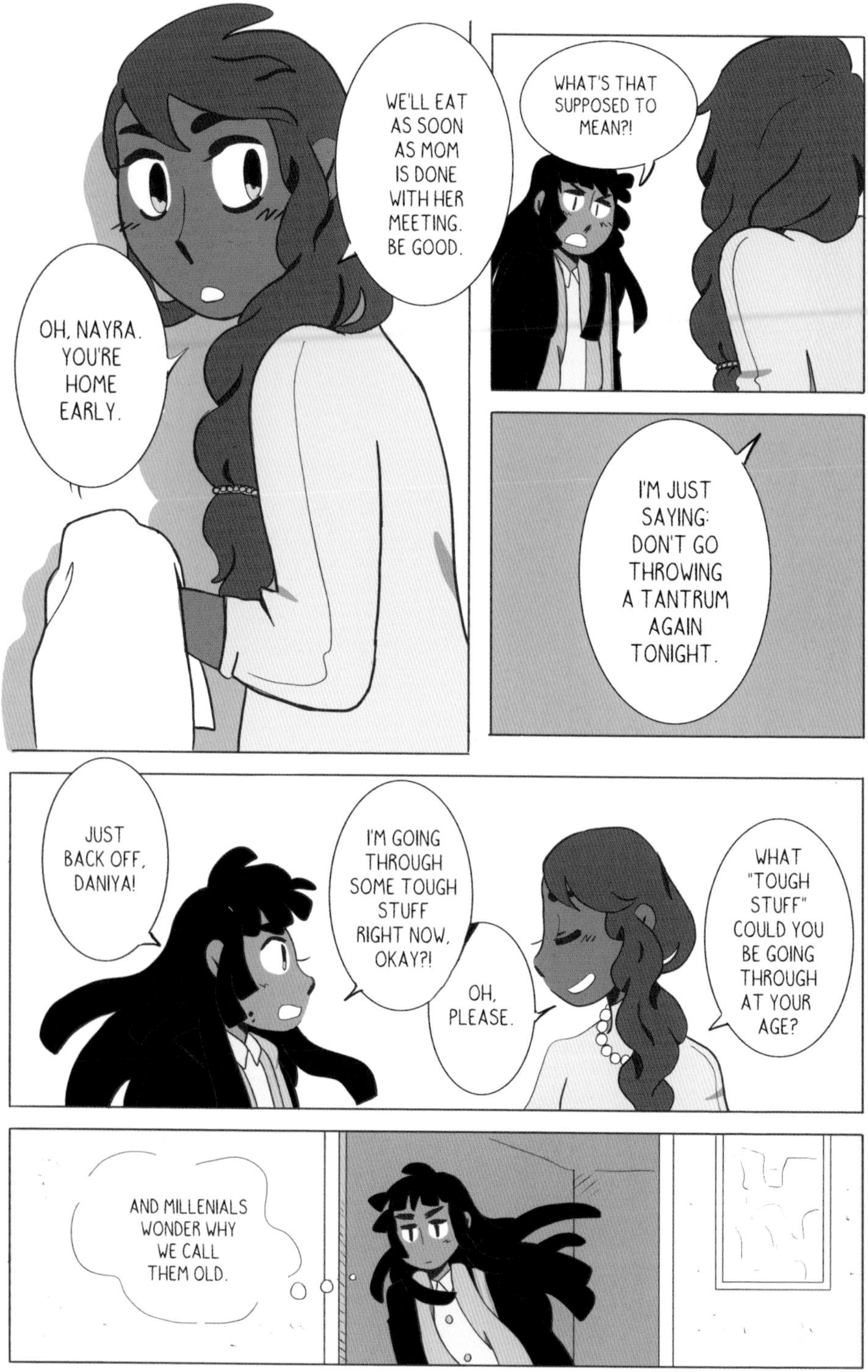
OH, NAYRA. YOU'RE HOME EARLY.
WE'LL EAT AS SOON AS MOM IS DONE WITH HER MEETING. BE GOOD.
WHAT'S THAT SUPPOSED TO MEAN?!
I'M JUST SAYING: DON'T GO THROWING A TANTRUM AGAIN TONIGHT.
JUST BACK OFF, DANIYA!
I'M GOING THROUGH SOME TOUGH STUFF RIGHT NOW, OKAY?!
OH, PLEASE.
WHAT "TOUGH STUFF" COULD YOU BE GOING THROUGH AT YOUR AGE?
AND MILLENIALS WONDER WHY WE CALL THEM OLD.

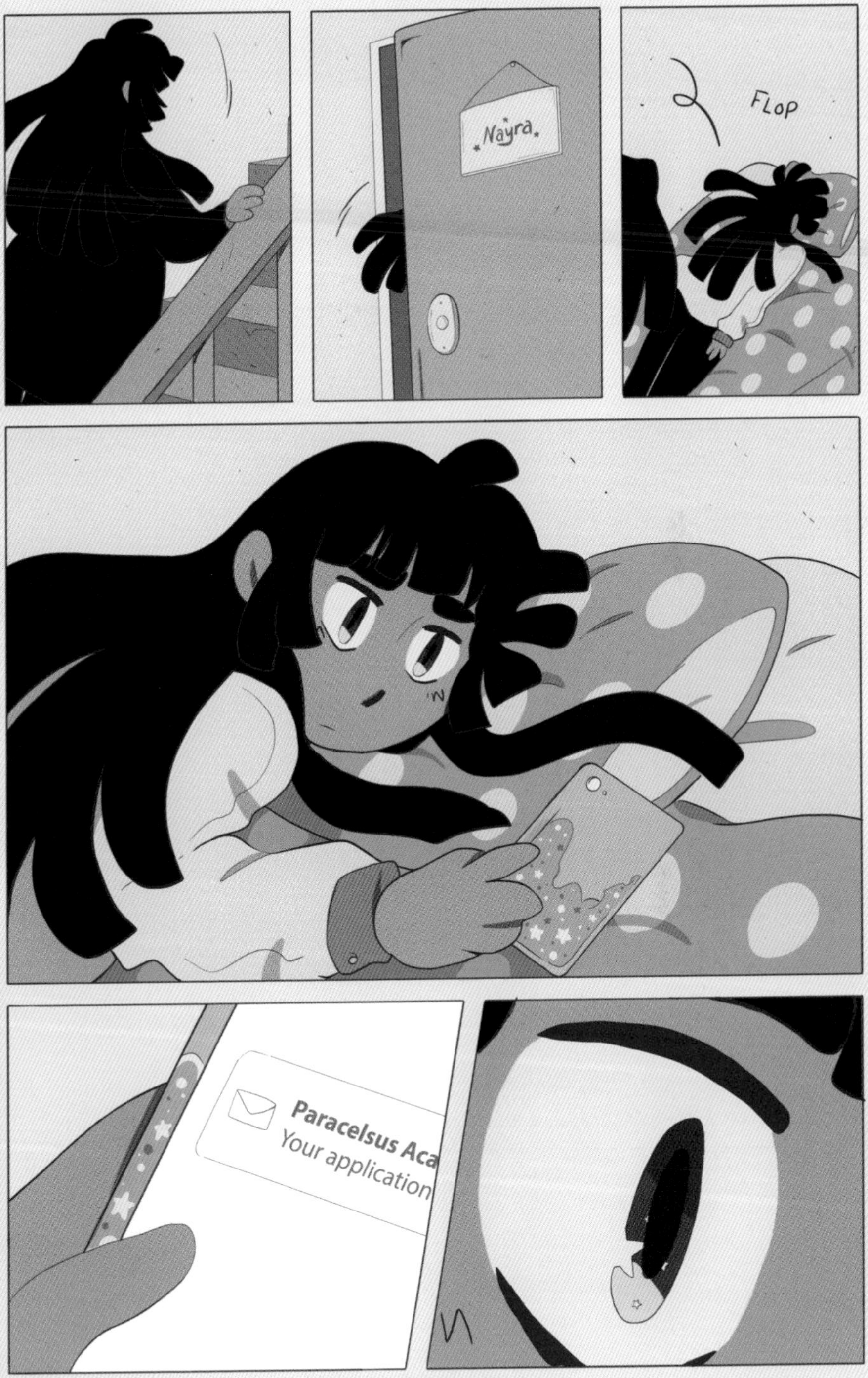
Nayra
FLOP
Paracelsus Aca
Your application

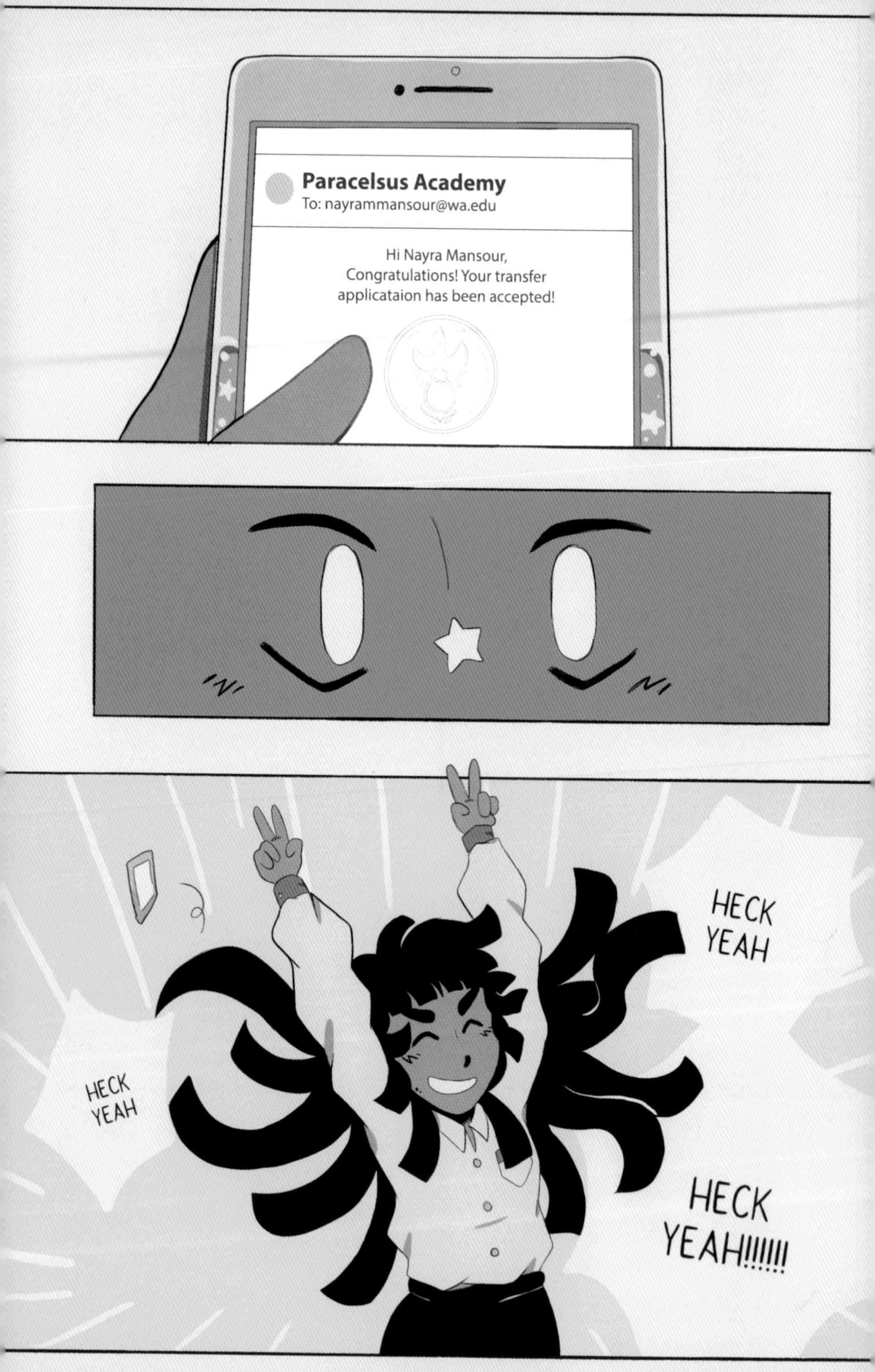
Paracelsus Academy
To: nayrammansour@wa.edu
Hi Nayra Mansour,
Congratulations! Your transfer applicataion has been accepted!
HECK YEAH
HECK YEAH
HECK YEAH!!!!!!!

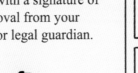

Please send the following e-forms with a signature of approval from your parent or legal guardian.

NOW, WHAT SHOULD I DO?! I SHOULD'VE KNOWN BETTER THAN TO APPLY IN SECRET...

MOM AND DAD WILL NEVER SIGN OFF ON THIS...

AND ON TOP OF THAT...

RAMI...

WHY IS EVERYTHING SO COMPLICATED?!

HNNN GHHH

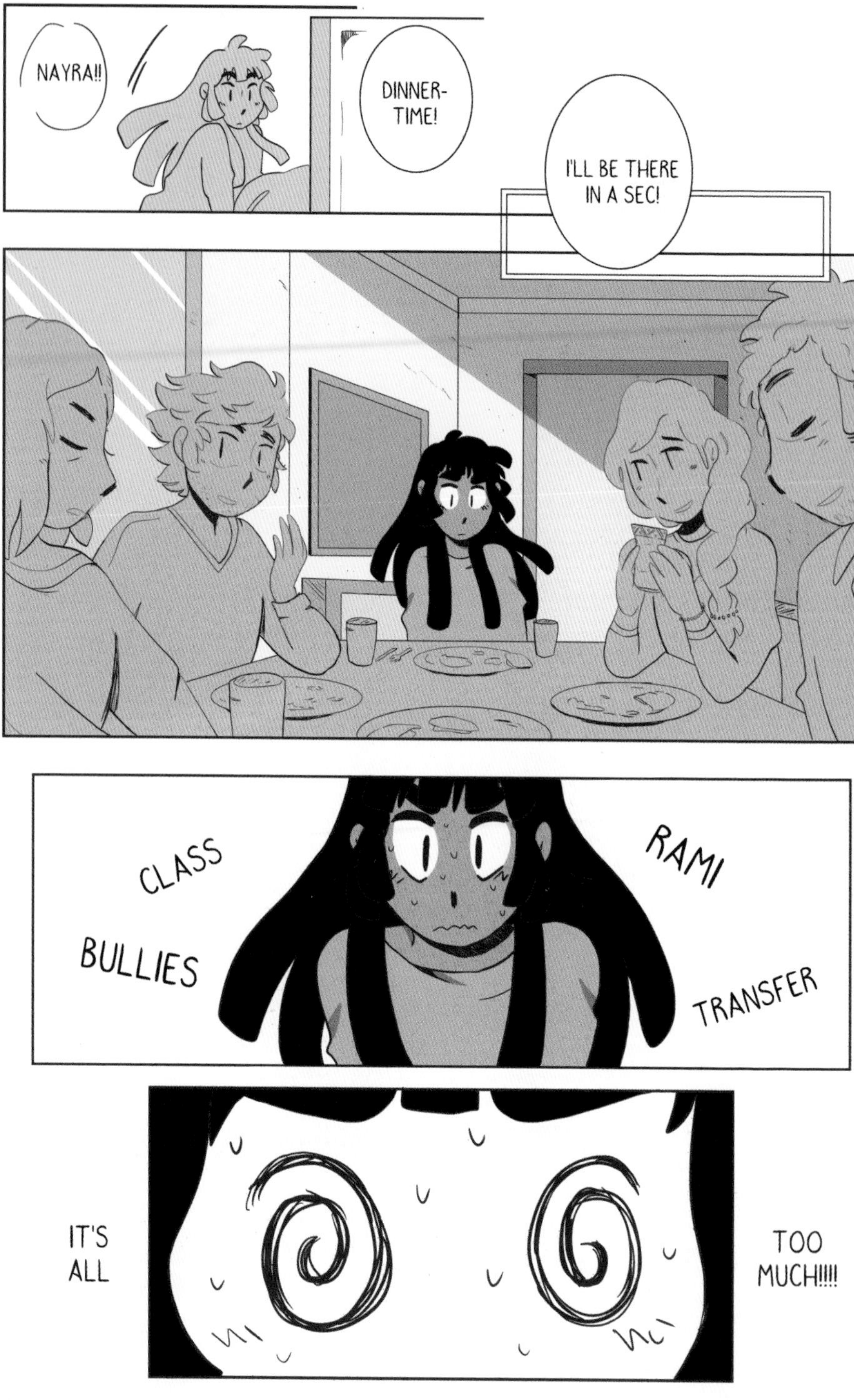
NAYRA!!
DINNER-TIME!
I'LL BE THERE IN A SEC!
CLASS
RAMI
BULLIES
TRANSFER
IT'S ALL
TOO MUCH!!!!

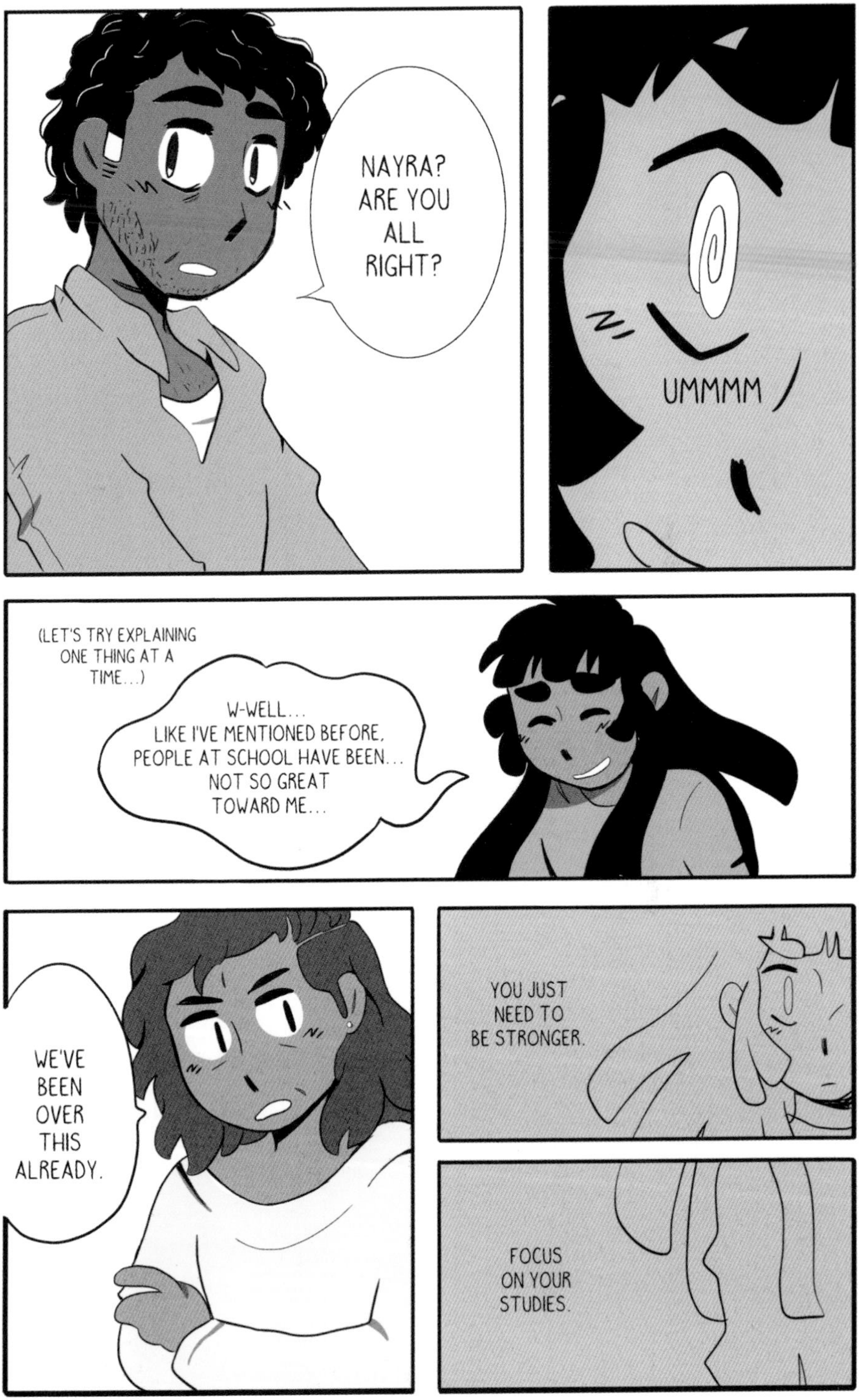
NAYRA? ARE YOU ALL RIGHT?
UMMMM
(LET'S TRY EXPLAINING ONE THING AT A TIME...)
W-WELL... LIKE I'VE MENTIONED BEFORE, PEOPLE AT SCHOOL HAVE BEEN... NOT SO GREAT TOWARD ME...
WE'VE BEEN OVER THIS ALREADY.
YOU JUST NEED TO BE STRONGER.
FOCUS ON YOUR STUDIES.

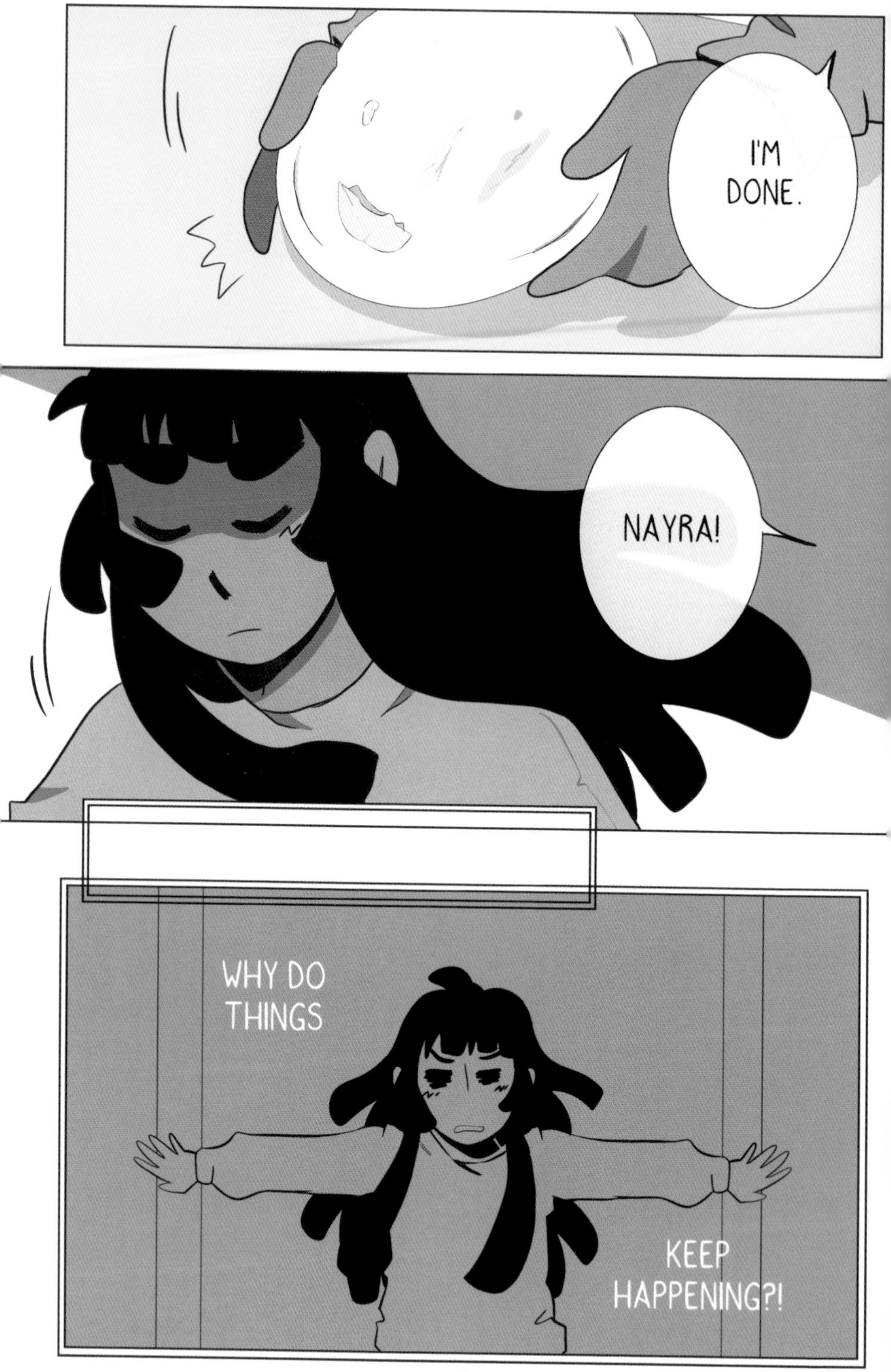
I'M DONE.
NAYRA!
WHY DO THINGS
KEEP HAPPENING?!

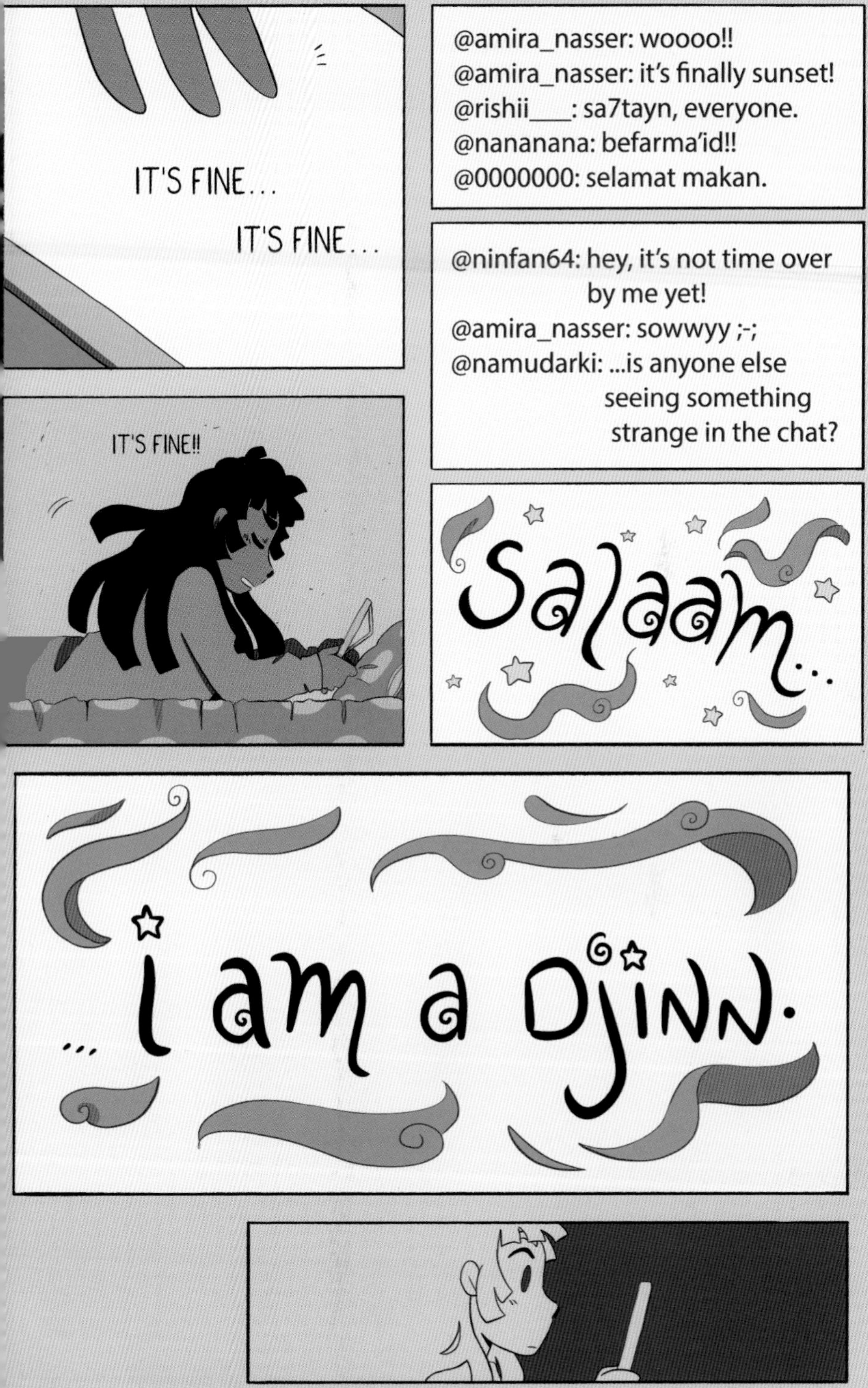
IT'S FINE...
IT'S FINE...
IT'S FINE!!
@amira_nasser: woooo!!
@amira_nasser: it's finally sunset!
@rishii___: sa7tayn, everyone.
@nananana: befarma'id!!
@0000000: selamat makan.
@ninfan64: hey, it's not time over by me yet!
@amira_nasser: sowwyy ;-;
@namudarki: ...is anyone else seeing something strange in the chat?
Salaam...
...I am a Djinn.

@amira_nasser: huhhh???
@namudarki: so it's not just me!
@000000: what's happening
@basickk: i'm so confused by this
I am currently posessing what you humans call "a computer" in an attempt to communicate.
I am looking for any human to help me hide out in the human world.
@nananana: namudarki is this you or what
@namudarki: i don't think it's possible for me to have smoke come out of your tablet
@mmarlenaa: ok so my laptop DOES look very sparkly and like firey all of the sudden
I can't explain why, but i had to leave the world of the djinn unexpectedly.
I know this may seem unlikely, but it is the truth. Please believe me.
Type message to #general...
my name is
@nayram: my name is nayra... and i believe you

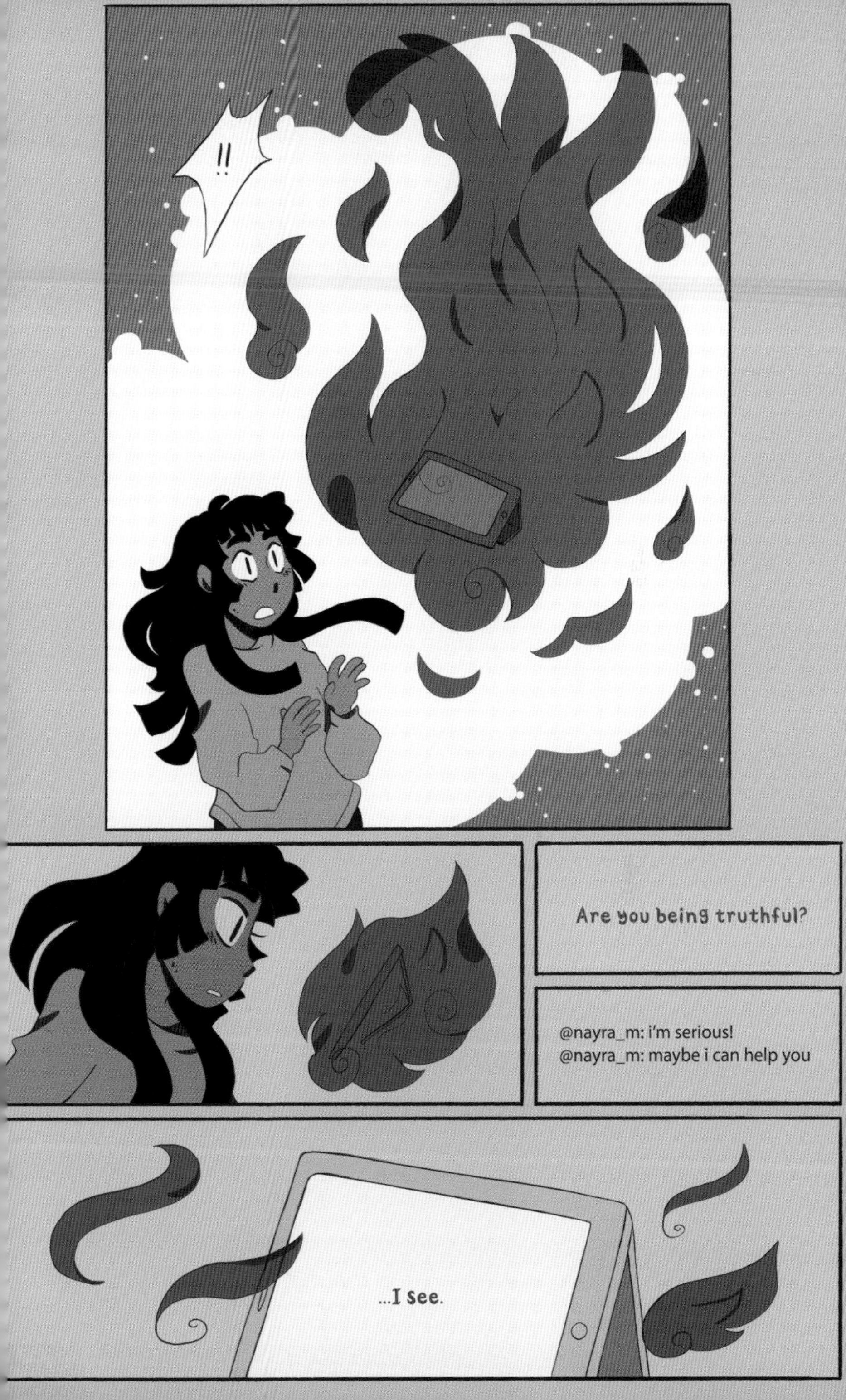

!!
Are you being truthful?
@nayra_m: i'm serious!
@nayra_m: maybe i can help you
...I see.

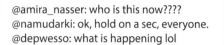

@amira_nasser: who is this now????
@namudarki: ok, hold on a sec, everyone.
@depwesso: what is happening lol

If that is something you can do, then I will happily accept.

Thank you for your graciousness.

I will appear to you shortly.
please wait for me.
Thank you.

@namudarki: ...
@namudarki: all that weird smoke and stuff disappeared.
@namudarki: so i have no idea what that was.

sickk: ooookkkkkkkk
awdi_saudi: Well, that was really, really strange.
@ninfan64: maybe i'm hallucinating from hunger...

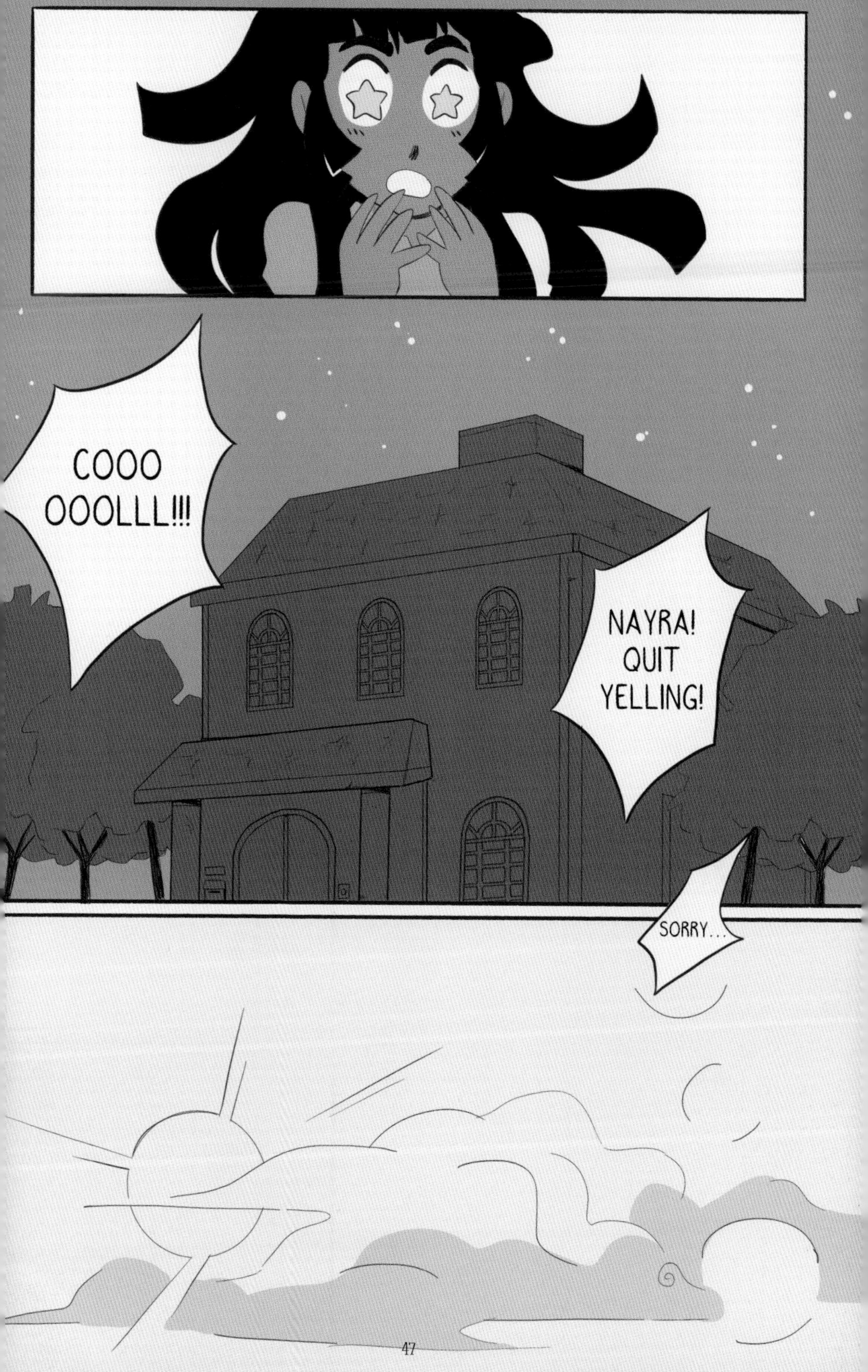
COOO
OOOLLL!!!
NAYRA!
QUIT
YELLING!
SORRY...

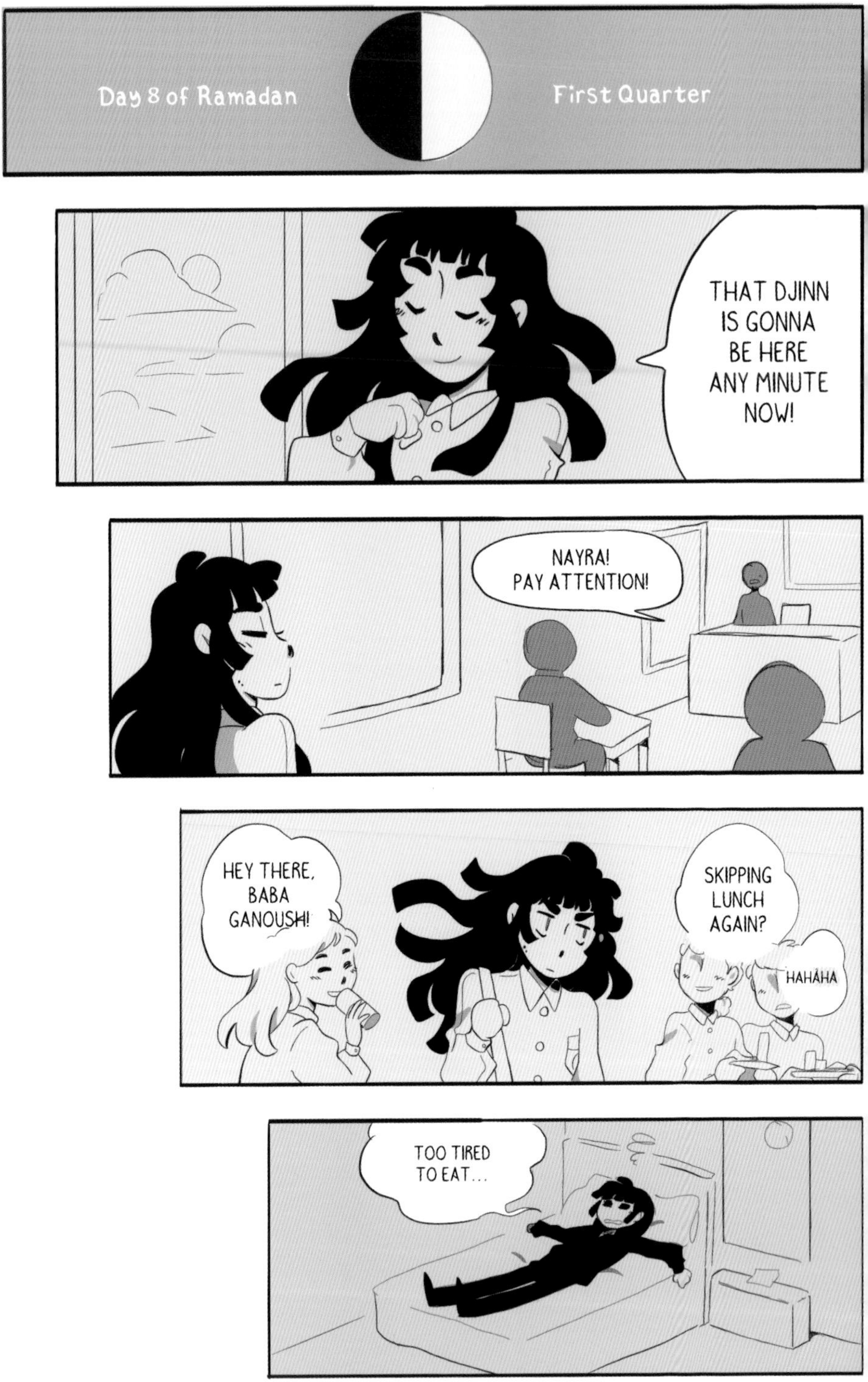
Day 8 of Ramadan
First Quarter
THAT DJINN IS GONNA BE HERE ANY MINUTE NOW!
NAYRA! PAY ATTENTION!
HEY THERE, BABA GANOUSH!
SKIPPING LUNCH AGAIN?
HAHAHA
TOO TIRED TO EAT...

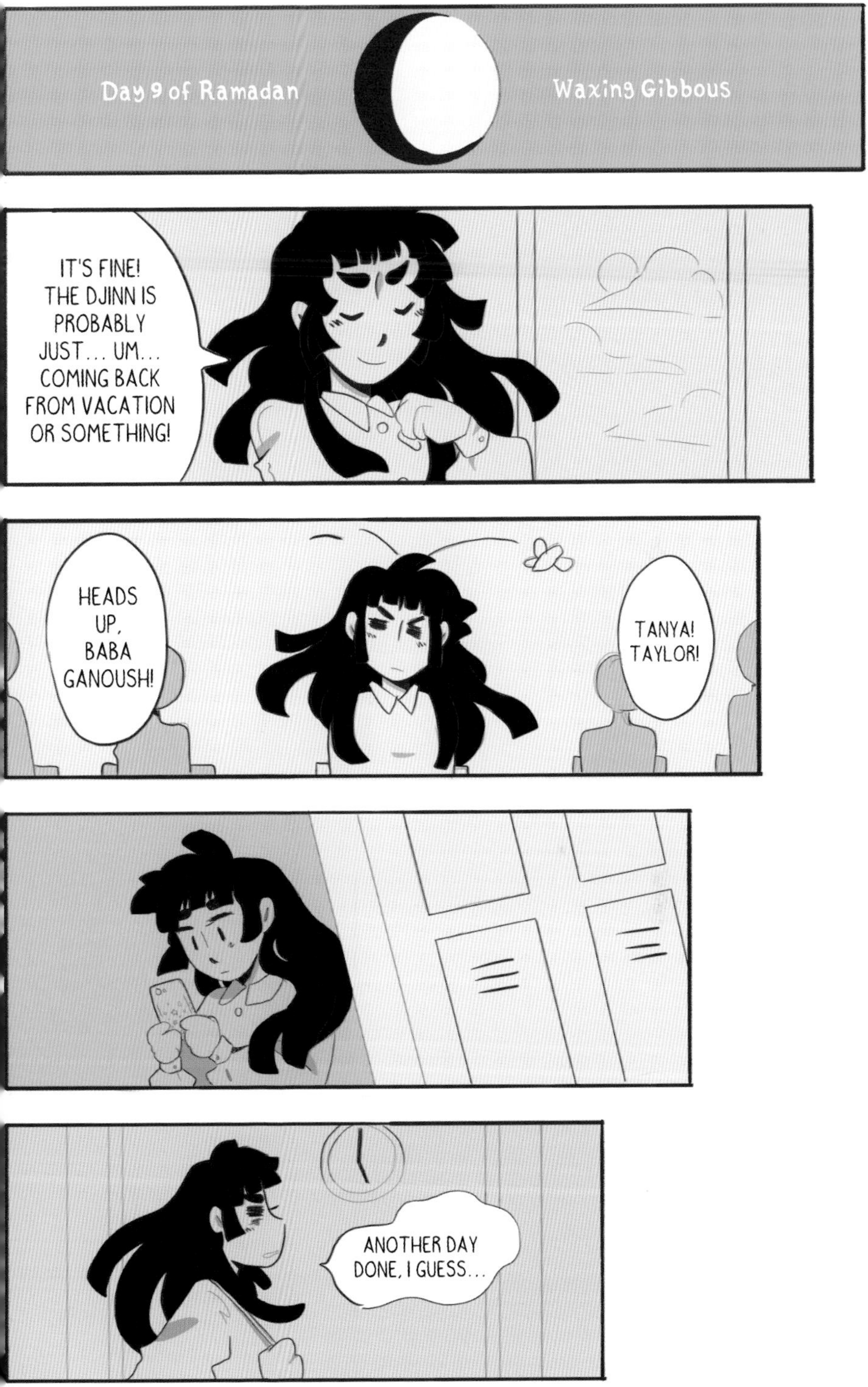
Day 9 of Ramadan
Waxing Gibbous
IT'S FINE! THE DJINN IS PROBABLY JUST... UM... COMING BACK FROM VACATION OR SOMETHING!
HEADS UP, BABA GANOUSH!
TANYA! TAYLOR!
ANOTHER DAY DONE, I GUESS...

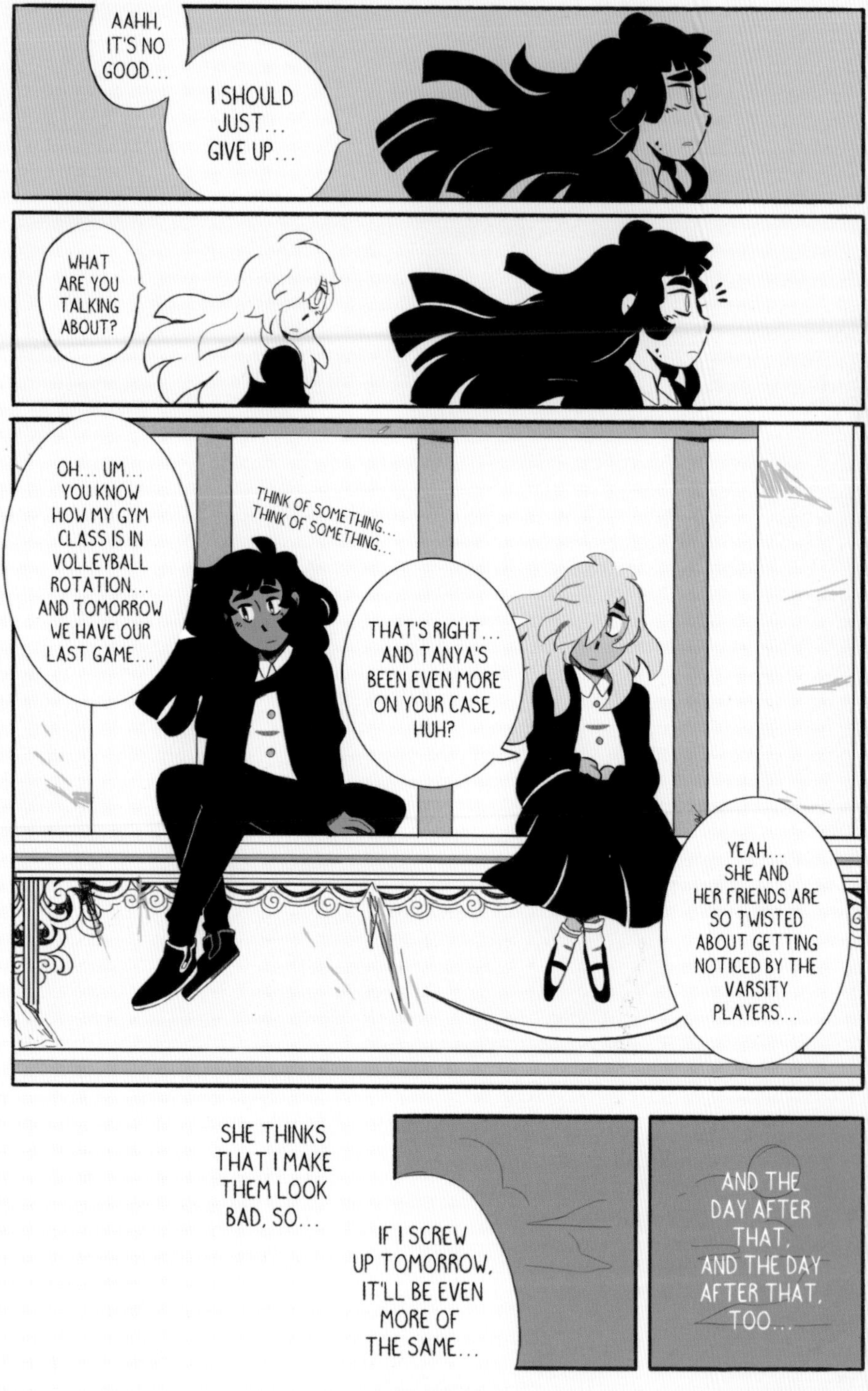
AAHH, IT'S NO GOOD...
I SHOULD JUST... GIVE UP...
WHAT ARE YOU TALKING ABOUT?
OH... UM... YOU KNOW HOW MY GYM CLASS IS IN VOLLEYBALL ROTATION... AND TOMORROW WE HAVE OUR LAST GAME...
THINK OF SOMETHING... THINK OF SOMETHING...
THAT'S RIGHT... AND TANYA'S BEEN EVEN MORE ON YOUR CASE, HUH?
YEAH... SHE AND HER FRIENDS ARE SO TWISTED ABOUT GETTING NOTICED BY THE VARSITY PLAYERS...
SHE THINKS THAT I MAKE THEM LOOK BAD, SO...
IF I SCREW UP TOMORROW, IT'LL BE EVEN MORE OF THE SAME...
AND THE DAY AFTER THAT, AND THE DAY AFTER THAT, TOO...

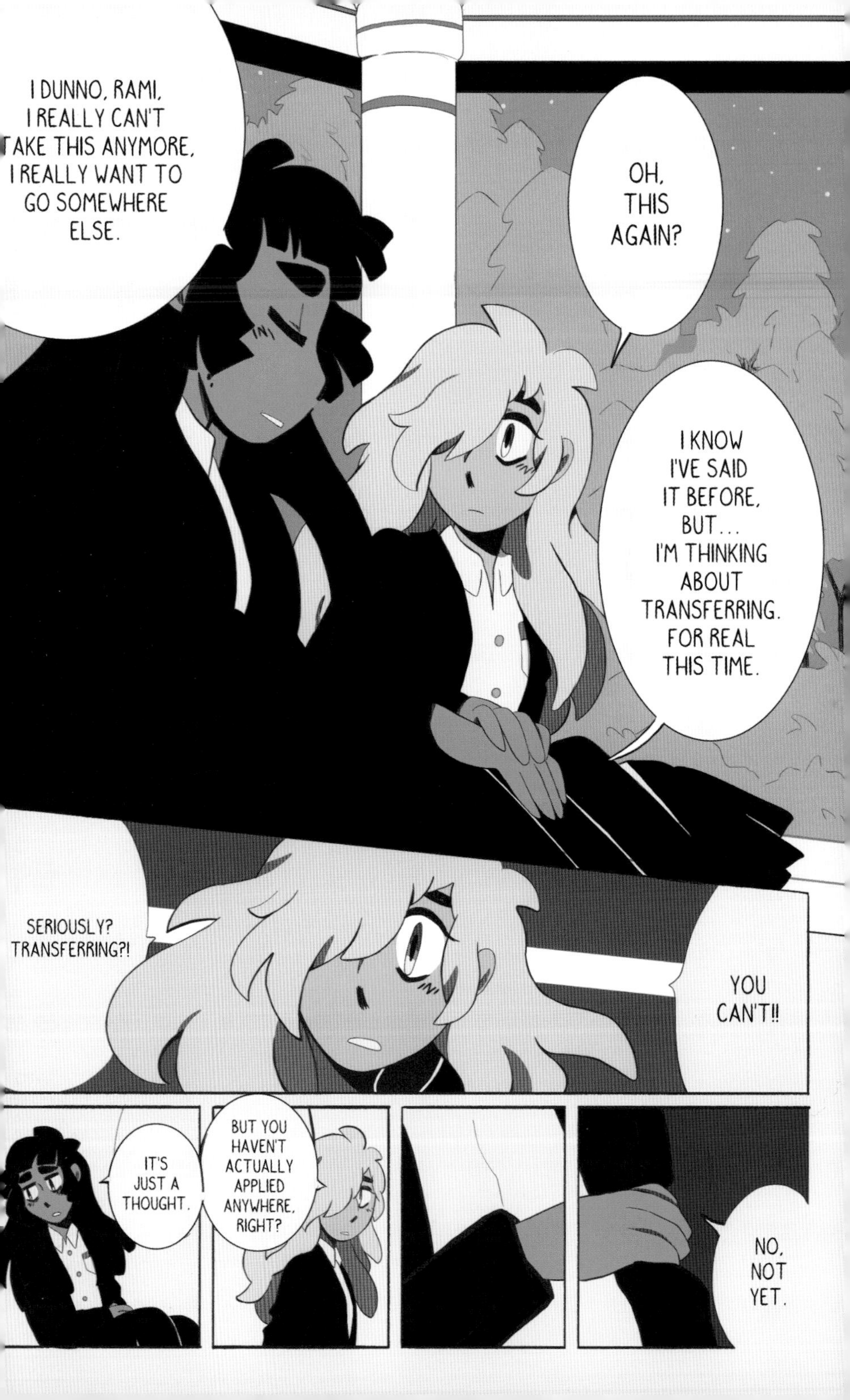
I DUNNO, RAMI, I REALLY CAN'T TAKE THIS ANYMORE, I REALLY WANT TO GO SOMEWHERE ELSE.
OH, THIS AGAIN?
I KNOW I'VE SAID IT BEFORE, BUT... I'M THINKING ABOUT TRANSFERRING. FOR REAL THIS TIME.
SERIOUSLY? TRANSFERRING?!
YOU CAN'T!!
IT'S JUST A THOUGHT.
BUT YOU HAVEN'T ACTUALLY APPLIED ANYWHERE, RIGHT?
NO, NOT YET.

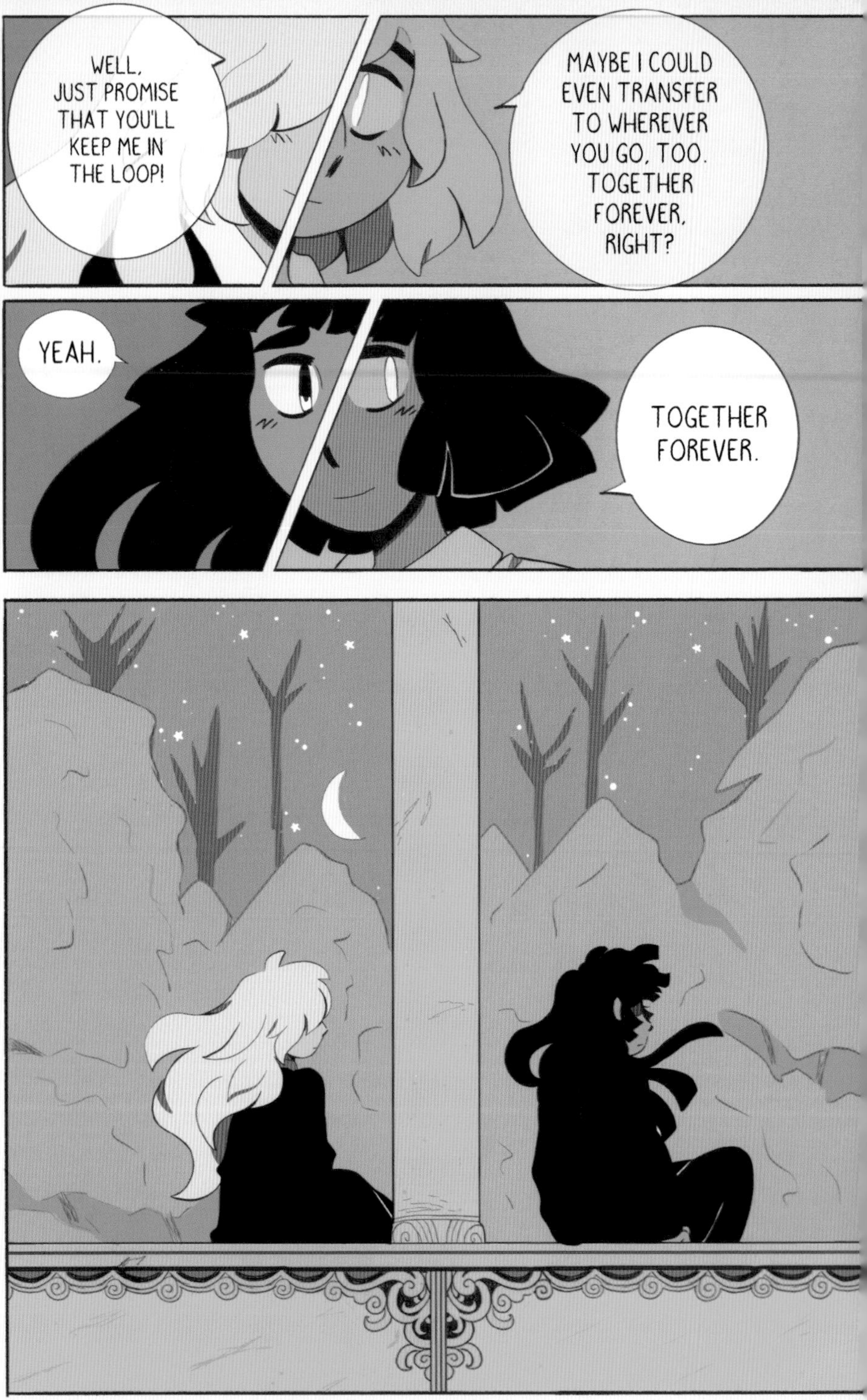
WELL, JUST PROMISE THAT YOU'LL KEEP ME IN THE LOOP!
MAYBE I COULD EVEN TRANSFER TO WHEREVER YOU GO, TOO. TOGETHER FOREVER, RIGHT?
YEAH.
TOGETHER FOREVER.

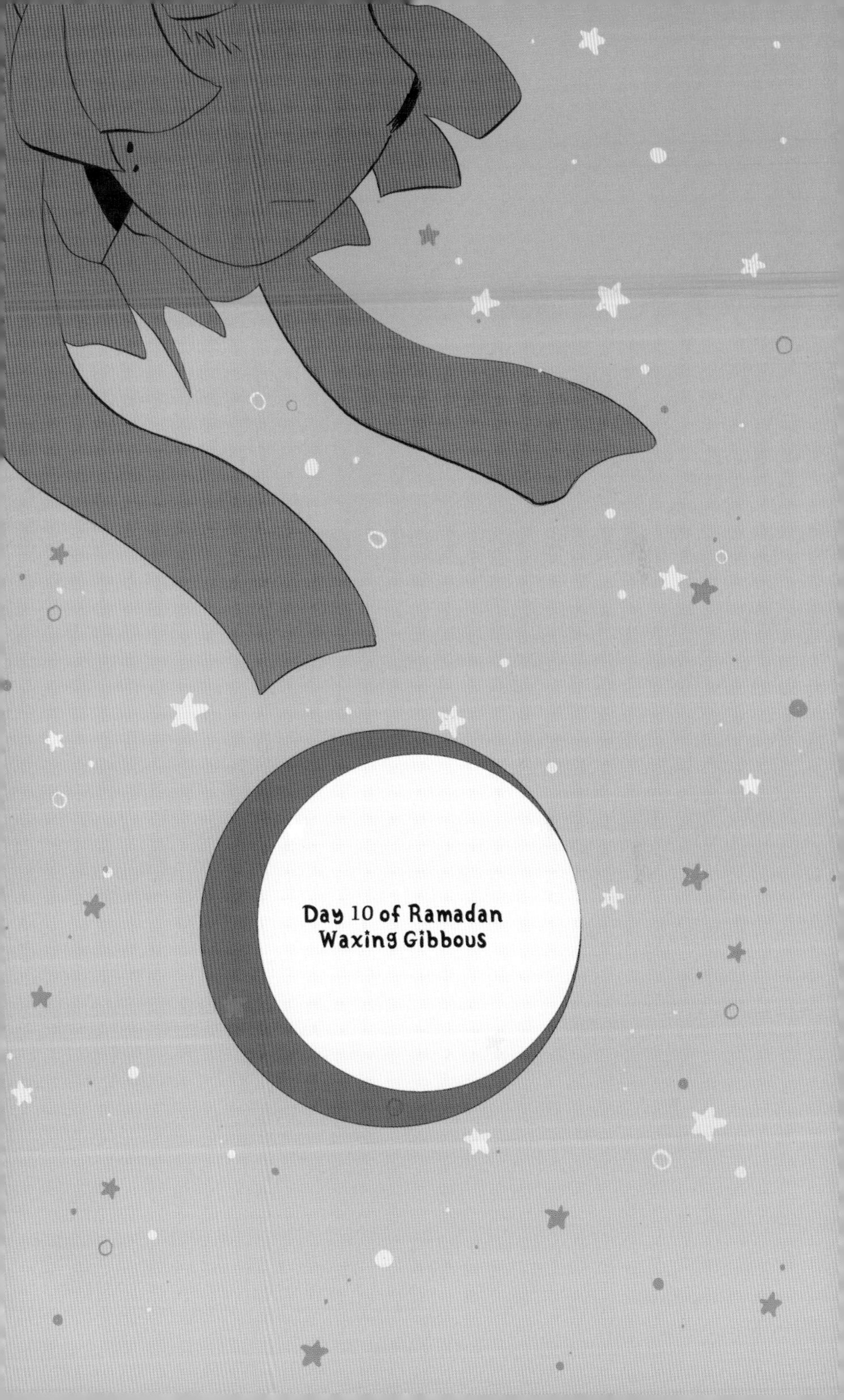
Day 10 of Ramadan
Waxing Gibbous

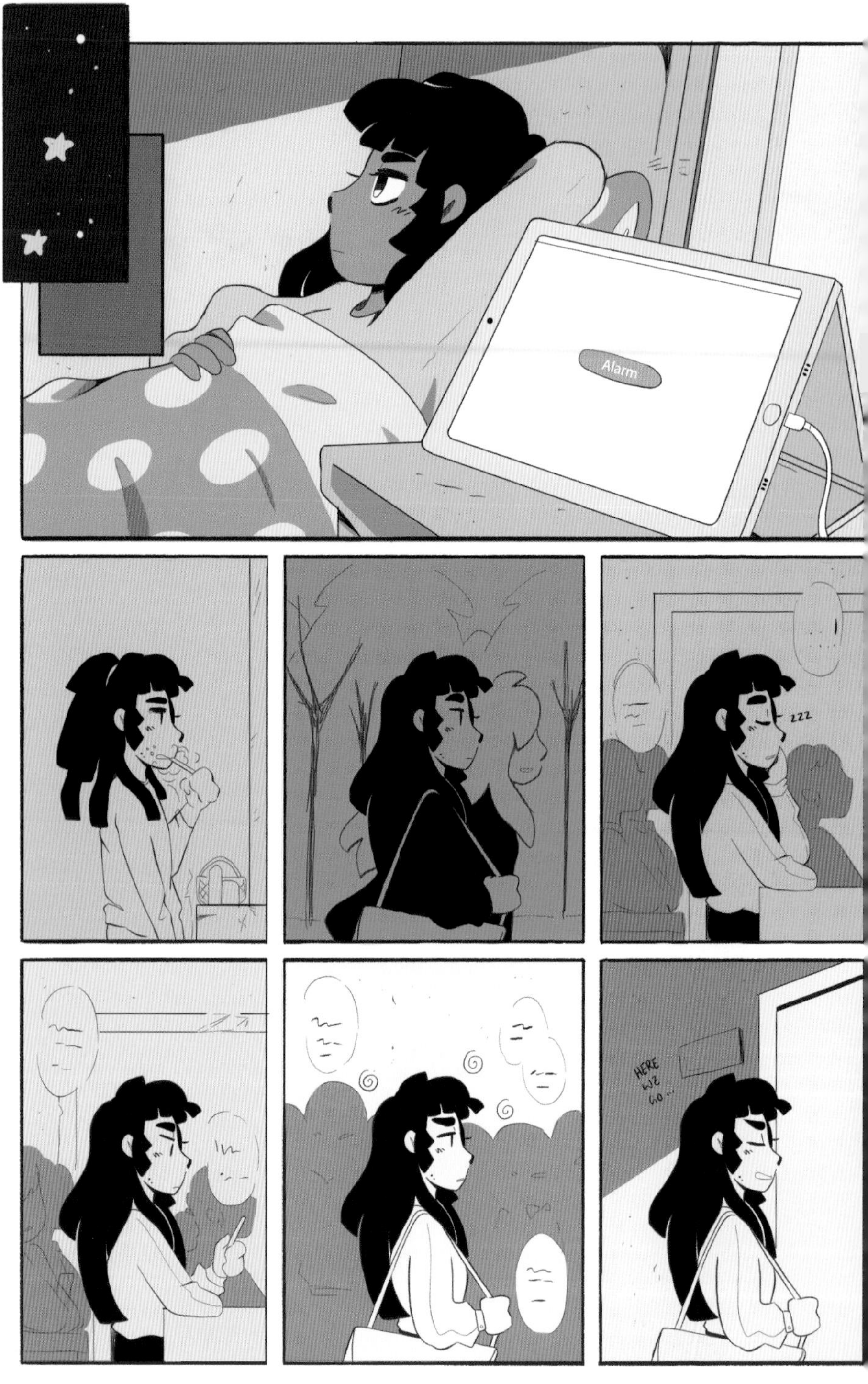
Alarm
zzz
HERE WE GO...

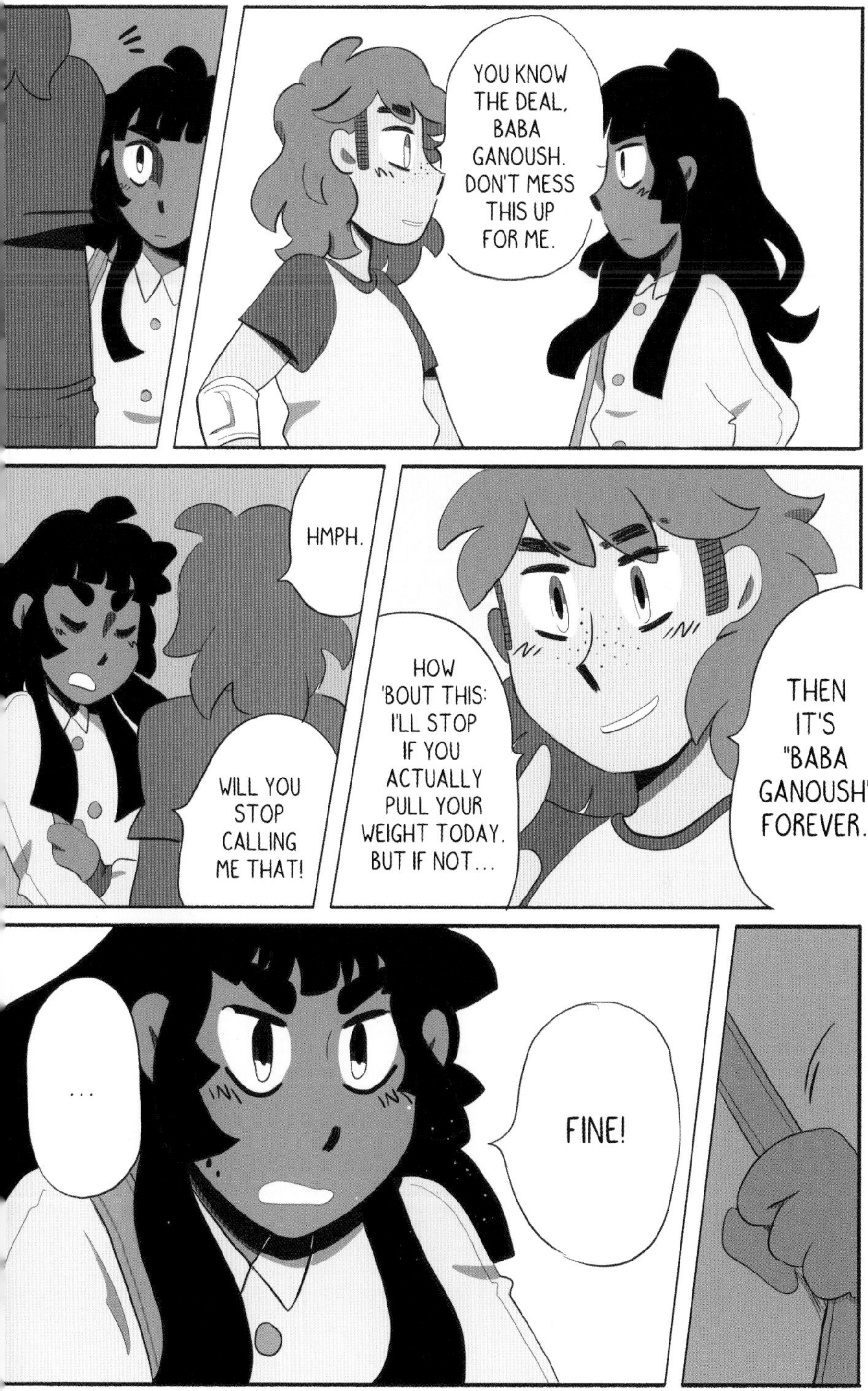
YOU KNOW THE DEAL, BABA GANOUSH. DON'T MESS THIS UP FOR ME.
HMPH.
WILL YOU STOP CALLING ME THAT!
HOW 'BOUT THIS: I'LL STOP IF YOU ACTUALLY PULL YOUR WEIGHT TODAY. BUT IF NOT...
THEN IT'S "BABA GANOUSH" FOREVER.
...
FINE!

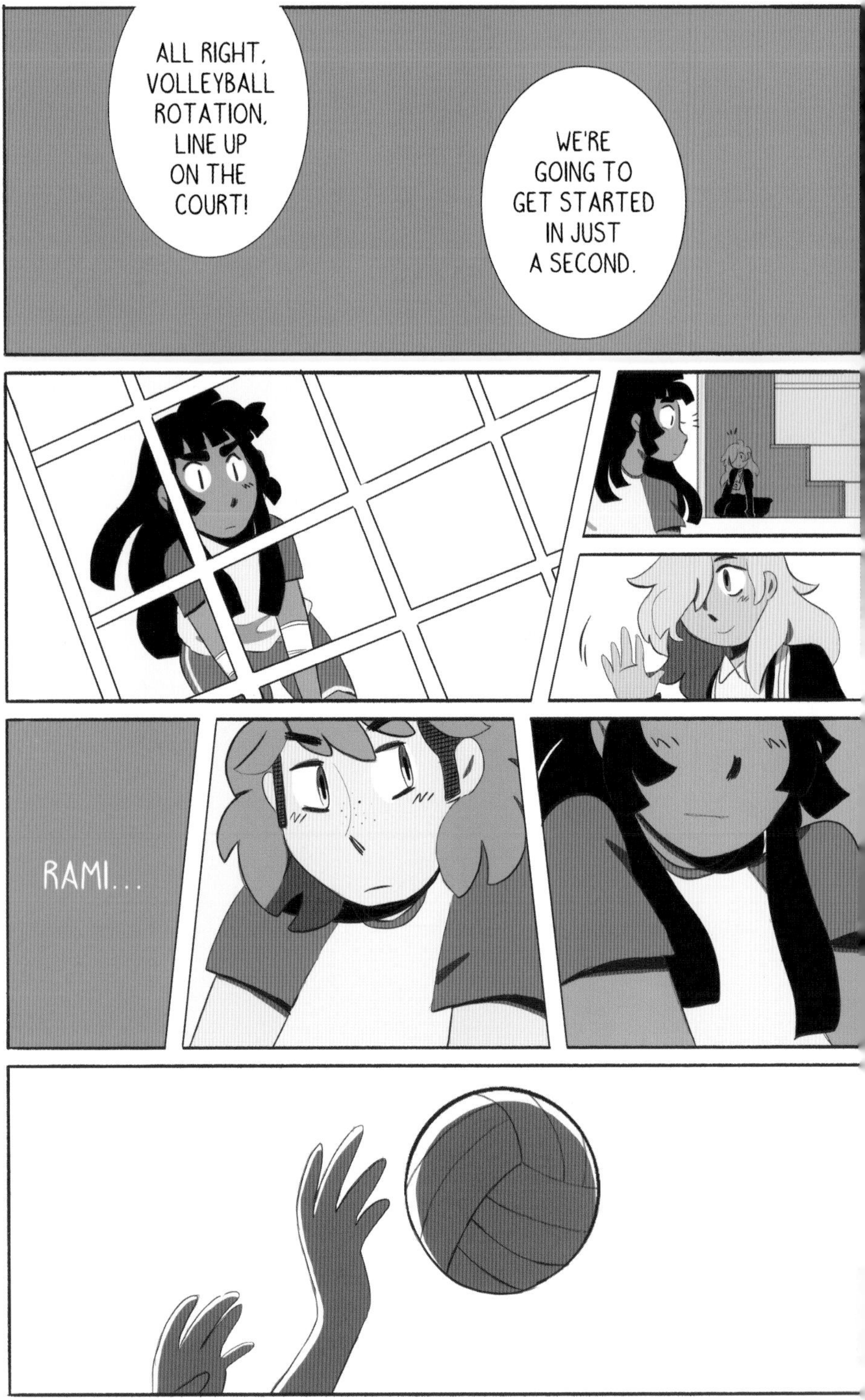
ALL RIGHT, VOLLEYBALL ROTATION, LINE UP ON THE COURT!
WE'RE GOING TO GET STARTED IN JUST A SECOND.
RAMI...

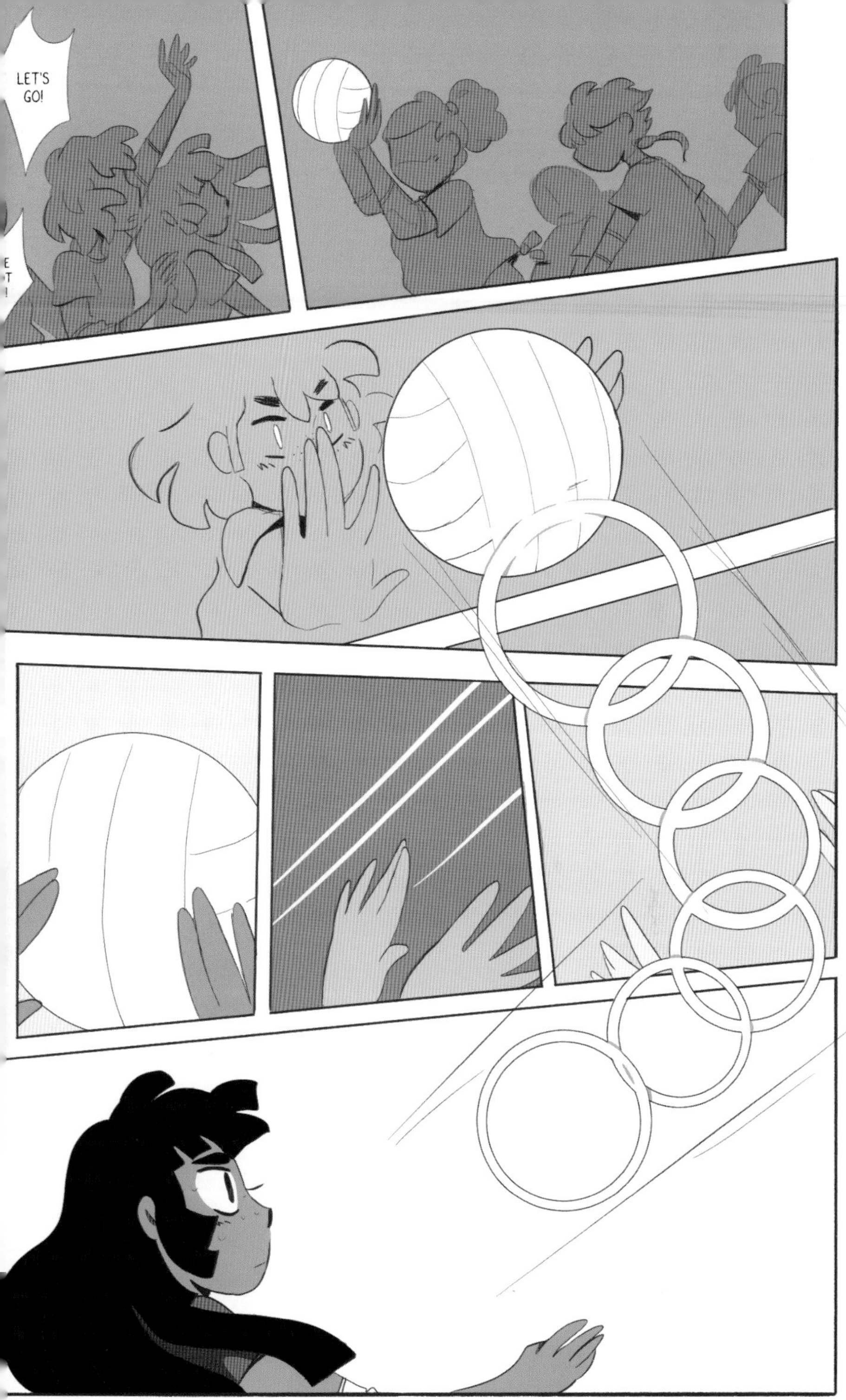
LET'S GO!

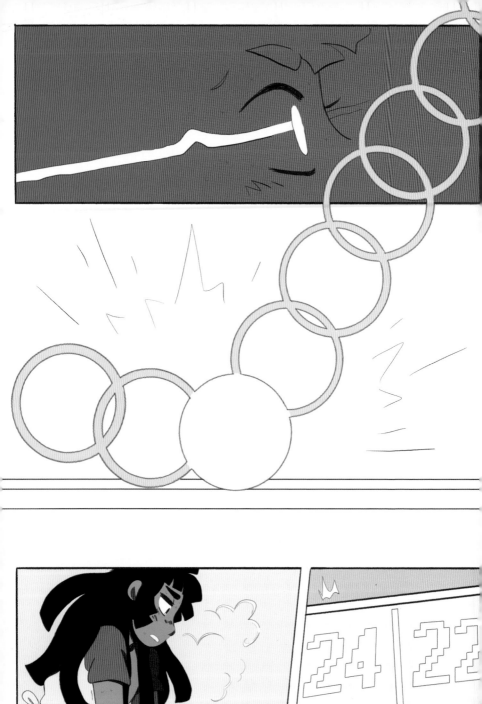

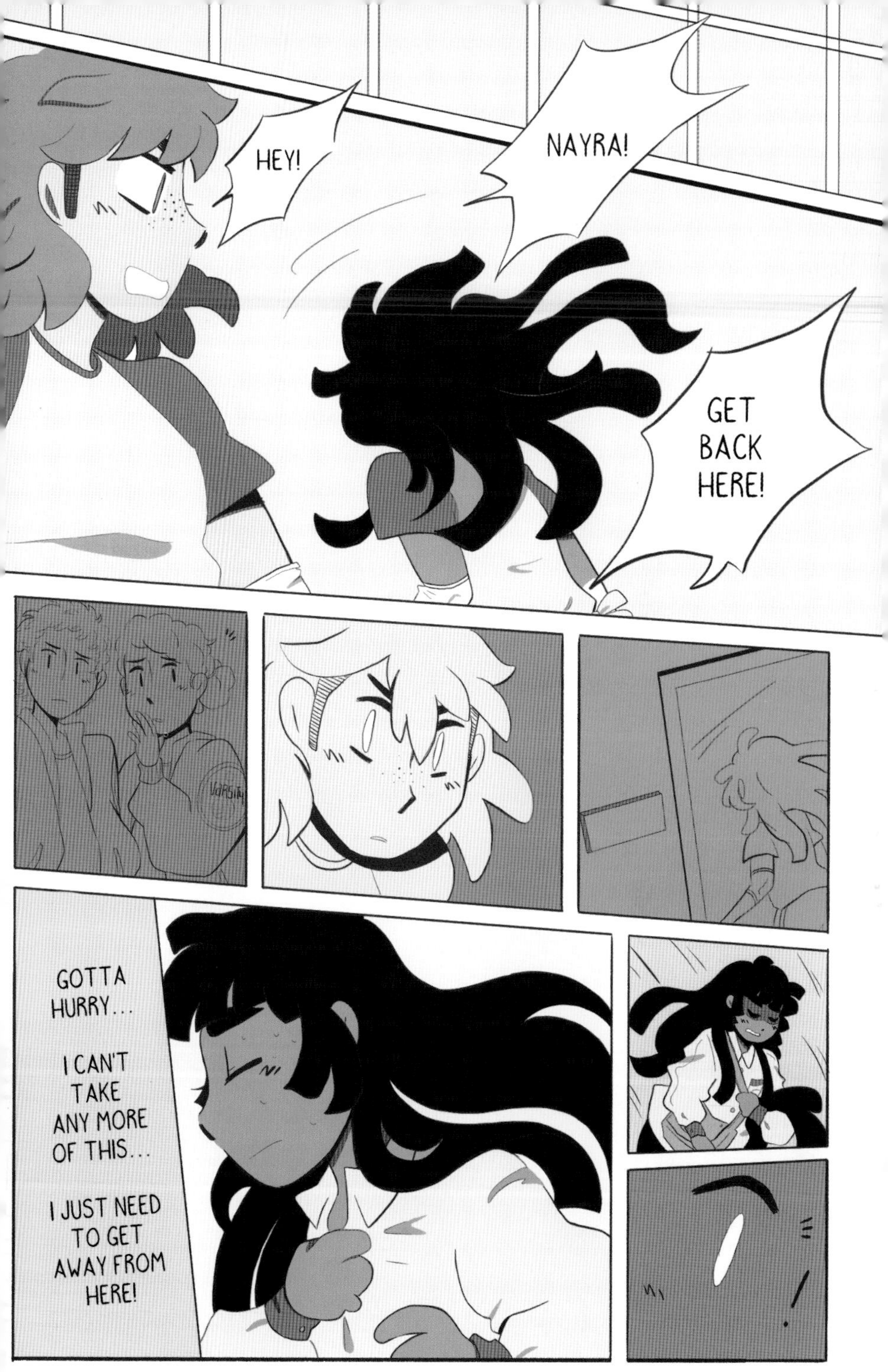
HEY!
NAYRA!
GET BACK HERE!
GOTTA HURRY...
I CAN'T TAKE ANY MORE OF THIS...
I JUST NEED TO GET AWAY FROM HERE!

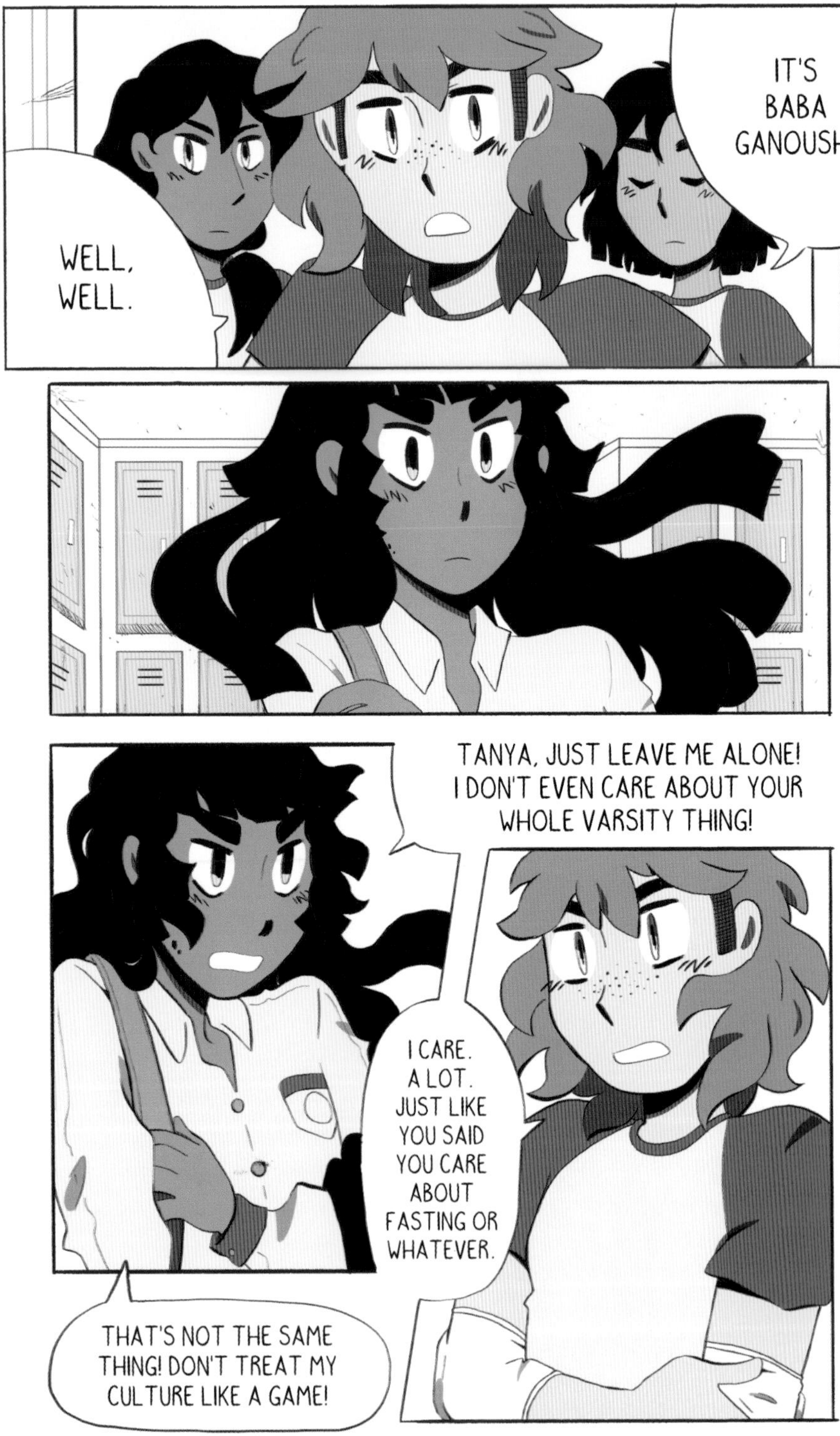
IT'S BABA GANOUSH.
WELL, WELL.
TANYA, JUST LEAVE ME ALONE! I DON'T EVEN CARE ABOUT YOUR WHOLE VARSITY THING!
I CARE. A LOT. JUST LIKE YOU SAID YOU CARE ABOUT FASTING OR WHATEVER.
THAT'S NOT THE SAME THING! DON'T TREAT MY CULTURE LIKE A GAME!

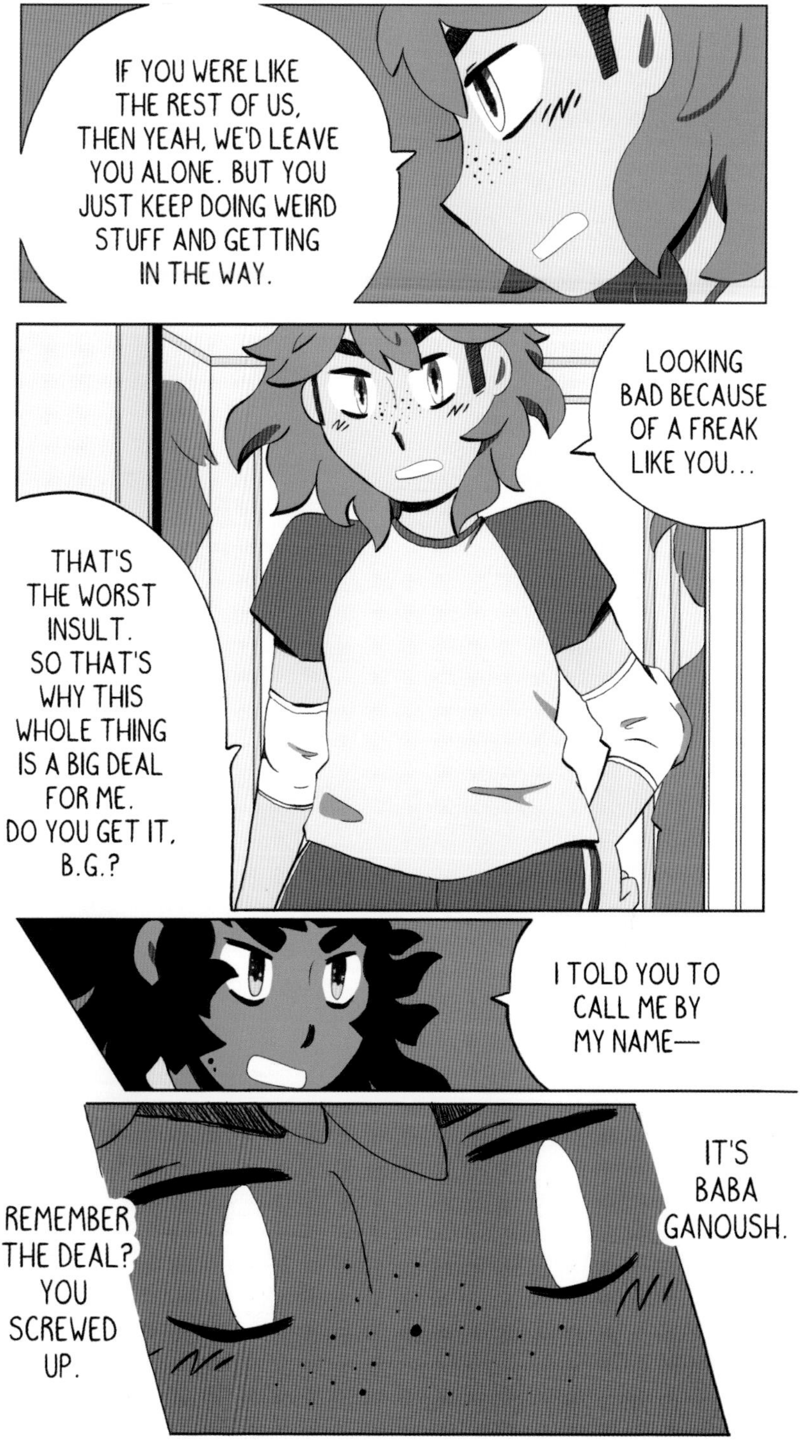
IF YOU WERE LIKE THE REST OF US, THEN YEAH, WE'D LEAVE YOU ALONE. BUT YOU JUST KEEP DOING WEIRD STUFF AND GETTING IN THE WAY.
LOOKING BAD BECAUSE OF A FREAK LIKE YOU...
THAT'S THE WORST INSULT. SO THAT'S WHY THIS WHOLE THING IS A BIG DEAL FOR ME. DO YOU GET IT, B.G.?
I TOLD YOU TO CALL ME BY MY NAME—
IT'S BABA GANOUSH.
REMEMBER THE DEAL? YOU SCREWED UP.

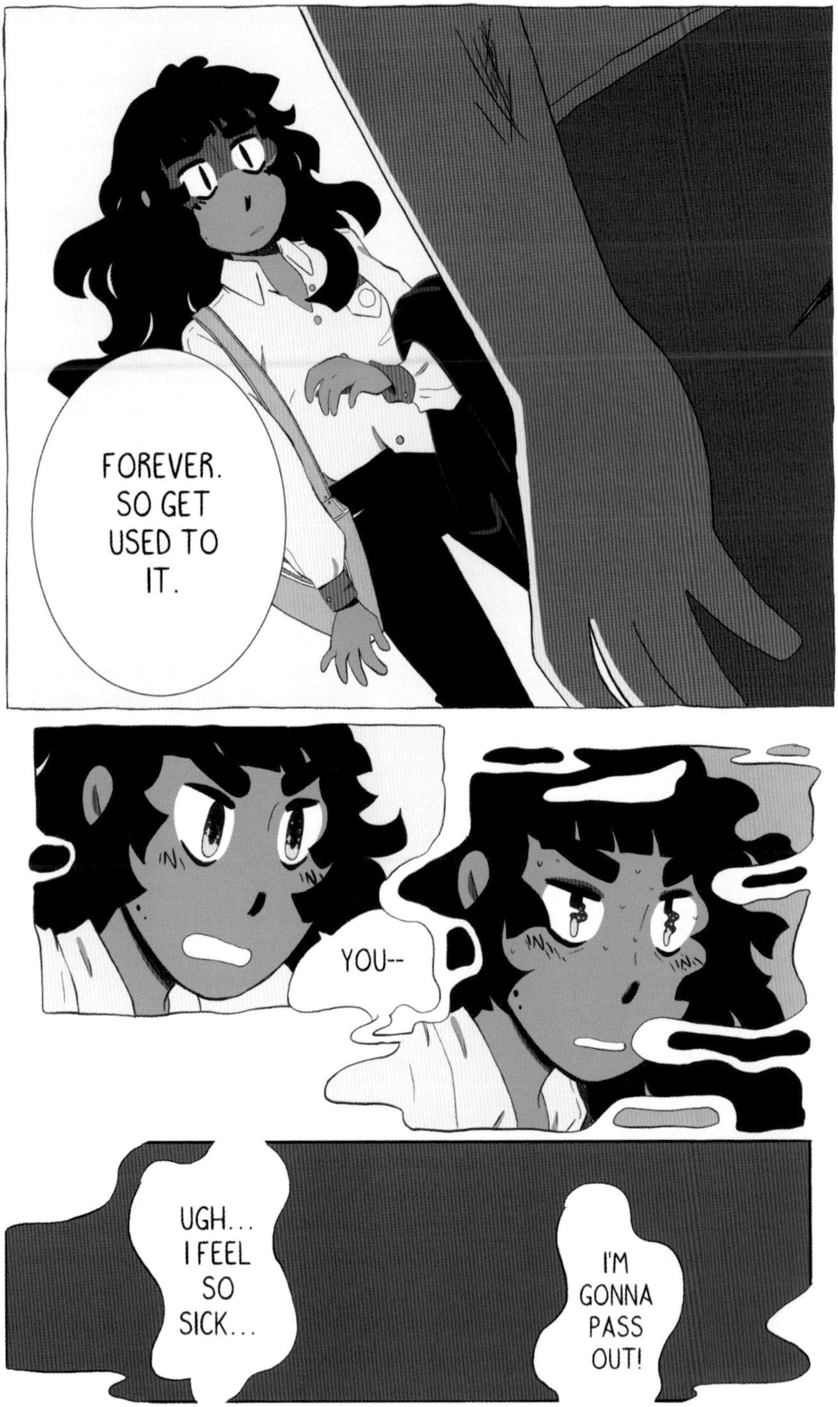
FOREVER. SO GET USED TO IT.
YOU--
UGH... I FEEL SO SICK...
I'M GONNA PASS OUT!

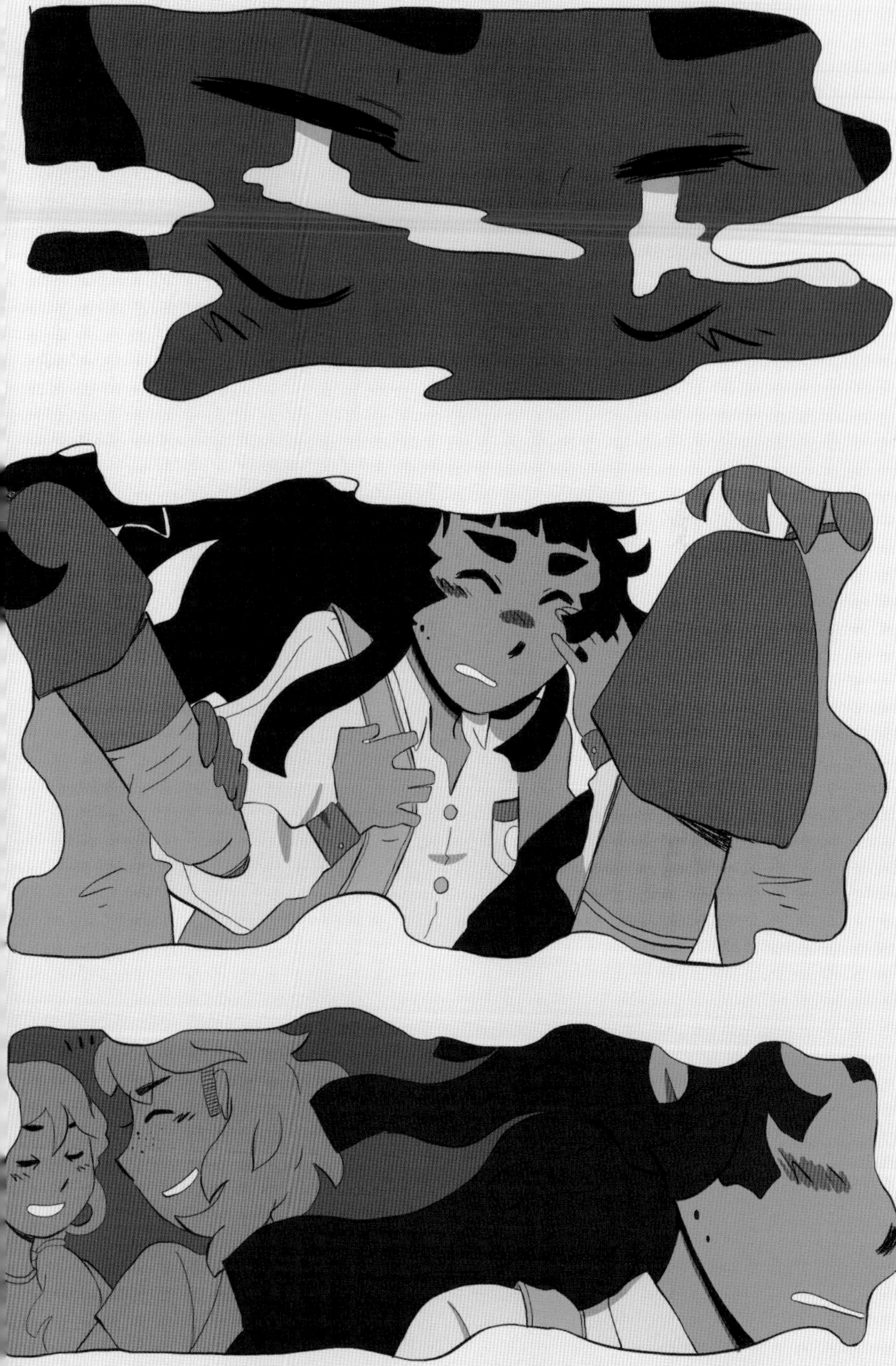

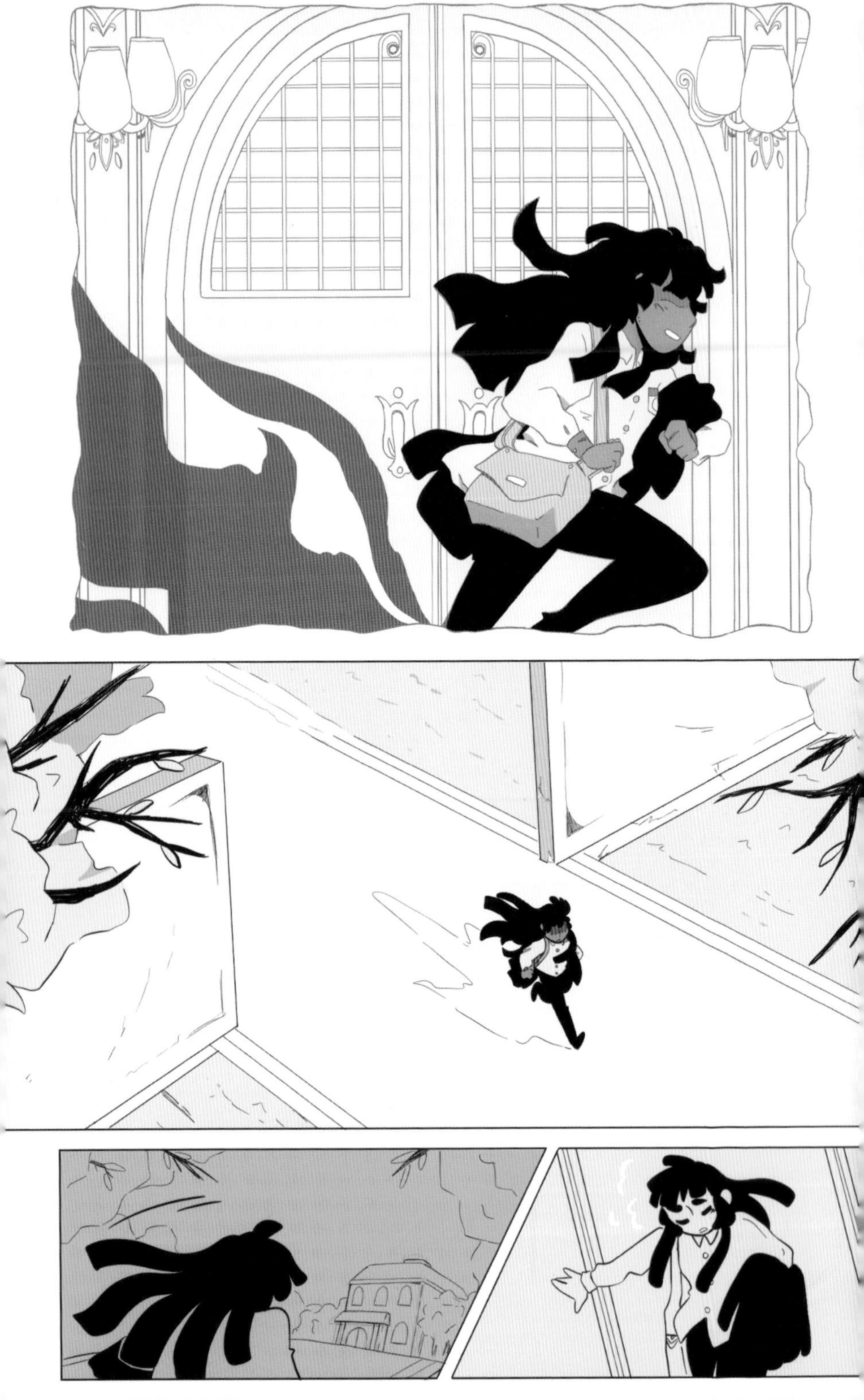

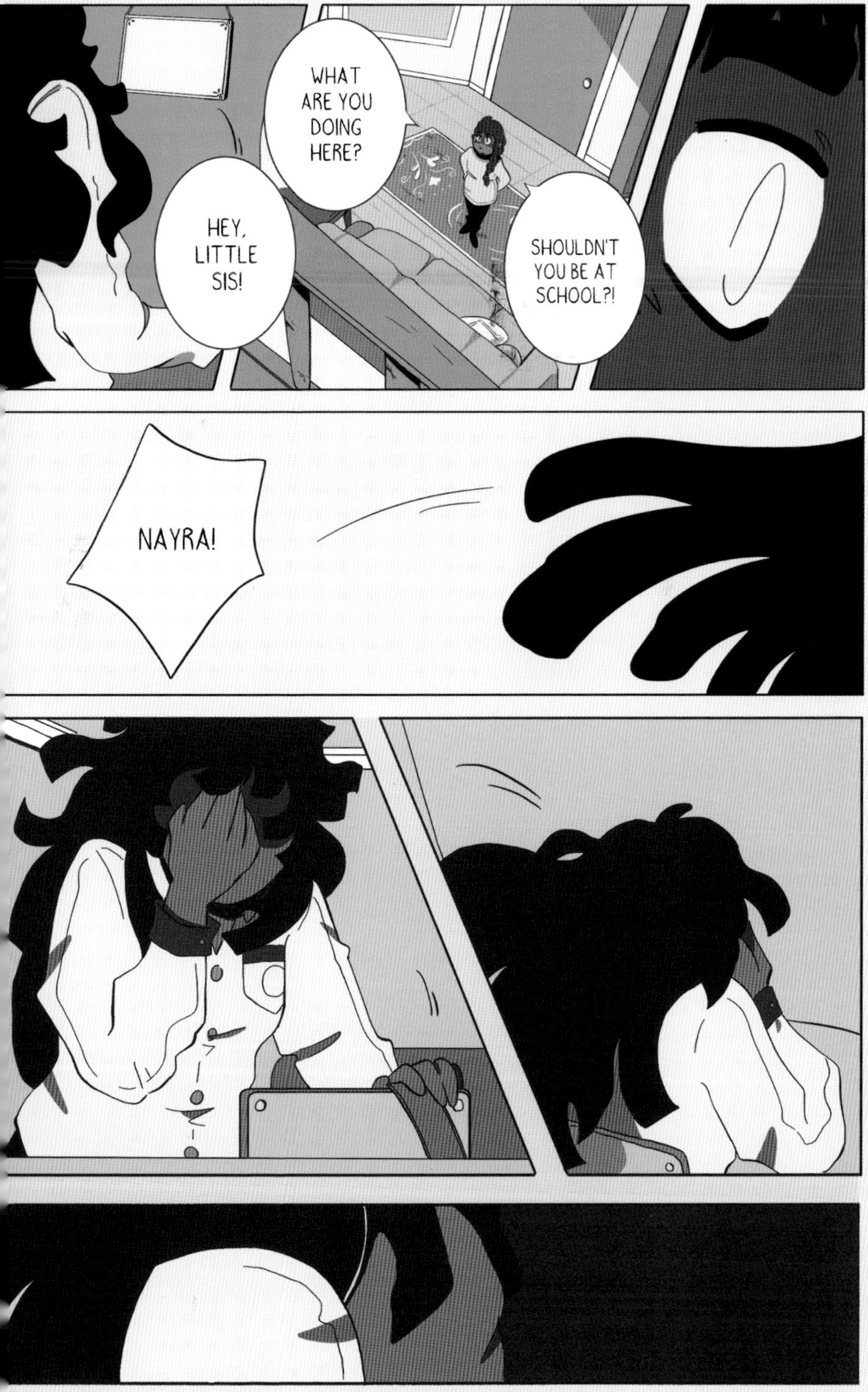
HEY, LITTLE SIS!
WHAT ARE YOU DOING HERE?
SHOULDN'T YOU BE AT SCHOOL?!
NAYRA!

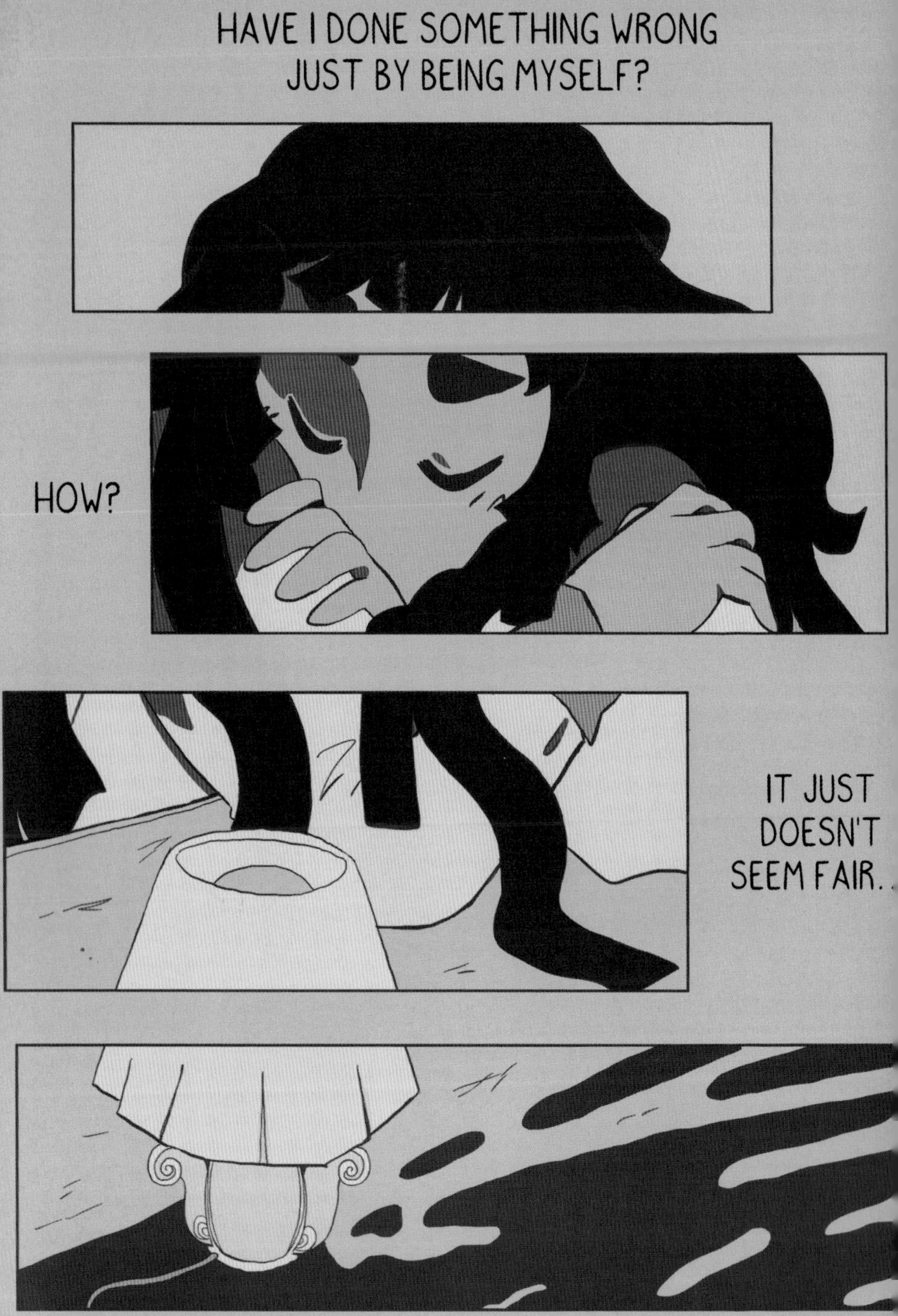
HAVE I DONE SOMETHING WRONG JUST BY BEING MYSELF?
HOW?
IT JUST DOESN'T SEEM FAIR...

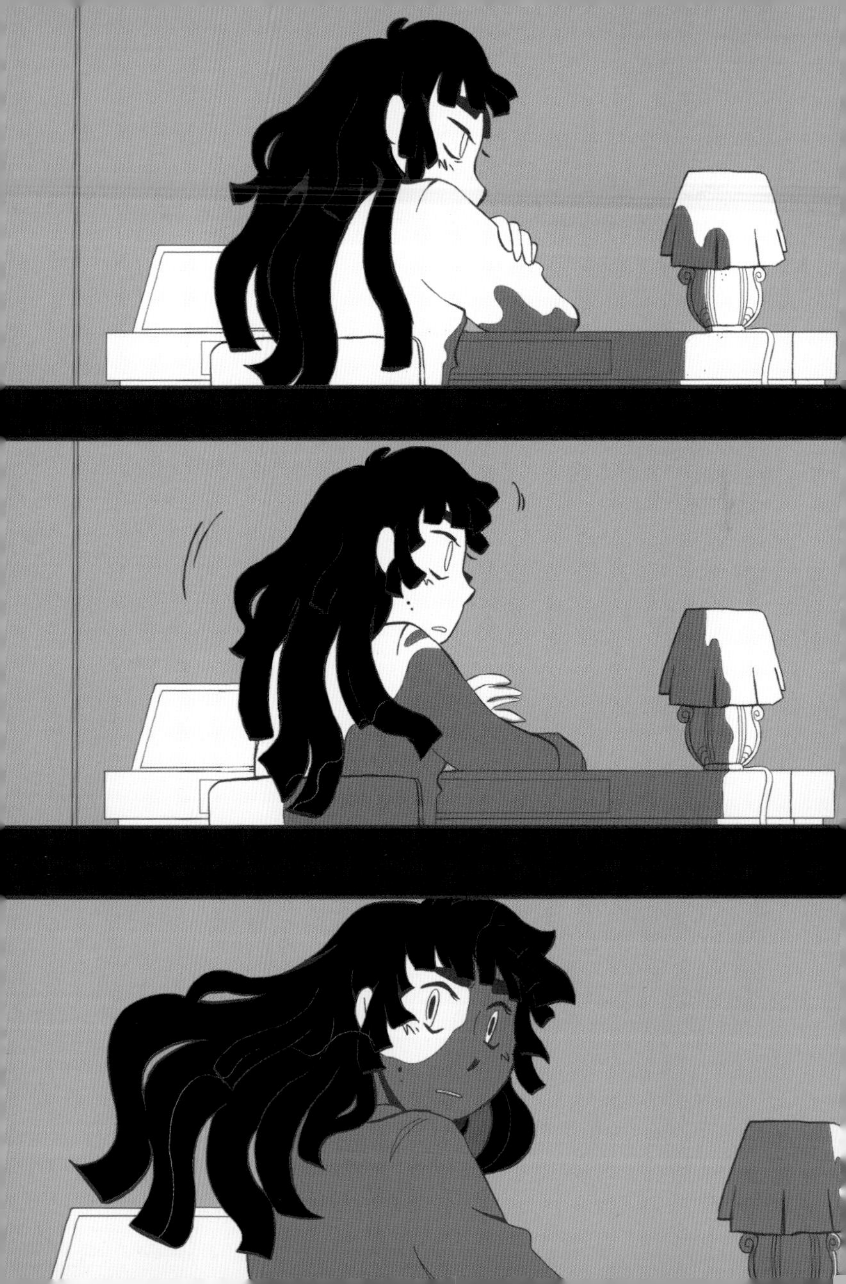

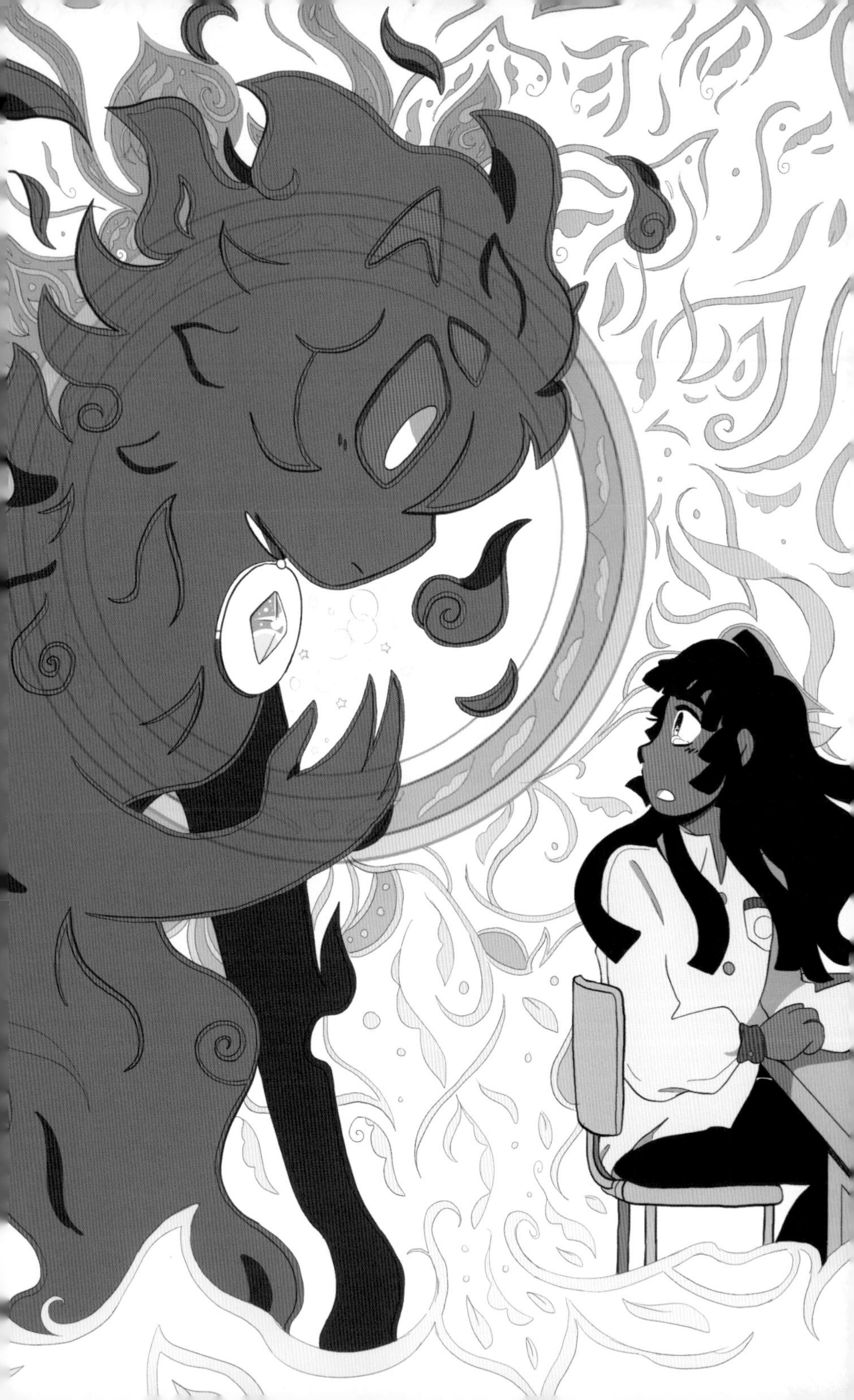

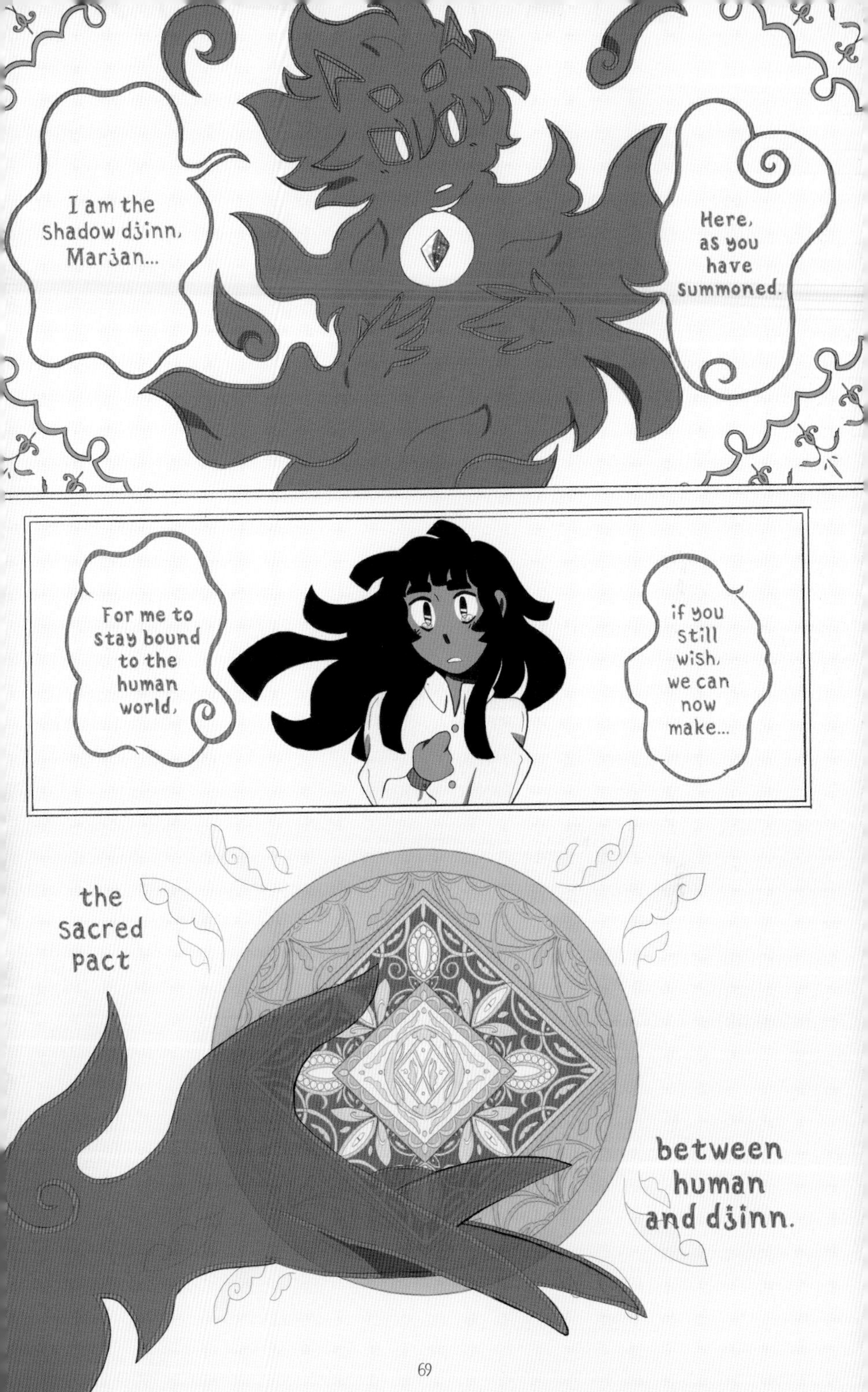
I am the shadow djinn, Marjan...
Here, as you have summoned.
For me to stay bound to the human world,
if you still wish, we can now make...
the sacred pact
between human and djinn.

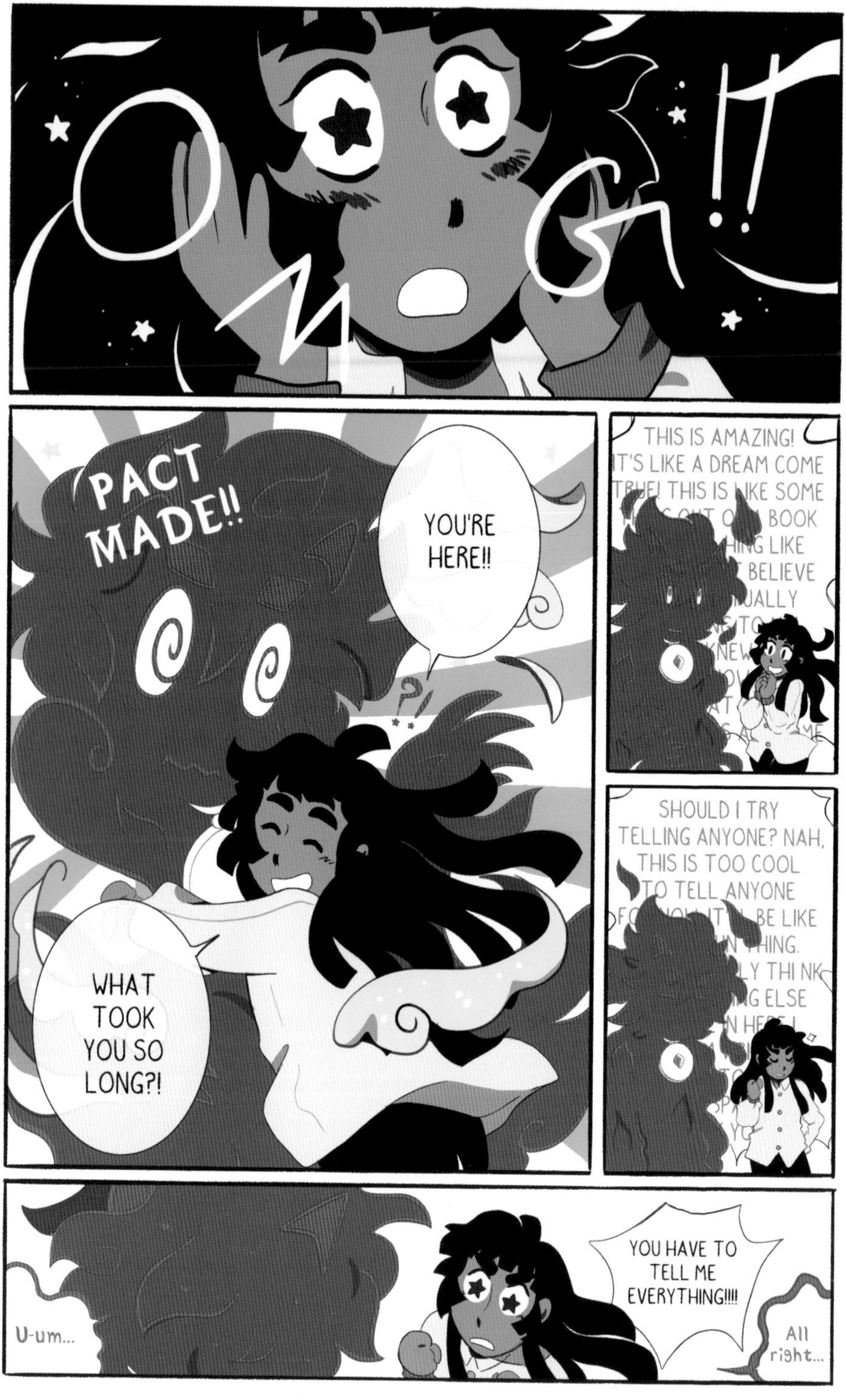
OMG!!
PACT MADE!!
YOU'RE HERE!!
WHAT TOOK YOU SO LONG?!
THIS IS AMAZING!
IT'S LIKE A DREAM COME
SHOULD I TRY TELLING ANYONE? NAH, THIS IS TOO COOL TO TELL ANYONE
U-um...
YOU HAVE TO TELL ME EVERYTHING!!!!
All right...

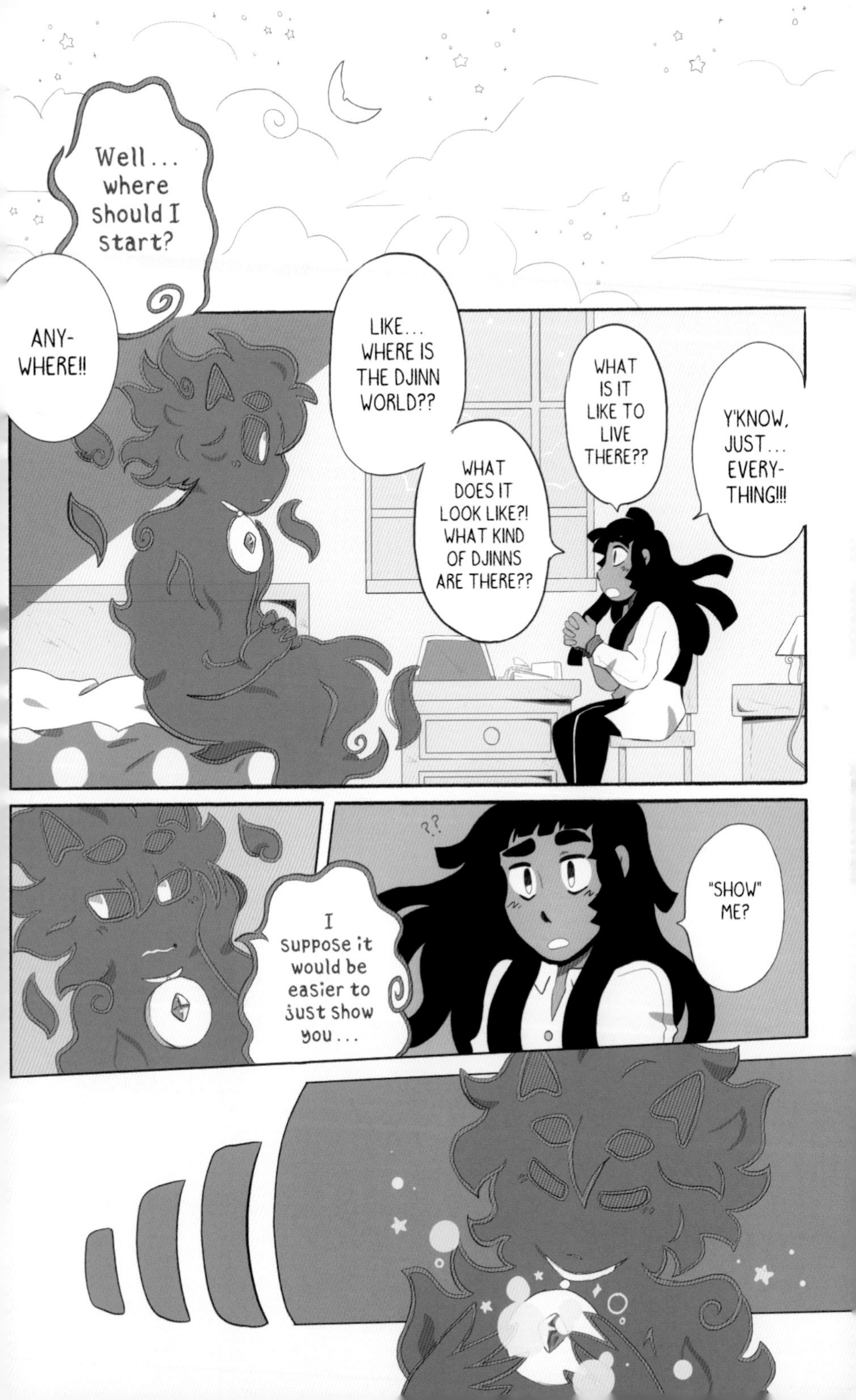
Well... where should I start?
ANY-WHERE!!
LIKE... WHERE IS THE DJINN WORLD??
WHAT DOES IT LOOK LIKE?! WHAT KIND OF DJINNS ARE THERE??
WHAT IS IT LIKE TO LIVE THERE??
Y'KNOW, JUST... EVERY-THING!!!
??
I suppose it would be easier to just show you...
"SHOW" ME?

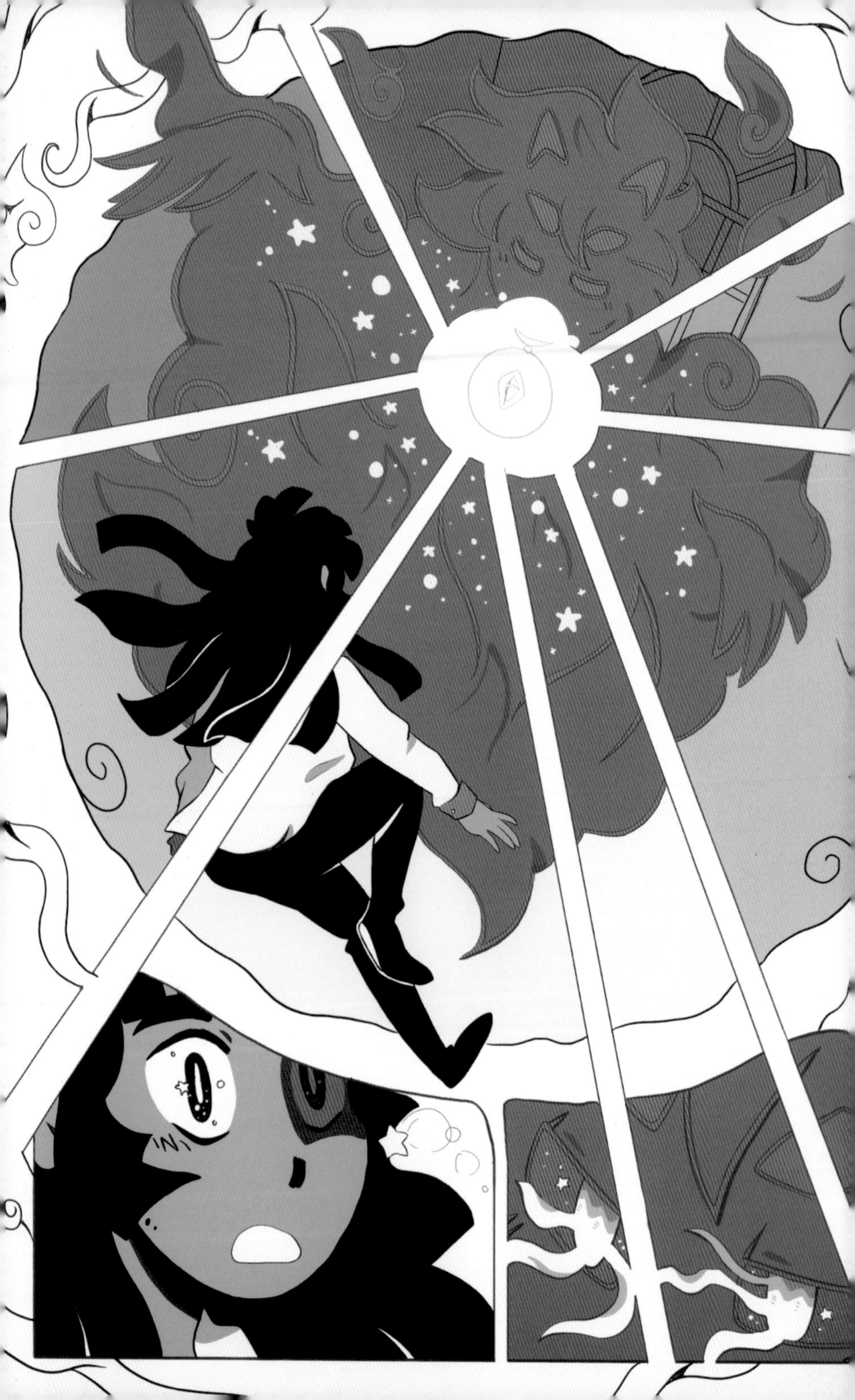

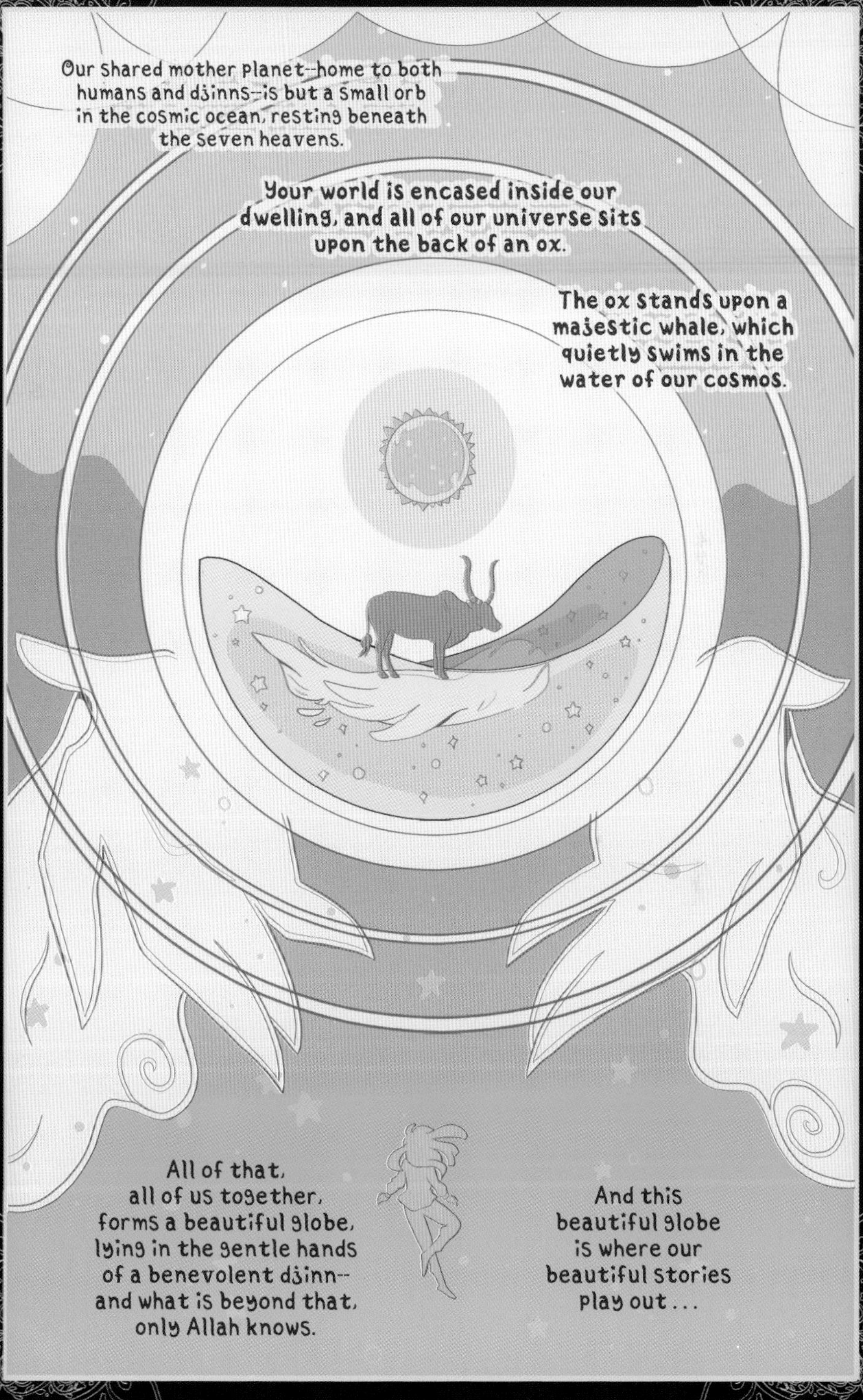
Our shared mother planet--home to both humans and djinns--is but a small orb in the cosmic ocean, resting beneath the seven heavens.
Your world is encased inside our dwelling, and all of our universe sits upon the back of an ox.
The ox stands upon a majestic whale, which quietly swims in the water of our cosmos.
All of that, all of us together, forms a beautiful globe, lying in the gentle hands of a benevolent djinn-- and what is beyond that, only Allah knows.
And this beautiful globe is where our beautiful stories play out . . .

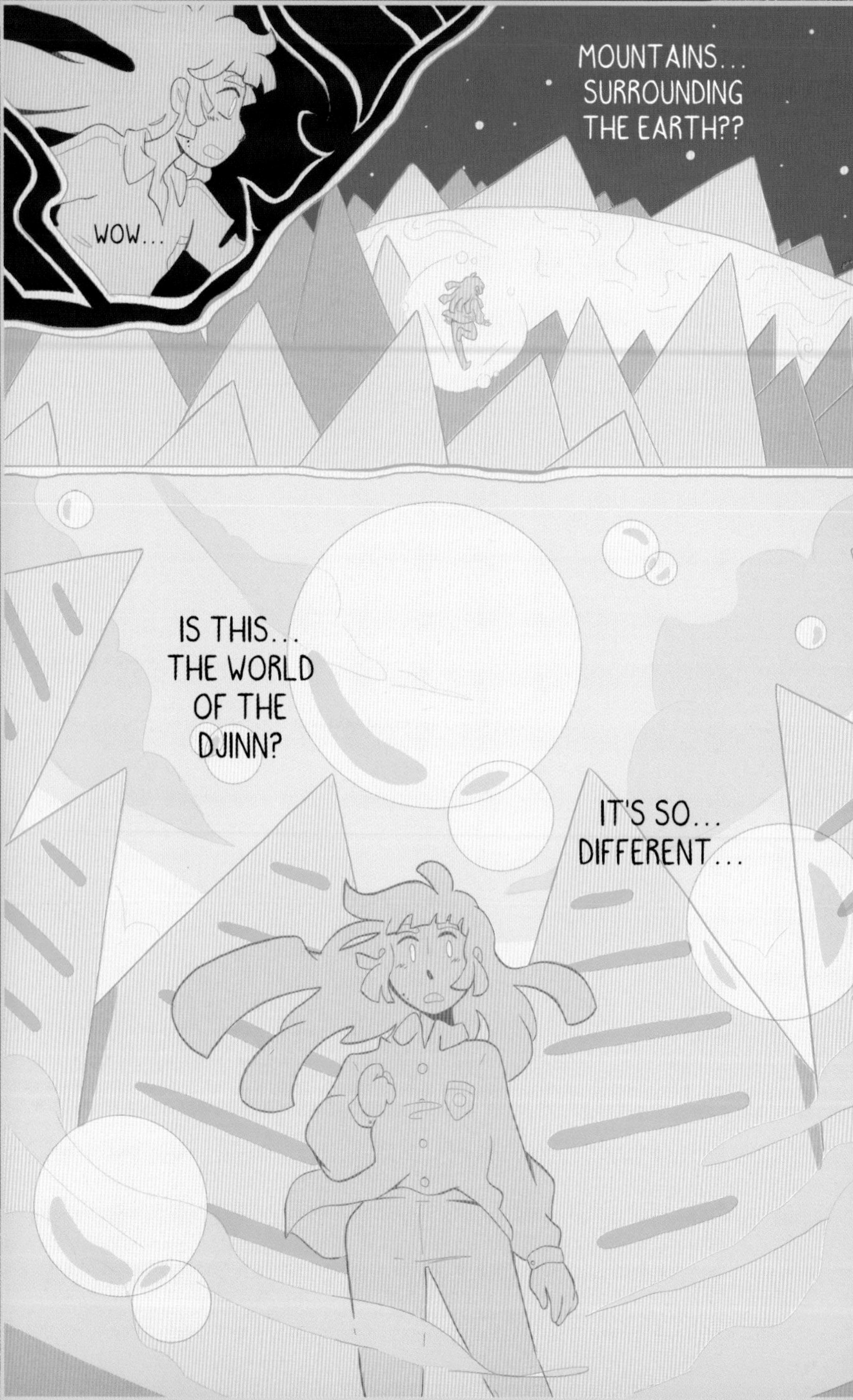
MOUNTAINS... SURROUNDING THE EARTH??
WOW...
IS THIS... THE WORLD OF THE DJINN?
IT'S SO... DIFFERENT...

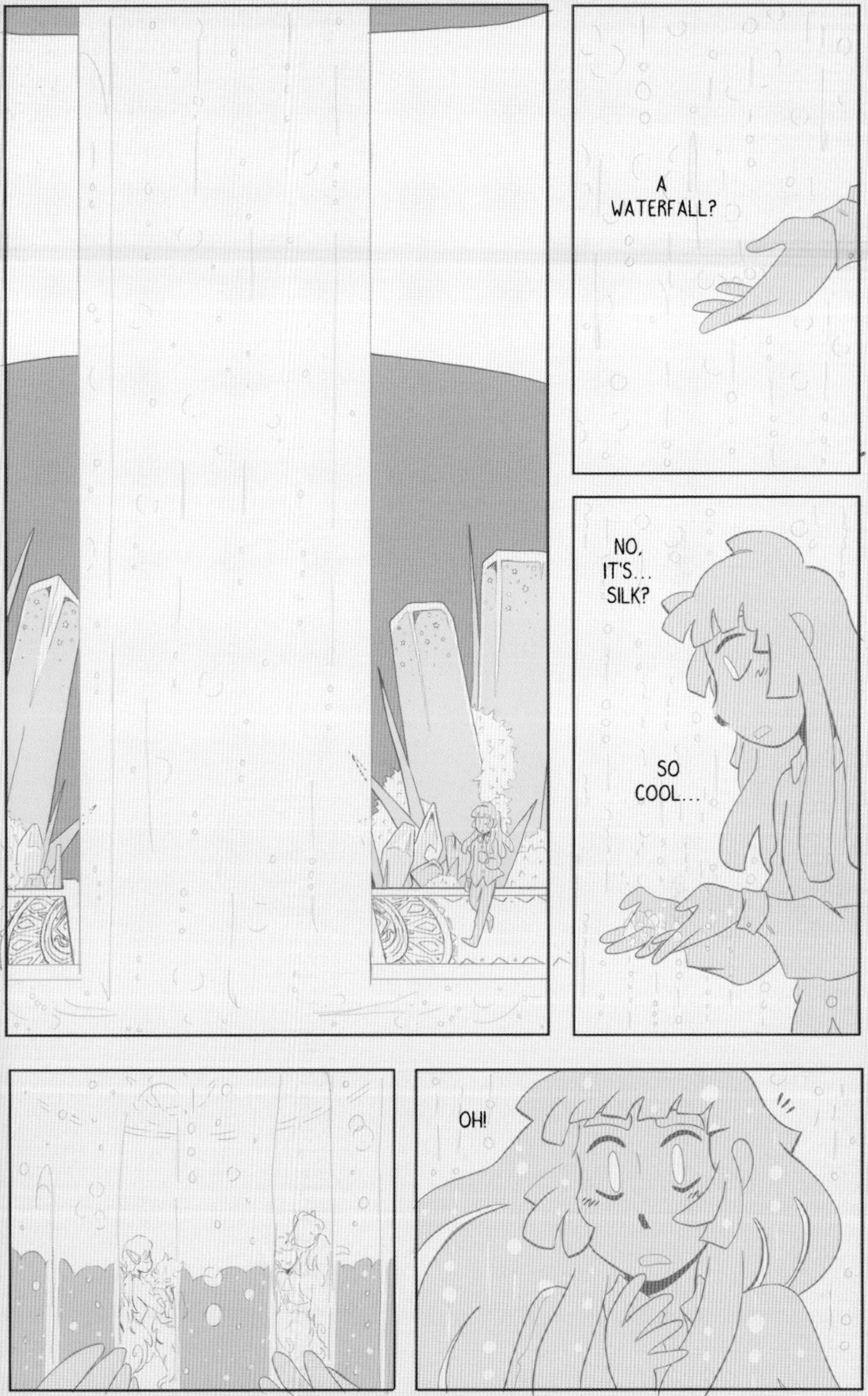
A WATERFALL?
NO, IT'S... SILK?
SO COOL...
OH!

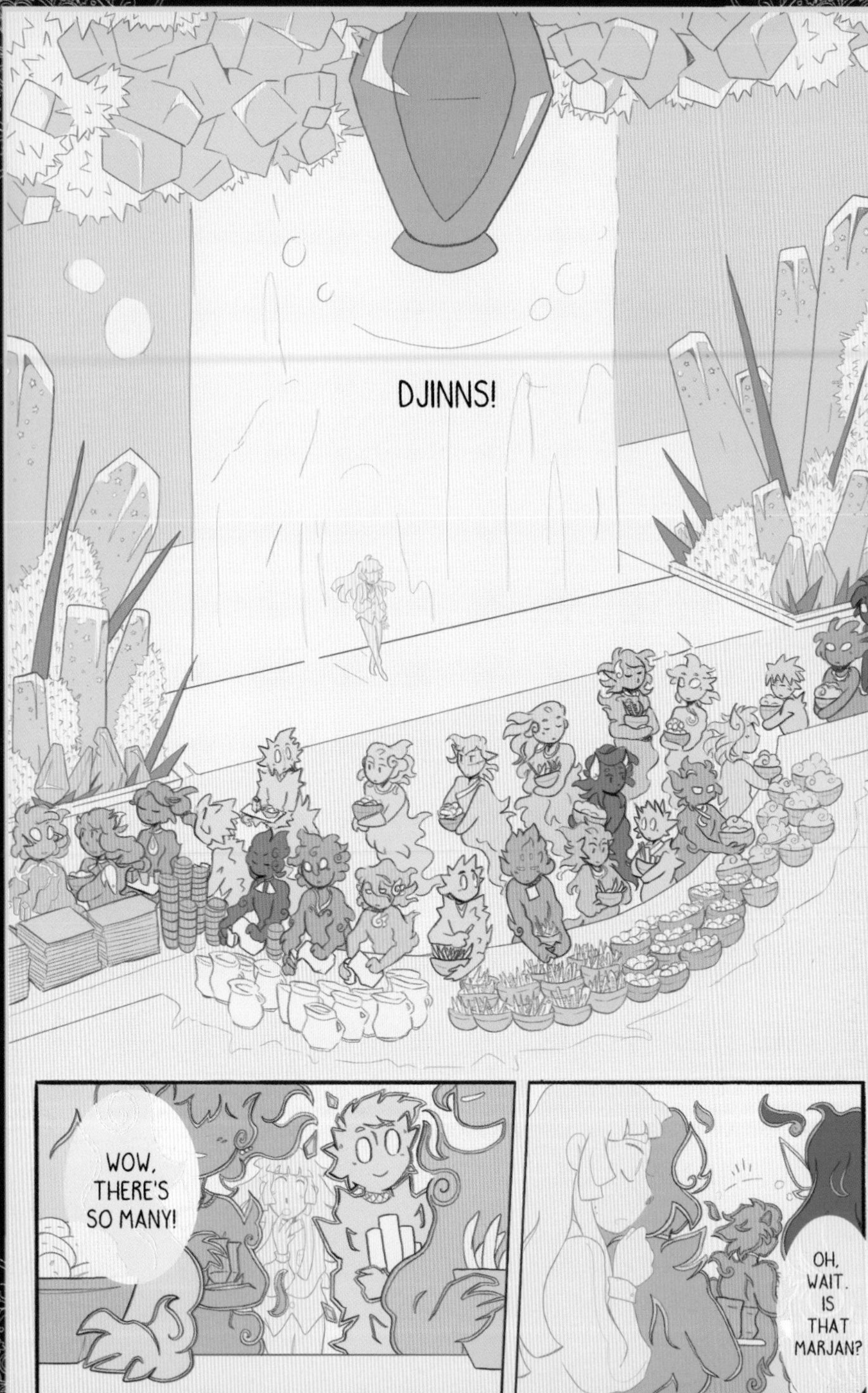
DJINNS!
WOW, THERE'S SO MANY!
OH, WAIT. IS THAT MARJAN?

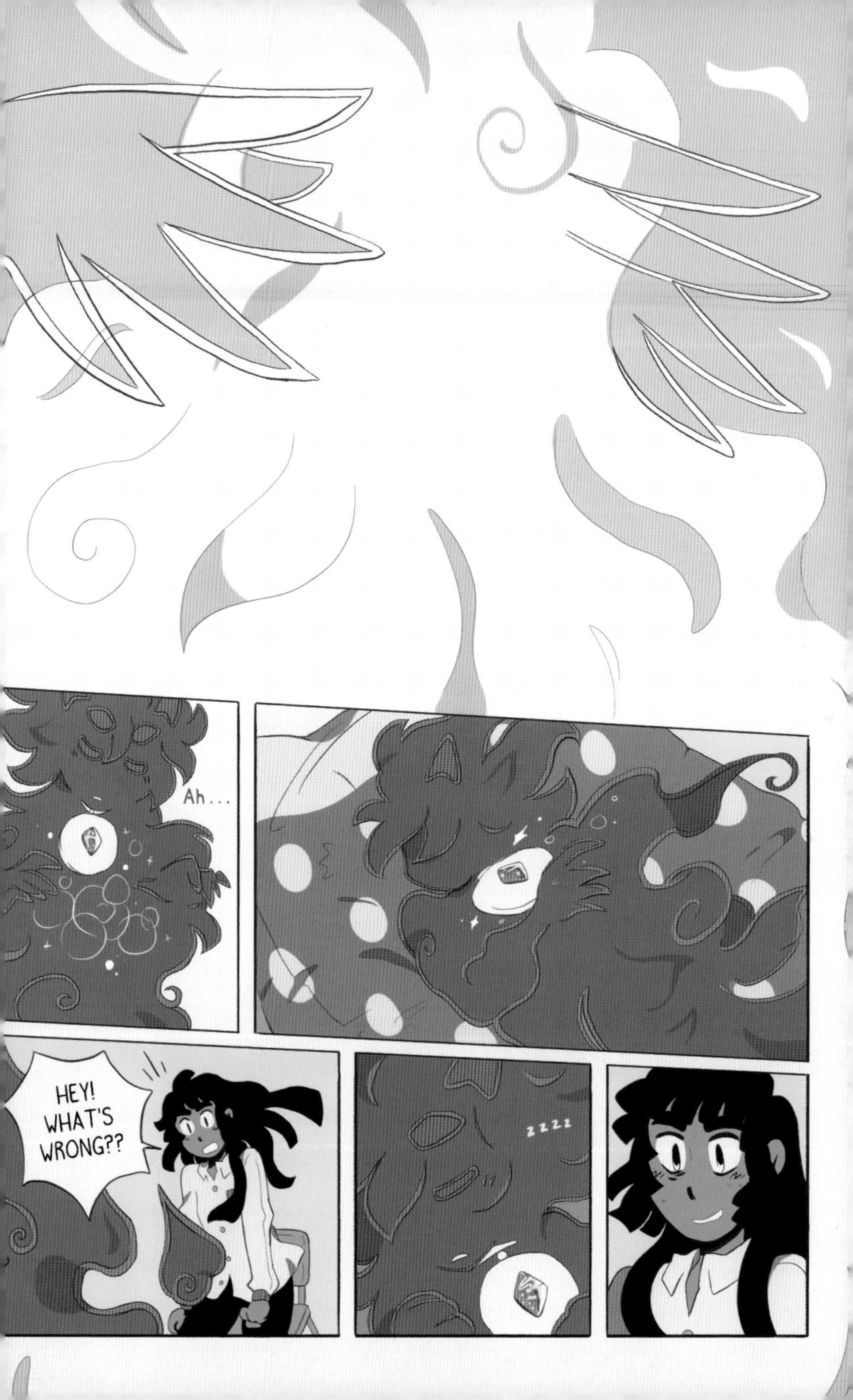
Ah...
HEY! WHAT'S WRONG??
zzzz

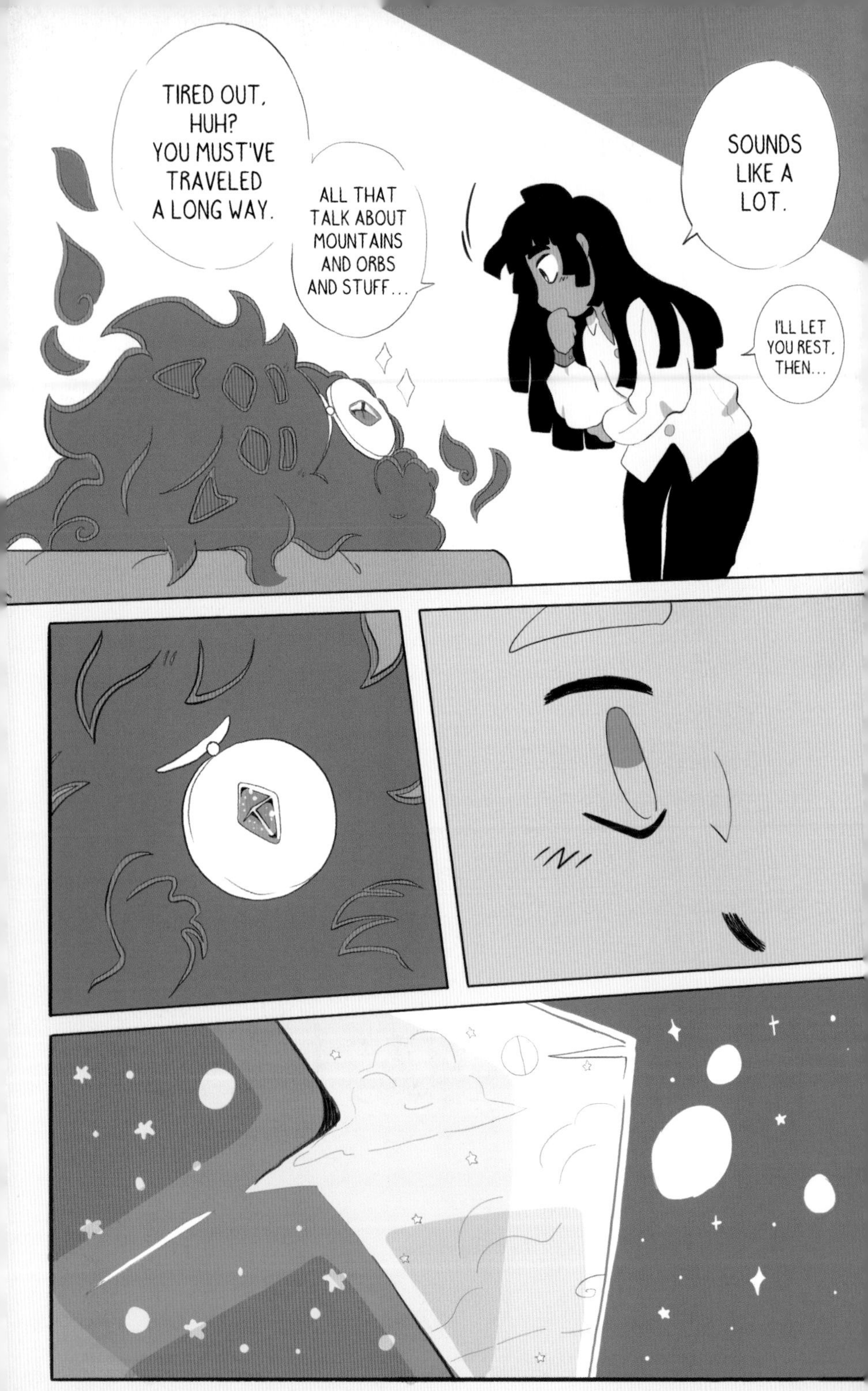
TIRED OUT, HUH? YOU MUST'VE TRAVELED A LONG WAY.
ALL THAT TALK ABOUT MOUNTAINS AND ORBS AND STUFF...
SOUNDS LIKE A LOT.
I'LL LET YOU REST, THEN...

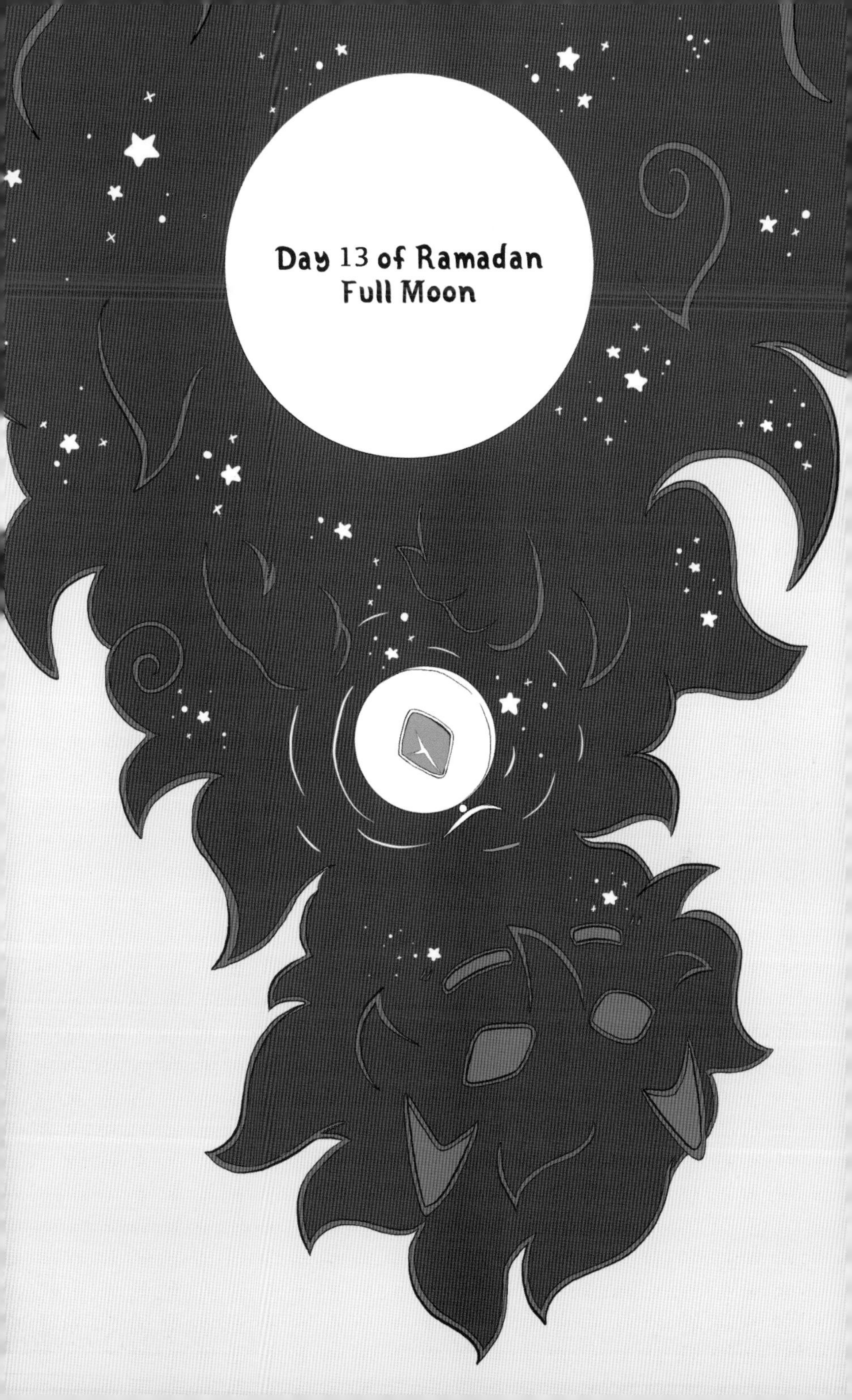
Day 13 of Ramadan
Full Moon

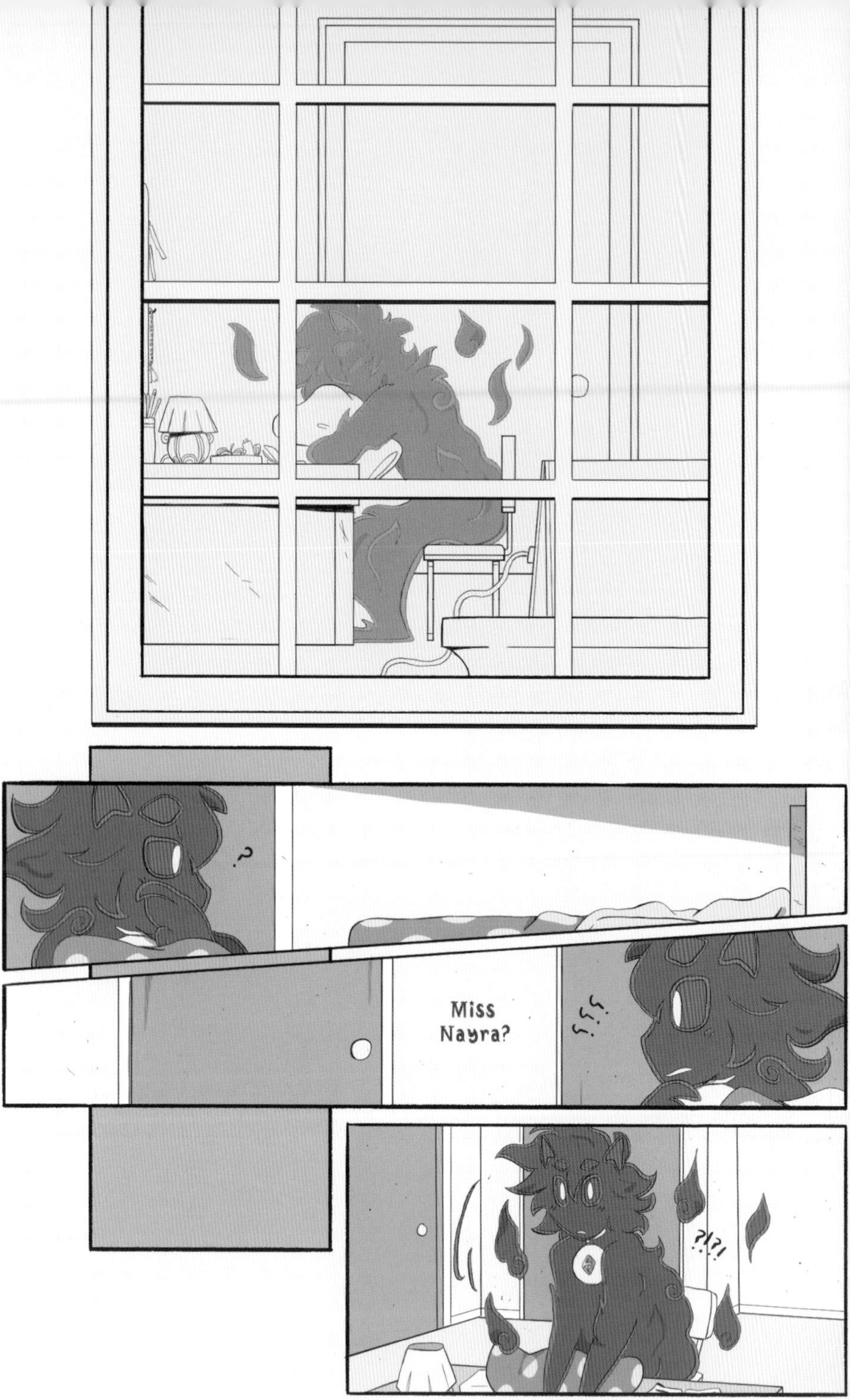
?
Miss Nayra?
?!?!

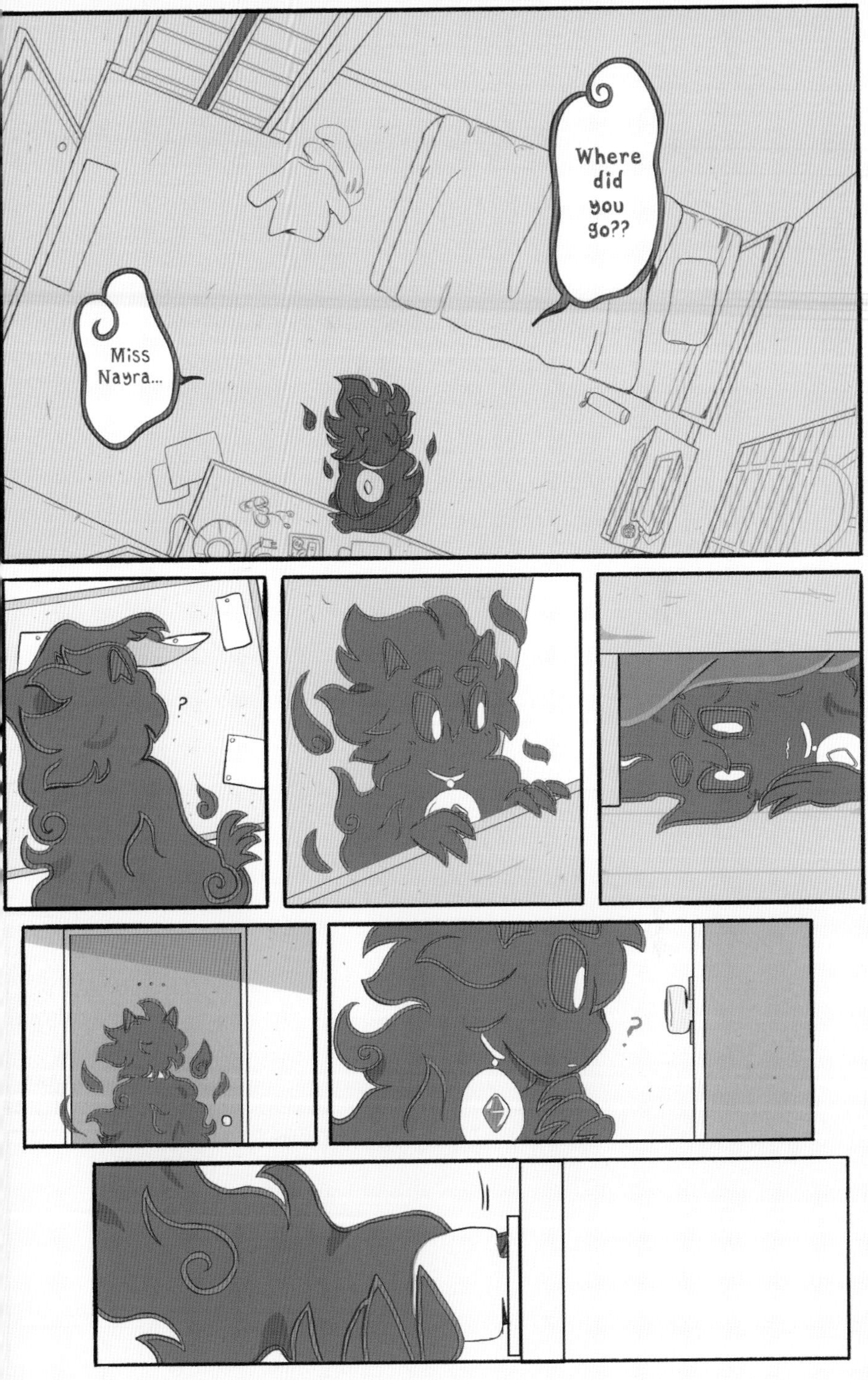
Where did you go??
Miss Nayra...
?
...
?

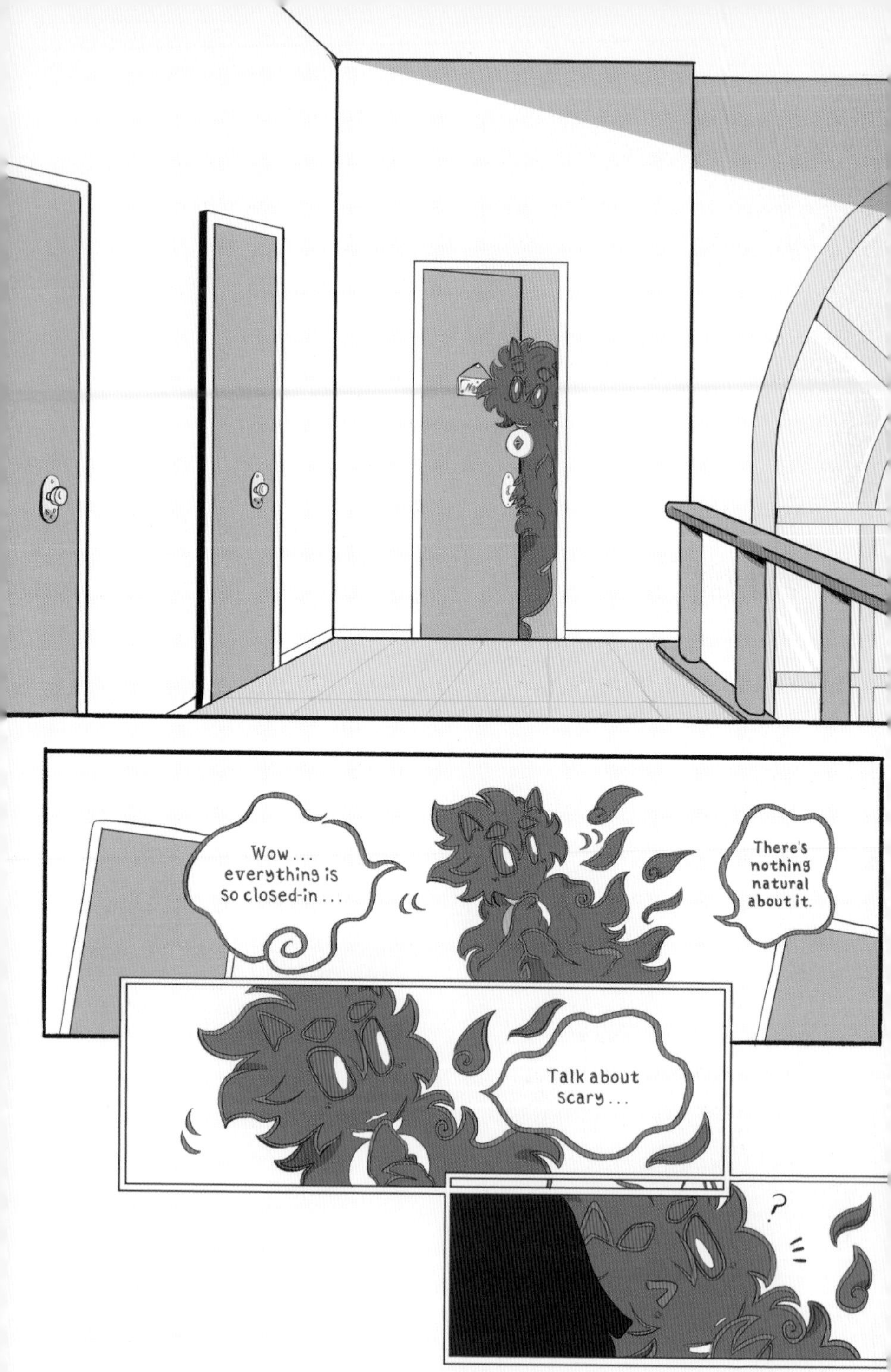
Wow... everything is so closed-in...
There's nothing natural about it.
Talk about scary...
?

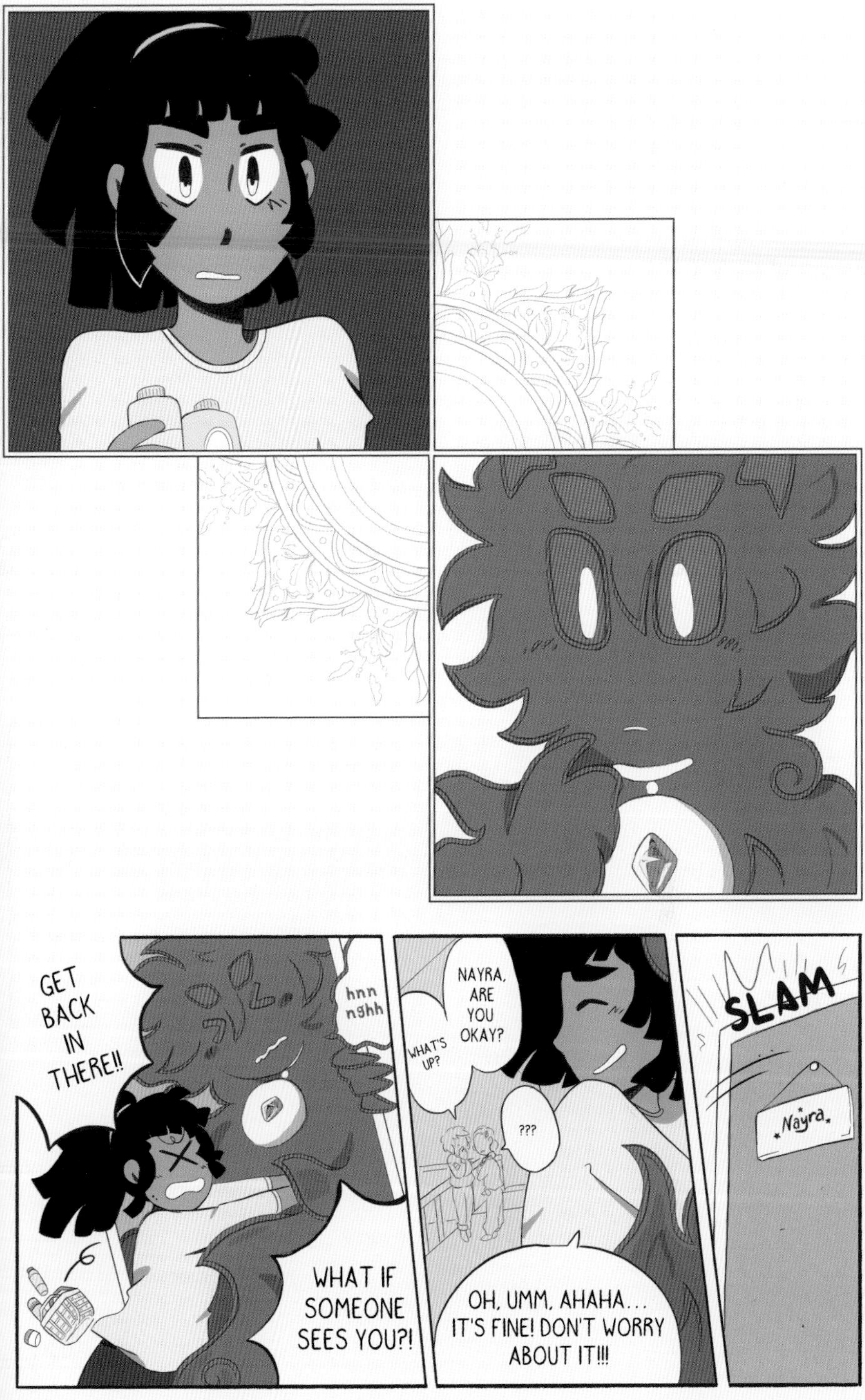
GET BACK IN THERE!!
hnn nghh
WHAT IF SOMEONE SEES YOU?!
NAYRA, ARE YOU OKAY?
WHAT'S UP?
???
OH, UMM, AHAHA... IT'S FINE! DON'T WORRY ABOUT IT!!!
SLAM
Nayra

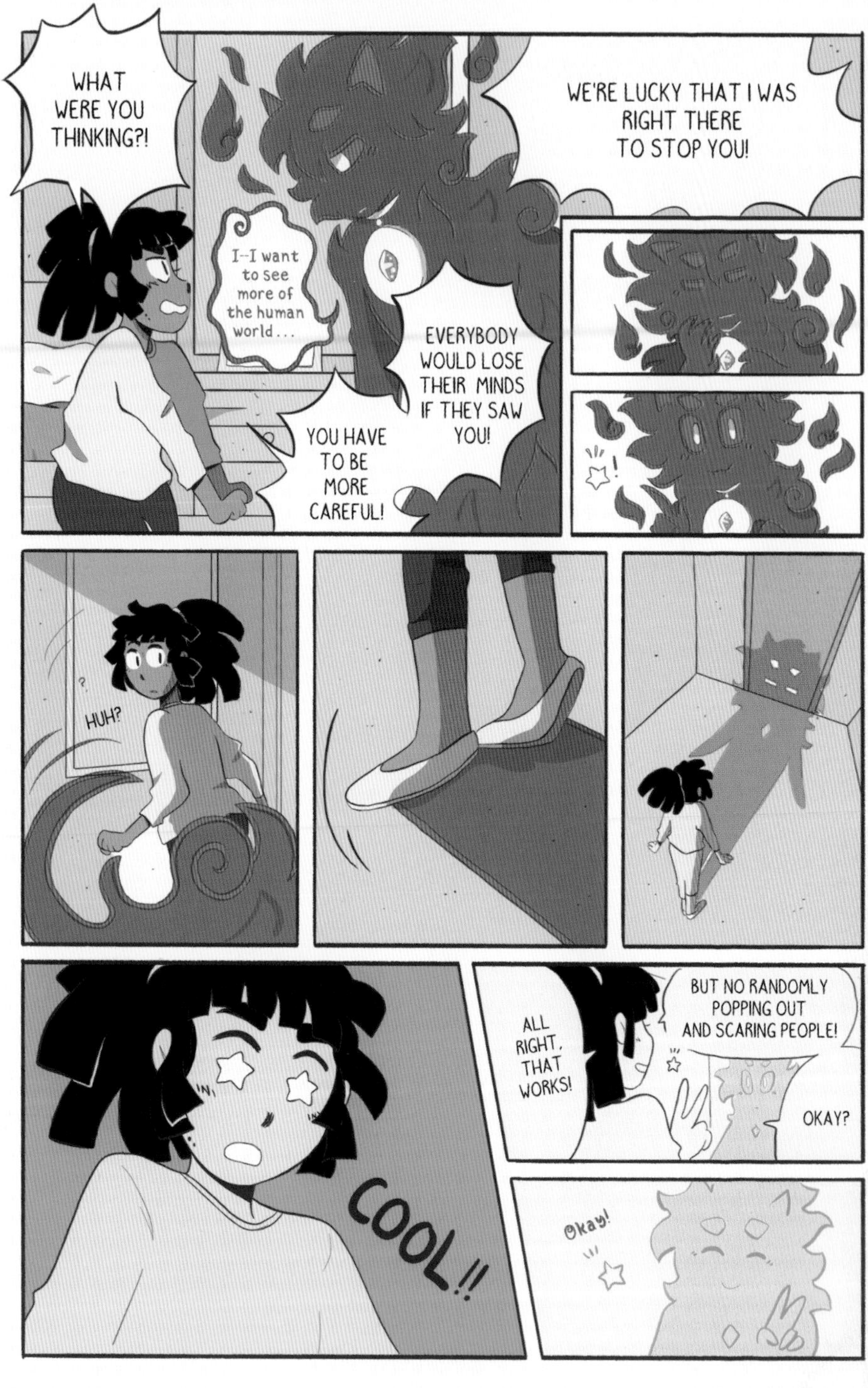
WHAT WERE YOU THINKING?!
WE'RE LUCKY THAT I WAS RIGHT THERE TO STOP YOU!
I--I want to see more of the human world...
EVERYBODY WOULD LOSE THEIR MINDS IF THEY SAW YOU!
YOU HAVE TO BE MORE CAREFUL!
!
HUH?
COOL!!
BUT NO RANDOMLY POPPING OUT AND SCARING PEOPLE!
OKAY?
ALL RIGHT, THAT WORKS!
Okay!

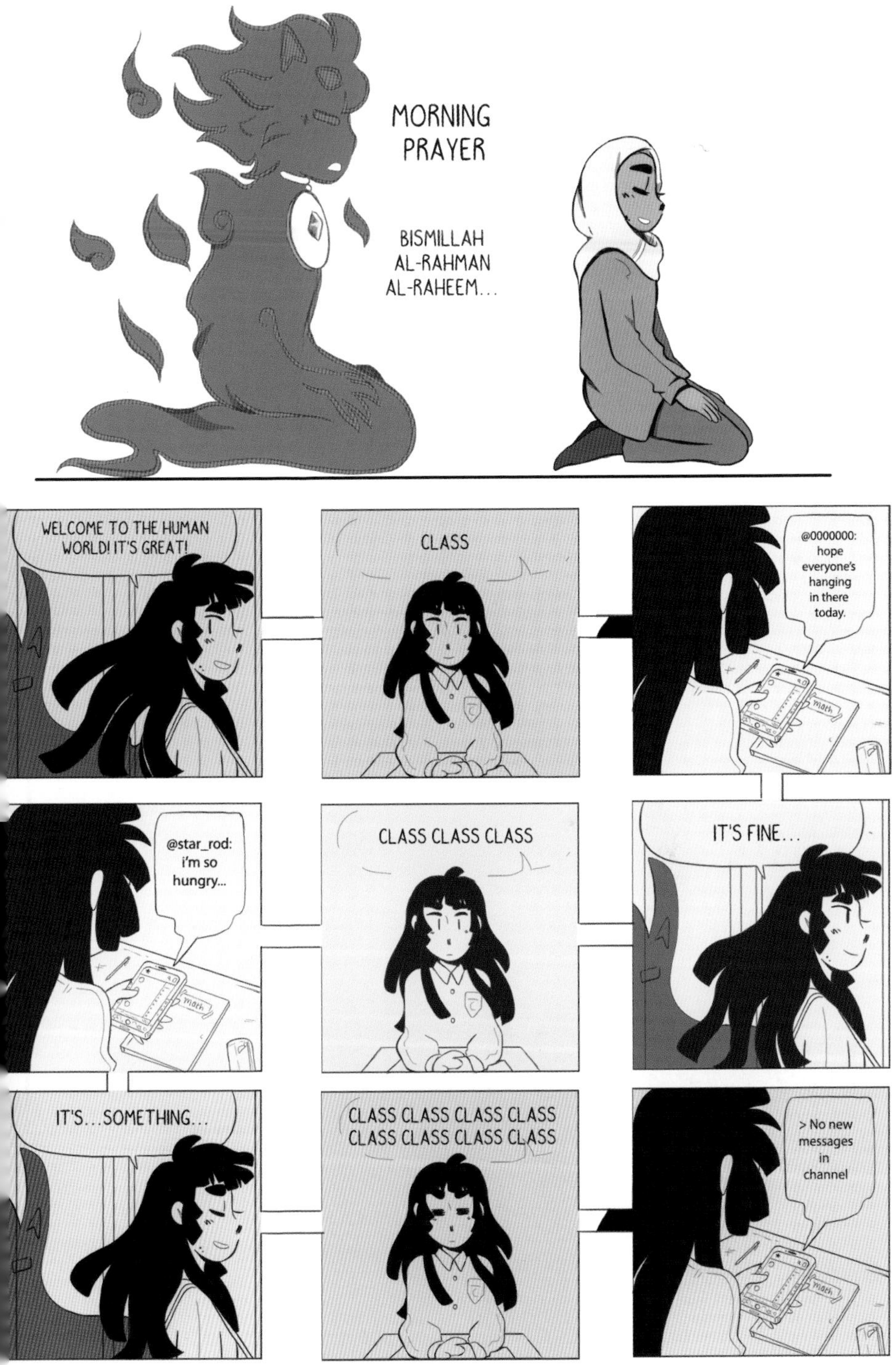
MORNING PRAYER
BISMILLAH AL-RAHMAN AL-RAHEEM...
WELCOME TO THE HUMAN WORLD! IT'S GREAT!
CLASS
@0000000: hope everyone's hanging in there today.
@star_rod: i'm so hungry...
CLASS CLASS CLASS
IT'S FINE...
IT'S...SOMETHING...
CLASS CLASS CLASS CLASS CLASS CLASS CLASS CLASS
> No new messages in channel

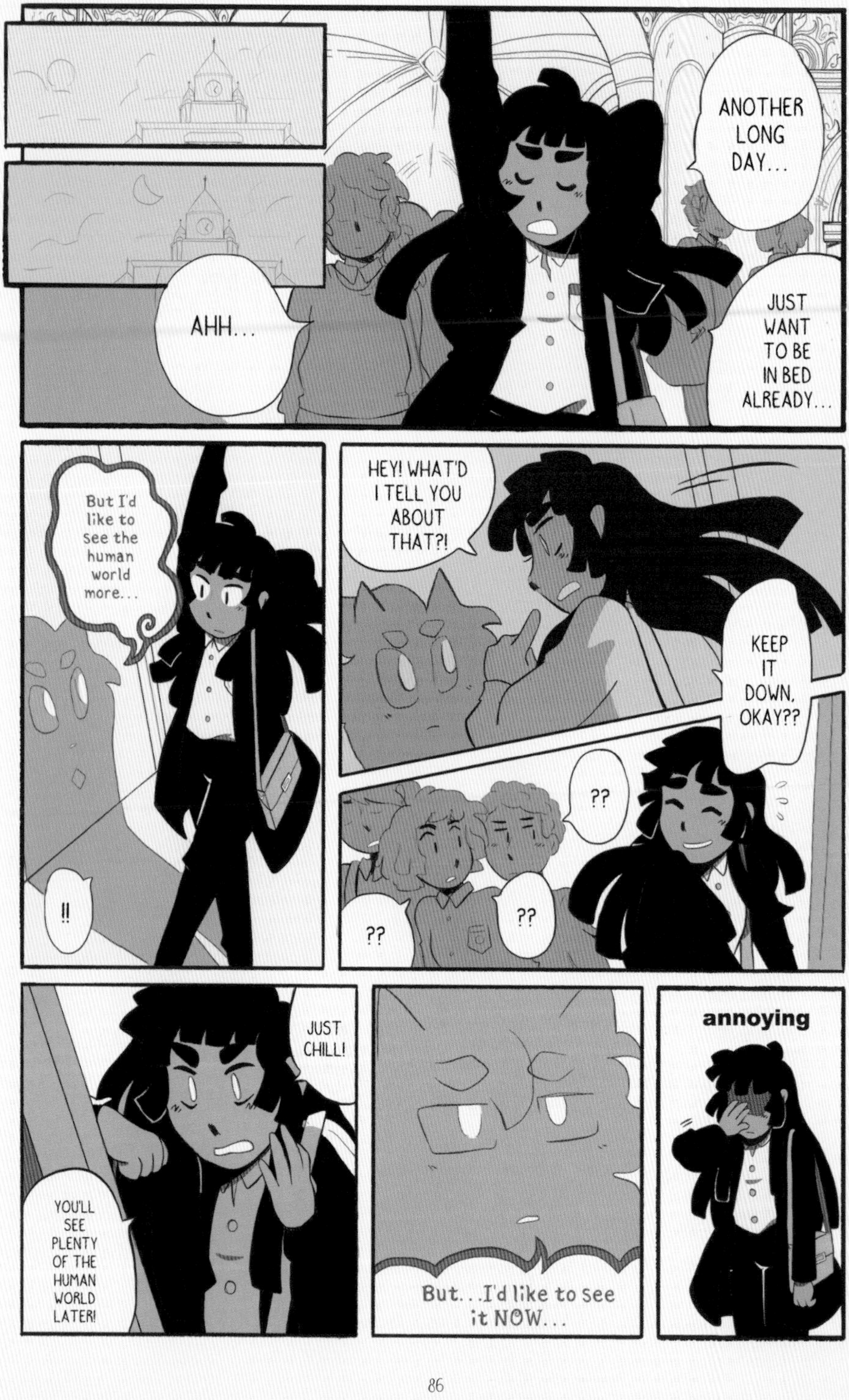
ANOTHER LONG DAY...
AHH...
JUST WANT TO BE IN BED ALREADY...
But I'd like to see the human world more...
!!
HEY! WHAT'D I TELL YOU ABOUT THAT?!
KEEP IT DOWN, OKAY??
??
??
??
JUST CHILL!
YOU'LL SEE PLENTY OF THE HUMAN WORLD LATER!
But...I'd like to see it NOW...
annoying

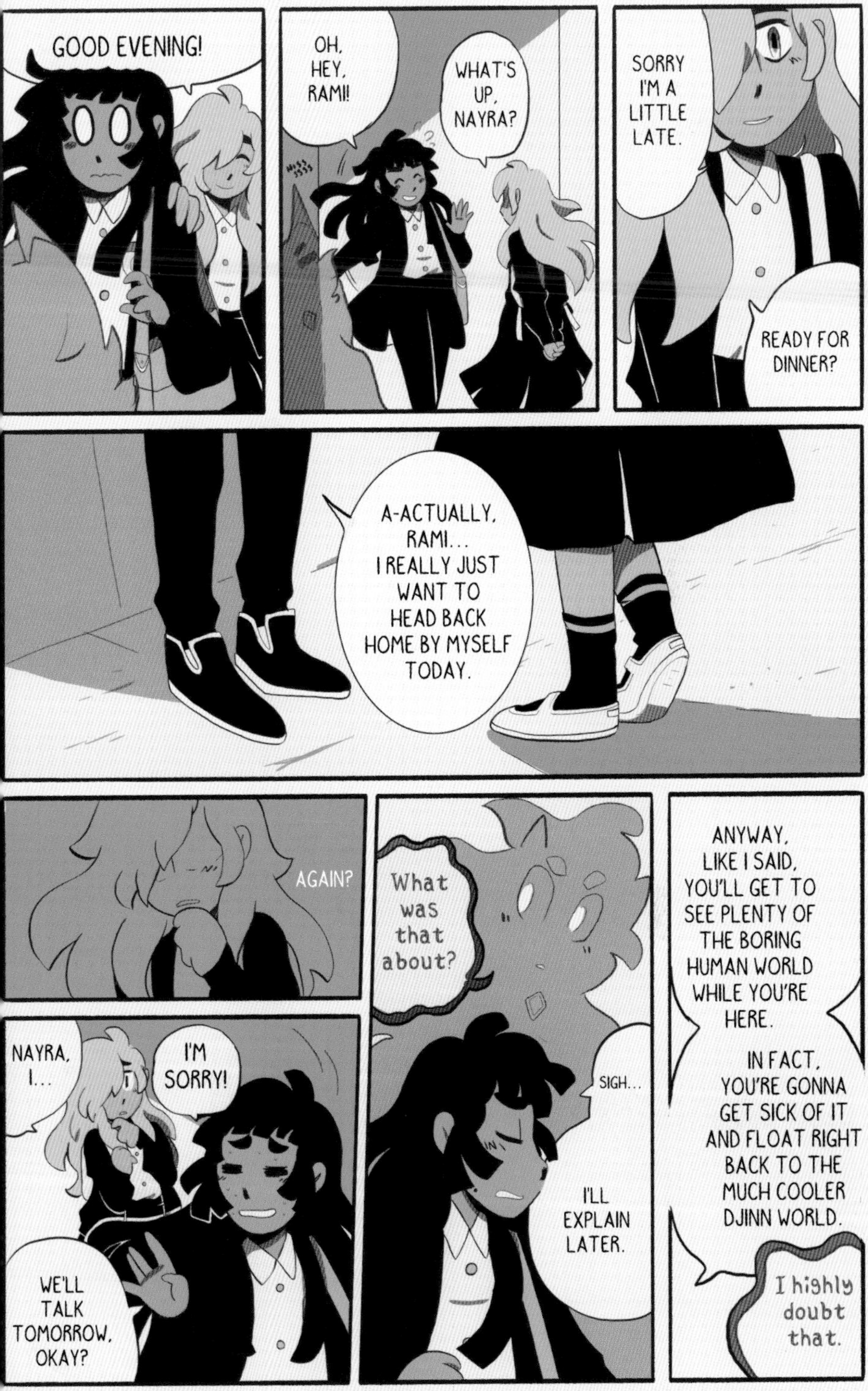
GOOD EVENING!
OH, HEY, RAMI!
WHAT'S UP, NAYRA?
SORRY I'M A LITTLE LATE.
READY FOR DINNER?
A-ACTUALLY, RAMI... I REALLY JUST WANT TO HEAD BACK HOME BY MYSELF TODAY.
AGAIN?
What was that about?
ANYWAY, LIKE I SAID, YOU'LL GET TO SEE PLENTY OF THE BORING HUMAN WORLD WHILE YOU'RE HERE.
IN FACT, YOU'RE GONNA GET SICK OF IT AND FLOAT RIGHT BACK TO THE MUCH COOLER DJINN WORLD.
I highly doubt that.
NAYRA, I...
I'M SORRY!
WE'LL TALK TOMORROW, OKAY?
SIGH...
I'LL EXPLAIN LATER.

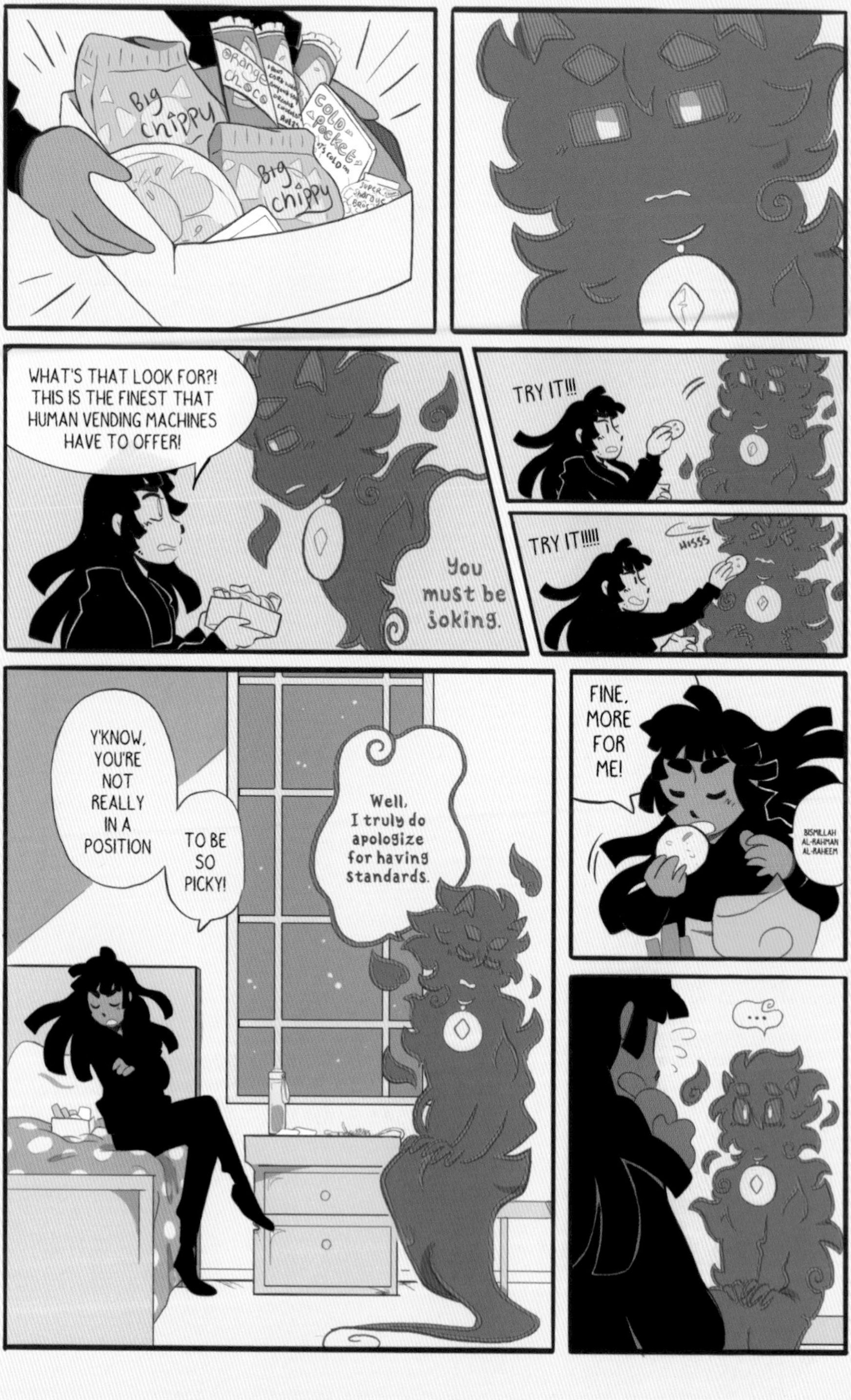
Big chippy
Orange choco
Cold Pocket
it's cold™
Big chippy
WHAT'S THAT LOOK FOR?! THIS IS THE FINEST THAT HUMAN VENDING MACHINES HAVE TO OFFER!
You must be joking.
TRY IT!!!
TRY IT!!!!!
HISSS
Y'KNOW, YOU'RE NOT REALLY IN A POSITION
TO BE SO PICKY!
Well, I truly do apologize for having standards.
FINE, MORE FOR ME!
BISMILLAH AL-RAHMAN AL-RAHEEM
...

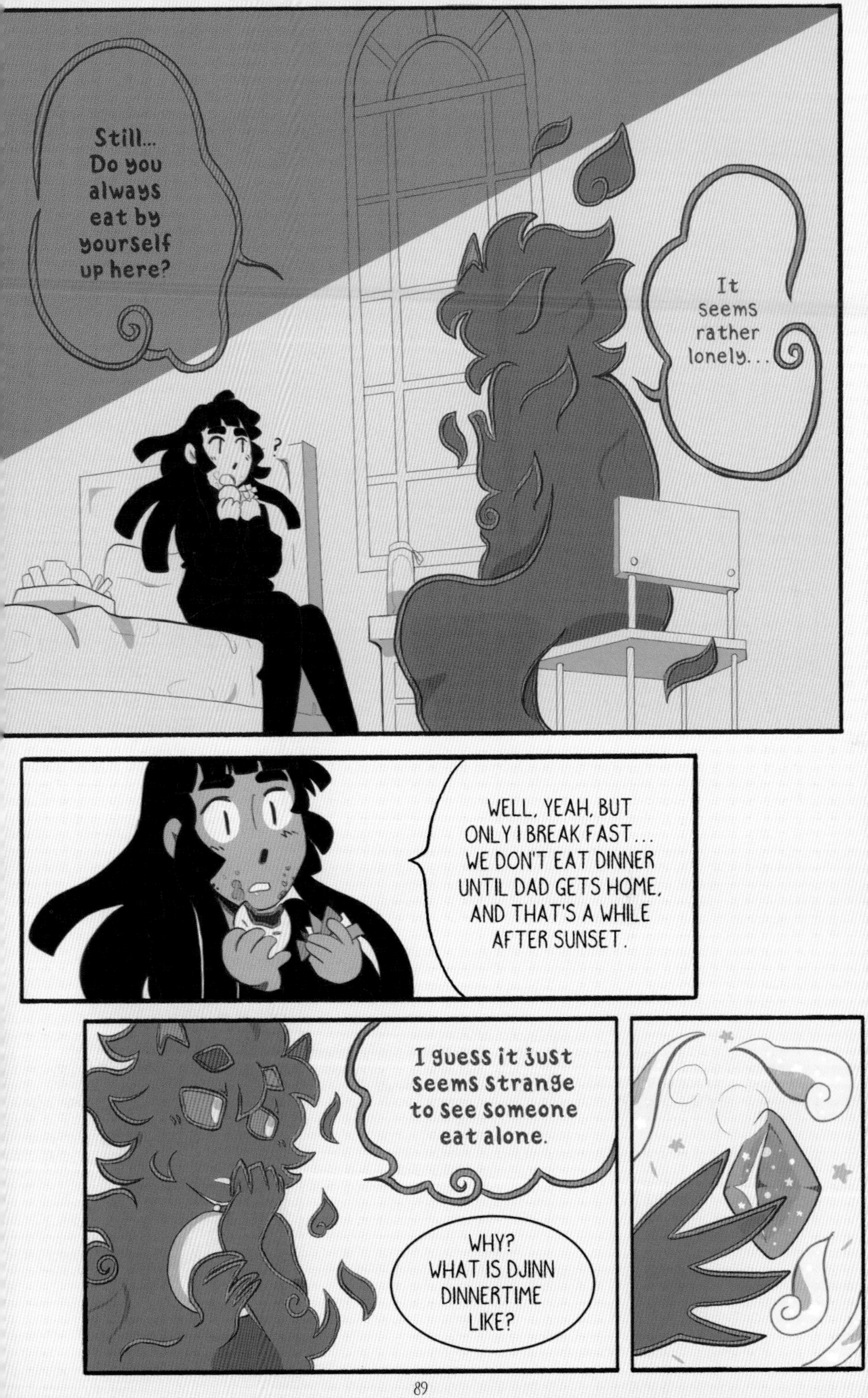
Still... Do you always eat by yourself up here?
It seems rather lonely...
WELL, YEAH, BUT ONLY BREAKFAST... WE DON'T EAT DINNER UNTIL DAD GETS HOME, AND THAT'S A WHILE AFTER SUNSET.
I guess it just seems strange to see someone eat alone.
WHY? WHAT IS DJINN DINNERTIME LIKE?

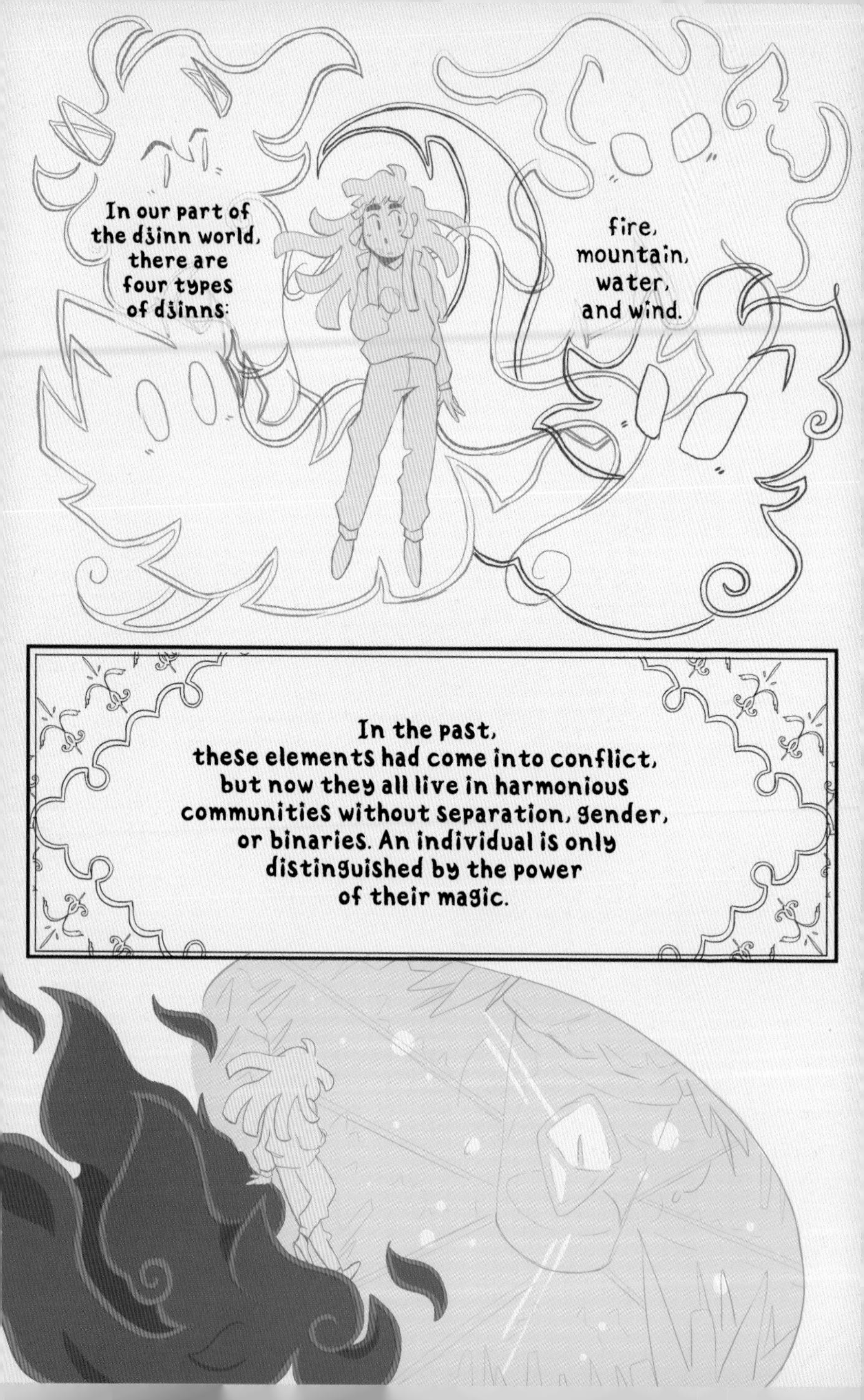
In our part of the djinn world, there are four types of djinns:
fire, mountain, water, and wind.
In the past, these elements had come into conflict, but now they all live in harmonious communities without separation, gender, or binaries. An individual is only distinguished by the power of their magic.

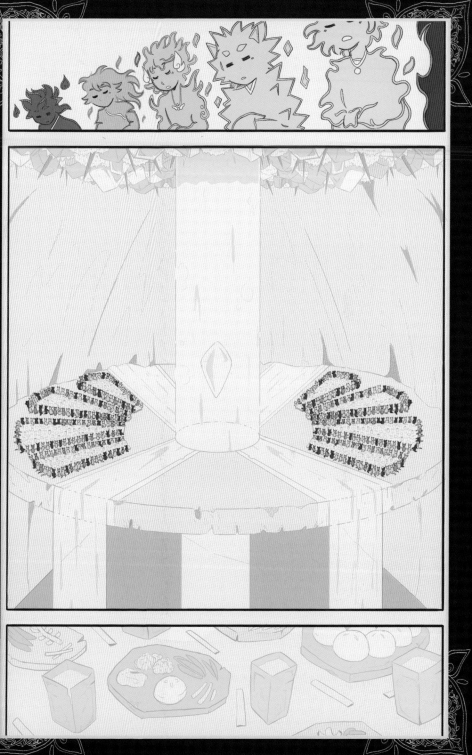

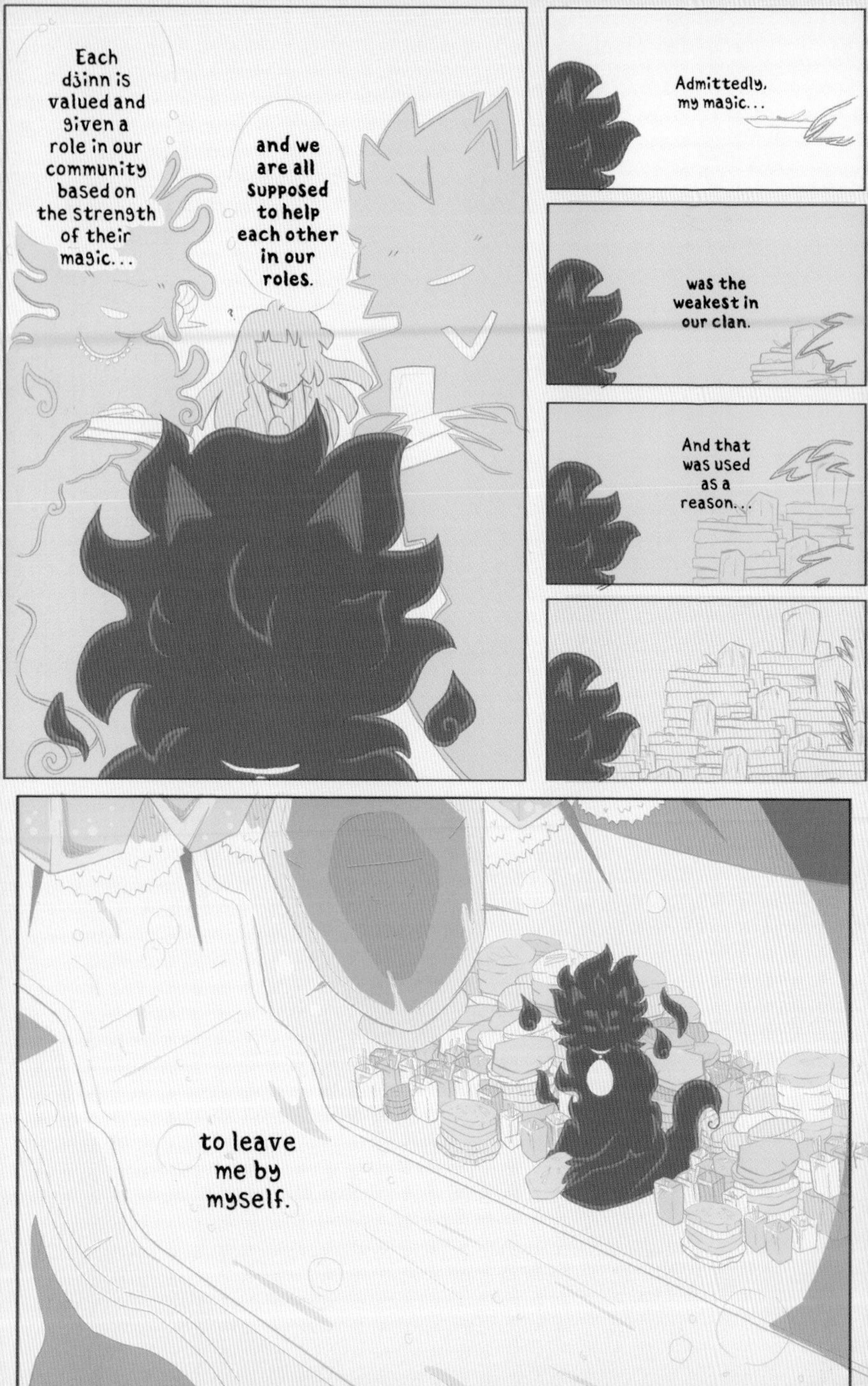
Each djinn is valued and given a role in our community based on the strength of their magic...
and we are all supposed to help each other in our roles.
Admittedly, my magic...
was the weakest in our clan.
And that was used as a reason...
to leave me by myself.

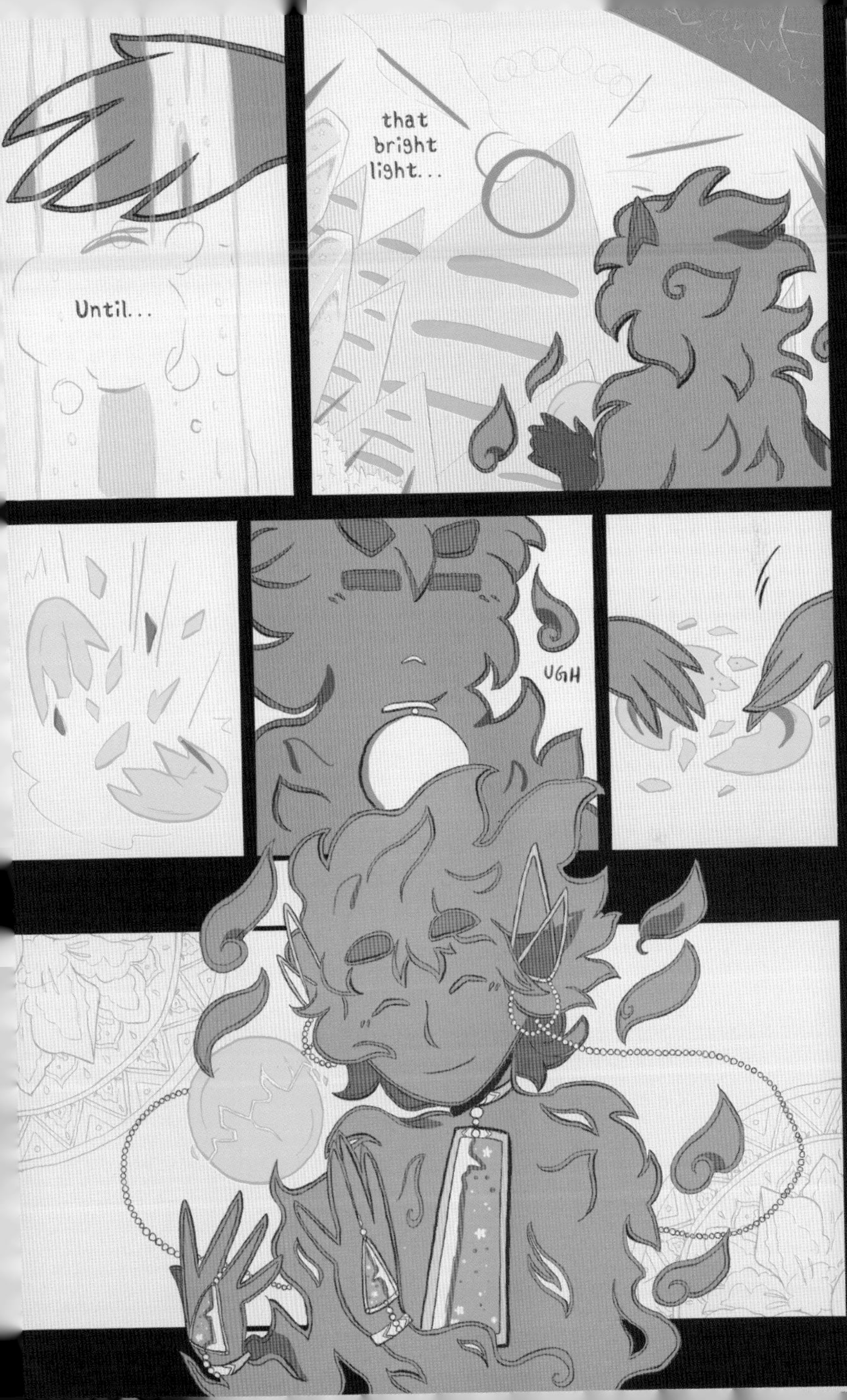
Until...
that bright light...
UGH

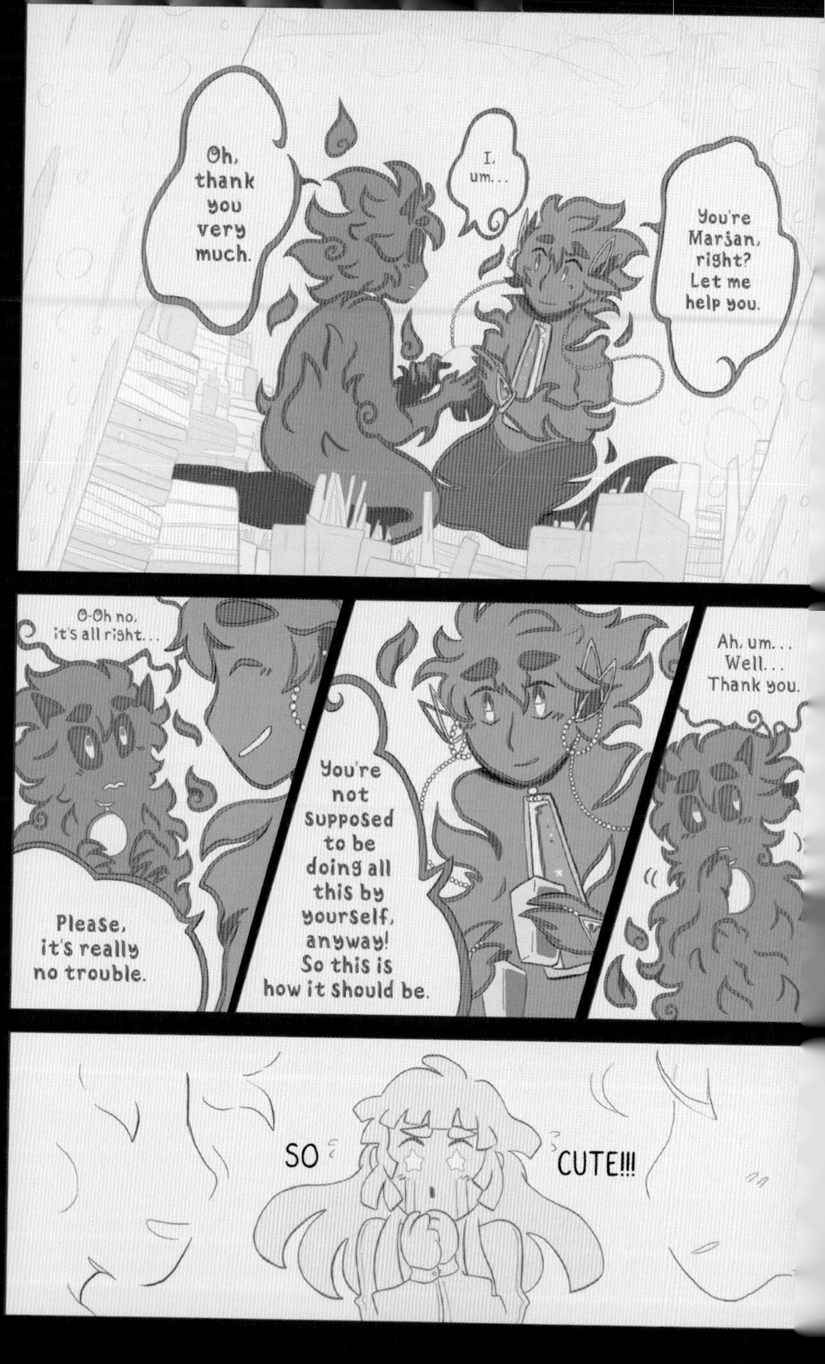

I, um...
Oh, thank you very much.
You're Marjan, right? Let me help you.
O-Oh no, it's all right...
Please, it's really no trouble.
You're not supposed to be doing all this by yourself, anyway! So this is how it should be.
Ah, um... Well... Thank you.
SO
CUTE!!!

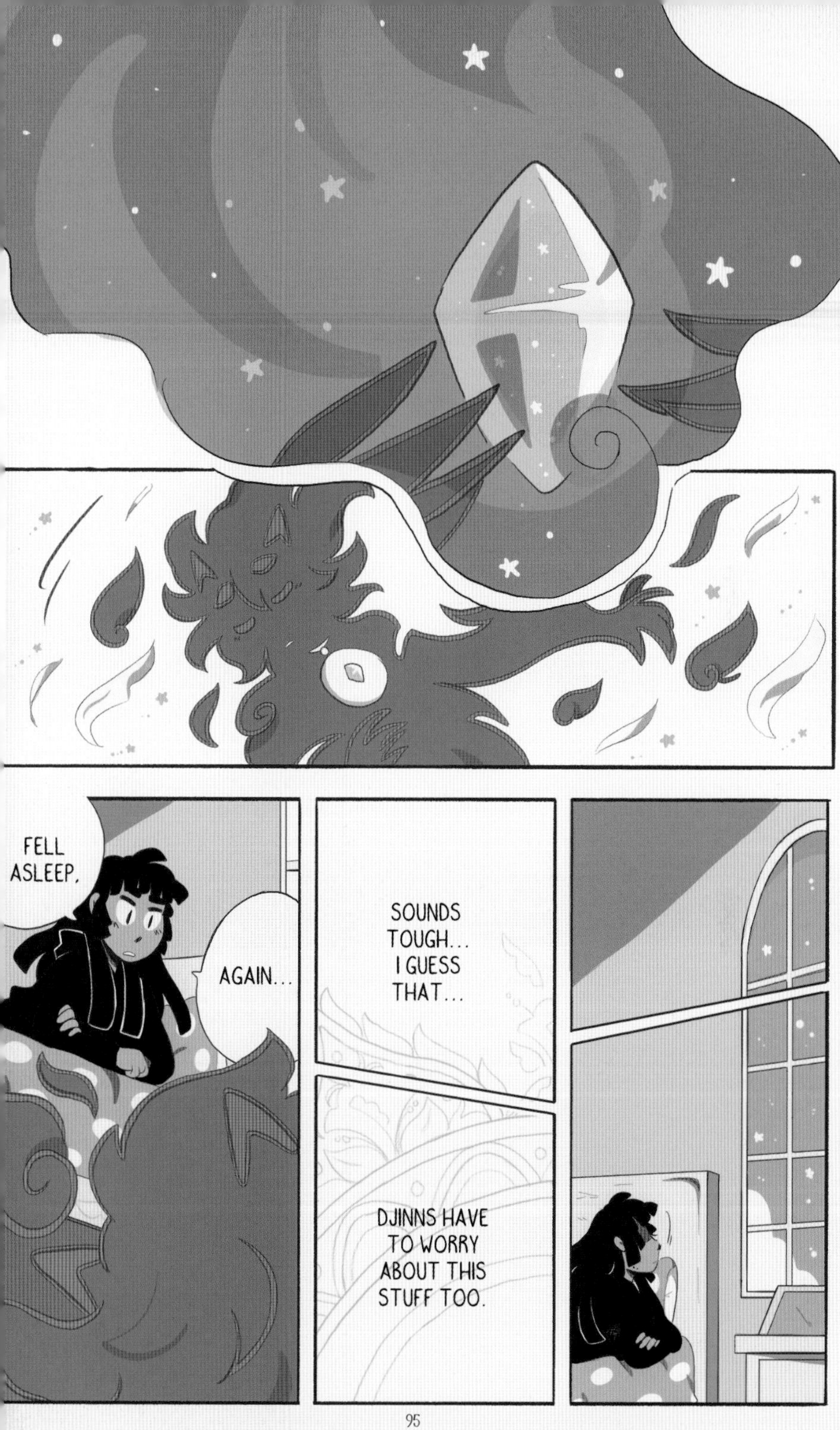
FELL ASLEEP,
AGAIN...
SOUNDS TOUGH... I GUESS THAT...
DJINNS HAVE TO WORRY ABOUT THIS STUFF TOO.

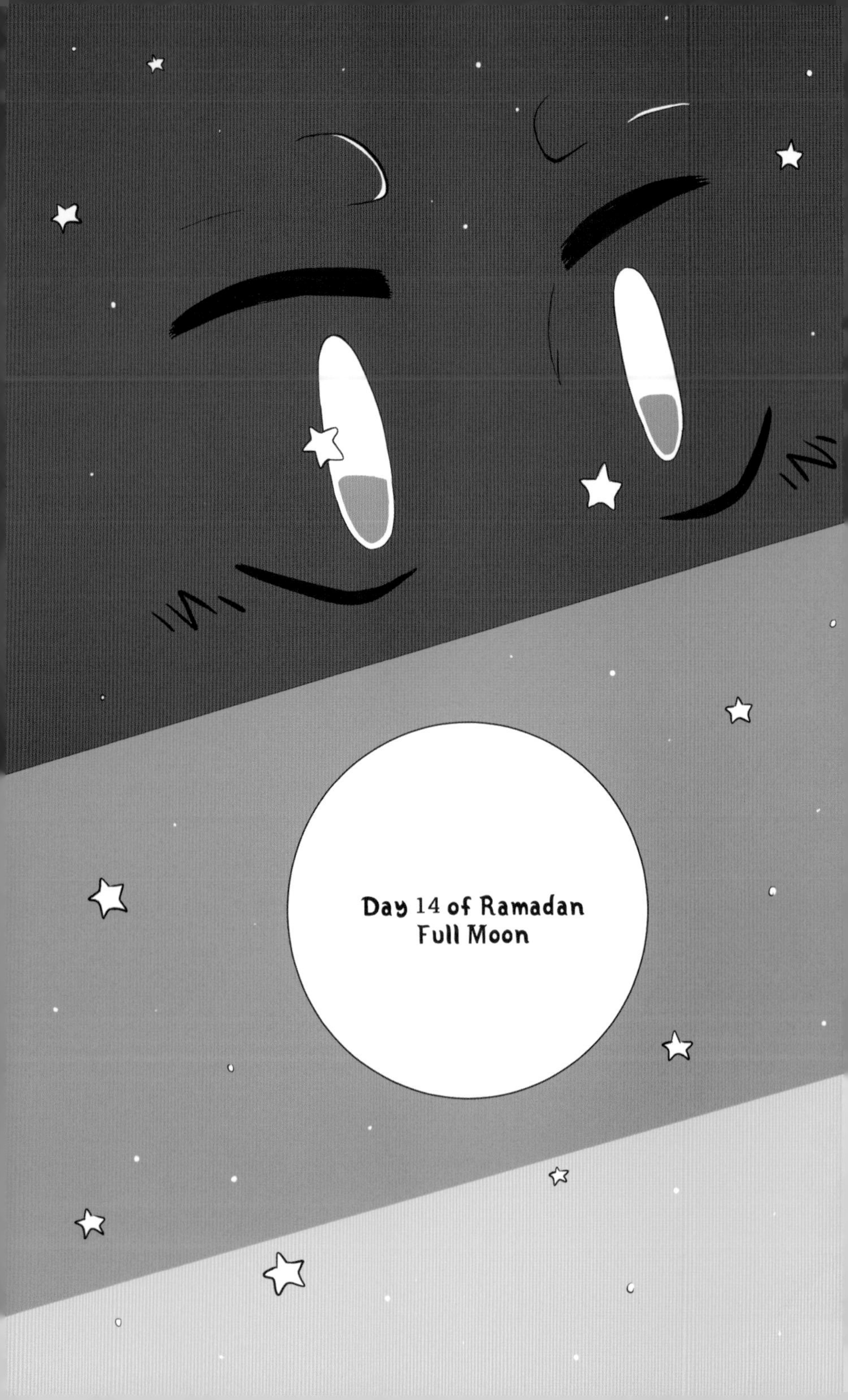
Day 14 of Ramadan
Full Moon

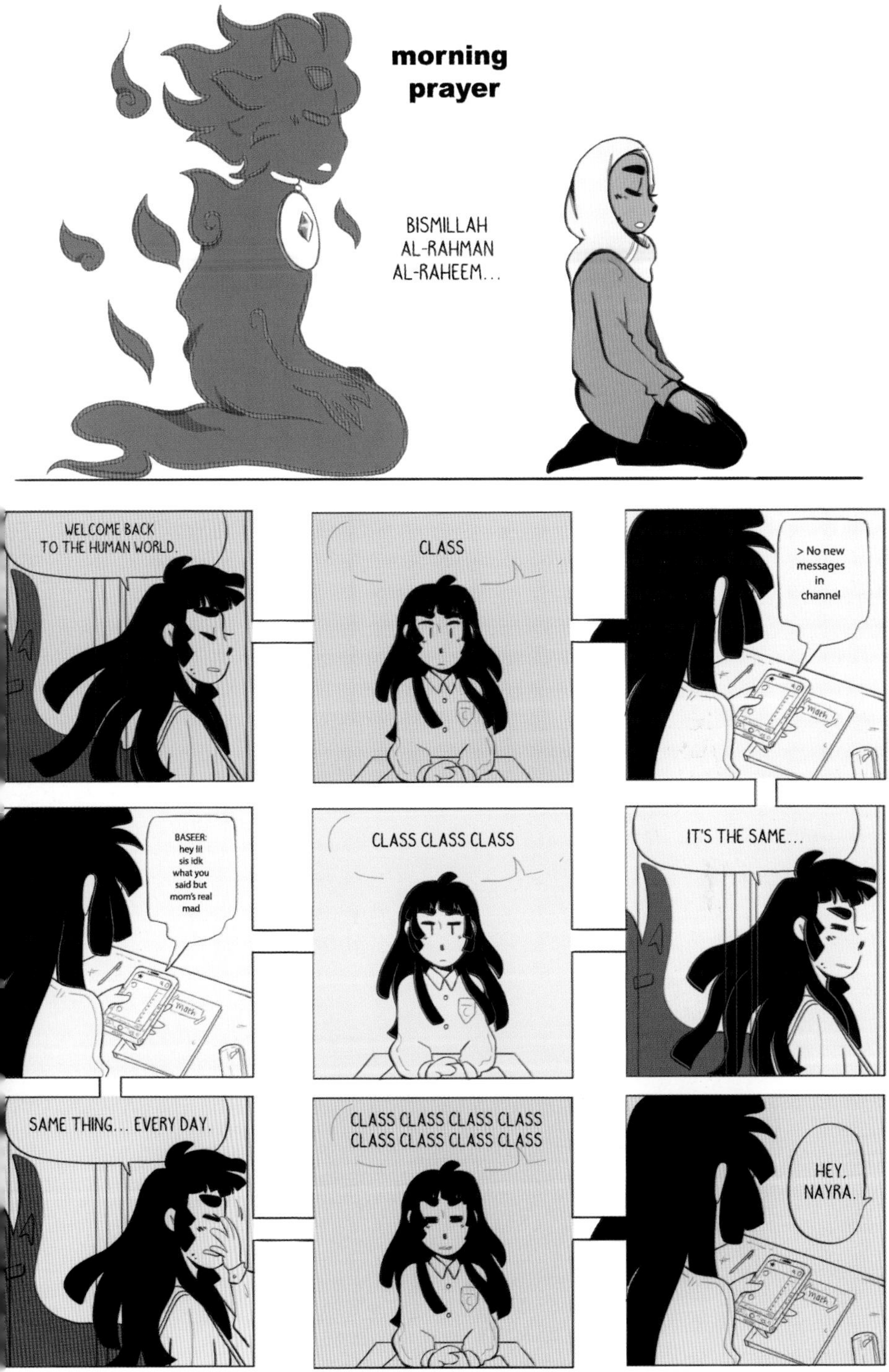
morning prayer
BISMILLAH AL-RAHMAN AL-RAHEEM...
WELCOME BACK TO THE HUMAN WORLD.
CLASS
> No new messages in channel
math
BASEER: hey lil sis idk what you said but mom's real mad
math
CLASS CLASS CLASS
IT'S THE SAME...
SAME THING... EVERY DAY.
CLASS CLASS CLASS CLASS CLASS CLASS CLASS CLASS
HEY, NAYRA.
math

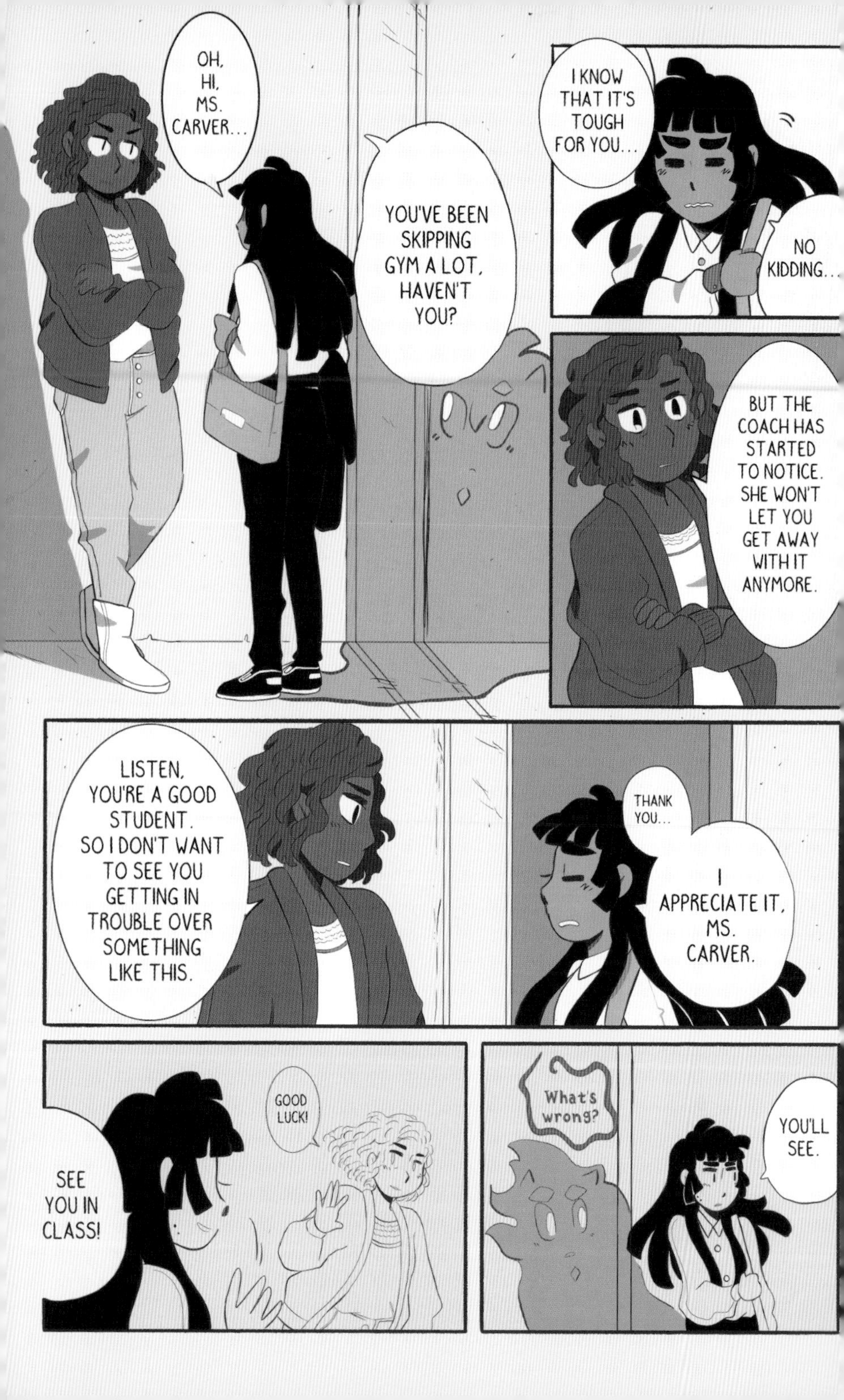

OH, HI, MS. CARVER...
YOU'VE BEEN SKIPPING GYM A LOT, HAVEN'T YOU?
I KNOW THAT IT'S TOUGH FOR YOU...
NO KIDDING...
BUT THE COACH HAS STARTED TO NOTICE. SHE WON'T LET YOU GET AWAY WITH IT ANYMORE.
LISTEN, YOU'RE A GOOD STUDENT. SO I DON'T WANT TO SEE YOU GETTING IN TROUBLE OVER SOMETHING LIKE THIS.
THANK YOU...
I APPRECIATE IT, MS. CARVER.
GOOD LUCK!
SEE YOU IN CLASS!
What's wrong?
YOU'LL SEE.

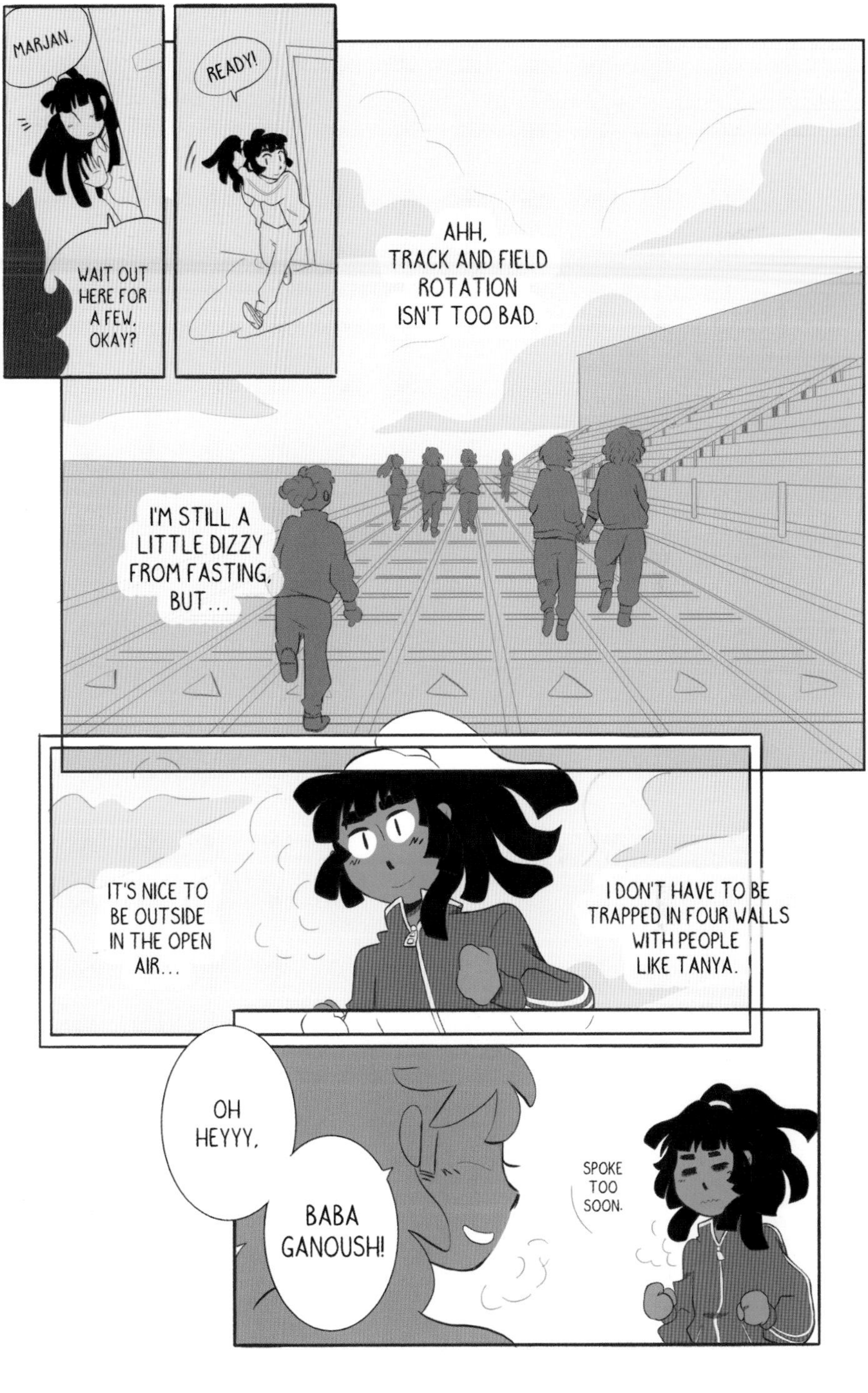
MARJAN.
WAIT OUT HERE FOR A FEW, OKAY?
READY!
AHH, TRACK AND FIELD ROTATION ISN'T TOO BAD.
I'M STILL A LITTLE DIZZY FROM FASTING, BUT...
IT'S NICE TO BE OUTSIDE IN THE OPEN AIR...
I DON'T HAVE TO BE TRAPPED IN FOUR WALLS WITH PEOPLE LIKE TANYA.
OH HEYYY,
BABA GANOUSH!
SPOKE TOO SOON.

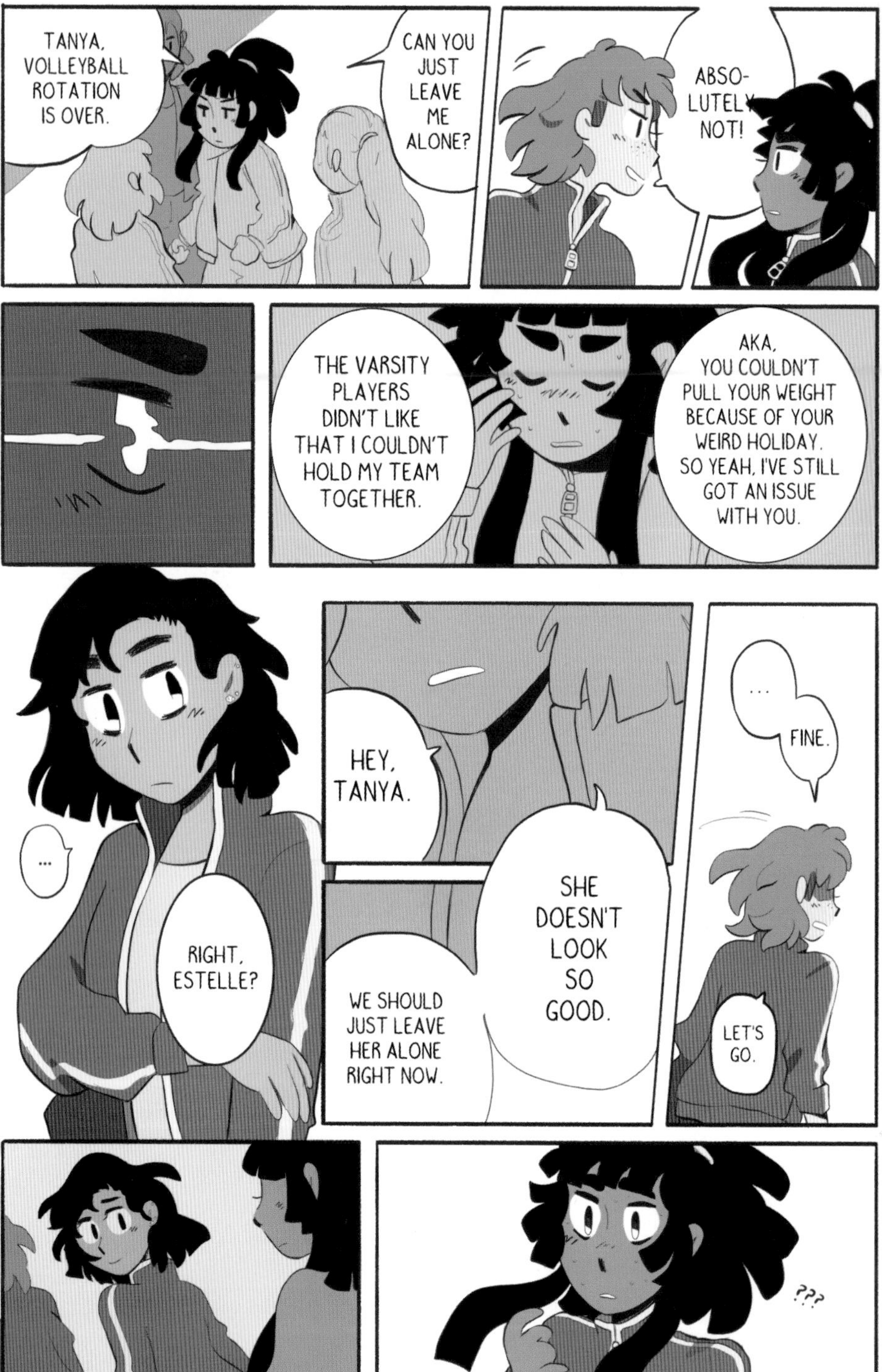
TANYA, VOLLEYBALL ROTATION IS OVER.
CAN YOU JUST LEAVE ME ALONE?
ABSO-LUTELY NOT!
THE VARSITY PLAYERS DIDN'T LIKE THAT I COULDN'T HOLD MY TEAM TOGETHER.
AKA, YOU COULDN'T PULL YOUR WEIGHT BECAUSE OF YOUR WEIRD HOLIDAY. SO YEAH, I'VE STILL GOT AN ISSUE WITH YOU.
...
HEY, TANYA.
SHE DOESN'T LOOK SO GOOD.
WE SHOULD JUST LEAVE HER ALONE RIGHT NOW.
RIGHT, ESTELLE?
...
FINE.
LET'S GO.
???

OH, NAYRA.

MY BROTHER WAS ASKING THE OTHER DAY...

ABOUT HOW YOUR FAMILY'S BEEN DOING LATELY.

Hungry...

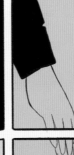

Thank you!!!

OK, HERE'S A DATE.

?

ARE YOU LISTENING?

UMM, HEY, DOESN'T SITTING HERE LIKE THIS...

MAKE YOU THINK...

ABOUT THE PAST?

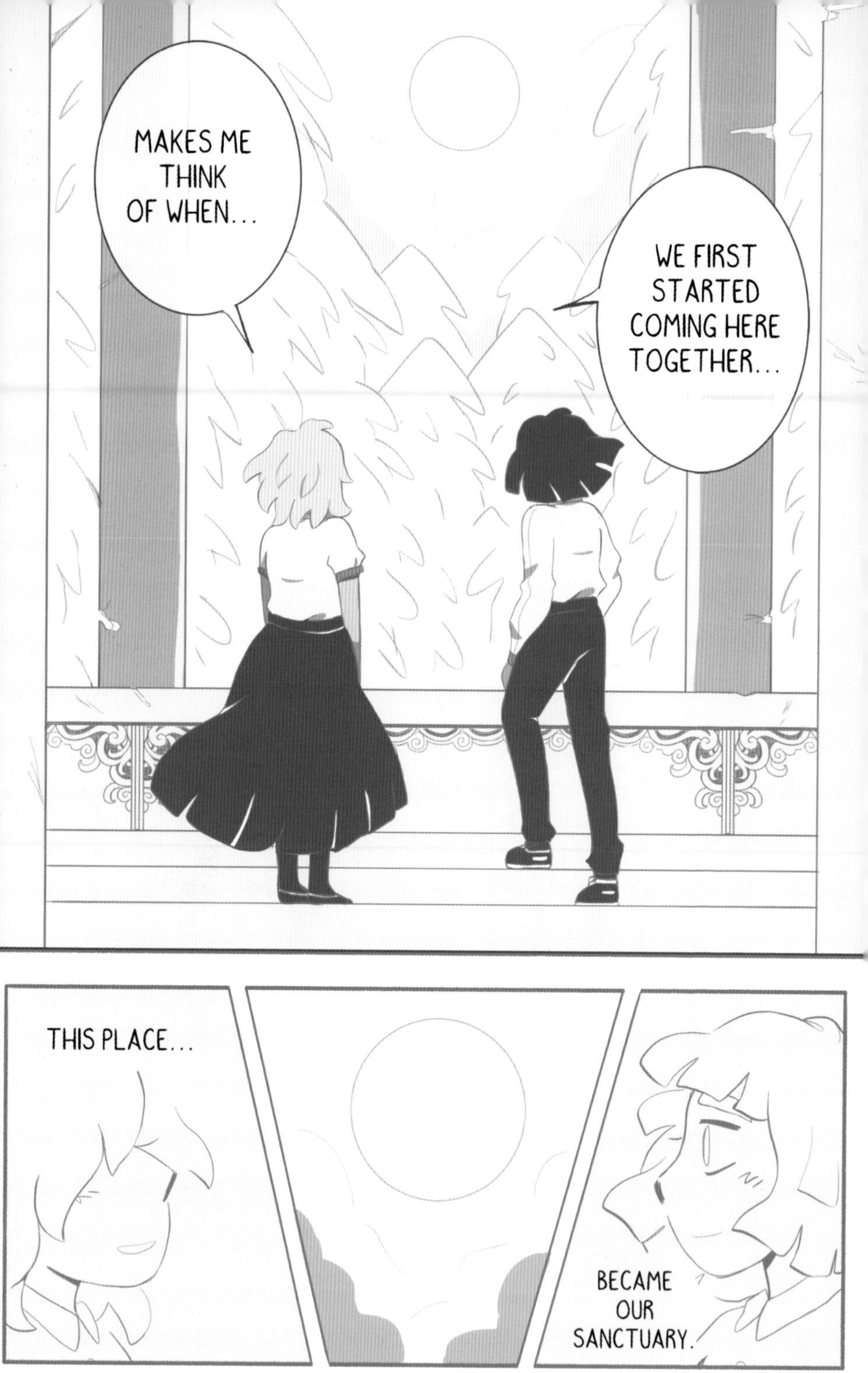
MAKES ME THINK OF WHEN...
WE FIRST STARTED COMING HERE TOGETHER...
THIS PLACE...
BECAME OUR SANCTUARY.

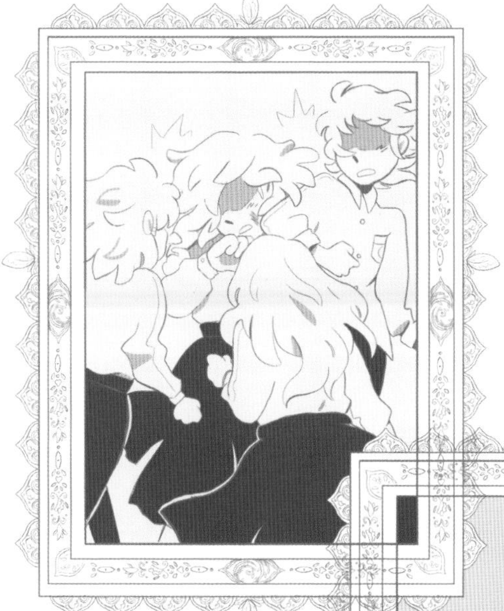

NO MATTER
WHAT HAPPENED
IN OUR
DAILY LIVES...

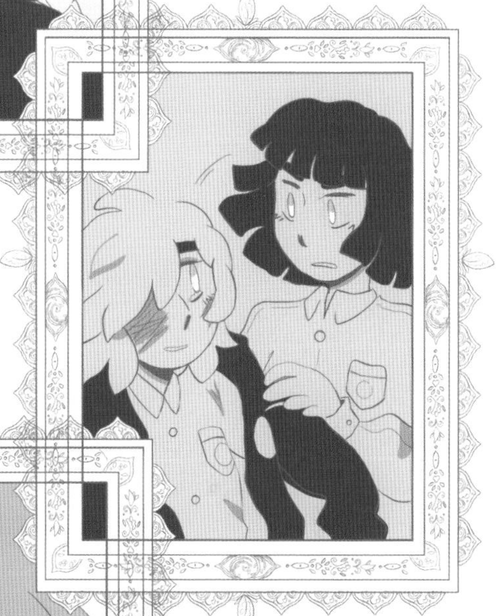

HOW OFTEN
WE'D GET INTO FIGHTS,
OR GET CALLED NAMES...

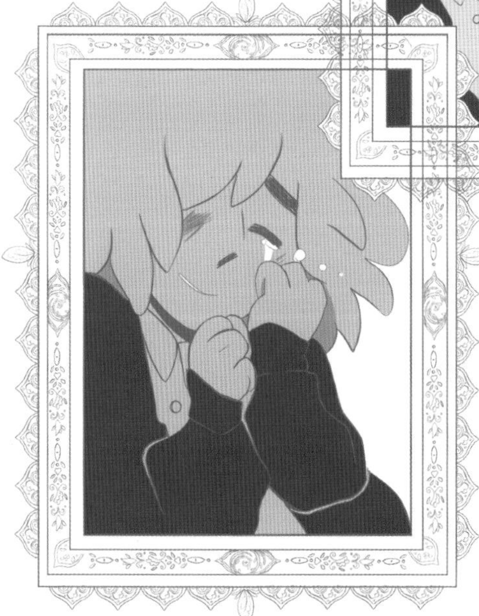

WE COULD
ALWAYS
COME BACK
HERE AND
HAVE A
MOMENT OF
PEACE.

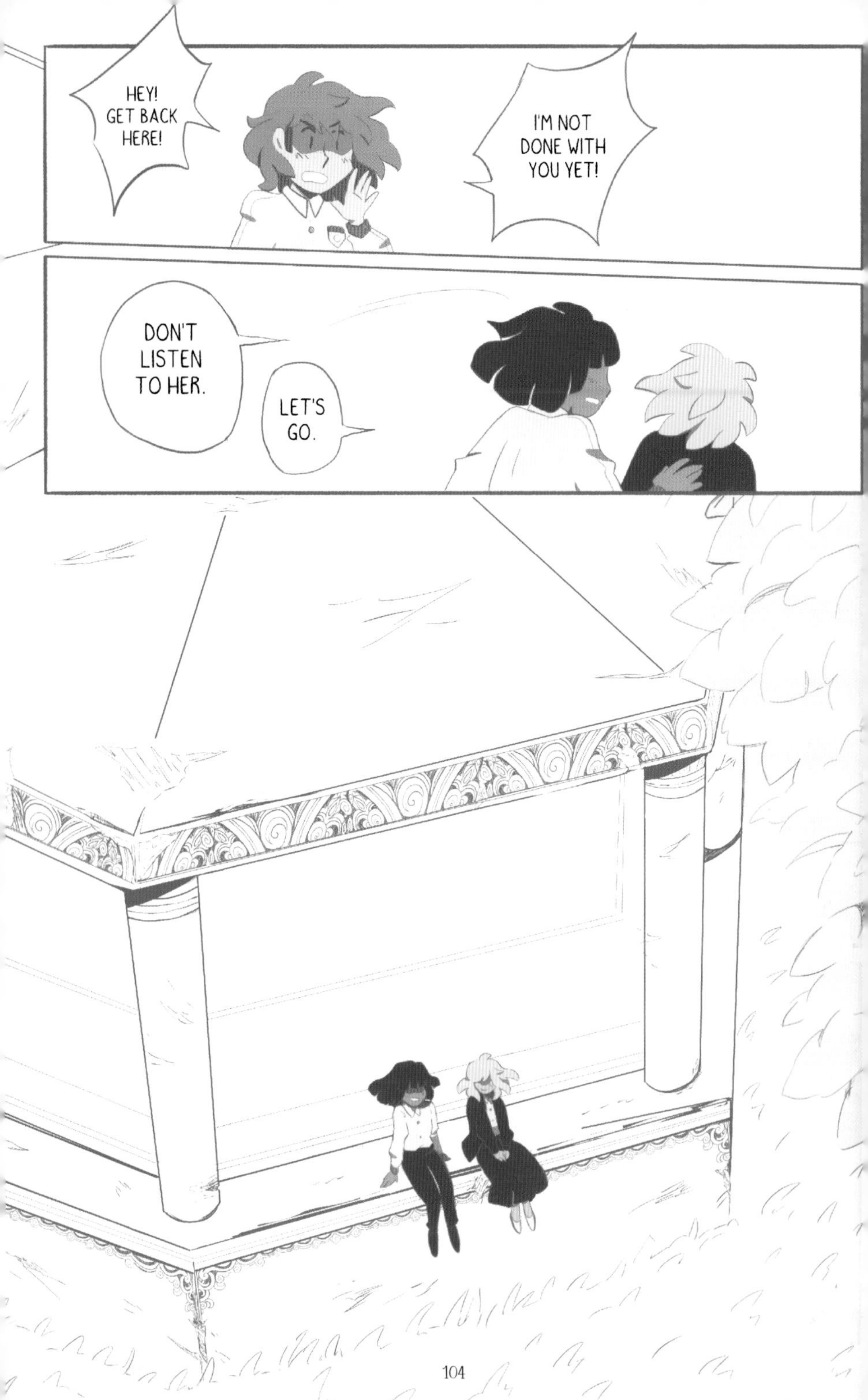
HEY! GET BACK HERE!
I'M NOT DONE WITH YOU YET!
DON'T LISTEN TO HER.
LET'S GO.

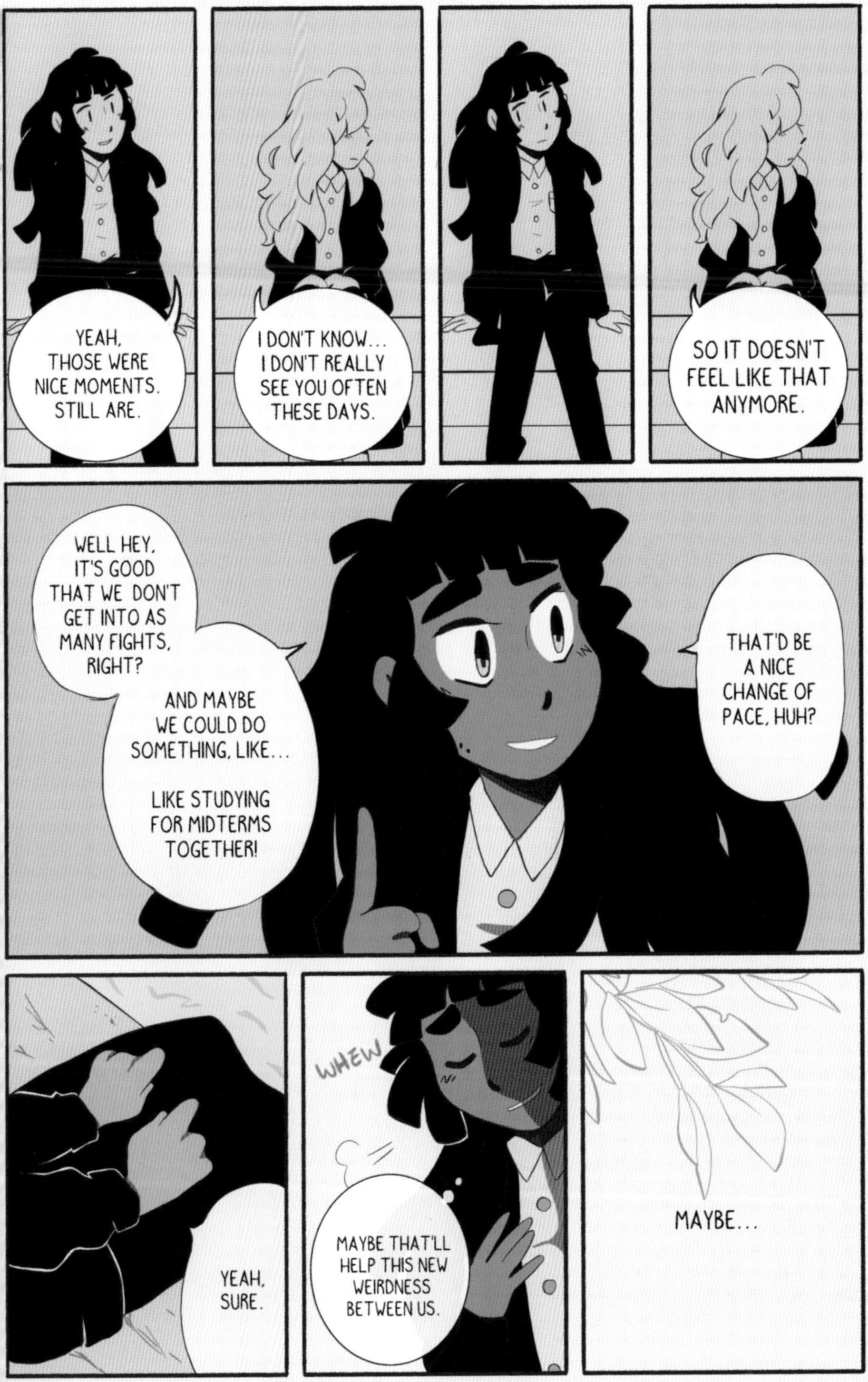
YEAH, THOSE WERE NICE MOMENTS. STILL ARE.
I DON'T KNOW... I DON'T REALLY SEE YOU OFTEN THESE DAYS.
SO IT DOESN'T FEEL LIKE THAT ANYMORE.
WELL HEY, IT'S GOOD THAT WE DON'T GET INTO AS MANY FIGHTS, RIGHT?
AND MAYBE WE COULD DO SOMETHING, LIKE...
LIKE STUDYING FOR MIDTERMS TOGETHER!
THAT'D BE A NICE CHANGE OF PACE, HUH?
YEAH, SURE.
WHEW
MAYBE THAT'LL HELP THIS NEW WEIRDNESS BETWEEN US.
MAYBE...

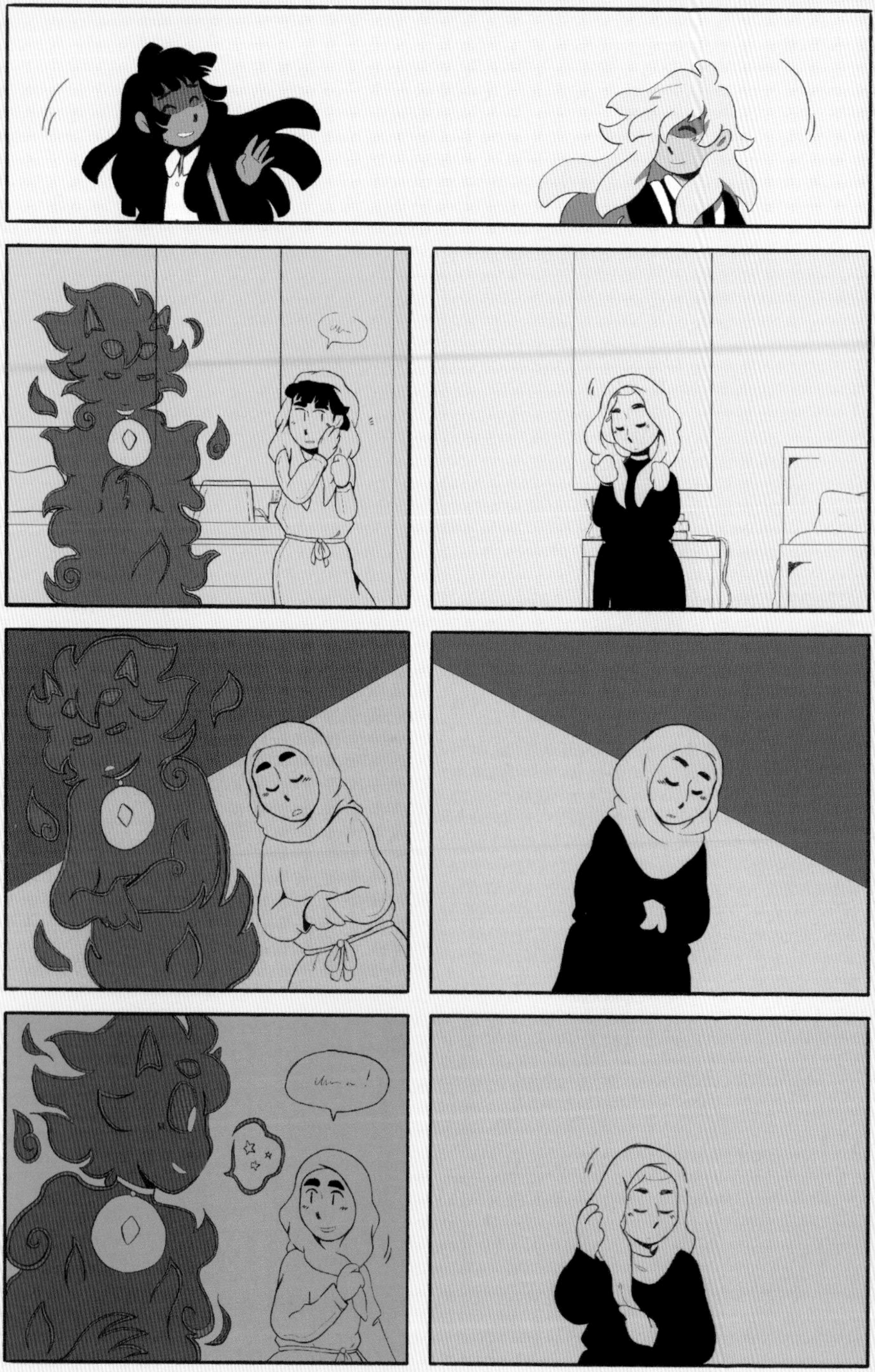

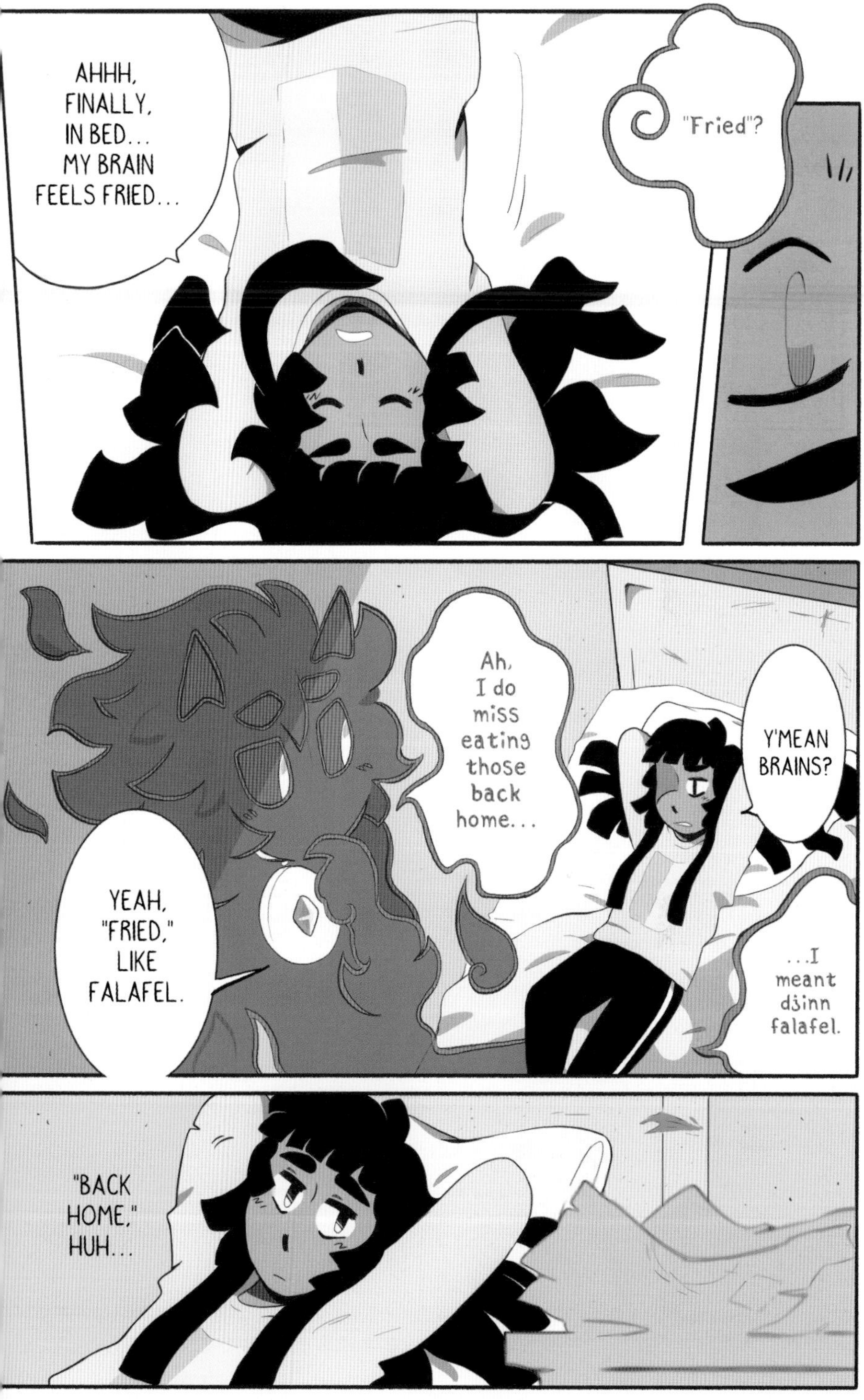
AHHH, FINALLY, IN BED... MY BRAIN FEELS FRIED...
"Fried"?
Ah, I do miss eating those back home...
Y'MEAN BRAINS?
YEAH, "FRIED," LIKE FALAFEL.
...I meant djinn falafel.
"BACK HOME," HUH...

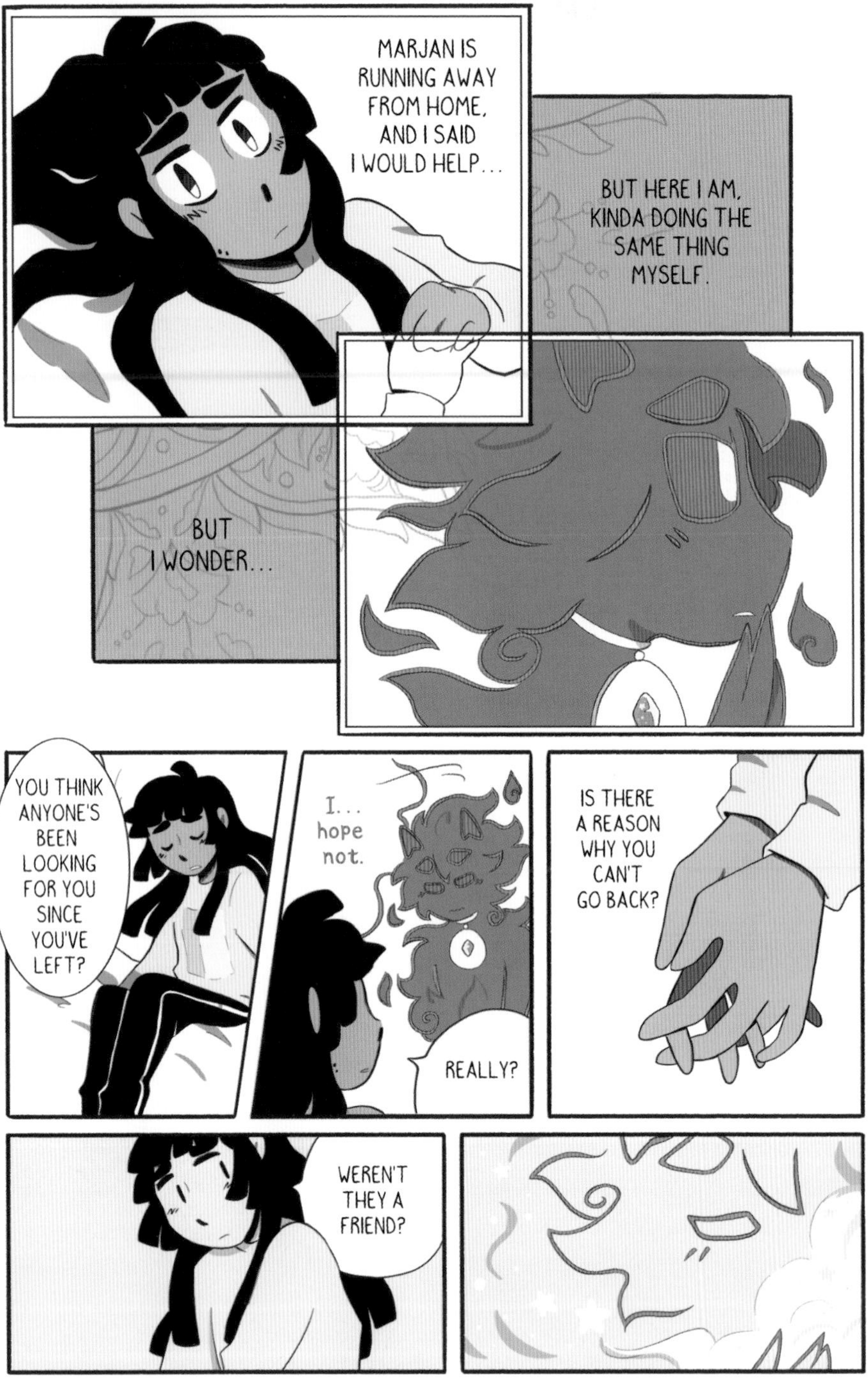
MARJAN IS RUNNING AWAY FROM HOME, AND I SAID I WOULD HELP...
BUT HERE I AM, KINDA DOING THE SAME THING MYSELF.
BUT I WONDER...
YOU THINK ANYONE'S BEEN LOOKING FOR YOU SINCE YOU'VE LEFT?
I... hope not.
REALLY?
IS THERE A REASON WHY YOU CAN'T GO BACK?
WEREN'T THEY A FRIEND?

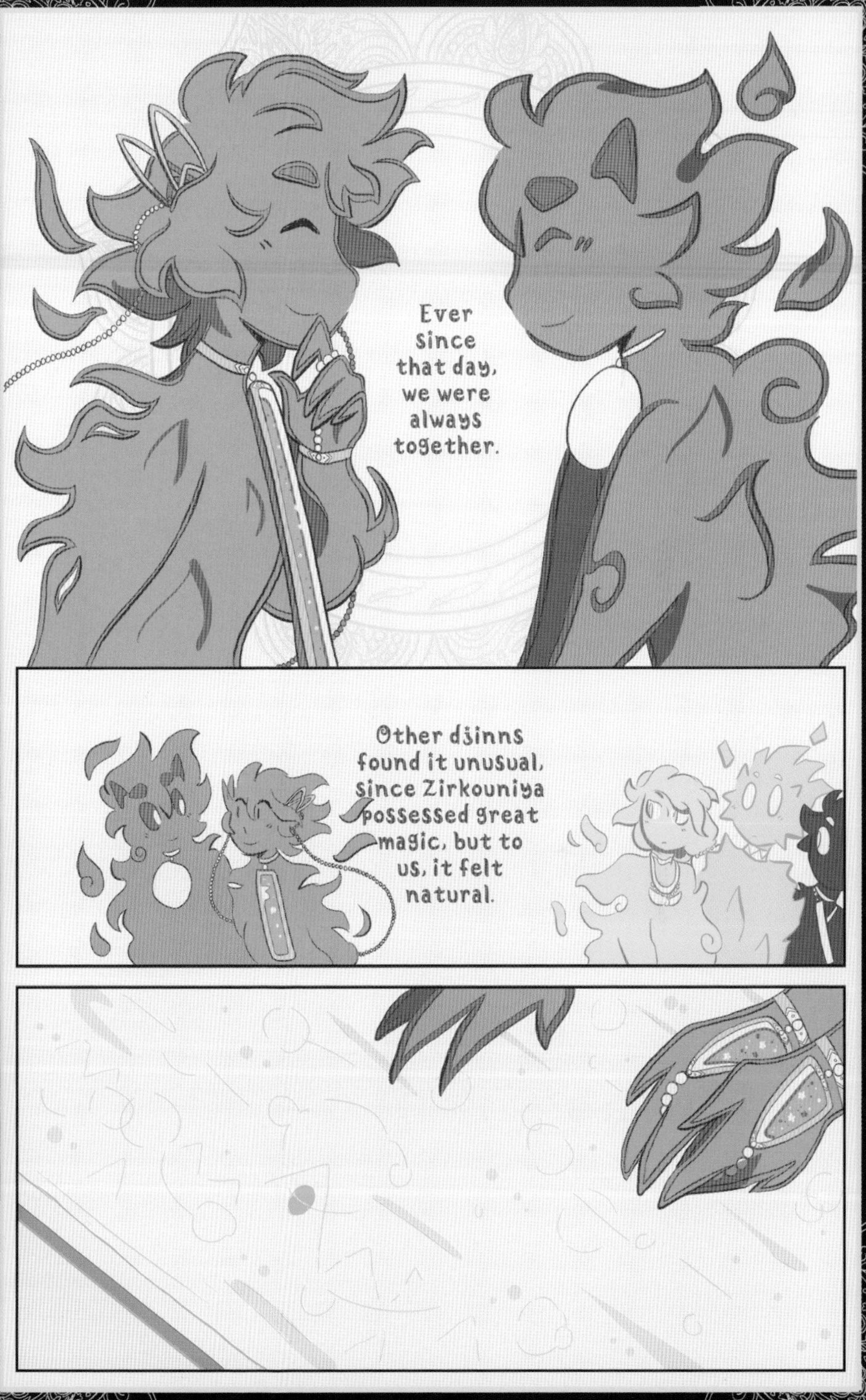
Ever since that day, we were always together.
Other djinns found it unusual, since Zirkouniya possessed great magic, but to us, it felt natural.

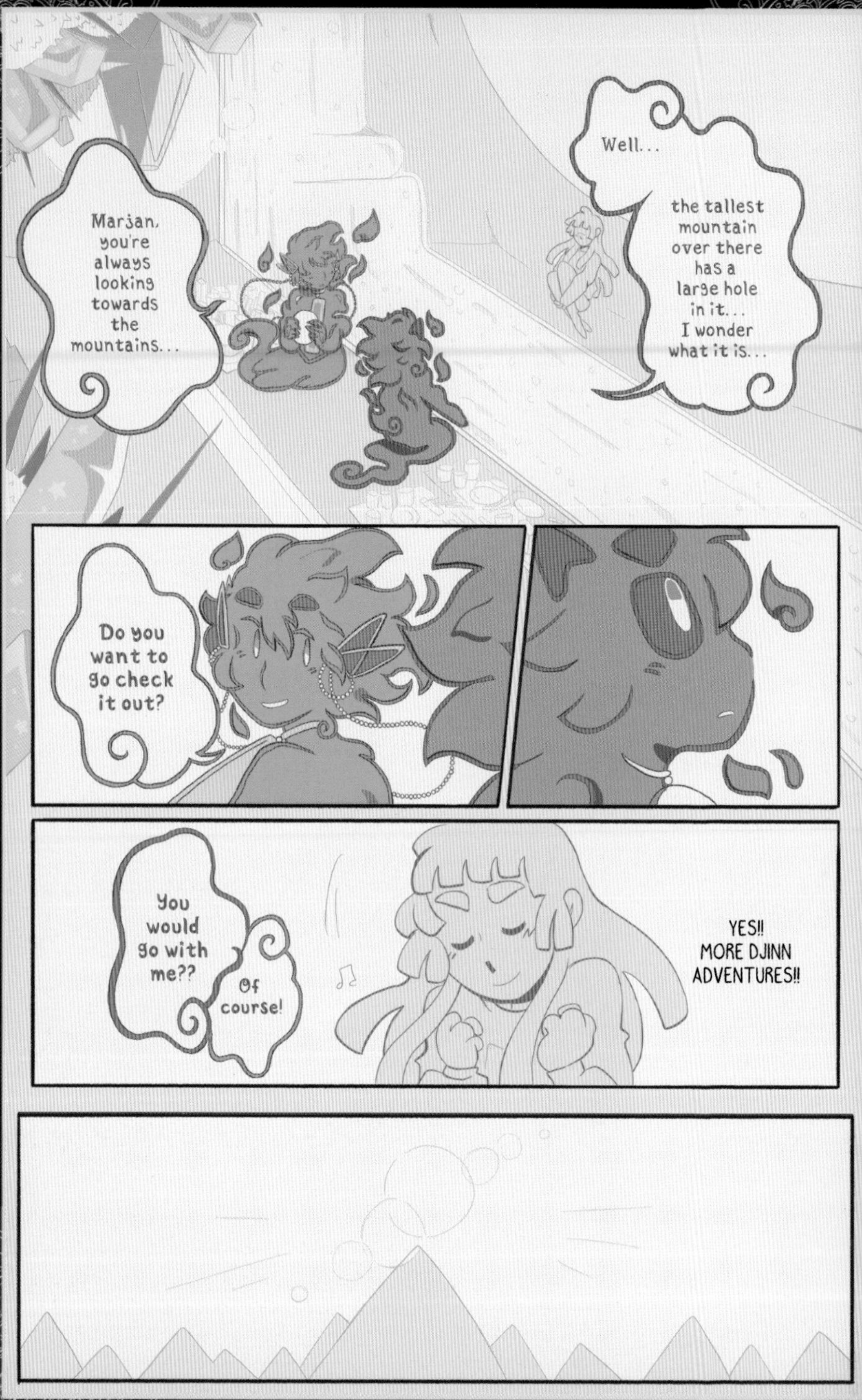
Marjan, you're always looking towards the mountains...
Well...
the tallest mountain over there has a large hole in it... I wonder what it is...
Do you want to go check it out?
You would go with me??
Of course!
YES!! MORE DJINN ADVENTURES!!

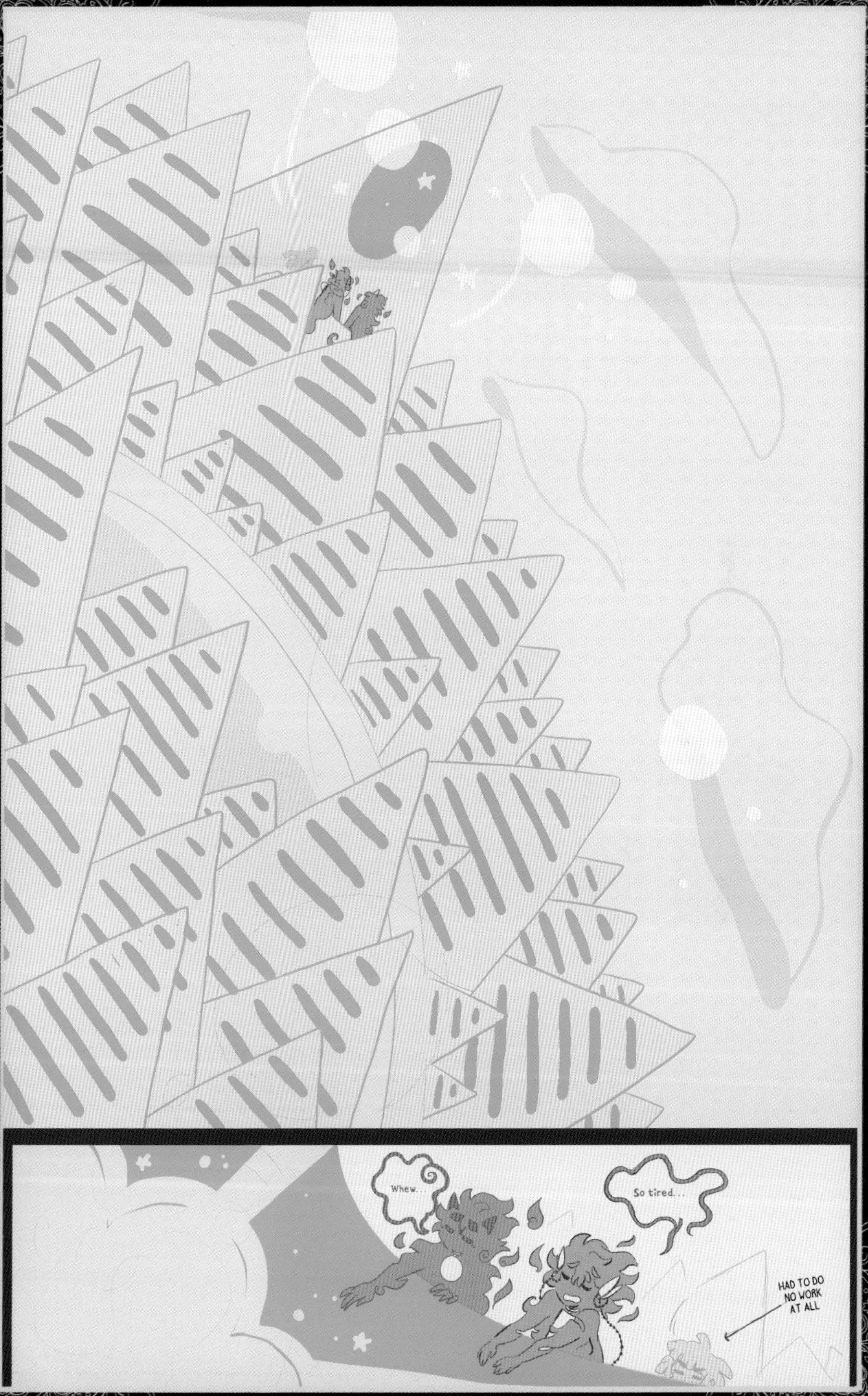
Whew...
So tired...
HAD TO DO NO WORK AT ALL

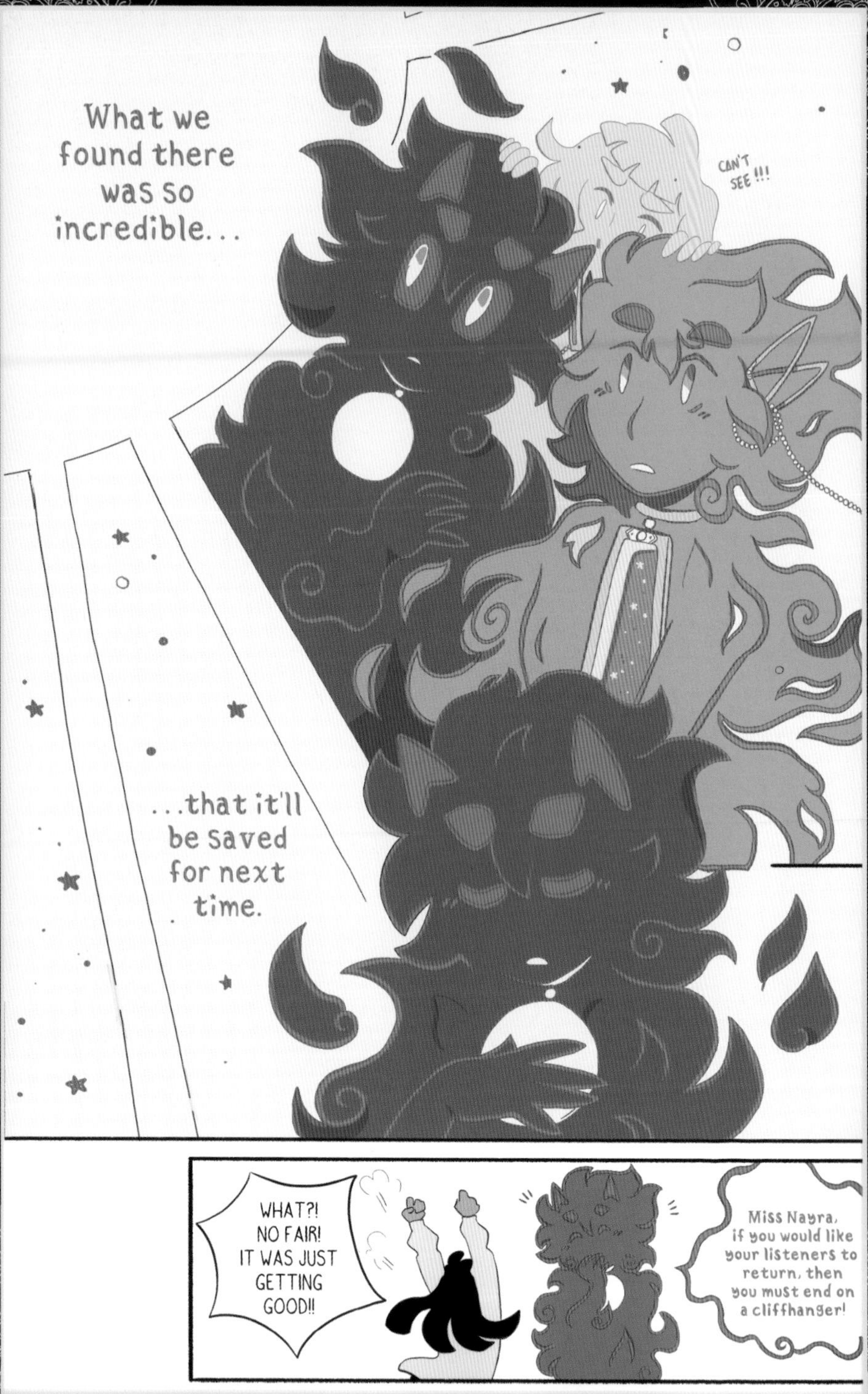
What we found there was so incredible...
CAN'T SEE!!!
...that it'll be saved for next time.
WHAT?! NO FAIR! IT WAS JUST GETTING GOOD!!
Miss Nayra, if you would like your listeners to return, then you must end on a cliffhanger!

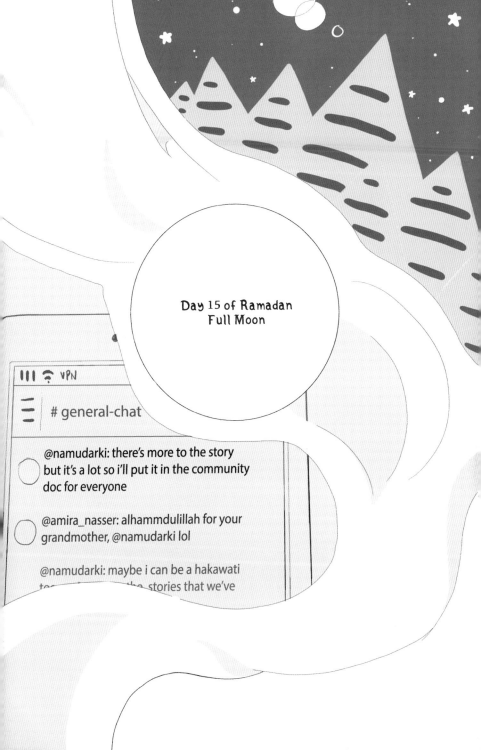

Day 15 of Ramadan
Full Moon

||| 📶 VPN

general-chat

@namudarki: there's more to the story
but it's a lot so i'll put it in the community
doc for everyone

@amira_nasser: alhammdulillah for your
grandmother, @namudarki lol

@namudarki: maybe i can be a hakawati
too, stories that we've

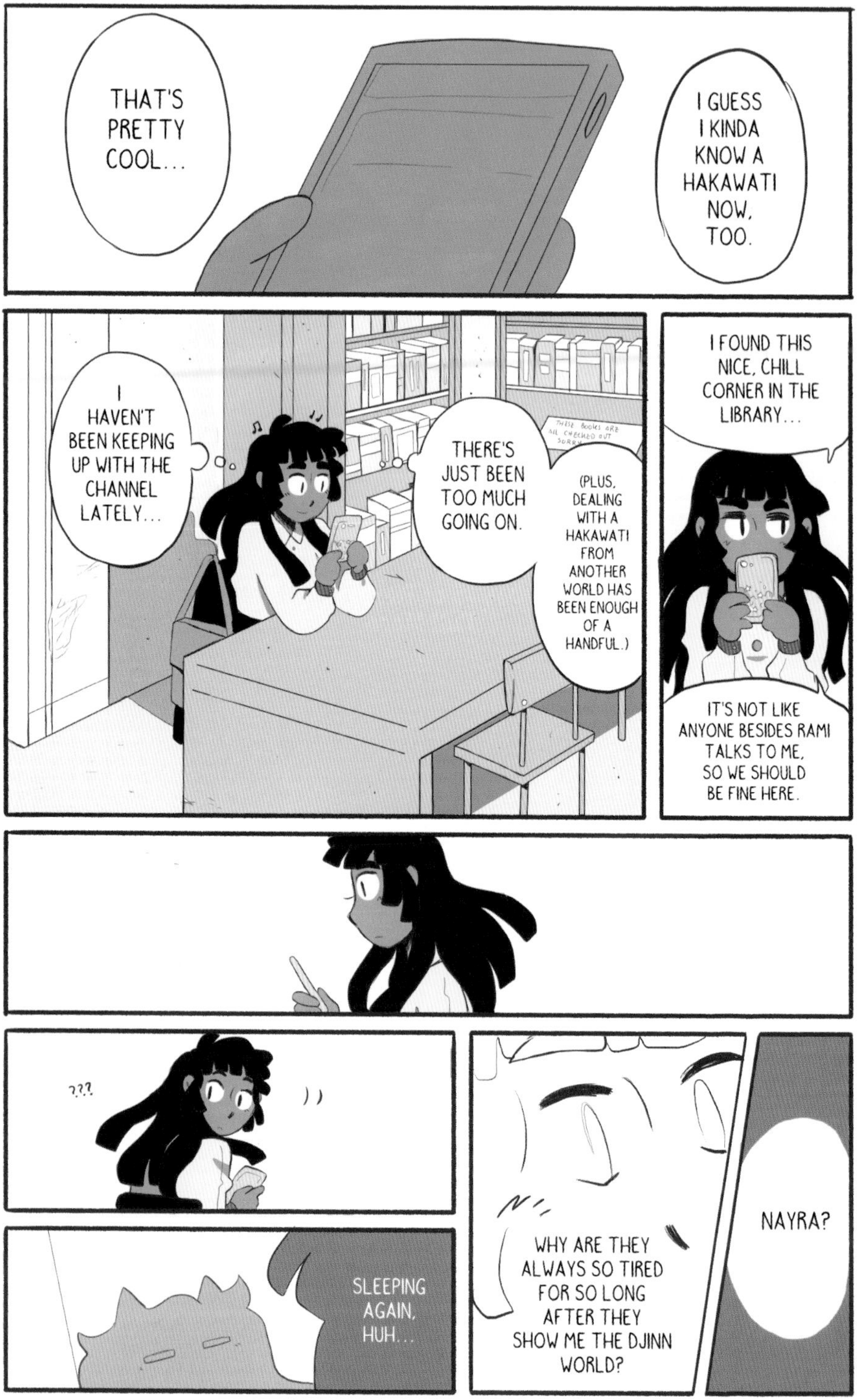
THAT'S PRETTY COOL...
I GUESS I KINDA KNOW A HAKAWATI NOW, TOO.
I HAVEN'T BEEN KEEPING UP WITH THE CHANNEL LATELY...
THERE'S JUST BEEN TOO MUCH GOING ON.
THESE BOOKS ARE ALL CHECKED OUT
(PLUS, DEALING WITH A HAKAWATI FROM ANOTHER WORLD HAS BEEN ENOUGH OF A HANDFUL.)
I FOUND THIS NICE, CHILL CORNER IN THE LIBRARY...
IT'S NOT LIKE ANYONE BESIDES RAMI TALKS TO ME, SO WE SHOULD BE FINE HERE.
???
SLEEPING AGAIN, HUH...
WHY ARE THEY ALWAYS SO TIRED FOR SO LONG AFTER THEY SHOW ME THE DJINN WORLD?
NAYRA?

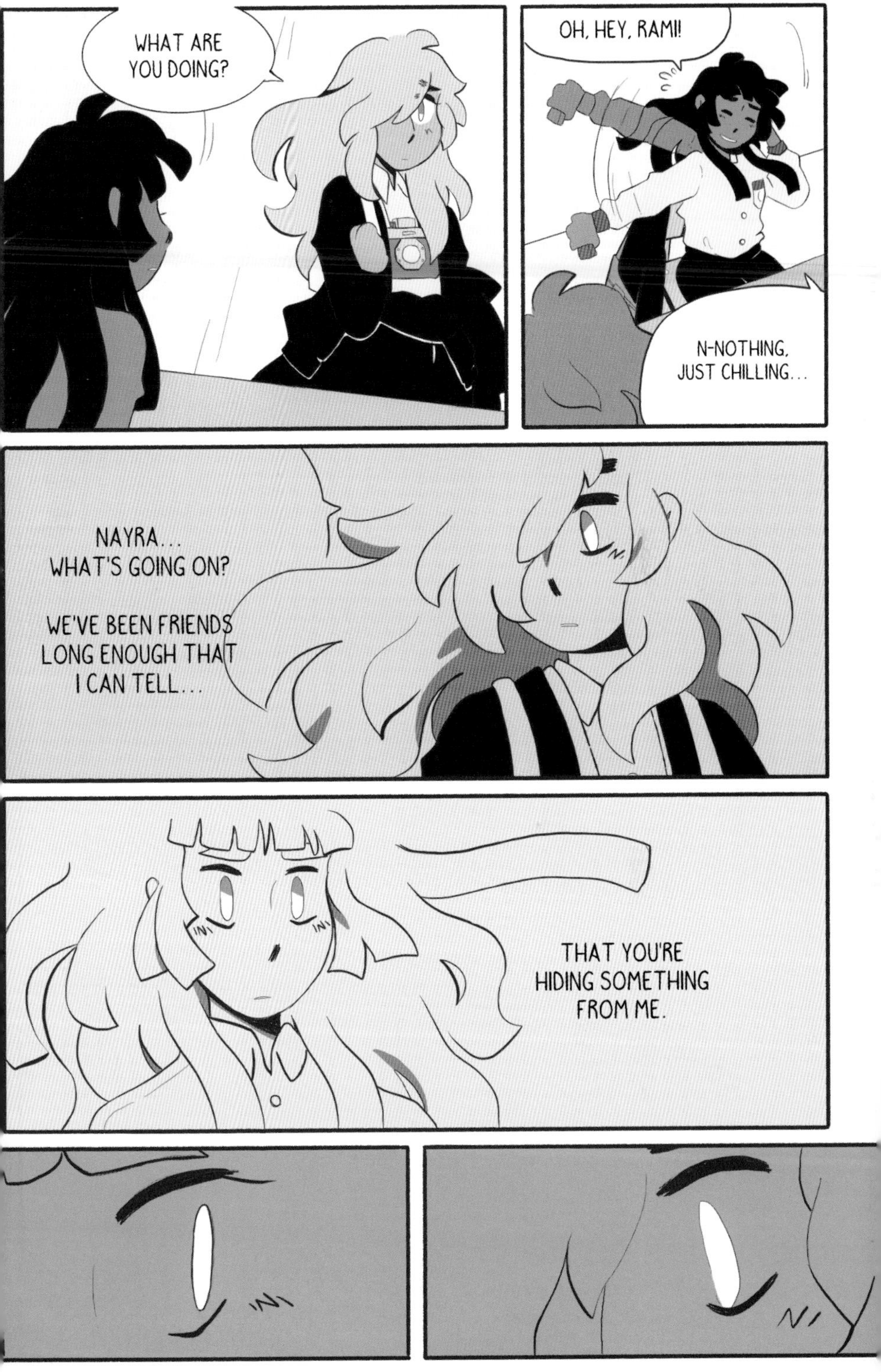
WHAT ARE YOU DOING?
OH, HEY, RAMI!
N-NOTHING, JUST CHILLING...
NAYRA... WHAT'S GOING ON?
WE'VE BEEN FRIENDS LONG ENOUGH THAT I CAN TELL...
THAT YOU'RE HIDING SOMETHING FROM ME.

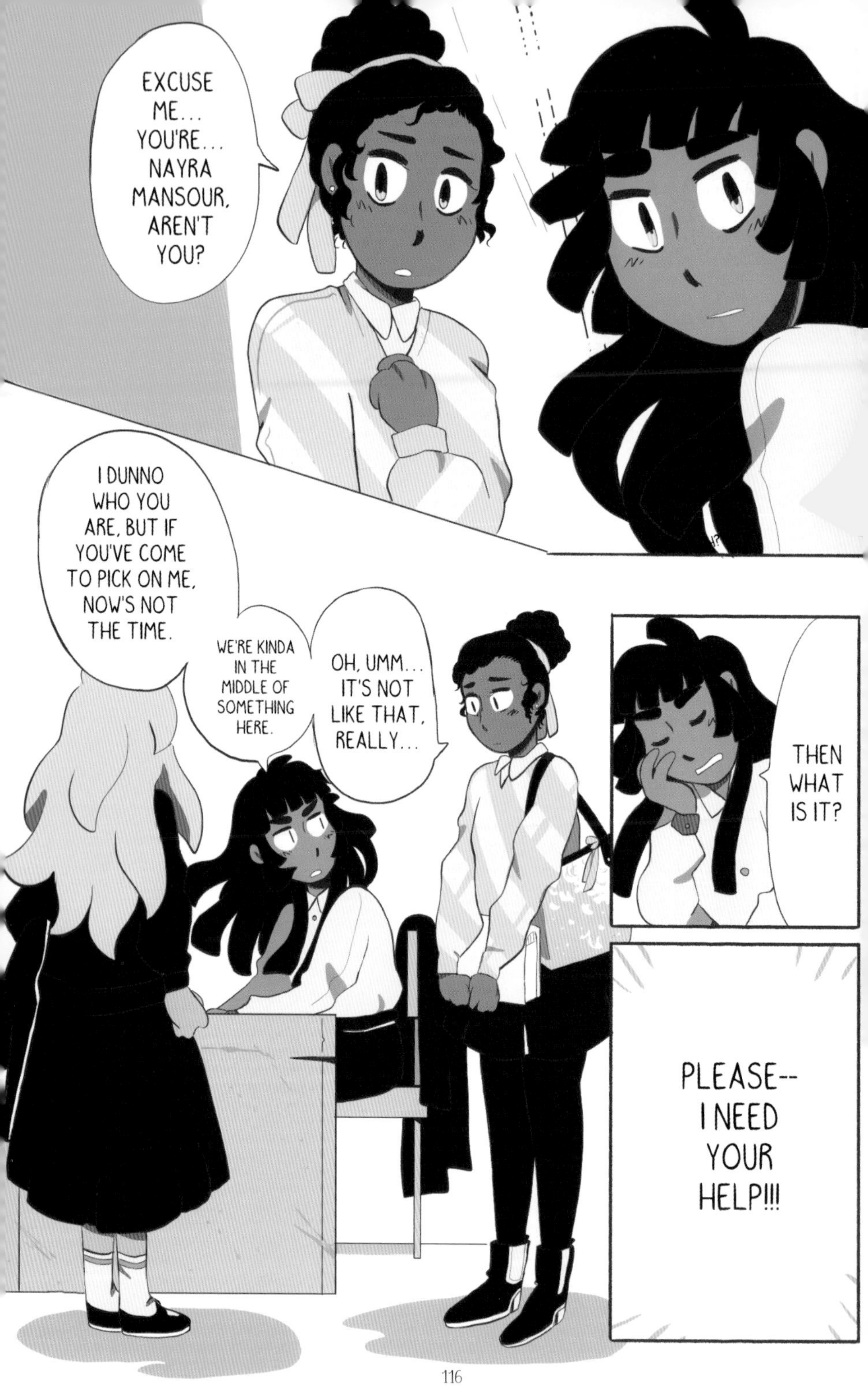
EXCUSE ME... YOU'RE... NAYRA MANSOUR, AREN'T YOU?
I DUNNO WHO YOU ARE, BUT IF YOU'VE COME TO PICK ON ME, NOW'S NOT THE TIME.
WE'RE KINDA IN THE MIDDLE OF SOMETHING HERE.
OH, UMM... IT'S NOT LIKE THAT, REALLY...
THEN WHAT IS IT?
PLEASE-- I NEED YOUR HELP!!!

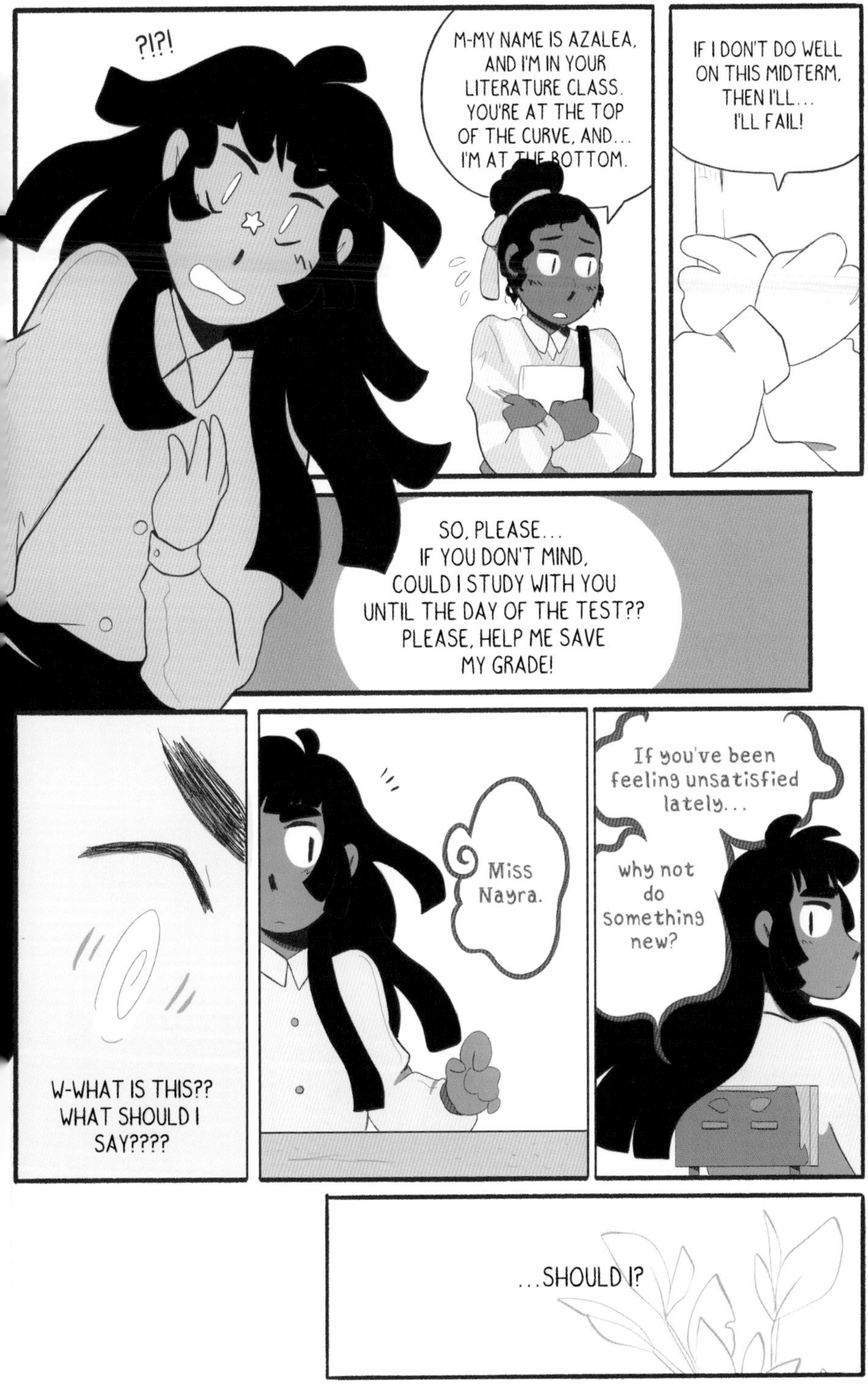
?!?!
M-MY NAME IS AZALEA, AND I'M IN YOUR LITERATURE CLASS. YOU'RE AT THE TOP OF THE CURVE, AND... I'M AT THE BOTTOM.
IF I DON'T DO WELL ON THIS MIDTERM, THEN I'LL... I'LL FAIL!
SO, PLEASE... IF YOU DON'T MIND, COULD I STUDY WITH YOU UNTIL THE DAY OF THE TEST?? PLEASE, HELP ME SAVE MY GRADE!
W-WHAT IS THIS?? WHAT SHOULD I SAY????
Miss Nayra.
If you've been feeling unsatisfied lately...
why not do something new?
...SHOULD I?

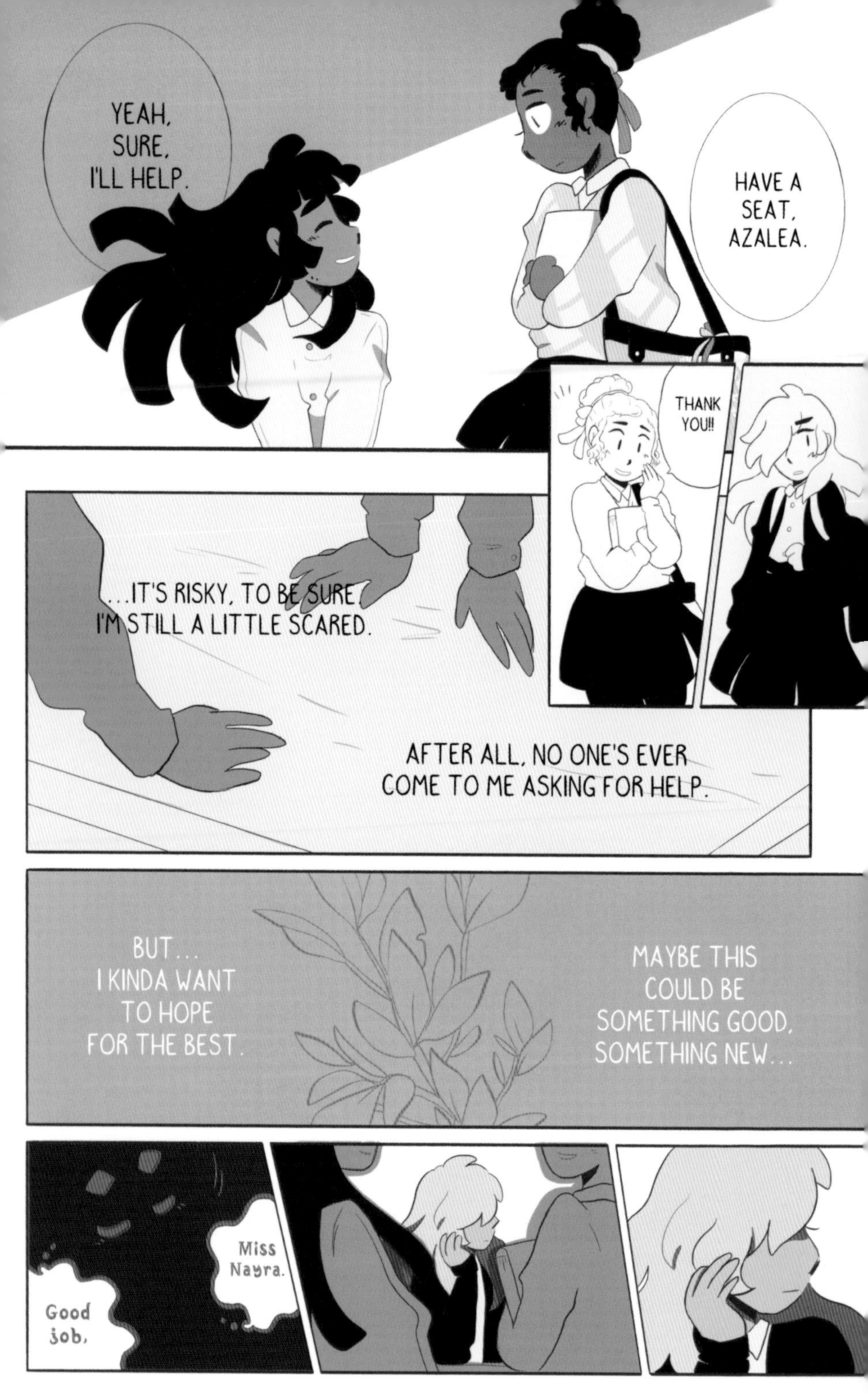
YEAH, SURE, I'LL HELP.
HAVE A SEAT, AZALEA.
THANK YOU!!
...IT'S RISKY, TO BE SURE. I'M STILL A LITTLE SCARED.
AFTER ALL, NO ONE'S EVER COME TO ME ASKING FOR HELP.
BUT... I KINDA WANT TO HOPE FOR THE BEST.
MAYBE THIS COULD BE SOMETHING GOOD, SOMETHING NEW...
Good job,
Miss Nayra.

That went well, did it not?

IT DID, BUT... RAMI DIDN'T SEEM TOO HAPPY ABOUT IT.

Perhaps it's best to focus on the positives here?

YEAH, YEAH.

IT'S NOT LIKE THERE AREN'T GOOD THINGS HAPPENING...

BUT IT ALL FEELS SO COMPLICATED. IT'S HARD TO KEEP TRACK OF WHAT MAKES ME HAPPY AND WHAT DOESN'T...

OH!!!

I ALMOST FORGOT!!!

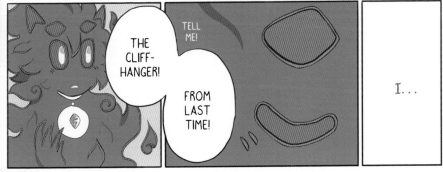

THE CLIFF-HANGER!

TELL ME!

FROM LAST TIME!

I...

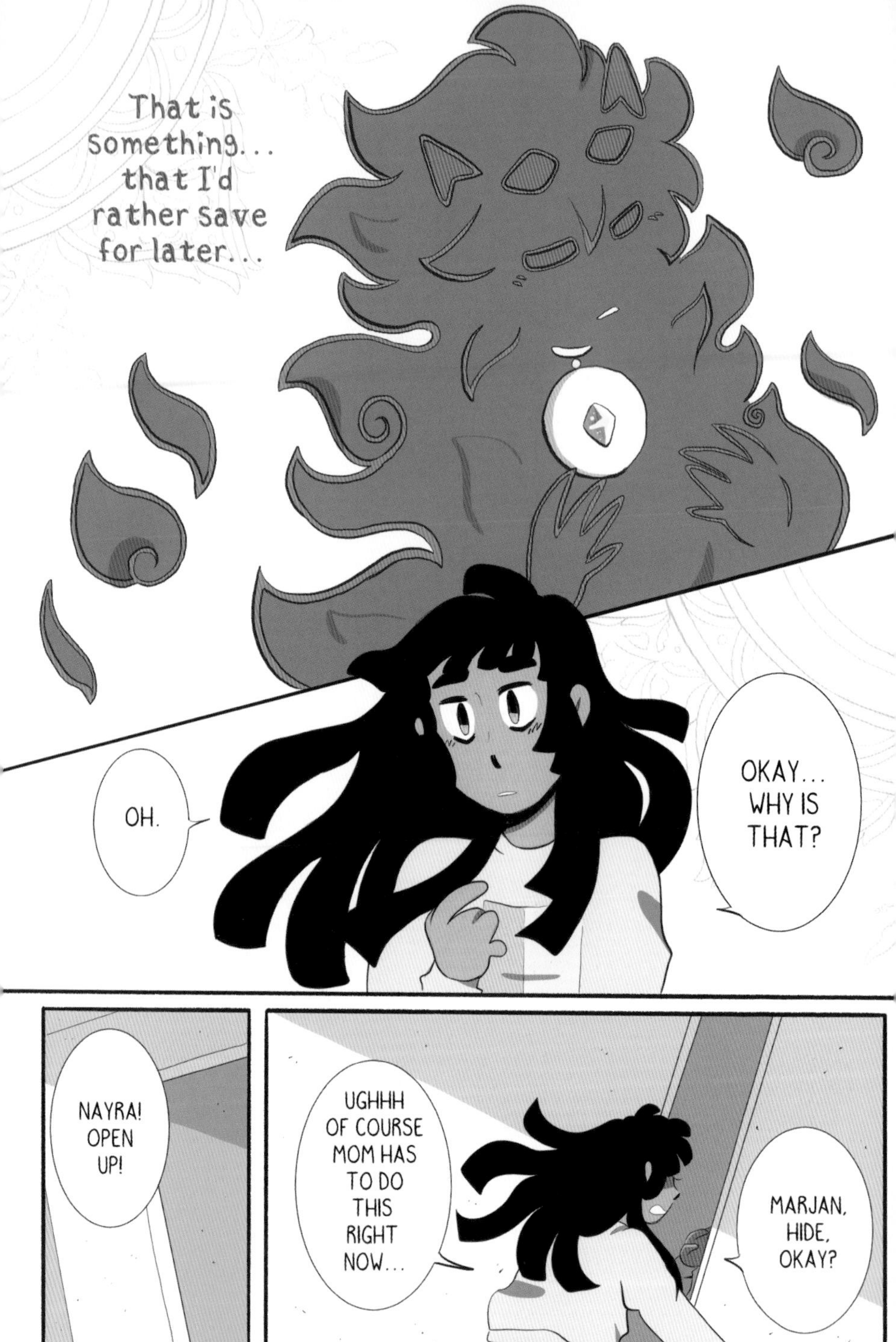
That is something... that I'd rather save for later...
OH.
OKAY... WHY IS THAT?
NAYRA! OPEN UP!
UGHHH OF COURSE MOM HAS TO DO THIS RIGHT NOW...
MARJAN, HIDE, OKAY?

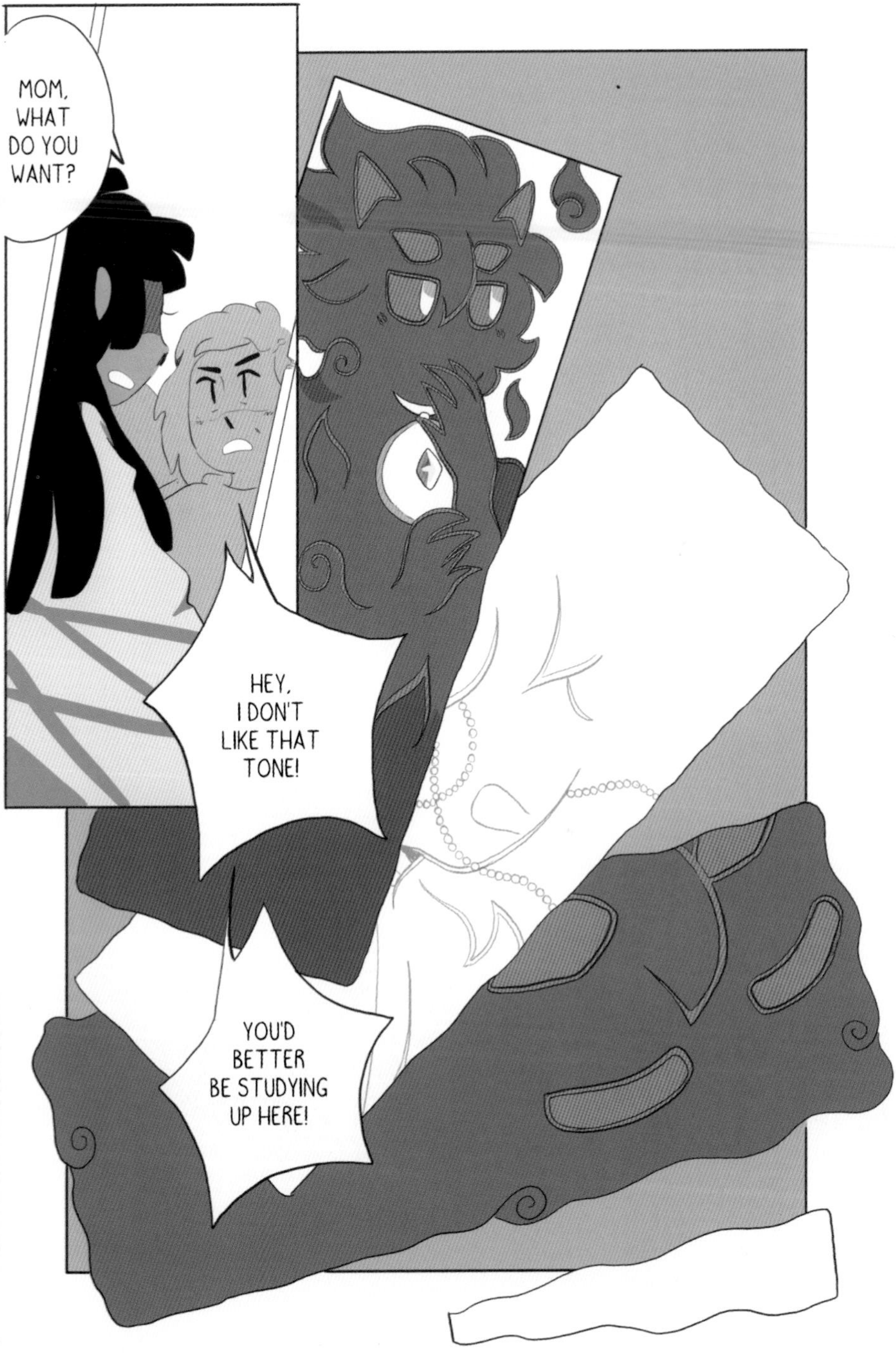
MOM, WHAT DO YOU WANT?
HEY, I DON'T LIKE THAT TONE!
YOU'D BETTER BE STUDYING UP HERE!

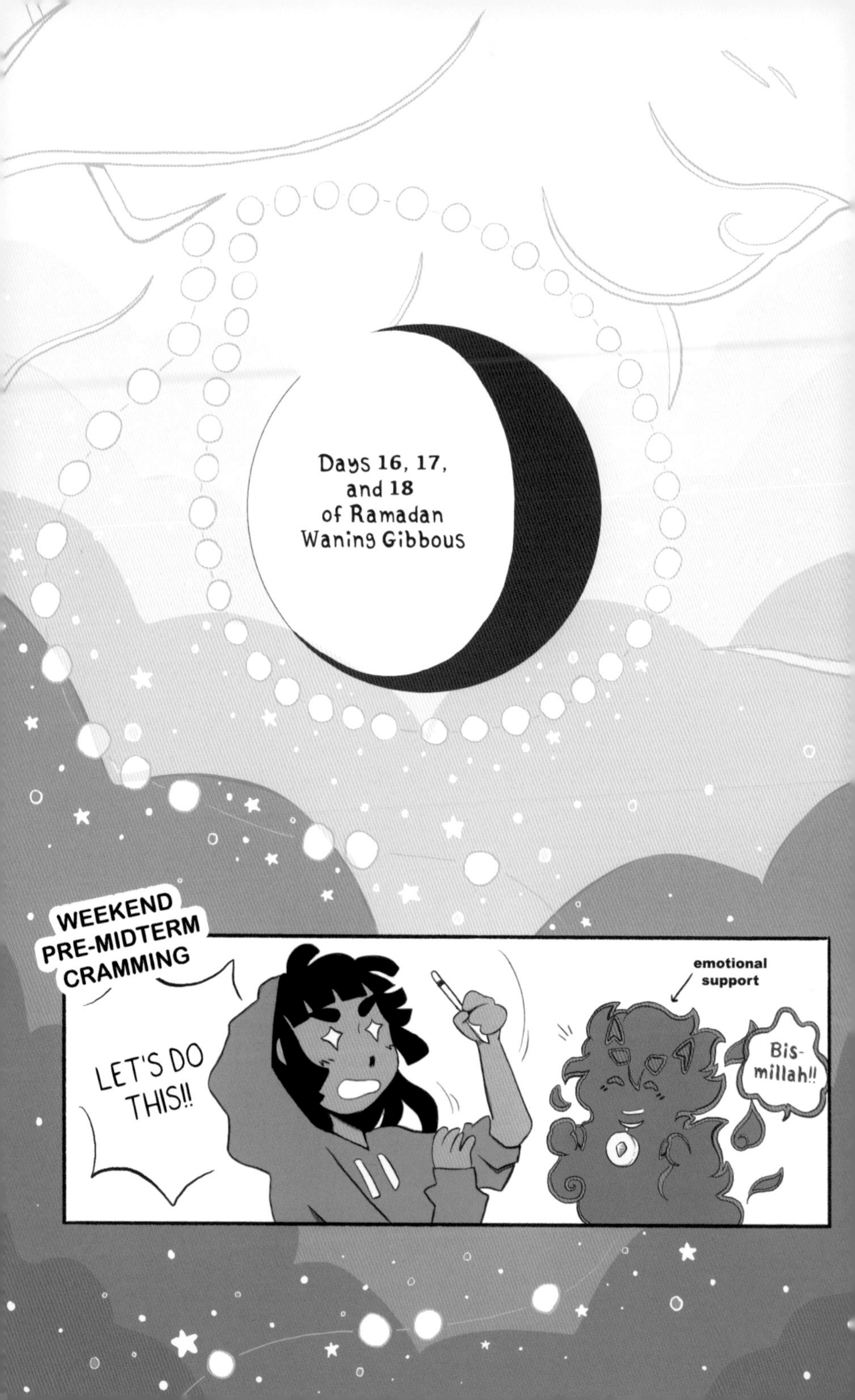

Days 16, 17, and 18 of Ramadan Waning Gibbous
WEEKEND PRE-MIDTERM CRAMMING
LET'S DO THIS!!
emotional support
Bis-millah!!

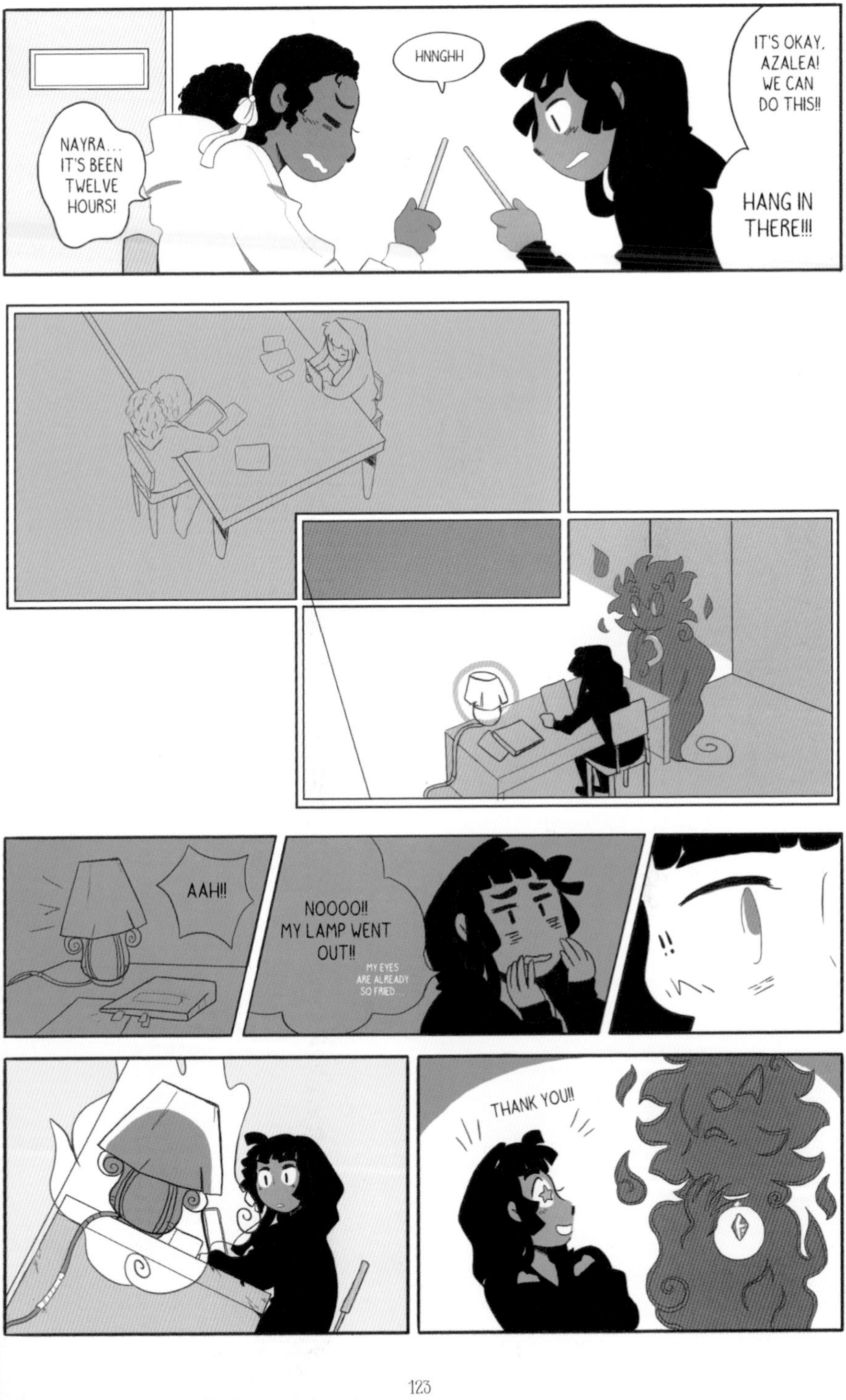
NAYRA... IT'S BEEN TWELVE HOURS!
HNNGHH
IT'S OKAY, AZALEA! WE CAN DO THIS!!
HANG IN THERE!!!
AAH!!
NOOOO!! MY LAMP WENT OUT!!
MY EYES ARE ALREADY SO FRIED...
!!
THANK YOU!!

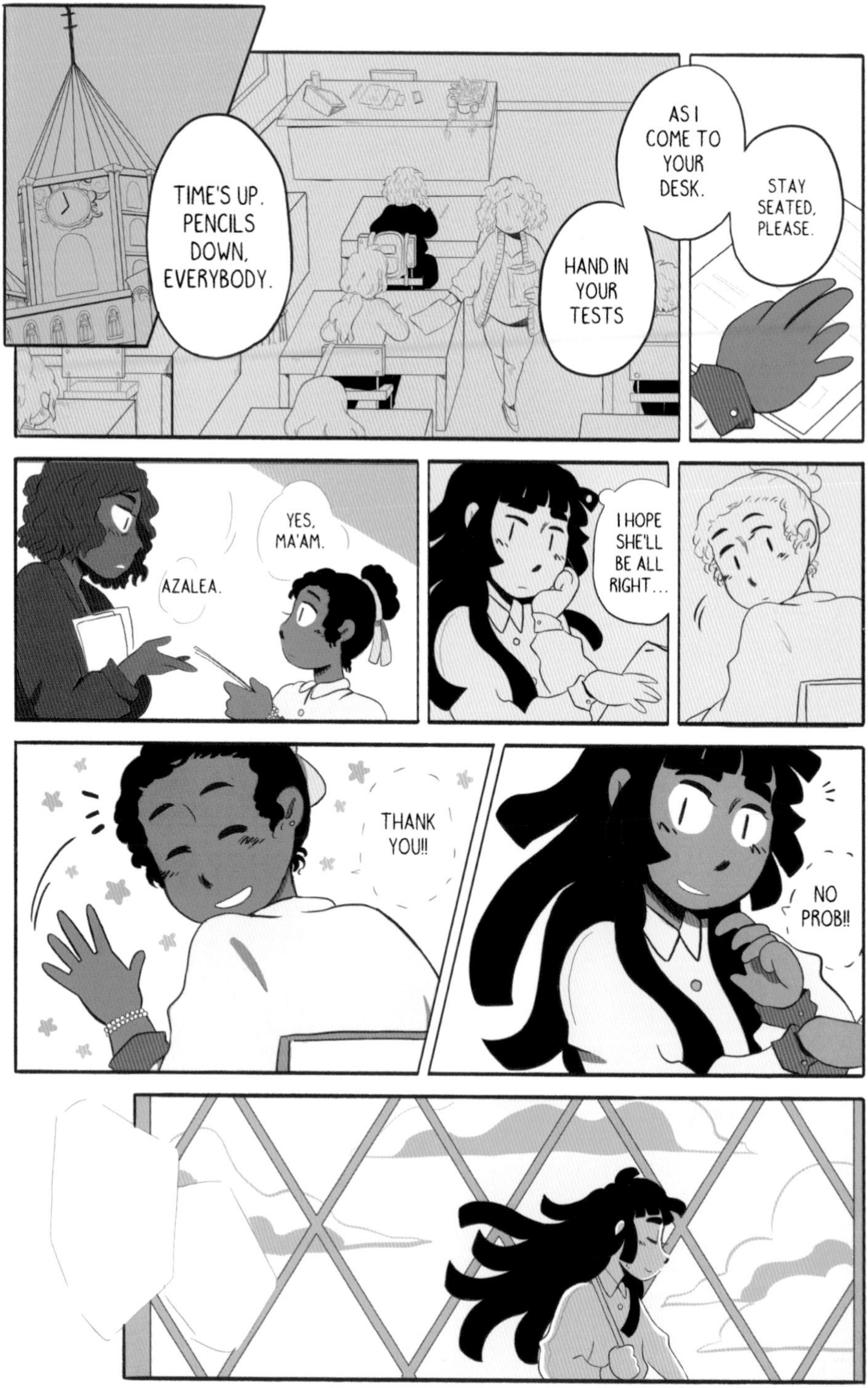
TIME'S UP. PENCILS DOWN, EVERYBODY.
HAND IN YOUR TESTS
AS I COME TO YOUR DESK.
STAY SEATED, PLEASE.
AZALEA.
YES, MA'AM.
I HOPE SHE'LL BE ALL RIGHT...
THANK YOU!!
NO PROB!!

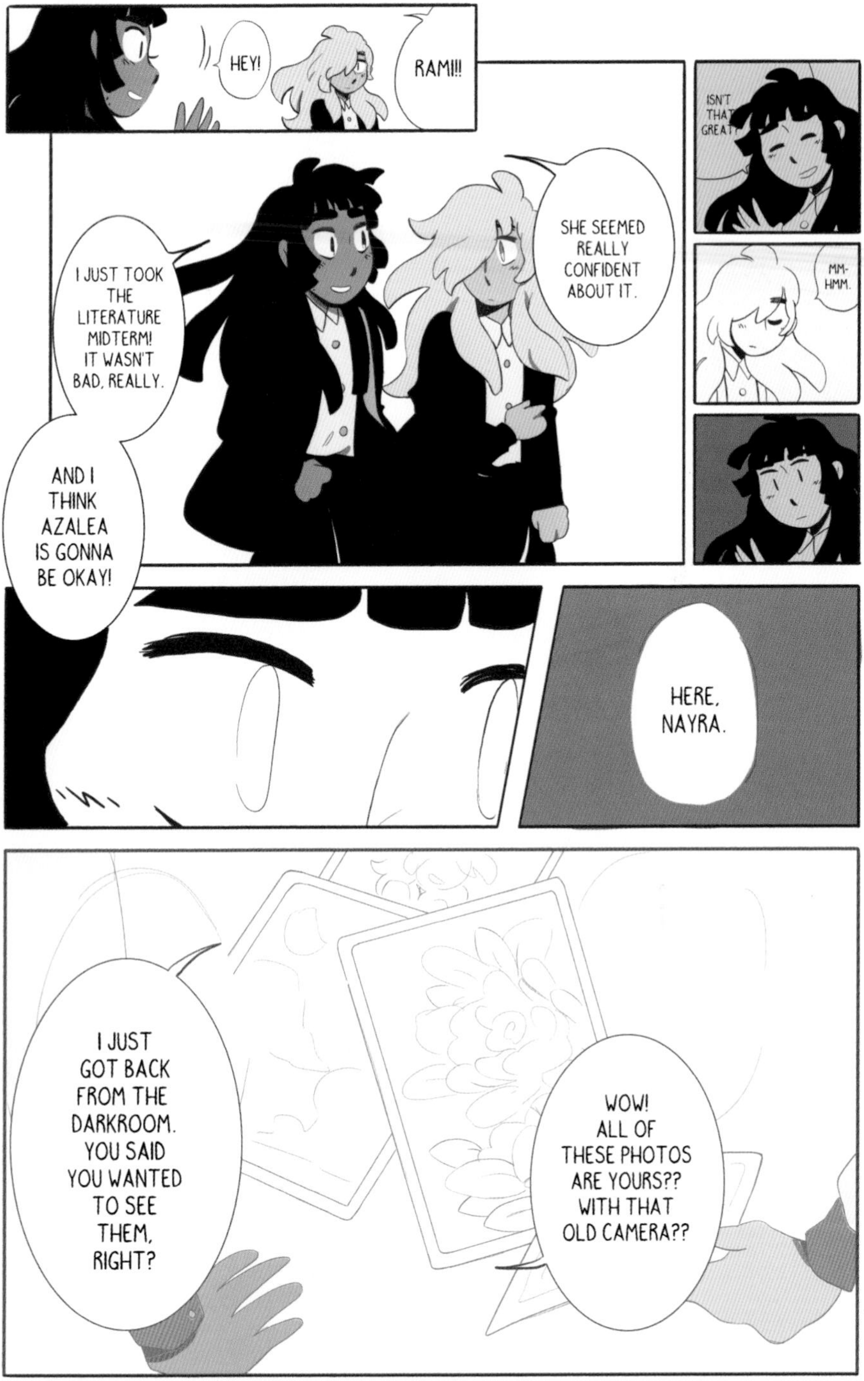
HEY!
RAMI!!
I JUST TOOK THE LITERATURE MIDTERM! IT WASN'T BAD, REALLY.
AND I THINK AZALEA IS GONNA BE OKAY!
SHE SEEMED REALLY CONFIDENT ABOUT IT.
ISN'T THAT GREAT?
MM-HMM.
HERE, NAYRA.
I JUST GOT BACK FROM THE DARKROOM. YOU SAID YOU WANTED TO SEE THEM, RIGHT?
WOW! ALL OF THESE PHOTOS ARE YOURS?? WITH THAT OLD CAMERA??

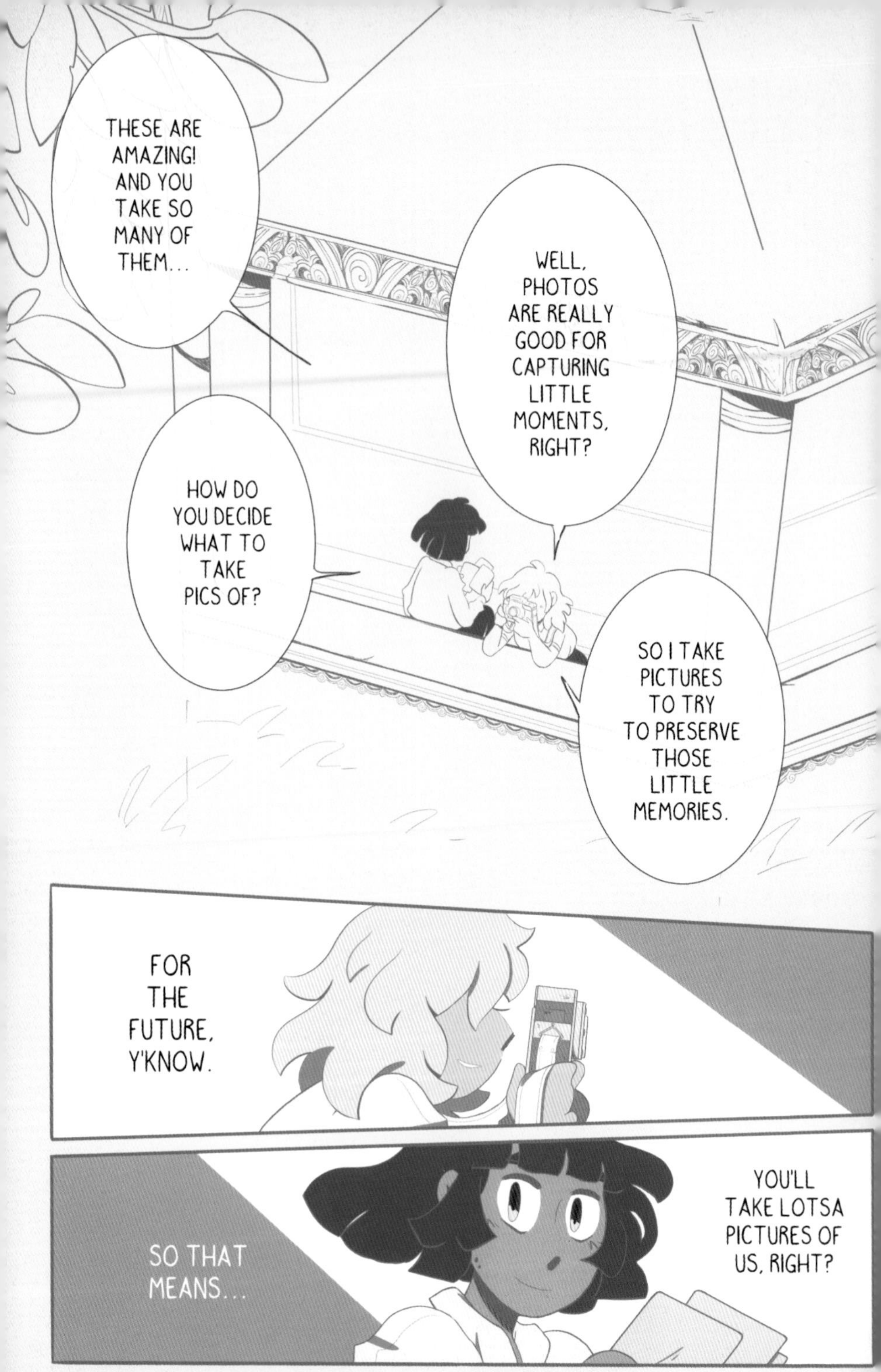
THESE ARE AMAZING! AND YOU TAKE SO MANY OF THEM...
WELL, PHOTOS ARE REALLY GOOD FOR CAPTURING LITTLE MOMENTS, RIGHT?
HOW DO YOU DECIDE WHAT TO TAKE PICS OF?
SO I TAKE PICTURES TO TRY TO PRESERVE THOSE LITTLE MEMORIES.
FOR THE FUTURE, Y'KNOW.
SO THAT MEANS...
YOU'LL TAKE LOTSA PICTURES OF US, RIGHT?

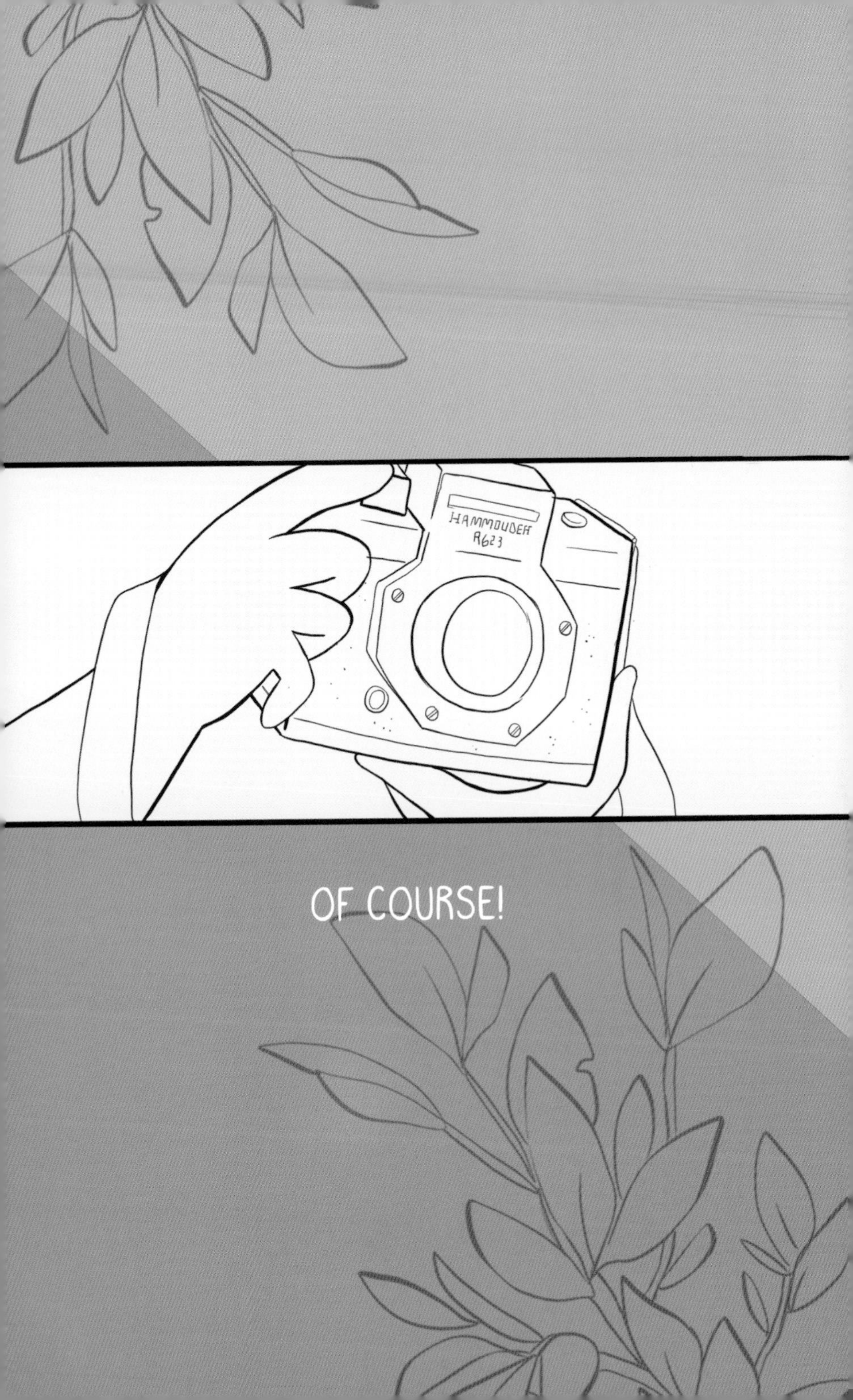
HAMMOUDEH
A623
OF COURSE!

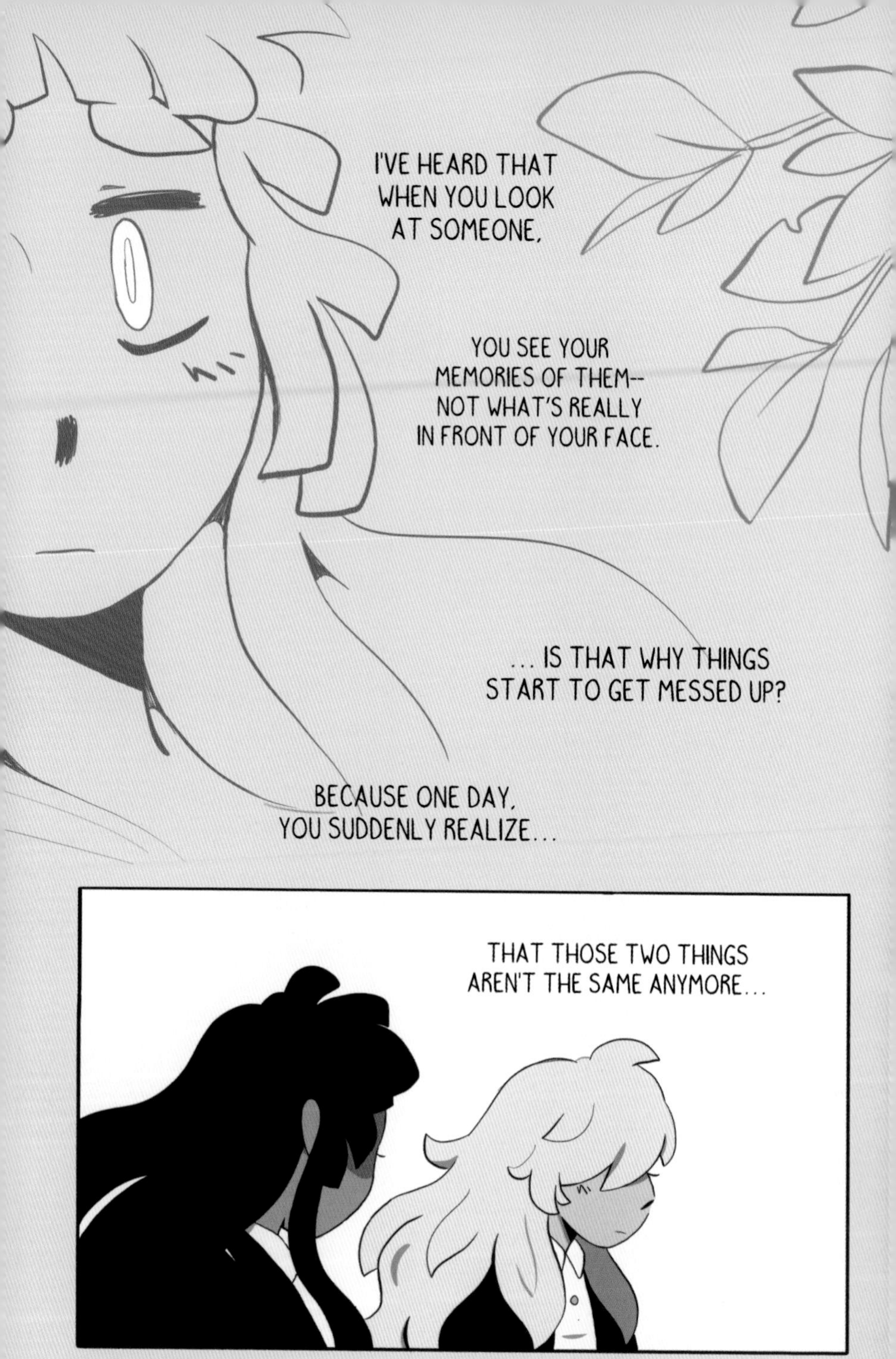
I'VE HEARD THAT WHEN YOU LOOK AT SOMEONE,
YOU SEE YOUR MEMORIES OF THEM-- NOT WHAT'S REALLY IN FRONT OF YOUR FACE.
... IS THAT WHY THINGS START TO GET MESSED UP?
BECAUSE ONE DAY, YOU SUDDENLY REALIZE...
THAT THOSE TWO THINGS AREN'T THE SAME ANYMORE...

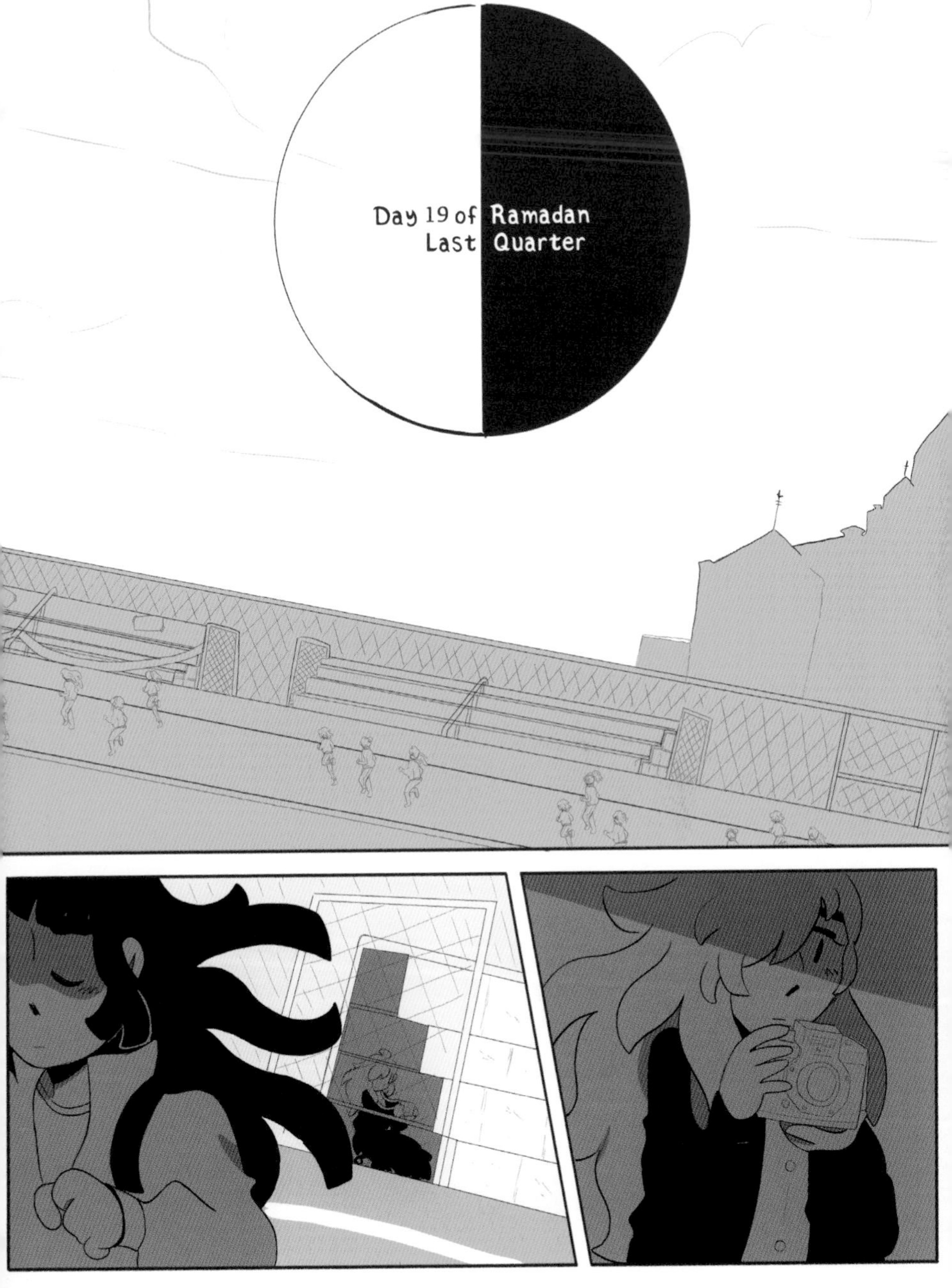
Day 19 of Ramadan
Last Quarter

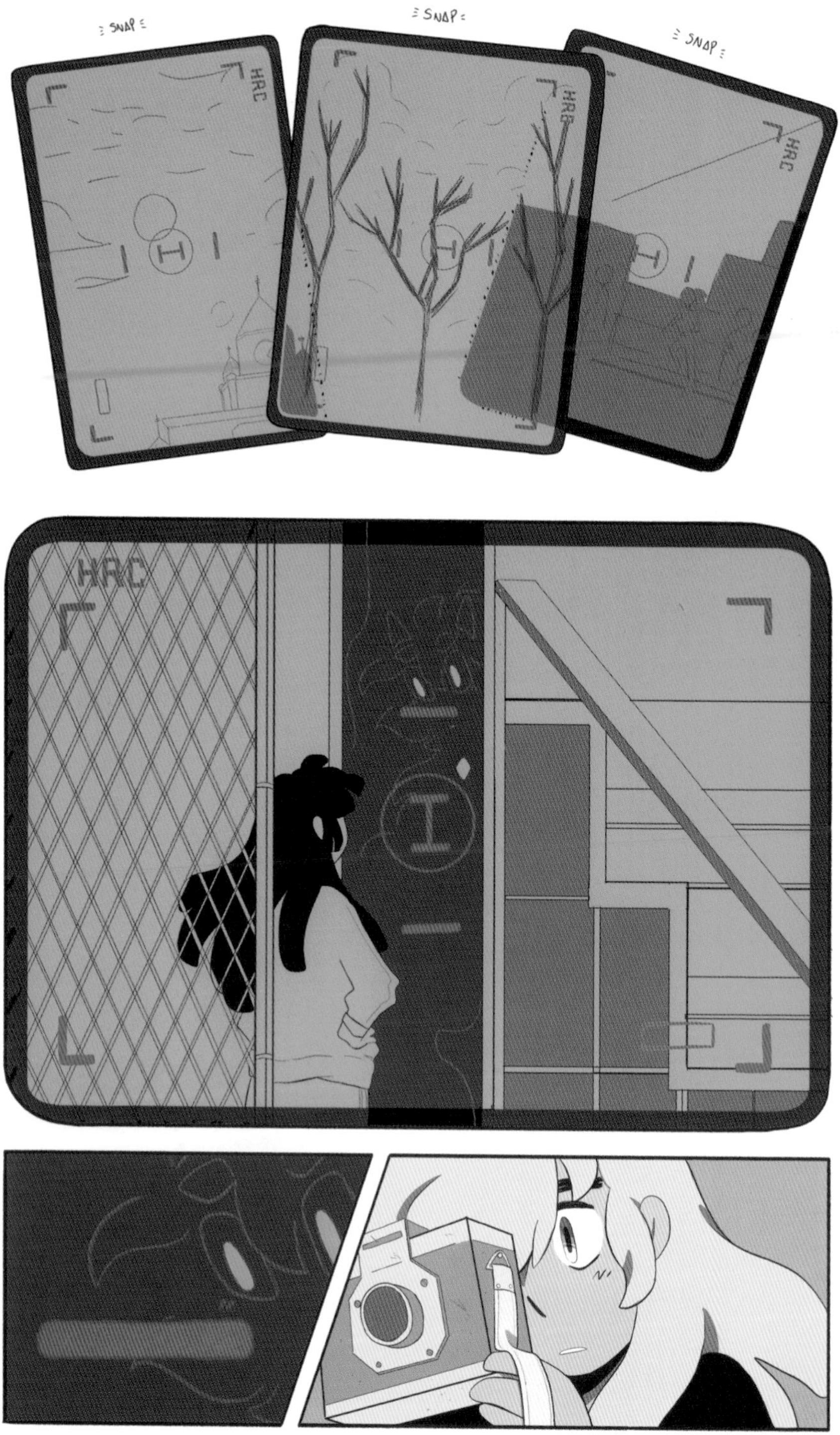
SNAP
HRC
SNAP
HRC
SNAP
HRC
HRC

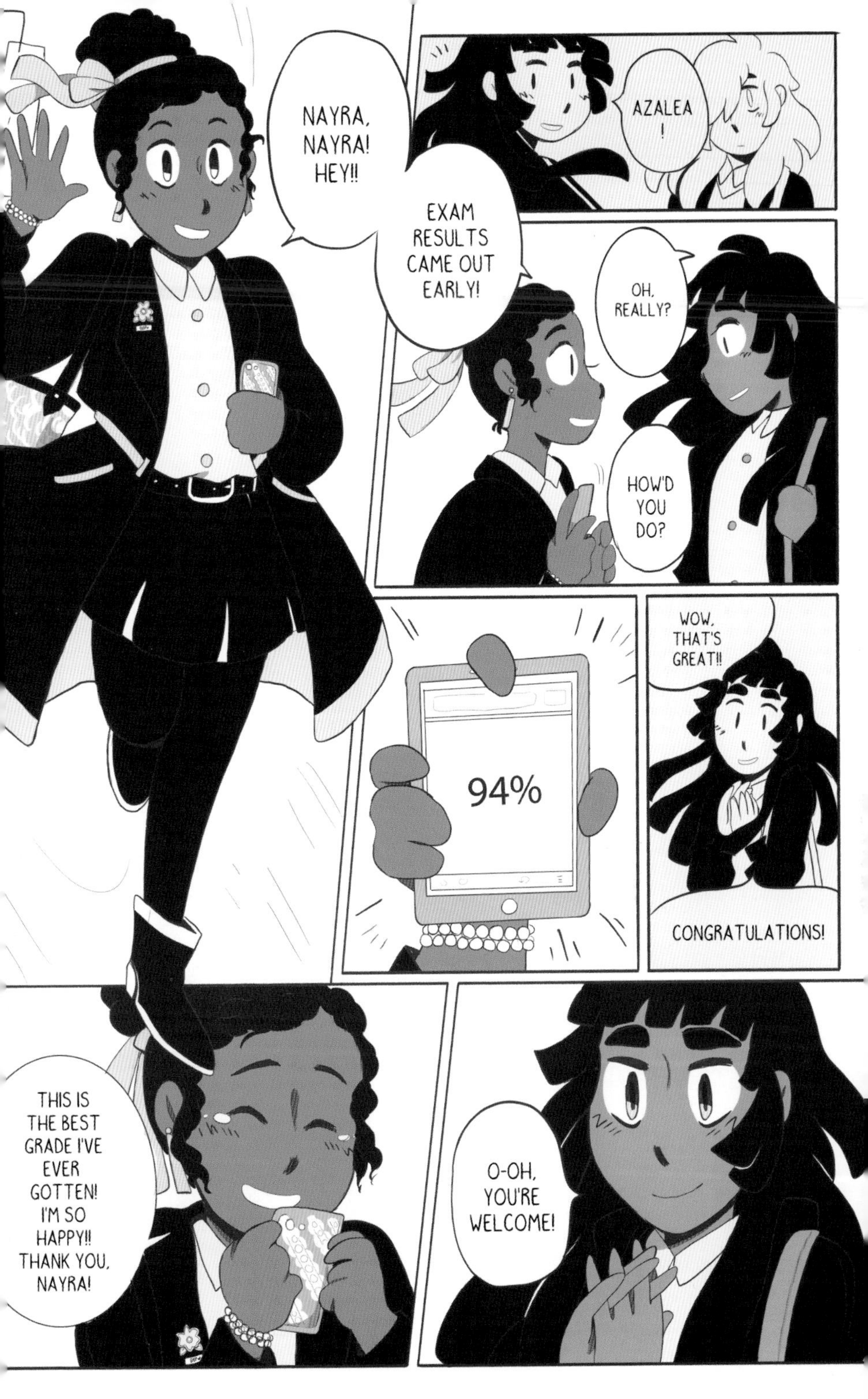

NAYRA, NAYRA! HEY!!
AZALEA!
EXAM RESULTS CAME OUT EARLY!
OH, REALLY?
HOW'D YOU DO?
94%
WOW, THAT'S GREAT!!
CONGRATULATIONS!
THIS IS THE BEST GRADE I'VE EVER GOTTEN! I'M SO HAPPY!! THANK YOU, NAYRA!
O-OH, YOU'RE WELCOME!

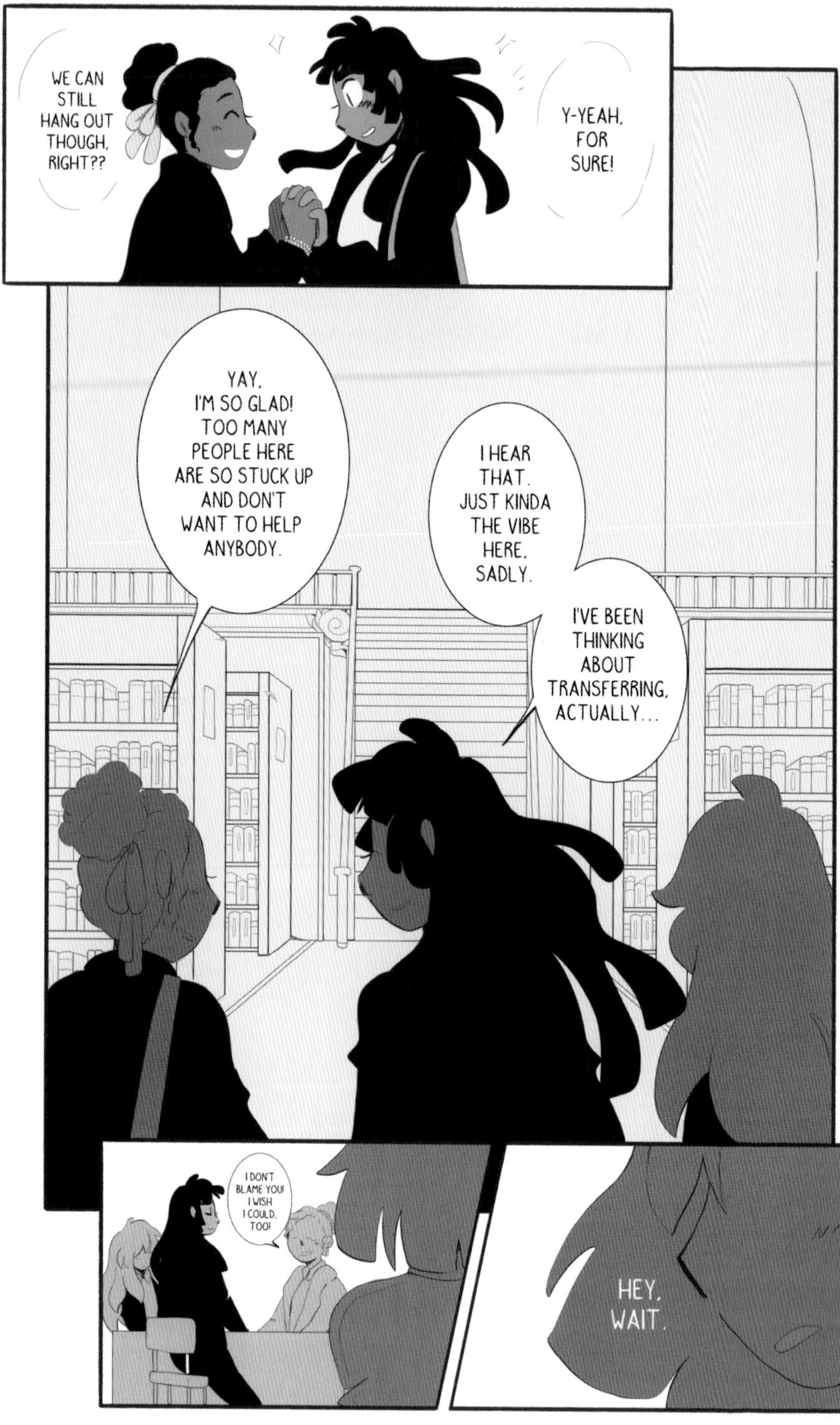
WE CAN STILL HANG OUT THOUGH, RIGHT??
Y-YEAH, FOR SURE!
YAY, I'M SO GLAD! TOO MANY PEOPLE HERE ARE SO STUCK UP AND DON'T WANT TO HELP ANYBODY.
I HEAR THAT. JUST KINDA THE VIBE HERE, SADLY.
I'VE BEEN THINKING ABOUT TRANSFERRING, ACTUALLY...
I DON'T BLAME YOU! I WISH I COULD, TOO!
HEY, WAIT.

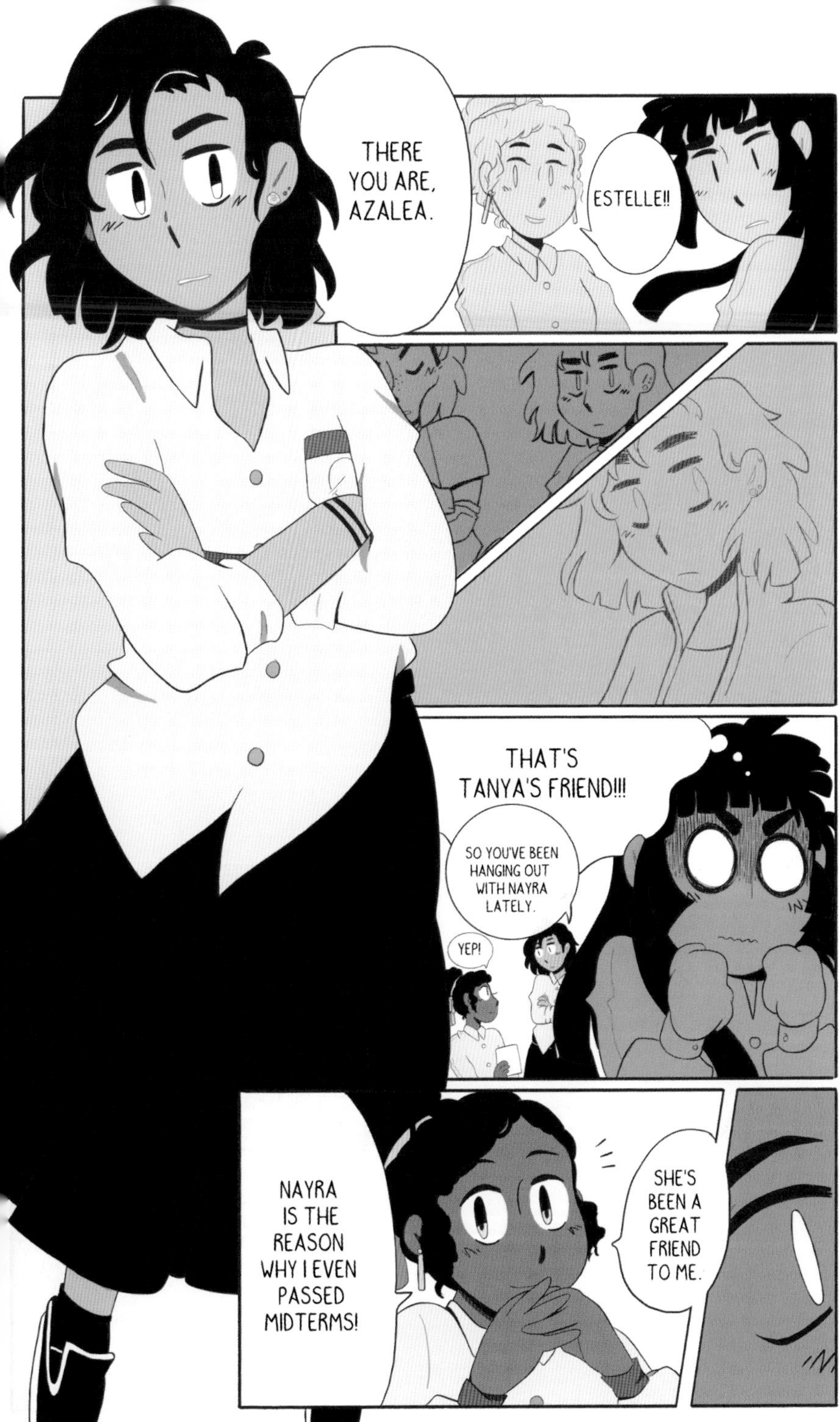
THERE YOU ARE, AZALEA.
ESTELLE!!
THAT'S TANYA'S FRIEND!!!
SO YOU'VE BEEN HANGING OUT WITH NAYRA LATELY.
YEP!
NAYRA IS THE REASON WHY I EVEN PASSED MIDTERMS!
SHE'S BEEN A GREAT FRIEND TO ME.

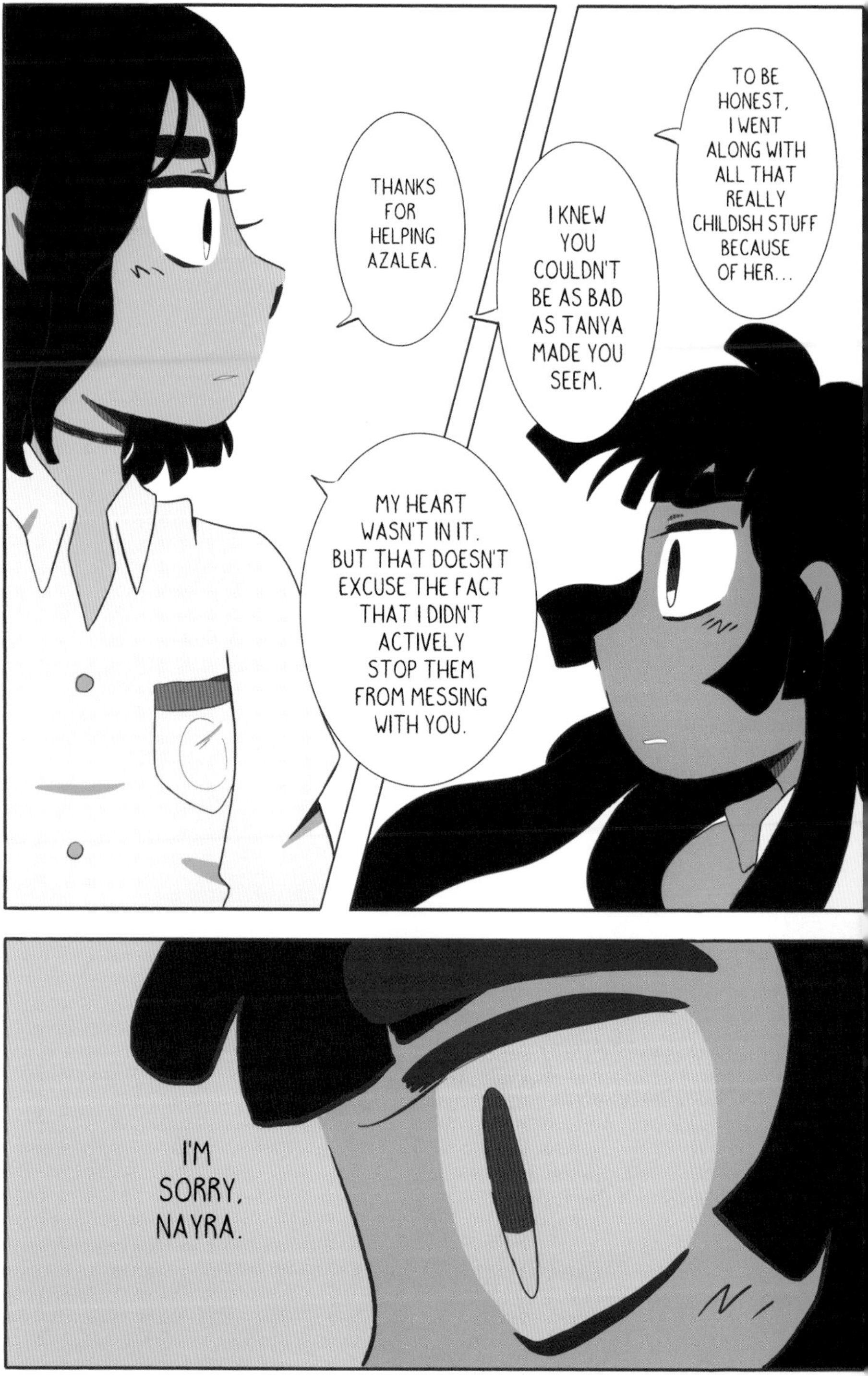
TO BE HONEST, I WENT ALONG WITH ALL THAT REALLY CHILDISH STUFF BECAUSE OF HER...
I KNEW YOU COULDN'T BE AS BAD AS TANYA MADE YOU SEEM.
THANKS FOR HELPING AZALEA.
MY HEART WASN'T IN IT. BUT THAT DOESN'T EXCUSE THE FACT THAT I DIDN'T ACTIVELY STOP THEM FROM MESSING WITH YOU.
I'M SORRY, NAYRA.

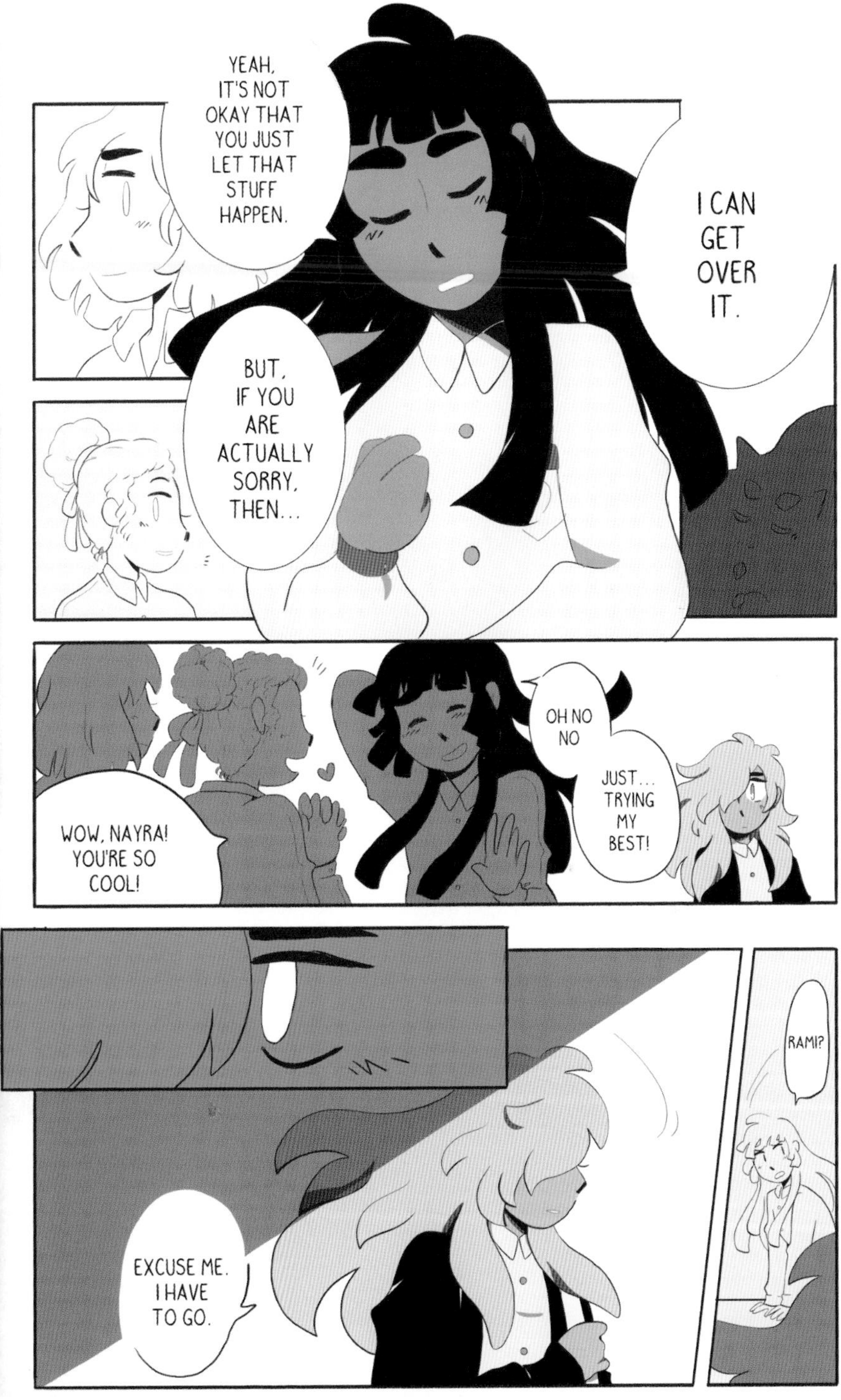
YEAH, IT'S NOT OKAY THAT YOU JUST LET THAT STUFF HAPPEN.
I CAN GET OVER IT.
BUT, IF YOU ARE ACTUALLY SORRY, THEN...
WOW, NAYRA! YOU'RE SO COOL!
OH NO NO
JUST... TRYING MY BEST!
RAMI?
EXCUSE ME. I HAVE TO GO.

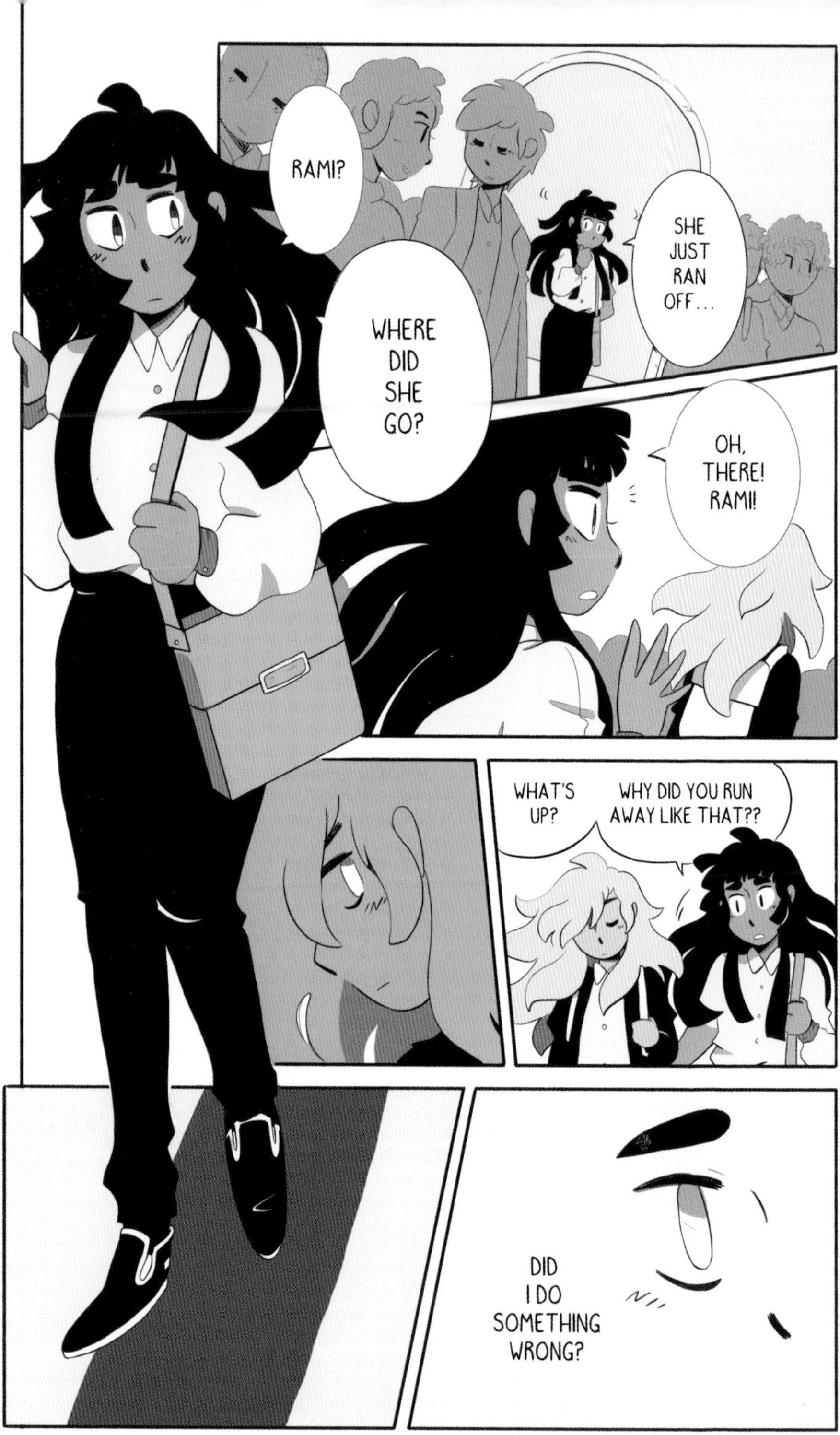
RAMI?
SHE JUST RAN OFF...
WHERE DID SHE GO?
OH, THERE! RAMI!
WHAT'S UP?
WHY DID YOU RUN AWAY LIKE THAT??
DID I DO SOMETHING WRONG?

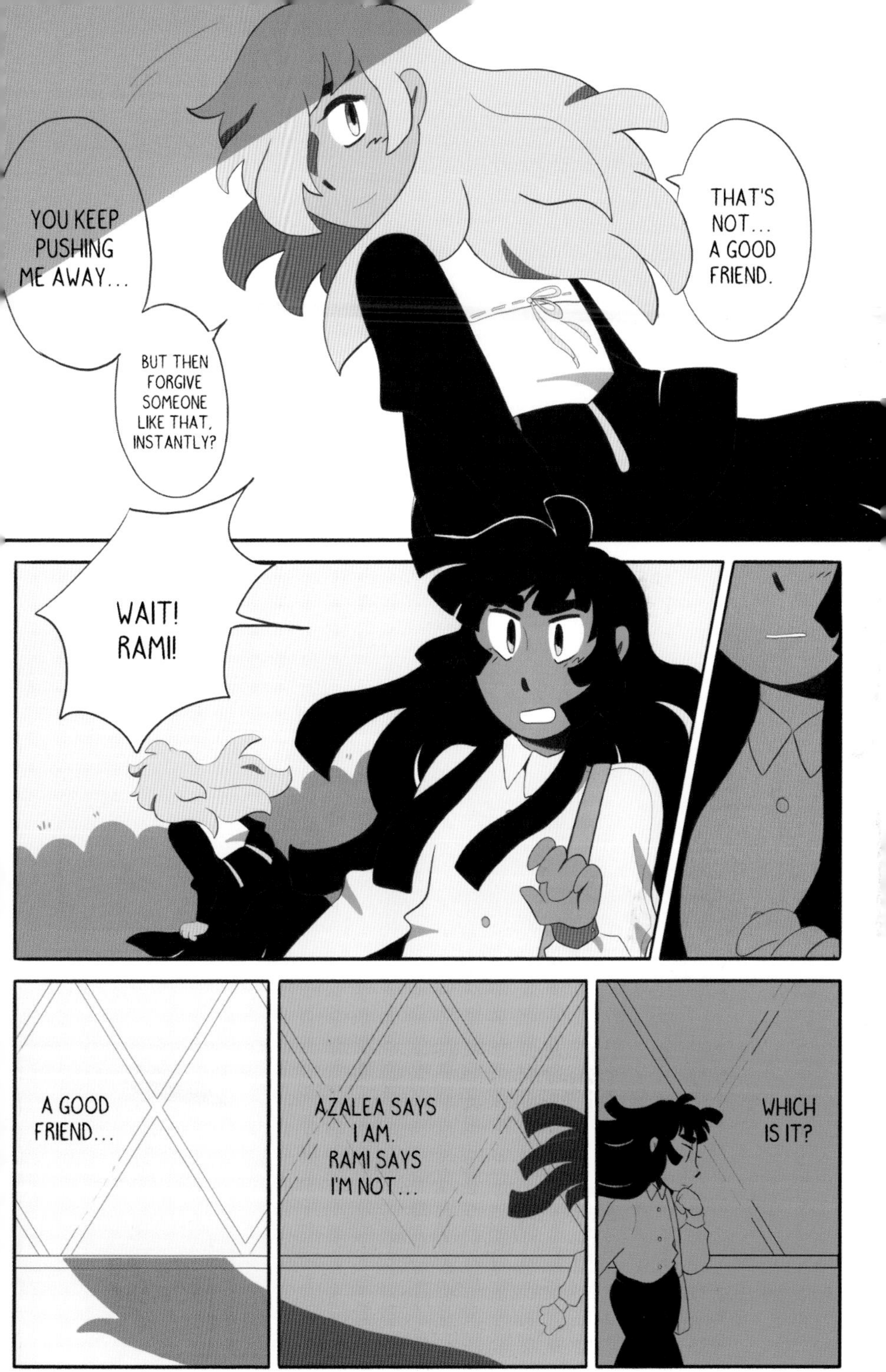
YOU KEEP PUSHING ME AWAY...
BUT THEN FORGIVE SOMEONE LIKE THAT, INSTANTLY?
THAT'S NOT... A GOOD FRIEND.
WAIT! RAMI!
A GOOD FRIEND...
AZALEA SAYS I AM. RAMI SAYS I'M NOT...
WHICH IS IT?

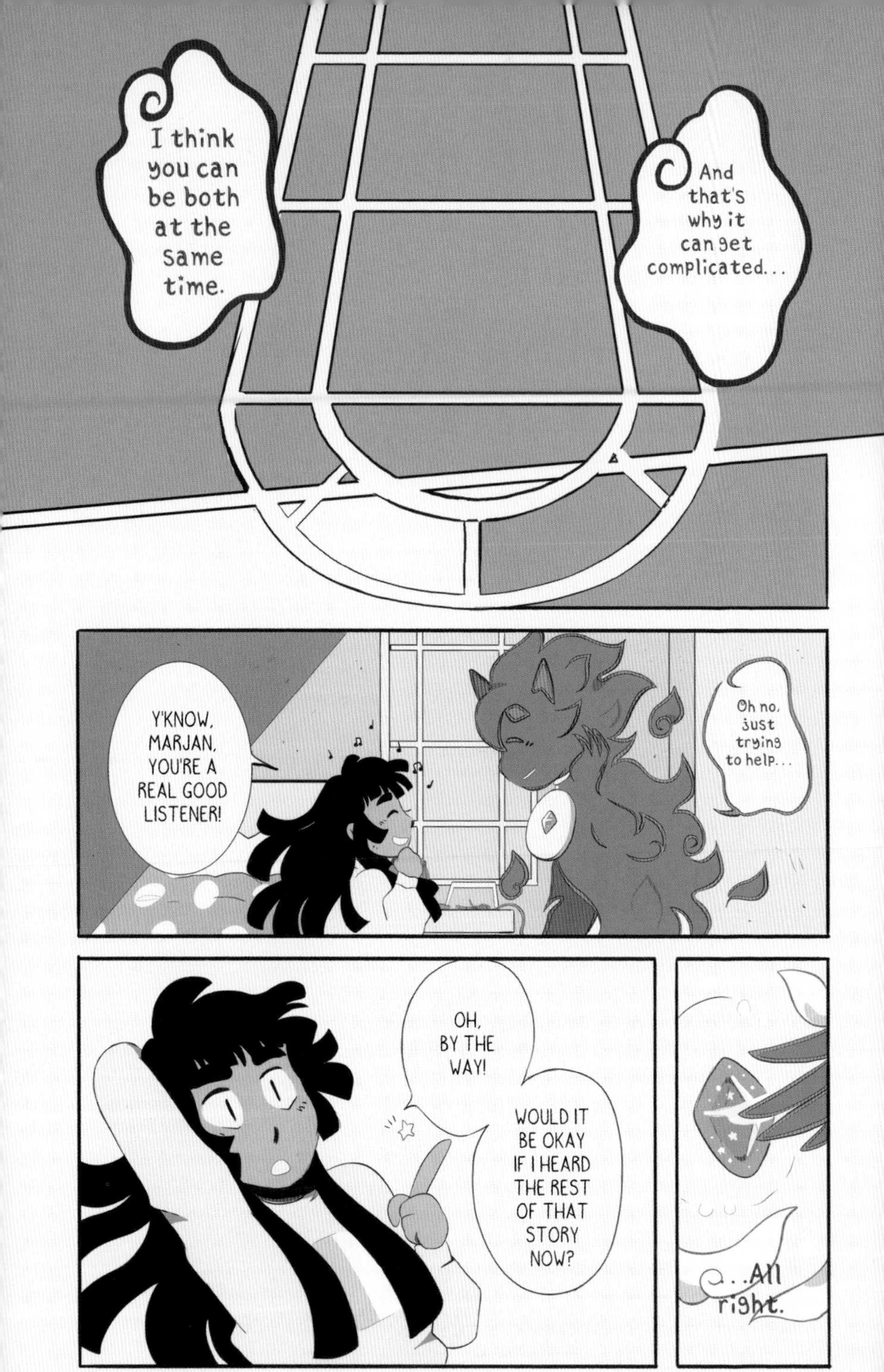
I think you can be both at the same time.
And that's why it can get complicated...
Y'KNOW, MARJAN, YOU'RE A REAL GOOD LISTENER!
Oh no, just trying to help...
OH, BY THE WAY!
WOULD IT BE OKAY IF I HEARD THE REST OF THAT STORY NOW?
...All right.

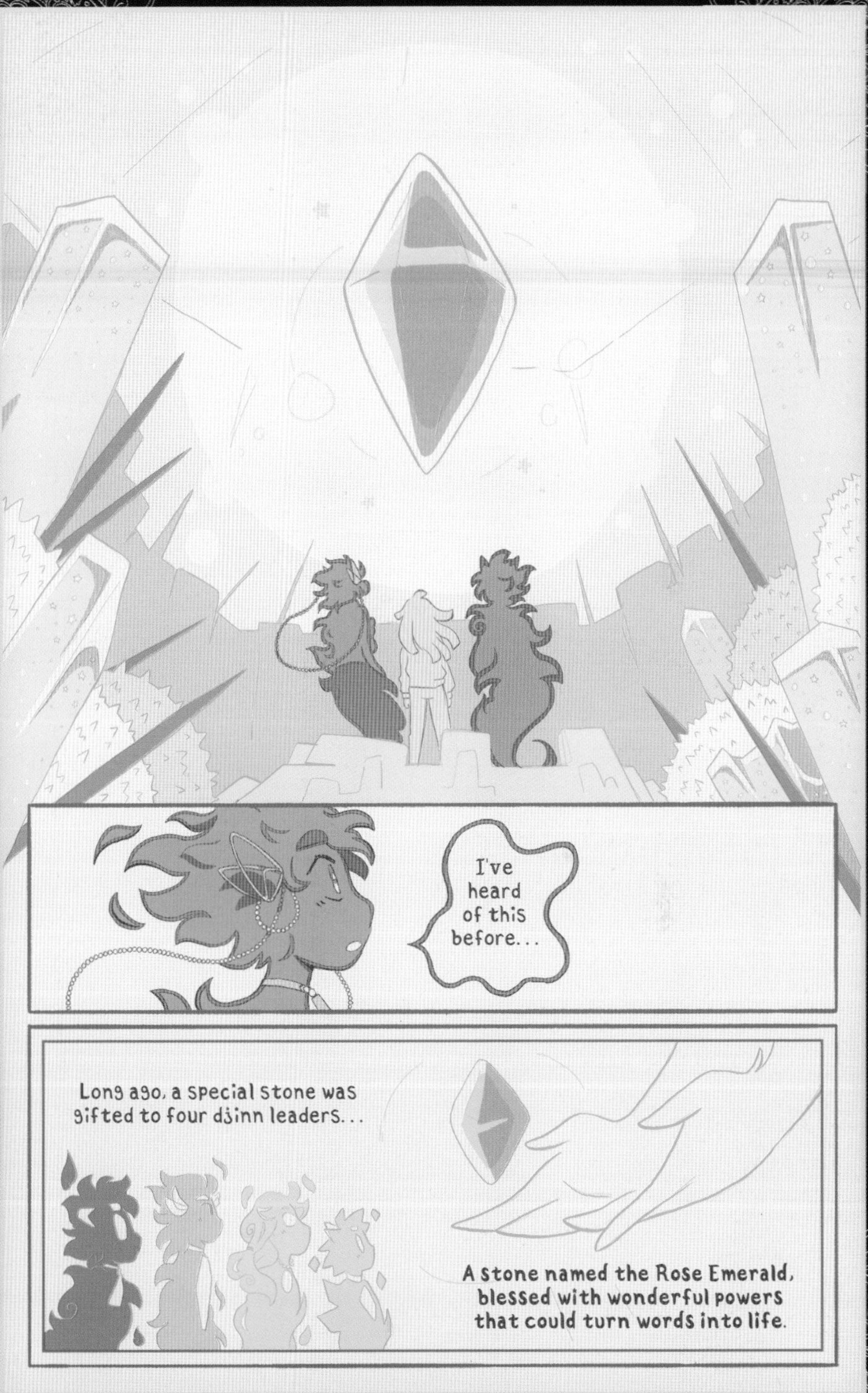
I've heard of this before...
Long ago, a special stone was gifted to four djinn leaders...
A stone named the Rose Emerald, blessed with wonderful powers that could turn words into life.

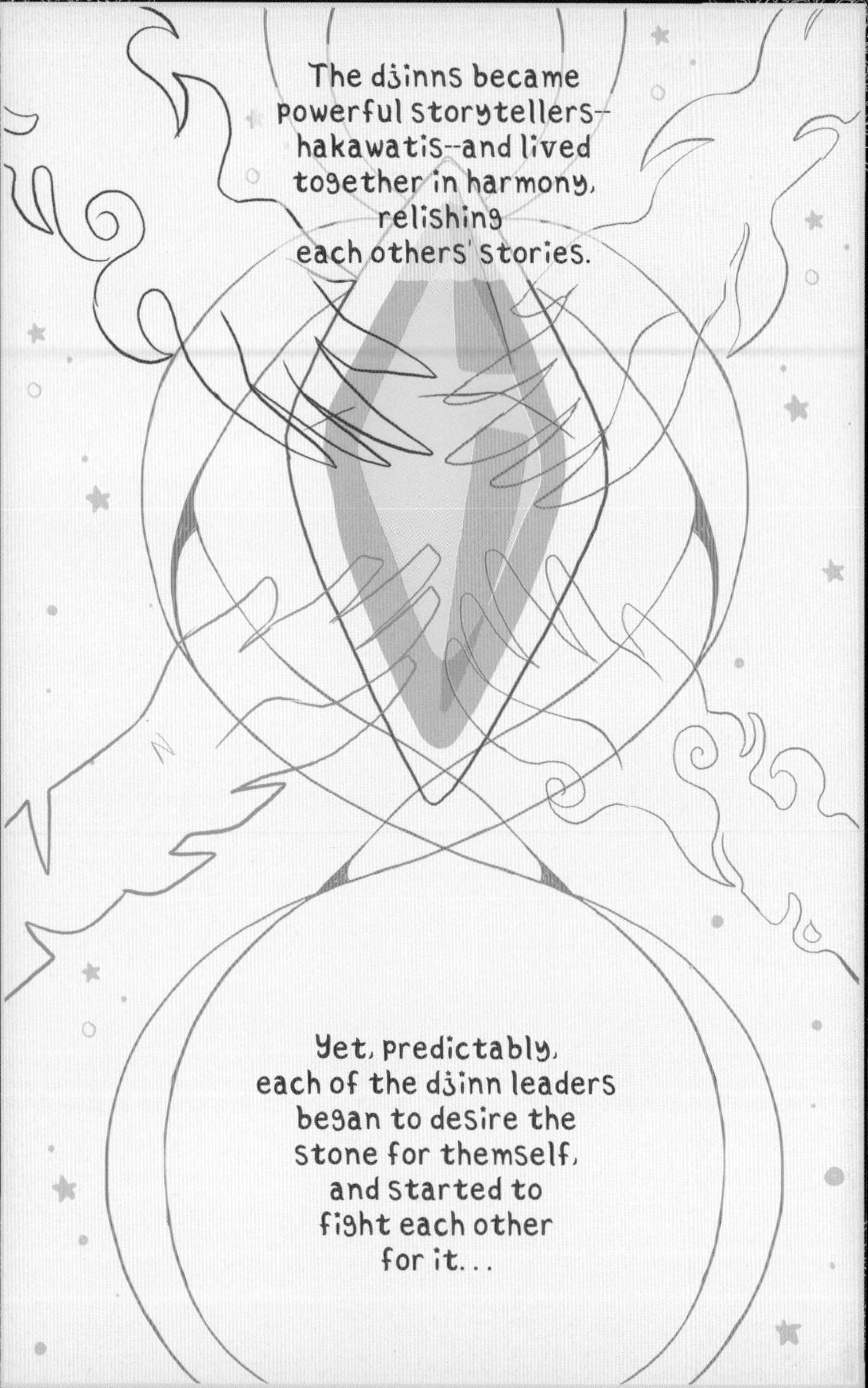
The djinns became powerful storytellers--hakawatis--and lived together in harmony, relishing each others' stories.
Yet, predictably, each of the djinn leaders began to desire the stone for themself, and started to fight each other for it...

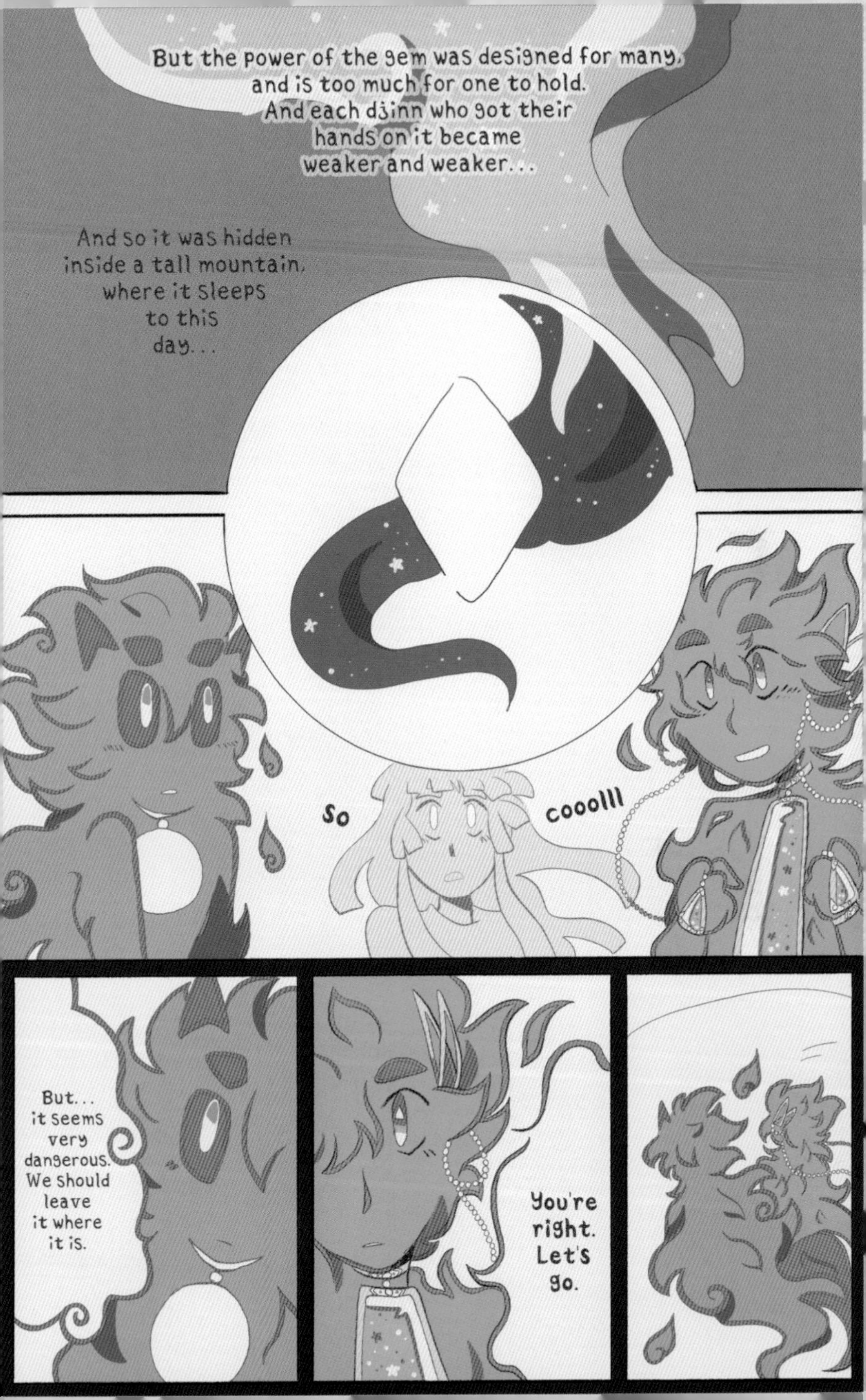
But the power of the gem was designed for many, and is too much for one to hold. And each djinn who got their hands on it became weaker and weaker...
And so it was hidden inside a tall mountain, where it sleeps to this day...
So
cooolll
But... it seems very dangerous. We should leave it where it is.
You're right. Let's go.

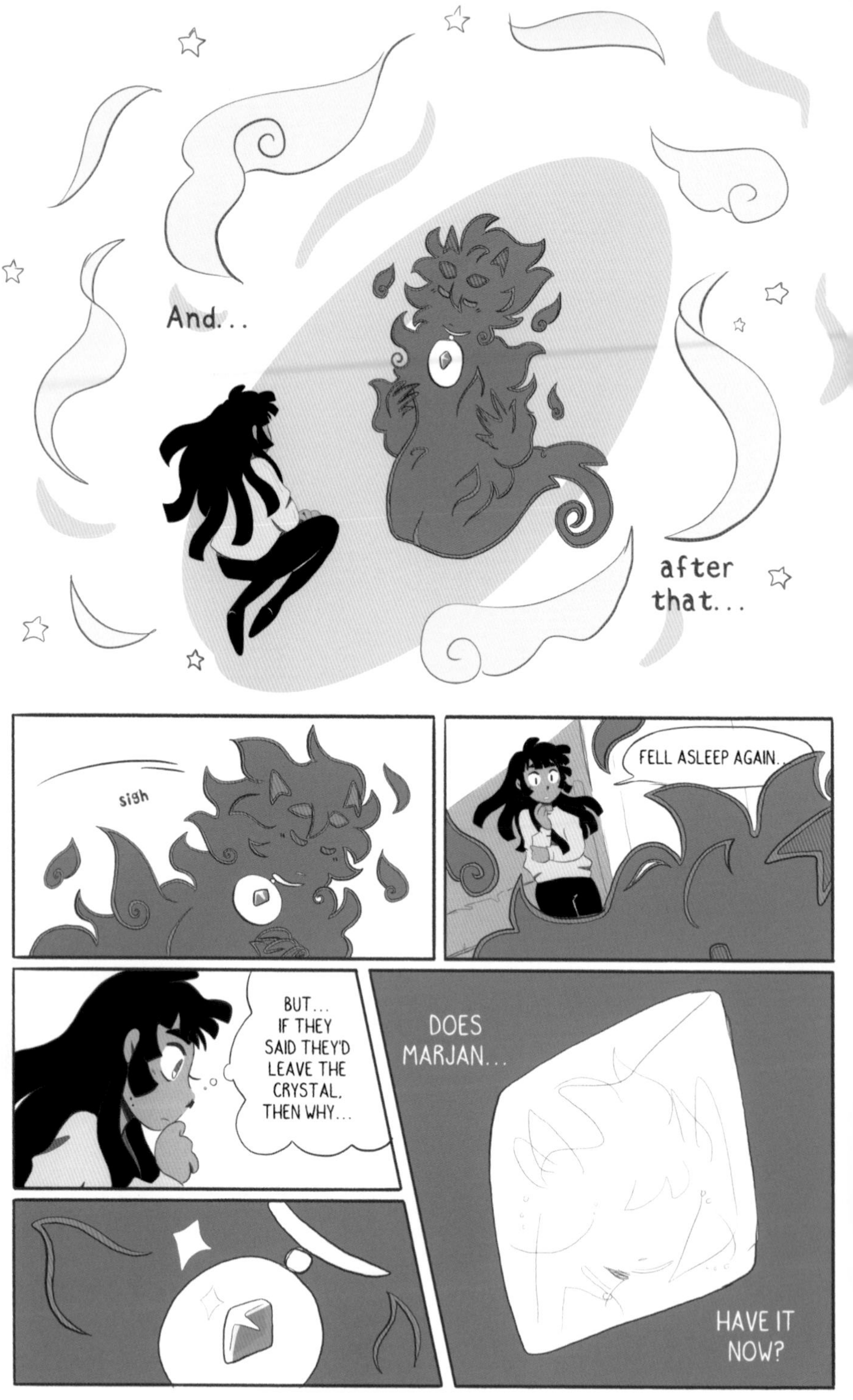

And...
after that...
sigh
FELL ASLEEP AGAIN...
BUT... IF THEY SAID THEY'D LEAVE THE CRYSTAL, THEN WHY...
DOES MARJAN...
HAVE IT NOW?

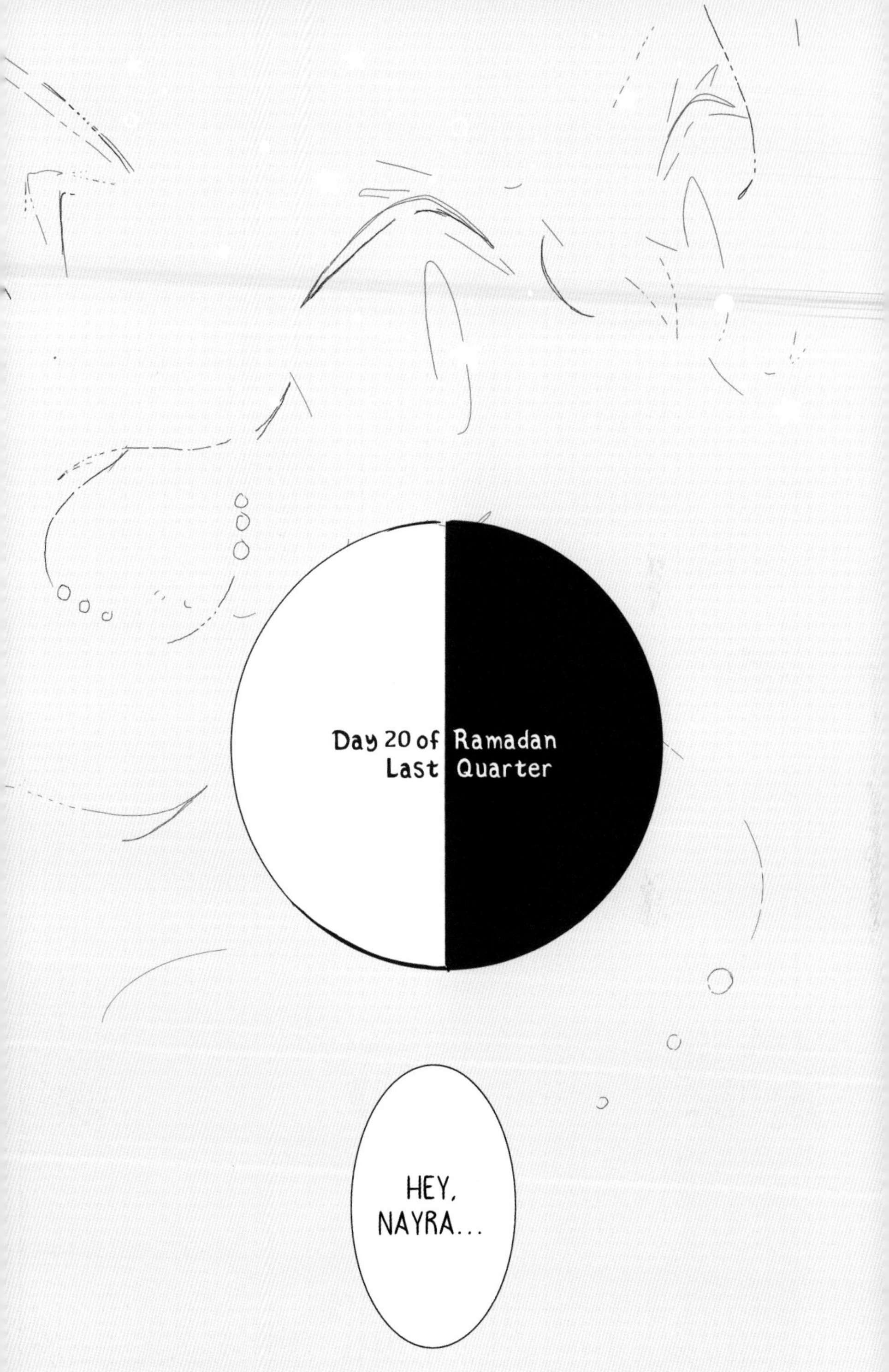
Day 20 of Ramadan
Last Quarter
HEY, NAYRA...

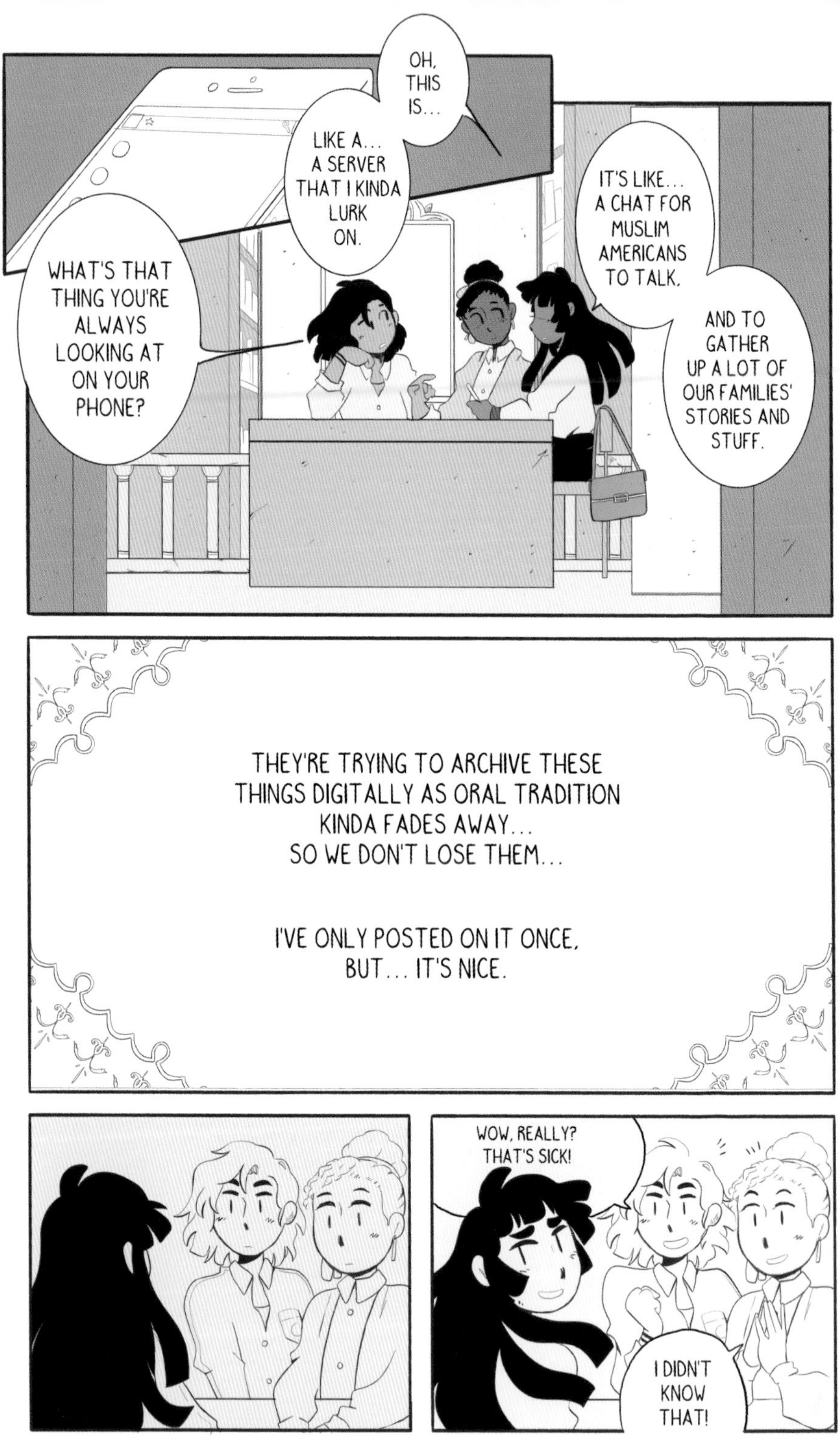
WHAT'S THAT THING YOU'RE ALWAYS LOOKING AT ON YOUR PHONE?
OH, THIS IS...
LIKE A... A SERVER THAT I KINDA LURK ON.
IT'S LIKE... A CHAT FOR MUSLIM AMERICANS TO TALK,
AND TO GATHER UP A LOT OF OUR FAMILIES' STORIES AND STUFF.
THEY'RE TRYING TO ARCHIVE THESE THINGS DIGITALLY AS ORAL TRADITION KINDA FADES AWAY... SO WE DON'T LOSE THEM...
I'VE ONLY POSTED ON IT ONCE, BUT... IT'S NICE.
WOW, REALLY? THAT'S SICK!
I DIDN'T KNOW THAT!

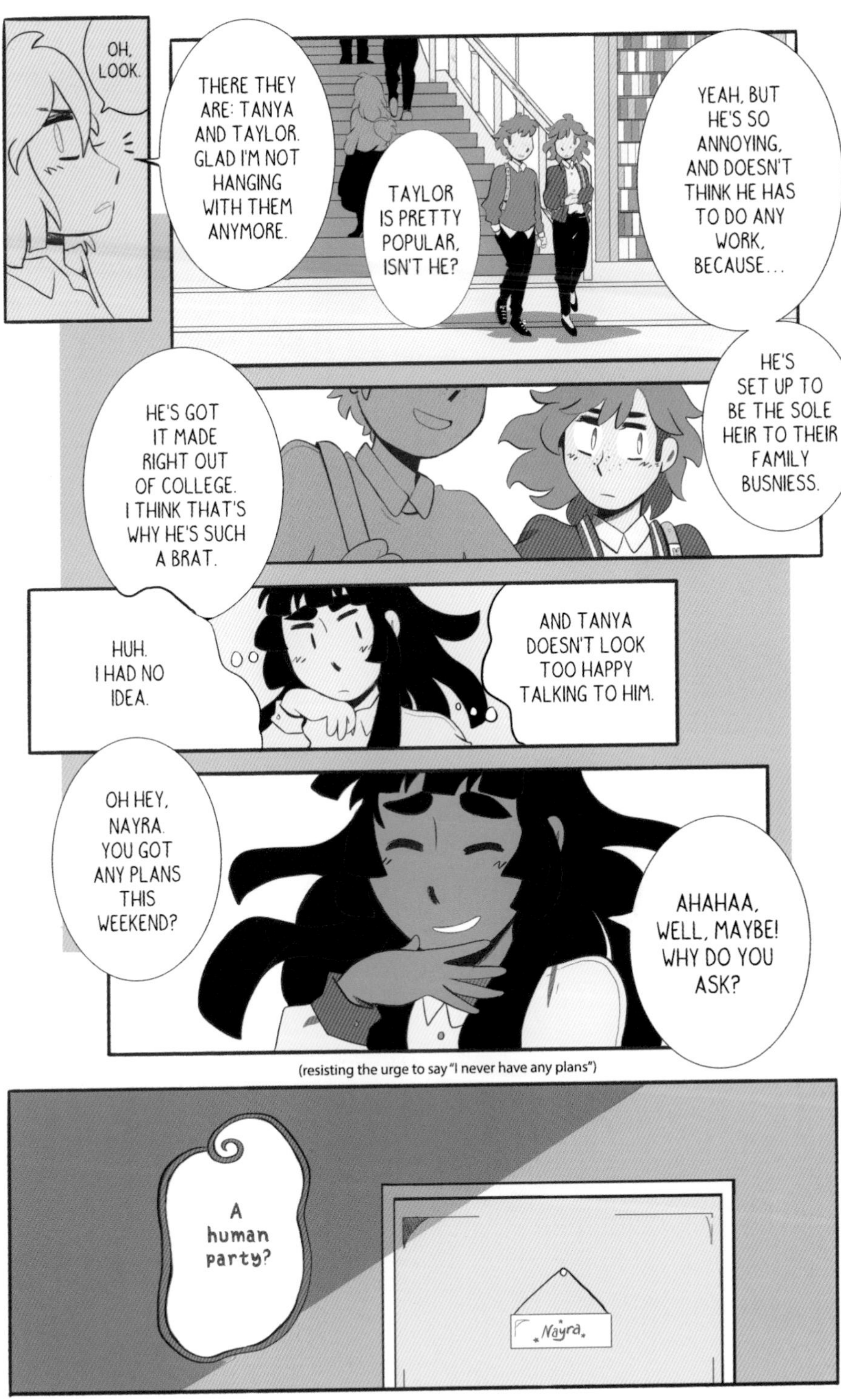
OH, LOOK.
THERE THEY ARE: TANYA AND TAYLOR. GLAD I'M NOT HANGING WITH THEM ANYMORE.
TAYLOR IS PRETTY POPULAR, ISN'T HE?
YEAH, BUT HE'S SO ANNOYING, AND DOESN'T THINK HE HAS TO DO ANY WORK, BECAUSE...
HE'S SET UP TO BE THE SOLE HEIR TO THEIR FAMILY BUSNIESS.
HE'S GOT IT MADE RIGHT OUT OF COLLEGE. I THINK THAT'S WHY HE'S SUCH A BRAT.
HUH. I HAD NO IDEA.
AND TANYA DOESN'T LOOK TOO HAPPY TALKING TO HIM.
OH HEY, NAYRA. YOU GOT ANY PLANS THIS WEEKEND?
AHAHAA, WELL, MAYBE! WHY DO YOU ASK?
(resisting the urge to say "I never have any plans")
A human party?
Nayra

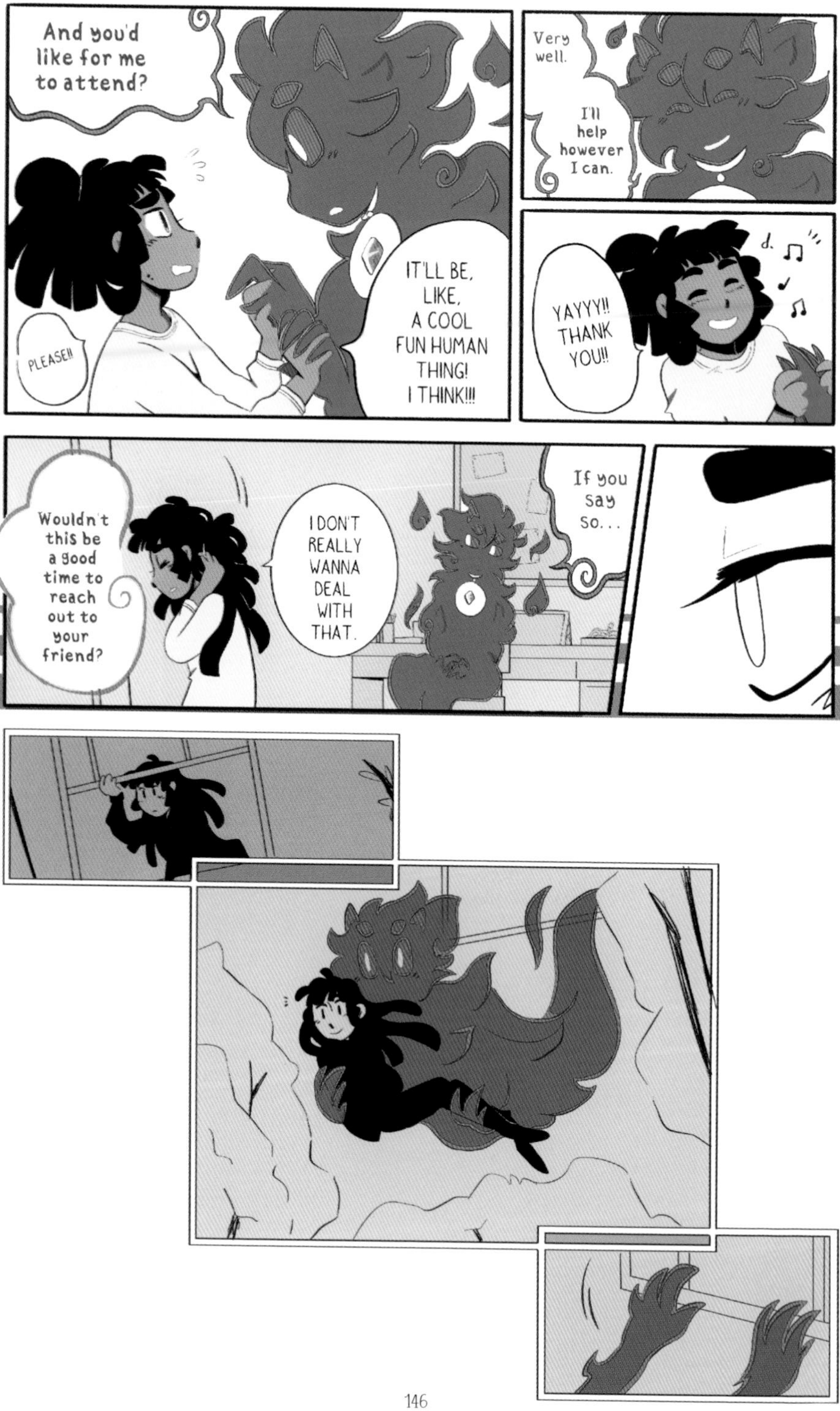
And you'd like for me to attend?
PLEASE!!
IT'LL BE, LIKE, A COOL FUN HUMAN THING! I THINK!!!
Very well.
I'll help however I can.
YAYYY!! THANK YOU!!
Wouldn't this be a good time to reach out to your friend?
I DON'T REALLY WANNA DEAL WITH THAT.
If you say so...

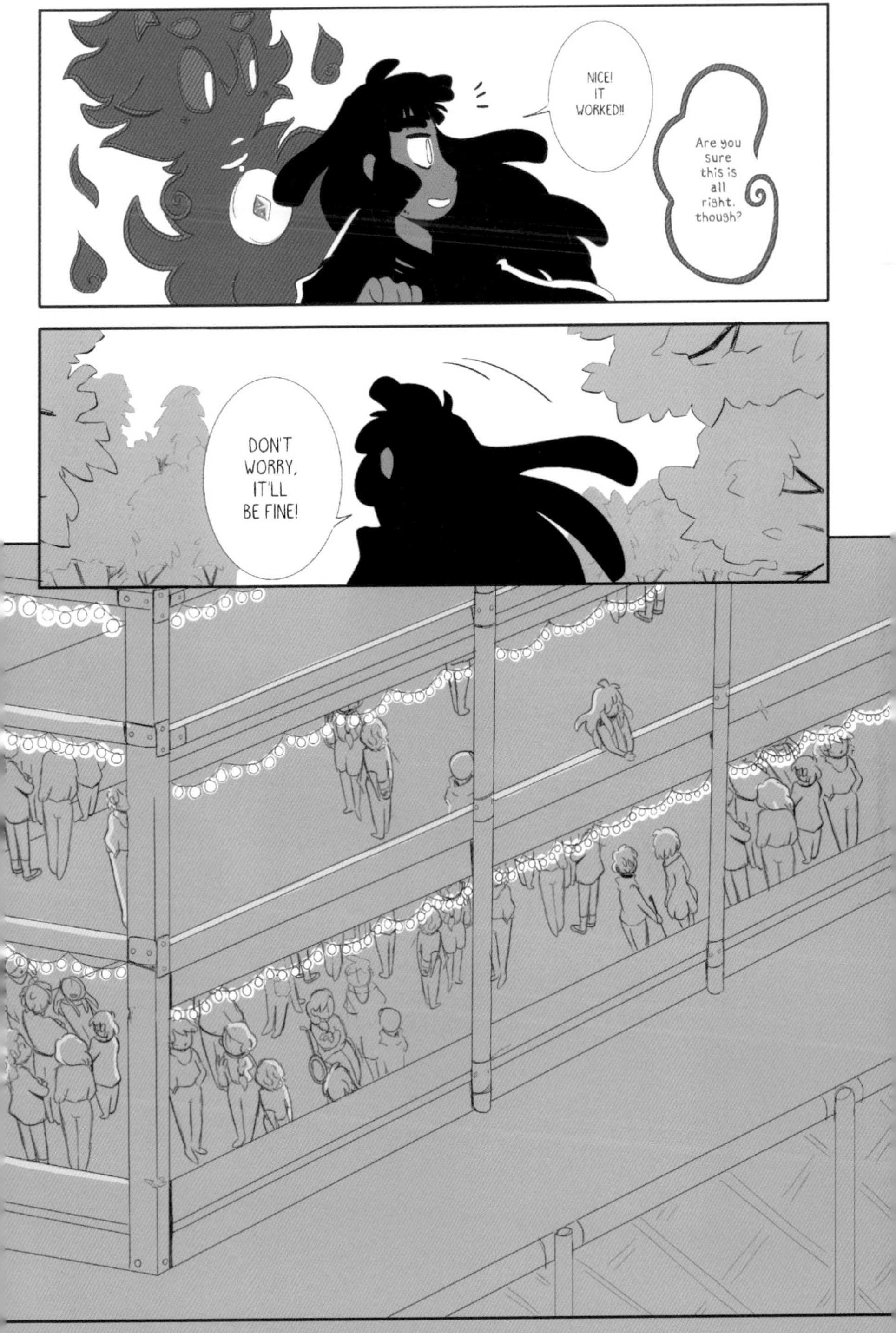
NICE! IT WORKED!!
Are you sure this is all right, though?
DON'T WORRY, IT'LL BE FINE!

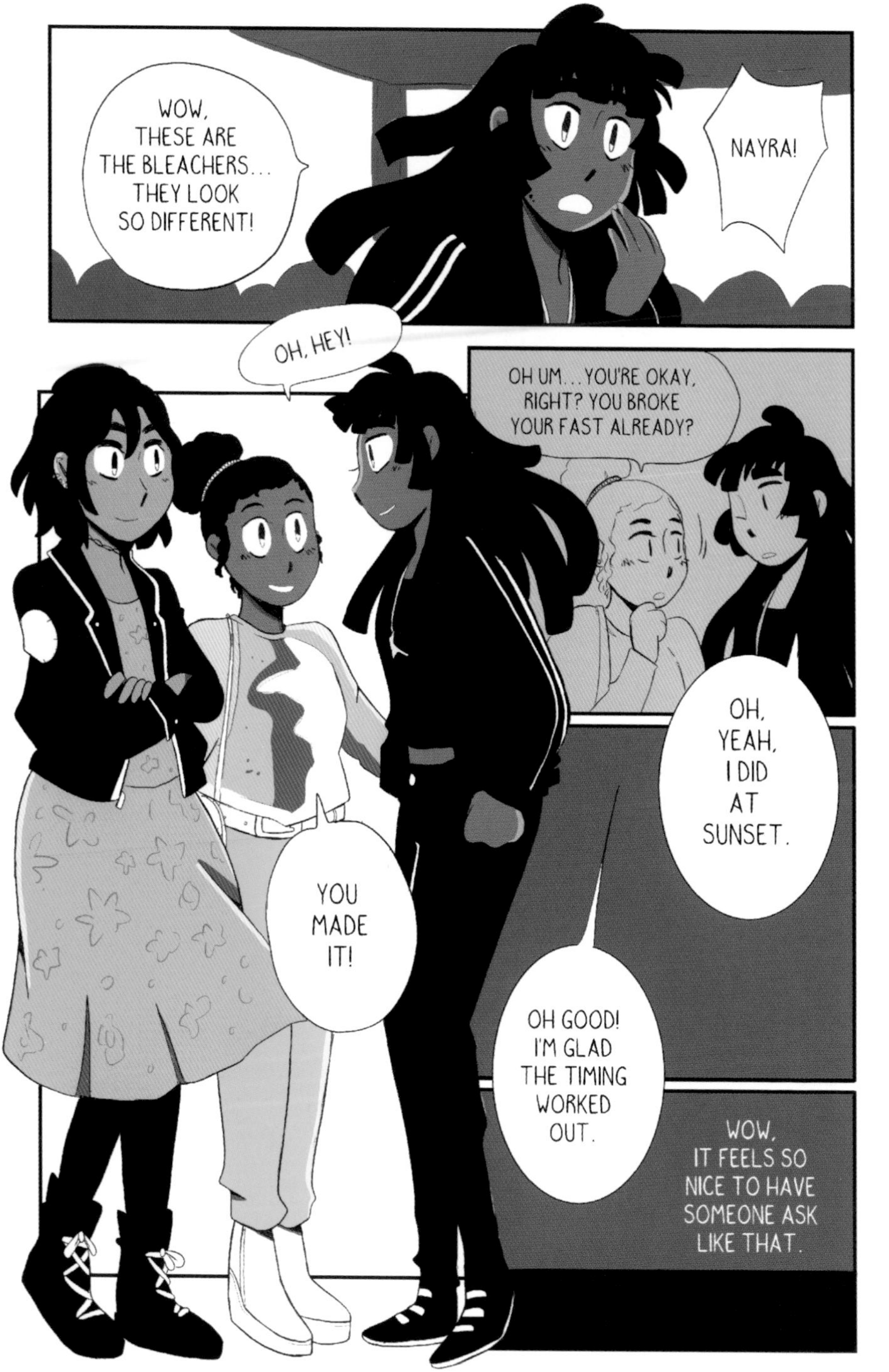
WOW, THESE ARE THE BLEACHERS... THEY LOOK SO DIFFERENT!
NAYRA!
OH, HEY!
YOU MADE IT!
OH UM... YOU'RE OKAY, RIGHT? YOU BROKE YOUR FAST ALREADY?
OH, YEAH, I DID AT SUNSET.
OH GOOD! I'M GLAD THE TIMING WORKED OUT.
WOW, IT FEELS SO NICE TO HAVE SOMEONE ASK LIKE THAT.

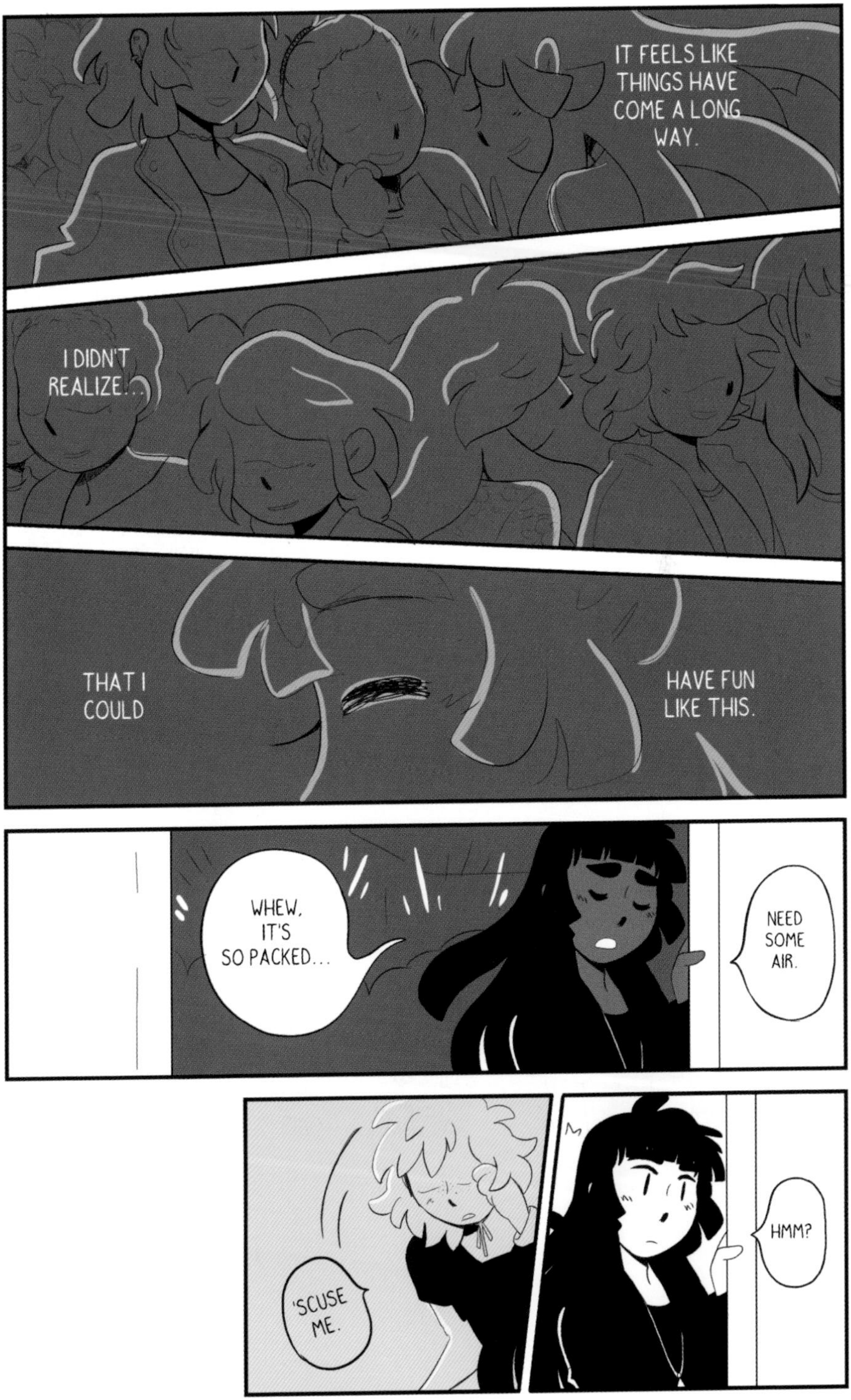
IT FEELS LIKE THINGS HAVE COME A LONG WAY.
I DIDN'T REALIZE...
THAT I COULD
HAVE FUN LIKE THIS.
WHEW, IT'S SO PACKED...
NEED SOME AIR.
'SCUSE ME.
HMM?

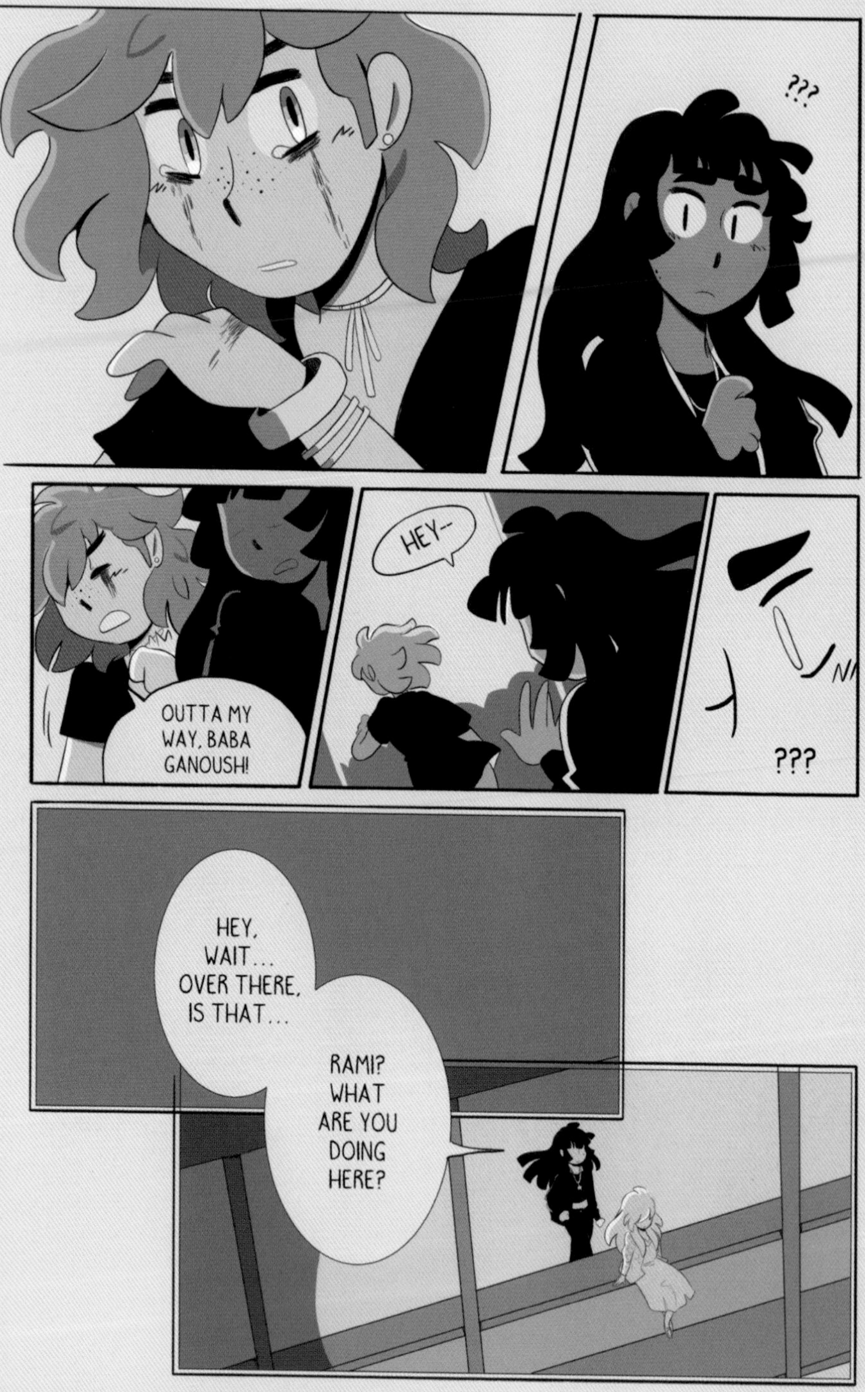
???
OUTTA MY WAY, BABA GANOUSH!
HEY--
???
HEY, WAIT... OVER THERE, IS THAT...
RAMI? WHAT ARE YOU DOING HERE?

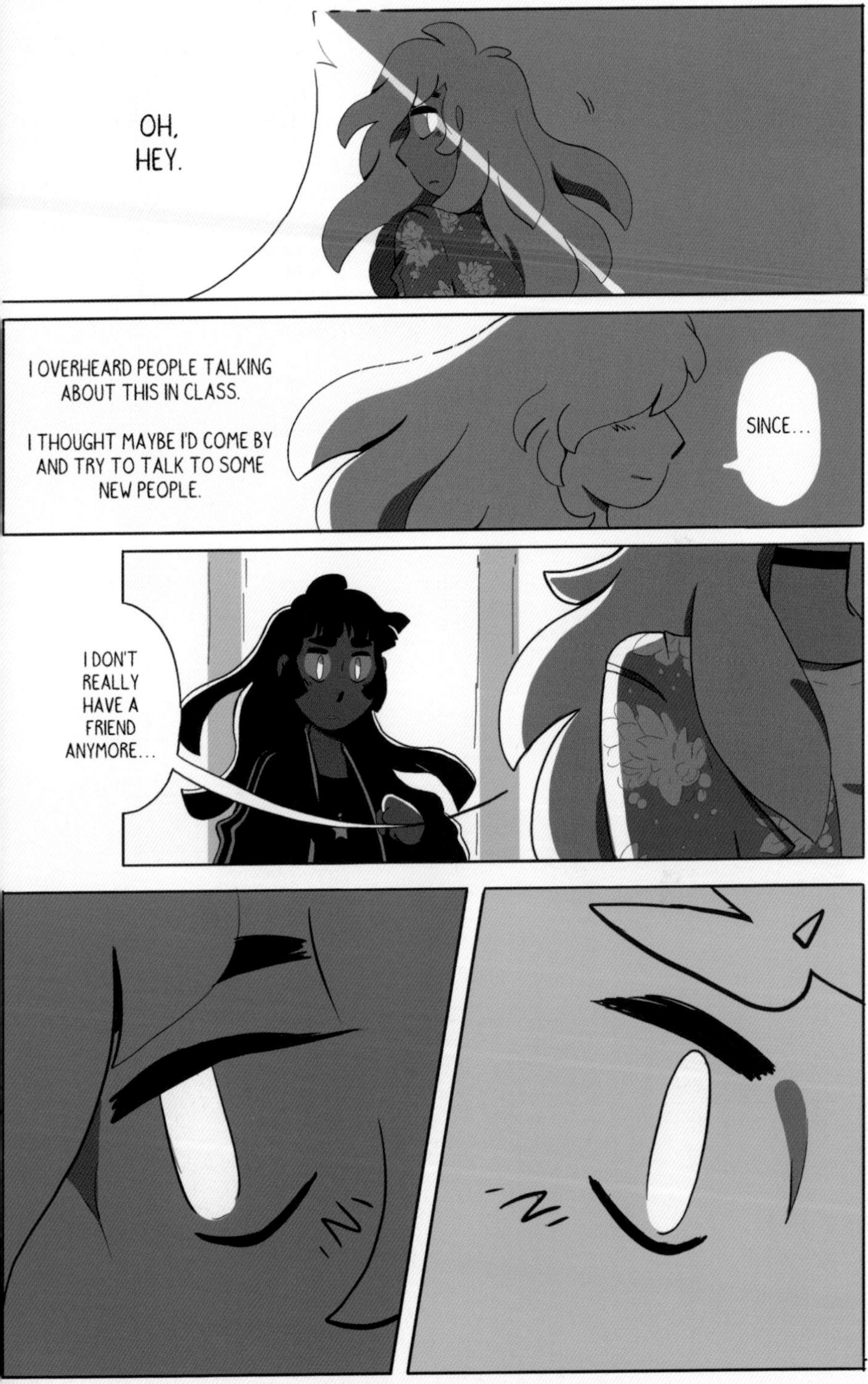
OH, HEY.
I OVERHEARD PEOPLE TALKING ABOUT THIS IN CLASS.
I THOUGHT MAYBE I'D COME BY AND TRY TO TALK TO SOME NEW PEOPLE.
SINCE...
I DON'T REALLY HAVE A FRIEND ANYMORE...

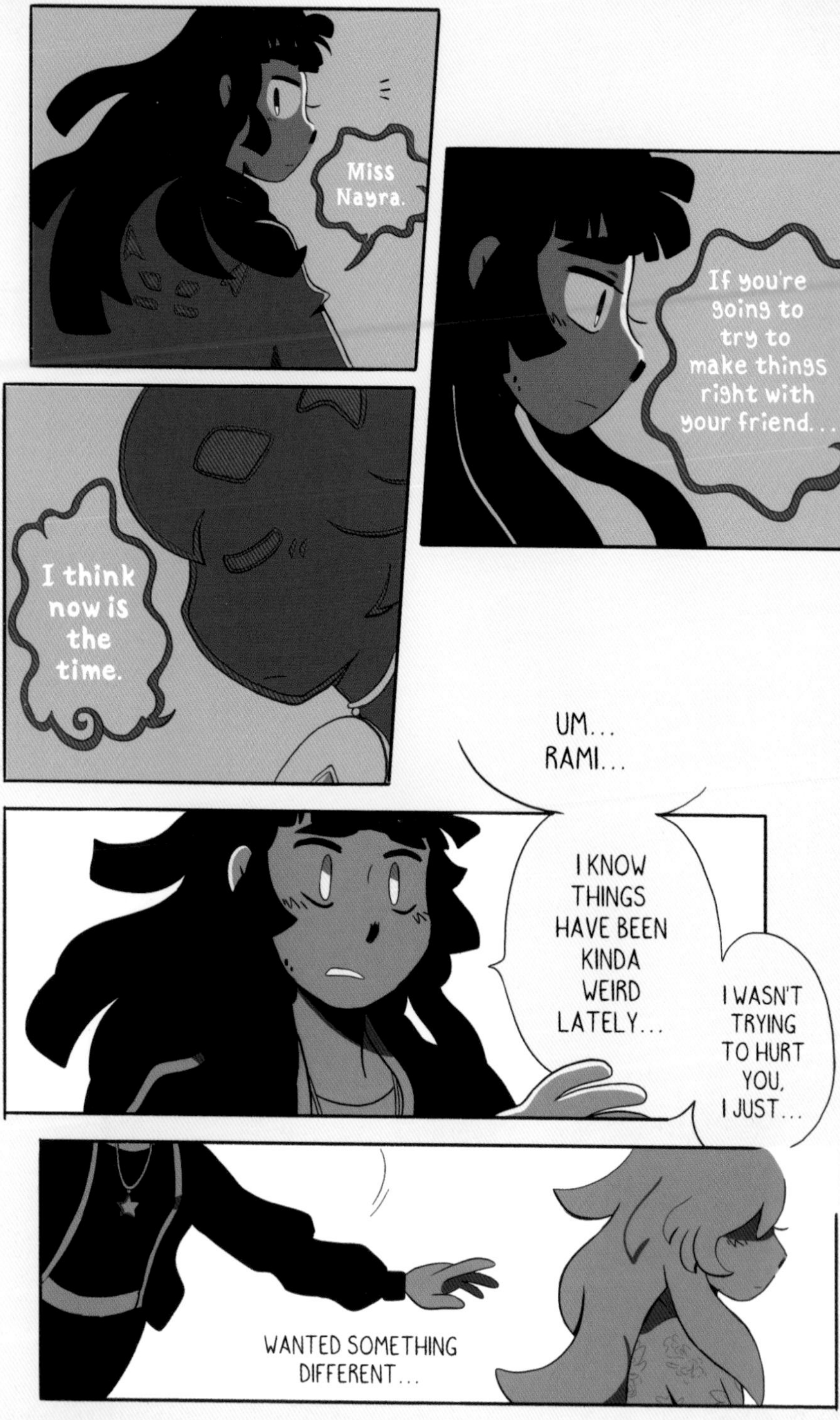
Miss Nayra.
If you're going to try to make things right with your friend...
I think now is the time.
UM... RAMI...
I KNOW THINGS HAVE BEEN KINDA WEIRD LATELY...
I WASN'T TRYING TO HURT YOU, I JUST...
WANTED SOMETHING DIFFERENT...

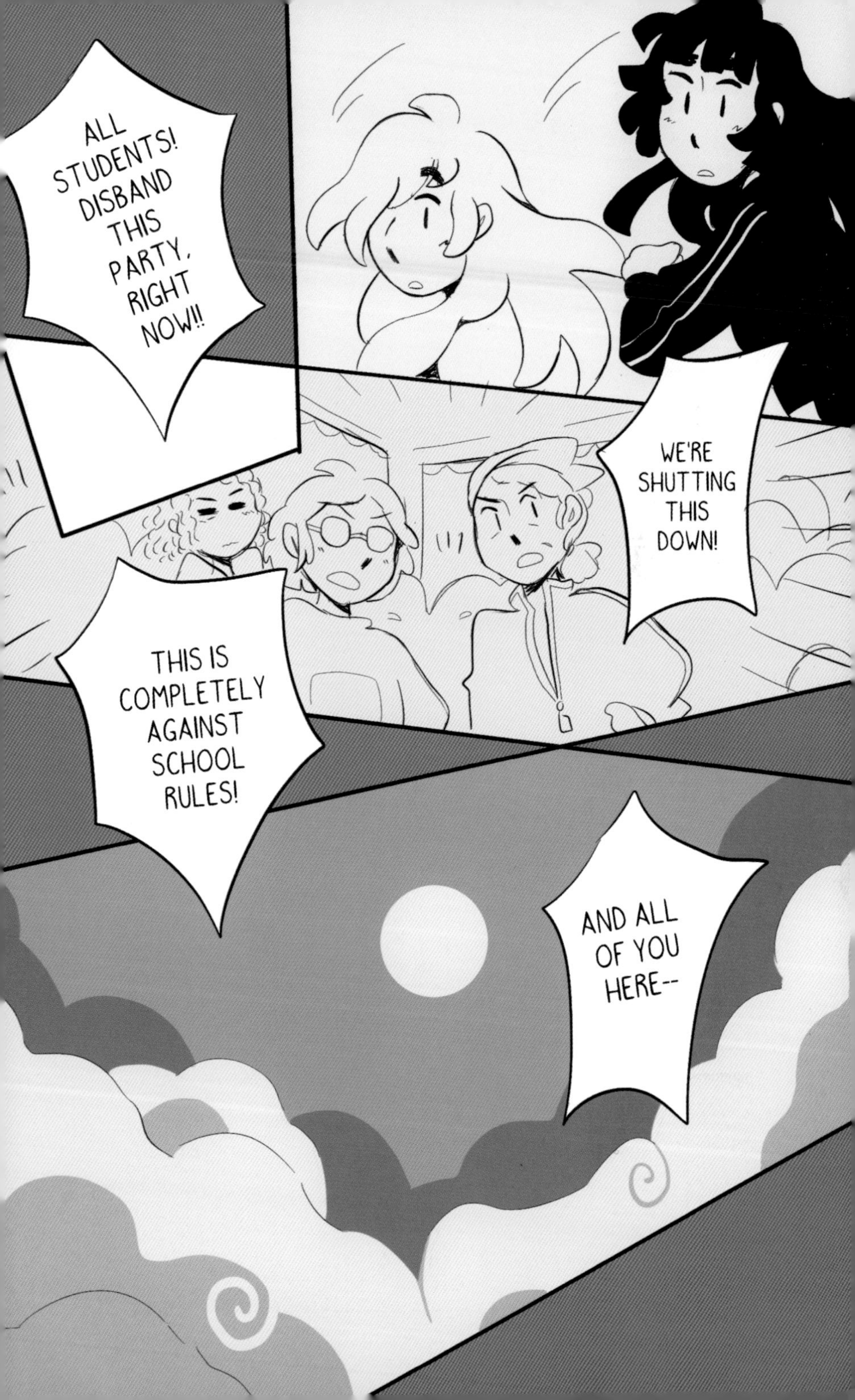
ALL STUDENTS! DISBAND THIS PARTY, RIGHT NOW!!
WE'RE SHUTTING THIS DOWN!
THIS IS COMPLETELY AGAINST SCHOOL RULES!
AND ALL OF YOU HERE--

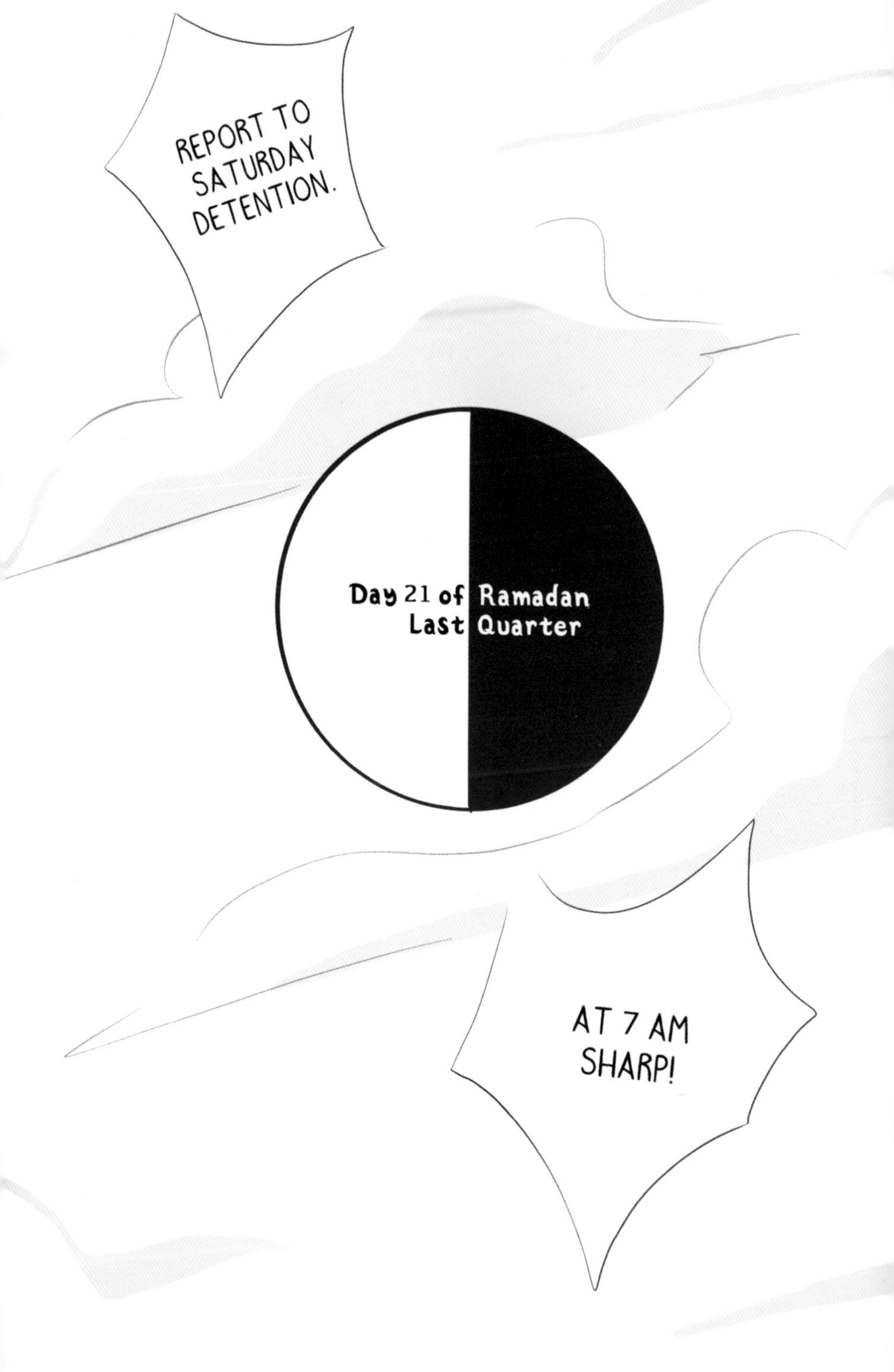
REPORT TO SATURDAY DETENTION.
Day 21 of Ramadan
Last Quarter
AT 7 AM SHARP!

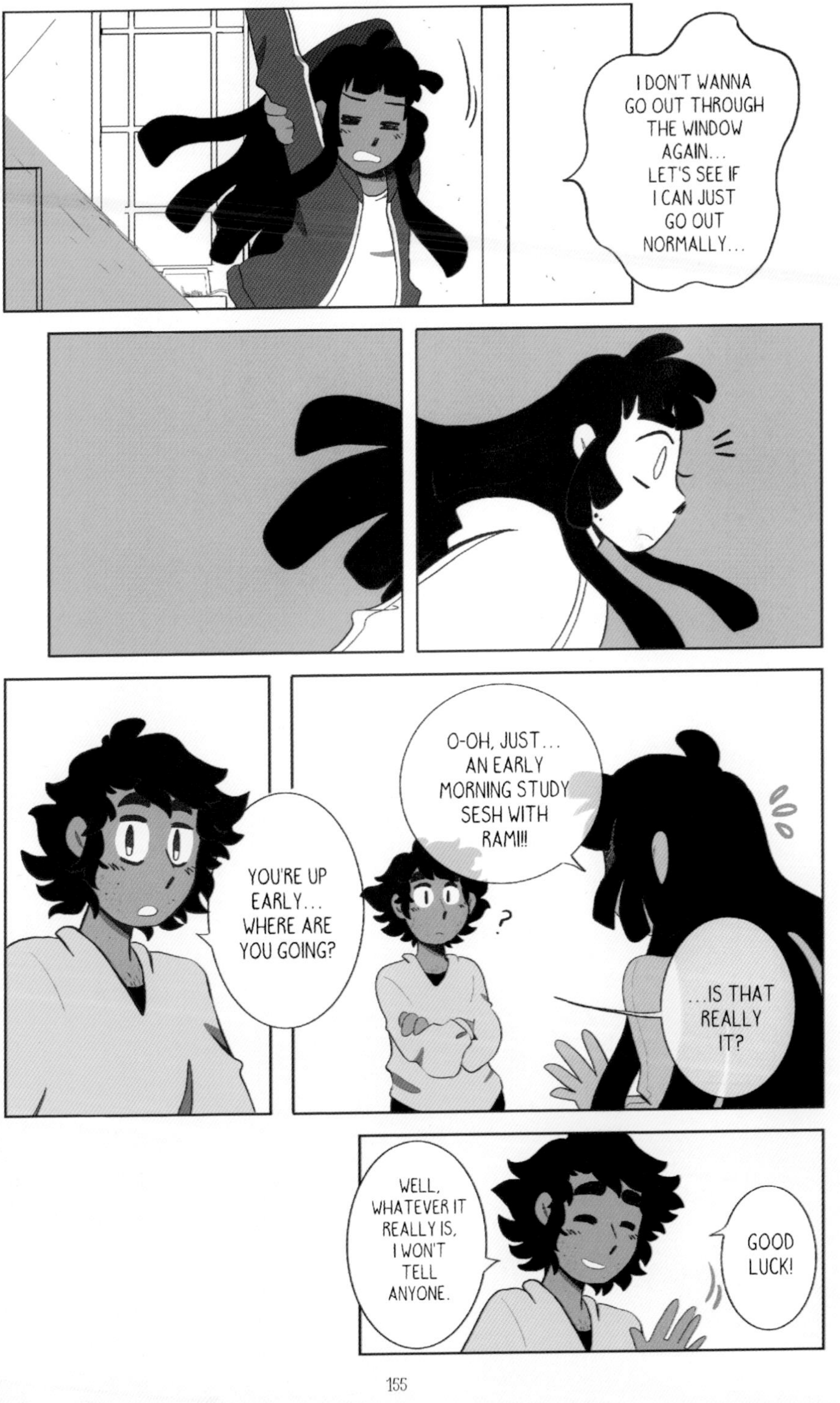
I DON'T WANNA GO OUT THROUGH THE WINDOW AGAIN... LET'S SEE IF I CAN JUST GO OUT NORMALLY...
YOU'RE UP EARLY... WHERE ARE YOU GOING?
O-OH, JUST... AN EARLY MORNING STUDY SESH WITH RAMI!!
?
...IS THAT REALLY IT?
WELL, WHATEVER IT REALLY IS, I WON'T TELL ANYONE.
GOOD LUCK!

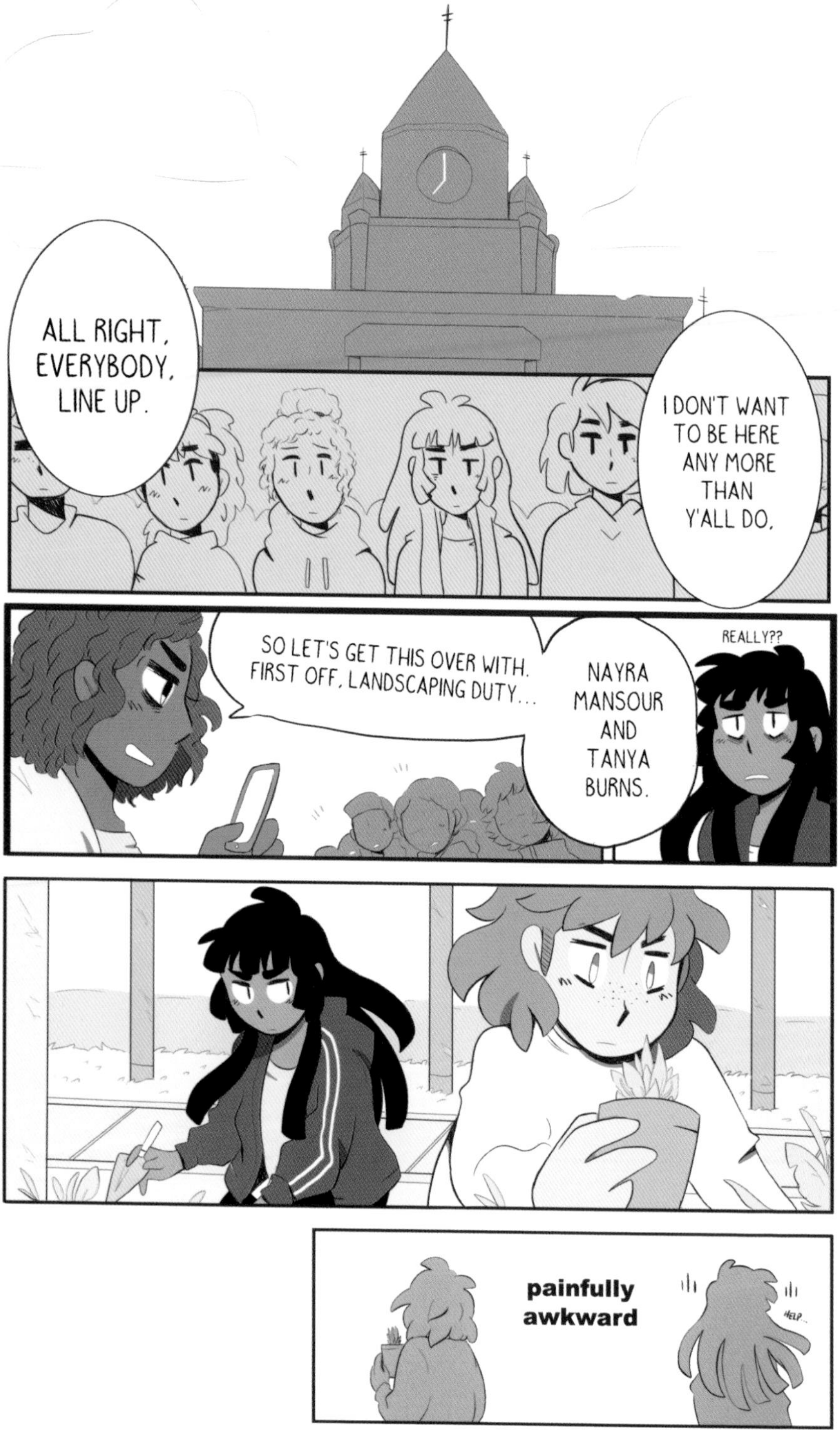
ALL RIGHT, EVERYBODY, LINE UP.
I DON'T WANT TO BE HERE ANY MORE THAN Y'ALL DO,
SO LET'S GET THIS OVER WITH. FIRST OFF, LANDSCAPING DUTY...
NAYRA MANSOUR AND TANYA BURNS.
REALLY??
REALLY??
painfully awkward
HELP...

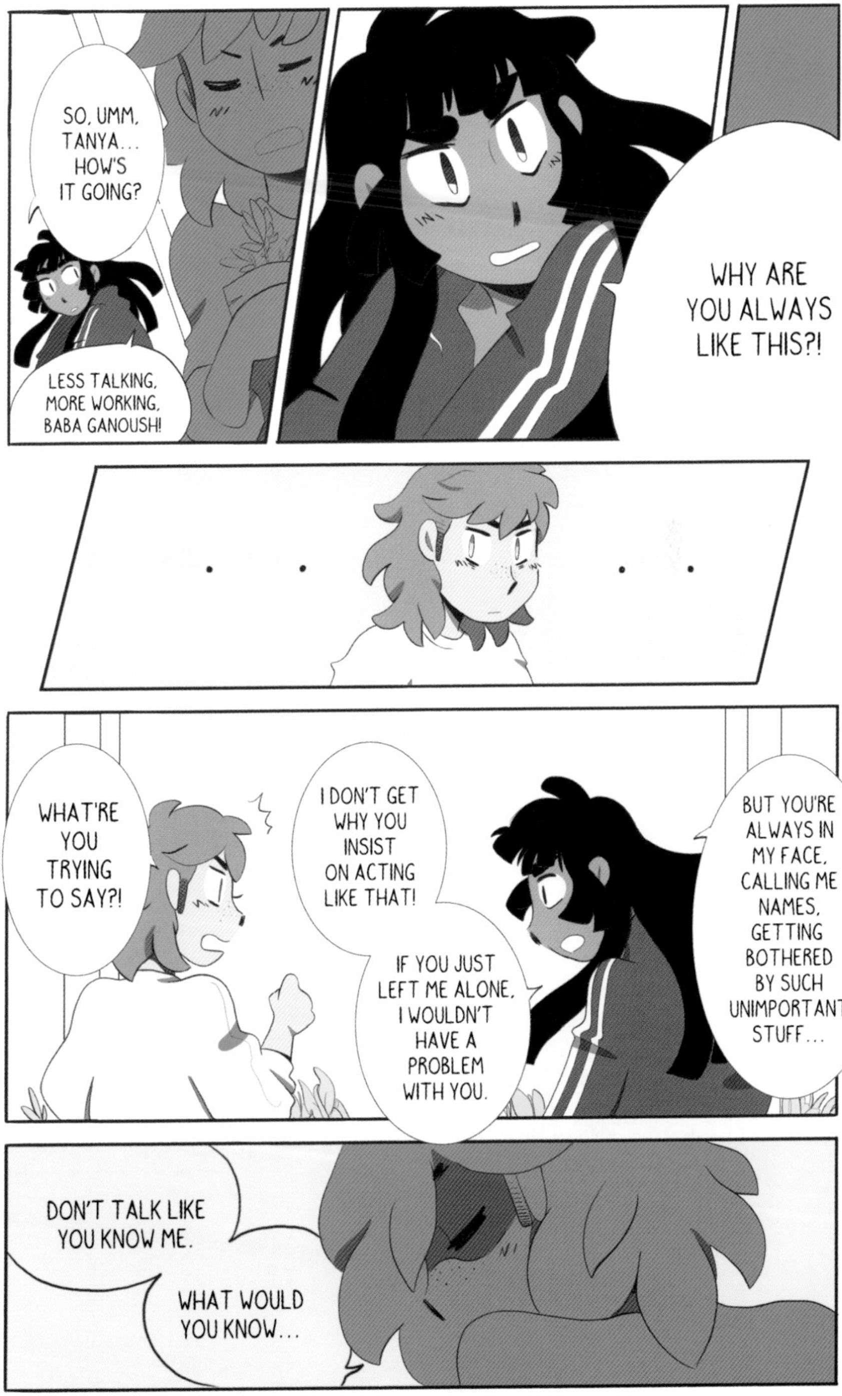
SO, UMM, TANYA... HOW'S IT GOING?
LESS TALKING, MORE WORKING, BABA GANOUSH!
WHY ARE YOU ALWAYS LIKE THIS?!
. . . . .
WHAT'RE YOU TRYING TO SAY?!
I DON'T GET WHY YOU INSIST ON ACTING LIKE THAT!
IF YOU JUST LEFT ME ALONE, I WOULDN'T HAVE A PROBLEM WITH YOU.
BUT YOU'RE ALWAYS IN MY FACE, CALLING ME NAMES, GETTING BOTHERED BY SUCH UNIMPORTANT STUFF...
DON'T TALK LIKE YOU KNOW ME.
WHAT WOULD YOU KNOW...

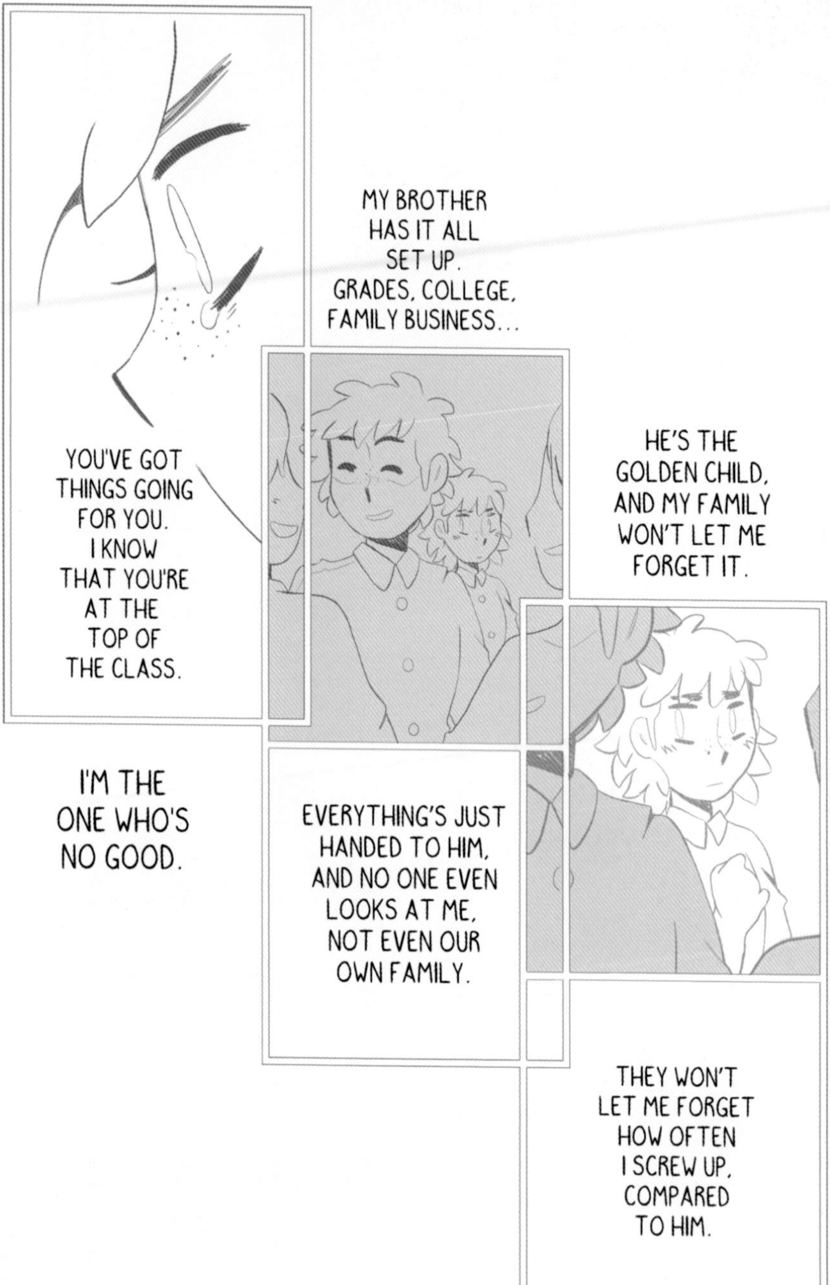
MY BROTHER HAS IT ALL SET UP. GRADES, COLLEGE, FAMILY BUSINESS...
YOU'VE GOT THINGS GOING FOR YOU. I KNOW THAT YOU'RE AT THE TOP OF THE CLASS.
HE'S THE GOLDEN CHILD, AND MY FAMILY WON'T LET ME FORGET IT.
I'M THE ONE WHO'S NO GOOD.
EVERYTHING'S JUST HANDED TO HIM, AND NO ONE EVEN LOOKS AT ME, NOT EVEN OUR OWN FAMILY.
THEY WON'T LET ME FORGET HOW OFTEN I SCREW UP, COMPARED TO HIM.

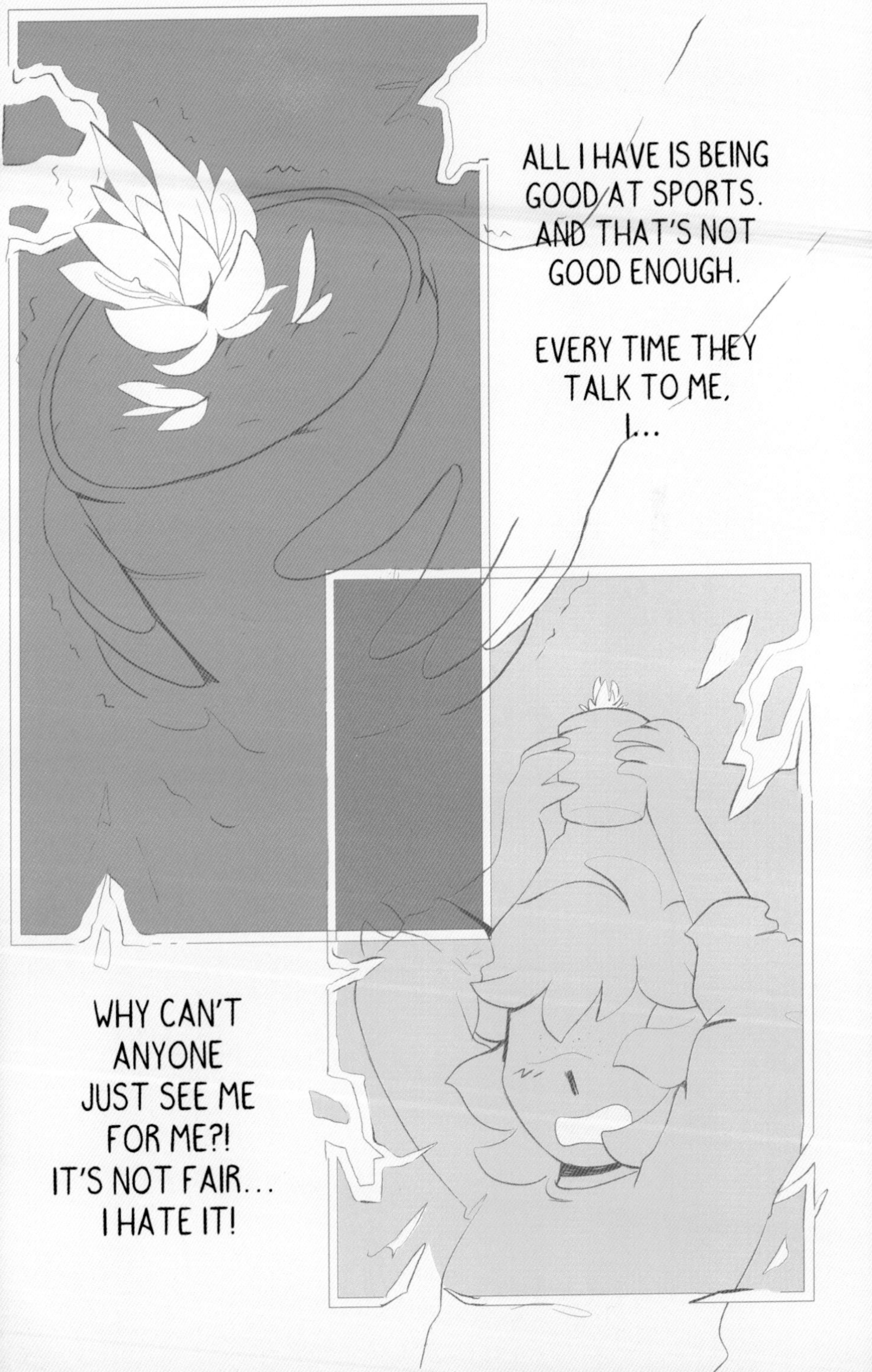
ALL I HAVE IS BEING GOOD AT SPORTS. AND THAT'S NOT GOOD ENOUGH.
EVERY TIME THEY TALK TO ME, I...
WHY CAN'T ANYONE JUST SEE ME FOR ME?! IT'S NOT FAIR... I HATE IT!

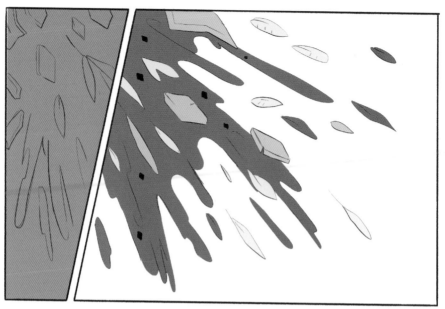

I have an idea.
Please lend me
a hand!

OKAY!

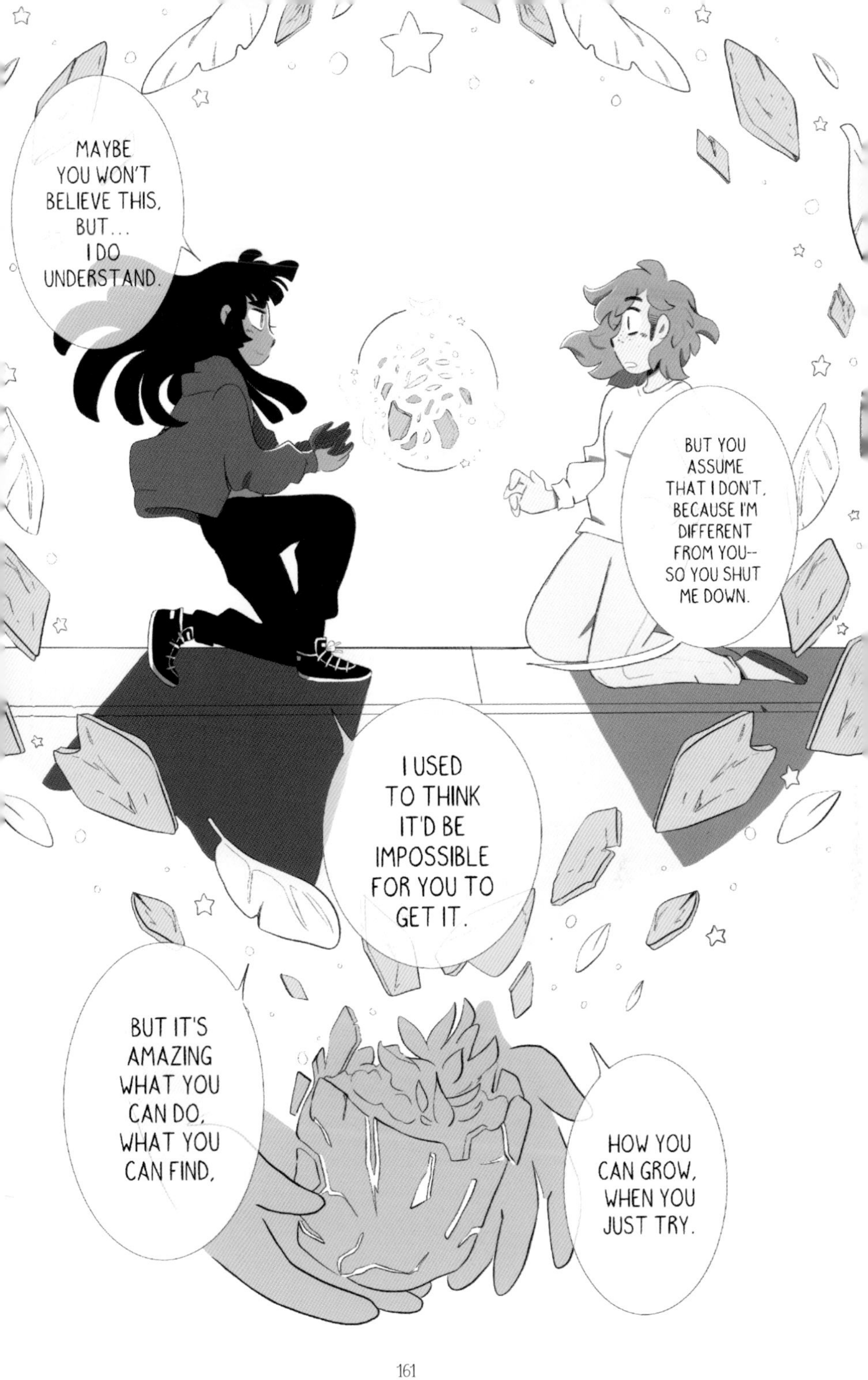
MAYBE YOU WON'T BELIEVE THIS, BUT... I DO UNDERSTAND.
BUT YOU ASSUME THAT I DON'T, BECAUSE I'M DIFFERENT FROM YOU-- SO YOU SHUT ME DOWN.
I USED TO THINK IT'D BE IMPOSSIBLE FOR YOU TO GET IT.
BUT IT'S AMAZING WHAT YOU CAN DO, WHAT YOU CAN FIND,
HOW YOU CAN GROW, WHEN YOU JUST TRY.

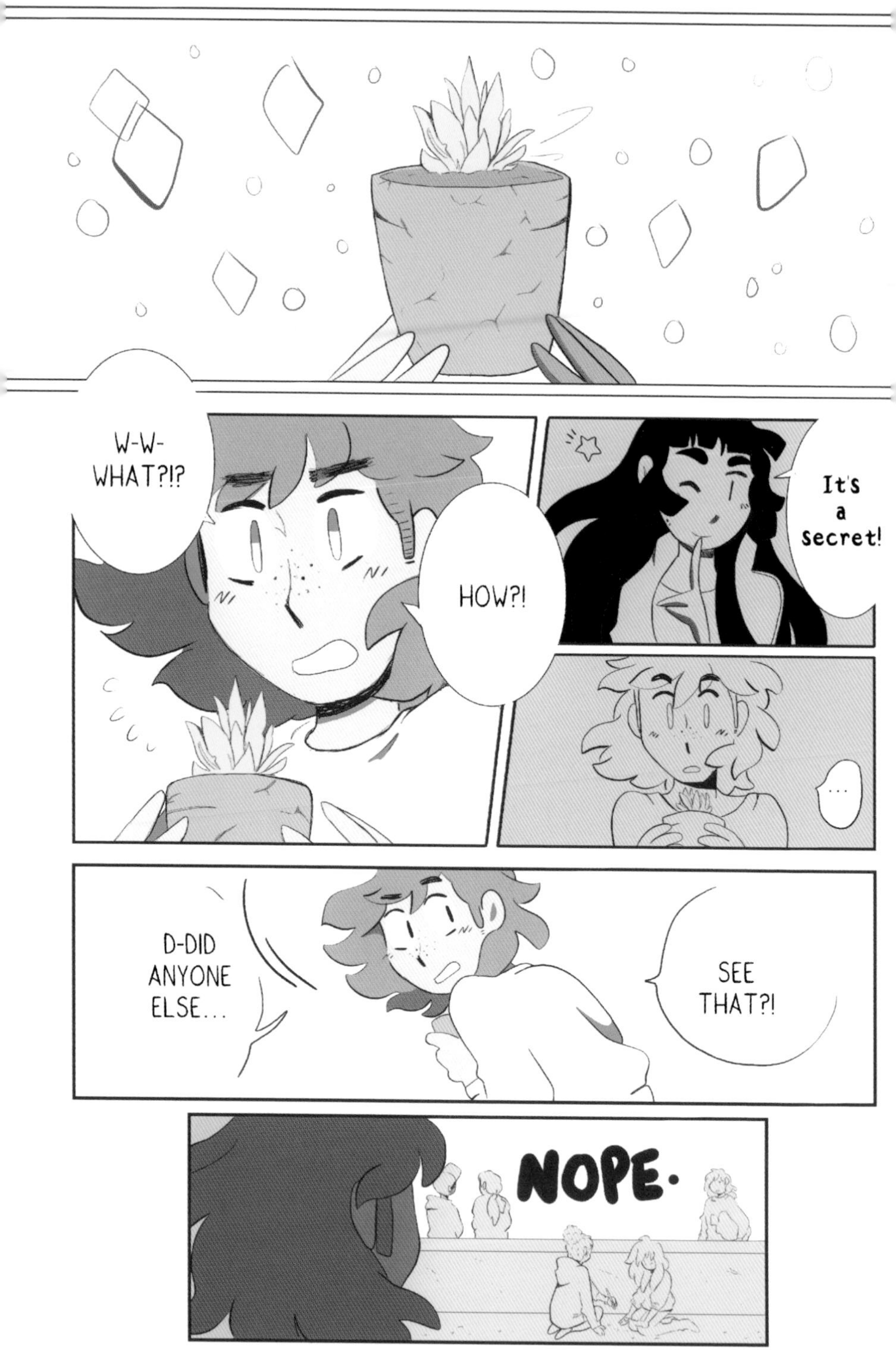
W-W-
WHAT?!?
HOW?!
It's
a
secret!
...
D-DID
ANYONE
ELSE...
SEE
THAT?!
NOPE.

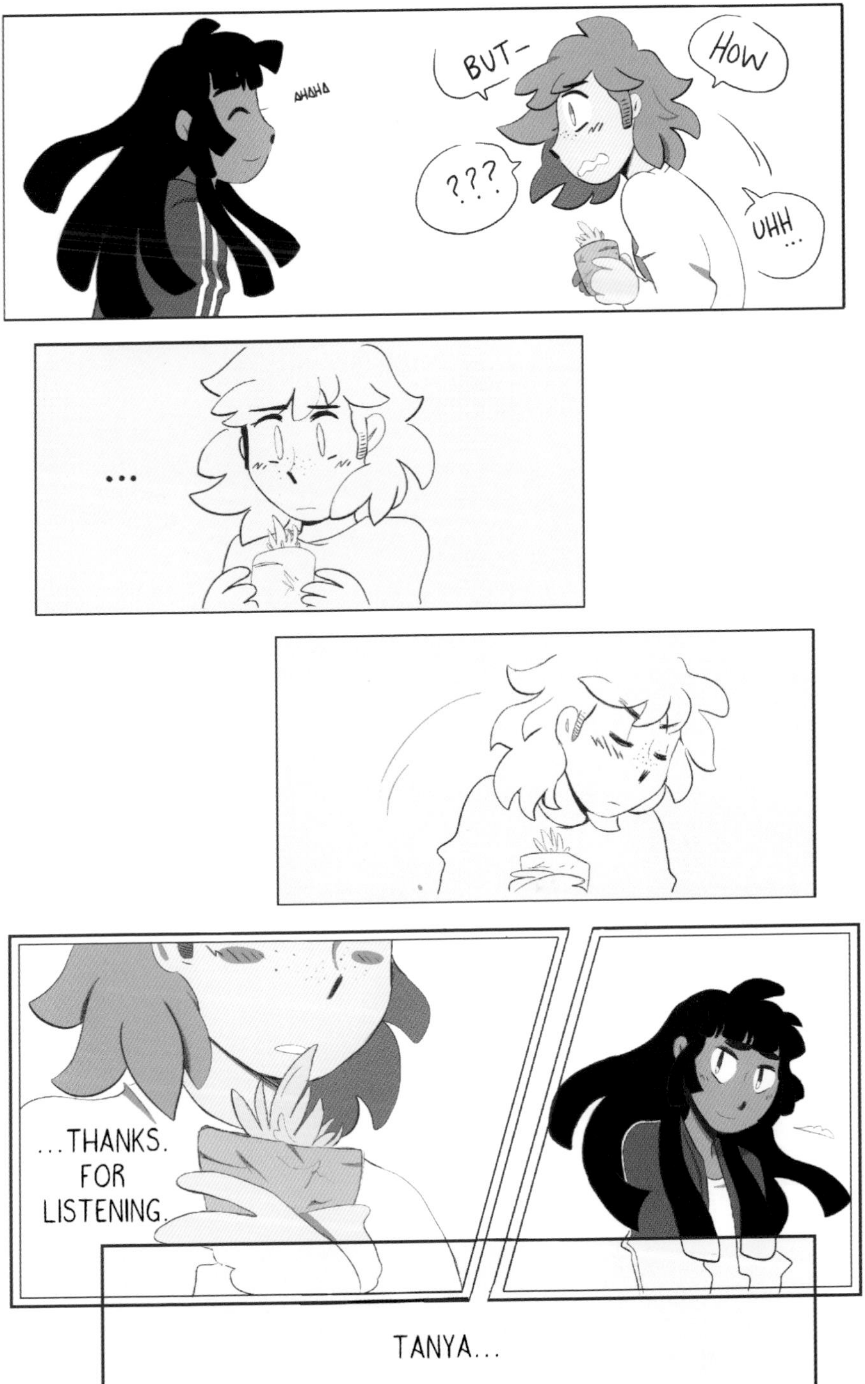
AHAHA
BUT-
HOW
???
UHH...
...
...THANKS. FOR LISTENING.
TANYA...

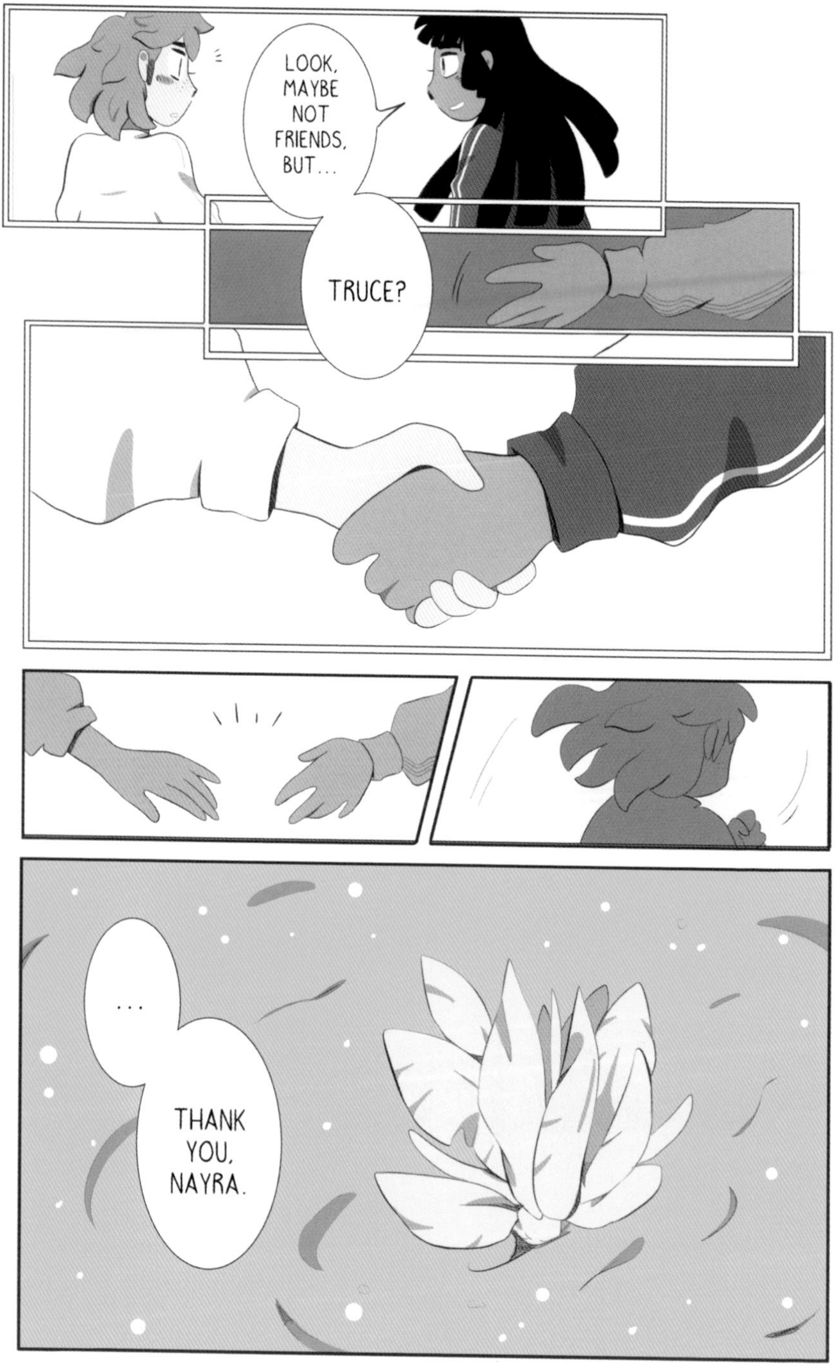
LOOK, MAYBE NOT FRIENDS, BUT...
TRUCE?
...
THANK YOU, NAYRA.

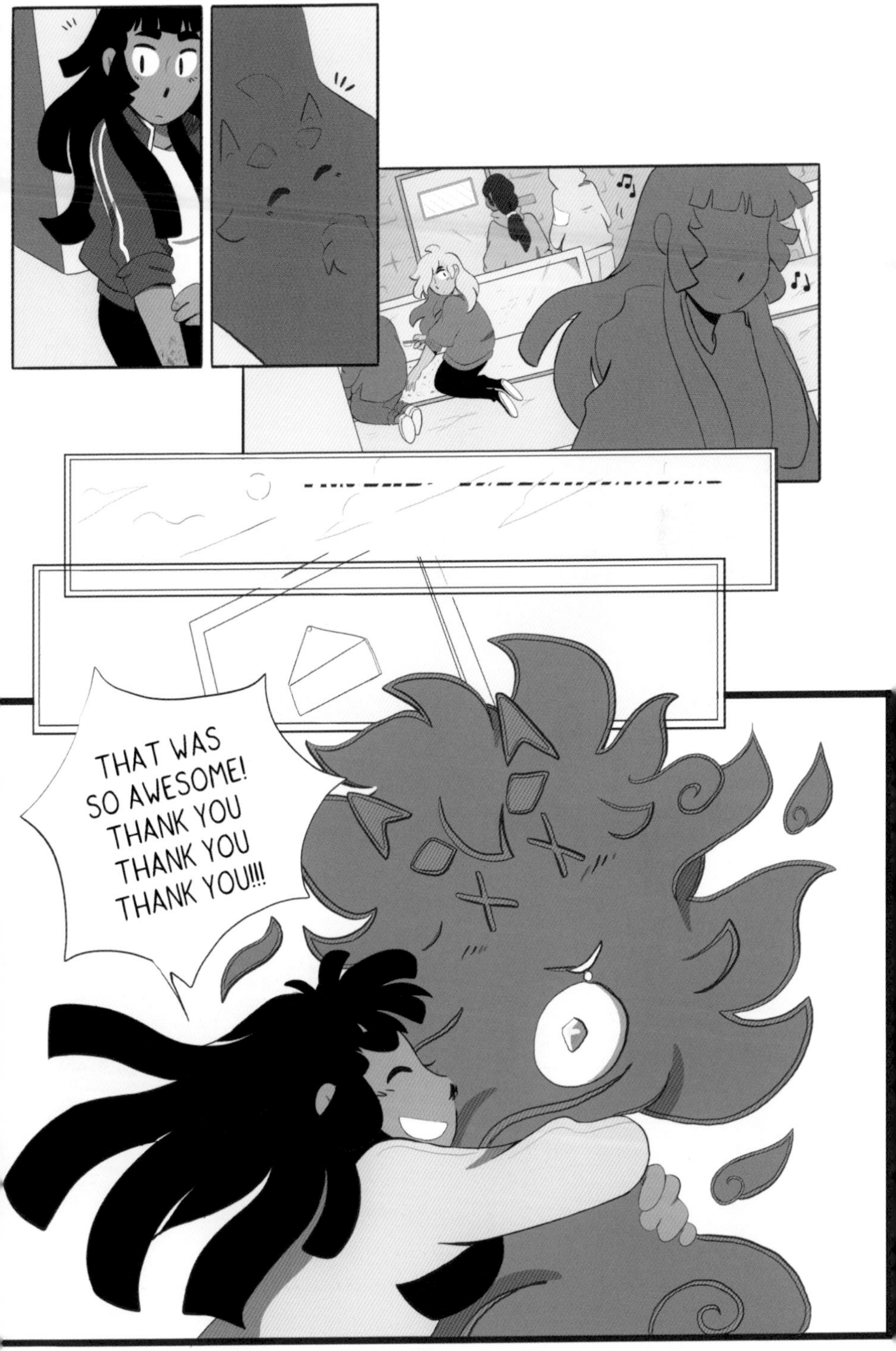
THAT WAS SO AWESOME! THANK YOU THANK YOU THANK YOU!!!

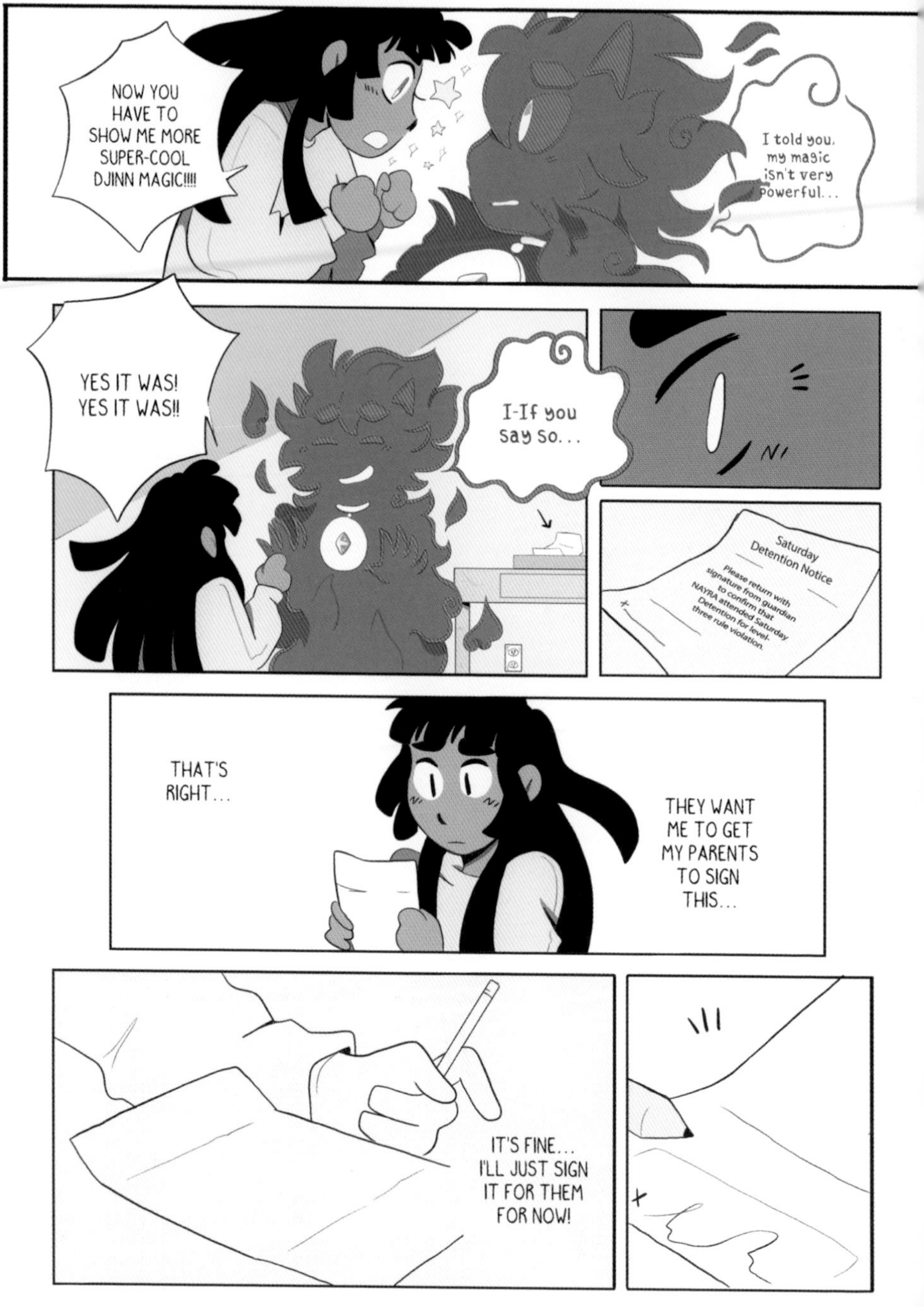
NOW YOU HAVE TO SHOW ME MORE SUPER-COOL DJINN MAGIC!!!!
I told you, my magic isn't very powerful...
YES IT WAS! YES IT WAS!!
I-If you say so...
Saturday Detention Notice
Please return with signature from guardian to confirm that NAYRA attended Saturday Detention for level-three rule violation.
THAT'S RIGHT...
THEY WANT ME TO GET MY PARENTS TO SIGN THIS...
IT'S FINE... I'LL JUST SIGN IT FOR THEM FOR NOW!

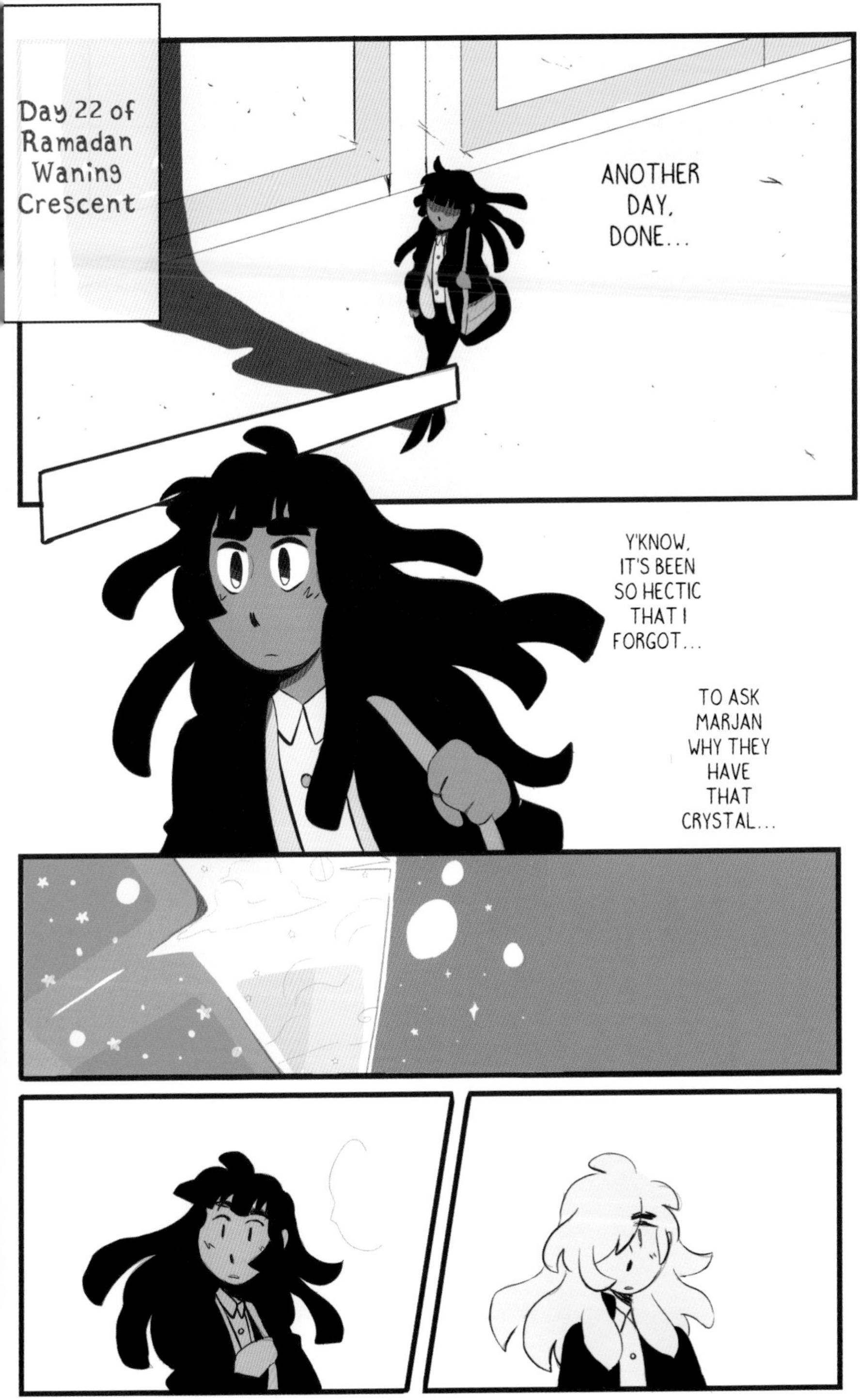
Day 22 of Ramadan Waning Crescent
ANOTHER DAY, DONE...
Y'KNOW, IT'S BEEN SO HECTIC THAT I FORGOT...
TO ASK MARJAN WHY THEY HAVE THAT CRYSTAL...

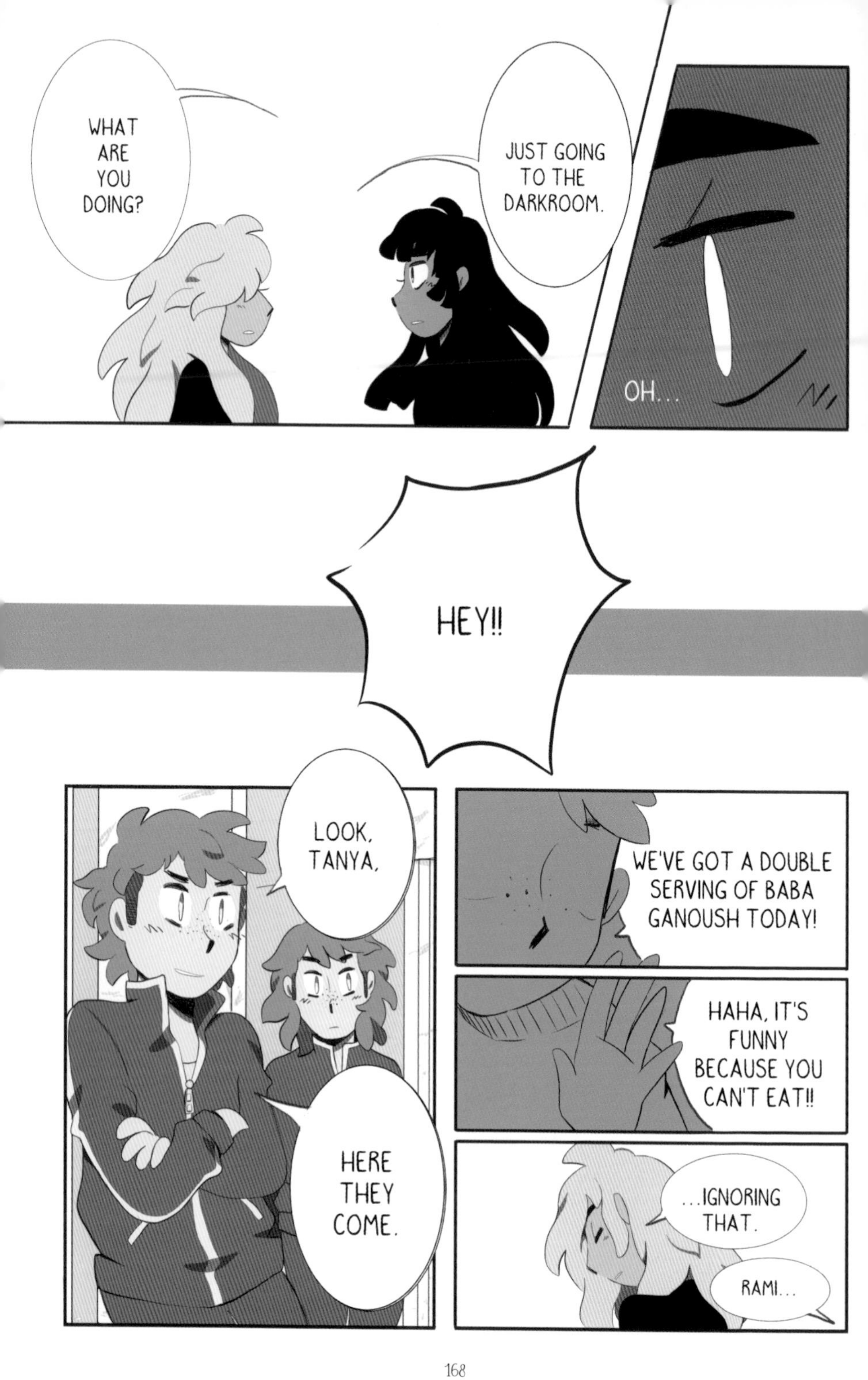
WHAT ARE YOU DOING?
JUST GOING TO THE DARKROOM.
OH...
HEY!!
LOOK, TANYA,
HERE THEY COME.
WE'VE GOT A DOUBLE SERVING OF BABA GANOUSH TODAY!
HAHA, IT'S FUNNY BECAUSE YOU CAN'T EAT!!
...IGNORING THAT.
RAMI...

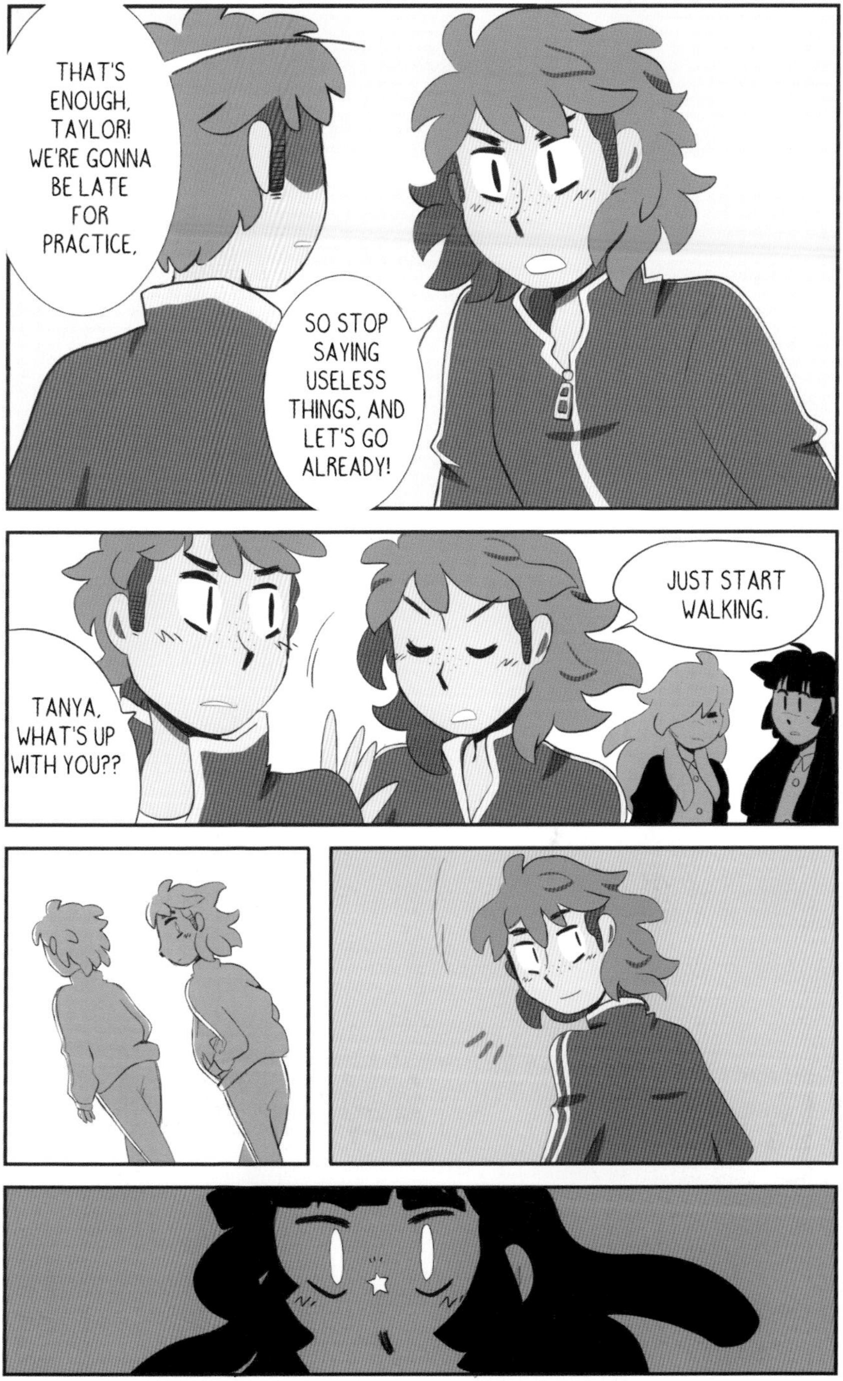
THAT'S ENOUGH, TAYLOR! WE'RE GONNA BE LATE FOR PRACTICE,
SO STOP SAYING USELESS THINGS, AND LET'S GO ALREADY!
TANYA, WHAT'S UP WITH YOU??
JUST START WALKING.

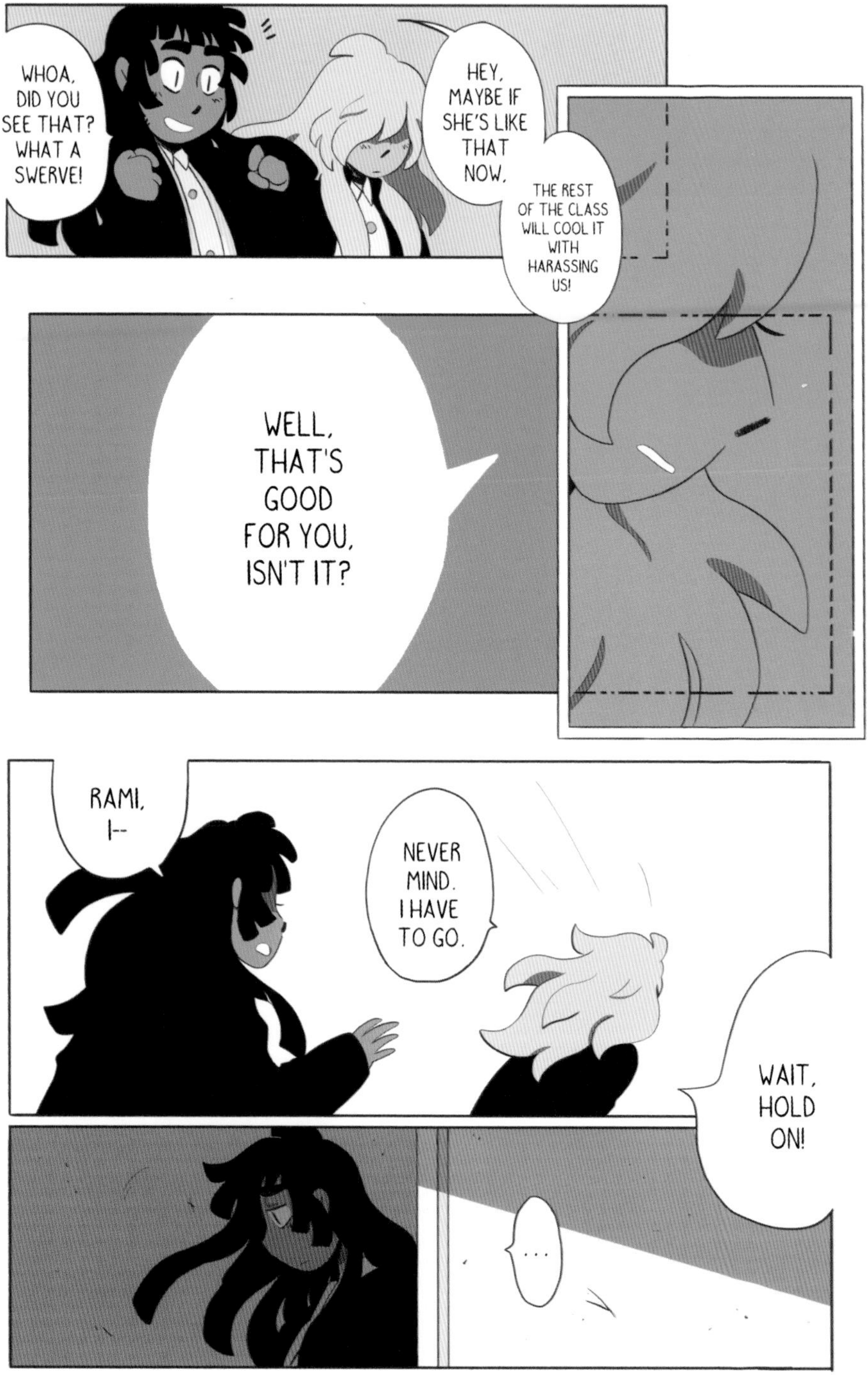
WHOA, DID YOU SEE THAT? WHAT A SWERVE!
HEY, MAYBE IF SHE'S LIKE THAT NOW,
THE REST OF THE CLASS WILL COOL IT WITH HARASSING US!
WELL, THAT'S GOOD FOR YOU, ISN'T IT?
RAMI, I--
NEVER MIND. I HAVE TO GO.
WAIT, HOLD ON!
...

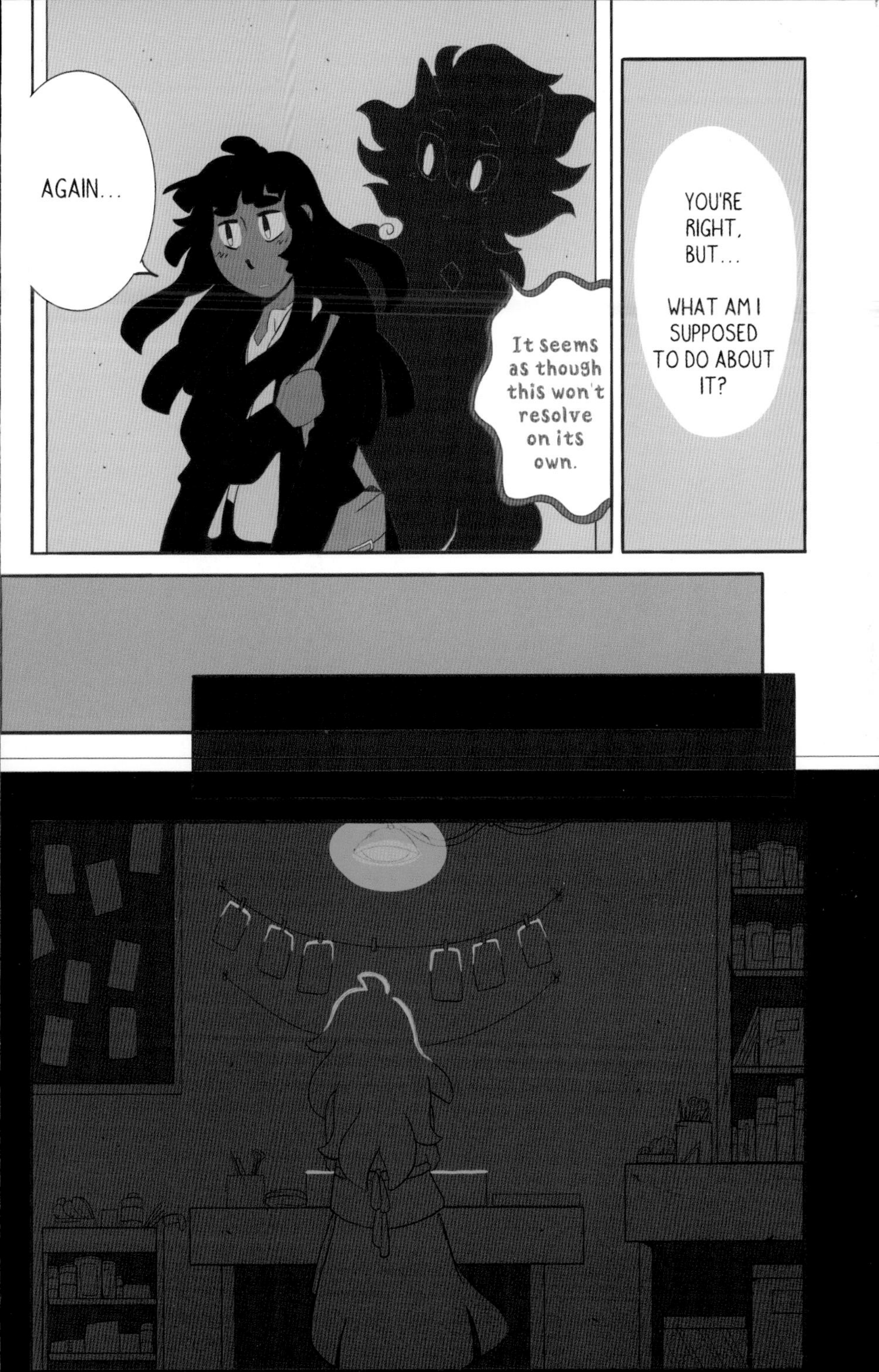
AGAIN...
It seems as though this won't resolve on its own.
YOU'RE RIGHT, BUT...
WHAT AM I SUPPOSED TO DO ABOUT IT?

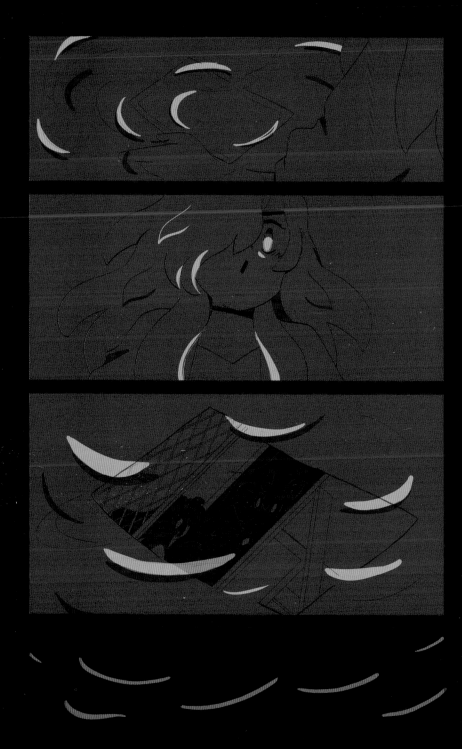

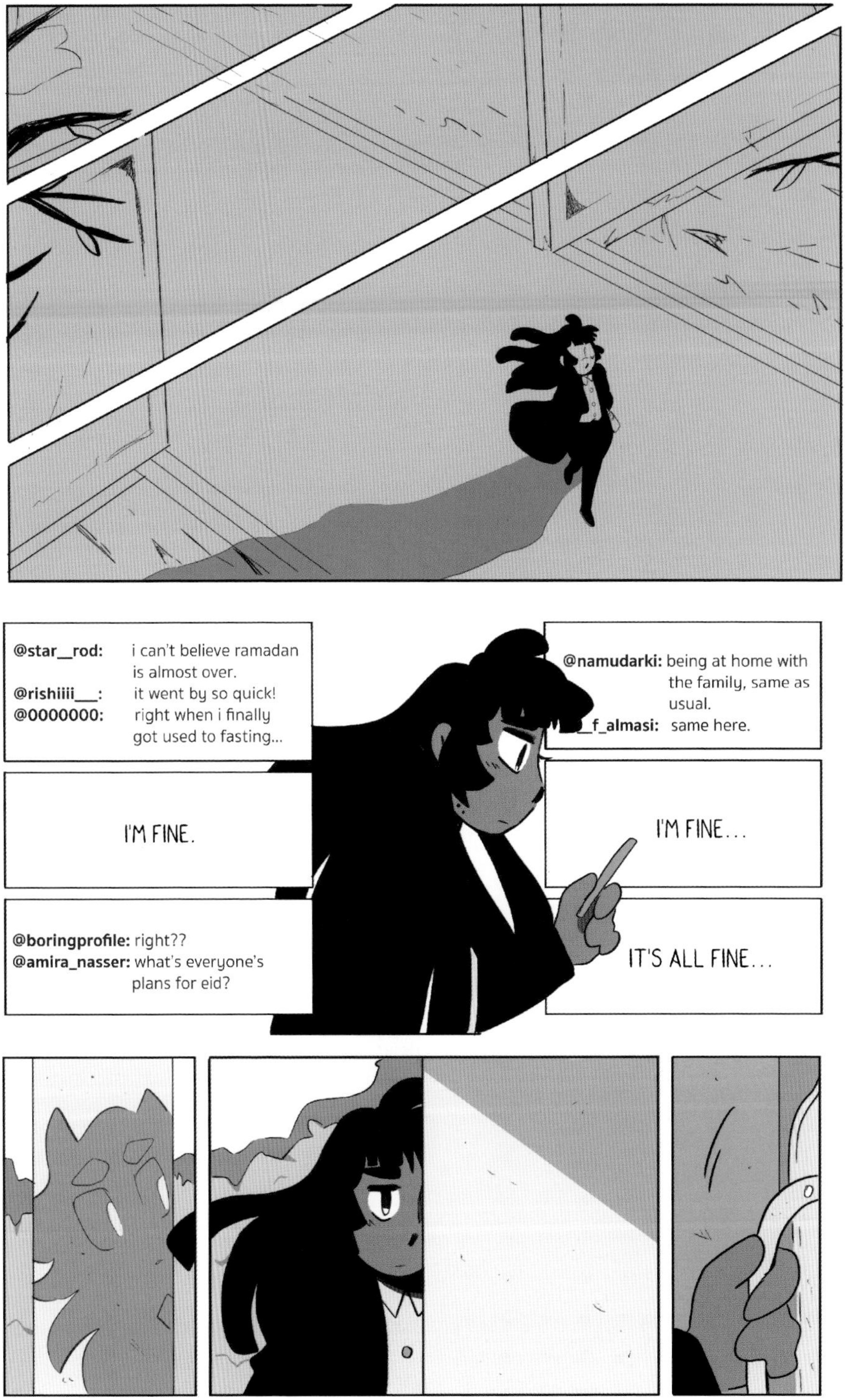
@star__rod: i can't believe ramadan is almost over.
@rishiiii___: it went by so quick!
@0000000: right when i finally got used to fasting...
@namudarki: being at home with the family, same as usual.
_f_almasi: same here.
I'M FINE.
I'M FINE...
@boringprofile: right??
@amira_nasser: what's everyone's plans for eid?
IT'S ALL FINE...

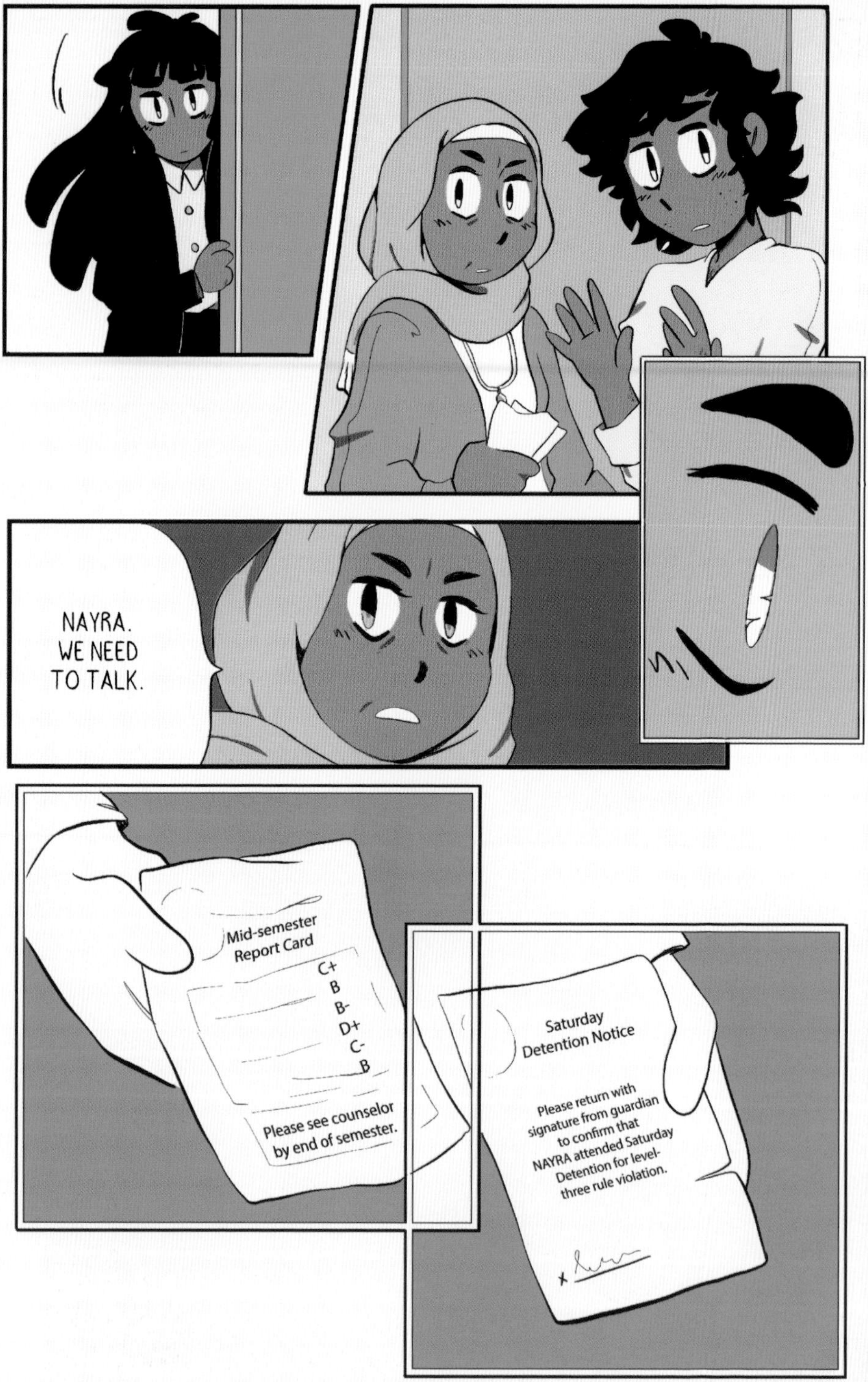
NAYRA. WE NEED TO TALK.
Mid-semester Report Card
C+
B
B-
D+
C-
B
Please see counselor by end of semester.
Saturday Detention Notice
Please return with signature from guardian to confirm that NAYRA attended Saturday Detention for level-three rule violation.

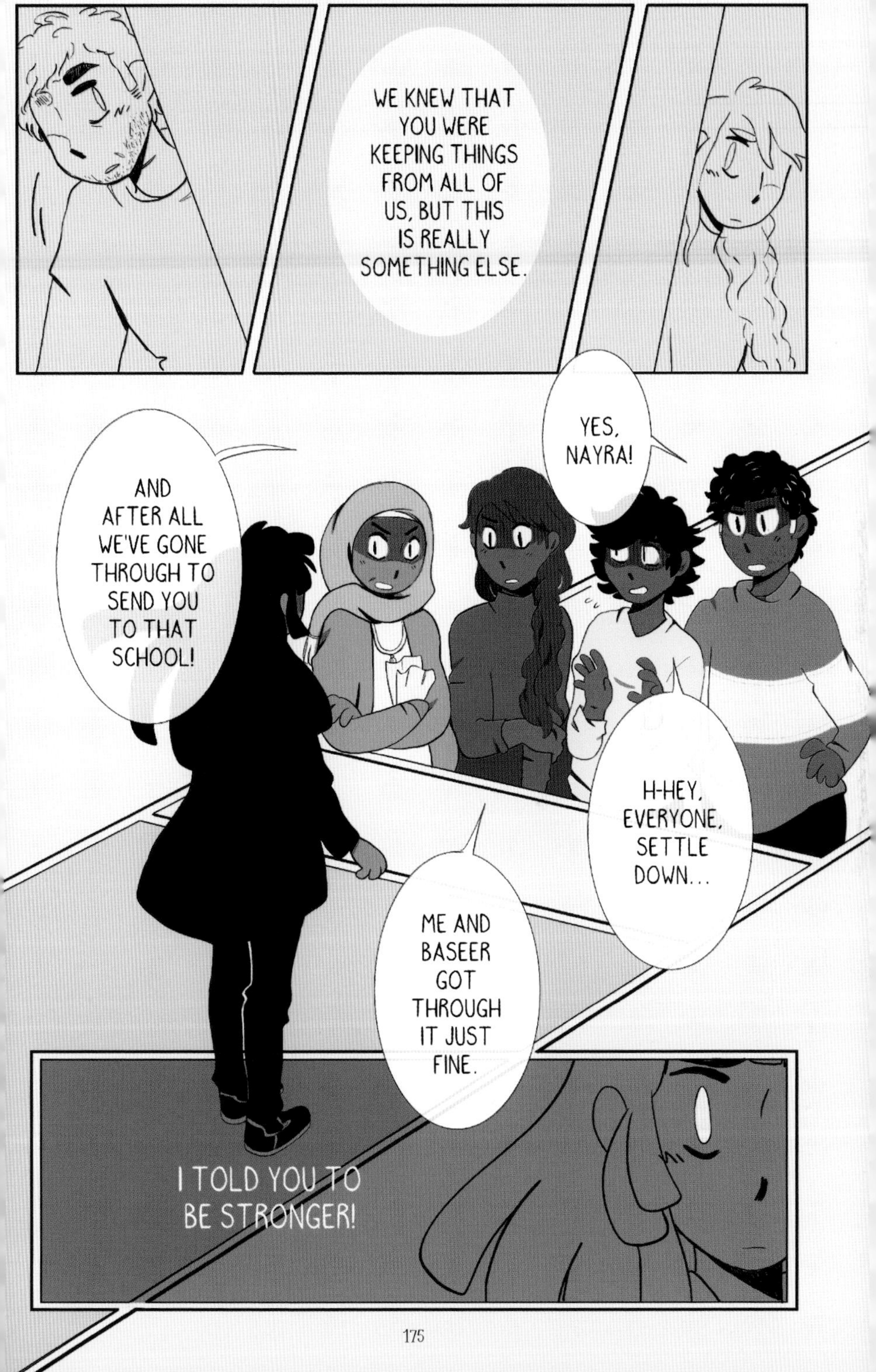
WE KNEW THAT YOU WERE KEEPING THINGS FROM ALL OF US, BUT THIS IS REALLY SOMETHING ELSE.
YES, NAYRA!
AND AFTER ALL WE'VE GONE THROUGH TO SEND YOU TO THAT SCHOOL!
H-HEY, EVERYONE, SETTLE DOWN...
ME AND BASEER GOT THROUGH IT JUST FINE.
I TOLD YOU TO BE STRONGER!

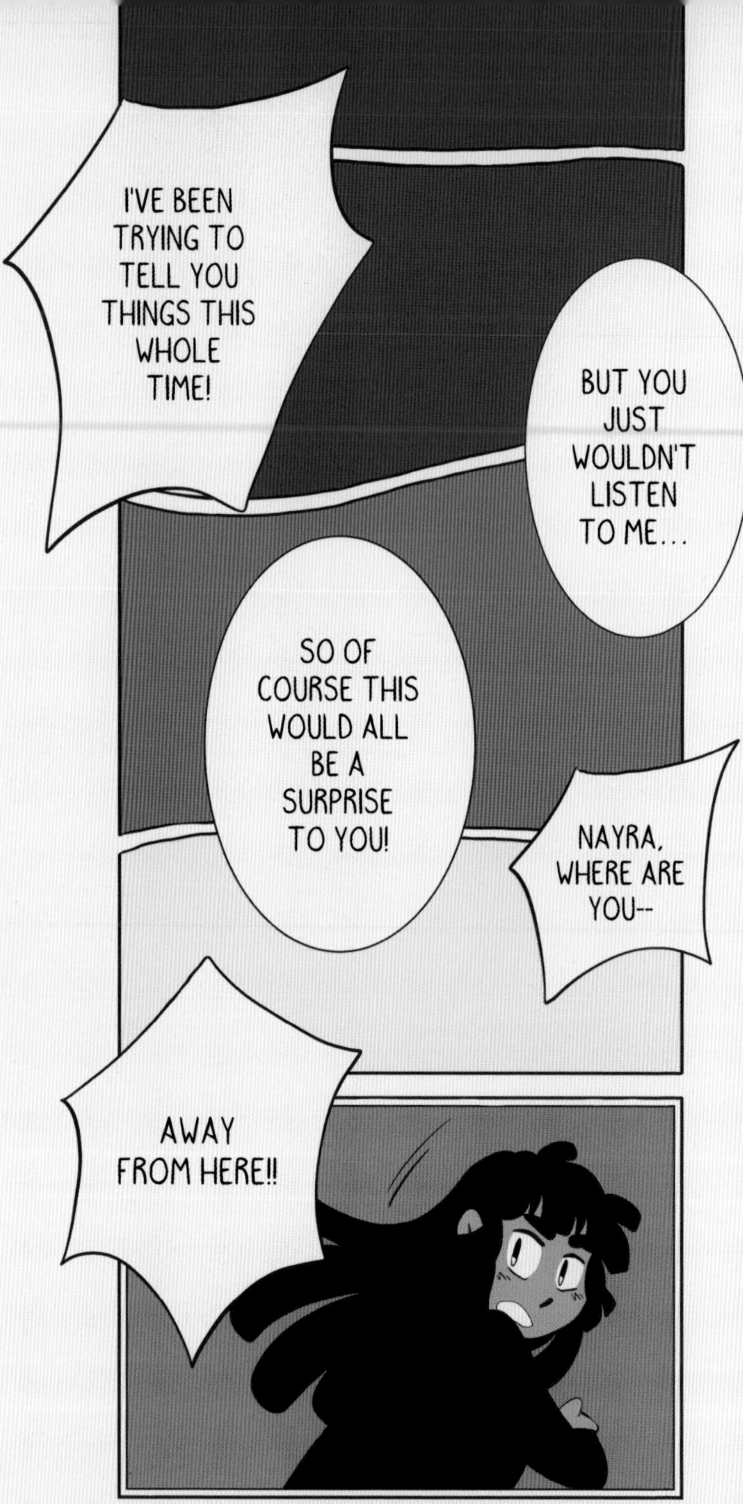
I'VE BEEN TRYING TO TELL YOU THINGS THIS WHOLE TIME!
BUT YOU JUST WOULDN'T LISTEN TO ME...
SO OF COURSE THIS WOULD ALL BE A SURPRISE TO YOU!
NAYRA, WHERE ARE YOU--
AWAY FROM HERE!!

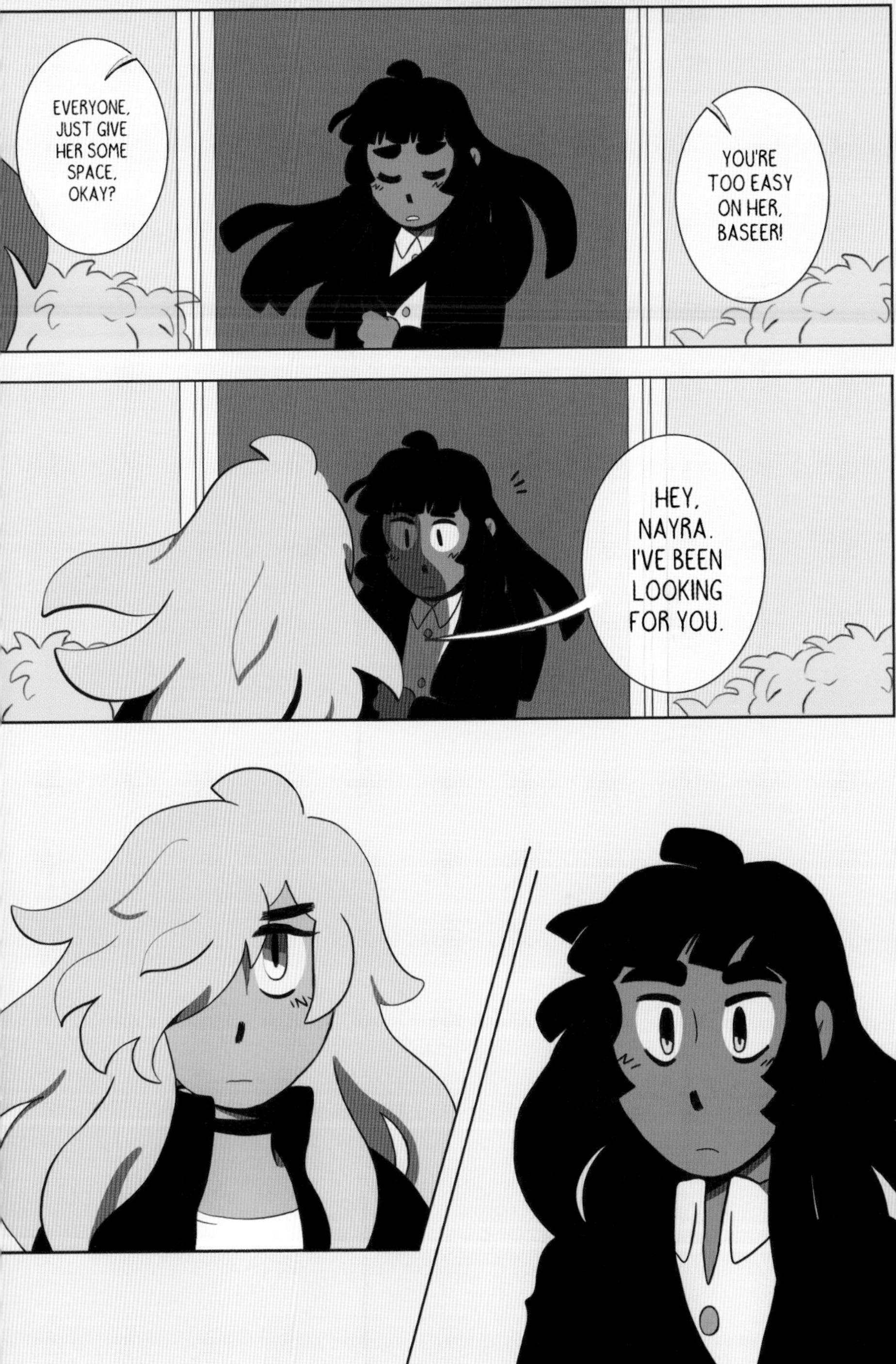
EVERYONE, JUST GIVE HER SOME SPACE, OKAY?
YOU'RE TOO EASY ON HER, BASEER!
HEY, NAYRA. I'VE BEEN LOOKING FOR YOU.

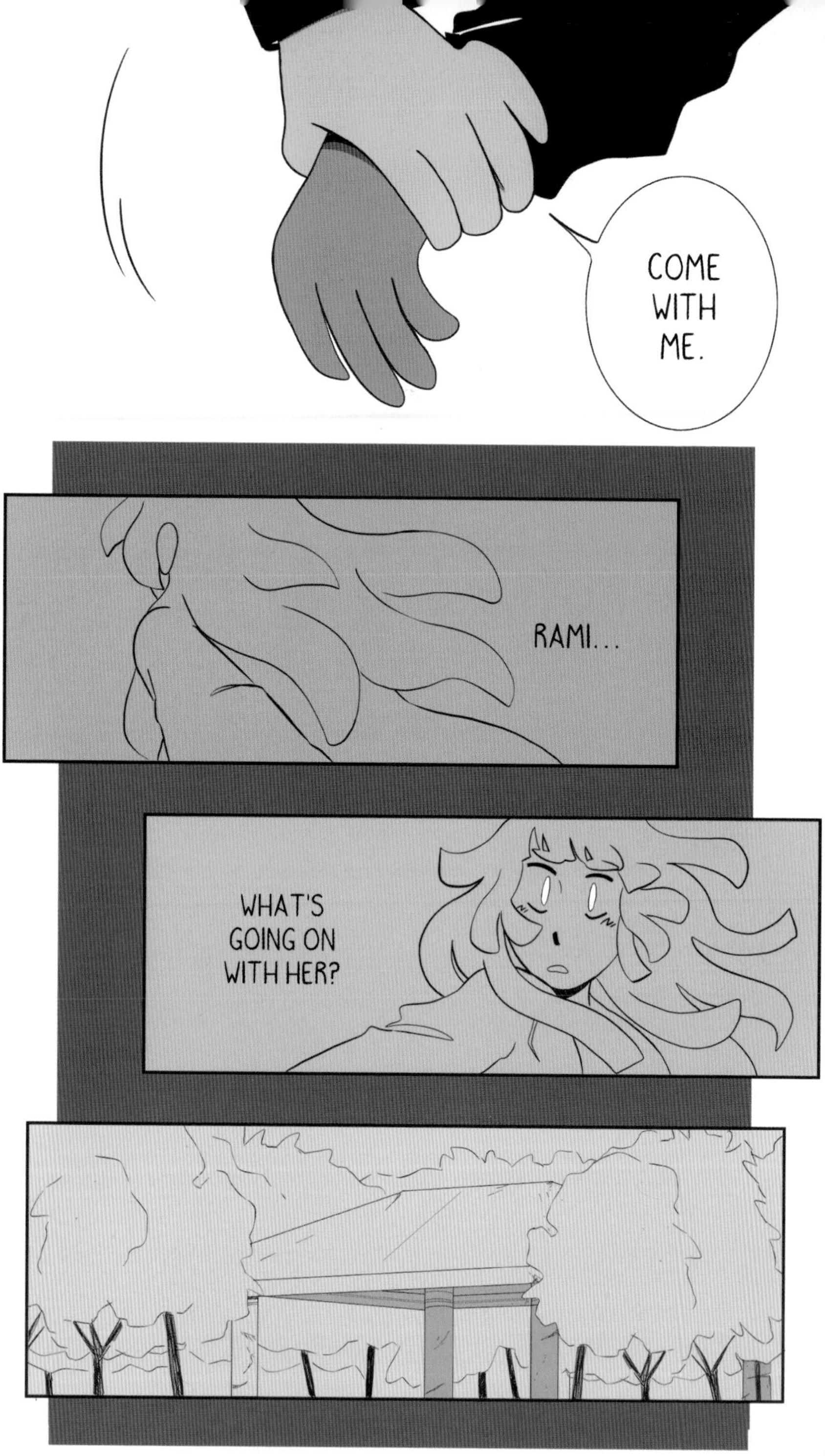
COME WITH ME.
RAMI...
WHAT'S GOING ON WITH HER?

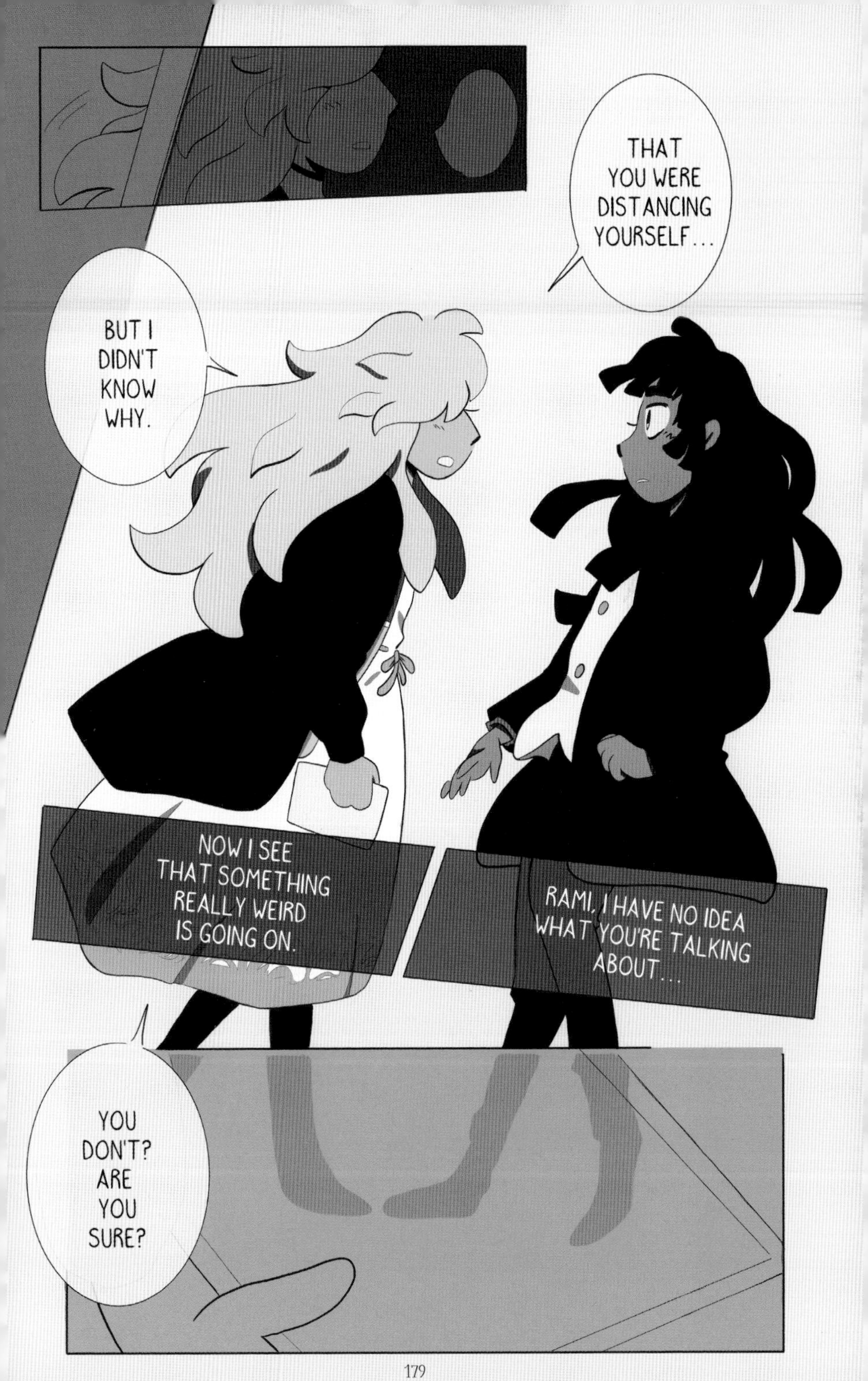
THAT YOU WERE DISTANCING YOURSELF...
BUT I DIDN'T KNOW WHY.
NOW I SEE THAT SOMETHING REALLY WEIRD IS GOING ON.
RAMI, I HAVE NO IDEA WHAT YOU'RE TALKING ABOUT...
YOU DON'T? ARE YOU SURE?

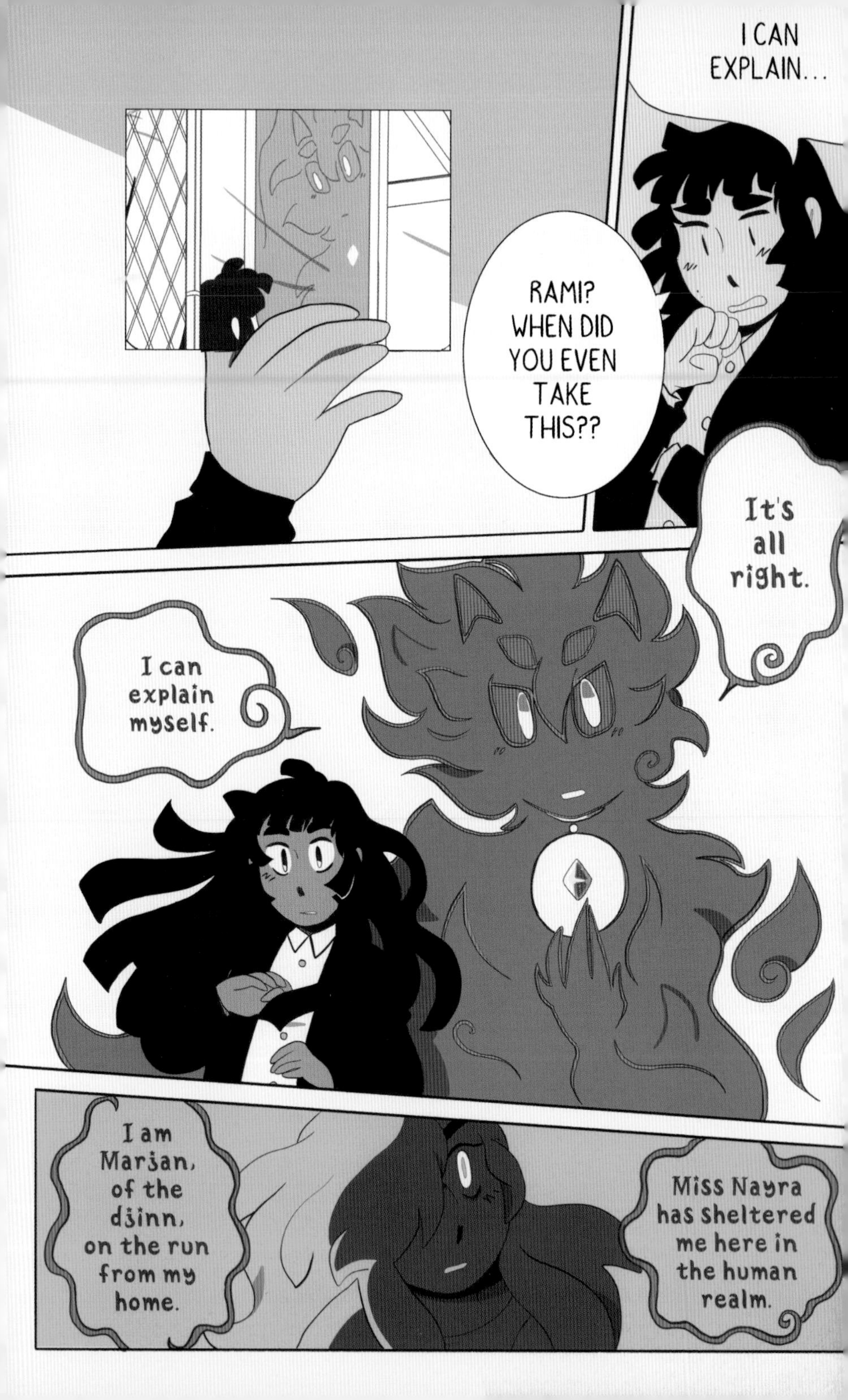
I CAN EXPLAIN...
RAMI? WHEN DID YOU EVEN TAKE THIS??
It's all right.
I can explain myself.
I am Marjan, of the djinn, on the run from my home.
Miss Nayra has sheltered me here in the human realm.

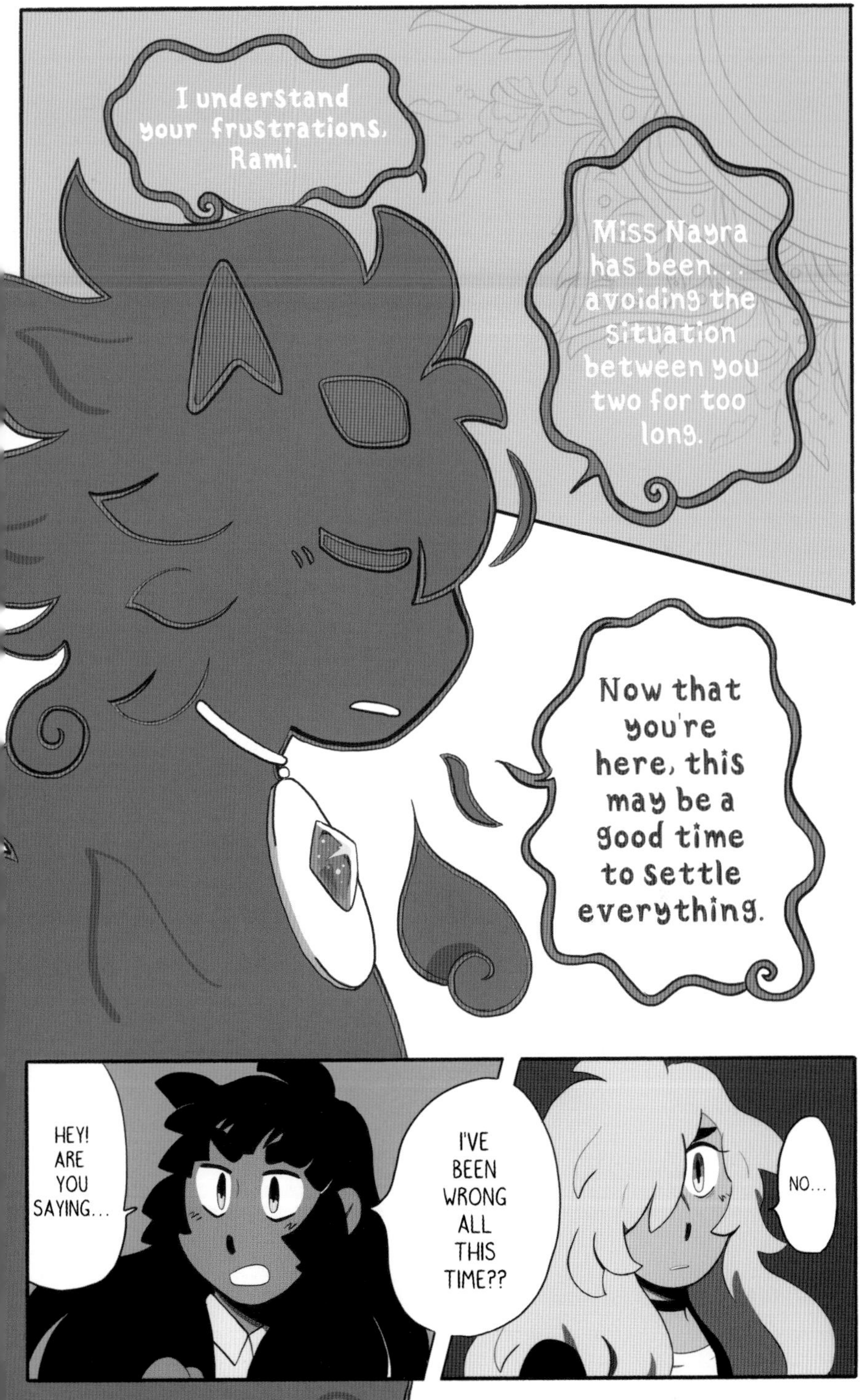
I understand your frustrations, Rami.
Miss Nayra has been... avoiding the situation between you two for too long.
Now that you're here, this may be a good time to settle everything.
HEY! ARE YOU SAYING...
I'VE BEEN WRONG ALL THIS TIME??
NO...

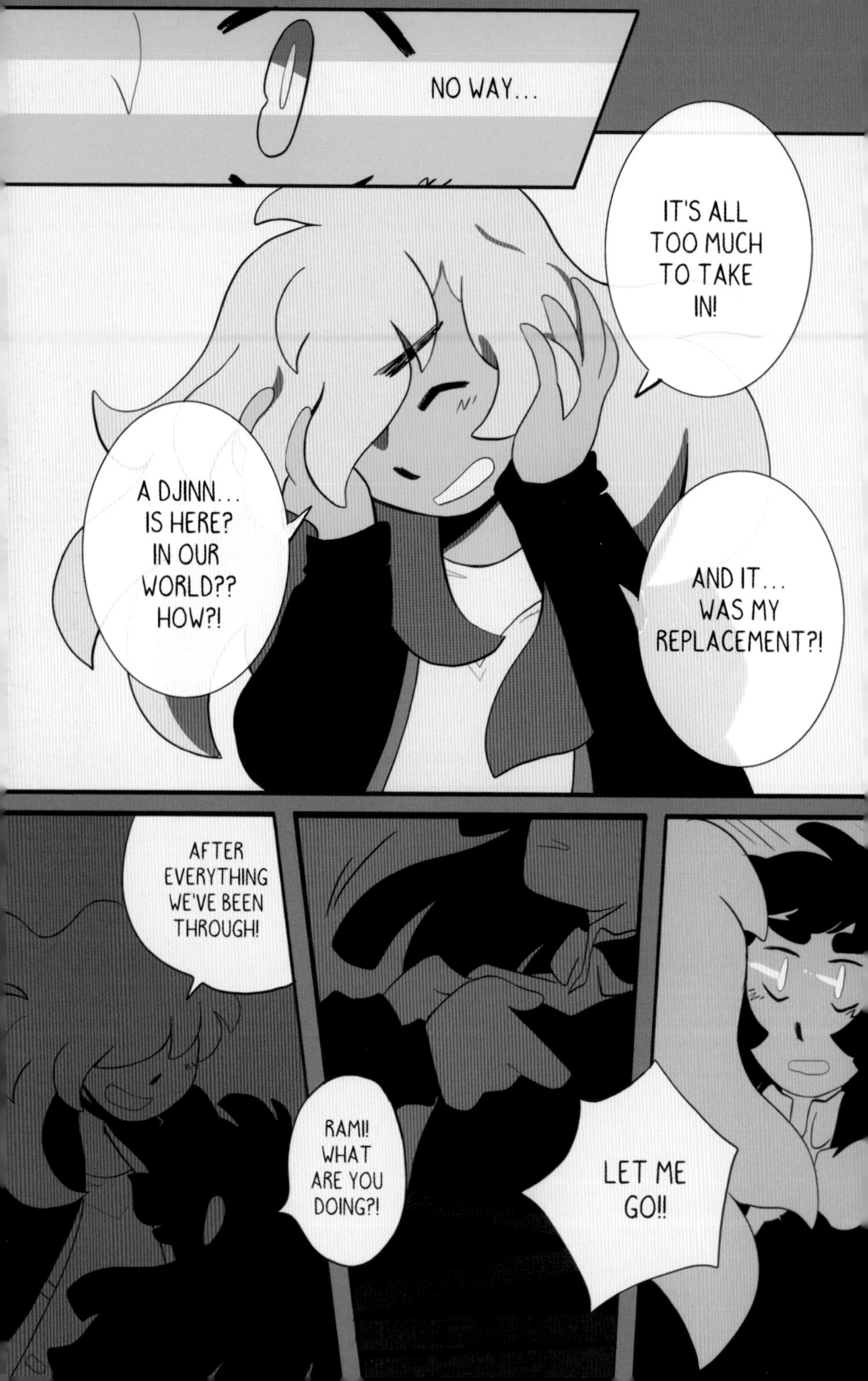
NO WAY...
IT'S ALL TOO MUCH TO TAKE IN!
A DJINN... IS HERE? IN OUR WORLD?? HOW?!
AND IT... WAS MY REPLACEMENT?!
AFTER EVERYTHING WE'VE BEEN THROUGH!
RAMI! WHAT ARE YOU DOING?!
LET ME GO!!

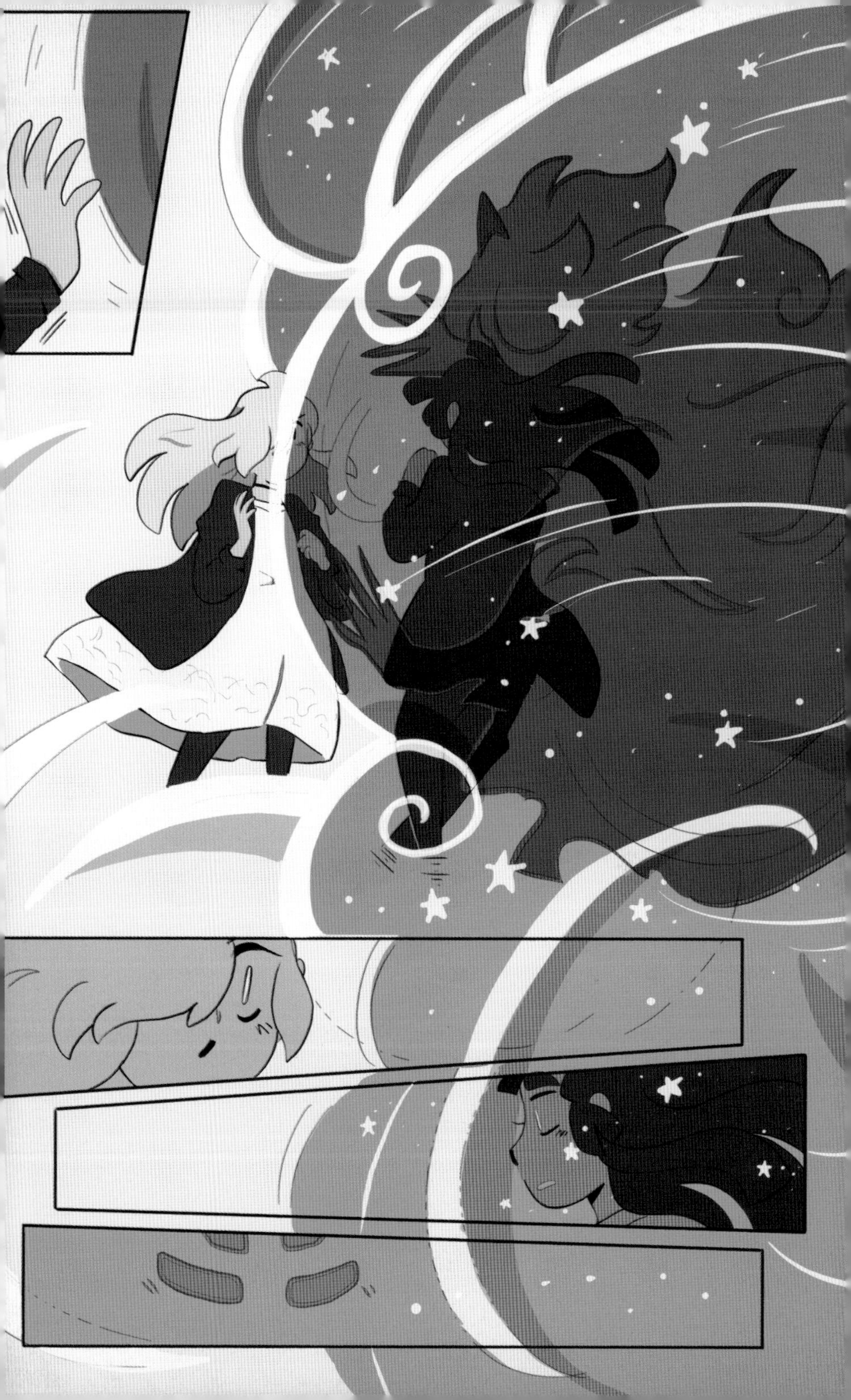

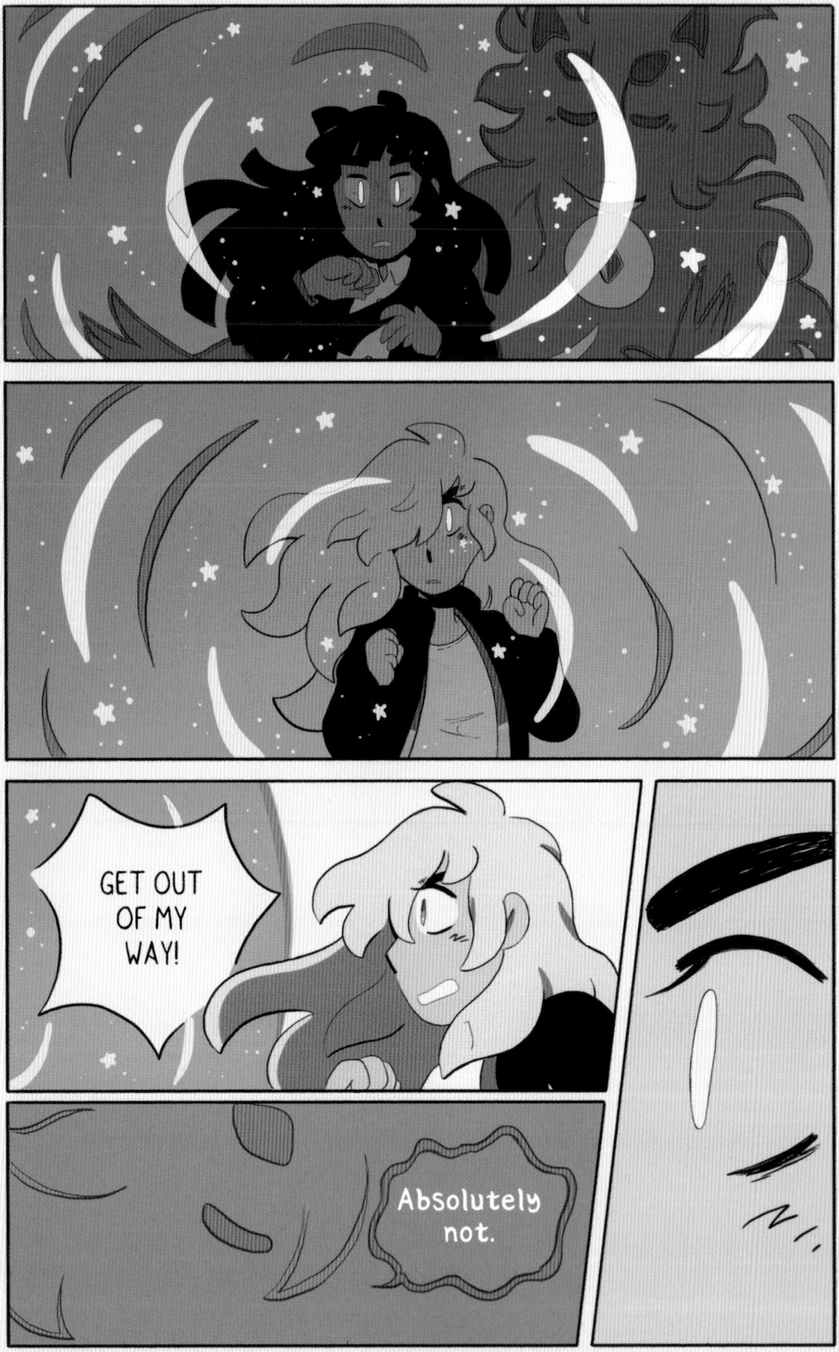
GET OUT OF MY WAY!
Absolutely not.

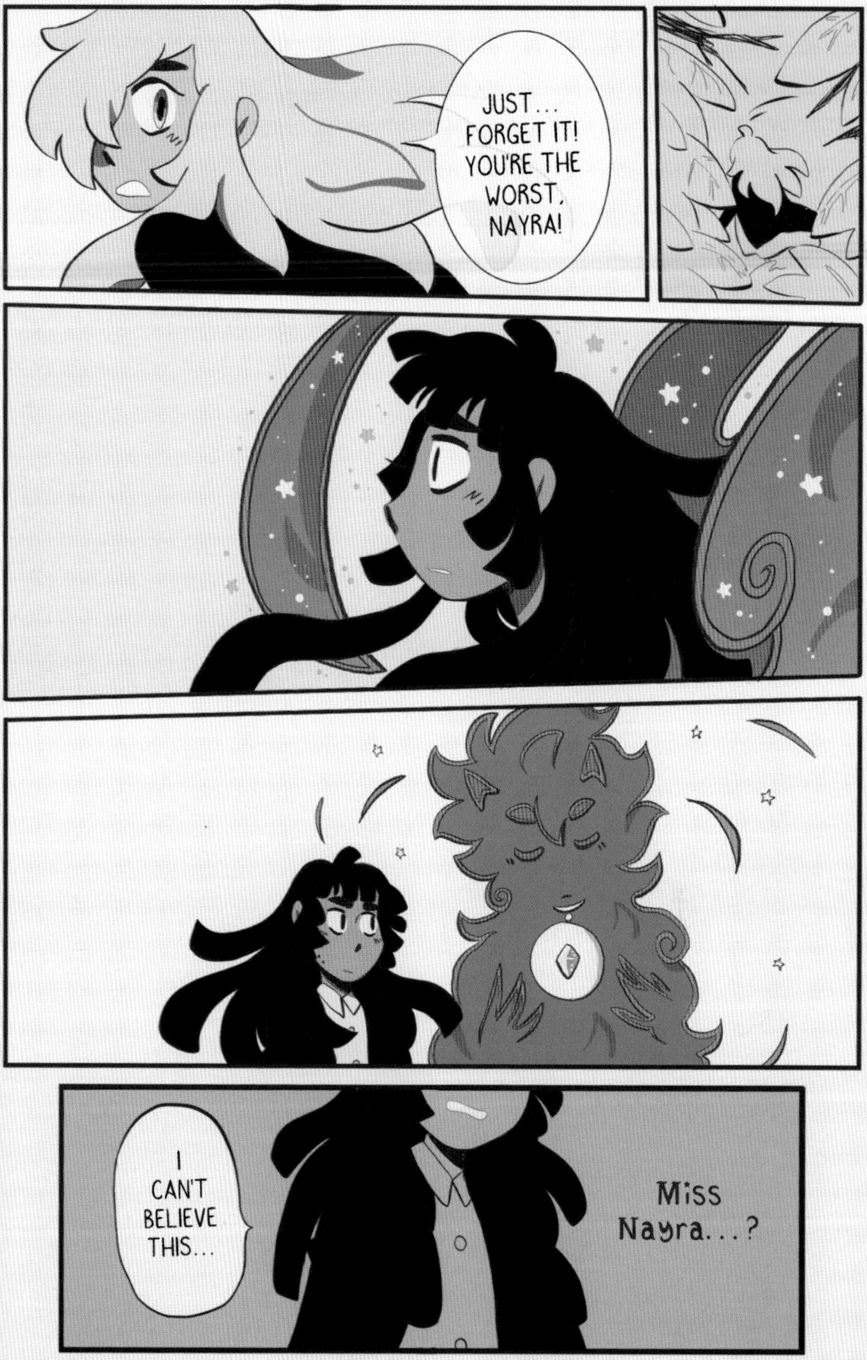
JUST... FORGET IT! YOU'RE THE WORST, NAYRA!
I CAN'T BELIEVE THIS...
Miss Nayra...?

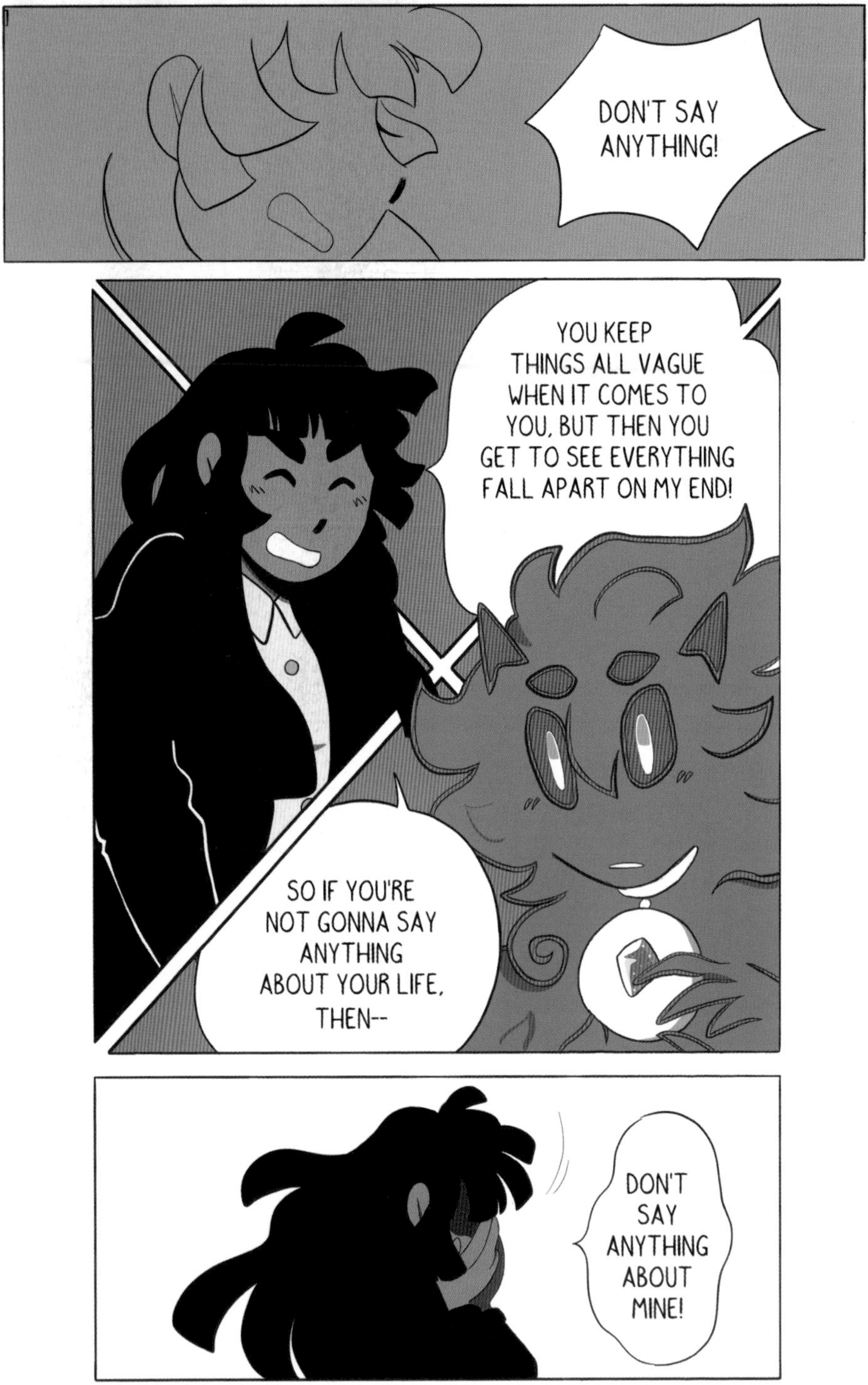
DON'T SAY ANYTHING!
YOU KEEP THINGS ALL VAGUE WHEN IT COMES TO YOU, BUT THEN YOU GET TO SEE EVERYTHING FALL APART ON MY END!
SO IF YOU'RE NOT GONNA SAY ANYTHING ABOUT YOUR LIFE, THEN--
DON'T SAY ANYTHING ABOUT MINE!

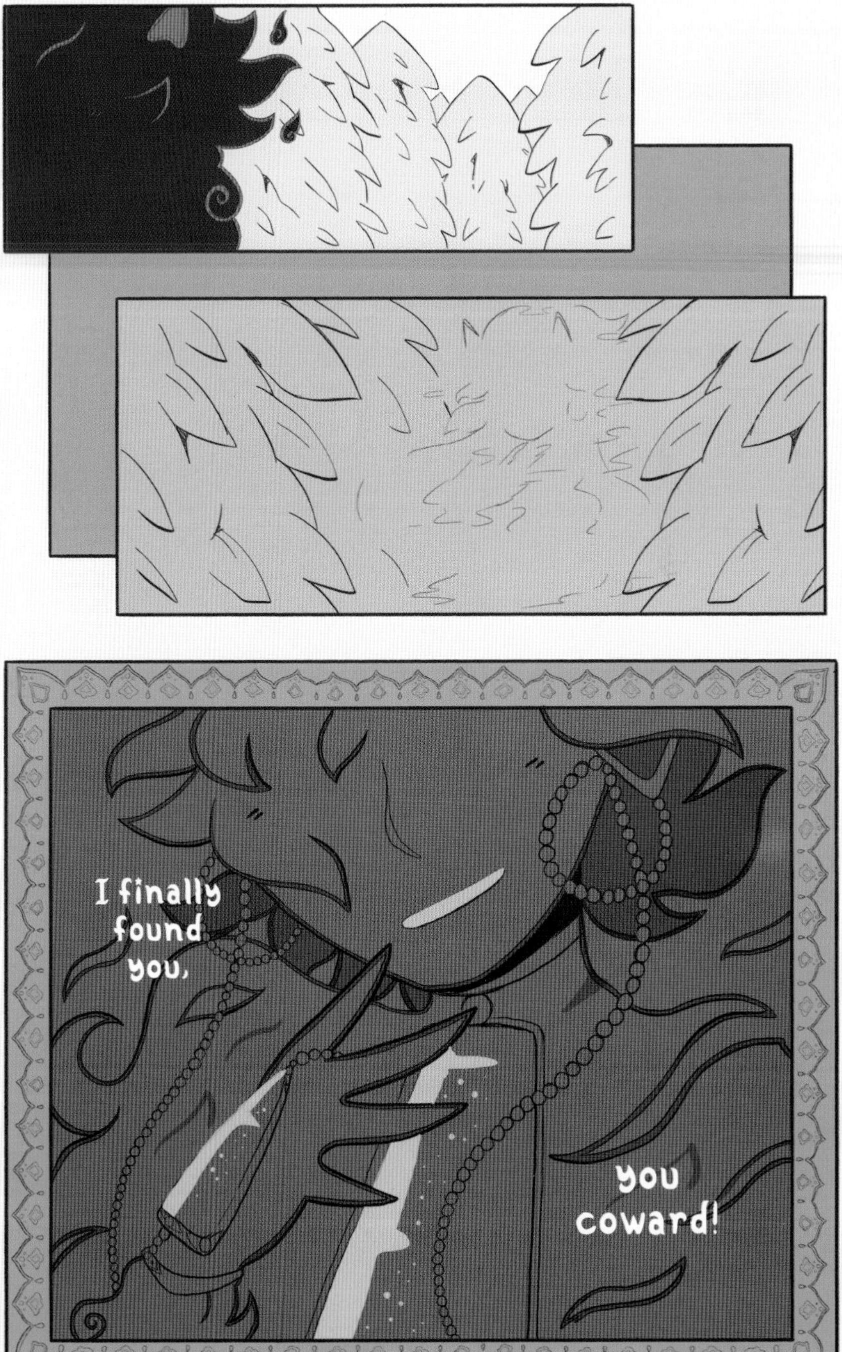
I finally found you,
you coward!

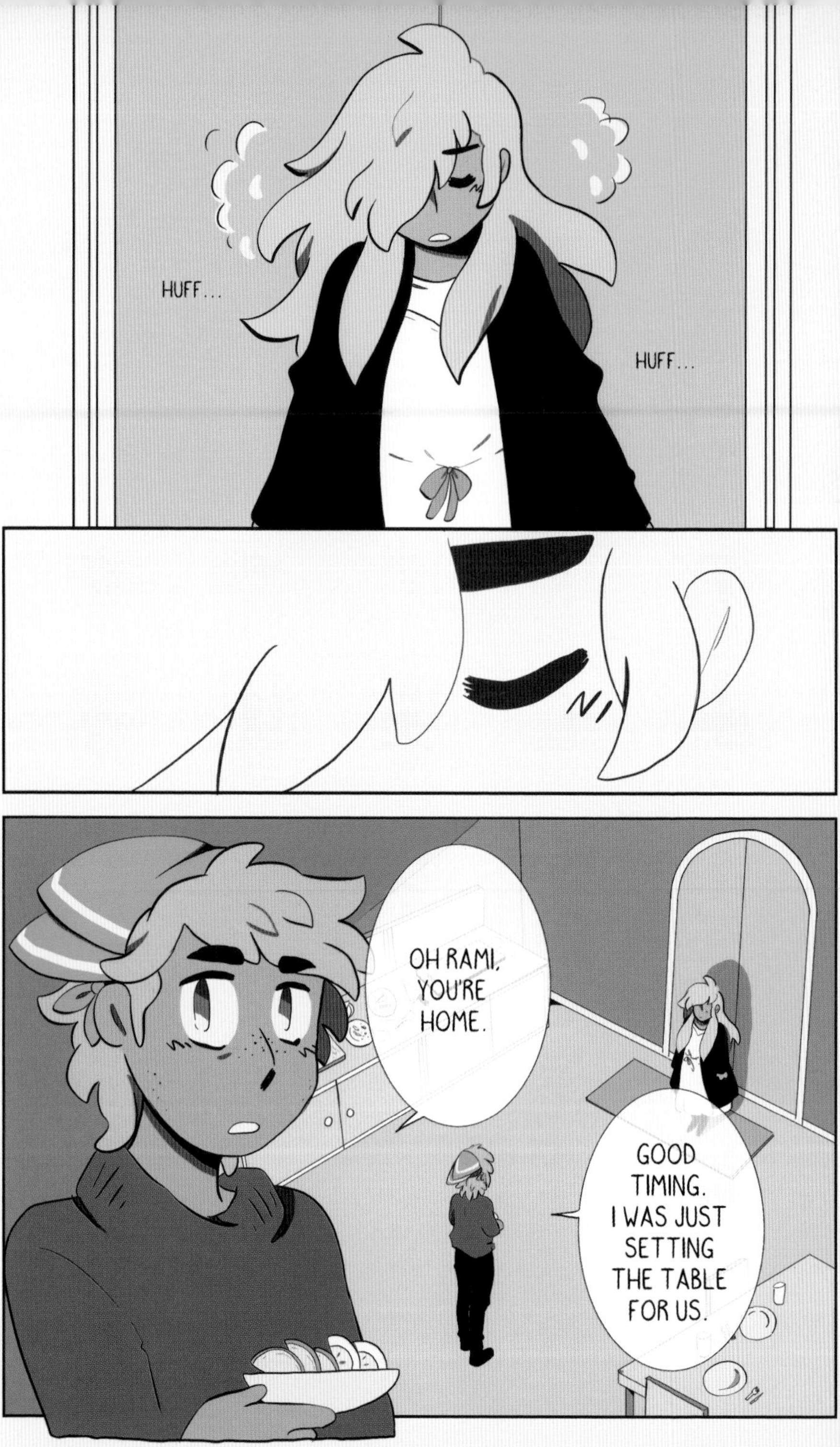
HUFF...
HUFF...
OH RAMI, YOU'RE HOME.
GOOD TIMING. I WAS JUST SETTING THE TABLE FOR US.

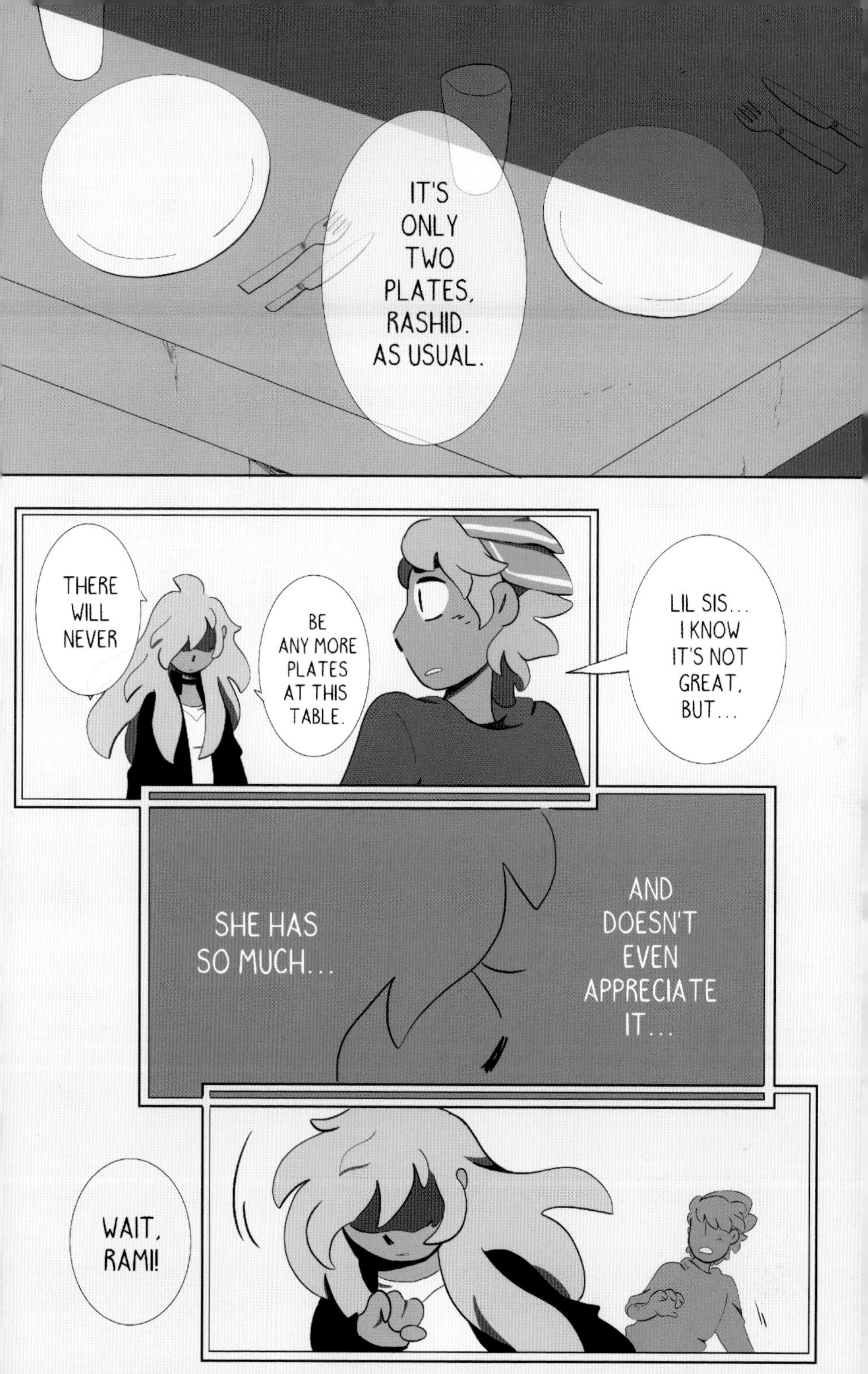
IT'S ONLY TWO PLATES, RASHID. AS USUAL.
THERE WILL NEVER
BE ANY MORE PLATES AT THIS TABLE.
LIL SIS... I KNOW IT'S NOT GREAT, BUT...
SHE HAS SO MUCH...
AND DOESN'T EVEN APPRECIATE IT...
WAIT, RAMI!

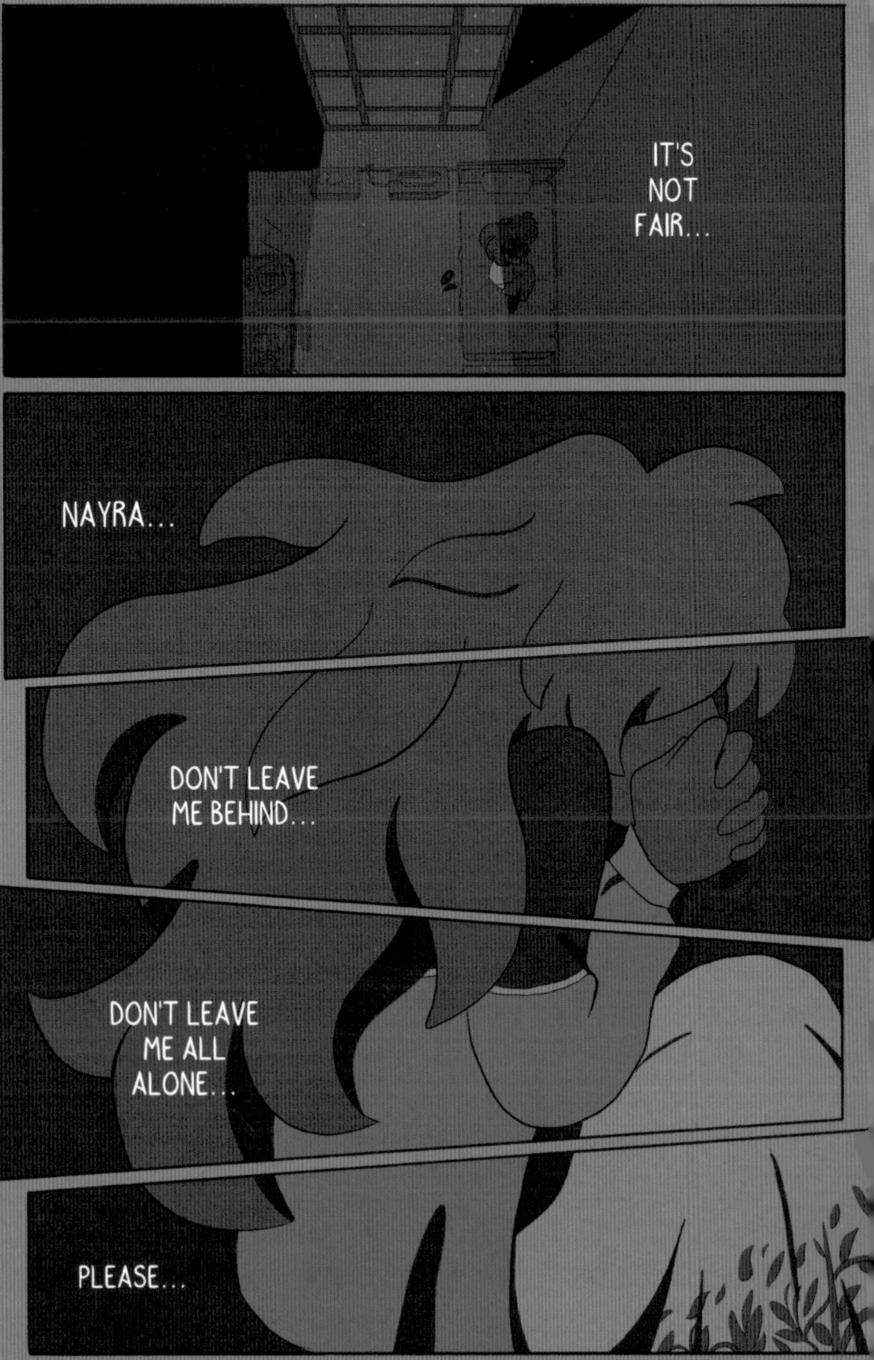
IT'S
NOT
FAIR...
NAYRA...
DON'T LEAVE
ME BEHIND...
DON'T LEAVE
ME ALL
ALONE...
PLEASE...

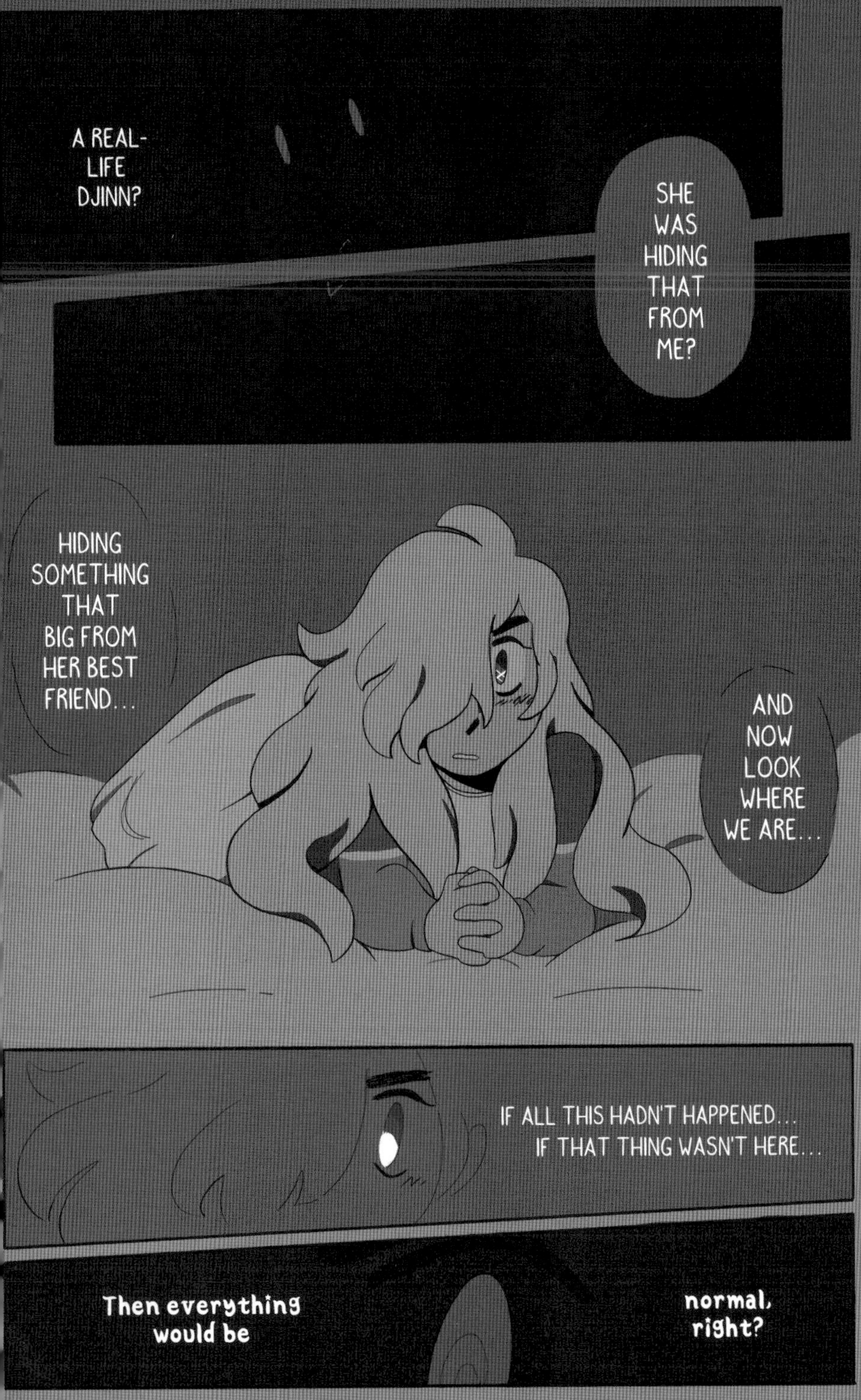
A REAL-LIFE DJINN?
SHE WAS HIDING THAT FROM ME?
HIDING SOMETHING THAT BIG FROM HER BEST FRIEND...
AND NOW LOOK WHERE WE ARE...
IF ALL THIS HADN'T HAPPENED...
IF THAT THING WASN'T HERE...
Then everything would be
normal, right?

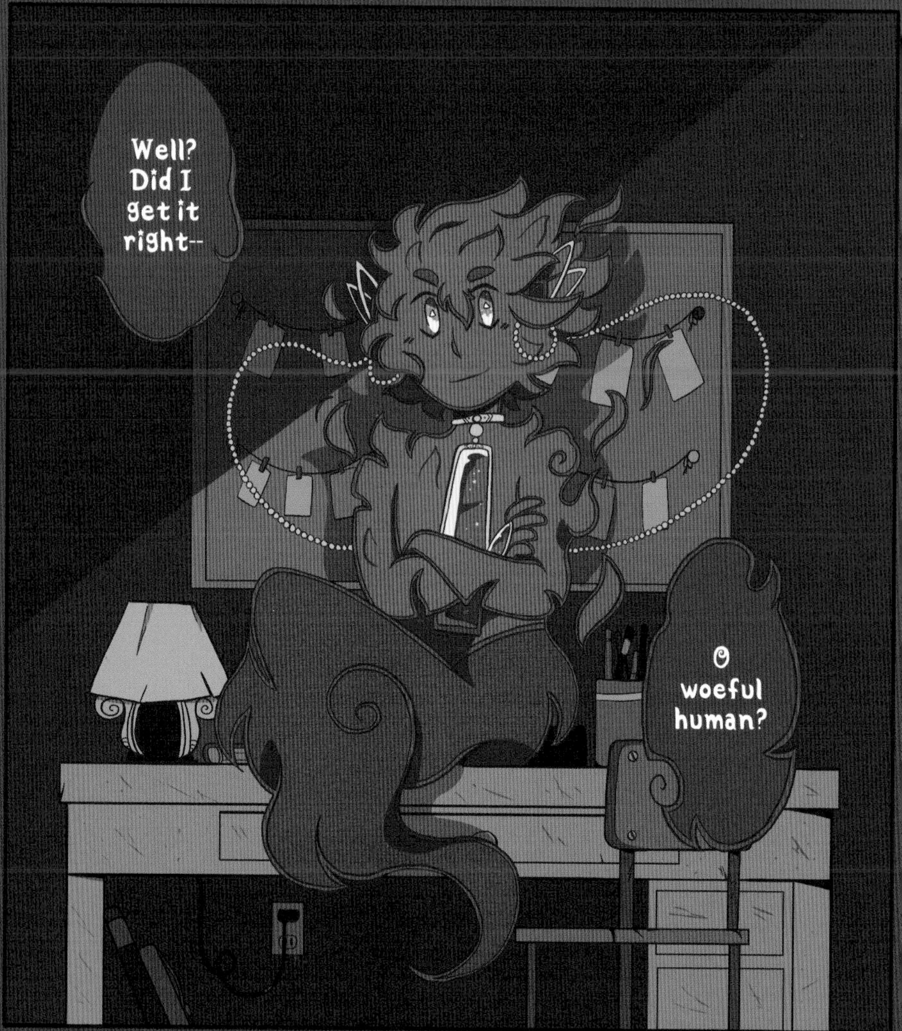
Well? Did I get it right--
O woeful human?

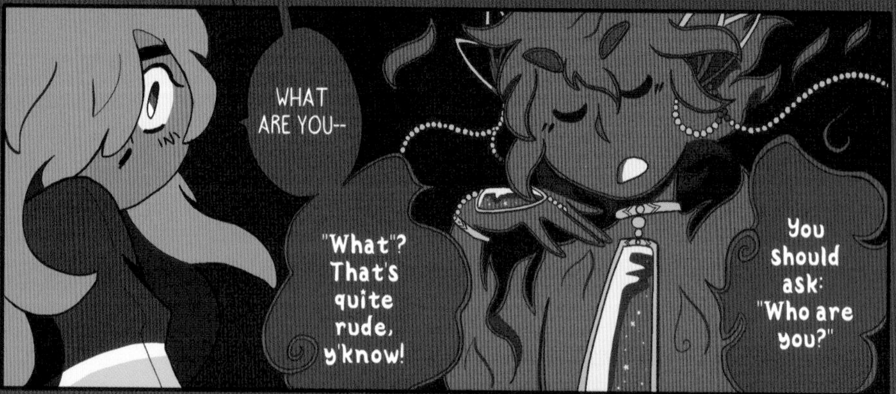
WHAT ARE YOU--
"What"? That's quite rude, y'know!
You should ask: "Who are you?"

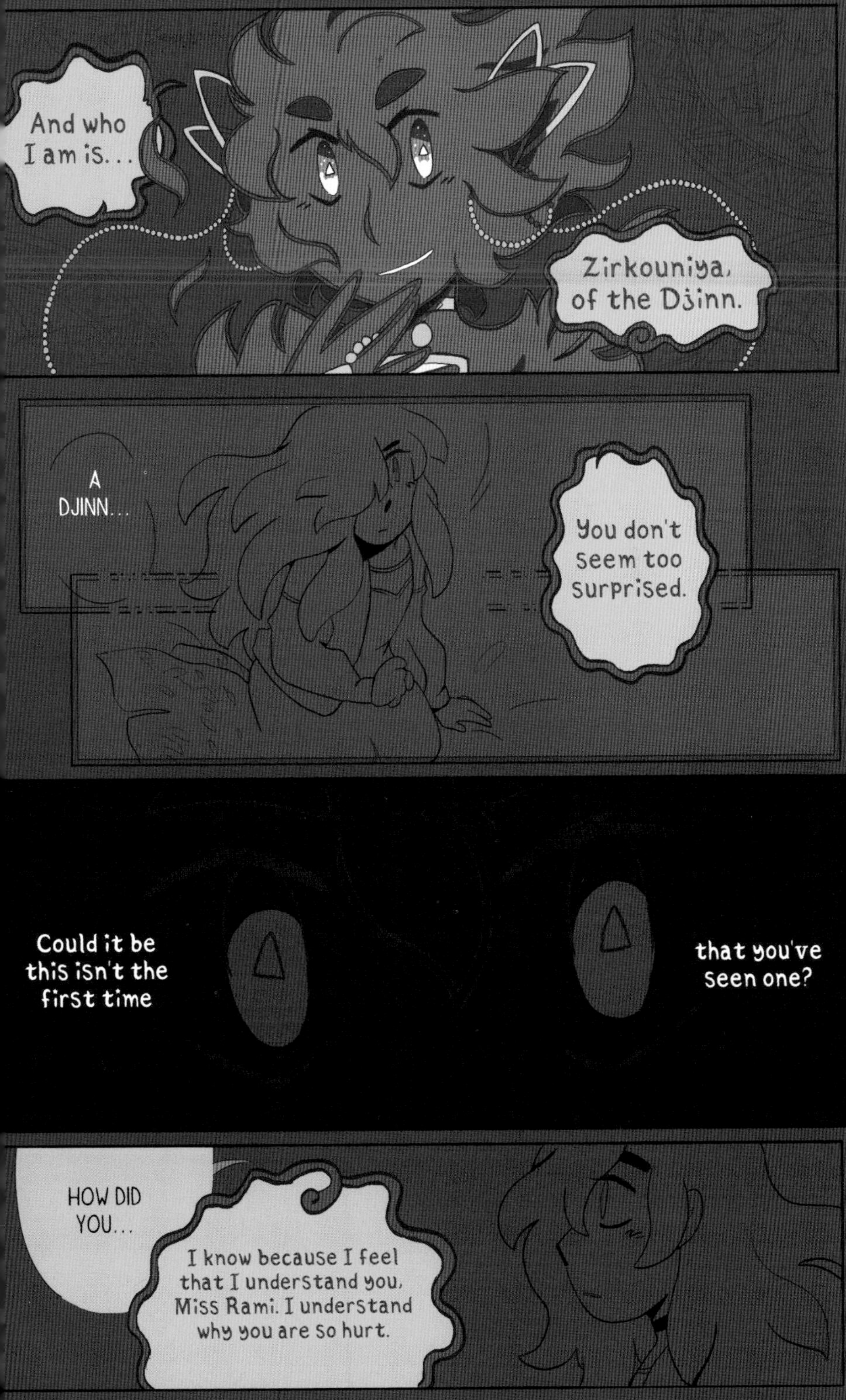
And who I am is. . .
Zirkouniya, of the Djinn.
A DJINN. . .
You don't seem too surprised.
Could it be this isn't the first time
that you've seen one?
HOW DID YOU. . .
I know because I feel that I understand you, Miss Rami. I understand why you are so hurt.

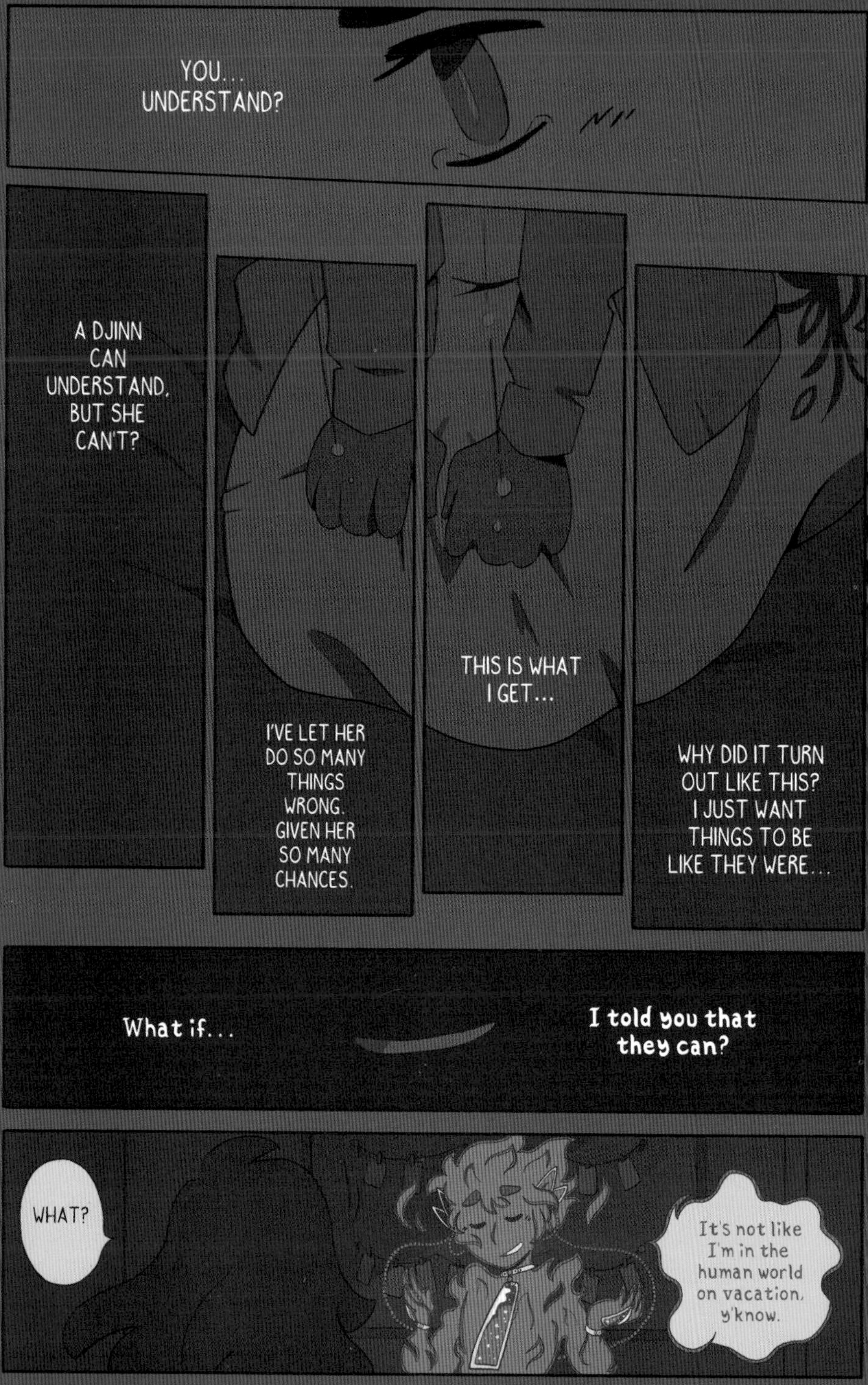

YOU...
UNDERSTAND?

A DJINN
CAN
UNDERSTAND,
BUT SHE
CAN'T?

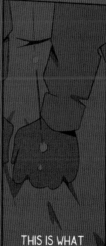

THIS IS WHAT
I GET...

I'VE LET HER
DO SO MANY
THINGS
WRONG.
GIVEN HER
SO MANY
CHANCES.

WHY DID IT TURN
OUT LIKE THIS?
I JUST WANT
THINGS TO BE
LIKE THEY WERE...

What if... I told you that
they can?

WHAT?

It's not like
I'm in the
human world
on vacation,
y'know.

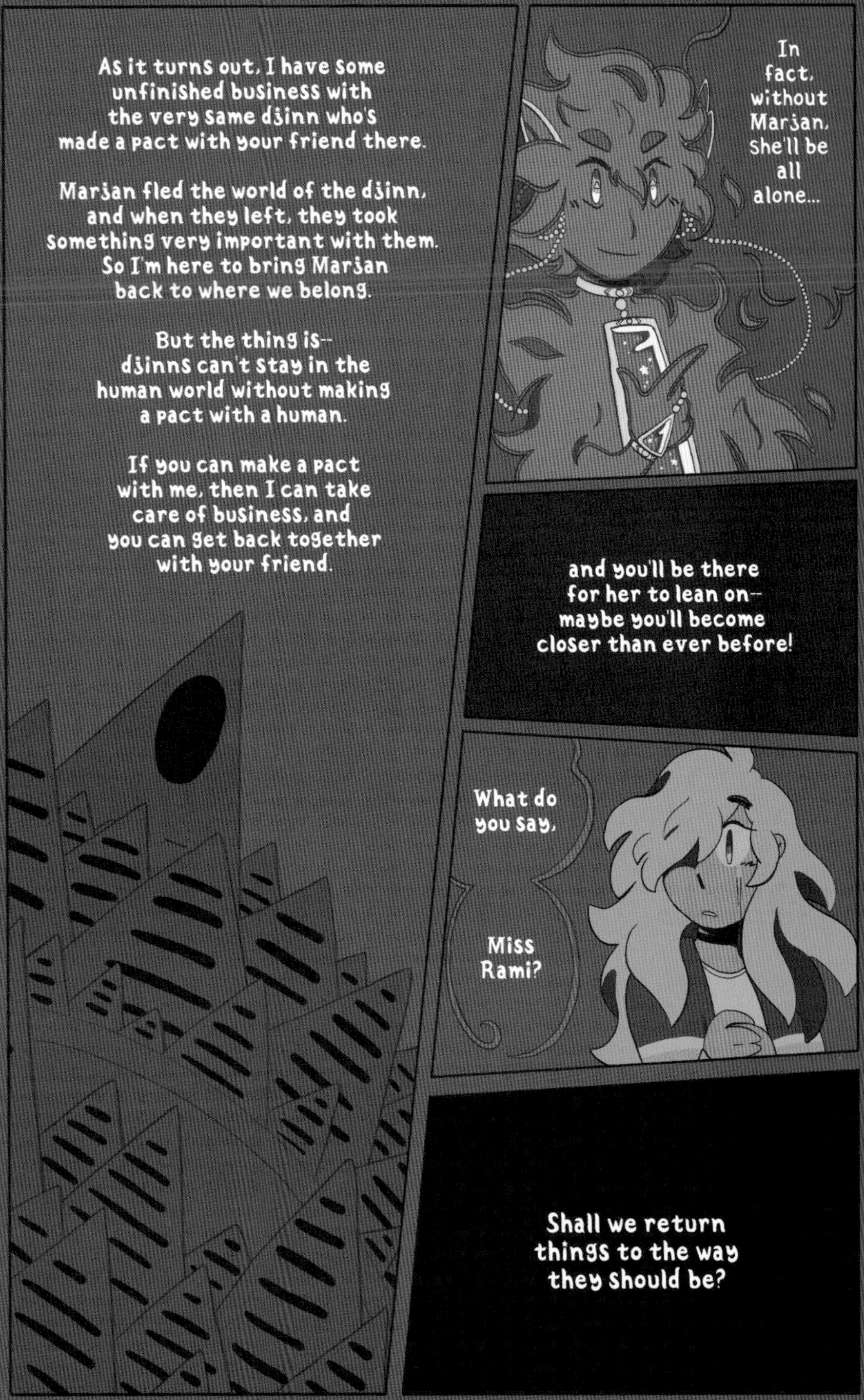
As it turns out, I have some unfinished business with the very same djinn who's made a pact with your friend there.
Marjan fled the world of the djinn, and when they left, they took something very important with them. So I'm here to bring Marjan back to where we belong.
But the thing is-- djinns can't stay in the human world without making a pact with a human.
If you can make a pact with me, then I can take care of business, and you can get back together with your friend.
In fact, without Marjan, she'll be all alone...
and you'll be there for her to lean on-- maybe you'll become closer than ever before!
What do you say,
Miss Rami?
Shall we return things to the way they should be?

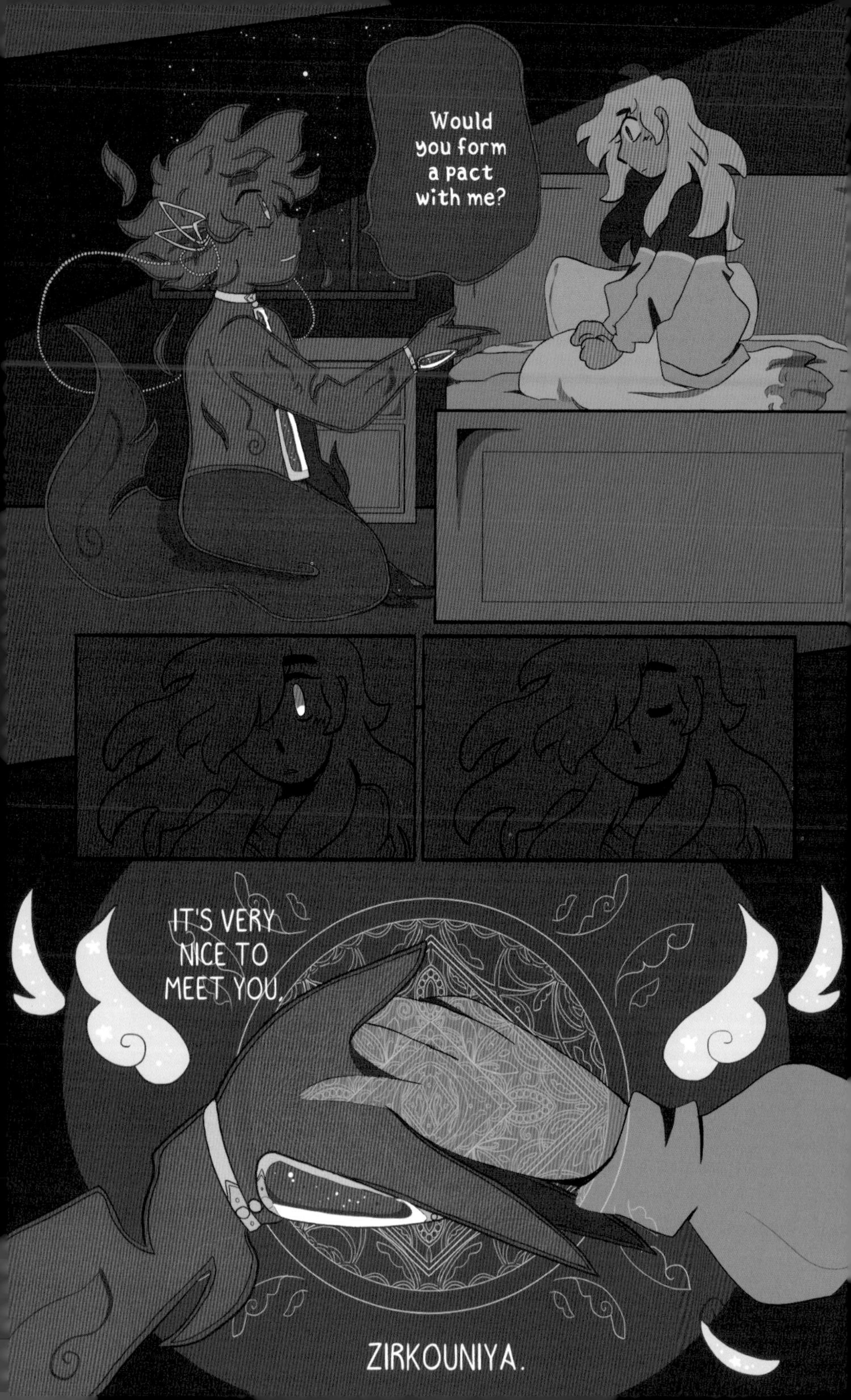
Would you form a pact with me?
IT'S VERY NICE TO MEET YOU,
ZIRKOUNIYA.

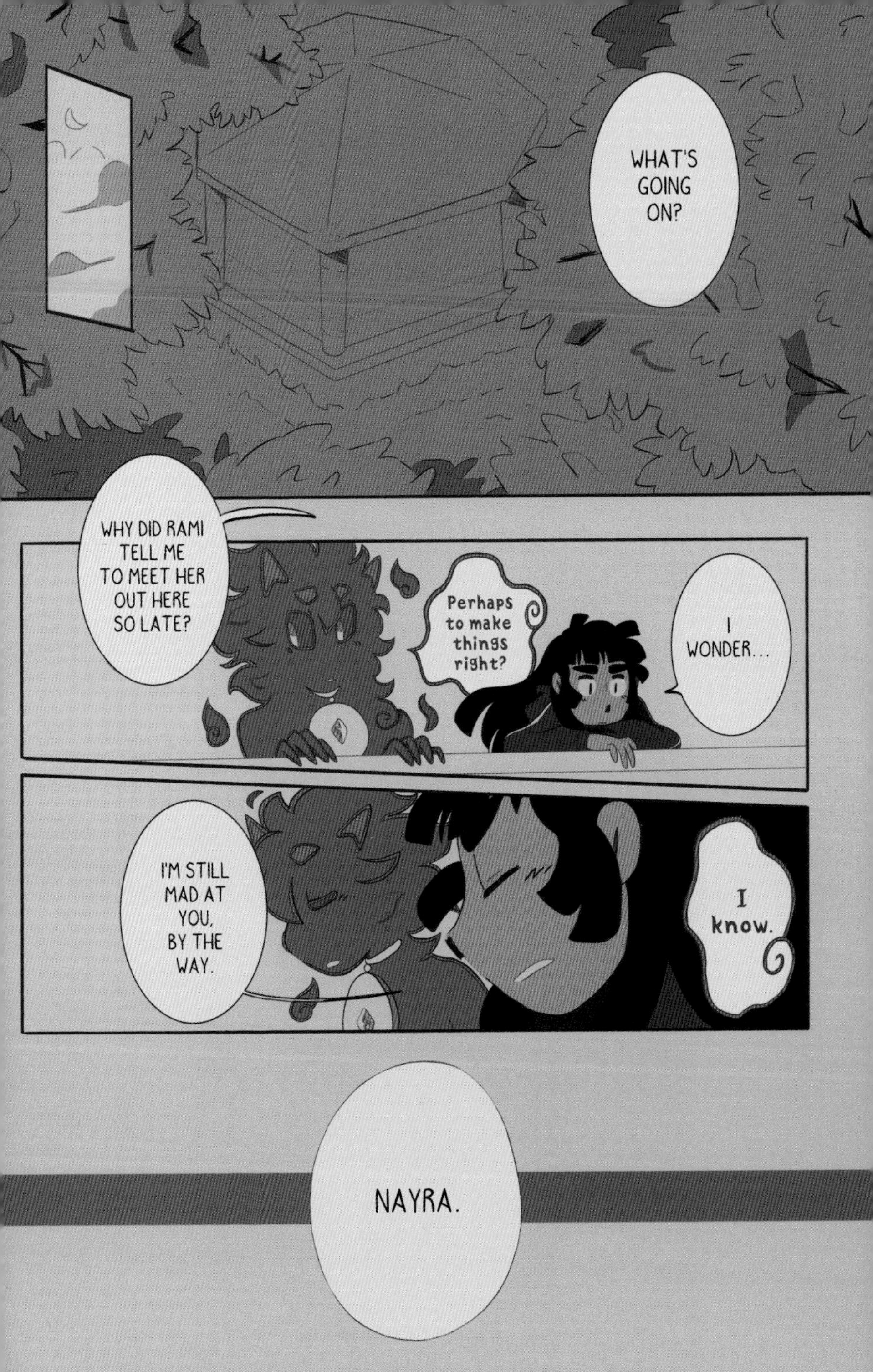
WHAT'S GOING ON?
WHY DID RAMI TELL ME TO MEET HER OUT HERE SO LATE?
Perhaps to make things right?
I WONDER...
I'M STILL MAD AT YOU, BY THE WAY.
I know.
NAYRA.

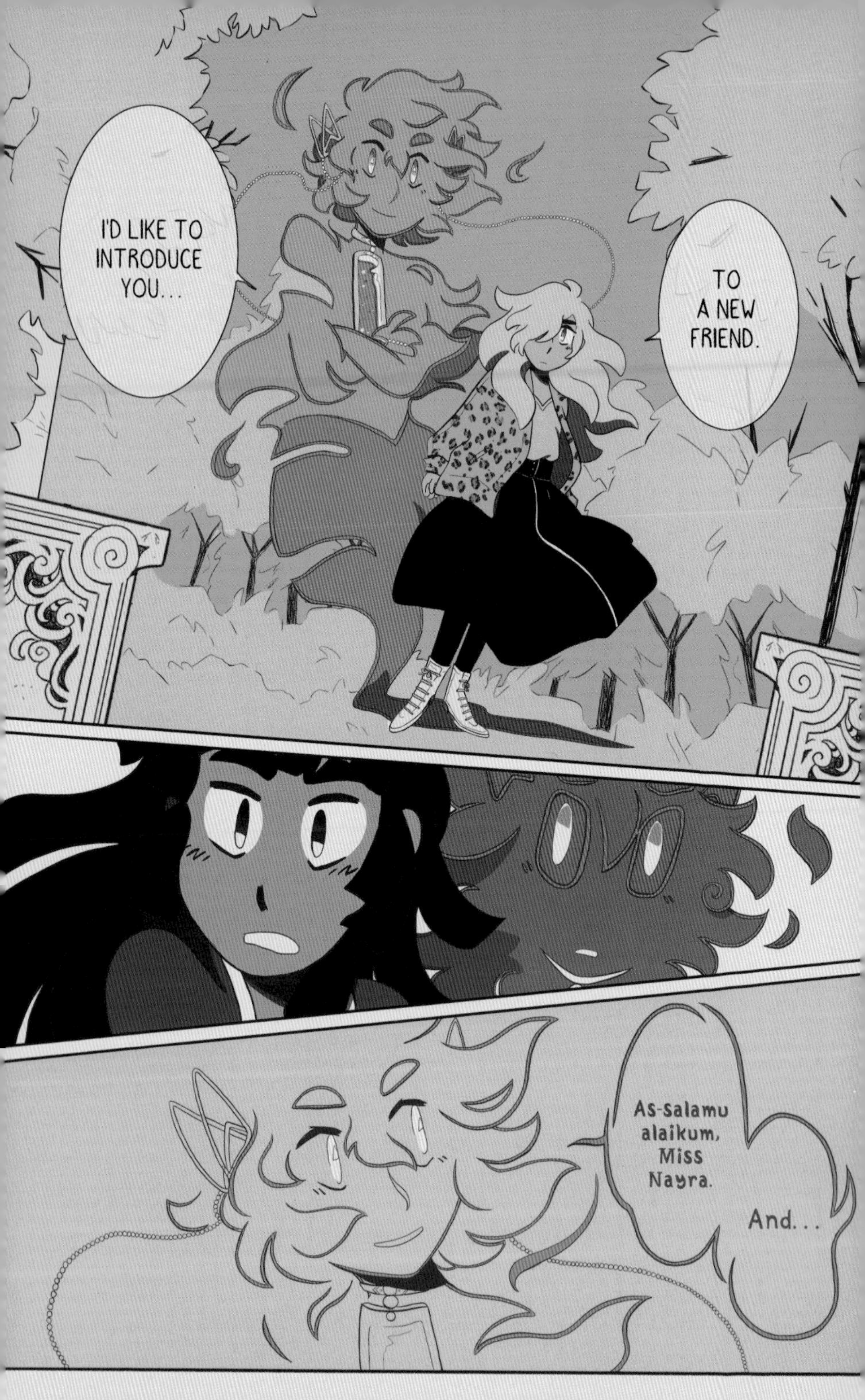
I'D LIKE TO INTRODUCE YOU...
TO A NEW FRIEND.
As-salamu alaikum, Miss Nayra.
And...

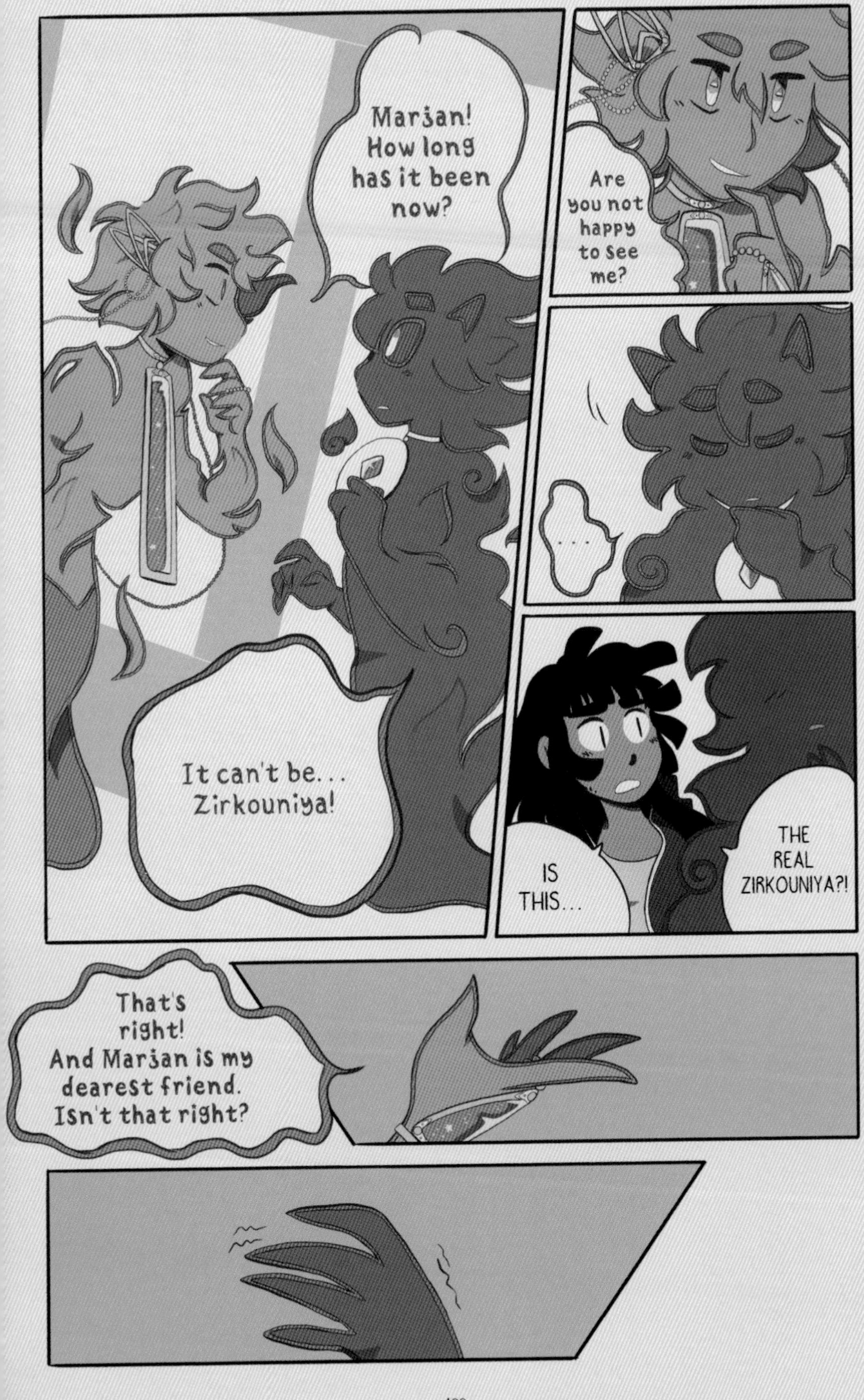
Marjan! How long has it been now?
Are you not happy to see me?
...
It can't be... Zirkouniya!
IS THIS...
THE REAL ZIRKOUNIYA?!
That's right! And Marjan is my dearest friend. Isn't that right?

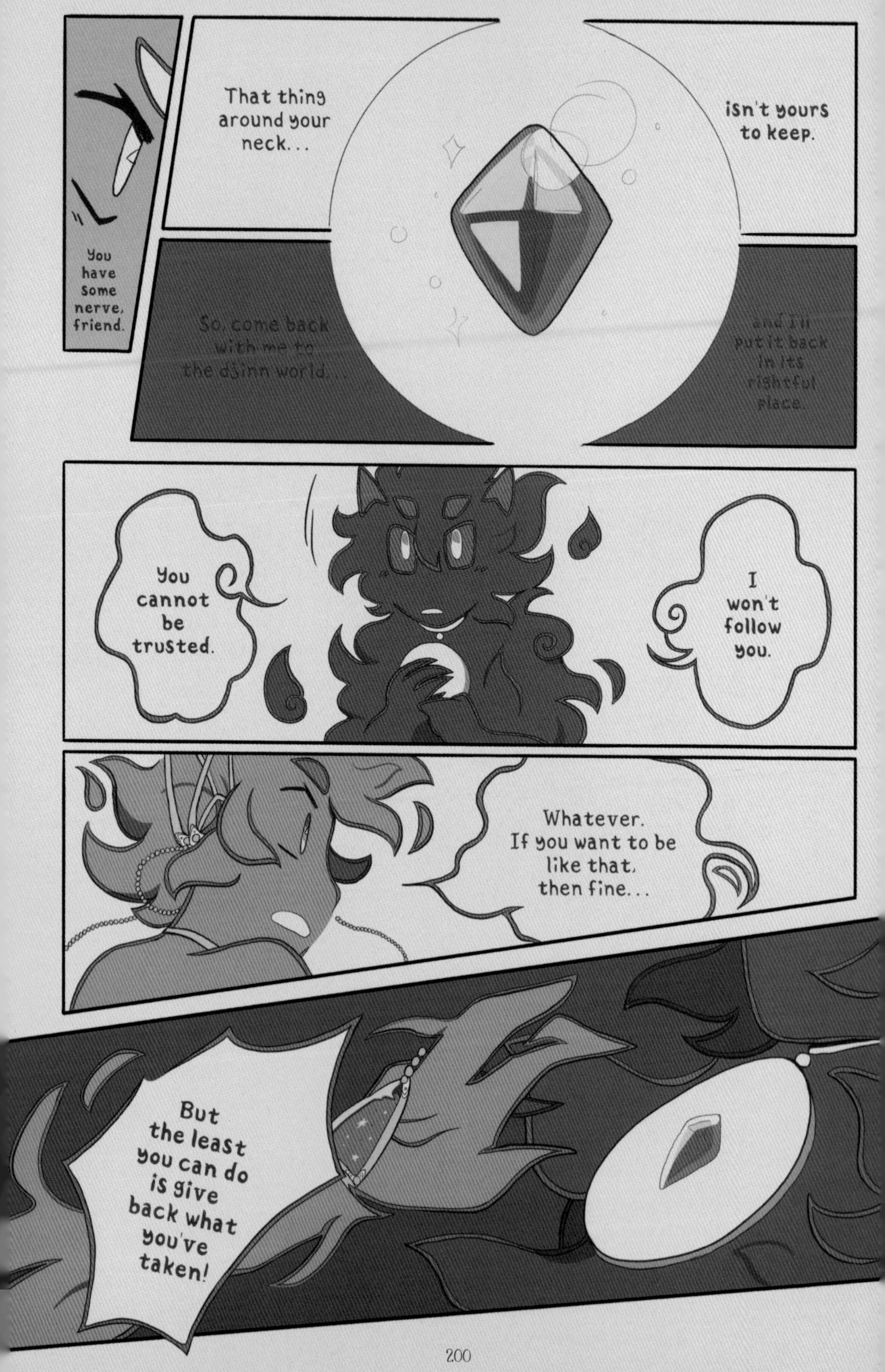
You have some nerve, friend.
That thing around your neck...
isn't yours to keep.
So, come back with me to the djinn world...
and I'll put it back in its rightful place.
You cannot be trusted.
I won't follow you.
Whatever. If you want to be like that, then fine...
But the least you can do is give back what you've taken!

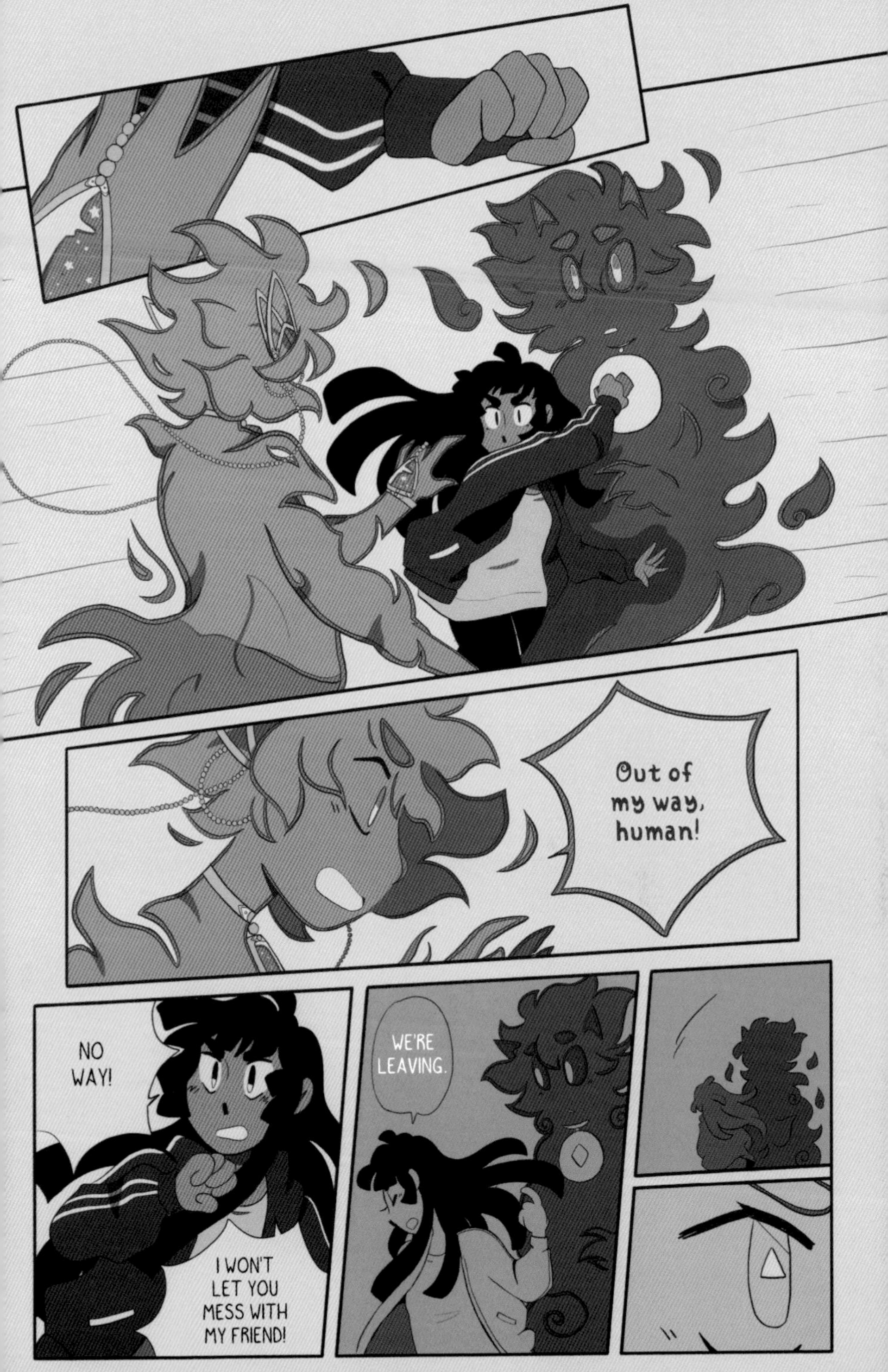
Out of my way, human!
NO WAY!
I WON'T LET YOU MESS WITH MY FRIEND!
WE'RE LEAVING.

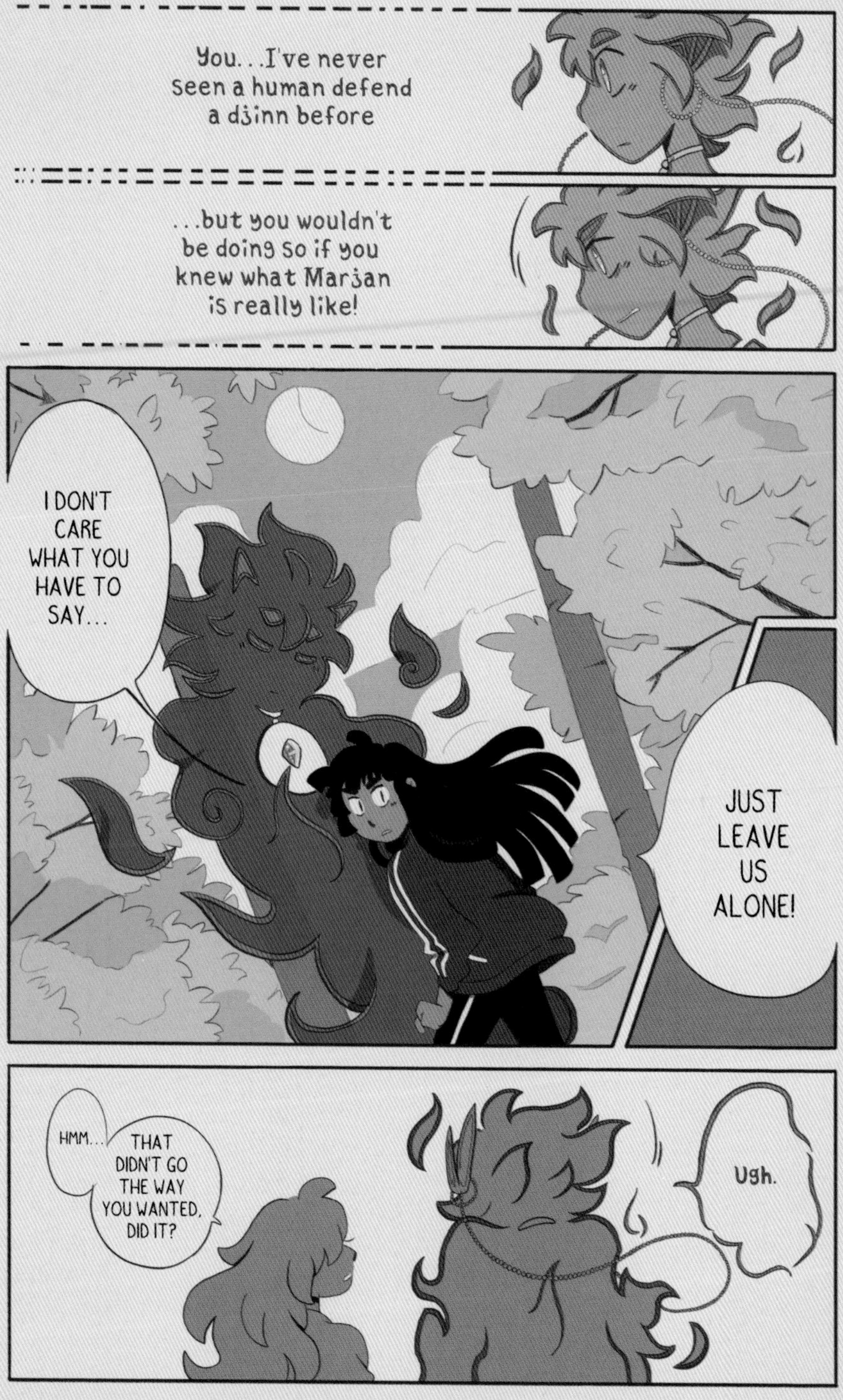
You. . .I've never seen a human defend a djinn before
. . .but you wouldn't be doing so if you knew what Marjan is really like!
I DON'T CARE WHAT YOU HAVE TO SAY...
JUST LEAVE US ALONE!
HMM...
THAT DIDN'T GO THE WAY YOU WANTED, DID IT?
Ugh.

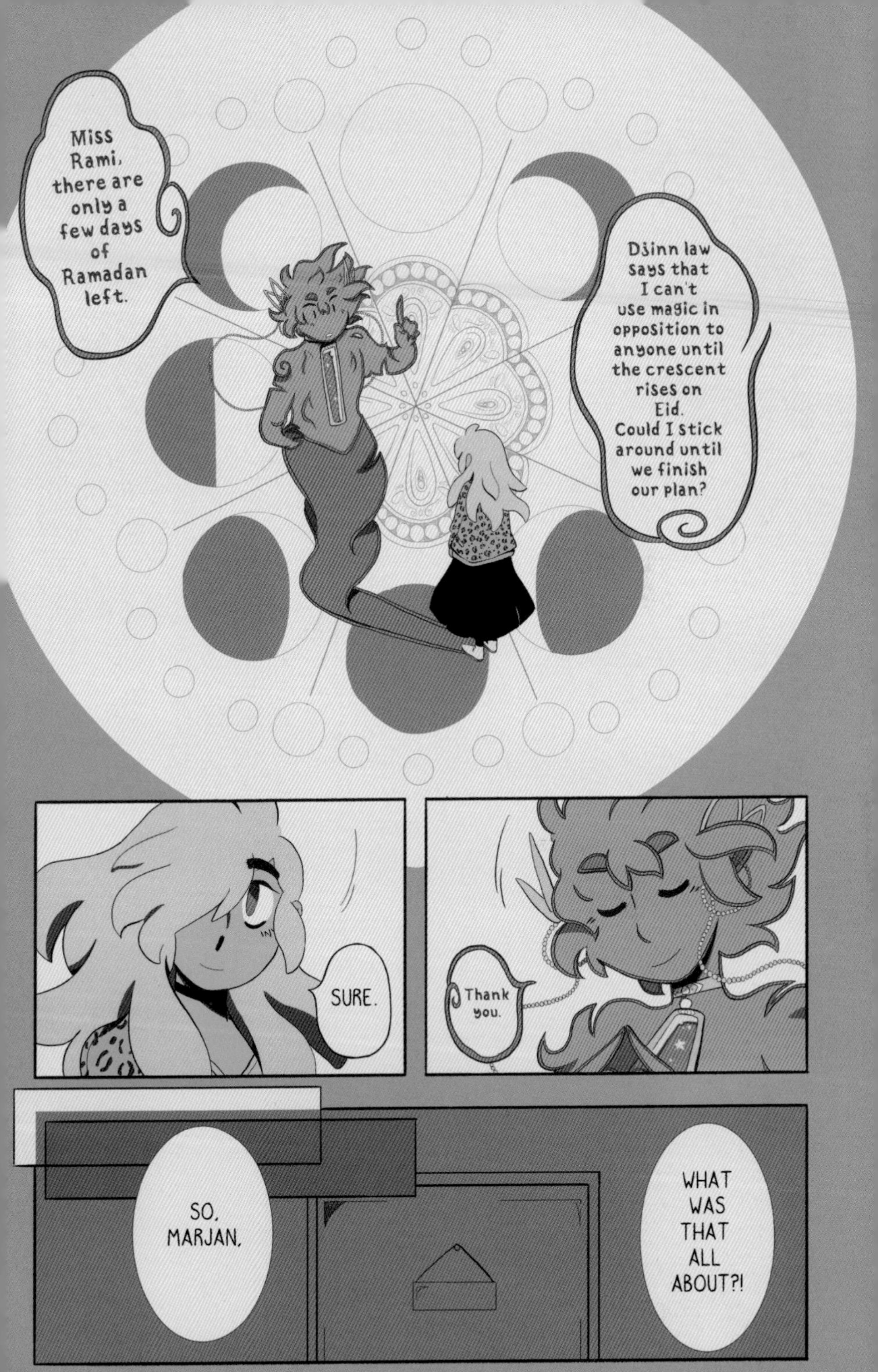

Miss Rami, there are only a few days of Ramadan left.
Djinn law says that I can't use magic in opposition to anyone until the crescent rises on Eid.
Could I stick around until we finish our plan?
SURE.
Thank you.
SO, MARJAN,
WHAT WAS THAT ALL ABOUT?!

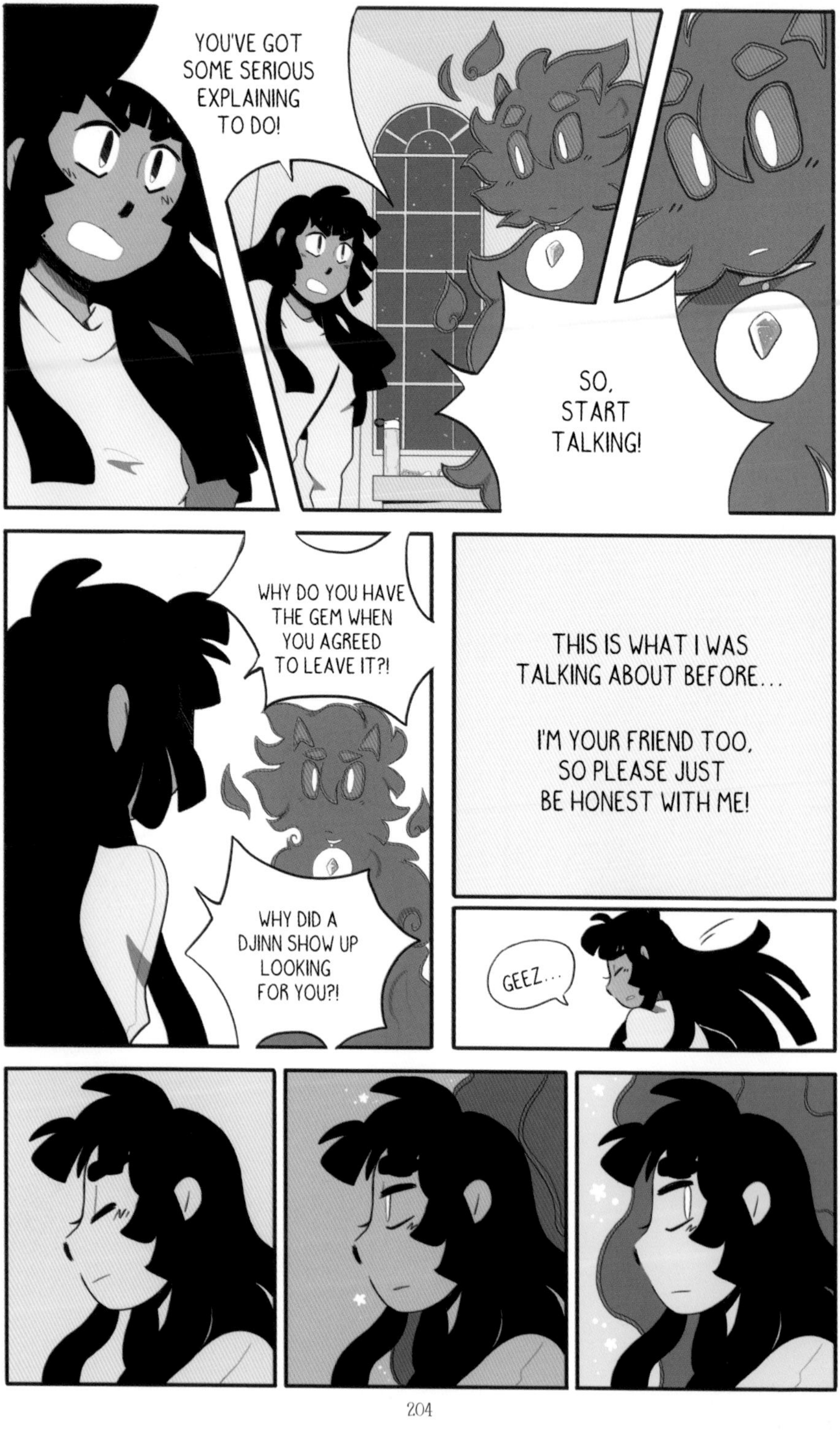
YOU'VE GOT SOME SERIOUS EXPLAINING TO DO!
SO, START TALKING!
WHY DO YOU HAVE THE GEM WHEN YOU AGREED TO LEAVE IT?!
WHY DID A DJINN SHOW UP LOOKING FOR YOU?!
THIS IS WHAT I WAS TALKING ABOUT BEFORE...
I'M YOUR FRIEND TOO, SO PLEASE JUST BE HONEST WITH ME!
GEEZ...

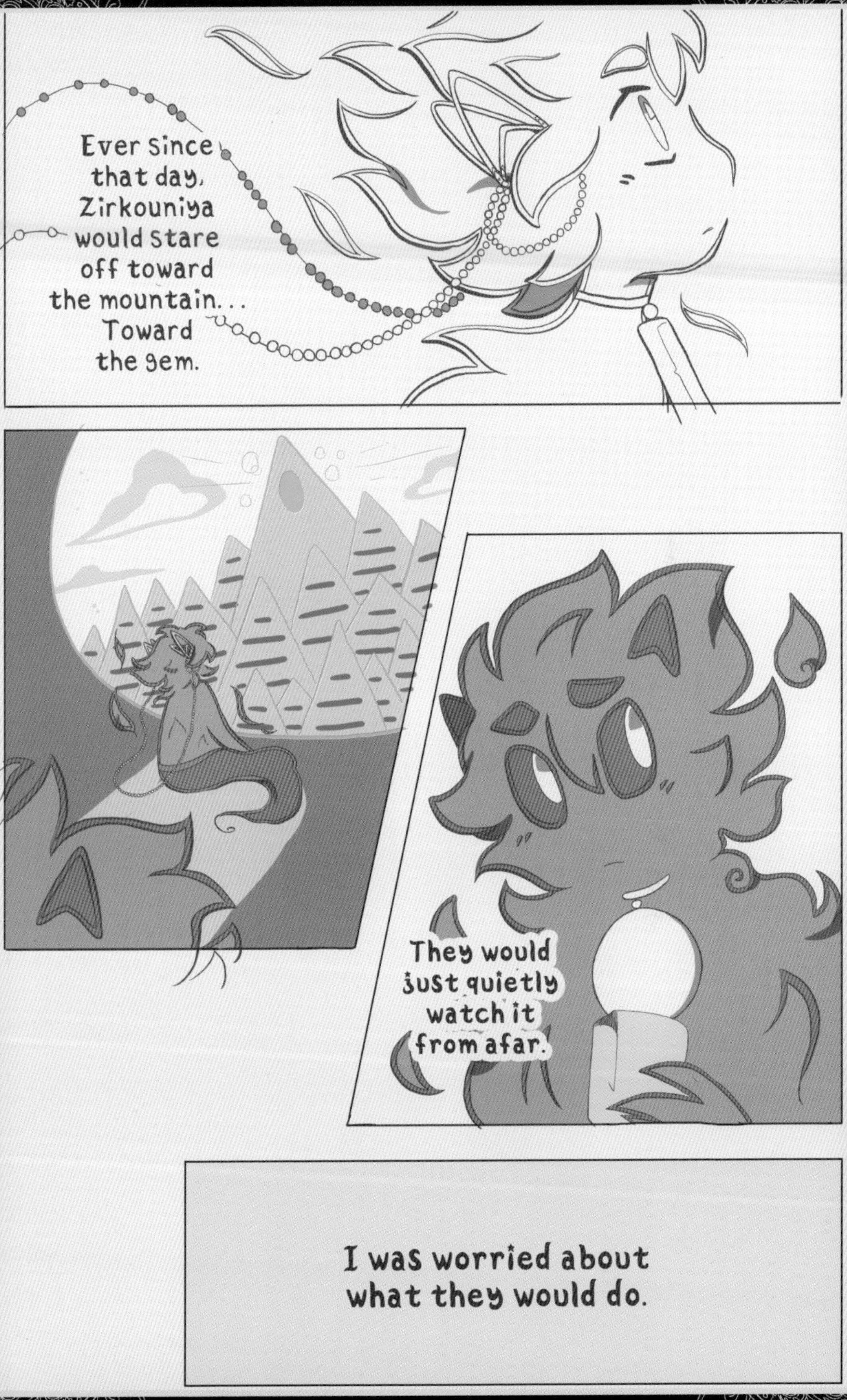
Ever since that day, Zirkouniya would stare off toward the mountain... Toward the gem.
They would just quietly watch it from afar.
I was worried about what they would do.

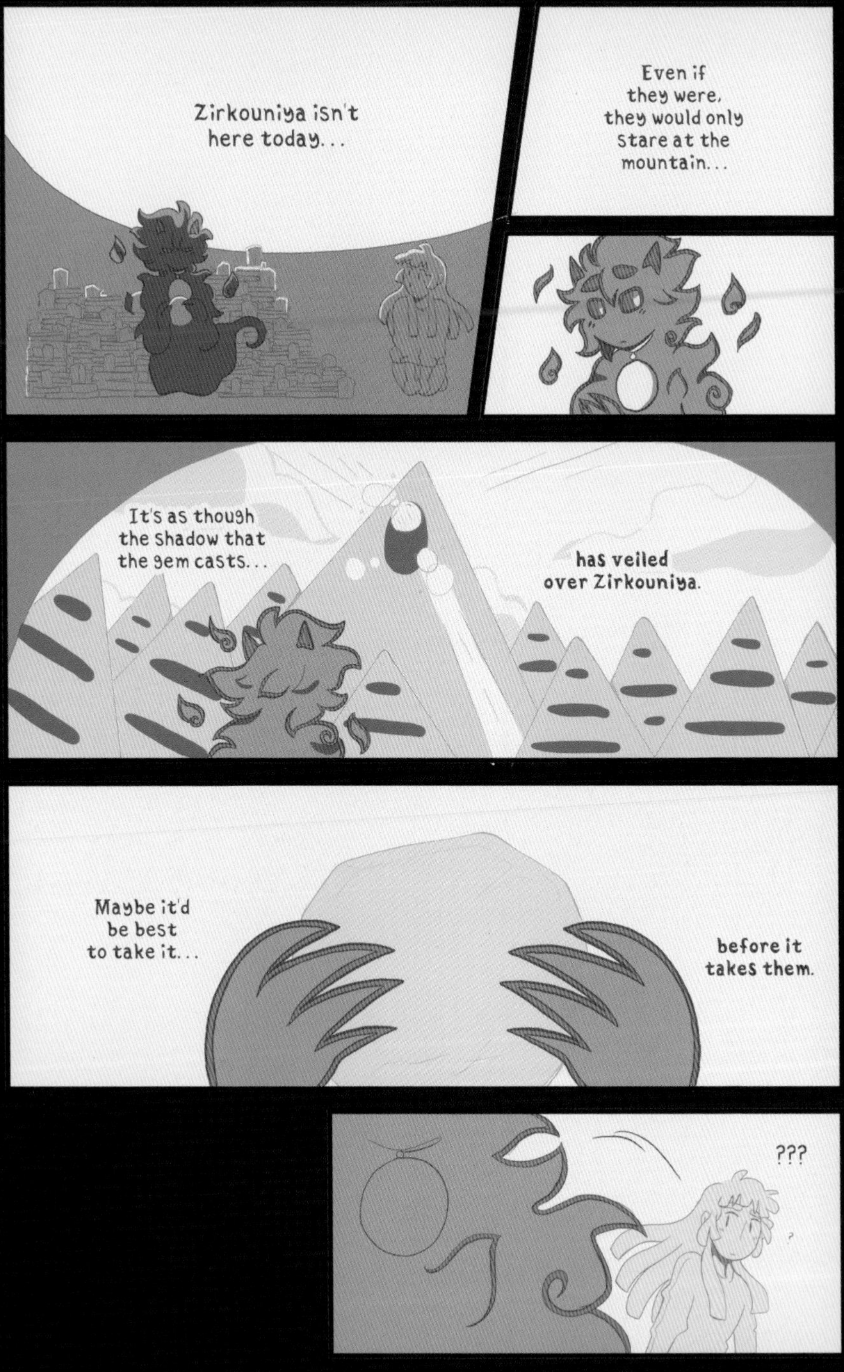

Zirkouniya isn't here today...
Even if they were, they would only stare at the mountain...
It's as though the shadow that the gem casts...
has veiled over Zirkouniya.
Maybe it'd be best to take it...
before it takes them.
???

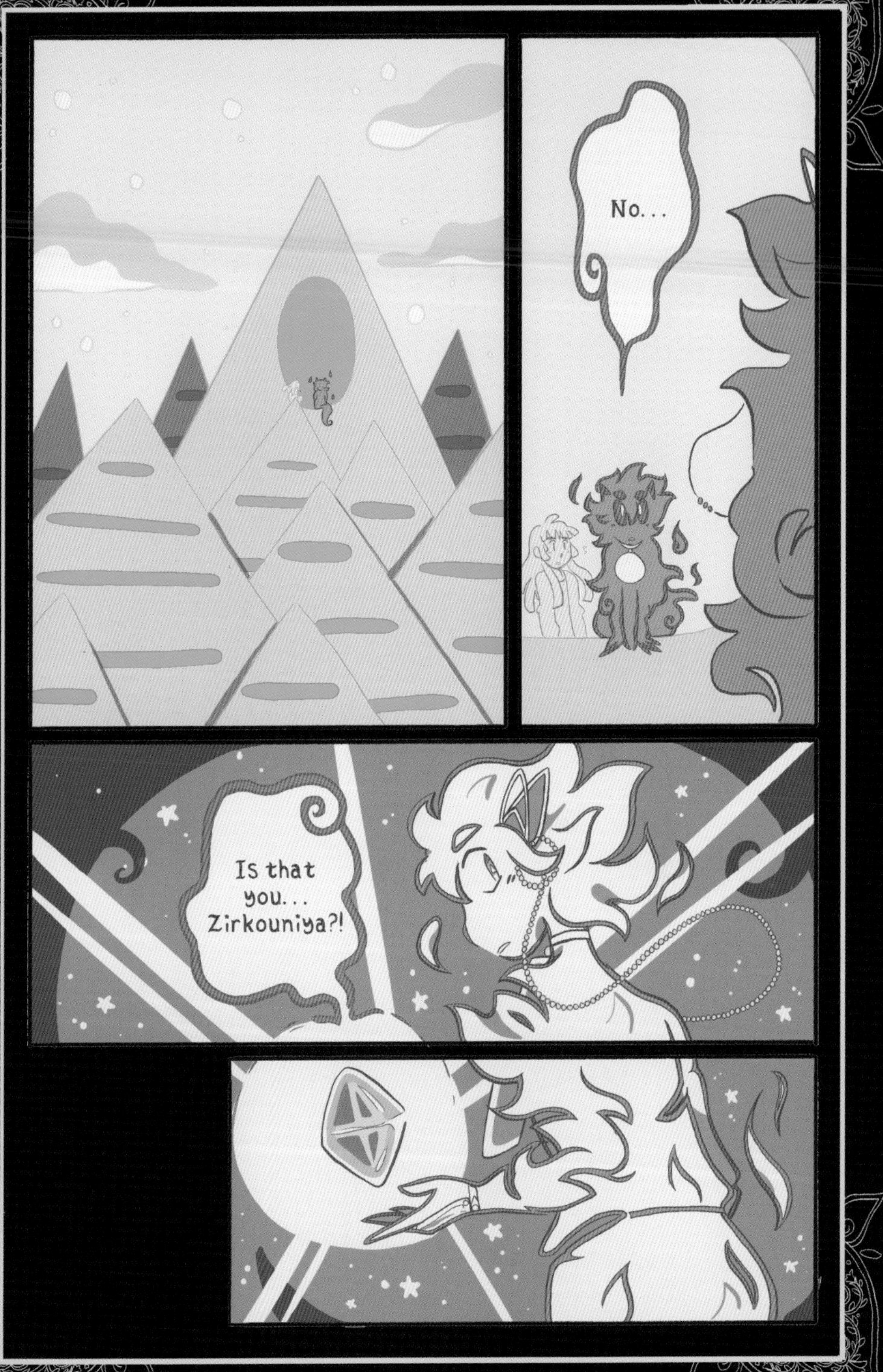
No...
Is that you... Zirkouniya?!

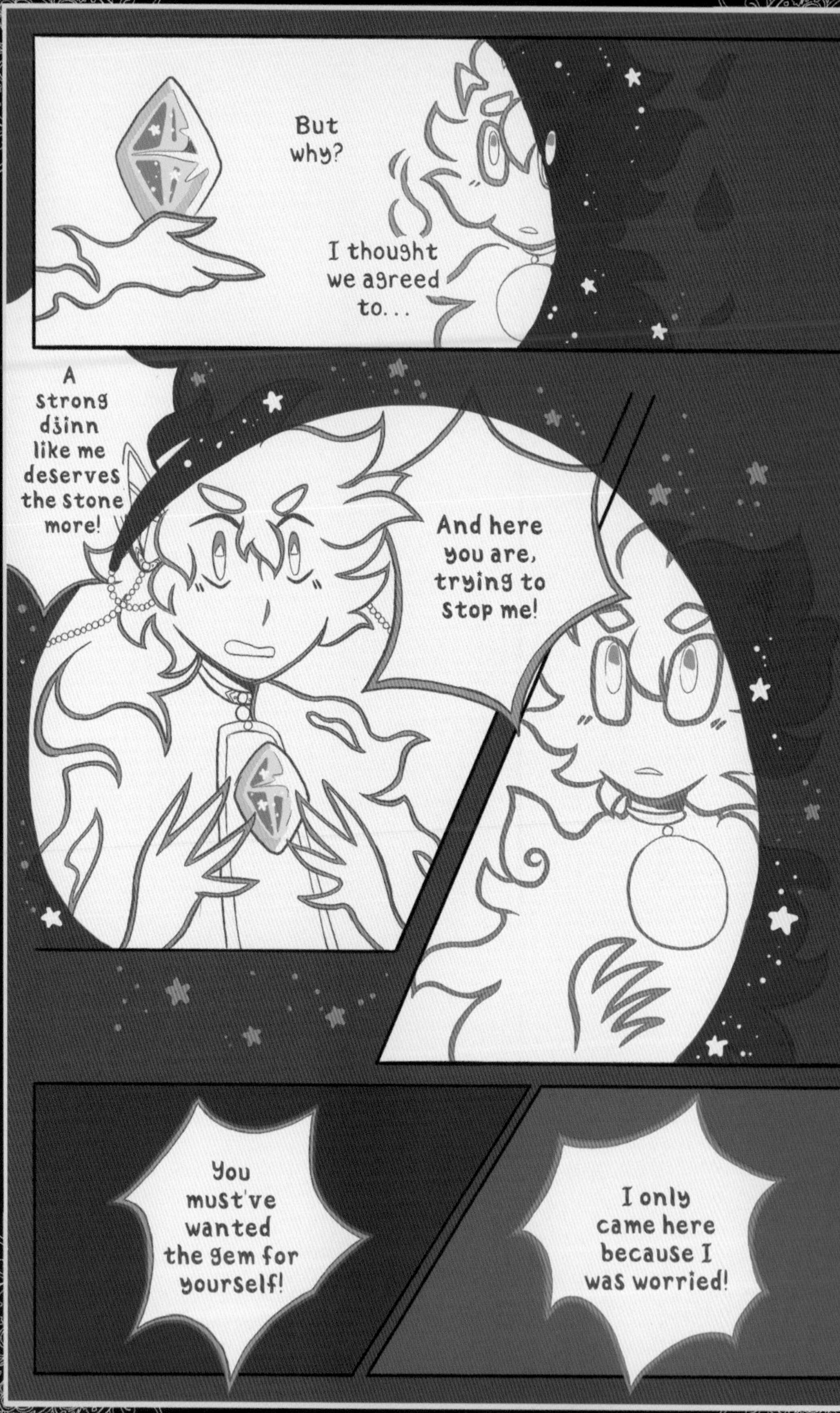

But why?
I thought we agreed to. . .
A strong djinn like me deserves the stone more!
And here you are, trying to stop me!
You must've wanted the gem for yourself!
I only came here because I was worried!

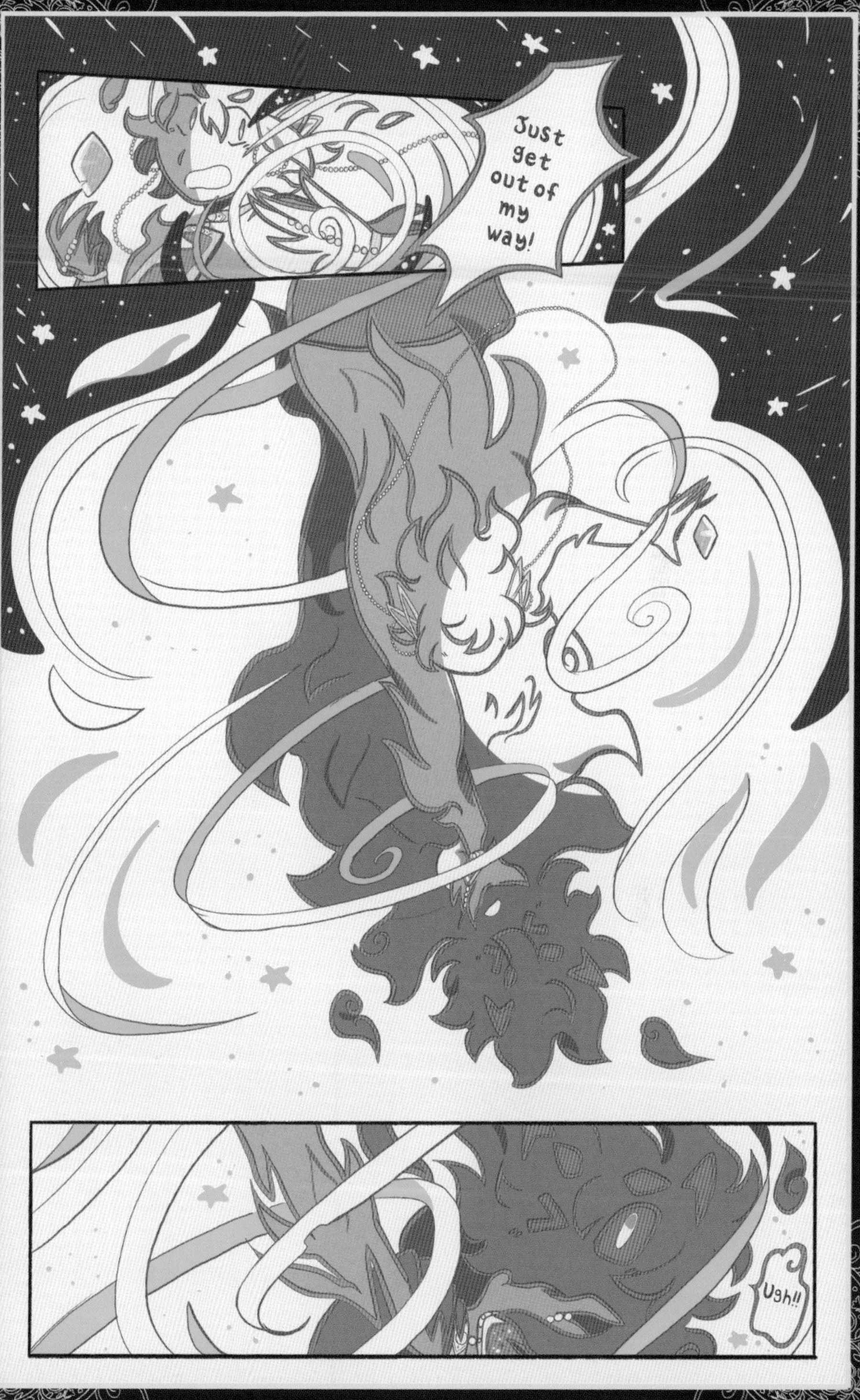
Just get out of my way!
Ugh!!

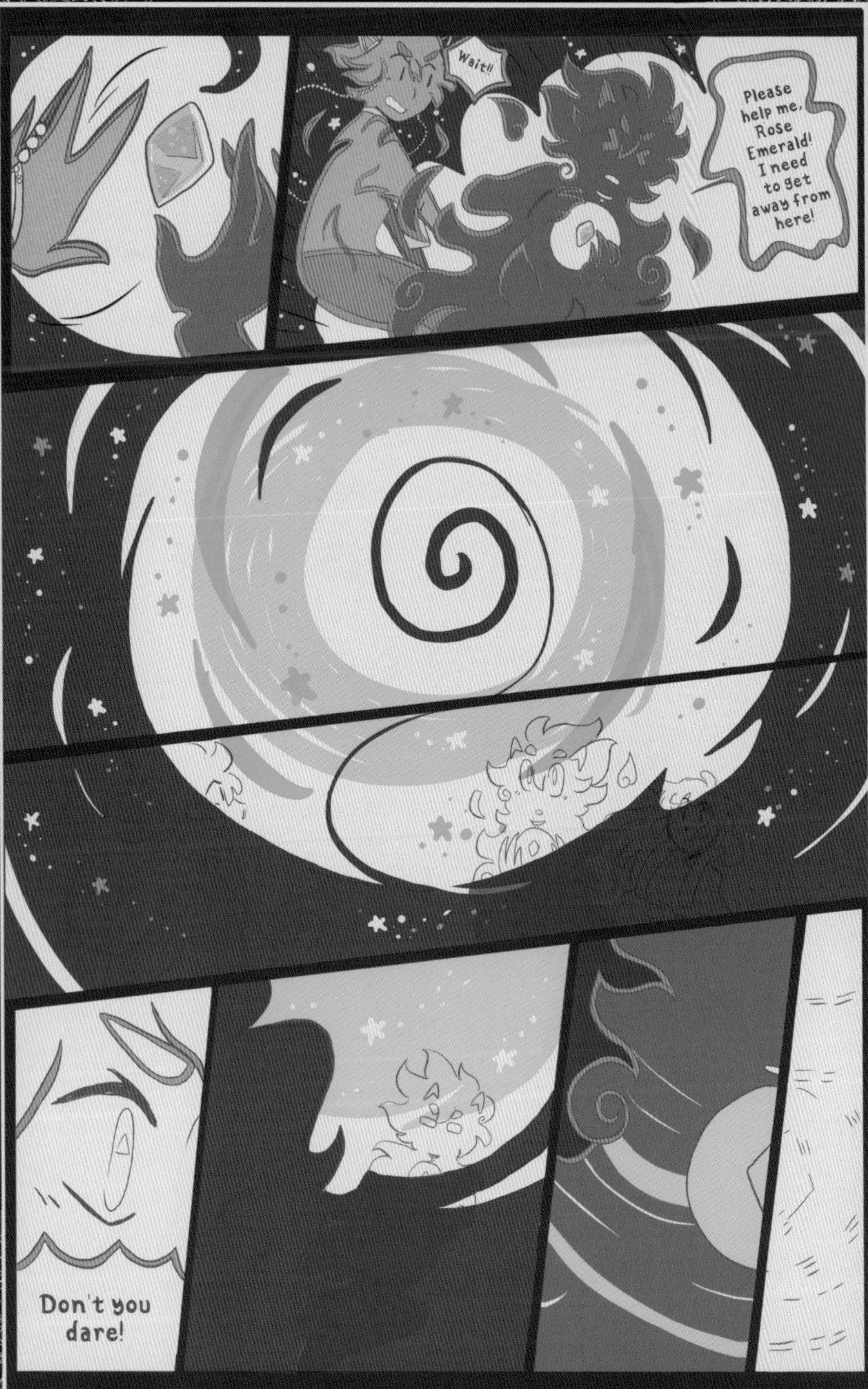
Wait!!
Please help me, Rose Emerald! I need to get away from here!
Don't you dare!

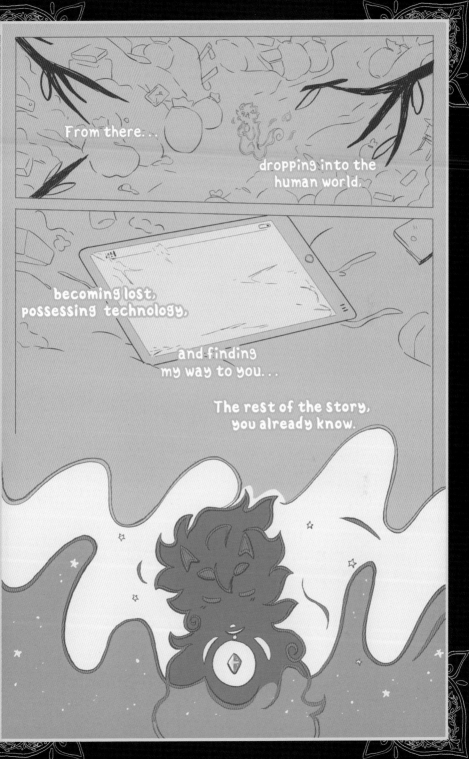

From there...

dropping into the human world.

becoming lost.
possessing technology.

and finding my way to you...

The rest of the story, you already know.

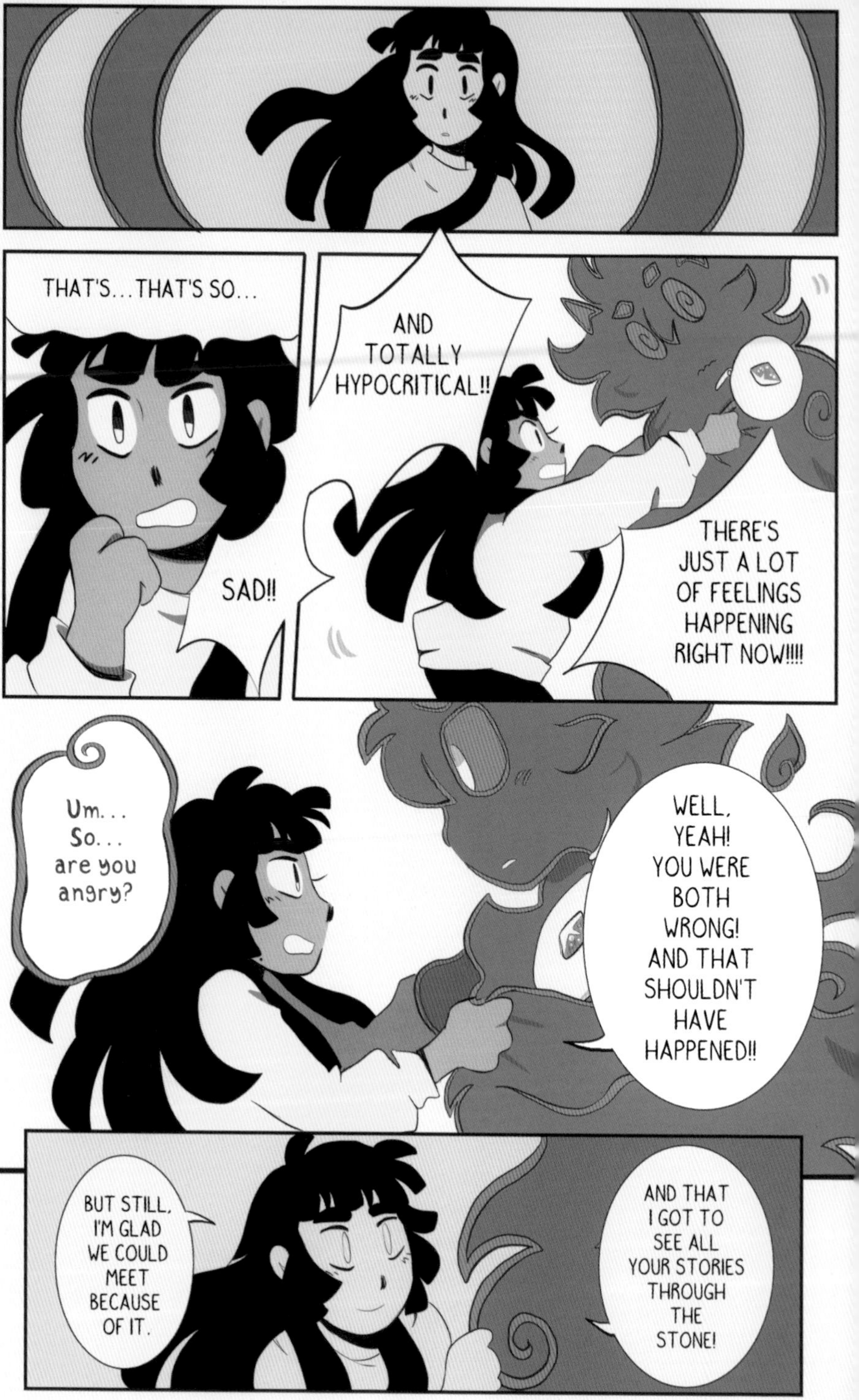
THAT'S...THAT'S SO...
SAD!!
AND TOTALLY HYPOCRITICAL!!
THERE'S JUST A LOT OF FEELINGS HAPPENING RIGHT NOW!!!!
Um... So... are you angry?
WELL, YEAH! YOU WERE BOTH WRONG! AND THAT SHOULDN'T HAVE HAPPENED!!
BUT STILL, I'M GLAD WE COULD MEET BECAUSE OF IT.
AND THAT I GOT TO SEE ALL YOUR STORIES THROUGH THE STONE!

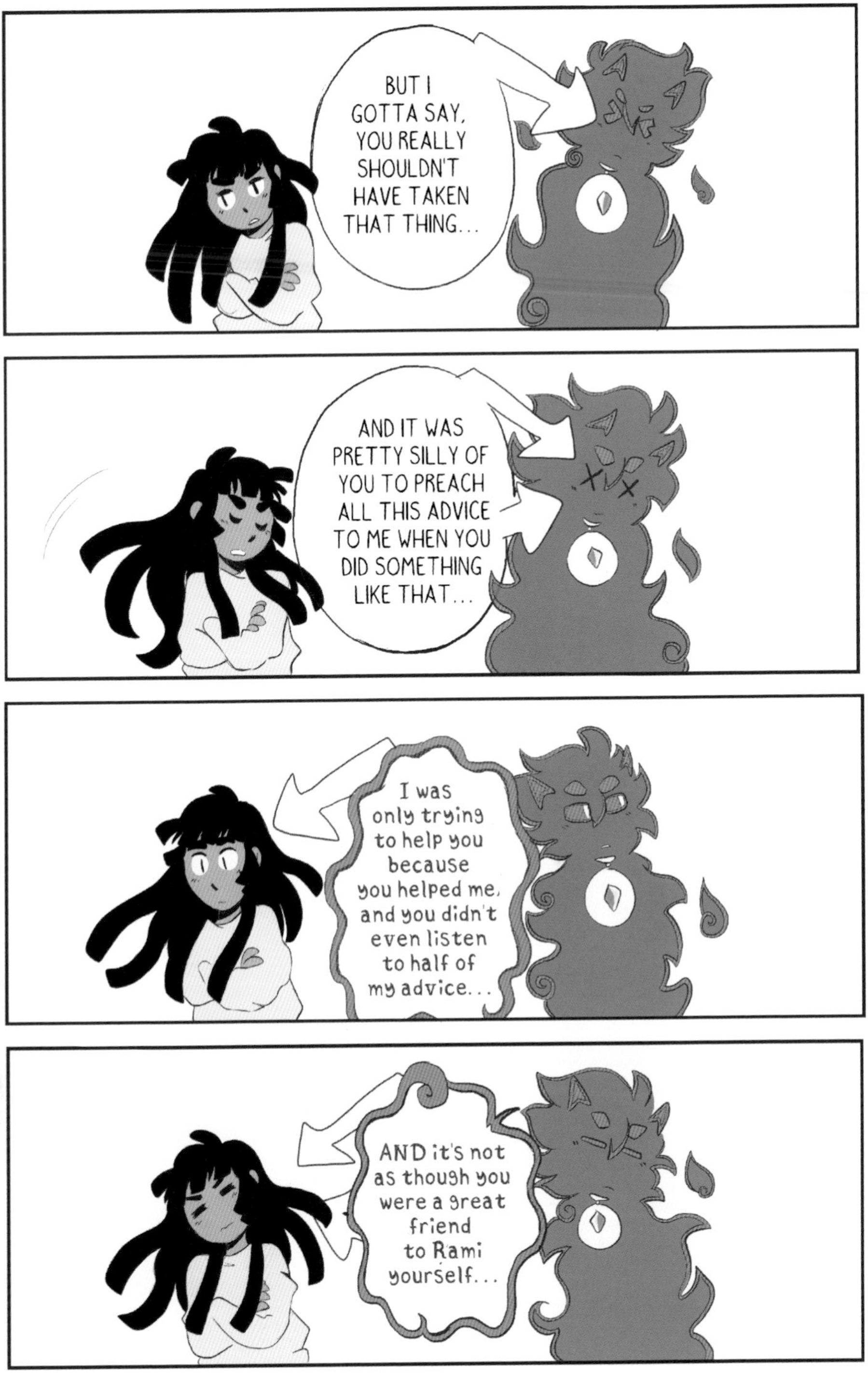
BUT I GOTTA SAY, YOU REALLY SHOULDN'T HAVE TAKEN THAT THING...
AND IT WAS PRETTY SILLY OF YOU TO PREACH ALL THIS ADVICE TO ME WHEN YOU DID SOMETHING LIKE THAT...
I was only trying to help you because you helped me, and you didn't even listen to half of my advice...
AND it's not as though you were a great friend to Rami yourself...

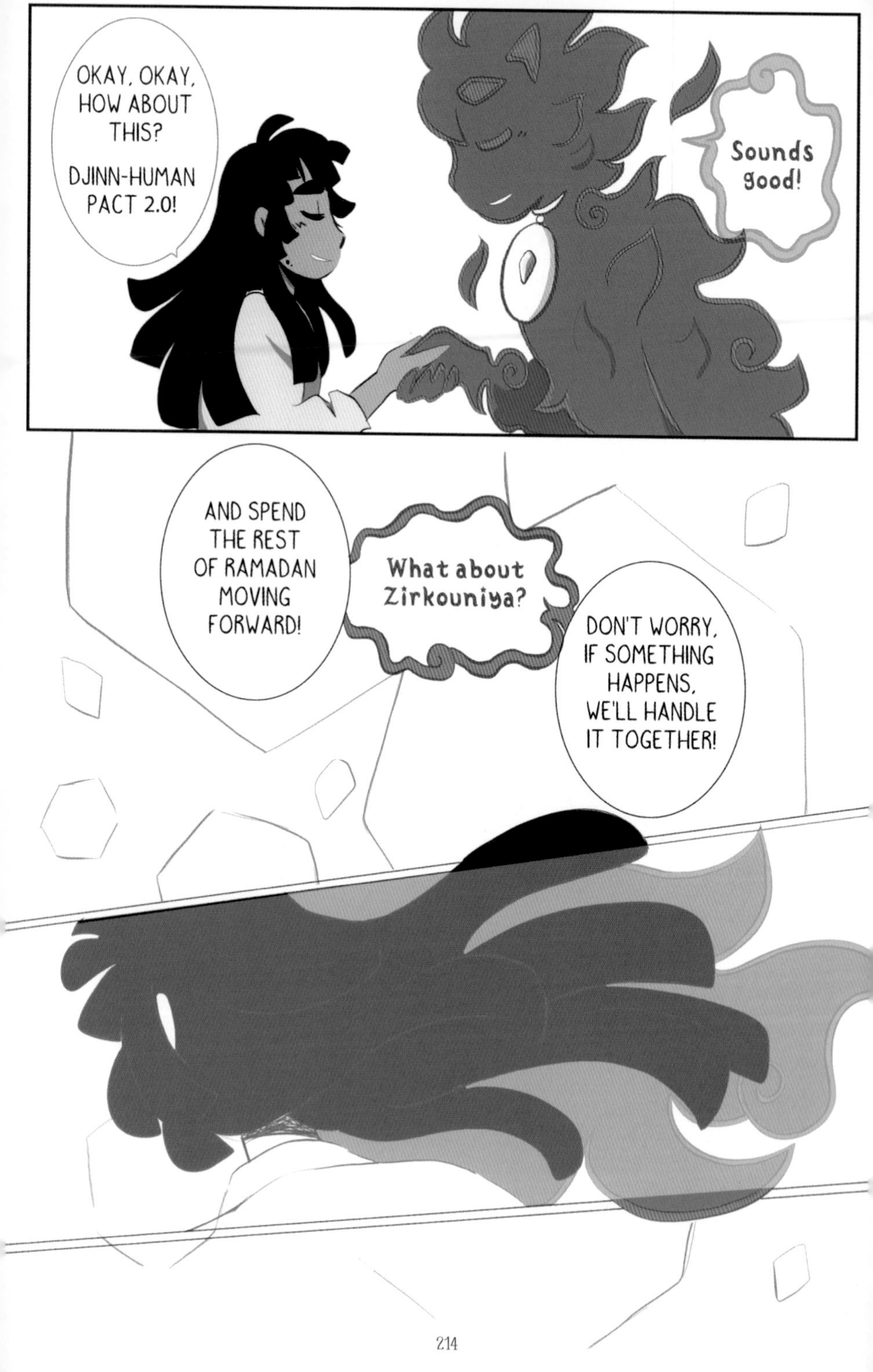
OKAY, OKAY, HOW ABOUT THIS?
DJINN-HUMAN PACT 2.0!
Sounds good!
AND SPEND THE REST OF RAMADAN MOVING FORWARD!
What about Zirkouniya?
DON'T WORRY, IF SOMETHING HAPPENS, WE'LL HANDLE IT TOGETHER!

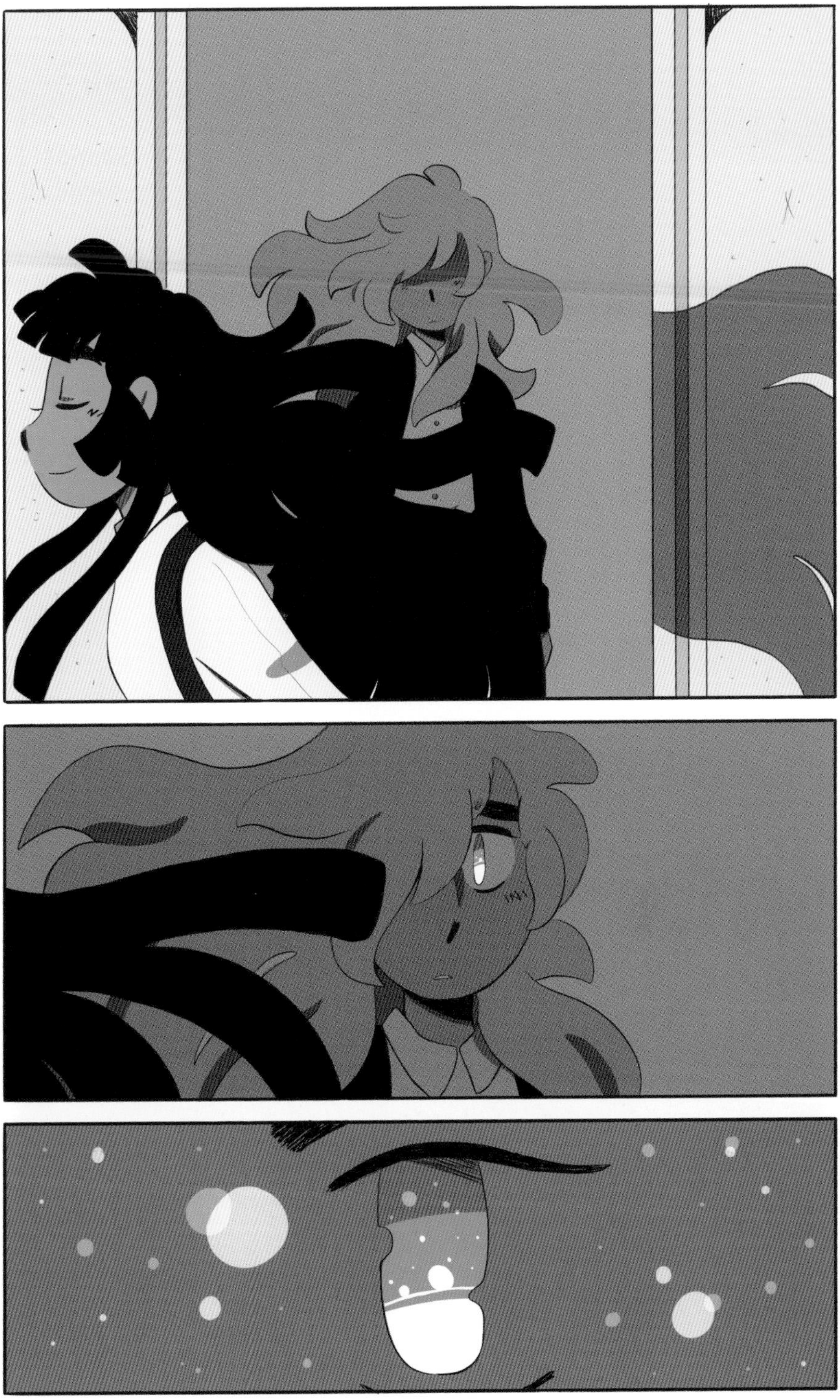

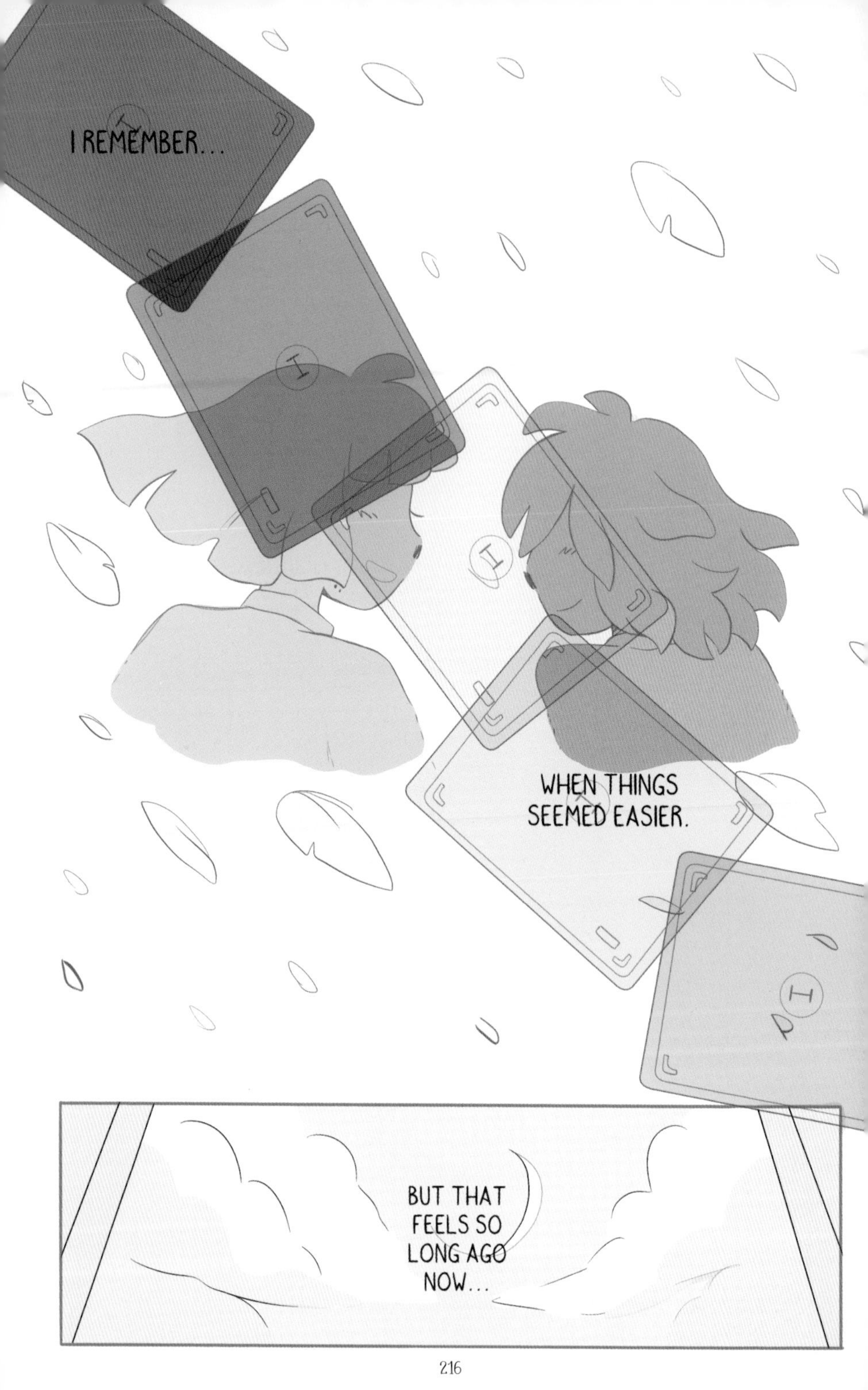
I REMEMBER...
WHEN THINGS SEEMED EASIER.
BUT THAT FEELS SO LONG AGO NOW...

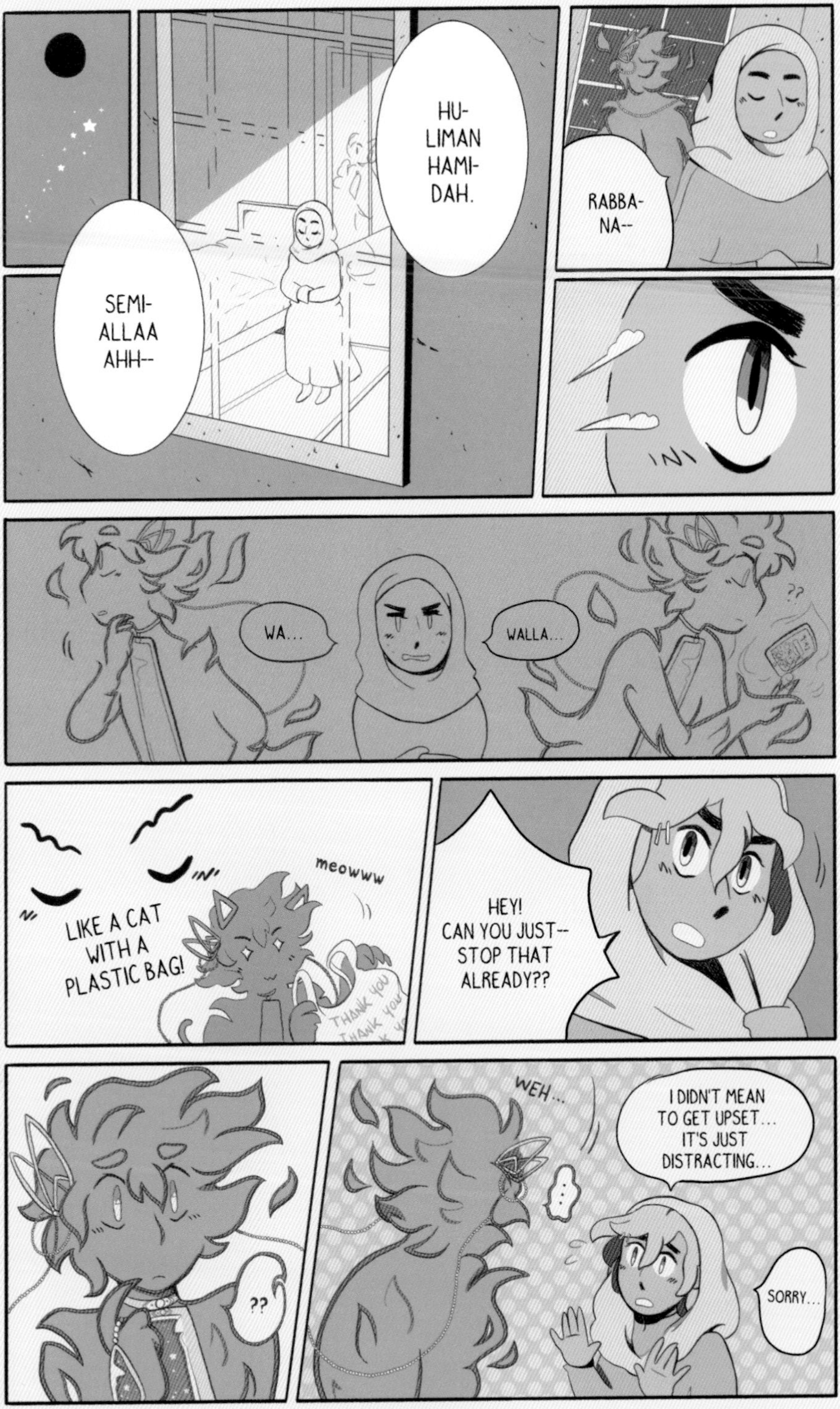
SEMI-
ALLAA
AHH--
HU-
LIMAN
HAMI-
DAH.
RABBA-
NA--
WA...
WALLA...
LIKE A CAT
WITH A
PLASTIC BAG!
meowww
THANK YOU
THANK YOU
HEY!
CAN YOU JUST--
STOP THAT
ALREADY??
??
WEH...
I DIDN'T MEAN
TO GET UPSET...
IT'S JUST
DISTRACTING...
...
SORRY...

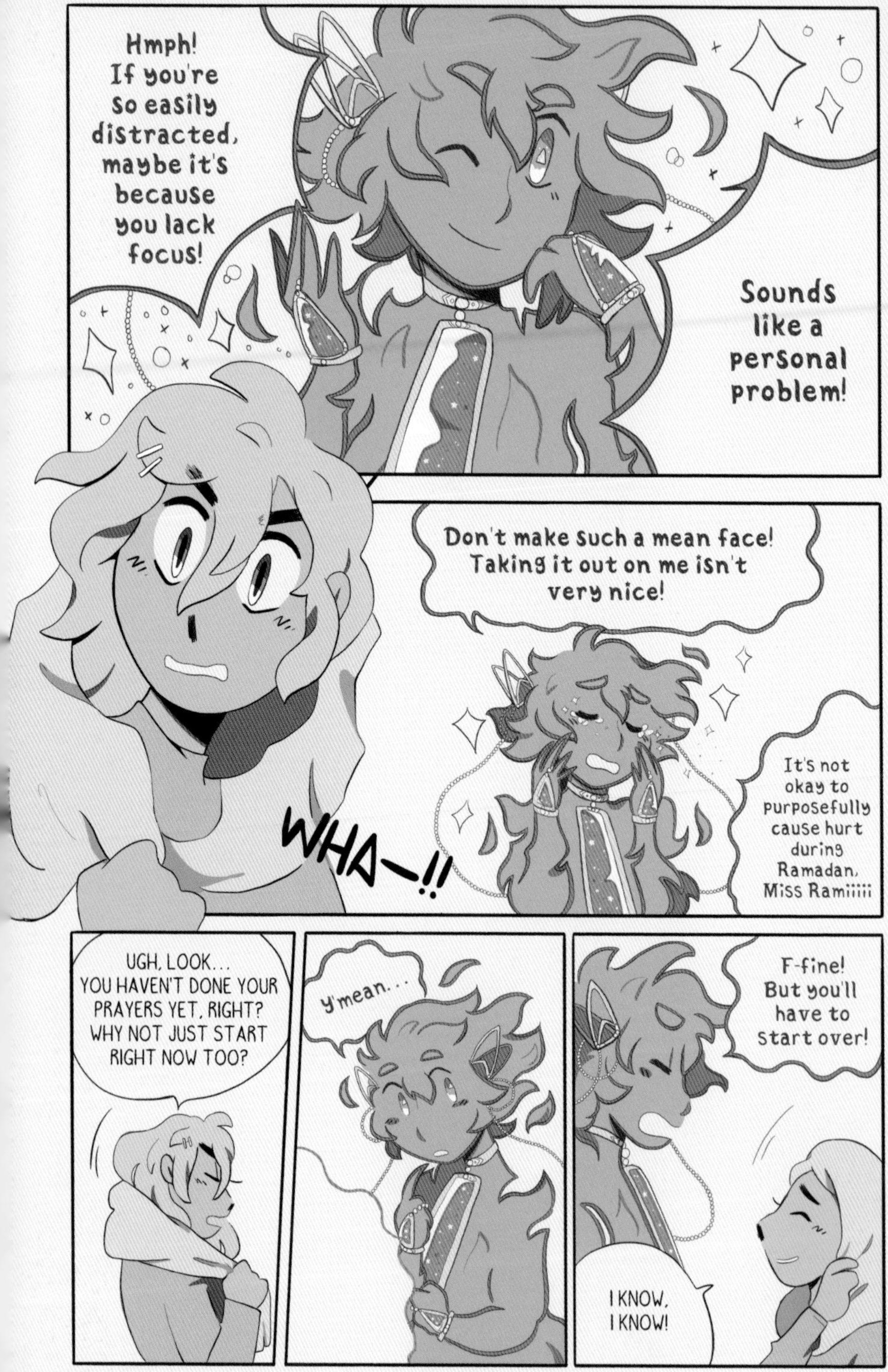
Hmph! If you're so easily distracted, maybe it's because you lack focus!
Sounds like a personal problem!
Don't make such a mean face! Taking it out on me isn't very nice!
It's not okay to purposefully cause hurt during Ramadan, Miss Ramiiiii
WHA—!!
UGH, LOOK... YOU HAVEN'T DONE YOUR PRAYERS YET, RIGHT? WHY NOT JUST START RIGHT NOW TOO?
Y'mean...
F-fine! But you'll have to start over!
I KNOW, I KNOW!

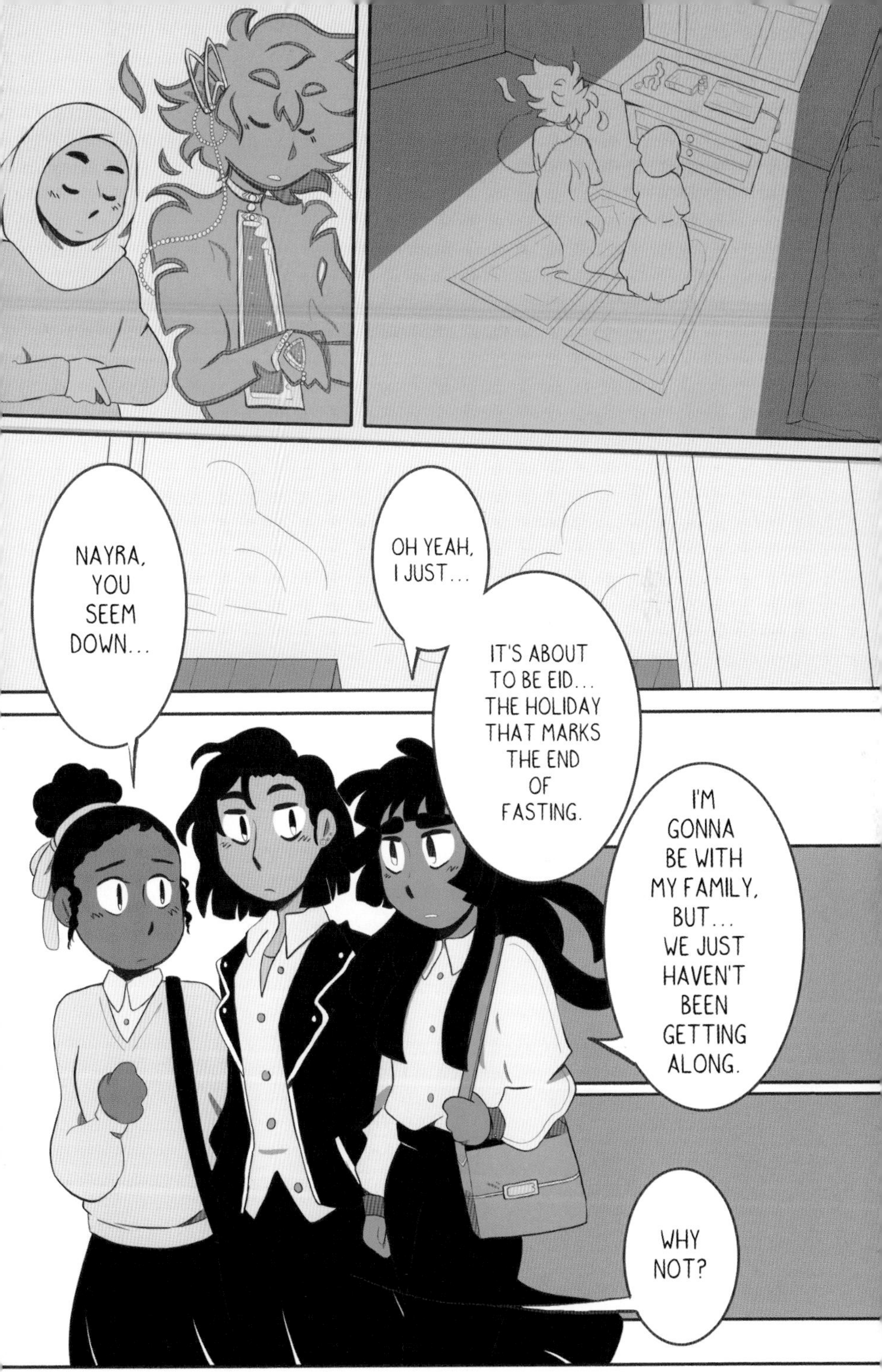
NAYRA, YOU SEEM DOWN...
OH YEAH, I JUST...
IT'S ABOUT TO BE EID... THE HOLIDAY THAT MARKS THE END OF FASTING.
I'M GONNA BE WITH MY FAMILY, BUT... WE JUST HAVEN'T BEEN GETTING ALONG.
WHY NOT?

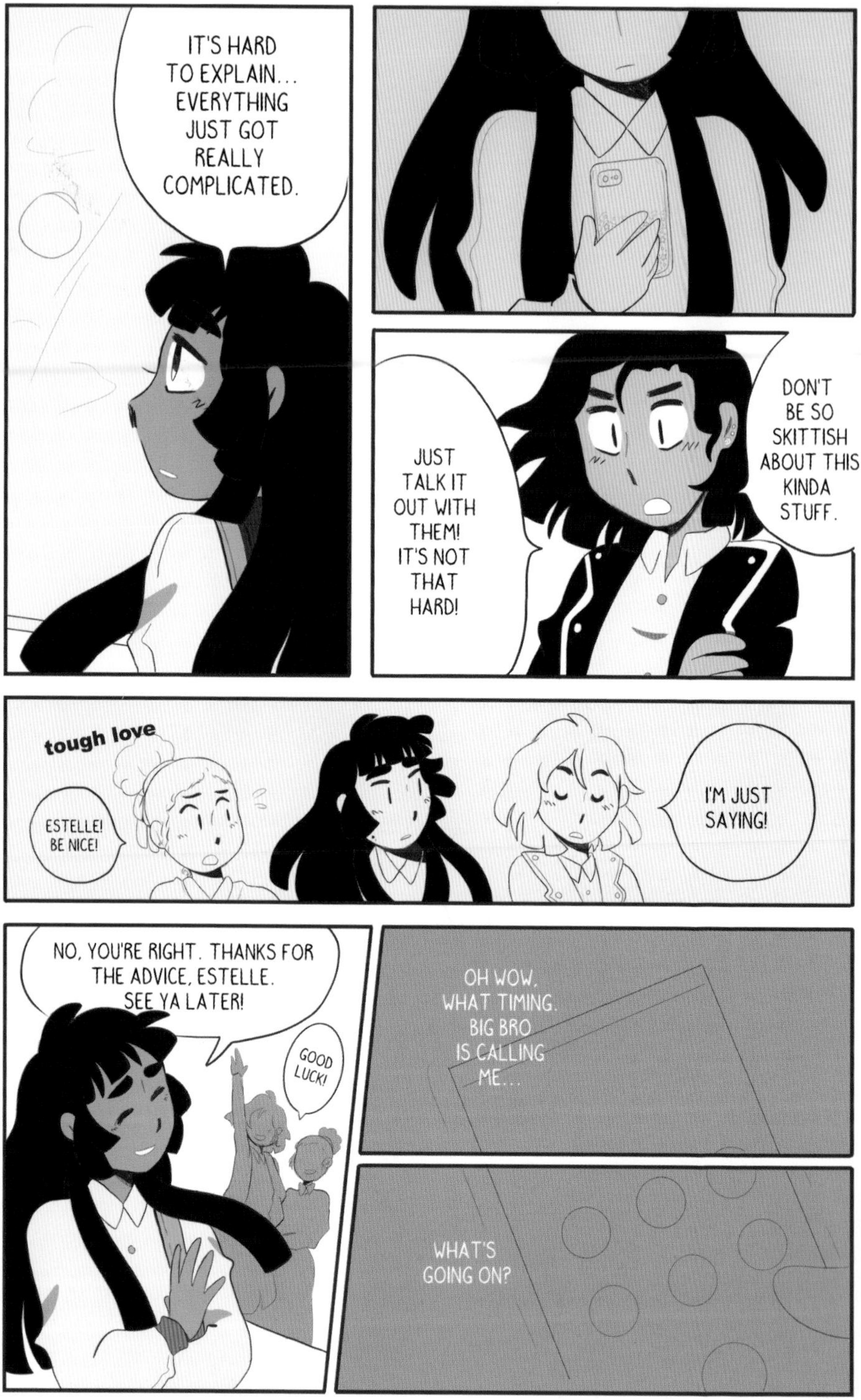
IT'S HARD TO EXPLAIN... EVERYTHING JUST GOT REALLY COMPLICATED.
DON'T BE SO SKITTISH ABOUT THIS KINDA STUFF.
JUST TALK IT OUT WITH THEM! IT'S NOT THAT HARD!
tough love
ESTELLE! BE NICE!
I'M JUST SAYING!
NO, YOU'RE RIGHT. THANKS FOR THE ADVICE, ESTELLE. SEE YA LATER!
GOOD LUCK!
OH WOW, WHAT TIMING. BIG BRO IS CALLING ME...
WHAT'S GOING ON?

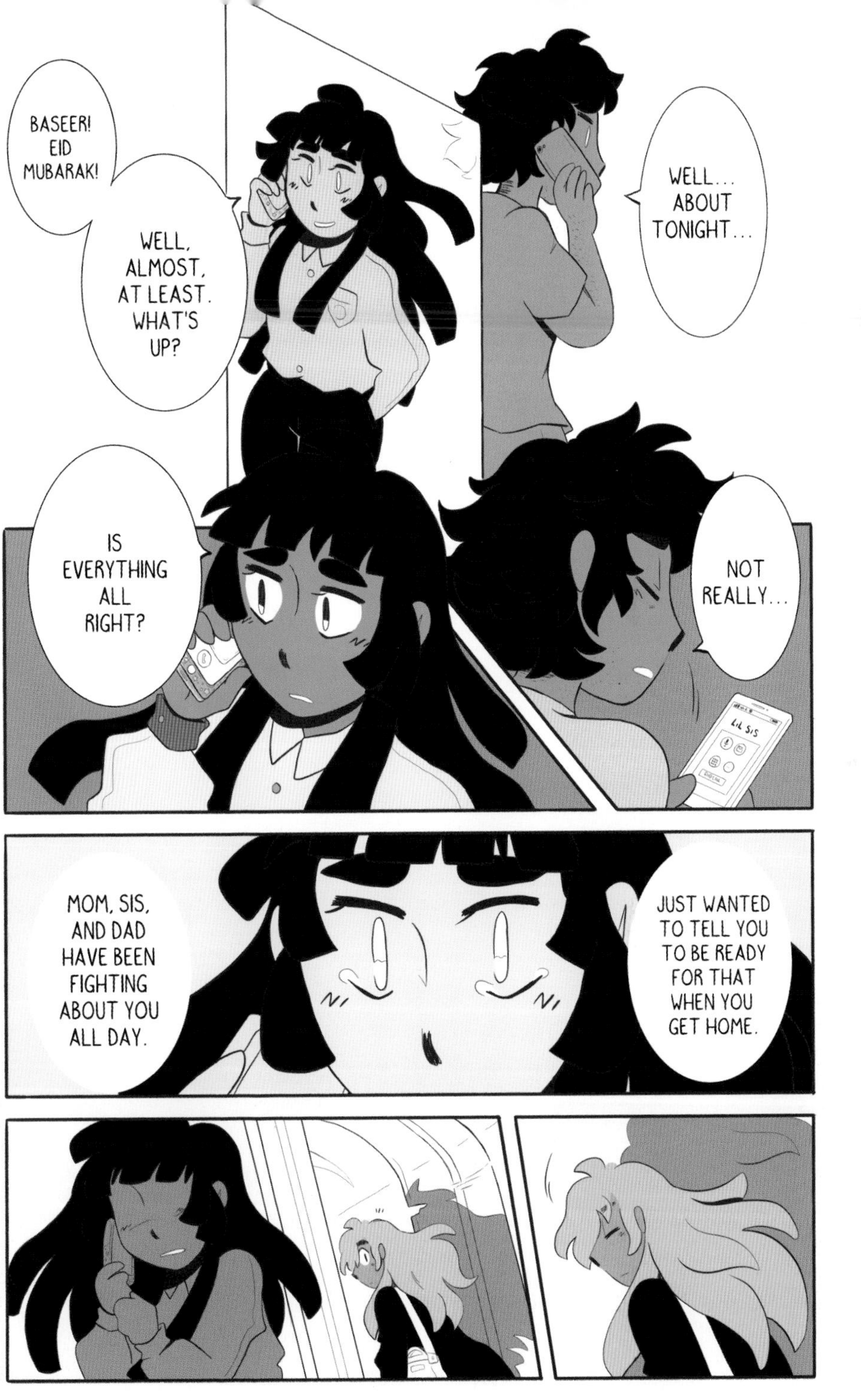
BASEER! EID MUBARAK!
WELL, ALMOST, AT LEAST. WHAT'S UP?
WELL... ABOUT TONIGHT...
IS EVERYTHING ALL RIGHT?
NOT REALLY...
MOM, SIS, AND DAD HAVE BEEN FIGHTING ABOUT YOU ALL DAY.
JUST WANTED TO TELL YOU TO BE READY FOR THAT WHEN YOU GET HOME.

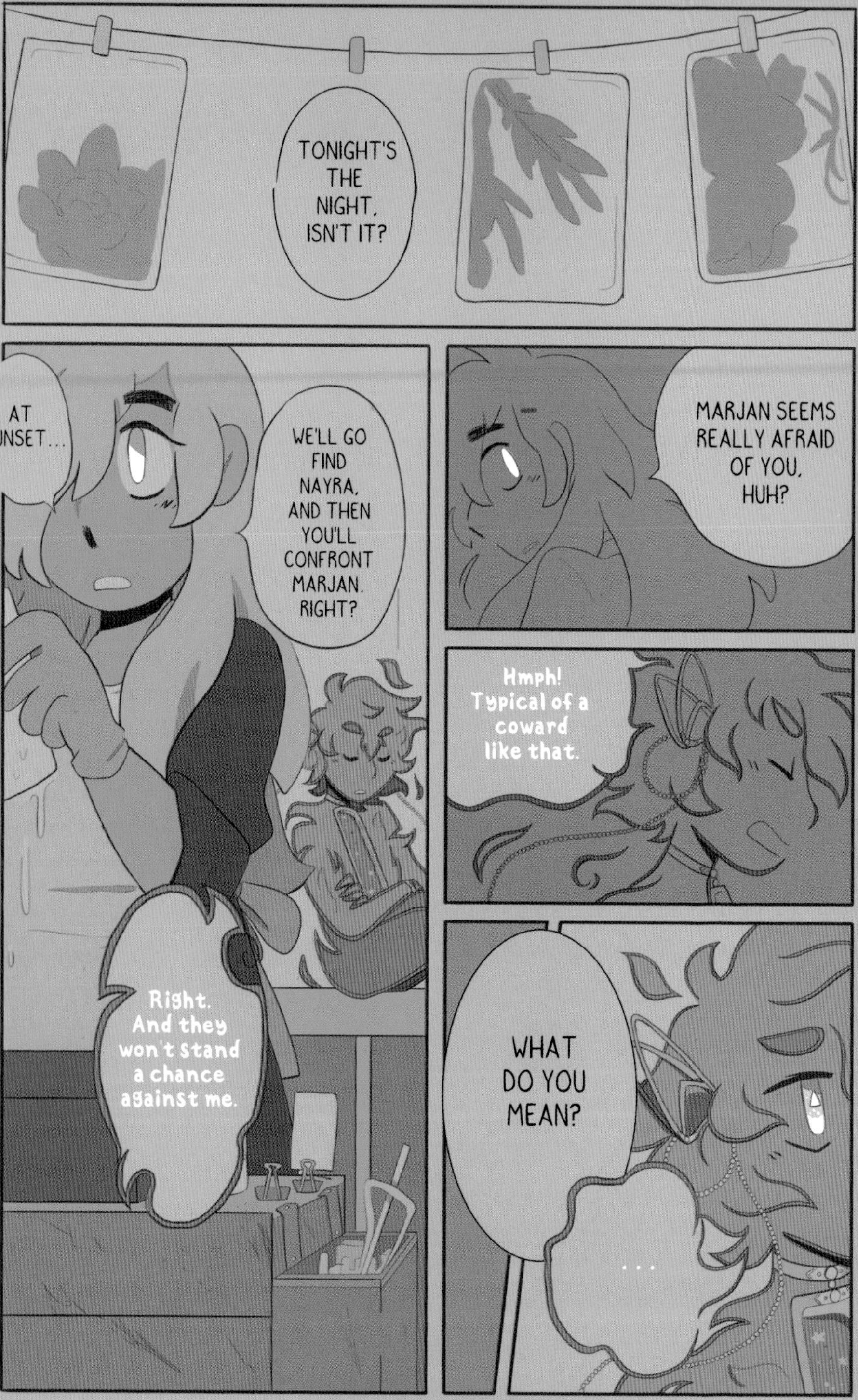
TONIGHT'S THE NIGHT, ISN'T IT?
AT SUNSET...
WE'LL GO FIND NAYRA, AND THEN YOU'LL CONFRONT MARJAN. RIGHT?
Right. And they won't stand a chance against me.
MARJAN SEEMS REALLY AFRAID OF YOU, HUH?
Hmph! Typical of a coward like that.
WHAT DO YOU MEAN?
...

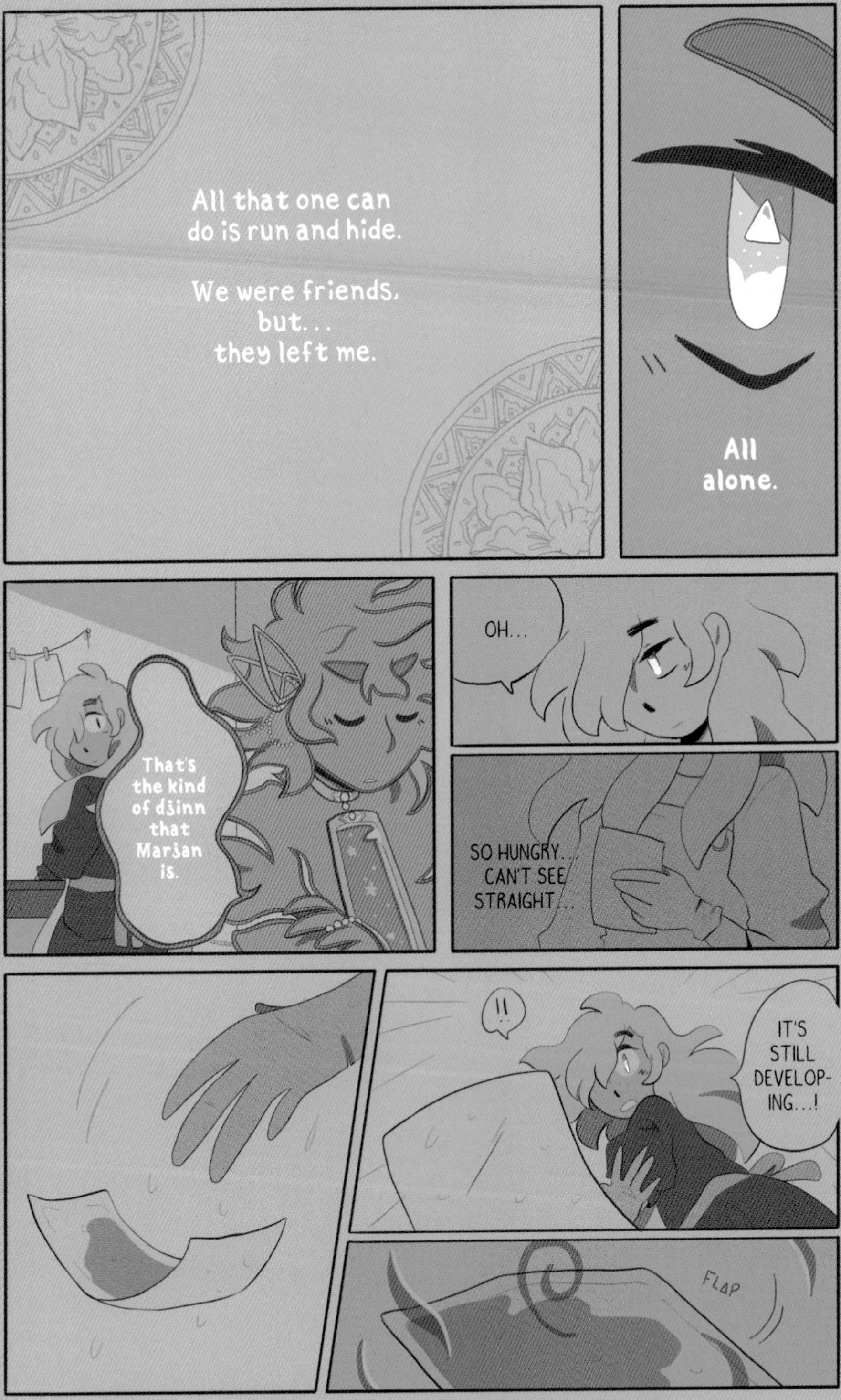
All that one can do is run and hide.
We were friends, but... they left me.
All alone.
That's the kind of djinn that Marjan is.
OH...
SO HUNGRY... CAN'T SEE STRAIGHT...
!!
IT'S STILL DEVELOP-ING...!
FLAP

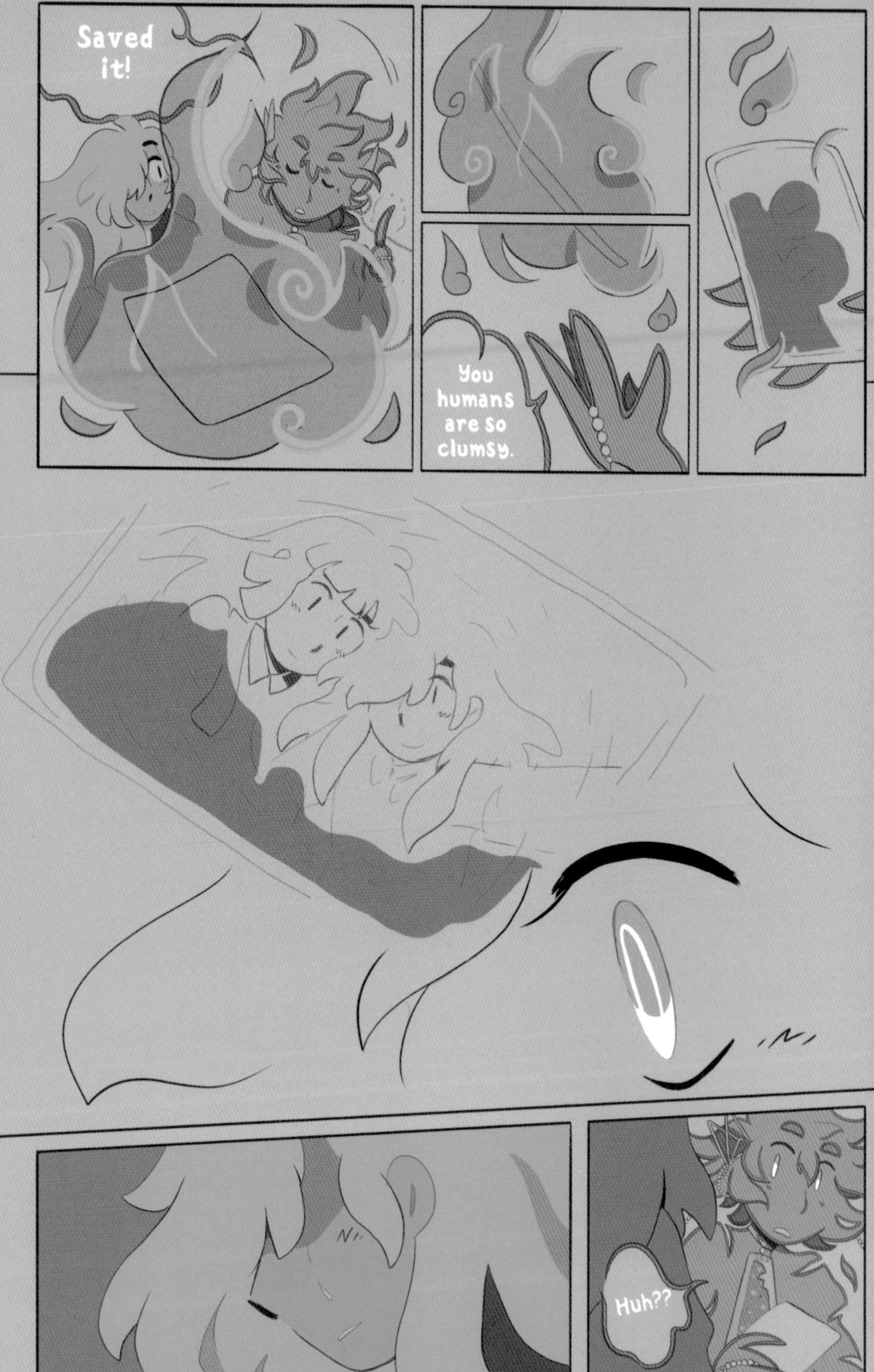
Saved it!
You humans are so clumsy.
Huh??

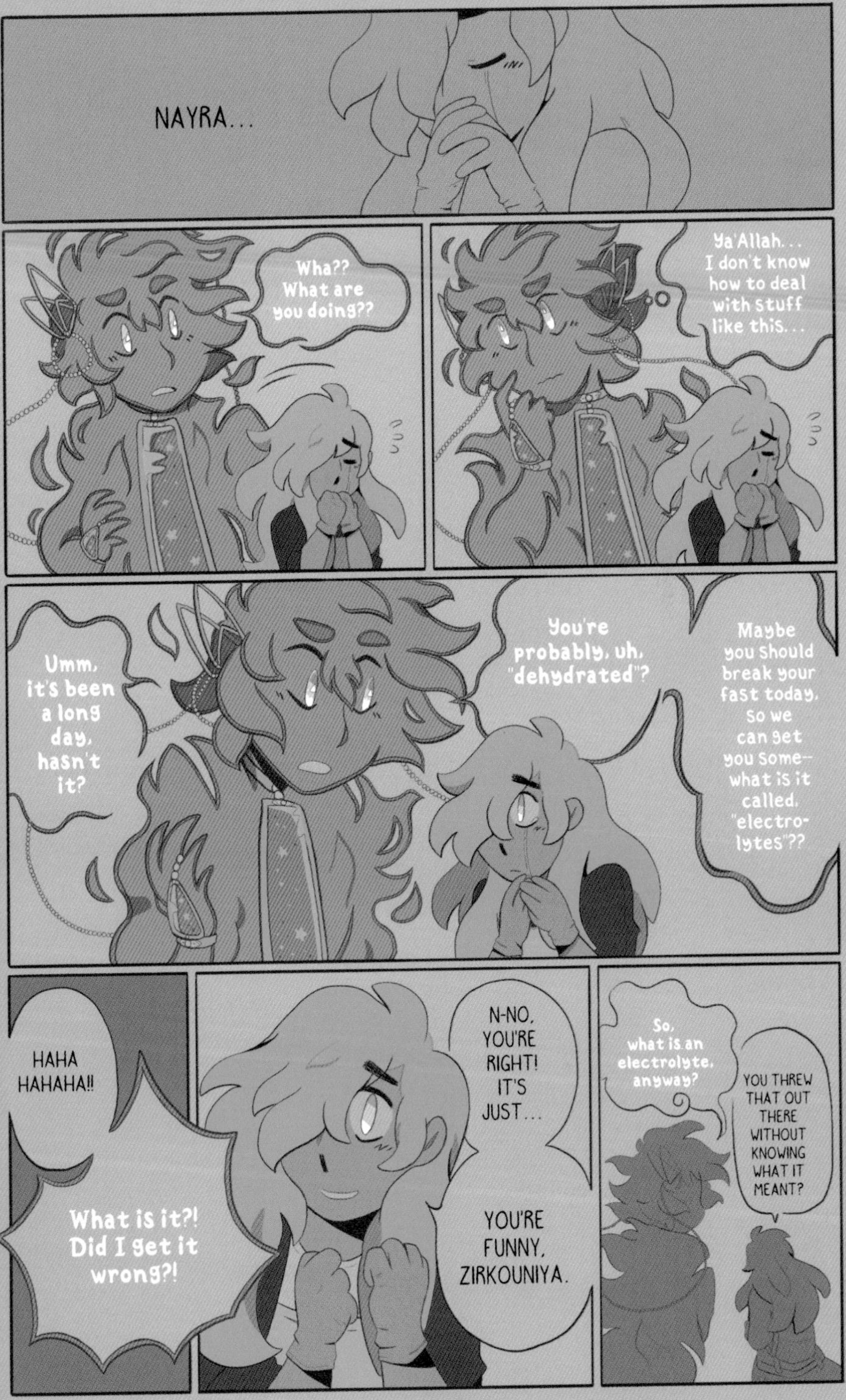
NAYRA...
Wha?? What are you doing??
Ya'Allah... I don't know how to deal with stuff like this...
Umm, it's been a long day, hasn't it?
You're probably, uh, "dehydrated"?
Maybe you should break your fast today, so we can get you some-- what is it called, "electro-lytes"??
HAHA HAHAHA!!
What is it?! Did I get it wrong?!
N-NO, YOU'RE RIGHT! IT'S JUST...
YOU'RE FUNNY, ZIRKOUNIYA.
So, what is an electrolyte, anyway?
YOU THREW THAT OUT THERE WITHOUT KNOWING WHAT IT MEANT?

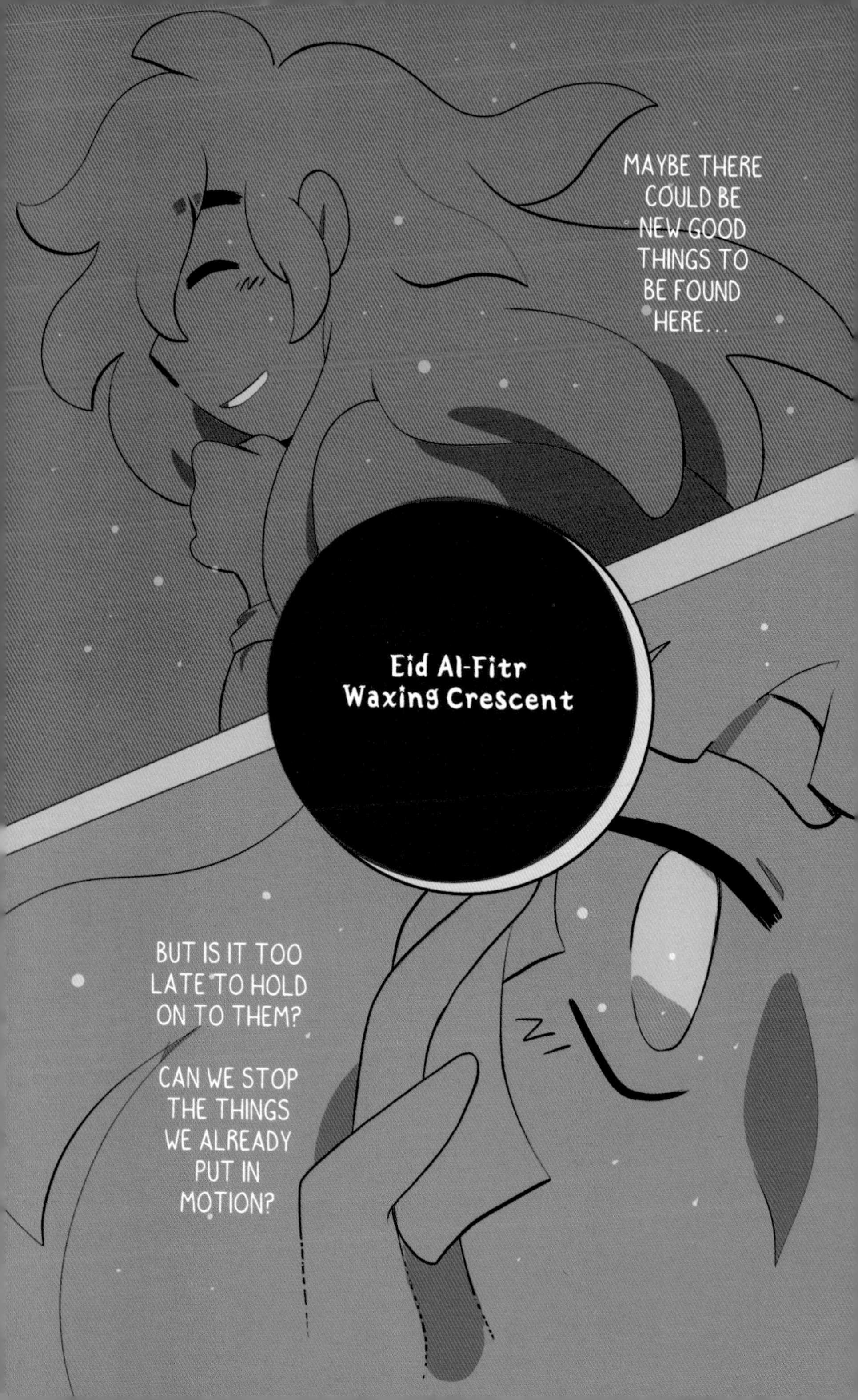
MAYBE THERE COULD BE NEW GOOD THINGS TO BE FOUND HERE...
Eid Al-Fitr
Waxing Crescent
BUT IS IT TOO LATE TO HOLD ON TO THEM?
CAN WE STOP THE THINGS WE ALREADY PUT IN MOTION?

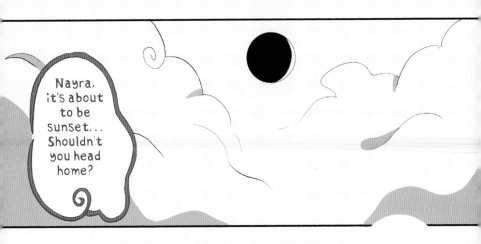

Nayra, it's about to be sunset... Shouldn't you head home?

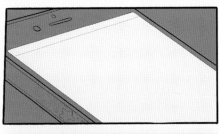

I DON'T KNOW.

MAYBE THEY DON'T EVEN WANT ME THERE...

FOR NOW, I GUESS I'LL JUST...

GO TO THE ONE PLACE I KNOW...

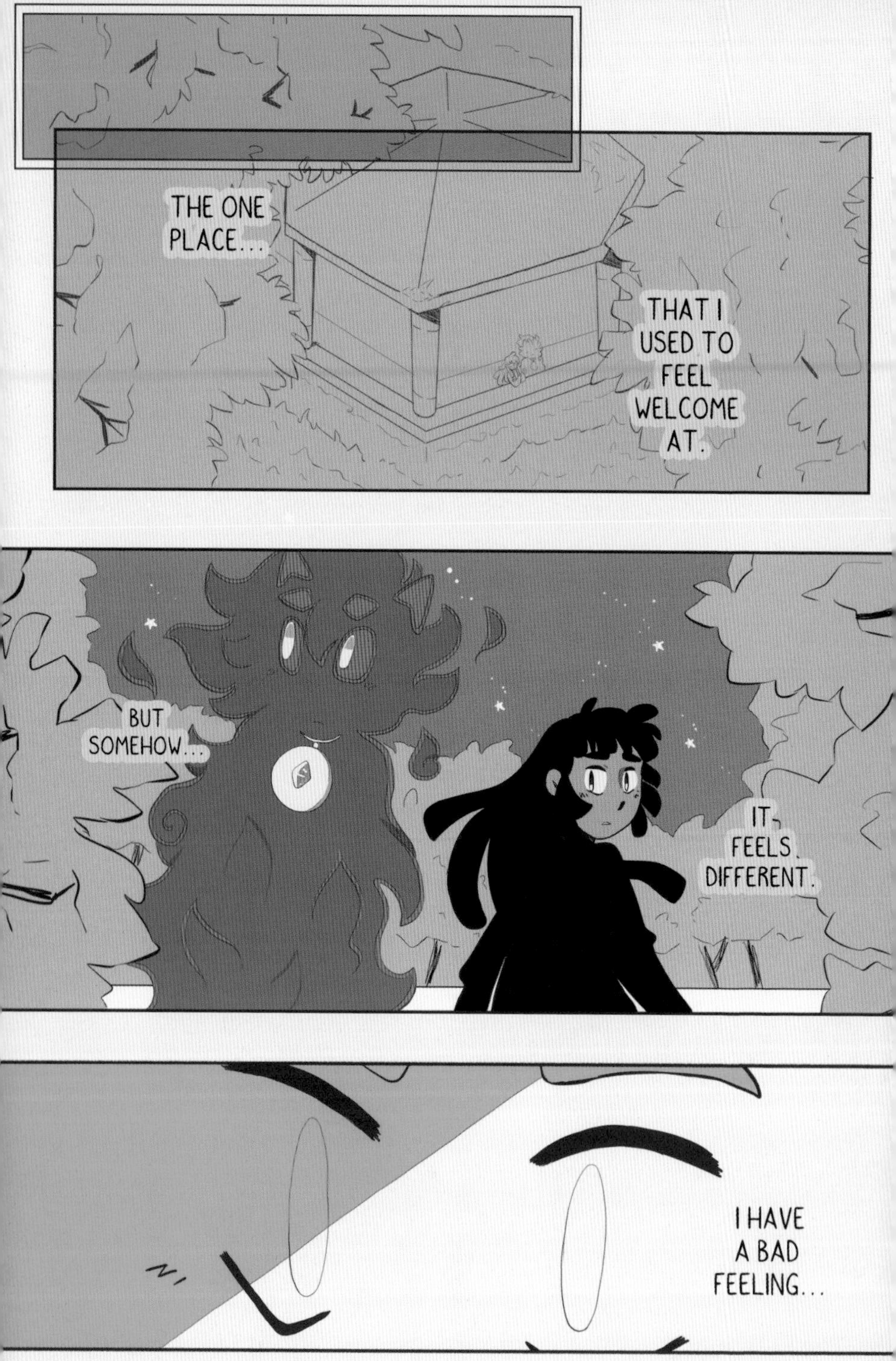
THE ONE PLACE...
THAT I USED TO FEEL WELCOME AT.
BUT SOMEHOW...
IT FEELS DIFFERENT.
I HAVE A BAD FEELING...

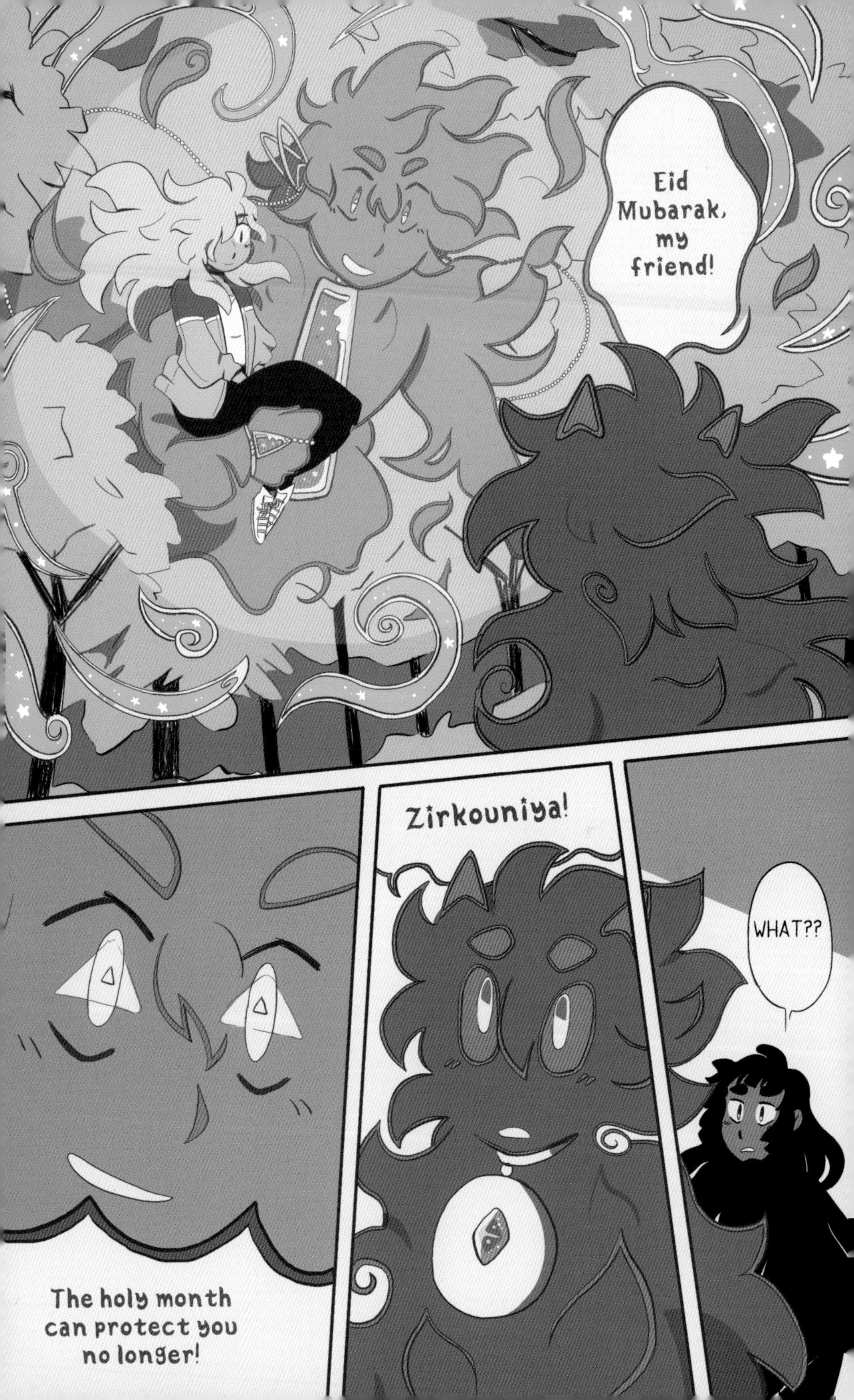
Eid Mubarak, my friend!
The holy month can protect you no longer!
Zirkouniya!
WHAT??

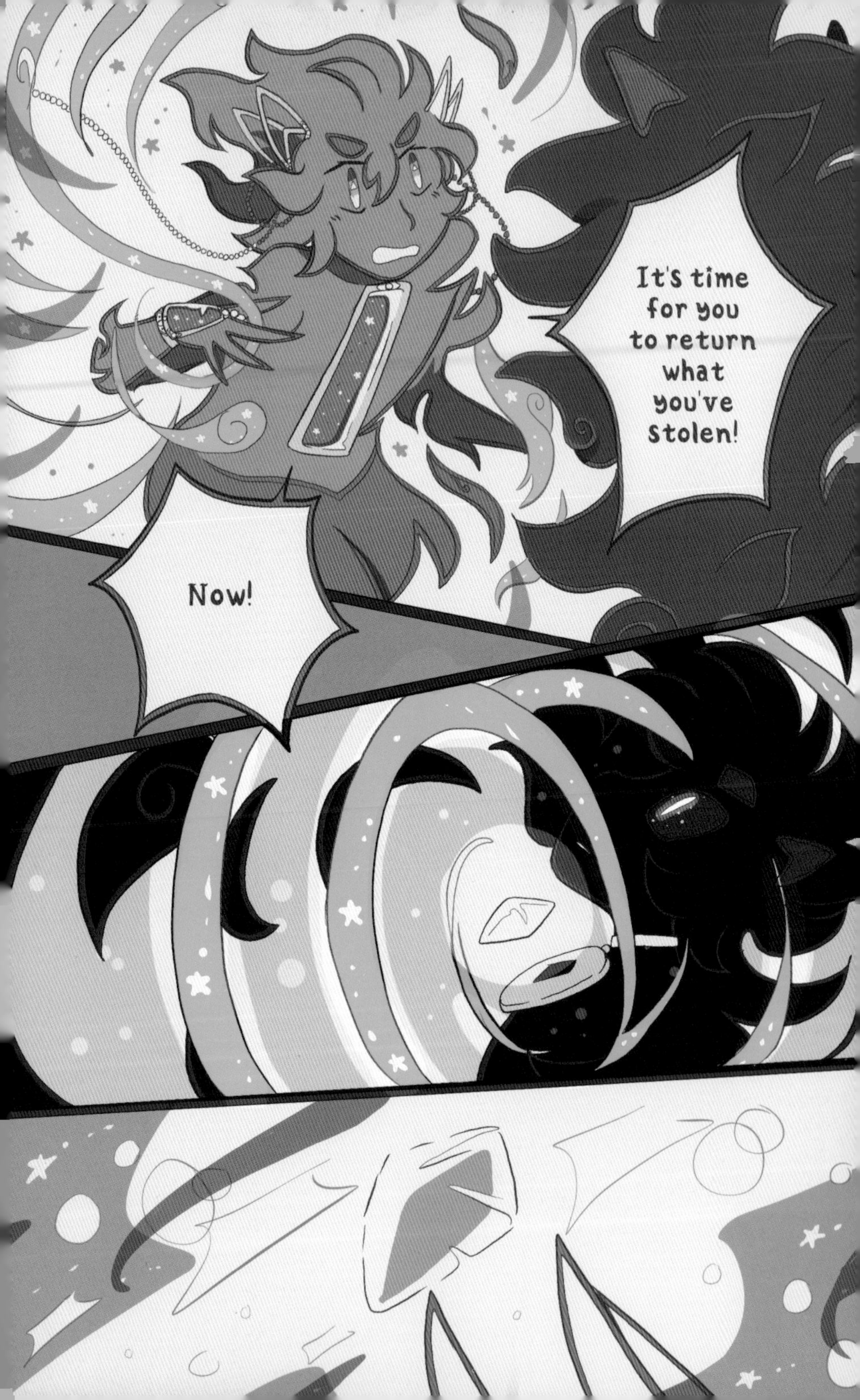
It's time for you to return what you've stolen!
Now!

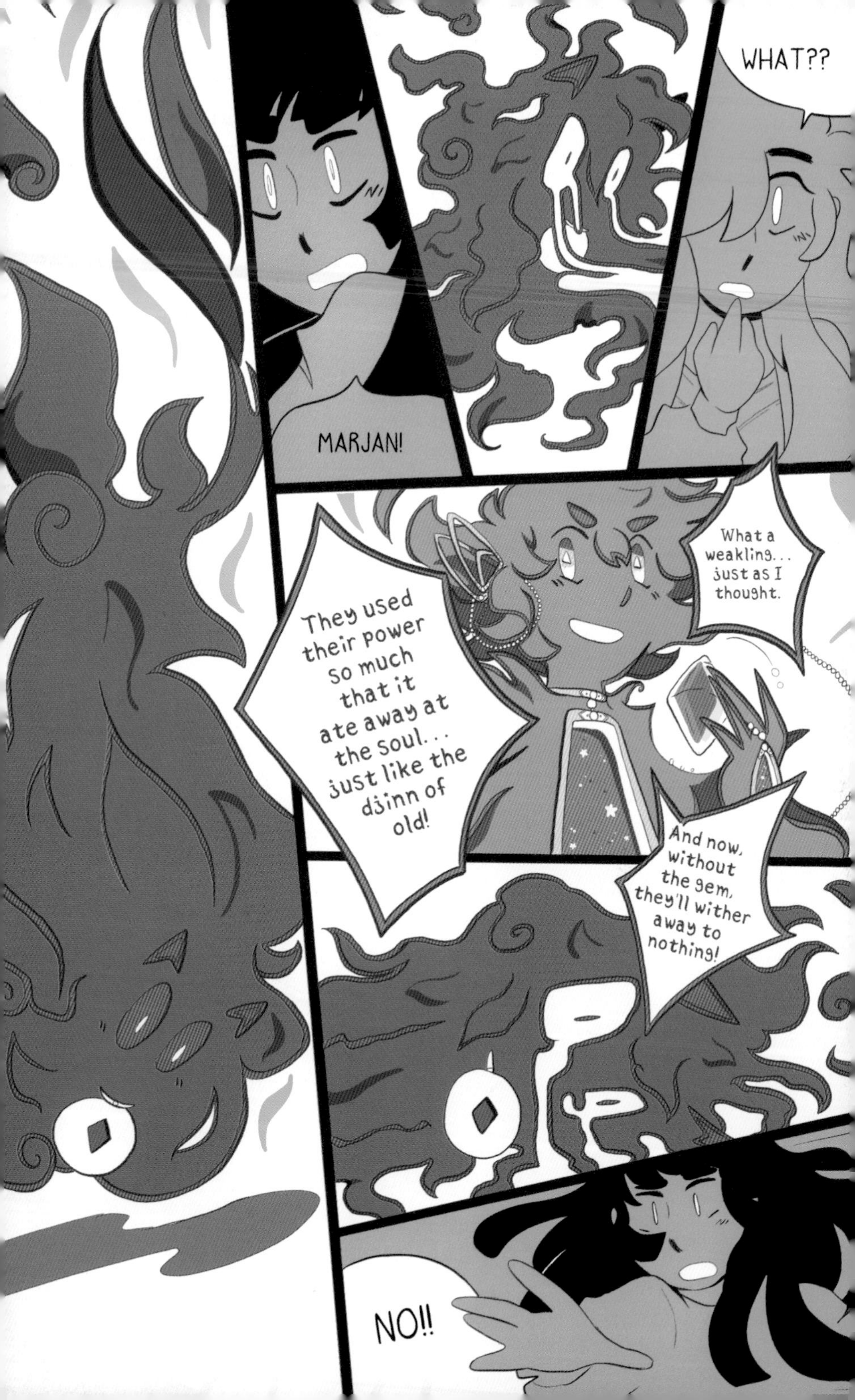

MARJAN!
WHAT??
They used their power so much that it ate away at the soul... the soul... just like the djinn of old!
What a weakling... just as I thought.
And now, without the gem, they'll wither away to nothing!
NO!!

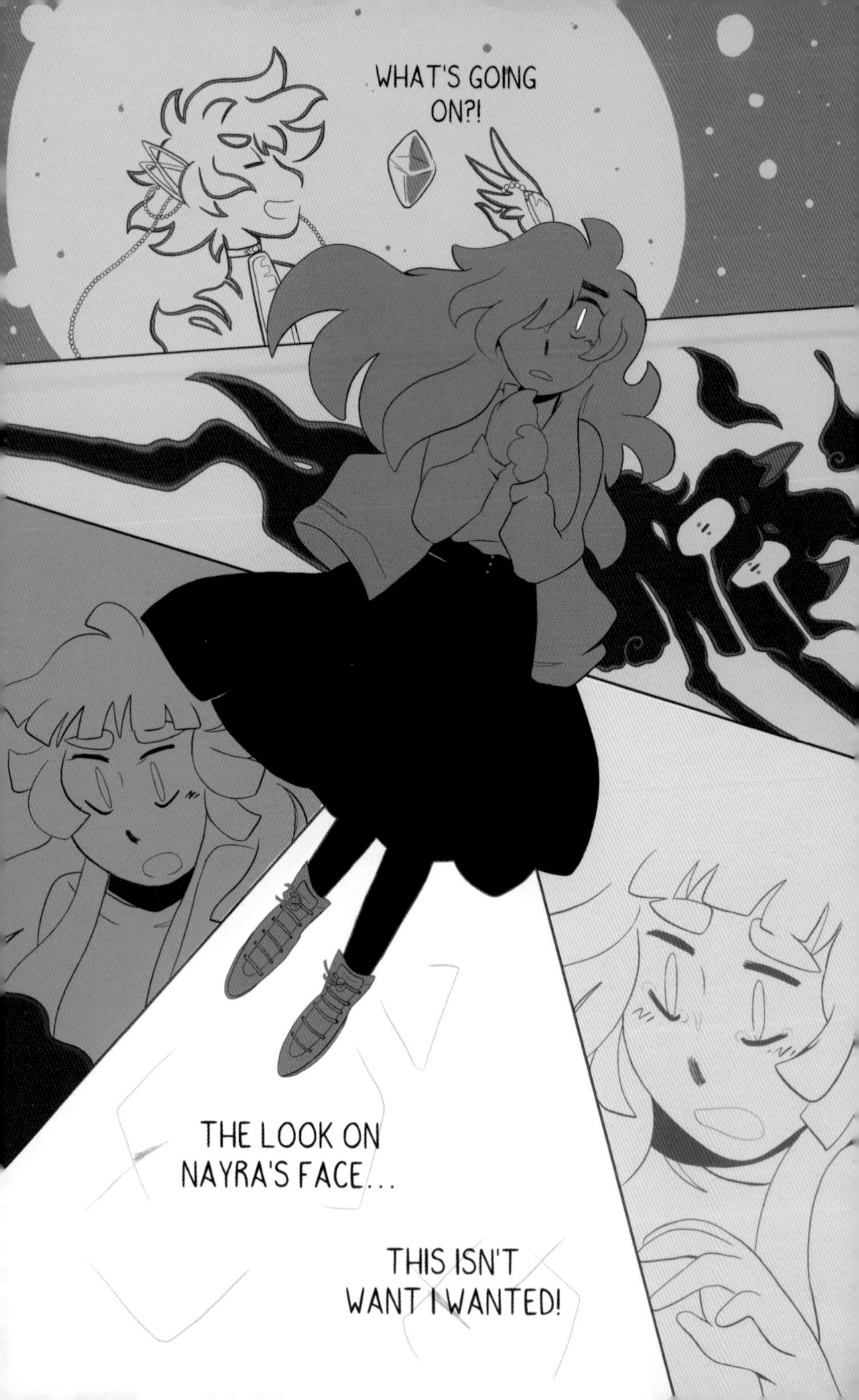
WHAT'S GOING ON?!
THE LOOK ON NAYRA'S FACE...
THIS ISN'T WANT I WANTED!

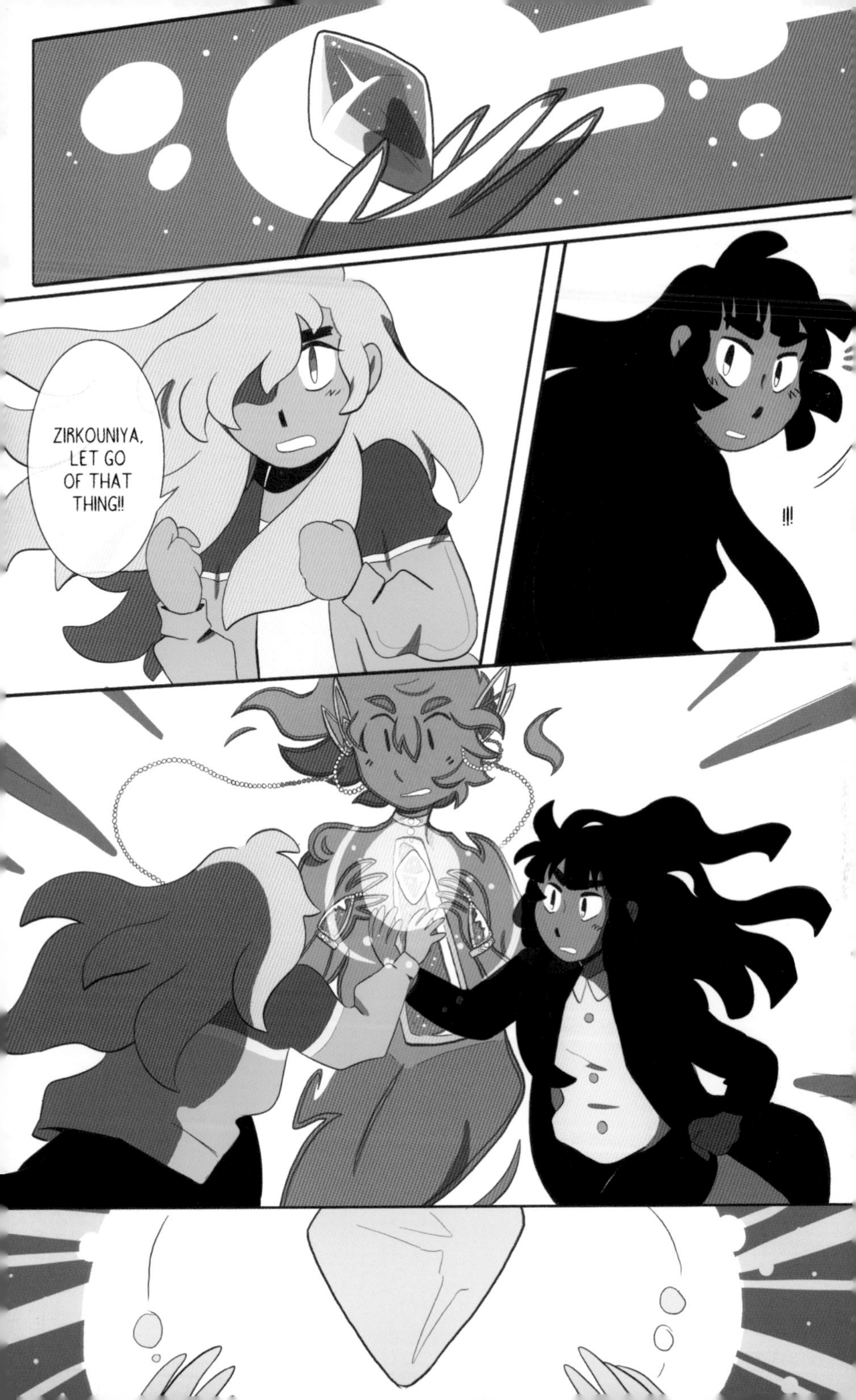
ZIRKOUNIYA, LET GO OF THAT THING!!
!!!

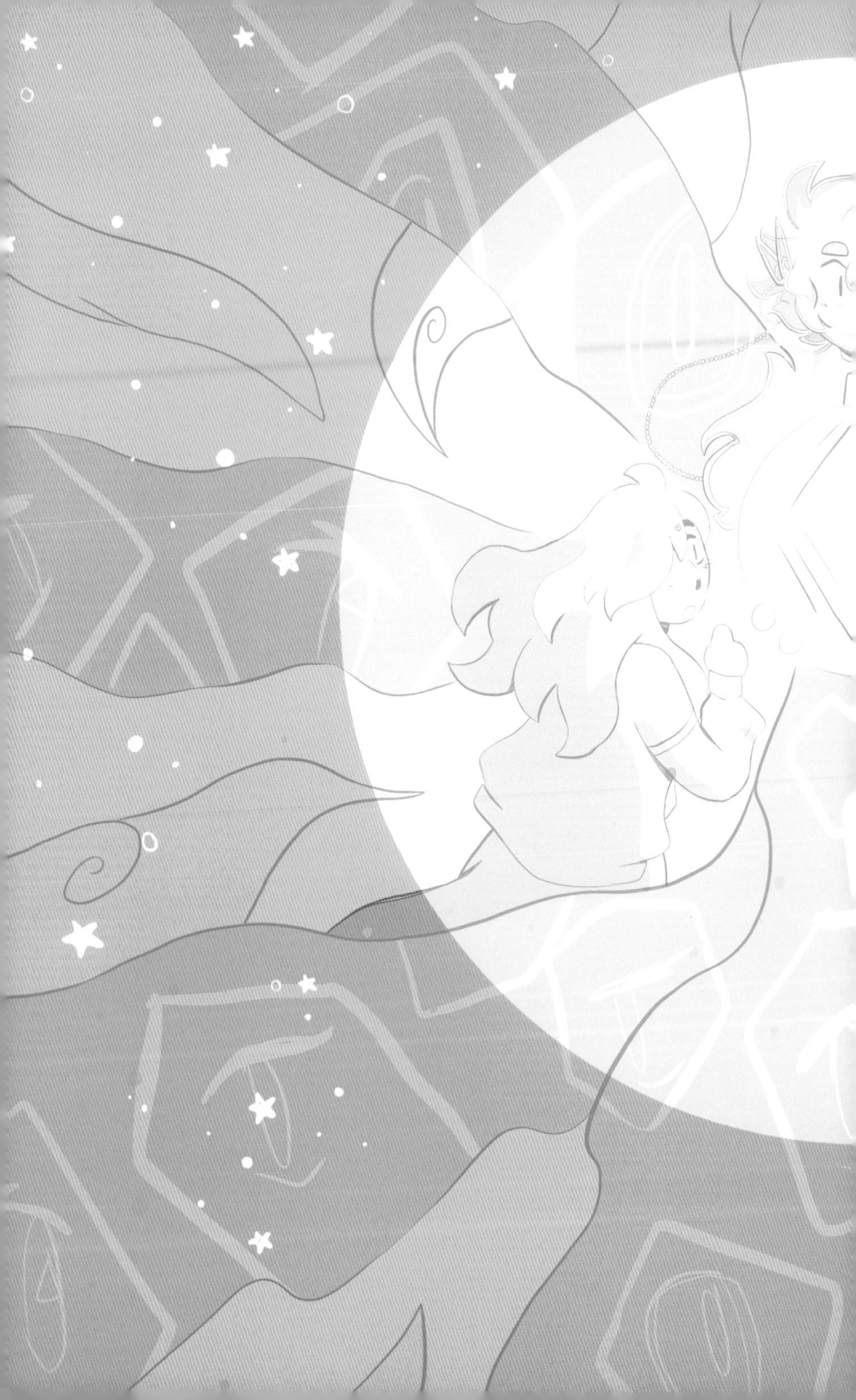

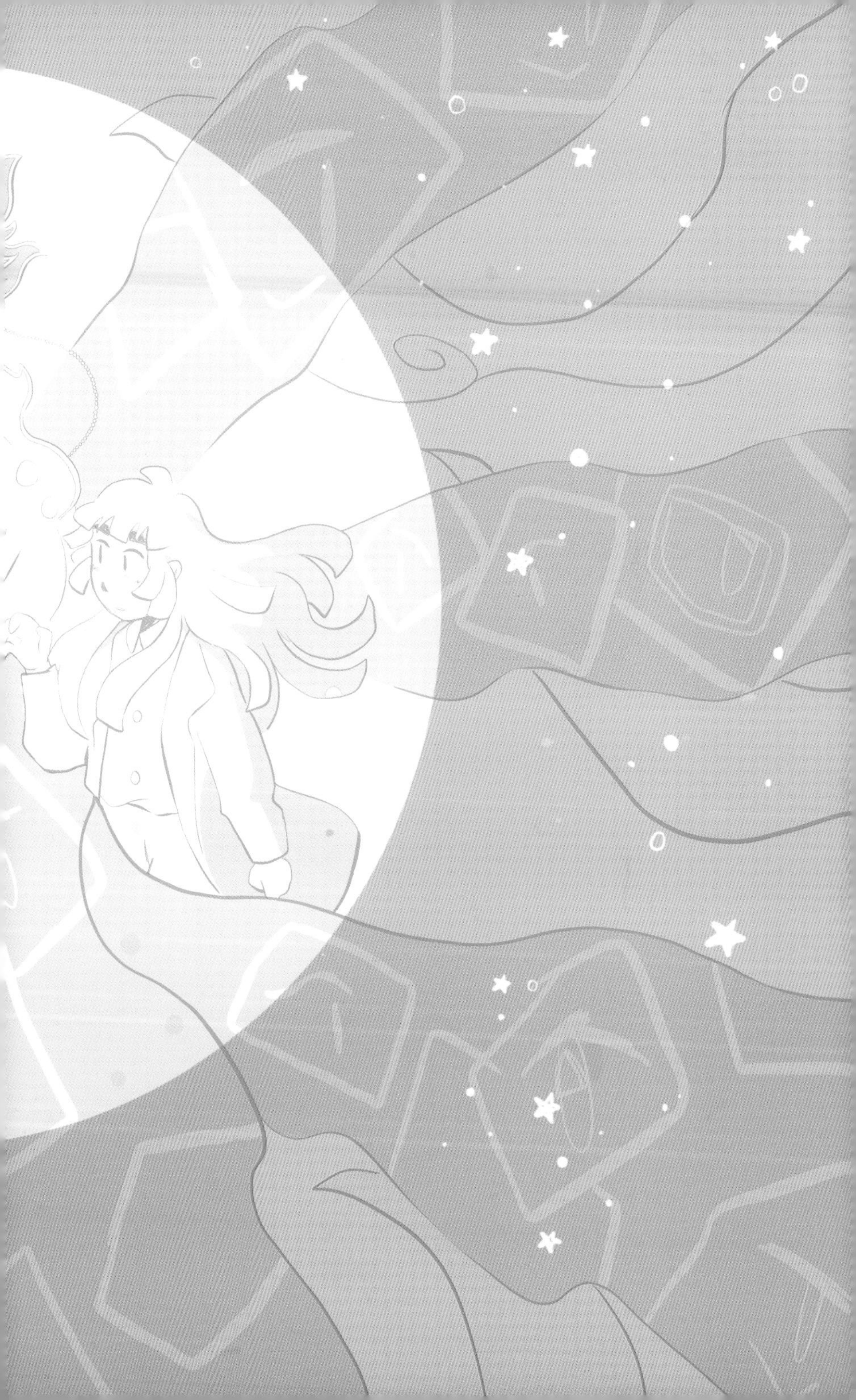

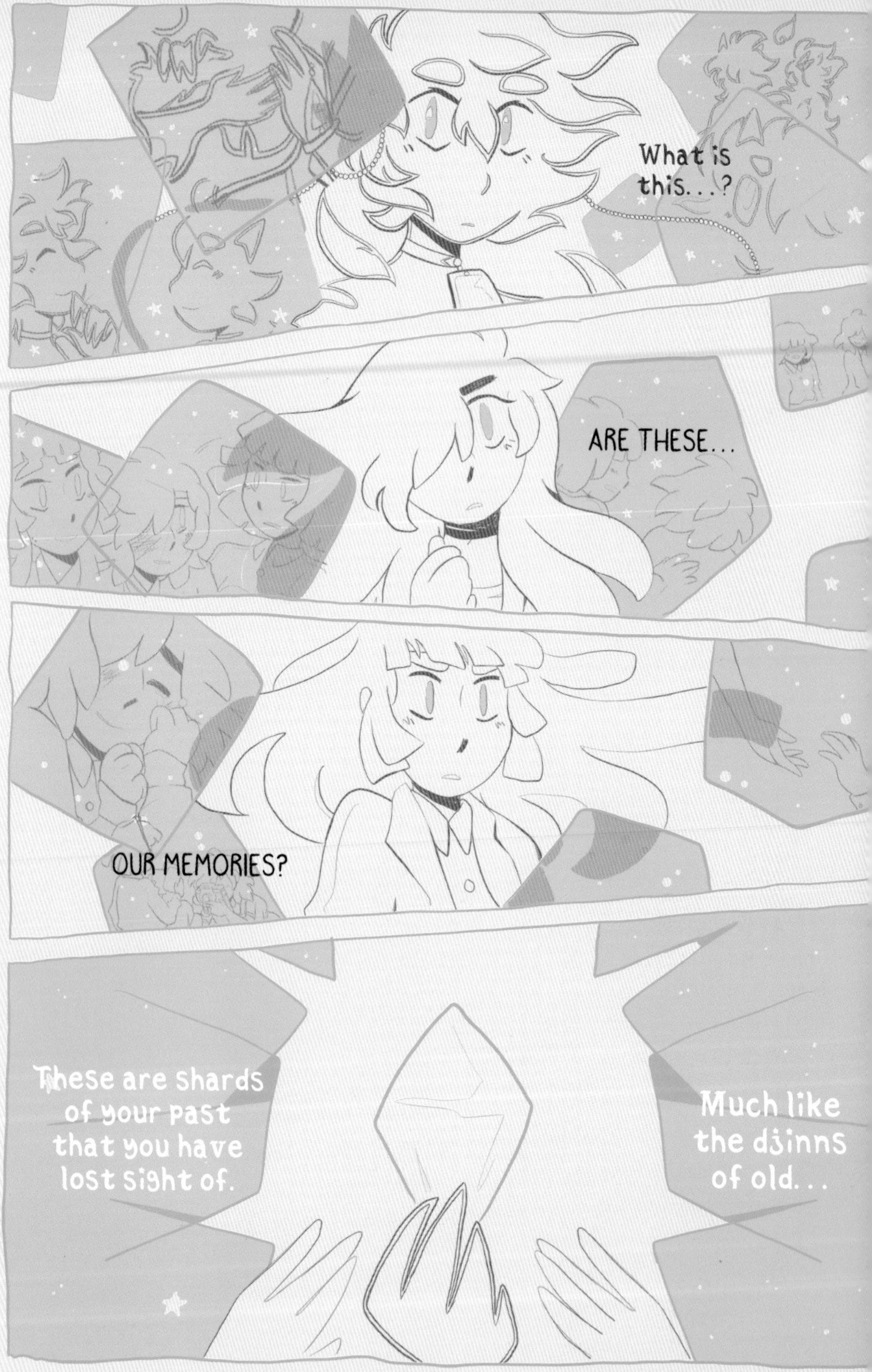
What is this...?
ARE THESE...
OUR MEMORIES?
These are shards of your past that you have lost sight of.
Much like the djinns of old...

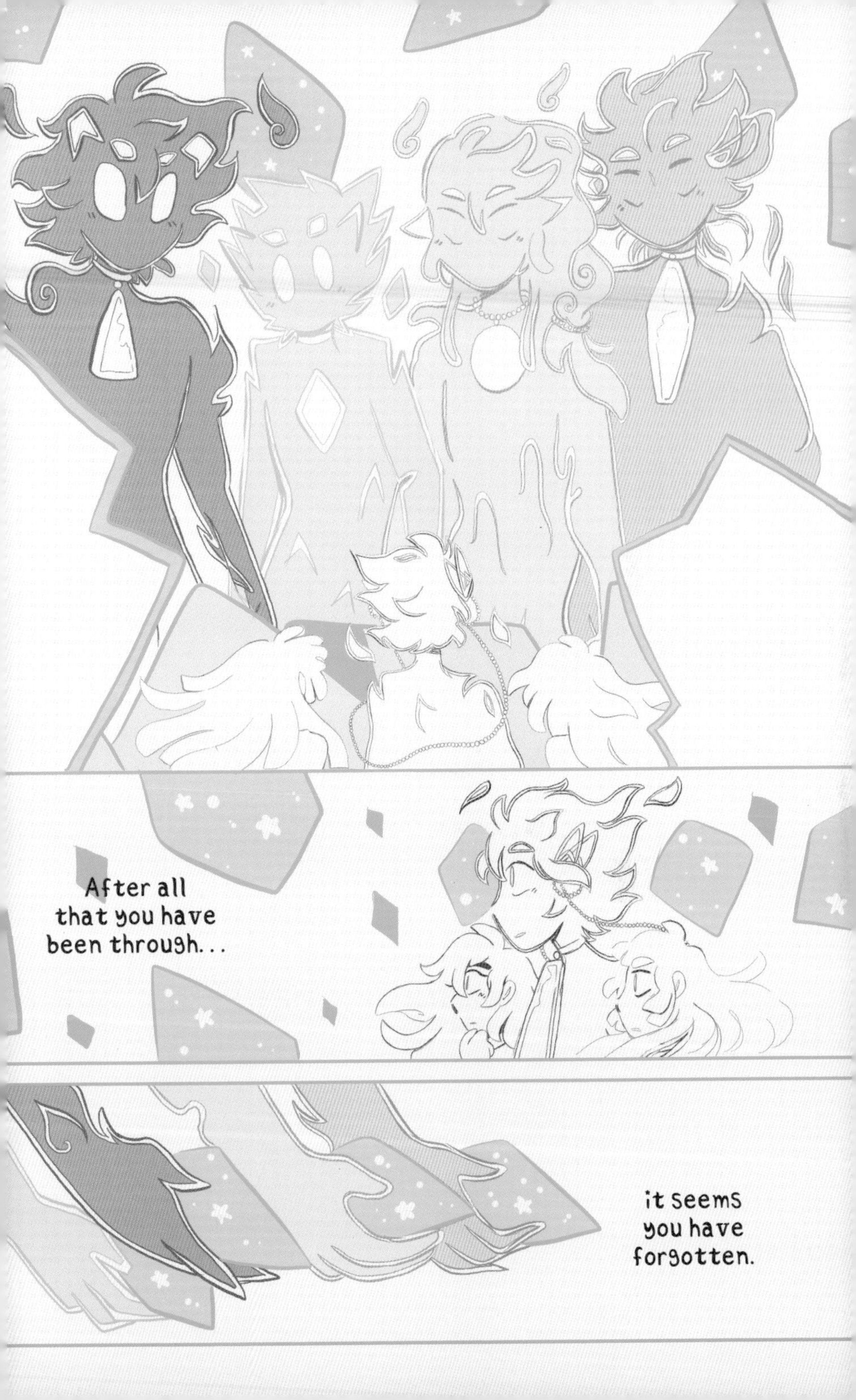
After all that you have been through...
it seems you have forgotten.

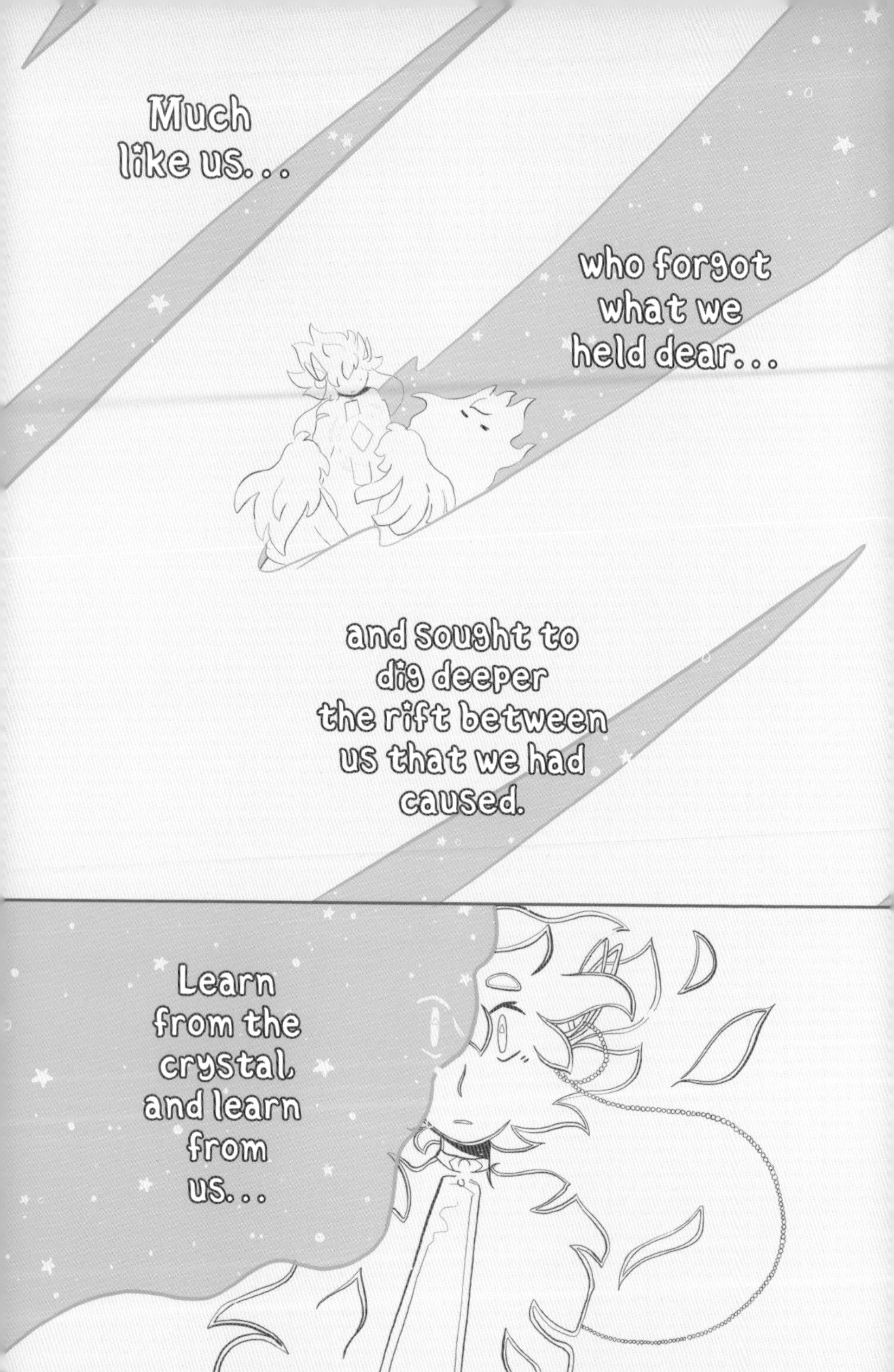
Much like us...
who forgot what we held dear...
and sought to dig deeper the rift between us that we had caused.
Learn from the crystal and learn from us...

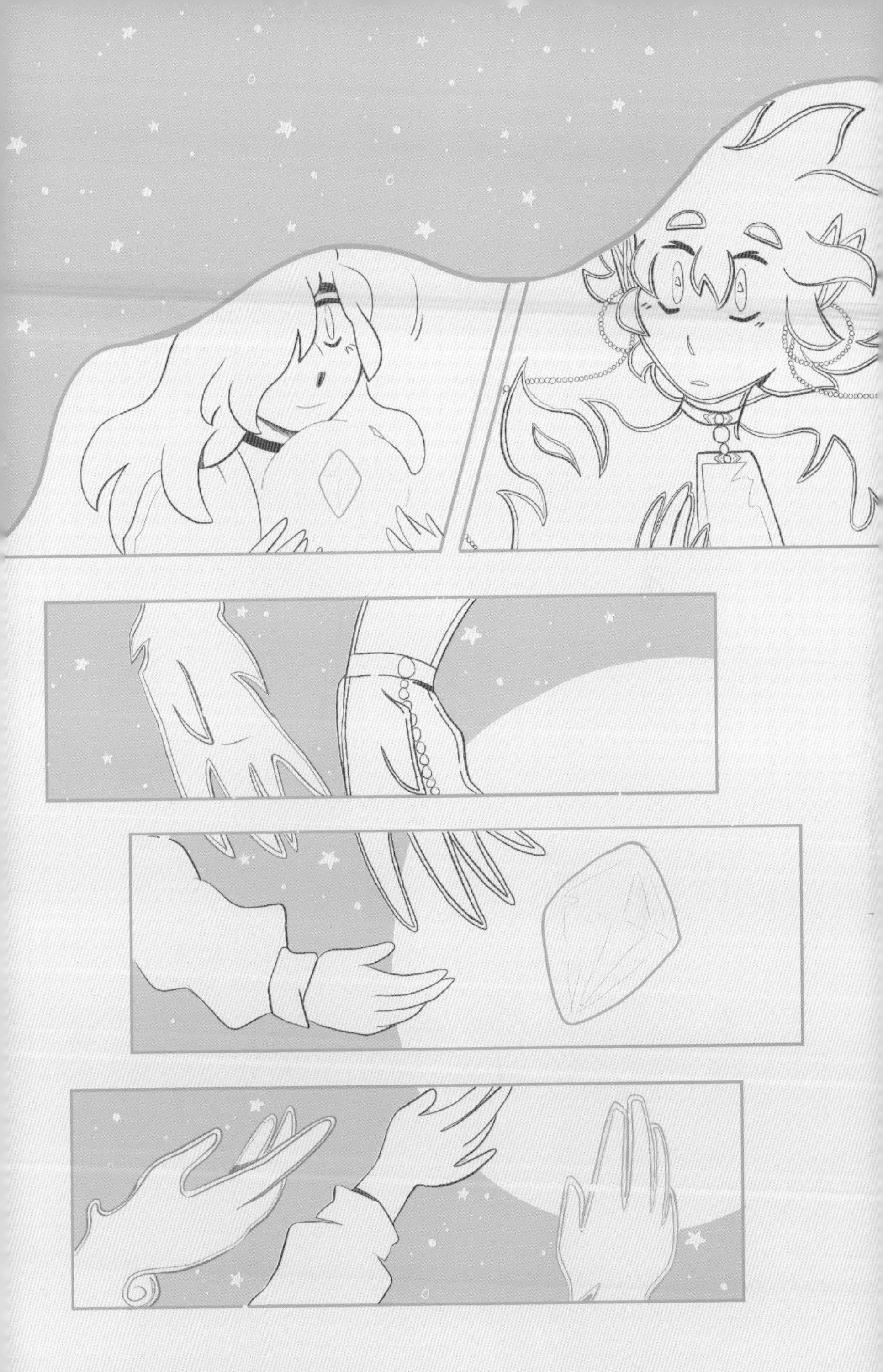

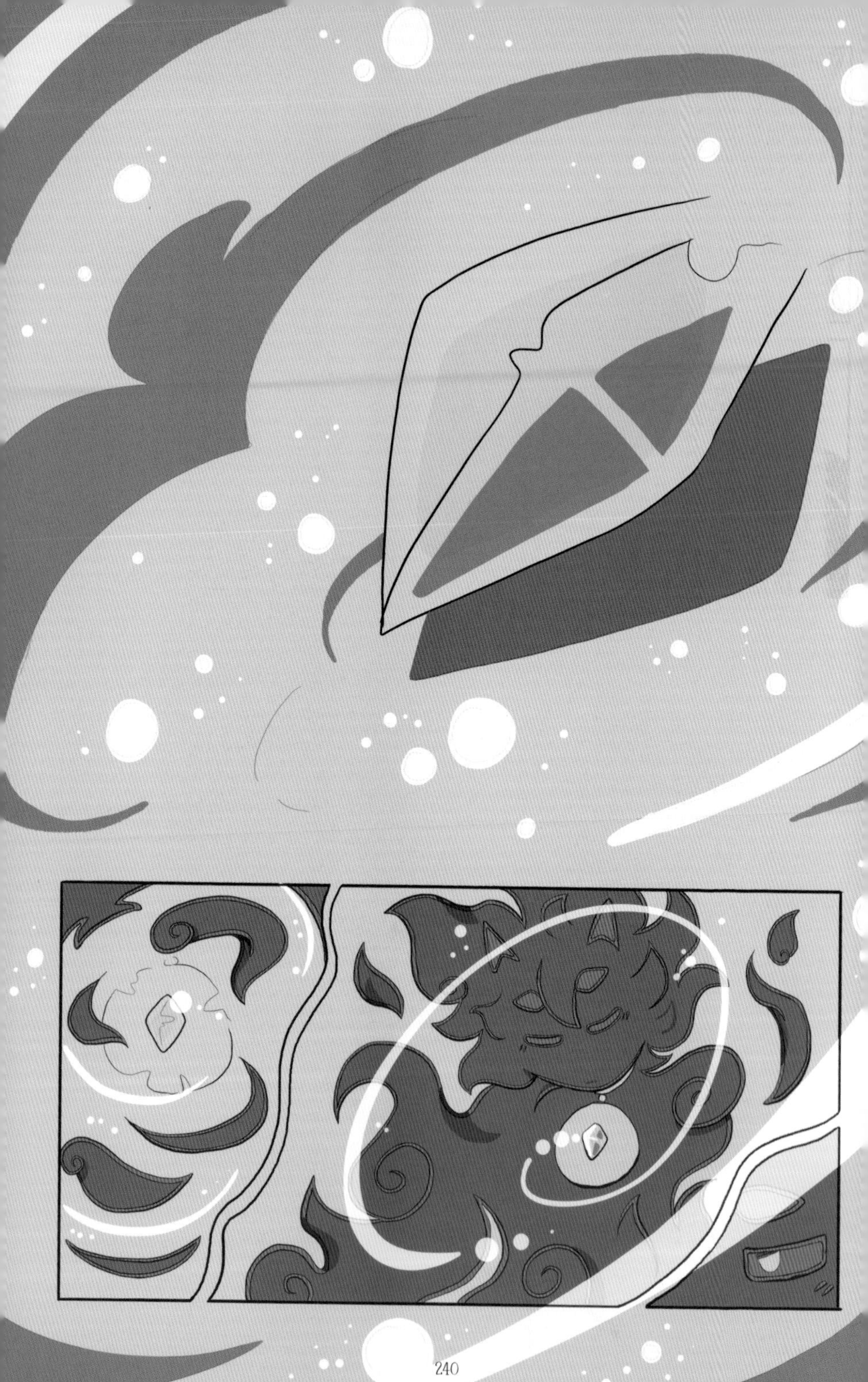

Marjan, I'm so sorry. The stone... I wasn't acting like myself...

It's all right. There was a good reason why the stone was hidden, after all.

RAMI... I DON'T THINK EITHER OF US MEANT TO HURT EACH OTHER...

I DON'T THINK SO EITHER.

MAYBE FROM HERE, WE CAN REBUILD, TOO.

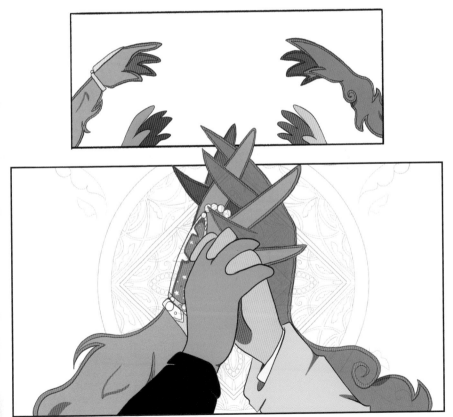

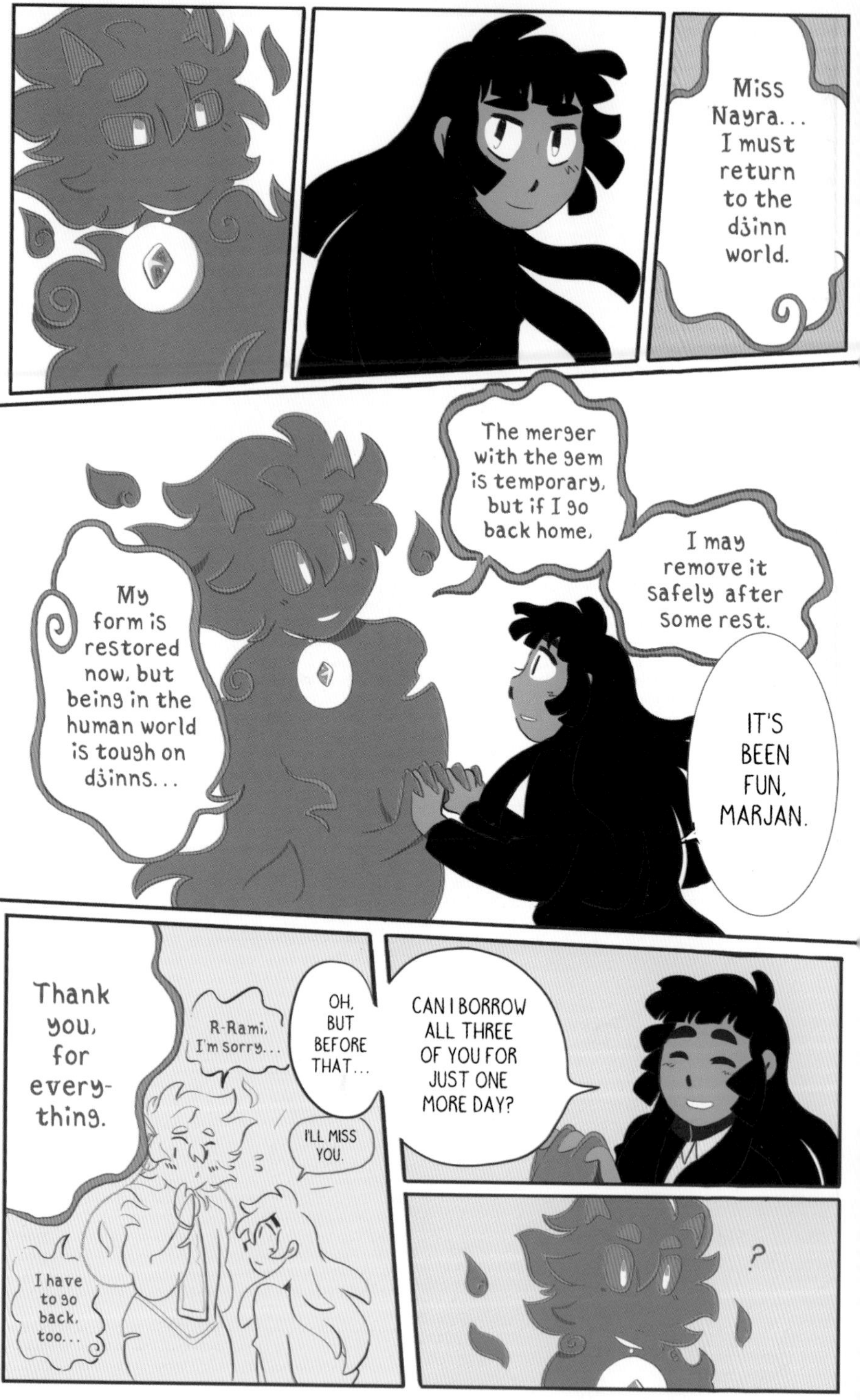

Miss Nayra... I must return to the djinn world.
The merger with the gem is temporary, but if I go back home,
I may remove it safely after some rest.
My form is restored now, but being in the human world is tough on djinns...
IT'S BEEN FUN, MARJAN.
Thank you, for every-thing.
R-Rami, I'm sorry...
I have to go back, too...
I'LL MISS YOU.
OH, BUT BEFORE THAT...
CAN I BORROW ALL THREE OF YOU FOR JUST ONE MORE DAY?
?

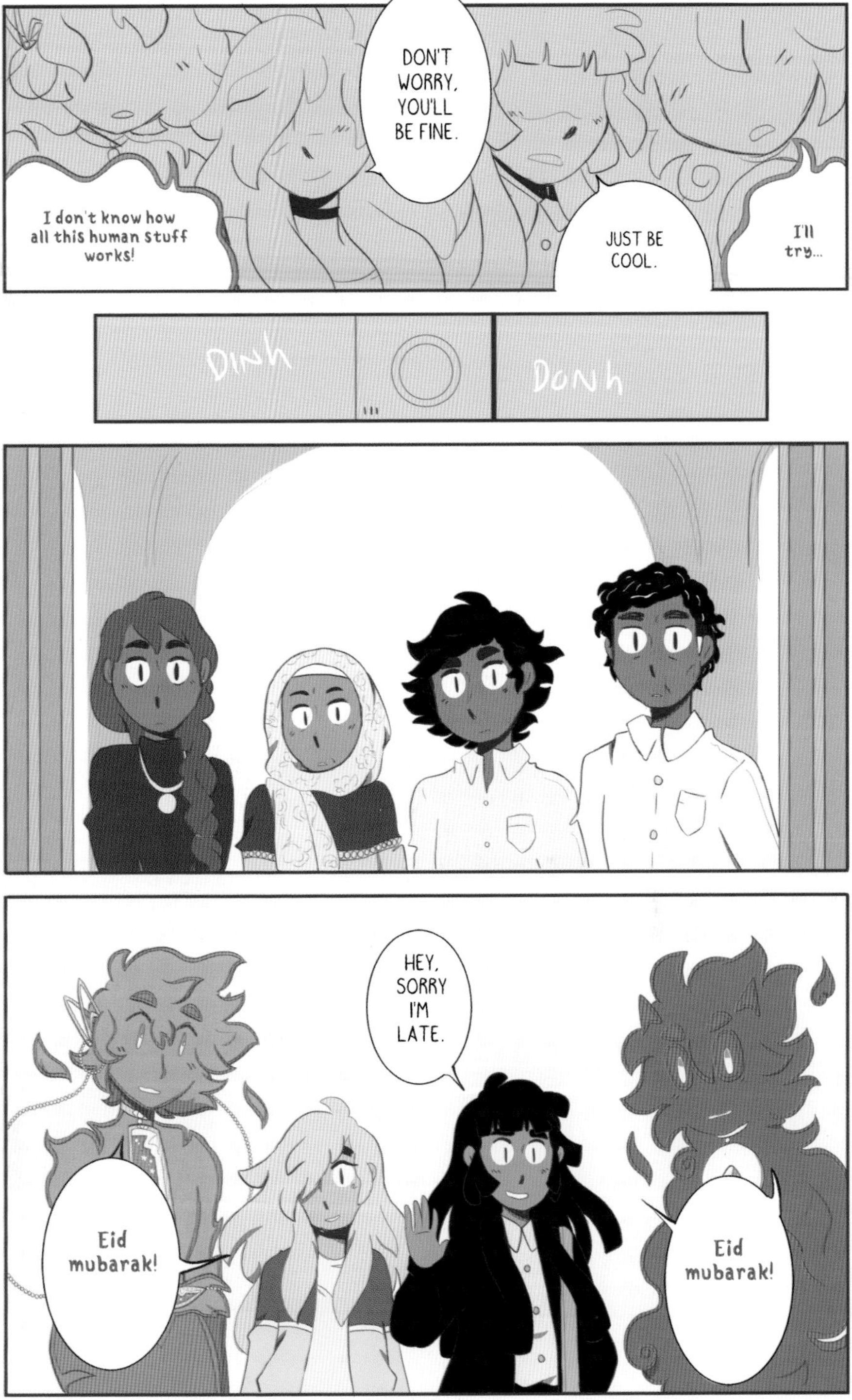
I don't know how all this human stuff works!
DON'T WORRY, YOU'LL BE FINE.
JUST BE COOL.
I'll try...
DINH
DONH
HEY, SORRY I'M LATE.
Eid mubarak!
Eid mubarak!

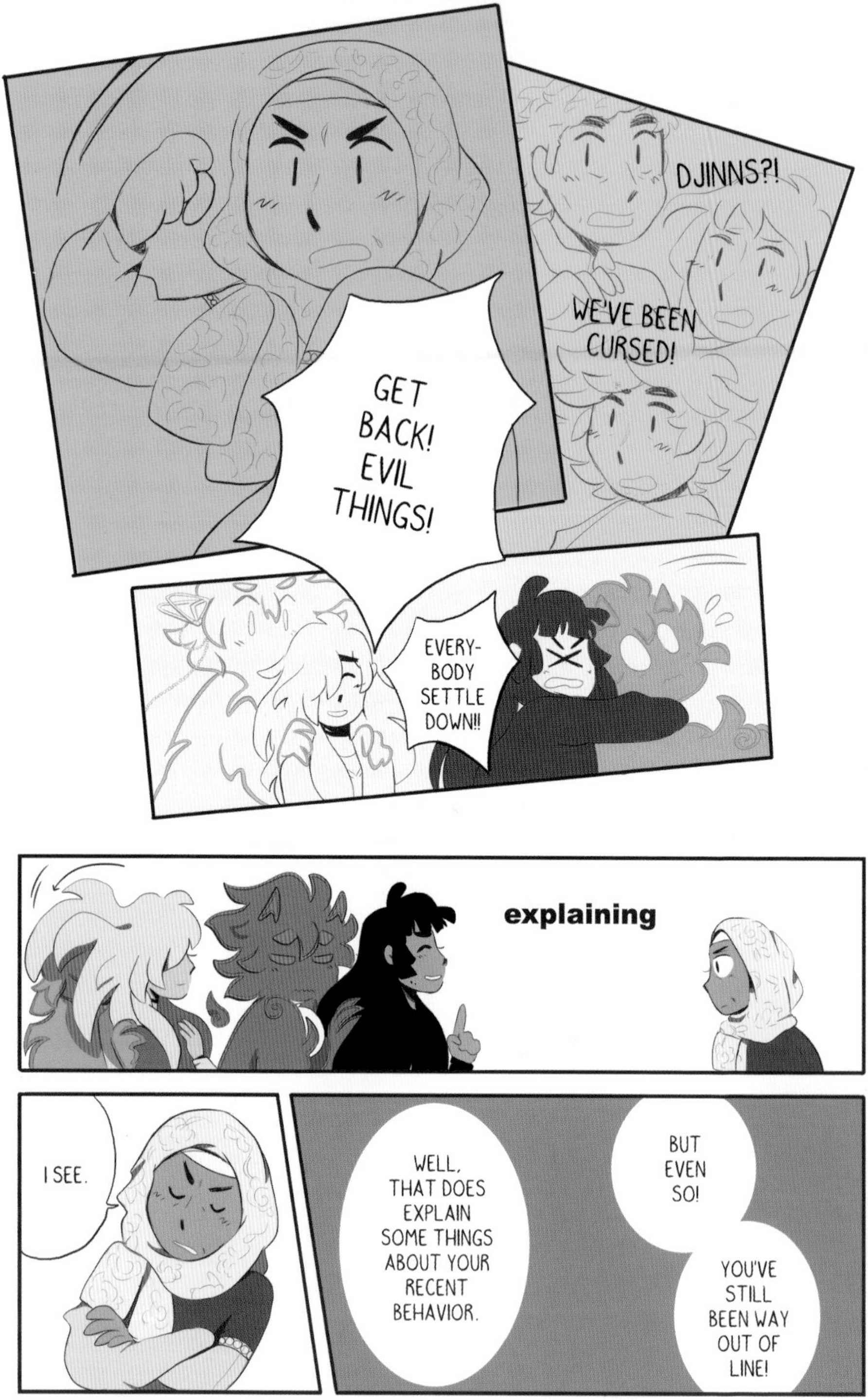
GET BACK! EVIL THINGS!
DJINNS?!
WE'VE BEEN CURSED!
EVERY-BODY SETTLE DOWN!!
explaining
I SEE.
WELL, THAT DOES EXPLAIN SOME THINGS ABOUT YOUR RECENT BEHAVIOR.
BUT EVEN SO!
YOU'VE STILL BEEN WAY OUT OF LINE!

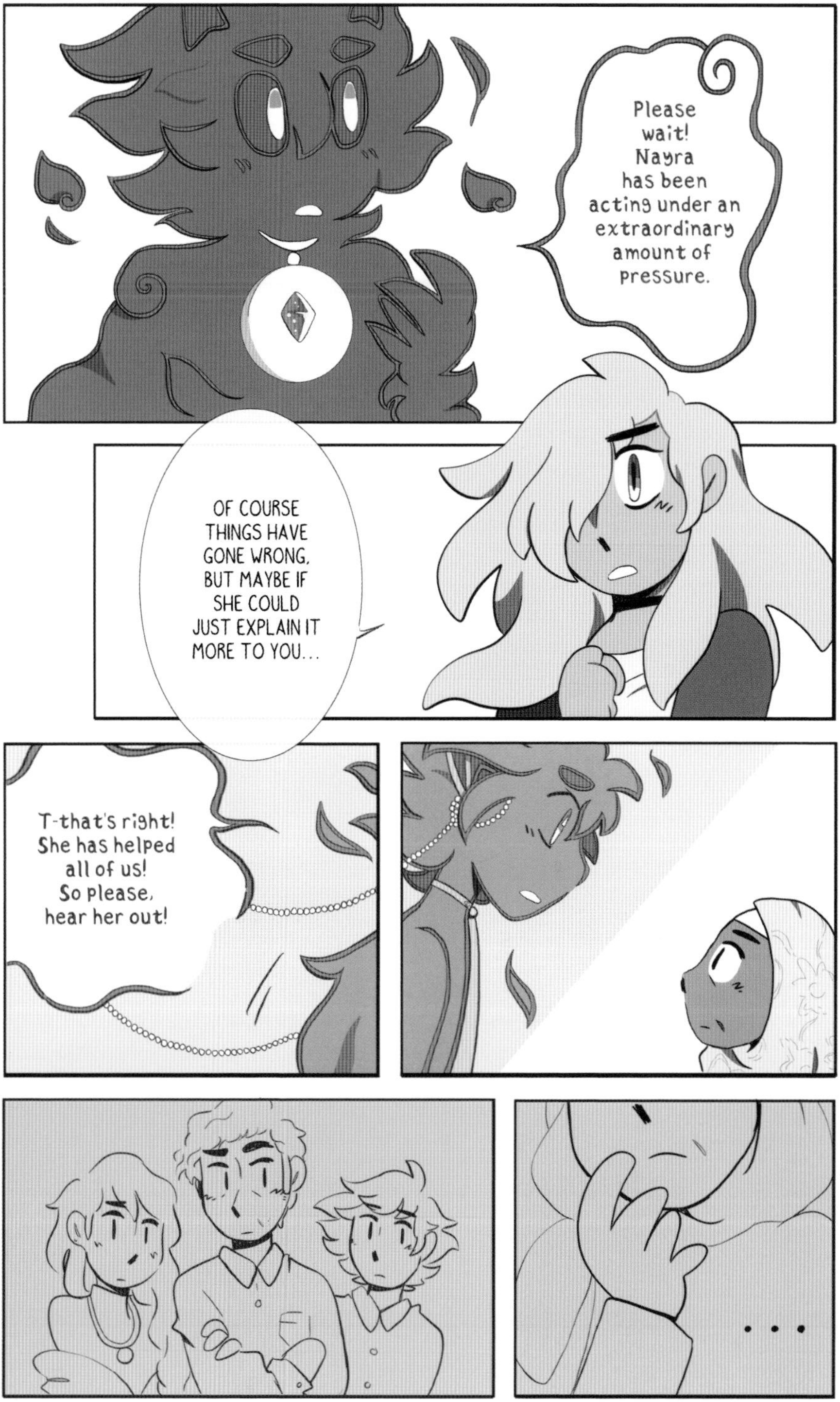
Please wait! Nayra has been acting under an extraordinary amount of pressure.
OF COURSE THINGS HAVE GONE WRONG, BUT MAYBE IF SHE COULD JUST EXPLAIN IT MORE TO YOU...
T-that's right! She has helped all of us! So please, hear her out!
. . .

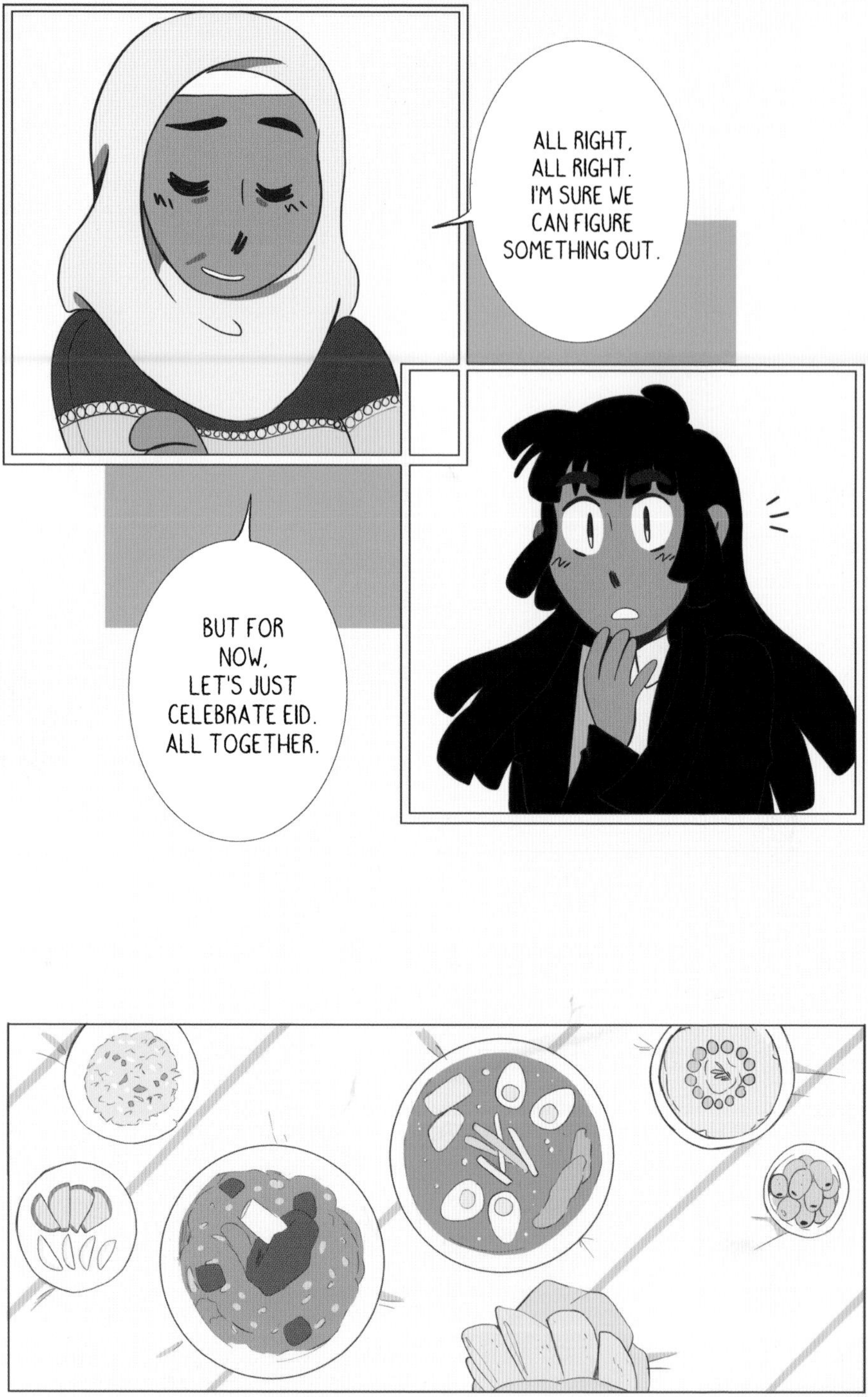
ALL RIGHT,
ALL RIGHT.
I'M SURE WE
CAN FIGURE
SOMETHING OUT.
BUT FOR
NOW,
LET'S JUST
CELEBRATE EID.
ALL TOGETHER.

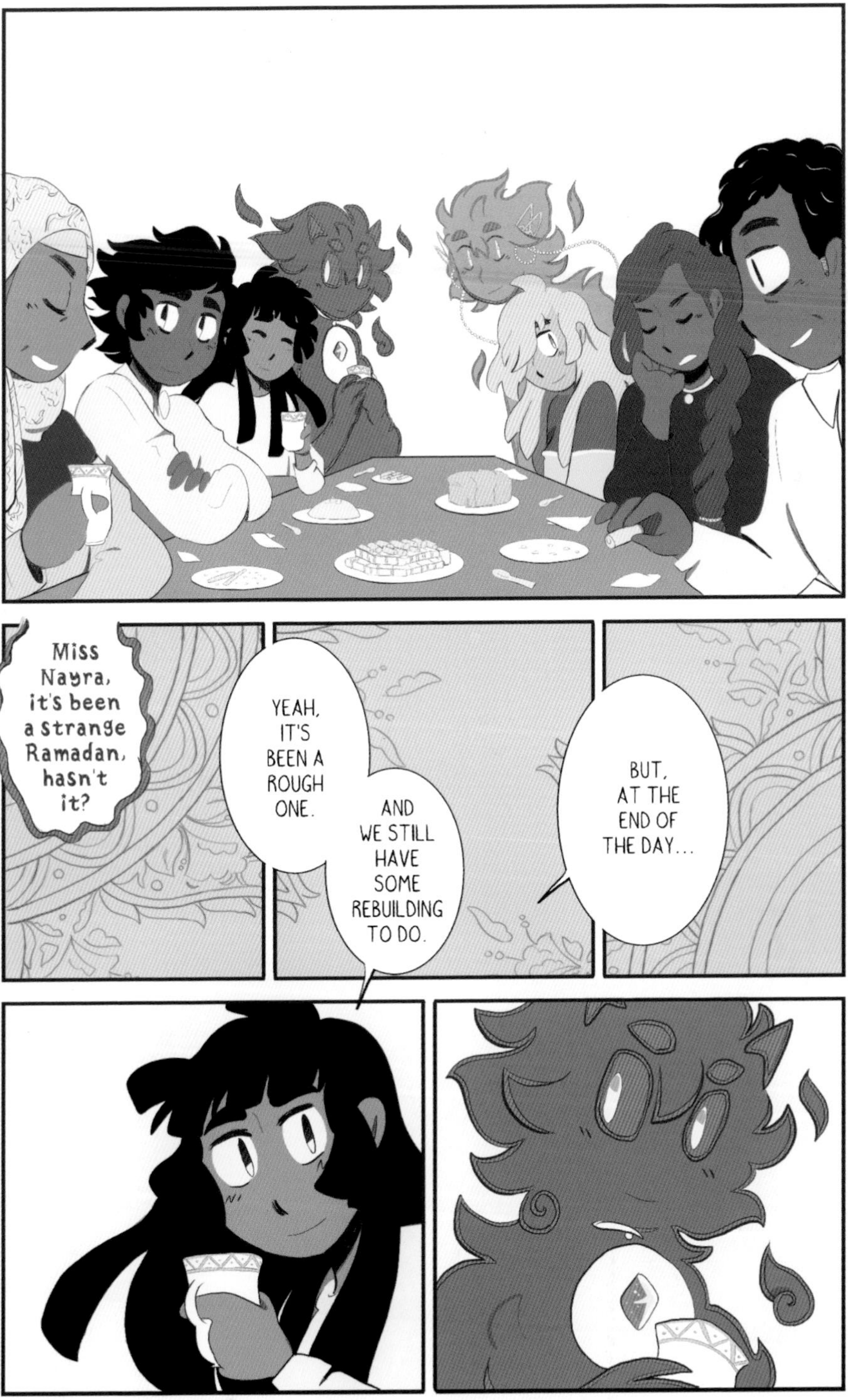
Miss Nayra, it's been a strange Ramadan, hasn't it?
YEAH, IT'S BEEN A ROUGH ONE.
AND WE STILL HAVE SOME REBUILDING TO DO.
BUT, AT THE END OF THE DAY...

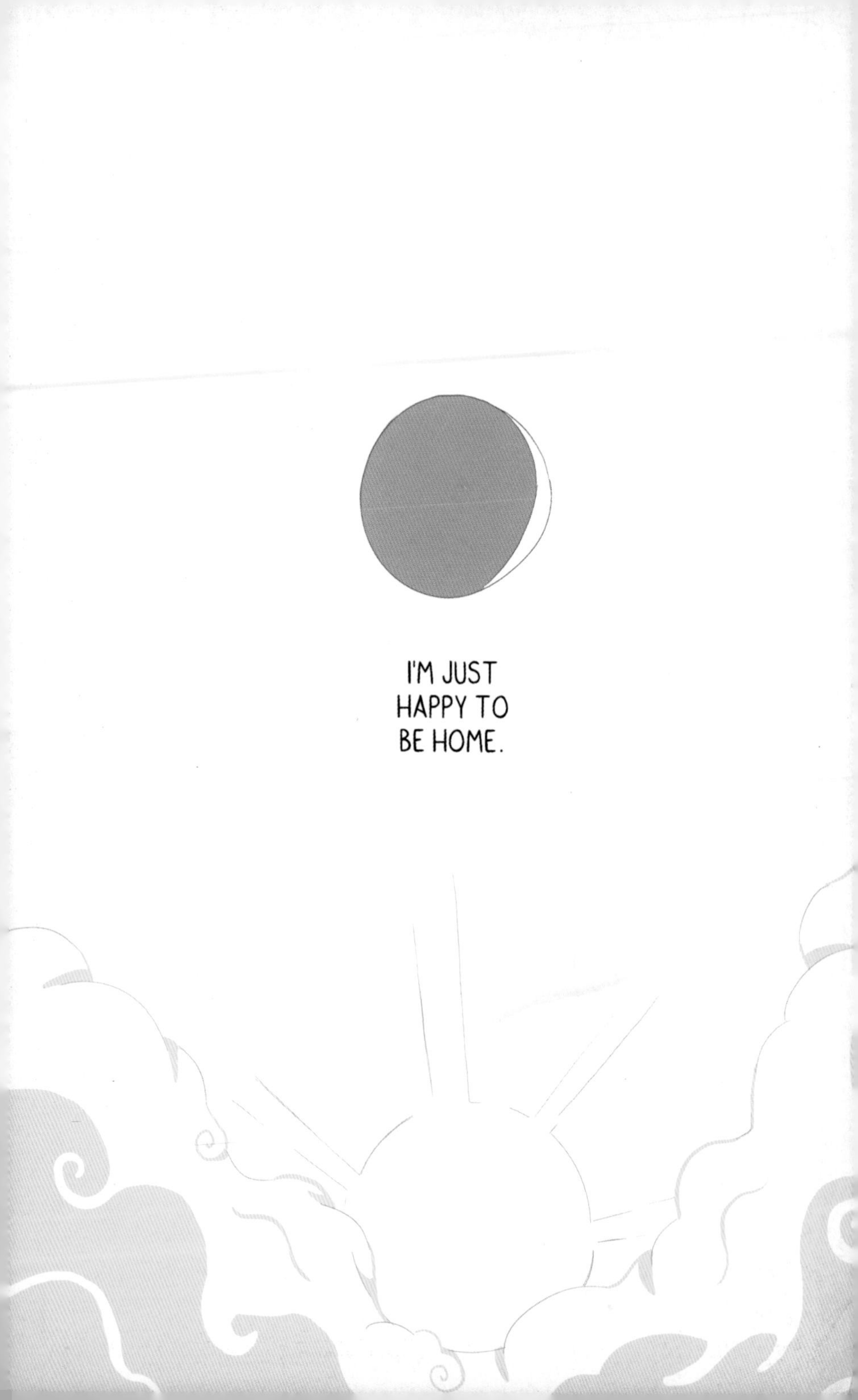
I'M JUST
HAPPY TO
BE HOME.